I DIED IN RIO

I DIED IN RIO

By

ARSEN PANKOVICH

A. PANKOVICH PUBLISHERS
NEW YORK

English Language Editor Melody Lawrence.

ISBN 0-9672101-0-0 (hardcover)
ISBN 0-9672101-1-9 (paperback)

Library of Congress Catalog Card Number: 99-90552

Published by A. Pankovich Publishers, New York

Design by Arsen Pankovich

Printed in the United States by R.R. Donnelly and Sons.

First Printing 1999

FIRST EDITION

10   9   8   7   6   5   4   3   2   1

for *NADA*

People
have the right
to be wrong

CHAPTER ONE

SATURDAY, 8 NOVEMBER 1997

This was to be just another ordinary Saturday. Arsen enjoyed these ordinary days, for the time belonged entirely to him. There was no early wake-up to rush to work at the Medical Division of the ARGO Company of New York or at the Brooklyn East Medical Office. On these ordinary days the morning routine usually started with a cup of coffee while Arsen read the newspapers, some delivered daily to the door of his apartment. 'Ordinary' did not mean quiet and dull. News, particularly in the international section, then Editorials and Op-Eds, could be satisfying or extremely annoying. On this eighth day of November, the papers had no great or depressing news or editorials. Most exciting was the slump in the Dow Jones of more than 100 points, which was boring anyway considering the undulation of the Dow in recent weeks.

Not a word on Serbia and a lot on Iraq. The similarity was remarkable between these two countries, Arsen thought. Their leaders reminded him of hogs that were clobbered constantly yet resisted stubbornly, made an awful noise and kept living. How long would the punishment last for crimes that were being committed all over the world at this very minute, Arsen murmured to himself. Yet no punishments for the crimes were forthcoming. It was not worth getting irritated about that repeatedly, he concluded.

The exchanges at the ceremonies for the opening of the Bush Library were boring. HIV care in the U.S. was a standard review. A short article reporting on the observations of a group of obscure Russian astronomers about a strange space object traveling in the direction of the Earth was interesting, although already denied by most prominent European and American astronomers. The Op-Ed articles were benign. Among the Editorials it was interesting to read that killers usually forgot their crimes.

Papers read, Arsen decided to write the narratives of two patients for

1

their lawyers. Though very lucrative, this was also very tedious work. As his friend, a psychiatrist, always said, 'In retirement you have to work to be recognized.' Obviously, the time was not entirely his as it was used today to earn money, not recognition.

The mail was delivered at noon, and Arsen sorted it out not expecting anything of interest. He separated out the usual junk mail. There were a few letters from Chase Bank. There were also two letters from some law offices, probably asking for copies of records or a narrative. A new catalog from MacWarehouse had arrived. A letter from the Forum on Foreign Policy in New York caught Arsen's attention. Probably advertising the meeting lectures. He had received similar invitations in the past. He never subscribed for the lectures. The letter, unopened, was thrown in the waste basket.

On second thought it would be interesting to find out who the speakers were for the coming year and what the topics were, Arsen thought, and he retrieved the envelope and opened it. Immediately he realized that this was a personal letter addressed to him.

November 5, 1997

Dear Dr. Pankovich:
    I was asked by the Program Board of the Forum on Foreign Policy to extend an invitation to you to present an hour long lecture on a subject of your choice at the regular Meeting of the Forum on Thursday, January 22, 1998 at seven o'clock in the evening at the Forum's quarters in New York.
    I would appreciate receiving your early response and the title of your topic.
    Your CV would help to introduce you at the meeting.

Sincerely yours,
Matthew Brown, Ph.D. , Secretary

Arsen was stunned. This was something completely unexpected and unbelievable, though it had occurred to him as an unachievable wish. Could this be a practical joke by someone? Very few people knew of his interest in international politics and ethnic problems. Even fewer people knew what his opinions and ideas were. Essentially nobody knew of his thoughts on solutions to ethnic problems. Must be a prankster, Arsen concluded. Must be, but who?

By now Arsen's distrust of people was at its height. His name had not appeared in any publications or articles on these subjects. Sure, he had written a couple of letters to the Editors of the local newspapers, but they had not been published or acknowledged. Only Steven Erhardt, a correspondent from Washington, had replied in response to Arsen's letter about his Op-Ed on Bosnia. Erhardt had answered a few months later and in polite phrases he had referred to the 'dignified expressions' in Arsen's letter, but had made no comments on his thoughts.

This was of no significance, and probably long forgotten by Erhardt. Yet, when Erhardt had accompanied the U.S. United Nations Ambassador on his first visit to Europe and Moscow, Arsen had been proud he had received that letter, as if it meant a recognition of Arsen's thinking, and that he had written something worthy of acknowledgment. This was how far Arsen's imagination traveled. Erhardt could not have had anything to do with this invitation.

Even a brief approving e-mail from Walter Adams, a recognized ethnic scholar, in response to Arsen's questions regarding a sudden agreement between Hungarians and Rumanians over Transylvania, was insignificant. Prof. Adams had agreed that this was an example of the cooperation of opposing nations when it was beneficial to their national interests, and that it removed the ethnic problems from their applications to NATO. These letters were Arsen's only contributions to international political thinking. Why would someone submit his name for the lecture? Someone had to do it. Someone obviously had done it. Who would that be and why had he done it? Arsen did not know a single political scientist or journalist or politician who would want to do it.

The letter appeared genuine, although obviously letters could easily be made on computers to look like originals, Arsen thought. A quick check of the address in the telephone directory confirmed that the address and phone number were correct. The only way to solve this puzzle was to call the Forum's office and find out if the letter was from them.

CHAPTER TWO

MONDAY, 10 NOVEMBER 1997

Monday was a very busy day at the ARGO. There were eight cases to be reviewed and each of them was complicated: either the problems were complex clinically, or it was difficult to determine whether the applicant could perform the prescribed duties or was permanently disabled. The decisions were difficult, and it was hard to be fair to the employer and to the ARGO Pension Board.

Arsen had no time to make a call to Mr. Brown at the Forum during office hours. He was thinking of calling Mr. Brown's secretary just to find out if they had sent the letter. He made the call late in the afternoon. The message on the answering machine indicated that the staff had gone home. He was ready to hang up when there was a click on the line, and a male voice answered.

"This is Mr. Brown at FFP. May I help you?"

Arsen had not expected to talk to Mr. Brown and he hesitated for a moment.

"This is Mr. Brown. May I help you?" The man was obviously impatient and Arsen thought it was better to call again in the morning. Then, his old confidence returned and he said in a firm voice:

"Mr. Brown, this is Dr. Pankovich. I received a letter from you, and I wanted just to make sure that I understand it correctly." And he added quietly, "Or perhaps to find out if there was a mistake of some sort."

"No mistake, Dr. Pankovich. I did send you the letter of invitation for a lecture," Mr. Brown confirmed. "Have you decided on the topic?"

"No, I have not. Now that I know you want me to give the lecture, I will choose the topic, and let you know. Also, I will send my CV, although I am not sure it is pertinent for the audience. I was an orthopedic surgeon until I retired a year ago. My bibliography is full of orthopedic papers - topics like the treatment of fractures. I am not sure that would fit too well with a political topic."

"Perhaps not," said Mr. Brown. "Still, people will be interested to know something about you since you're not widely known in the circle of political scientists."

"They never heard of me, I assure you," Arsen said.

"You would be surprised, very surprised, about what people know, and how they find out," Mr. Brown said and laughed. "In any event we want you to give the lecture."

"Who recommended me?"

"It is the policy of the Board to withhold that information," Mr. Brown said. "Let me just say that you were recommended by someone who knew you or about you, and who believed that your lecture would be of interest to our members. Isn't that enough?"

"I am very curious," Arsen said. "It is true that I have given many lectures on orthopedic subjects over the years; some would call them stimulating and others controversial. This will be the first lecture in the political arena. I will give it a try."

"I'm sure you will," Mr. Brown said.

"Good night, Mr. Brown. I will be in touch," Arsen said quietly.

"Good night, Dr. Pankovich. Do keep in touch." Mr. Brown hung up.

Arsen held the receiver for a moment, then lowered it slowly to the set. "This is it," Arsen said aloud and returned to the medical office room. His colleagues noted that he looked absent minded.

At home, Nada was preparing dinner when Arsen arrived; he was too tired and nervous to eat. After the six-thirty news with Bradley Adams, he went to the Vertical Club for his usual fifty-minute/four-mile walk. By the time he got home, took a shower, and dressed, it was nine-thirty. Arsen was exhausted, but not ready to sleep. A movie, a standard detective story, made him sleepy, and he was ready for bed at the movie's end.

CHAPTER THREE

TUESDAY, 11 NOVEMBER 1997

Arsen spent the morning calling the offices of several plastic surgeons to find one qualified to take care of a problem his friend's daughter had - something that could not be treated in Belgrade. It became clear that such a specialist was not to be found in New York, either. Arsen downloaded two papers on the subject from the Medline web site and realized that there was only one surgical option, and it was a complicated one. The authors were from Virginia and the Mayo Clinic. A very expensive plastic surgeon from Norfolk was available, yet her fees were exorbitant and unaffordable. The plastic surgeon from the Mayo Clinic was most helpful, very knowledgeable, and his package deal was quite reasonable. It was such a good feeling to realize that there were still places where greed was not the primary motivation, as it appeared to be in Norfolk. A heavy responsibility Arsen had felt, disappeared. There was no doubt that he would recommend the Mayo Clinic to his friend.

The Forum lecture was constantly on Arsen's mind. He knew that the topic would be ethnicity as a global problem, and the situation in the former Yugoslavia before and after the disintegration of the Communist States. The problem was how to present such material to a group of knowledgeable people, many of them probably experts on ethnic problems. Arsen remembered his lectures about fracture treatment that he had given to orthopedic surgeons, who were often knowledgeable on the subject. To keep them interested he would present controversial topics, often from the frontiers of the subject, and add some personal touch, enough to make them jump, and revolt during the discussion. It would not be such a bad idea to present the ethnic material from a different angle, and provide new solutions, Arsen thought. They should be stirred to revolt. They should become indignant and excited. Then they would listen and think. Some might even agree in the end.

CHAPTER FOUR

WEDNESDAY, 12 NOVEMBER 1997

Wednesday was a hard working day. Nineteen patients came up for examination at Brooklyn Medical. It was too much for one day, plus traveling by subway at least an hour in each direction.

It was amusing to read in the paper about a young woman's interest in a professor in Paris whom she had met on the Internet. In the future, Arsen thought, people will meet, fall in love, propose and get married before ever meeting each other physically, because of the distances between them in space. Traveling would be prohibitive as it would disrupt the workstation of the prospective traveler, and employment at the destination would not be insured. Sperm and eggs could be sent to a lab somewhere in space for fertilization, brought to term in a recipient or tube, and delivered wherever and however required. Children would grow in a wonderful nursery and kindergarten somewhere in space, and be brought up and educated according to their abilities and their parents' means. Maybe all of them would eventually meet.

What about the actual physical sexual act, Arsen wondered. Pleasure and satisfaction would be available in a beautifully designed setting, with an individual of fantasized beauty and intelligence, without a chance for failure and with no need for performance - actual masturbation in a virtual cyber space; not expensive, timed on demand, repeated as desired, and without attachments and obligations. The real intellectual relationship, in a Platonic sense, would be reserved for that real person somewhere in space. This sounded crazy, but virtual sex was not a novelty. Masturbation and fantasies must have existed from the moment the first individual felt and recognized his or her own sexuality, and had served well young and old, happy and miserable, poor more often than rich, lonely and shy individuals and many other categories. Arsen laughed at his crazy thoughts.

It was nine o'clock when Arsen arrived home that evening. Nada and her mother wondered if something had happened on his way home. It was too late for the Vertical Club and walking. A light supper was all he could eat. Tomorrow was another day, he decided. Tonight, only a movie, a glance at the market and a scan of the papers. The Dow Jones had plunged another hundred points. A headline caught Arsen's attention:

MUSLIMS KILLING SERBS IN SARAJEVO DURING WAR

The story from 'Nasha Borba' out of Belgrade on the Internet the day before was now confirmed. He wished only Muslims had done all killings.

The movie was good. Some dead, some alive, and justice prevailed at the end. The American way. Arsen noticed the light in the bedroom, and realized that Nada was probably reading. Both of them were sleepy, and the conversation did not last long. They talked mainly about their daughters, in Belgrade and Pamplona. Nada had talked to both of them that morning. The new baby in Belgrade, a granddaughter, was fine and so was the mother. The daughter in Pamplona had reported her lack of progress in arranging a medical rotation in New York for December. As suspected, the problem was her lack of malpractice insurance. Crazy but real.

It was midnight. Arsen could not fall asleep as he was thinking of dying in bed, perhaps of a stroke. He could not dispel the horrific story of Bauby, a man who had suffered a major paralysis--so called lock-in-syndrome--and had been able only to close and open his left eye, while his intellect and memory were intact. Bauby had written a book about his paralysis, dictated by blinking his left eye, and had died a few days after the book was published. Recently, Arsen had read a paper from the Mayo Clinic which described a very effective treatment for lock-in syndrome; Bauby could have lived if the treatment had been available to him.

Eventually, Arsen sank into the nothingness of a sleep without dreams.

CHAPTER FIVE

WEEKEND 14-16 NOVEMBER 1997

Arsen's thoughts wandered to his main mental preoccupation - the Forum lecture.

After some vacillation Arsen decided on a general title for his lecture, and he wrote a letter to Mr. Matthew Brown at the Forum:

14 November 1997

Dear Mr. Brown:

Though surprised, I am pleased to accept the invitation to present a lecture at the meeting of the Forum on 22 January 1998.

Global Ethnic Problems and their Possible Solutions:

real and utopian, short and long term goals.

As you requested, enclosed is my C.V.

I will call you before the meeting, and if you should have any questions, please do not hesitate to call me.

Sincerely,

Arsen M. Pankovich, M.D.

Now I have to prepare my lecture, Arsen thought. It should not be a difficult job considering that he had read so much on the subject and that he had a clear idea what should be done to resolve these problems.

CHAPTER SIX

WEEK OF 17-23 NOVEMBER 1997

The week was rather dull. Arsen covered two days at the ARGO Pension Board, on Monday and Tuesday. In the papers, world politics was dominated by the American-Iraqi confrontation. The Russians made a deal with Iraq, though nobody knew exactly what was promised at the high-level meeting. Mutual interests were obvious.

Other news was not interesting to Arsen, except for a long article about corruption in the Congo. Kabila had talked about Mobutu's corruption during the rebellion, and now his own administration was accused of the same. Corruption kept people fighting to stay in office, Arsen reasoned, so that more money could be stolen, and larger fortunes made. It seemed that if you audited all Presidents, Premiers, and their Ministers, many would wind up in jail. Who could do the auditing, then conduct trials, and imprison the guilty? A headline out of Frankfurt in Germany was pertinent.

STATES' OFFICIALS SHOULD NOT BE BRIBED
ANY MORE 29 NATIONS AGREE

It was hilarious that the main provision of the treaty was to force countries to prosecute their own companies for paying bribes to officials in other countries, although bribing of their own officials was illegal. They were saying that if companies are not allowed to commit crimes in their own countries they should not be doing it abroad either. That was aimed at Europe and Japan where the attitude 'Do not bribe at home; it is okay to do it abroad' was pervasive. In some places expenses for foreign bribes were tax deductible. No wonder, then, that it was happening in the Congo, and elsewhere, and that it had always existed. Enforcement was and would be a problem. This was more important than disarmament, Arsen thought.

Removing the crooks would attract honest and idealistic people into the governments. Something was missing here - the enforcer in some sort of World Government. This was too far out of the field.

A package from a relative in Zagreb contained a small Croatian-English dictionary, and clippings of translations of a series of articles from the memoirs of the German General von Horstenau. The General had been Hitler's emissary in Croatia during WW II. It was incredible that this had been published in Croatia. The events, and the participation and guilt of various individuals were already known; of interest were the General's personal observations and his descriptions of conversations with Hitler and his staff.

In Saturday's edition of the papers there was again a short report on the object in space, that was supposedly flying in the direction of the Earth. Again, Russians claimed the object existed, and everybody else denied it. Arsen was puzzled but paid no further attention to it.

CHAPTER SEVEN

MONDAY, 24 NOVEMBER 1997

Monday was the usual day at the ARGO Pension Board; usual conversations, usual applicants, usual decisions, and the usual trip home by train.

There were several messages on the answering machine. A patient was looking for an orthopedic surgeon. There was a call from a lawyer's office; Brooklyn Medical had a question; and someone, speaking in Serbian, wanted to talk to Arsen, but the message was blurred and Arsen could not recognize the name or hear the phone number. He would call again if he needed something, Arsen thought. As he was going to the living room, the telephone rang. Arsen pressed the speaker.

"This is Dr. Pankovich."

"Good evening Arsen. This is Ivo Stipich," a male, with a pleasant, deep voice, said in SerboCroatian. "I hope you still remember me from the distant past? To remind you, that was in Banja Luka, after the war: in forty-seven and forty eight."

As if through a fog, Arsen saw the face of a soldier whom he had met in Ban's Court, the building that had served as office and home for the Ban- -the Governor of Vrbas Province--before World War II, but which was being used a Cultural Center for Army Officers by that time. On weekend evenings the building's large banquet hall was used for dancing. Arsen remembered those days. He was a dancing regular in the Ban's Court. But it was not always easy to get an entrance pass, and without a pass, one had to bypass a guard--some of whom were more difficult to negotiate than others. Again as if through a fog, Arsen remembered a young guard who was very tough to bypass, yet he always let Arsen and his girlfriend in, while halting others. Vaguely he remembered his first name was Ivo, but the last name was obscure. Arsen's thoughts flew back in time to his days in high school in Banja Luka. Anna was his dancing partner, and an unsteady girlfriend. Anna was a Croatian, a few years older than Arsen, already working in a construction company, 'Krajina', and she liked to dance with him. Arsen was not in love, but liked having a girlfriend like most of his friends. Having a girlfriend was almost a status symbol; it showed that one was not weird. Arsen remembered a Saturday evening when they were trying to get in past a very stubborn guard. He would not let them in. A few times they tried to sneak by, when the guard was looking in the other direction and arguing with another couple, and always he managed to stop them. Arsen remembered Ivo, and asked the adamant guard if he knew where Ivo was. The guard became mellow immediately.

"Why do you want to know? Is he your friend, or something?" The guard was annoyed, but less unfriendly.

"Actually, he is a friend of mine. He always lets me in."

"How come he is your friend?"

"Why don't you ask him?"

The guard was not persuaded, and still refused to let them in. Just then, Ivo showed up. The guard stood up. Arsen noticed the single stripe of a corporal on Ivo's sleeve. Ivo turned to Anna and Arsen, and showed them in.

"Stupid jerk," Ivo said. "He should have let you in. Sorry about this. Go and dance. I am working tonight and cannot join you." Ivo went back to the front door.

Arsen wondered why Ivo had been so nice to him. Anna asked the same question. Arsen remembered vaguely a young partisan who was captured by his unit somewhere in Bosnia late in '44, when he was in the Royal underground; Arsen had not wanted to see him executed and had helped him escape by cutting the rope around his wrists. Was that partisan Ivo? Arsen did not know and Ivo never made reference to the incident. It was not something either Ivo or Arsen would ever bring up, Arsen thought.

There was no time to think any more about all that, as they were entering the dance hall where couples were dancing an English waltz.

"We missed this one," Arsen said.

"We did. They will probably play another one later. Shall we drink something?"

"Get something for me, too. I will check our coats. "

This incident was very vivid in Arsen's mind, as he answered the question the caller had asked.

"Ivo Stipich? Do I know you? Would this be the corporal from the Ban's Court, who was always nice to me and my girlfriend on Saturday nights? I saw you last one evening, must have been in 1948, as we were getting into the dancing hall. You were helpful. I don't remember ever seeing you again. Where have you been all these years? How did you find me, and why?"

"This is the same corporal from the Ban's Court," Ivo Stipich said. "I remember our last encounter. It seems as if it happened yesterday, yet it was forty years ago. What happened to me? It is a long story, forty years long, complicated, fragmented by interruptions, some happy and many more not. This is not something to talk about over the phone. Would it be possible that we meet somewhere, maybe in a restaurant? When, and where?"

Ivo Stipich expected him to come, Arsen thought. What did he want after all these years? What had become of him? He might be a criminal trying to kidnap him, or blackmail him for something. He could not think of anything compromising. Or he wanted him in a business deal, probably a scam to steal his money. Arsen remembered Ivo's kindness years ago, and despite his doubts decided to accept the invitation.

"Smith and Wolinsky, 49th Street and Third Avenue. I will make the reservation for Thursday evening. Okay?"

"We could not meet earlier?" Ivo Stipich asked.

"Tonight is already too late. Tomorrow I will be attending a formal dinner with my wife. On Wednesday I work, often until late in the evening, and afterwards I am usually too tired," Arsen said firmly.

"If it has to be Thursday, let it be. There is not much for me to do in New York but hang around for three days."

"What do you mean by hanging around? Are you telling me that you came to New York just to talk to me?"

"Yes that is what I am trying to tell you. Would you reconsider and have dinner with me tonight at Smith and W...? I don't remember the name."

"Smith and Wolinsky," Arsen said.

"Yes, Smith and Wolinsky, at Forty-Ninth Street and Third Avenue. At eight o'clock. Now it is six. I will wait for you there. Is that okay?" Ivo Stipich was persistent.

Arsen was puzzled and curious. Who was this man from his distant past, coming from the cold, and asking to have dinner with him tonight? Why was he in such a hurry? He came from who knew where, just to have dinner with him? Why hadn't he called in advance? Arsen would find out when they meet, he thought. He decided to accept the invitation.

"Okay, eight o'clock. How will I recognize you?" Arsen asked.

"I will be waiting for you in the restaurant. They will direct you to my table. Thank you for agreeing to come. See you later." Ivo Stipich hung up.

Arsen told Nada about the call and his decision to accept the invitation.

"Are you sure you should go? You don't know this man. You have no idea what he wants," she cautioned Arsen.

"You are right. But I will find out what he wants. It makes no difference if it is tonight or Thursday. Just as well, let it be tonight, to get it over with."

Arsen took a shower, and dressed in his usual: a white shirt and blue tie, his favorite gray trousers and a navy blue jacket. There was plenty of time to watch the news, to finish reading the papers, and to look for e-mail.

Arsen decided to walk to the restaurant. The evening was pleasant: the sky was clear, and it was warm out. He liked to stroll in the neighborhood. The restaurant was not too far, only thirteen short blocks. At that hour there were many people walking the sidewalks, particularly between Sixtieth and Fifty-seventh streets. On the west side of the avenue was Bloomingdale's, which always attracted many people, and on the east side were the movie theaters, which often had lines to buy tickets. The sidewalks were crowded, and one was hardly able to keep up with the traffic lights at the corners. The lights changed and one crossed the street and paced down the block to the next corner only to find that light had already changed. A 30-second wait was then inevitable, as there were many cars trying to get through. After the light changed one would then hurry to the next corner, and wait again. It was amusing to watch people rushing from corner to corner, only to have to stop and wait. Many people stepped into the street, almost inviting cars to hit them. That sometimes happened.

Below Fifty-Seventh Street there were fewer people, and Arsen moved on faster, yet still had to wait for the light at each corner. Past the Post Office he could beat the lights a few times. Smith and Wolinsky's Restaurant was at the corner of Forty-Ninth Street. He walked into a rather dark waiting area where a tall, husky man, well-dressed and inquiring, was looking after the customers.

"Can I help you, Sir?"

"Yes, a friend of mine should be somewhere in the restaurant. His name is Mr. Stipich. He may be seated somewhere."

"I presume he had a reservation. Oh, I remember him. He is in the upper room. Let me see. Go upstairs, and ask for table fifteen. You will find him there."

Arsen climbed to the upper floor, and was shown to the table, where Ivo Stipich was already sipping a drink. Arsen did not recognize Ivo. He remembered a lightly built, rather skinny man with burly, dark brown hair, inquisitive large eyes, a prominent nose and chin, high forehead, and a deep voice that did not fit his appearance. The man seated in the chair had a prominent, square chin. His nose looked as if someone had flattened it in a fight. That turned out to be the case. The forehead was lost in the baldness of the head, where the hair grew from around the ears and on the occiput, and the eyebrows accentuated the borders of the face. The eyes were still inquisitive, with a serious look radiating from them. The man looked muscular though slightly heavy. His dark blue suit, and a light blue shirt with a matching tie, looked elegant.

Ivo Stipich stood up, shook hands with Arsen, and again thanked him for accepting the dinner invitation.

"It would be somewhat boring to stay in New York for three days, and wait for the meeting with you. I would have waited, if you hadn't come tonight. Now, I can fly out in the morning."

"What is the hurry?" Arsen could not resist the question.

"Oh, I have to meet some other people in the next few days," Ivo Stipich said. "Can I order a drink for you?"

"Tonic water with a twist."

After the drink was served, Arsen started the conversation. He was determined to find out if this man was who he said he was, the corporal Ivo whom Arsen had known in Banja Luka.

"It has been a long time since we last met in Banja Luka. Do you still remember our last encounter?"

"Yes, I remember it very well," Ivo Stipich said, and he told the story of getting Anna and Arsen into the dance exactly the way Arsen remembered it.

Arsen was now convinced that this was the Ivo he once knew. He still had not found out the purpose of this meeting.

"What happened to you after that? Where did you go?" Arsen asked.

"Where but to jail." Ivo Stipich replied. "That was the time of the Inform Bureau and confrontation with the SSSR and Stalin. The split was inevitable. I decided to support the pro-Russian camp, and we lost. Those comrades who were exposed as Inform Bureau sympathizers were sent to the Island of Goli Otok, as you know. Extensive reeducation and indoctrination were upon us, and we succumbed to it, some genuinely and others by pretending. I pretended and convinced my ideologues that I was converted back to the Titoist mainstream. Eventually, they let me go.

"When I returned home I quickly realized that I was a marked man, without a future. I could not get a job or any support and depended on my family's support. That was degrading and unacceptable. I knew I had to do something, go somewhere, where my past could be overlooked or even appreciated. I think you get the picture. Where would my background be appreciated? Of course, in other communist countries. I managed to escape to Bulgaria, where people like me were tolerated but not appreciated very much. Still, I enrolled at the University of Sofia, and graduated in Political Studies. It took much pushing for four years to be permitted to go to SSSR.

"I thought that was my resurrection, when I was on the train to Moscow. Very quickly, I was again disillusioned. Mother Russia was no different from Yugoslavia. They used the same political language, and the same methods, though perhaps more crude and cruel than at home. Stalin was dead. Do I have to explain? Then, with a bit of luck, I found a job as a driver for a government functionary in the Ministry of Heavy Industry. He was a young and ambitious man. After Stalin's death my boss had advanced rather rapidly. Being a Ukrainian, he moved to the NKVD in Kiev, and I went with him. He knew my background and by then trusted me. He appointed me his personal secretary, and I did most of his work. I advanced along with him. When Khrushchev came to power in Moscow we transferred back there. My boss moved into the Counterintelligence Department, which was very secretive, and very powerful.

"His power rose as the presidents changed. We were in charge of ethnic problems, and of people dealing with ethnic problems on the scene. That is the spot from which we have followed changes in Russia, the rise of Gorbachev and Yeltsin. This was a traumatic experience for both of us, since we handled much staff when the SSSR disintegrated, and the new ethnic states emerged. My boss and I have had a very smooth relationship. He made sure that our position in the Department was secure politically, and I handled day-to-day problems. Actually, he made sure that we knew everything about everybody in the NKVD, and the government. That was our insurance policy for a long life. Also, we knew our ethnic staff very well, and took care of the problems, small and large, as the higher-ups wanted. Often they sought our advice." He was talking rapidly, not giving Arsen a chance to ask any questions.

Ivo Stipich's story was interrupted by the serving of dinner. He had ordered salmon, despite Arsen's urging him to take a rib steak. Wine was ordered and Ivo Stipich started drinking it as soon as it was served. Arsen wondered what the rest of the story would be, and what his explanation would be for the dinner invitation and the meeting. It was unlikely that he wanted only to visit an old acquaintance.

The restaurant was packed, and the room was warm. The tables were a bit too close to each other, but the noise level was not too high to interfere with conversation. They had no problems with privacy, since they spoke in their native SerboCroatian. The service was fast and efficient although the waiters were hurried and remote, and somewhat edgy.

As they finished their entrees, Ivo Stipich continued his story.

"You can imagine the magnitude of ethnic problems as the SSSR disintegrated. Yet, I think things worked out generally okay, except in Chechnya. If they had listened to us there would have been no disaster there either. But they did not."

Ivo Stipich stopped for a moment, to give Arsen a chance to digest the story, and ask questions. Arsen was quiet and listened attentively, but asked no questions.

"I am sure you are wondering what this meeting is all about," Ivo Stipich said. "Let me come to the point. Certain people in Russia, and in other countries, are trying to bring together people interested in global ethnic problems. These people believe that ethnic disagreements are responsible for a great number of problems in the world, and that they have to be dealt with, and soon. By ethnic disagreements we mean antagonism that is based on the differences in peoples' ethnic histories, and also in their racial histories. That in itself would not be a problem if all groups had the same power.

Unfortunately, the stronger ethnic group usually exploits the weaker. That is the law of the jungle, isn't it? But that would not be a problem, if the two groups were separated and kept at a distance. The real problems are, how to separate these entities from each other, how to keep them separated, and how to prevent them from oppressing and killing each other. We feel that once separated, independent, and sovereign, and - very important - prevented from attacking each other, these people would find a common ground and mutual respect. Old hatreds would disappear sooner or later. The big question is, how can we accomplish that?" Ivo Stipich paused again, expecting Arsen to ask questions, but he again remained silent.

Arsen's mind was flying all over the world to places where conflicts existed. The list had no end, only the degree and depth of conflict were different. And wise men had always talked about the need for understanding and tolerance among those who had been killing each other just the day before. Hundreds of thousands were being killed right now by the intolerant population of the Earth, while the world was watching, almost boringly and cynically preaching peace.

"World Government could do it," Arsen suddenly pronounced.

"Arsen, you are so right."

They were silent for awhile, each deep in his own thoughts. Ivo Stipich finished his bottle of wine, and Arsen sipped from a glass of water.

"I wanted to tell you what happened to me, after we saw each other in Banja Luka in May of 1948. I also wanted you to know about my life in Russia, and my background. I think you have now a good idea what kind of life I led, and what I did. Obviously, you have no idea what kind of a man I have become. I dedicated my life to my boss, and to my work. I never married, although I had a few opportunities which ended only as affairs. Partially that was the instinct for survival in a very hostile environment; but also curiosity and the thrill of the important things that were happening around me, and in which I was a participant, kept me from family life. The boss has retired, and so have I. We are now associated with the Institute for Ethnic Studies in Moscow.

"However, something important is happening - right now only in Russia, but it will eventually spread all over the world. I am not allowed to tell you exactly, and there are still things I don't know myself. However, we need people with an interest in ethnic problems who will take responsibility when the time comes. This may happen sooner than you think. There is not much you would have to do if you joined us now, nor would you have to be involved. We would like you to study ethnic problems in the Balkans, in the Middle East, in Turkey, in Southwest Asia, and in part of East Asia. Your study would not be restricted by anybody. We would only like to provide some assistance in finding sources and materials of importance to you, so that you would not lose any time. From time to time we would provide information that we thought you should have. You may also want to travel to these countries to gain firsthand impressions, and to meet certain people. We would facilitate these contacts for you, and of course, we would pay traveling expenses - modest ones. You would not get rich by these travels, but I am sure you would enrich your impressions and gain experience which would be useful to you later.

"Although we have a good idea of your thinking, which is incidentally very close to our own, we would hope that you would present your ideas to us as they have evolved so far, and as they develop later. And another thing. You should not waste any time. We would like to know what you want to do, and when, and what you need. You can tell me right now, or when I call you in a day or two. You may want to rent an office and hire a staff, a secretary in the beginning, and additional people as you need them. Just tell me. You may want to think about all this, before we continue this conversation, or ask questions right now." Ivo Stipich looked inquisitively at Arsen, obviously waiting to hear what he had to say.

Arsen wanted answers to two major questions before proceeding any further.

"Is this a secret, underground organization?"

"Not at all," Ivo Stipich replied. "The Institute for Ethnic Studies in Moscow is a respected institution, which traces its origins to the works of Lenin and his deep concerns about ethnic problems in Russia, long before the Revolution. Stalin had the same concerns, and he supported the Institute over the years, though in those days, Stalin's ideas dominated, and rarely did anyone dare come up with an idea of his own. Despite that, much good work came out of the Institute, and it consisted of the collection and analysis of ethnic groups and their demography, their history, their cultural background, and their activities and strivings at that time.

19

Unfortunately, those groups that were out of line with the reality of the system were completely ignored.

"The policies of the Institute slowly changed after Stalin's death. More independent studies were conducted, since later leaders did not pay as much attention to ethnic problems as Lenin and Stalin had. As you can imagine, my boss and I kept an eye on the Institute, since we were in charge of ethnic problems in the Counterintelligence Department. Somehow people were bored with ethnic problems and assumed they did not exist. That was good for us, as the competition and rivalry in the Counterintelligence community was in the political sector and in the International Division.

"As I mentioned, our moment of truth came when the SSSR began to disintegrate, and ethnic states were created. Further, democratization in Russia allowed greater independence for the Institute, which now operates like any similar institution in the West. My boss and I are members of the Institute. The name of my boss is Grigor Kravchenko. He is a senior member of the Institute, and a member of its Policy Board. His connections in the Government, which are still very extensive, make him indispensable. Information on the ideas developed at the Institute, though not always widely circulated, are available to any interested individual or organization. Does this give you an idea of the Institute I represent?"

This sounded quite interesting and acceptable to Arsen; he had been thinking of joining such an institute although he knew nobody who would extend an invitation.

"It is puzzling to me that you have found me, and even more so, why have you selected me. Why?" Arsen insisted.

"That was one of those coincidences that sometimes happen. Of course, I remembered you from the old country and from Banja Luka. Although I have known where you were, and what you were doing in Chicago and New York, I did not want to approach you during the Cold War, to spare you any problems you might encounter from association with me. I traveled repeatedly to the States, but I limited my activities to our Embassy and dealt mainly with our various representatives, who were collecting the information we needed. I checked on you several times, and I knew you were a successful orthopedic surgeon. That pleased me, and I enjoyed it from a distance."

"Why such an interest in me?"

"I will tell you some day about a favor you did for me. You will not remember it, but I do, and I always will." Ivo Stipich obviously did not want to talk about that any more. "As for the coincidence, it happened in London last year. I was at a dinner with people who were attending a seminar on NATO and Ethnic Relations which was organized by an American visiting professor from the London School of Economics. There was some discussion about the relations of Hungarians and Rumanians in Transylvania. He cited a letter you sent him about the reason why these opposing ethnic groups were suddenly pushing for the resolution of mutual conflicts, unsolvable only recently. You suggested that they were trying to hide an obstacle to their admission to NATO. The Professor thought that was a clever observation. So did I.

"I did not mention that I knew you, but it occurred to me that I did not know what you were doing then. It turned out you were retired, and deep in the study of ethnic problems. It was easy to find out what you were thinking. The next step was to present your name to the Policy Board of our Institute, and to convince them of your potential usefulness. You must understand, Arsen, I am not a scientist, but an operative. I understand ethnicity, and I know how to use information, but I don't create it. I knew of your administrative abilities, as the Department Head, and your reputation as a straight shooter. Combine your new interest with your administrative experience, and you have the answer to your question."

Ivo Stipich made a positive impression, and Arsen believed what he said. It was not entirely clear to him why his abilities were of interest to the people at the Institute.

"Did you submit my name as a lecturer before the Forum on Foreign Policy?" Arsen asked.

"Definitely no! This is great. I assume you will pick up an ethnic topic. Will you?"

"Of course, what else? Perhaps I will be able to answer your questions on my current thinking. It is still a mystery who arranged that invitation."

"Should I assume you are telling me that you will accept our invitation?" Ivo Stipich asked.

"If everything you say is true, it would be difficult to turn you down. Let me think about it for a day or two before I give you my final answer. There is so much I don't understand, and so much is happening to me. Ethnicity seems simple by comparison. If I decide to accept, I will let you know what I need."

"I am delighted that we have had such a good conversation and that you have a positive attitude toward the future. I will call you on Thursday morning."

Arsen looked around the restaurant. It was empty, and waiters were clearing the tables. It was time to leave. Ivo Stipich agreed. They descended to the main floor, shook hands on the street, and parted. Arsen had a strange feeling about the whole encounter. At the very least, it was incredible. He walked back home.

Nada was not asleep when Arsen came in. He went into the bedroom, where she was reading, and told her what had happened at the dinner with

Ivo Stipich. She was just as puzzled and curious about the whole thing as he was, and she was quite suspicious of and cautious about the Russian Ethnic Institute.

"Maybe they are who they say they are," Nada said. "Maybe they are not. They are obviously planning something big regarding ethnic problems. They are secretive. They are hiding behind the facade of the Institute for Ethnic Studies. Who knows who is really behind all this, who is building an organization for who knows what purposes. Maybe they plan to conquer the world."

"Wouldn't that be preposterous? I think they want a global organization and to be able to deal with ethnic problems from a position of strength. Something like a human rights organization, only on a larger scale, and more powerful."

"Do you think you will join them? It might be interesting to travel, and see some places where you would never go. They could help you find, get, and analyze the ethnic material, something you could never find time to do on your own. Would they let you leave their organization, if you wanted to? Probably not, until they win or lose. Always there is a quid pro quo. Nothing is free of charge."

"You are probably right. I doubt they need me only to do ethnic studies and to meet people in distant lands. There must be a purpose behind all that. What is the purpose? This appears more like the work of an organization than an institute. The Institute is only a facade; you are right." Arsen was perplexed.

"We should go to sleep, as we will not solve this puzzle tonight," Nada said; and she turned off the light on her side of the bed. Arsen did the same.

CHAPTER EIGHT

TUESDAY, 25 NOVEMBER 1997

Tuesday was his day off. Ivo Stipich and his proposals were constantly on Arsen's mind. He admitted being in the Russian Counterintelligence. There was no reason to doubt that part of his story, although it was unbelievable that a Croat, a foreigner in Russia, could have penetrated the power tower of the government.

Arsen confirmed the existence of the Institute for Ethnic Studies by looking it up on the Internet. And he found the name Grigor Kravchenko listed among the Board's Directors. The list of the members was not provided, and Arsen could not verify that Ivo Stipich was a member. The Institute's web site was attractively designed and easy to connect to. The history of the Institute was provided in outline and in depth. The roles of Lenin and Stalin in the development of the Institute were well presented. In the Search section, one could find much information on ethnic topics, particularly on the history of the different ethnic groups in Russia. Even small and insignificant tribes were presented, often with much detail. The Index listed all the written material that had been published by the Institute's members or submitted by them in manuscript form, and all the photographs in the collection. All scientific papers could be read and downloaded from the web site, although there were only summaries of the full-length papers in English and French. A few photographs could be projected, but most of them were only indexed. Arsen was impressed after his inquiry.

The fact that the Institute existed did not answer Arsen's questions about what it was. He suspected it must be operational, and that it was recruiting new members. The purpose of the organization was also unclear.

Arsen was perplexed about this whole episode. What did he need potential troubles for, if the organization was illegal in the U.S.? What if this was a terrorist organization? Should he consult the FBI ? Arsen did not want to exaggerate things and panic, but it would be stupid to become associated with an illegal organization. Finally, he decided to go along.

CHAPTER NINE

THURSDAY, 27 NOVEMBER 1997

Thursday was Thanksgiving. Arsen had finished his first cup of coffee and was copying the clippings from the papers when Nada and her mother went to the kitchen. Arsen joined them for coffee and talk about the situation in Serbia and Bosnia.

Mother-in-law asked him if he would like to visit Belgrade next year.

"Since you like Serbia so much, why don't you come after I return to Belgrade. I know you would like it there, as you did during your last visit in '88. You don't have to stay there more than a few weeks. You could visit your daughter and her husband and see your grand-daughter. You could visit with your friends. Why don't you come?"

"This is the wrong day to ask me to come. Visiting you and the children would be okay. My friends are better off not seeing me at all, ever again," Arsen replied.

"Why?" Mother Zlata was surprised.

"I have been thinking about my friends and the intellectuals I knew in Banja Luka. I cannot say I have much respect for them. What have they done for the troubled country and the Bosnian Serbs. Plain nothing. All of them made sure they were far away from Bosnia. Of course, they had to save their own skins, but then who was left to fight for the Serbs they love so much?" Arsen was speaking with obvious cynicism.

"My friends are not patriots. If they were, the outcome in Bosnia would have been different. Where were they when Karadzic and Mladic were fighting in Bosnia? If they had been in the Pale, perhaps they would have been the leaders. At least they would have been in a position to influence the leadership. That required courage and desire, patriotism and self-sacrifice. They had none.

"Only Nikola Koljevic was involved, and he is dead now. Maybe he committed suicide. Perhaps someone killed him to get him out of the way.

The fact is that he lost his life because of that involvement. I am sure he would be alive today if he had escaped to Serbia. Whatever his role, and whether he contributed a little or a great deal, he was there. My friends did nothing. I would tell them that, and they would probably dislike that very much.

"In return they would ask me where I was and why I had not come to fight for Bosnia? You know, they would be right. Where was I during the Bosnian war? Making money in New York. That is where I was. And it is not that it didn't occur to me that I should go to Bosnia to fight. Somehow, I could not see myself on the periphery of things, say treating patients in the hospital in Banja Luka. My experience and expertise, and even some of my money would have helped.

"The only excuse I have is my participation in the Second World War, in the Royal Army under Mihajlovic, and my retreat through Bosnia and capture by the Communists. I did fight for the Serbian cause. But I survived, and that was a long time ago. This time around I abstained."

"You are too hard on yourself," his mother-in-law said.

"You may be right, but it hurts anyway. The best thing for me is to go nowhere from New York. I should concentrate on writing my book, making some money, and trying to stay alive. In New York, I have the sources of information I need for my writing. I should not be going places and criticizing people. It is enough that I feel the way I do."

The conversation was interrupted by the ringing of Arsen's phone, which he answered. Ivo Stipich was on the line.

"Good morning Arsen. Hopefully, I did not wake you up."

"Not at all. I already finished my coffee, read my newspapers, and had a long political conversation with my mother-in-law. Where are you calling from?"

"From Paris," Ivo Stipich said. "I have finished the business part of my trip. Before going back to Russia, I thought, I would spend a few days in Paris. I know some people here, Croatians, who have been here since the end of the war. I will visit with them today, do some sightseeing and shopping for a couple of days, then fly back home."

"Moscow is home for you, isn't it?" Arsen remarked.

"Like New York for you. I would not know what to do in Banja Luka or Zagreb. Most of the older people I knew have died, and I keep in touch with only a few of my friends. You must be celebrating Thanksgiving today, are you?"

"Yes, we are," Arsen said. "Turkey and the rest. For me this is a different day only because my son will come for dinner, and we will probably spend the afternoon talking. I have been thinking about our meeting the other day, and what you told me. Very perplexing, I must say. I still have no idea what the purpose of your invitation is. I don't know why you have invited me. And what are you planning to do and accomplish in the future? I know only that it all has something to do with ethnic problems. What is the eventual goal, the aim, the purpose? I have no idea. Can you tell me that?"

"That is a long story, and not a simple one. In the immediate future your role will be to read, study, and travel to meet people. In a capsule, the eventual goal of this group is to influence the global ethnic situation. At the moment we are getting a number of people together. Some of them are political scientists, some, like yourself, are proven administrators who have a good grasp of ethnic problems and their solutions. We may take a more active role in the United Nations and push for the realization of our goals. Timing for that is not clear as yet."

"Timing for what?" Arsen asked impatiently.

"Timing to press for talks in the United Nations," Ivo Stipich said firmly. "As you know, there is the Commission for Human Rights in the United Nations, which is not as effective as we would like it to be. Most of all, they are very slow in their deliberations, and impotent in translating their decisions into action. Therefore, not enough is done in the field. Only revolts, rebellions, and revolutions change things. That is not the best way to accomplish anything.

"Look what happened in neighboring Zaire and Rwanda with their Hutu-Tutsi problems. The net result is one million killed. Look at Bosnia. Hundreds of thousands have become refugees or have been killed. What about Northern Ireland, the Middle East, Kurdistan, Kosovo and so on. Nothing was done in time to prevent disaster.

"Solutions are too often implemented against the wish of those involved - the people. The solutions are often the seeds of future problems. I am sure you understand what I am talking about. We would like to change that with the help and support of the United Nations. Once that is negotiated we will need individuals, like yourself, to effect changes in the field. I have outlined to you the geographic area that would be your responsibility."

"You mean I would change things in Bosnia, Turkey, Iraq and other countries with the support and blessing of the United Nations? You think that is possible?" Arsen was stunned.

"Yes, it is possible. We are working on that right now, but I cannot tell you how long it will take. It will depend a great deal on the global situation and on the willingness of the governments to participate. You will not have to be involved with that."

"That sounds like creation of a World Government with broad powers." Arsen was probing further to get some concrete answers, but Ivo

Stipich was not willing to discuss it any more. He asked Arsen if he had decided to accept the invitation, or whether he needed more time to decide.

"The decision is already made. I accept because I think this is an opportunity to do some good for many people. It would make my preparation for the job much easier if I knew exactly what my responsibilities will be, and how broad my authority will be in decision making. The way I work, I need to be told what I am expected to accomplish, the time frame, and the general rules of action. I will tell you what I need to do it. If we agree, I am ready to do the job. If not, it would be better to ask someone else. And another thing. I play a fair game, and expect the same from above. I need about ten minutes to clear my desk and pack before leaving without questions asked. I am an unpleasant tiger if mistreated. That is about all I have to say." Arsen felt that he had to make his position clear.

Ivo Stipich was discernably pleased with the conversation. He told Arsen that he would report to the group what they had just discussed, and suggested that Arsen should come to Moscow for further discussions. Arsen interrupted him abruptly and impatiently:

"Ivo, I am dealing with you and I don't have time to waste traveling to Moscow. You will keep me informed, and you may want to come and visit me in New York, if you think the meeting would be useful. When the time comes that you, and the group in Moscow, want to talk to me, I will come. Another thing. How do we correspond? You asked me to list items I will need immediately, and in the future. It will be better if I submit that in writing. Where shall I send it? By mail, by fax, or by Internet?"

"Internet is the most efficient way."

"You probably know my address, don't you? You know everything else," Arsen asked with some jocularity, which had a note of seriousness in it.

"You won't believe me but I don't know it." Ivo Stipich paused for a moment. "Arsen, it was my real pleasure to meet with you, and to deal with you. I will keep you informed about important happenings, issues and decisions, particularly those that are concerned with your activities. It is of utmost importance that you keep us informed of the progress of your studies, of conversations with people you meet when you start traveling, and of your thoughts on the solutions of the problems which will face us in your domain. Keep in touch. And Arsen, I know you have made the right decision. I will talk to you soon." Ivo Stipich hung up.

Arsen was pleased with this conversation. Now he knew what had to be done and how it would have to be done.

Arsen continued thinking about the job that was awaiting him, about the organization of an office he would soon need in New York, and about travels which were ahead of him. He decided to outline for the group in

Moscow his ideas for dealing with ethnic problems in an ideal situation, and solutions that would resolve these problems. Ideas for the individual countries would be developed after he had studied their problems in more detail, and after he had met the individuals and officials in the different countries.

"Now is the time to eat dinner," Arsen decided, and went into the living room where Nada and her mother were talking with Mark.

"When are we going to eat? I am hungry, and the smell from the kitchen is inviting."

"Another half an hour or so. The turkey has to cool off a bit." His mother-in-law was the supreme expert on cooking.

The rest of the day was quiet and digestive. Mark left in the evening.

CHAPTER TEN

After the morning routine of reading the papers and copying interesting clippings, Arsen was set to write a letter to Ivo Stipich. He wanted to present his thoughts about global ethnic problems and their possible solutions, and to submit the list of items for the office. It occurred to him that, by joining the Moscow Group, he would become an agent of a foreign organization. Registration with an Agency of the Federal Government was probably a wise step. He decided to look into it.

28 November 1997

Dear Ivo:

This letter will be waiting for you when you return to Moscow. I wanted to express my ideas about ethnic problems as you requested.

My basic idea is that in the global ethnic jungle, every legitimate ethnic group has the right to meaningful autonomy or independent sovereignty. They also have the right to the territory on which they live. When I speak of meaningful autonomy, I assume that it would exist not only on the books but in fact, and that it would be enforced. This will easily be determined for some groups, like the Basques in Spain and France. For other areas, like parts of Zaire - or call it the Congo if you like - it may be a major hurdle, though not impossible through negotiations. I am also saying that all borders will have to be redrawn, new ones negotiated among the concerned parties, and in some cases the new ones will have to be decided by a plebiscite. There is nothing to add to this basic principle. You will note that I have used the term 'territory' instead of 'state' or 'country.' I would hope that your group would agree with this principle.

The problem that will immediately arise, after the basic principle is implemented, is the political organization of the created autonomous, or sovereign, territory. I do not see how anyone would have the right to dictate to the people how to run their own territory. That would simply deny them freedom. However, there are, and always will be, individuals and groups who will try to usurp the will of the rest of the people. As much as we should not interfere with their political inclinations, people will have to be assured of periodic free elections, in which everyone would have the right to vote so that the electoral process reflects the desires and the will of the people. If the majority wants to have a government based on super fundamentalist Islamic principles, as is favored in Afghanistan by Taliban, they should vote for it. Who are we to tell them that they cannot have it? Our job will be to ensure freedom of political expression even if the resulting government is not based on democratic principles as we know them. Otherwise, we will be imperialists who prescribe to other people what we think is best.

The next obvious problem will be to preserve the borders of the created territories. Who will provide enforcement? That question will be answered after we find out who will implement the changes. Other questions, about issues such as relations among the territories, economic organization and support for poor territories, **and other issues** will have to be decided by a governing Board of the world. Therefore, I see no hope for a project like this one without the creation of a World Government that has broad powers in defined areas, and no power over the internal processes of the individual territories. I can see major broad powers of World Government in preserving the integrity of individual territories, broad powers in providing and ensuring the basic, agreed upon levels of living standards, broad powers in provision of health care, but no powers in decisions on religion, education, and political structure. I cannot imagine the World Government telling a territory to change the President they have elected, no matter how obnoxious he may be, but I can see the enforcement by the World Government of the essential ecological laws.

One major task of the World Government and its regional administrators will be to effect the total disarmament of the population and of existing or prospective governments. Of course, this will be a single major obstacle in any negotiations for establishment of the World Government. The present-day major powers will fight tooth-and-nail against disarmament, and argue for their national interests and about their vulnerability to attack, although there would exist only the Military of the World Government whose job would be only to preserve the borders of the established territories.

As much as I can see the existence of a World Government as a clear precondition to anything happening anywhere along the lines I outlined above, the vision is rather foggy as to who would initiate, select, and install the World Government and even that such a government is a possibility - in the near future, or ever.

If the World Government should become a reality, in any way, I see my role very clearly. My job will be to establish the territories in the domain you assigned to me. I will have to disarm whoever does not want to be disarmed, and I will have to supervise the election process and actual voting. My role will end thereafter. I will want it to end at that time.

I am obviously at a loss as to what has been done, if anything, so far.

As for my present needs, I will be needing the following:

A small office in Manhattan with an office for me, another for a secretary, and a larger room to accommodate three additional individuals, files, and office needs. The secretary will keep track of appointments, if I should have any, and of mail, and she will gather source materials for my studies. Two computers will do in the beginning, a fax machine, several phone lines, basic furniture which will probably be rather expensive, and some money for supplies.

You may want to decide how much money you will allot for my trips - which, you thought, would be essential - and where I should go. Your advice and help will be necessary in planning these trips. Your contacts in the proposed countries will be indispensable and critical.

My first trip should be to the former Yugoslavia. This could be a good exploratory trip since it is to a country I know very well, although I do not know any officials personally.

Sincerely,

Arsen Pankovich

Arsen spent the rest of the day reading, answering a letter to a friend in

Serbia, browsing over the Internet, and reviewing a voluminous chart for the ARGO. The evening news was more entertaining than exciting. The four-mile/fifty-minute walk had become routine, but was necessary. The TV movie that night was also a standard, a rerun about the capture of a train somewhere in Colorado by a terrorist group. This was a hi-sci blackmail for money. Quite electrifying even seeing it for the third time. Of course, the good guys won at the end.

It was time for bed. Arsen always checked his e-mail before going to sleep. There were two important letters. A relative from Zagreb provided his new telephone number, as Zagreb was converting to a new, more modern, telephone system. The other letter was from Ivo Stipich. Arsen remembered that he had not given Ivo his e-mail address, which meant that he had somehow received the e-letter he had sent to Moscow at noon, even though he was still in Paris. The mystery of this letter was soon resolved.

Ivo's letter was short and to the point:

28 November 1997

Dear Arsen:

I received your e-letter through my office in Moscow.

You expressed ideas that are almost identical with our own. There will not be much to explain to you about the principles. We believe, as you do, in the right to self-determination of any legitimate group and in their political rights. We agree with your idea of a World Government. You have described your role so well that I have nothing to add. I will be able to confirm your appointment by our Executive Board on Saturday. The Board Members are aware of our discussions, even of the contents of your letter, and their comments are very favorable.

An account will be established for your use at the Chase Manhattan Bank, in the branch near your home. $100,000.00 will be deposited in the account.

I am very encouraged by and pleased with the progress of our association.

Sincerely,

Ivo Stipich

Arsen loved this kind of efficiency.

CHAPTER ELEVEN

The weekend promised to be quiet. Reading, answering some letters, and working on his book was all Arsen was planning to do. That was not the way it turned out to be.

Arsen woke up early, and eagerly climbed out of bed. He was full of energy, and ready to work. He looked out the window and saw the clear sky among the towering buildings, blue and bright from sun rays, which were already penetrating the room. Walking in Central Park on a day like this might actually be pleasant, Arsen thought. He rarely walked in the Park, or anywhere else, unless there was a purpose for the walk; walking, for him, was a way of reaching a destination and not a physical satisfaction.

Today was different, Arsen thought. Today he was happy with himself and with the way life was unfolding. Some important and interesting things would soon be happening. Who knew where all this would lead?

He made coffee and poured himself a cup, took the delivered daily paper from the hall, and positioned himself comfortably in the armchair in his study. There was no news of interest to him. Smoke pollution from forest fires in Indonesia, the resignation of the Indian Premier, a ban on fox hunting in England and an impasse in negotiations with Iraq were not thought-provoking news.

Three old men had made news, as reported in *The Times*, each in his own colorful and allegorical way. Racial history was always of interest and so was the obituary of Buck Leonard, the black baseball player and the star of the Negro Leagues in the '30s and '40s, who had never made the major leagues because of racial prejudice.

The perennial Senator Robert Byrd, at eighty years of age, was described as one of the best orators the Senate had ever witnessed, although not a legislative big gun by his accomplishments.

The headline 'From Prison, Old Militant Struggles On' and the story about Philip Berrigan, the Vietnam era and anti nuclear arms militant, was inspiring. He was still fighting for the old causes at the age of seventy-four.

Arsen was thinking of the lives these three men had led. Each man was intelligent and talented in his own way. While skin color had kept the first man from national achievement and fame, the second man was raised in political circles that were still prejudicial to blacks, and the third man had set God aside and fought for what he thought was right, but with methods that had landed him repeatedly in jail. Why couldn't all three of them have lived harmoniously with a society that professed democracy during their tenures on the Earth? Why? Arsen asked the question aloud.

There were really only three global principles that were important, and that would have changed the lives of these three men: the enforced right of self-determination for each ethnic group, the right to hold free elections, and total disarmament of all countries of the world. Symbolic, indeed.

At noon Arsen decided reluctantly to take a walk in Central Park. The day was still beautiful, as it had been in the morning, and the sun was shining in the bright, clear sky. It was not cold, and the streets were crowded with pedestrians, who were after bargains offered by the merchants to induce a buying spree.

Arsen was going west on the Sixty-Second Street, and just as he crossed Lexington Avenue, he run into an old acquaintance - Sabrina Harley. He almost did not recognize her. Sabrina was a secretary in the office of the lawyer who had represented Arsen in a malpractice case a few years earlier. Arsen had thought she was an exceptional secretary; he had liked her understanding of the issues and her knowledge of the details of the case. Sabrina was neat and cheerful though not pretty, she dressed modestly but with taste, and she was clearly intelligent. She had visited Arsen a few times in his Whitestone office for a shoulder problem.

Now Sabrina appeared to have gained weight, her face was rounded and much older looking and her cheerful expression had been replaced by one of sadness.

"Hi, Doctor," Sabrina greeted Arsen, and she proceeded to the cross walk, obviously not intending to stop and talk.

Arsen was interested in talking to talk to her and finding out about the changes he had noticed.

"Sabrina, is that you? I almost didn't recognize you. It has been such a long time since I saw you last. How are you?"

Sabrina hesitated for a moment, then turned to Arsen with a smile on her face.

"I am doing just fine. How are you?"

Arsen shook her hand, pulled her to the side, and kissed her. He smelled alcohol on her breath, and the acid odor of alcoholics.

"How is everything at Lifshutz and Barnes? Busy as usual?" Arsen inquired.

"I don't work for them anymore," she replied, her voice somewhere between crying and screaming.

"How can they exist without you?" Arsen was sincerely surprised.

"Nothing is permanent, as you know," Sabrina said. Her face became even sadder than before.

"You never go to the office anymore?"

"No."

"Oh, you must tell me everything that has happened to you," Arsen insisted. "Let me buy you a cup of coffee somewhere, so we can talk in peace. Are you in a hurry?"

"Not really."

"Let us go to a Brazilian restaurant, around the corner on Lexington Avenue."

"Okay," Sabrina agreed.

The restaurant "Circus" was open for lunch, and almost all tables were taken. Arsen asked Sabrina whether she wanted to have lunch. She just nodded in agreement. A small table in a corner was available. They ordered *Salada Tropical* and *Befe Acebolade*, a dish of medallions of filet mignon. Sabrina ordered a glass of white wine, and Arsen his usual tonic water with a twist of lime.

Arsen could not wait for the food to be served before starting his inquiry.

"Sabrina, tell me about yourself. Where are you working now? In a law firm? You knew them all, and they knew you. You must have had many offers. Which one did you choose?"

"I simply don't have a job right now." Sabrina's voice changed again, and became quiet and sadder. "I am not looking for a job right now. I have enough to do."

Arsen could not believe what she was telling him, as he could not believe that she she had not been grabbed by someone the day after she left Lifshutz and Barnes.

"I don't understand something. Are you telling me that nobody offered you a job, even before you left the firm?"

"No, I am not telling you that."

"Then how come you don't have a job right now?"

"That is a long story. I'll tell you about that sometime--"

"Sometime when?" Arsen interrupted her. "I would like to hear it now, because I don't believe it. Why don't you tell me now, please?"

A waiter approached their table and started arranging the silverware and plates. A beautiful young waitress served the food expertly and graciously; she inquired about the arrangement of the table, and wished them bon appétit. The food was exquisite: prepared right, cooked right, and it tasted right. The inviting smell of the food and the quiet atmosphere of the restaurant helped them to relax and to feel hungry. They looked at each other. Arsen saw the first smile on Sabrina's face and the recovery of some of her old charm. They had almost finished the entree before they said anything. Arsen broke the silence.

"Sorry for my earlier excitement. It was just inconceivable and unacceptable to think that you have retired. I would really like to hear what happened to you since we met last time. Could you tell me?"

Sabrina again hesitated and Arsen did not insist. The conversation ceased again, and both of them became uncomfortable. Sabrina broke the silence this time.

"I am not as talkative these days as I used to be, and I don't like to talk about myself. There is nothing much to say, especially nothing pleasant to talk about. Can you understand that?"

"Not really," Arsen replied. "Not when it concerns you."

Sabrina realized that Arsen was not about to change the subject and talk about the weather. She was lonely and depressed. She needed someone to talk to, to get some things off her chest. Why not talk to Arsen? Why not tell him what happened? She had kept it too long inside herself.

"Since you insist so much," she began, "I will tell you what happened to me. The story is rather ordinary. Do you remember John Barnes in our office? He handled your case. I worked exclusively for him as his executive secretary. About two years ago his wife suddenly left him for another man. I don't think he ever thought that was possible. They had been married more than thirty years. The story was that the man was a trainer in her health club.

"John never talked about her afterwards, and he would become angry if anybody asked him anything about her. I certainly never did. The divorce proceedings were a mess, since she asked for much of the property and a great deal of money. He could not stand her anymore, and he wanted the divorce at almost any price. Bob Lifshutz, who represented him, saved him from ruin.

"Obviously, I became involved. I tried to make him feel better by working even harder and longer hours, and making sure everything ran very smoothly. I shielded him from problems whenever it was possible. One day last year, at the beginning of the summer, he invited me to visit his estate on Long Island near Hempstead over a weekend.

"I guess I was always a little bit in love with him, probably from the time he hired me to work in his office. Nothing had ever happened because he paid little attention to me as a woman; I was his secretary who took care of all his business needs, and he paid me very well to do that. He was in love with his wife. So, when he invited me, I knew what would happen, and I was looking forward to being with him."

Sabrina halted her story and sank deep in her thoughts. She was thinking of Hempstead Summer, as she called the visits to the estate during that summer of 1996. She remembered the first visit. She had taken the bus to Hempstead, then a taxi to the estate. John had already been there for a few days, while she had had to finish the work in the office.

When she finally arrived on Saturday, late in the afternoon, she found John impatient for her arrival. He helped her with the luggage, brought into the hallway by the taxi driver, and showed her to a bedroom which had been made ready for her stay. Both of them were uneasy; something never felt before in their relationship. He was the boss, and she was a secretary. Now she noticed that he was awkward in his attempt to show her into the bedroom, and in behaving as the boss and at the same time as the host to a friend. The role did not fit him very well. He was more natural as the boss. He left the bedroom after explaining that he had made arrangements for the two of them to have dinner in Hempstead. She was delighted with this invitation, never offered to her as a secretary. She knew this was different, and she decided to let him lead wherever he wanted to go.

Even their conversation was different. John wanted to talk about anything except business, but that was difficult for him as he knew nothing about her interests outside the office. Sabrina was a graduate of Barnard College. After college she had changed secretarial jobs a few times before becoming John Barnes's executive secretary. Quickly she had made the operation of the office smooth and efficient, and had become indispensable to him. The job took a toll on her time. There was not much time left for anything by the time she got home to her modest apartment. Dinner alone, newspapers to read to keep up with John, and reading before going to bed. Her idea of entering a Ph.D. program had been postponed several times, and eventually became just a contingency idea. Five years had flown in a breath, unnoticed.

This evening she was alone with John, and everything was different. He drove her to a restaurant in Hempstead where he knew many people, probably many a friend among them. They greeted them as they were walking into the restaurant, and many stopped by the table. He introduced her as a friend, not as his secretary. That was new, too. They ate vichyssoise, her favorite; roasted duck, specially prepared; fruits, served at the end; and they drank much light white wine between. They did not talk much. Still, there was something in the air, in the whole atmosphere of the restaurant, its dimmed lighting just bright enough to look around. The wine made her slightly dizzy and light-headed, yet happy inside.

John was charmingly helpful and awkward. Not much was said on the way to the estate. John was whistling an old tune. After they returned to the house she told him she wanted to retire, and he escorted her to the bottom of the stairs that led to the upper floor. She thanked him for the pleasant evening, and a delicious dinner. He kissed her hand and let her climb the stairs alone. Sabrina was still reading in bed when she heard a knock on the door. Obviously it was John. She asked him to come in. He came in holding two glasses of red wine, and he said that his excuse for knocking was the light in the bedroom, and his need of company. She assured him she did not mind. He gave her one of the glasses of wine, and sat in an armchair next to her bed. He was looking at her without speaking, and she responded in the same soundless way. Ten minutes must have passed, and it seemed to her that the momentum of his visit and the delight of the silence would perish if she did nothing. She got out of bed and walked to the window, from which the back garden was visible under bright lights. The view was wonderful, she said, and asked John to come and look. He got up from the chair and walked deliberately slowly. As he stood next to her, it was inevitable that their bodies would touch. She wanted him very much and was glad to feel his hand on her arm. He was standing behind her as if to avoid seeing the refusal of his advance. She did not move. Slowly he caressed her arm, then the other, until he finally kissed her neck. She remained still even at that. He inched closer to her until she felt his body trembling slightly. When she turned to face him, he embraced her and they kissed. He carried her to bed, undressed her, and took her in a most gentle and poignant delight. She let him have her any way he wanted, and he was insatiable in his desire for her body and very ingenious at getting her to enjoy his continuous love making. She had not expected him to be so sexual. It was a truly unforgettable weekend.

Sabrina had almost forgotten she was in a restaurant, and that Arsen was sitting across the table.

"Oh, the weekend was wonderful," Sabrina continued her story. "We talked a lot, ate in good restaurants, and, as you expected, made love. I found out that I was really in love with the man - who was twenty years my senior. I was not planning to marry him, although the thought did occur to me. The summer was wonderful. We were together continually, in the office and out. He was admirable in his attention to me and his desire for me. I almost thought he was falling in love with me. Well, maybe he actually did. Other people, and particularly his son and daughter, ruined everything that was built between us. I was approached by the daughter and offered a sum of money to leave him and the job. I felt awful and indignant but said nothing to John. A month or two later I noticed that John was changing. His mood changed, and he was often annoyed, even sarcastic on occasion, and our affair was surely dying down. I withdrew into myself.

"Things became worse, and we stopped meeting out of the office. There was always a reason. One day in October he called me into his office, and asked me to close the door. This was ominous and unusual. Without ceremony and straight to the point he told me that our affair was over and that it would be better for everybody concerned that I leave the firm. He assured me that I would be compensated handsomely. Compensated for what? For being his mistress, a whore with 'compensation.' He hurt me irrevocably.

"I asked him whether there was something else. He replied that there was nothing else. I left his office, packed my belongings from my desk, and went home. That was the last time I saw him. I never went to the office again. A brief letter and a check for $100.000 just confirmed my worst whore graduation wish, and completely overwhelmed me. I kept the letter and returned the check voided with the word 'ERROR'. The next and the last letter I received from John I returned unopened. That is my story. I am still recovering, or at least trying to." Her face expressed a deep dejection.

Sabrina and Arsen sat in silence for a while.

Arsen finally broke the silence.

"Sabrina, I have a proposition for you. I am supposed to establish an office here in New York, and will need people to help me do the job. First, I will need one secretary, later we will hire more people. Everything will depend on the progress of our project--"

"And that is?" Sabrina interrupted him.

Arsen explained the connection with the Institute in Moscow, and the purpose of and need for the office.

"Do you think you would want this job?"

"Do you pay a salary and benefits?" Sabrina asked.

"Yes, we do. How much I don't know yet, but I should have an answer by tomorrow. How much do you want?"

"Sixty and benefits," Sabrina said unconvincingly.

"I think I will be able to get it for you. Do I understand that you accept the deal?" Arsen was pushing her to accept.

"I will take it for whatever you can get. I need a change, and something to occupy my mind," she admitted. "I have been without a job and without any responsibilities too long."

Arsen was delighted. He knew that a well functioning office was on the way.

"We have to find an office, and that is our first priority. Then, furniture that must be above average, attractive and elegant, if for no one else than ourselves. We need at least four telephone lines, an intercom system, a security system for the office itself and for the office entrance, file cabinets,

and computers. Don't forget an Internet provider - I would like to continue with Interport. Think of a possible future web site. And think of things
I have not mentioned. Keep in mind the budget until we find out how
much it will be. Oh, I almost forgot, get yourself a cellular phone and a
beeper so that we can be in touch when I need you."

"This is a long list. It seems we have to start from scratch." Sabrina
laughed, and she sounded more like herself from the past.

"I was told I would have the money by Monday. If it is not here by
then, that will be the end of this project."

"What is the project all about? Am I supposed to know?"

"Of course you should know. Let me explain it briefly. After I retired,
I started to study ethnic problems globally and in my native Yugoslavia. I
managed to come up with some ideas of my own. Certain people found
out about my interests. Don't ask me how they found out. In any event, in
the Ethnic Institute in Moscow there is a group of important people who are
thinking of turning ideas into action. How they are going to do it I have no
idea. These people invited me to join them as an associate, with the responsibility of studying and overseeing an area extending from the Balkans to
China. My immediate task is to become familiar with conditions in these
countries, and I have already done some of that on my own. I will also travel to the area and meet some of the local leaders.

"How they are going to start the project they envision as the way to
change things in those areas, I don't know. I am not sure they know either.
It is unimportant, as long as I can continue my studies. It will be even more
interesting to meet some of the people in countries like Turkey, Iran, Greece,
Israel and others.

"Your research will be for materials I will need in my work, and you
will procure copies of those materials; you will communicate with Moscow
and coordinate our activities with theirs, particularly when I am out of New
York; and, you will schedule my activities in New York and organize my
trips abroad. I don't believe you will be able to travel much, if at all. I hope
you have an idea where we stand right now. We will find together where
we will be going from now on. You will have to be familiar with every
aspect of our operations."

"Sounds quite interesting."

"Before we leave, I would like to tell you that it is good to have you on
board. I would like you to come tomorrow to our apartment and meet my
wife. I hope you would find time. It is important also that you become
familiar with things in my study, as I anticipate that there will be occasions
when you will have to find something there, and even work from there.
Come in the afternoon if you can."

"I will be there at four, if that's a good time," Sabrina agreed.

"Excellent."

Arsen signed the credit card billing slip, and they went out onto Lexington Avenue. It was already three o'clock. Sabrina flagged a taxi to take her home, and Arsen walked slowly back home, up Sixty-Second Street.

Nada and her mother wondered where he had gone. He told them about Sabrina and the invitation for the following day.

Arsen went to his study, and checked his e-mail. An e-letter from Ivo Stipich was on the list of the Eudora 'in box'.

11/29/97

Dear Arsen:

I have arrived in Moscow and have immediately set to work to resolve some questions you raised in your letter.

My report on our conversations in New York and afterwards was well received. Mr. Kravchenko was impressed, and so were the other members of the group including Gen. Alexei Shagov. As you might have heard the General is a well known computer scientist and an astronomer. Recently, he discovered an object in space which is heading towards the earth. The discovery caused an unpleasant reaction among disbelieving astronomers in Europe and America.

I was asked to invite you to Moscow. They really want to talk to you. They feel that your ideas are excellent and very close to their own, and in many ways more practical in the area of global affairs and global relations. They are very impressed with your basics and your approach to solutions. Not least, they like your organizational ideas.

Let me know when would you like to come to Moscow, so that I can make arrangements for your visit.

Sincerely,
Ivo Stipich

Arsen was again pleased with the efficiency and speed of Ivo's responses. He concluded that he would be able to work with him and that he would use him as a liaison with the other members of the group.

1/29/97

Dear Ivo:

I appreciate your prompt answer.

I have managed to hire a secretary who will, I am sure, prove to be very valuable to us. I trust she will have our office operational within a week.

As for my trip to Moscow, I would prefer not to go now, unless you tell me I must. Then I will have time to stay there only a day or two. Let me know.

Sincerely,

Arsen Pankovich

Before going to sleep Arsen found another e-letter from Ivo Stipich.

11/29/98

Dear Arsen:

Yes, I think you should come to Moscow. Let me know what date.

Bank Info: Chase Manhattan, 2nd Avenue and 64th Street

Acc. # PPP6 4W32 3678 5599. You are authorized to sign checks.

The deposit was made as discussed, and the amount will be the same next month.

Regards,

Ivo Stipich

Indeed very impressive, Arsen concluded as he was getting into bed.

CHAPTER TWELVE

SUNDAY, 30 NOVEMBER 1997

The Sunday papers were unusually bland. Again, there was a short article on the finding of the Russian astronomers. Gen. Alexei Shagov was quoted as saying that he was not entirely sure of the nature of the object, but he had no doubt that it was on a collision course with the Earth. Another Russian observatory reported that they had also spotted the object, but they were not sure of its trajectory.

Sabrina came punctually at four. She and Nada found common ground quickly, and were discussing *God is a Verb*, a book Nada had recently bought. Arsen had no idea what the book was all about, and he did not want to find out.

Sabrina looked noticeably different from the day before. Her face was not sad any longer; Arsen would almost swear she had lost weight. She again looked neat, wearing a simple and well-fitting Navy blue dress, and high heel shoes.

After talk about the book was finished, Sabrina came into the study. She looked at the books on the shelves, and picked a few and browsed through them. She looked at the two computers, several copiers, the printer, the Sony TV-VCR set, the label writer and the Bose radio.

"This is a technological citadel. You have everything," Sabrina said.

Arsen showed Sabrina his sources of information. The files consisted of newspaper clippings mostly from the New York papers. Keesing's *Record of World Events* was handy on the shelf, along with the World and Wall Street Journal almanacs. A multitude of web sites was neatly lined up in the CiberLink folder. These sources covered everything Arsen thought important for his studies. The Bosnian and Zairean files were the thickest, as both countries were in the news continually. The ethnic problems were also the most interesting. Arsen tried to explain some of the conflicts, but realized that would be purposeless. Sabrina would have to catch up on her own. He told her about the Ethnic Institute in Moscow and the mysterious interest Ivo Stipich had in him, and about his forthcoming trip to Moscow.

"I will go to Moscow after the office is organized and functioning. How long will it take, do you think? I have to give a date to Ivo Stipich."

"I would think about two weeks," Sabrina said. "I saw an office this morning on Lexington Avenue near Fifty-Sixth Street, on the twentieth floor. The building has doormen, and all visitors are screened. The office is the second on the left from the elevator. It is very nice, and requires only minor repairs. There is a reception area, and there are two offices on each side. There are also two additional rooms: a smaller one for supplies, and a dinette. I don't see the need for a separate file room. We'll keep file cabinets in the offices. The rent is about forty thousand a year; not so bad anywhere. We will rent furniture until we decide what to buy. Telephone lines will be ready in a day or two. I already have a cellular phone and a beeper. Receipts will be filed in the office. I gave the manager a thousand in advance. I surely will need that money soon."

"You will have it right now." Arsen wrote a personal check.

"We need a credit card for the office to keep track of expenditures. I already called American Express."

"Do you ever forget anything?" Arsen was really impressed. "We also have to decide about your salary. Sixty-five, benefits, and expenses. Would that do?"

"Very much so," Sabrina answered cheerfully and appeared satisfied with the offer. "I will have to organize my household too."

Dinner was dominated by conversation about the coming project and about ethnic problems in the former Yugoslavia.

Sabrina was falling into the ethnic net.

CHAPTER THIRTEEN

MONDAY, 1 DECEMBER 1997

Monday was Arsen's ARGO Pension Board day. There were several interesting cases and much unrelated talk with Marvin and Dave. Arsen talked to the Lieutenant and explained that he would have to resign his position on the Board as of next week. Soon the Chief Surgeon and the Inspector came to talk to Arsen and to find out what was happening. Obviously, it would be impossible to work on the project, as Arsen started calling his new engagement in the ethnic circle, and to carry on any other activities.

Later in the day Arsen talked to David Milstein about quitting Brooklyn Medical. Reaction was the same as at the ARGO. Arsen was firm, although he was sorry to leave them; they had been good to him in the past year.

Unpleasant things behind, Arsen called Sabrina on the cellular phone.

"Doctor, this must be you? Who else would know to call me at this number." Not waiting for an answer she began to report the day's events. "You won't believe it. We have telephone lines installed. I also called Mr. Paladino, at Office Communications Company, whom I knew, and he promised to install the internal lines and the phone systems for the office."

"Marvelous," Arsen said. "I should be able to go to Moscow next week and get that done."

"If you wish, but there is still much to be done right here." Unmistakably Sabrina was not for an early Moscow trip. "You should let them wait a bit."

"With me it does not work that way. I like to get things done yesterday, not tomorrow. I don't play games. There is no positioning, there are no delays, no second thoughts, there is no long decision-making. What has to be done, had better be done today, as thinking about the unknown will only delay things and not resolve them. I should go to Moscow next Thursday."

"What about your vacation in Puerto Rico?"

"Hell, I completely forgot about the vacation. The Moscow trip will have to be postponed for a week. I will send an e-letter to Ivo Stipich to let him know about this change. By the way, I assume you have worked on the Internet."

"Our office was on the Net in 1992," Sabrina assured Arsen. "Do you have a lap top computer for the trip? I think you should take it with you. Do you have an address on AOL? They have local connections everywhere. You can then work on the Internet from anywhere. Also it is less expensive."

"I had better order a Power Book from MacWarehouse tonight; I will have it tomorrow. To connect to AOL is easy. They will give me connection numbers abroad. I wonder if they operate in Moscow. We'll find out."

Arsen thought how lucky he was to have found Sabrina on the street last Saturday. She was just plain excellent.

"Another thing," Sabrina said. "I talked to the Public Library about getting copies of materials we'll need when we start the studies. There will be no problems. Originals don't leave the library, but we can make copies. Are there other sources we would need to look into?"

"Yes, we will have to connect to WNS over the Internet. This is a subscription service from the Commerce Department. They publish translated newspaper articles from all over the world. That is the way to obtain current information. It costs about fifty dollars per month. Which computers are we going to have?"

"You work on Macs at home. Why change it?"

"Done," Arsen said. "I will order two Macs tonight and the basic software. We may as well get two printers, and a label writer. Why don't you order a fax machine and keep it in your office. I hate fax machines -- bureaucratic inventions that cause you to waste time by first faxing a letter then mailing the original. What is the hurry in this world?"

"Anyway, it's nice to have a fax," Sabrina said. "Can you come to the office tomorrow?"

"Only in the morning. I have to be at ARGO at one for my last Pension Board meeting" Arsen said. "I will come to the office about nine."

"Okay, Doctor. I will see you in the morning." Arsen really liked that she called him 'Doctor' rather than by first name; their relationships was in that way close enough, and nonetheless there was a respectable distance between them.

Back at home, Arsen looked through the mail. There was a letter from the Forum on Foreign Policy, from Mr. Brown's secretary, Arlene Strumpf.

28 November 1997

Dear Dr. Pankovich:

Enclosed you will find the Program for the Forum Meeting on 22 January 1998. Dr. Brown asked me to invite you to the reception prior to the meeting, and to the dinner afterwards.

Please let me know whether you will attend these functions.

Sincerely,
Arlene Strumpf
Secretary to Matthew Brown, Ph.D.

There it was, Arsen thought, the Program for the Meeting, which introduced him as the speaker and the topic as he had submitted it 'Global Ethnic Problems and their Possible Solutions'. Unbelievable but there was no turning back. The lecture must be delivered. The mystery of the person who had submitted Arsen's name as the potential lecturer was not solved. The few suspects had already denied involvement.

At home that evening Nada reported the news from their daughters in Belgrade and Pamplona, and the progress of the latest-grand daughter in Belgrade.

Arsen fell asleep while watching a Cinemax movie after dinner. The only option to sleeping in the chair in front of the television was to sleep in bed. Reluctantly, Arsen chose the latter option.

CHAPTER FOURTEEN

TUESDAY, 2 DECEMBER 1997

Arsen was in the office at nine. He liked the building, the elevator man, and the entrance to the office. Two men were installing telephone lines. Sabrina was drinking coffee and offered a cup to Arsen.

"We will have telephones and a fax operational today -- and they will be sitting on the floor because the desks will not be in until tomorrow or Thursday. I rented the furniture so that we can decide what we really want, before we order it. Sometimes getting the furniture takes a few months. In the other office, all the furniture was rented, and changed as needed. Executive Furniture Rental is the best rental company and has an excellent selection. And it is not very expensive. Perhaps we should just rent?"

Arsen ignored the question.

"Let me show you the rooms." Sabrina led Arsen to his office. Hers was the second on the right. "The window will be behind your chair," she said. "The computer area will be to your left, and the file cabinets on the right. We need two chairs for visitors and a nice Picasso print for the wall, unless you have something at home--"

"I have something at home," Arsen interrupted.

"...a small chest for a few figurines and a vase, and, of course, bookshelves on the right wall, next to the file cabinets."

As they returned to the reception area Sabrina suggested that they should get a receptionist soon, as the work would expand quickly. "Answering the phone is time-consuming. Once we determine the volume of library copying, we may need someone to do research, and to go to the library."

"Go ahead, I am in favor," Arsen said.

"I know a girl who is looking for a job. Do you want to interview her?"

"Not really. That is up to you."

Sabrina inquired further about the ethnic ideas and problems, about the Russian Group and the projects they were planning.

"I don't understand how they think they will be able to realize these ideas," Sabrina said. "They'll need the support of many people, like the whole United Nations. That's impossible. Big powers will not give up their advantages and prerogatives; medium size powers won't want to lose any power, and territory is part of power; and, small countries will resist being even smaller. As for the ethnic groups, who will listen to them?"

"You are entirely right. I have the same questions, and the same doubts as you do."

"You must have asked these questions, in your conversations with them."

Arsen explained his discussions with Ivo Stipich.

"I have not had a chance to talk to the leaders of the project. That must be the reason for my invitation to Moscow. I simply don't know yet."

Arsen looked at his watch. It was close to eleven.

"We had better go to the bank. I don't want to be late at ARGO."

As they were parting after arranging things at the bank, Sabrina asked, "When should I start this girl if she wants the job? Tomorrow?"

"Tomorrow is fine."

Arsen took the R train and read a chapter of his latest book acquisition as the train made its way to the Woodhall station. The book. *The Serbs and their Leaders in the Twentieth Century* was edited by two Serbian intellectuals who lived and taught in Australia -- Peter Radan and Aleksandar Pavkovic. The book was informative and Arsen realized that he knew only the Serbian myths and nothing of substance about Serbia and the Serbs in the last two centuries. The essays were controversial, and reflected the authors' subjective feelings, though they were probably historically accurate. Accurate or not, the pictures of the personalities they painted were mostly ugly, and the events these leaders had effected were a salad of personal promotion and intrigue -- and often cruelty and sheer stupidity. King Peter I, a decent individual who was truly loved and appreciated by his subjects, was pushed aside by the aggressive younger generation led by his own son, Aleksandar.

On the train Arsen read about Gen. Draza Mihajlovic, another honorable leader and an inept politician, who played his Serbian roots during World War Two expecting other nationalities to bow to Serbian supremacy. The General lost the battle, and in the end he lost his own life. Arsen concluded sadly that he could have lost his own life while he was a teenage participant in Mihajlovic's guerrilla movement.

The Pension Board meeting was stormy and unpleasant, because of a disagreement among the members on a procedural matter. At least it was not boring as it sometimes had been.

The evening was quiet and provided a balance to the rest of the day.

CHAPTER FIFTEEN

On Wednesday Arsen was in Queens working for Brooklyn Medical. Michael was substituting for Sarah, and things were not going as smoothly as usual, but there were no real problems.

Sabrina called.

"The computers have not arrived. Have you ordered them?"

"No, I have not. I will do it as soon as I get back home. Did the furniture arrive?" Arsen inquired.

"They promised to deliver them first thing in the morning. You didn't write down our new phone numbers. You have a separate, individual line. Then there's the main number and several cascading numbers. The Internet line is an ICD line. Oh, don't forget modems."

Arsen put the office numbers on his watch file.

"Are you coming to the office tomorrow?" Sabrina asked.

"I may come later in the day to unpack the computers, if they deliver them tomorrow. I have many things to do, mostly unanswered letters awaiting replies. Some of them will soon be coming your way. I hope, anyway. I have had no time even for the newspapers. I must keep up, now more than ever. I will call. Let me know if there is a problem."

Finally at home, he ordered the computers and software, and caught up with *The New York Times*. A cute article on Livonians in Latvia, a vanishing nation, whose language was 'the tongue of the sea,' and the subject of a researcher's question: Mara Zirnite queried why it was more important to save a tiger than an old culture. There were only a few Livonians left, and their nation was on its death bed. What was the point of the song about the Livonian language:

> I shall never forget it
> As I cannot forget my mother...

when the last Livonian was preparing to die. The poet must have thought his soul would not forget the language when it joined the rest of the Livonians somewhere in the Universe.

Arsen was thinking of many dying tribes, and of oppressed ethnic groups, abused, demeaned, denied the right of self determination in acceptable democracies; he was thinking of the Basques in Spain and France, the Gypsies in the Czech Republic, the Aborigines in Australia. There must be a way to change that effectively.

CHAPTER SIXTEEN

THURSDAY, 4 DECEMBER 1997

Arsen decided to go to the office after lunch. The computer equipment and the furniture had been delivered. Phones were operational and in place on the desks. Arsen unpacked the Mac in his room, connected the wiring, and installed the software. It was very easy to connect to the Internet via Interport. The first message went to Ivo Stipich:

4 December 1997

Dear Ivo:

Just a note on our new e-address and the address of the office and our phone numbers.

I will leave New York on the way to Moscow on 18 December 97: Air France will take me to Paris then to Moscow. I should be there on Friday in the afternoon. I would like to be back in New York on Tuesday, at the latest.

Sincerely, Arsen

"Sabrina, our first e-mail is gone. I want to make sure you check the e-mail three times a day when I am out of the office. It should be loosely confidential. I don't expect it to become secret. When a problem arrives in the mail and you know how to handle it, just do it. Keep me informed. Copy all messages into the e-mail database. You should arrange for my trip to Moscow in the morning."

"Understood," she replied. "Is there anything you're taking with you, or do you need anything collected and organized?"

"Nothing that I can think of. I have no idea why they need me in Moscow. Most likely they just want to meet me. That is Russian stupidity."

"Michelle Brigens will start tomorrow," Sabrina said. "I could use some help organizing the office. Also, she'll have to do some shopping for the office. I opened an account with a stationary store. A small refrigerator will arrive tomorrow. We're almost set."

"Let us try again to find out how our Internet connection is functioning." Arsen launched Eudora; surprisingly, there was new mail form Ivo Stipich.

12/4/97

Dear Arsen:

Your letter has been received, and your plans for coming to Moscow understood.

Please cancel all plans for the trip.

Gen. Alexei Shagov will arrive in New York on Sunday, 7 Dec 97, and will leave for Washington on Thursday, 11 Dec 97. He would like to meet with you on Sunday, 7 Dec 97 at 8pm in his room at the Plaza Hotel. Please confirm. On Monday the General will visit the U.N. to discuss his findings before the Space Committee. He will also give a talk and have informal meetings with the members of the American Astronomical Society. Try to keep your schedule open. Please postpone your trip to Puerto Rico.

Sincerely, Ivo.

"Sabrina, we have problems." Arsen showed her the letter from Ivo Stipich.

"Are you ready to meet the General?"

"Of course, I am ready," Arsen said. "It is better that he is coming to New York than that I travel to Moscow. He will want to talk about the future of the project, and probably my role in it. I know what to do although I am not sure what they will do to make it possible. We'll find out what he wants from us. Do you think he might need secretarial help? Ivo did not say whether he was bringing a secretary with him."

"We will do whatever is necessary," Sabrina said.

"Would you mind sending Michelle to help if he needs someone? How about hiring a temp?"

"We don't need outside help," Sabrina said. "Besides there will be some confidential staff to handle. We can't take just anybody from the street."

Arsen thought he saw anger on her face when he mentioned secretarial help for the General. It lasted just a moment, like a flash. She probably thought he wanted her to do it, Arsen thought. She was sensitive.

"We will have a few hectic days during his stay. I wonder what is he like? I don't think I have ever met a general." Arsen was verbalizing his thoughts. "Should I address him as 'General' or 'General, Sir,' or just "Sir,' or perhaps 'Mister Shagov.' I don't think 'Comrade Shagov' would be appropriate any more. I think I will use only 'General.' That sounds the best to me."

"'General' sounds the best to me, too," Sabrina agreed.

Arsen went home thinking about the forthcoming meeting with the General.

Days were flying by too fast, and quiet days had become a rarity, Arsen thought. Everything had started with the Russian project. Now he had the office, and two secretaries, telephones and a fax machine, cellular phones and beepers. This was worse than when he was in practice. If he only knew where he was heading...

CHAPTER SEVENTEEN

FRIDAY, 5 DECEMBER 1997

When Arsen got up Nada and her mother were still asleep. He made coffee, poured a cup, and went to the study with Friday's papers, which were delivered to the entrance door. There was not much for Arsen to do in the office. Sabrina wanted to talk to Michelle, to get the supplies for the office and to attend to many details. Arsen had promised to come in the afternoon and to bring the picture for the wall in his office; it was a drawing of a woman in the nude in charcoal crayon by an unknown artist from Mexico, that he had bought in Cancun.

There was nothing to prepare for the meeting with the General. Arsen knew his unreachable vision of the ethnic world too well.

The newspapers were there to be read.

Winnie Mandela was denying everything before the Truth and Reconciliation Commission, even the crimes she had been convicted for, and accusing thirty witnesses of lying. People often denied the obvious.

'Former Italian Premier Found Guilty' a headline read since he was setting a slush fund. Influence and greed, Arsen concluded, attracted too many crooks into politics. What would happen if politicians were audited randomly, as athletes or policemen were tested for drugs, during the term in office and afterwards for five years? Would the political panorama be changed by the loss of the crooks and by the advent of honest individuals encouraged by the change in the political climate. Who knew, maybe they would become greedy, corrupt and cruel when opportunities arose? Finally, Arsen had time to visit Tito's web site in Ljubljana. That had been an old communist tune about a happy and united nation. Why had it fallen apart so rapidly? From ethnic love? Arsen moved on as if he had been burned by the old propaganda.

Nazi Gold was still a headline.

Arsen also brushed up on the publications of Walker Connor and Ruth Lapidoth, two well known ethnicists whose writings were pertinent to his forthcoming talks with Gen. Shagov. He felt that the issues were in his bones, and he knew exactly what had to be done.

In the office in the afternoon, Arsen met Michelle, a pleasant girl, skinny, and with a melodic voice; an excellent choice for a receptionist. Sabrina showed the office proudly to Arsen: it was ready for business.

"Doctor, Ivo Stipich, calling from Moscow, is on line two," Michelle announced over the intercom. "Do you want to take the call?"

"Of course," Arsen said and picked up line two. "Ivo, finally we can talk. The office is ready and functioning. I am looking forward to meeting the General. Is he coming on Sunday?"

"Yes, he will be there," Ivo Stipich said. "We wanted him to bring a secretary with him but he just refused. He thought you would take care of him."

"The General is right. The office will give him any support he wants. You are paying good money to have this office - why not use it? How much commotion would you expect during a visit to the United Nations and to the Astronomical Society? Why would he need anybody?"

"You don't know the General," Ivo Stipich said. "He can stir things up quickly. Besides, he has important information for the scientific community. Do you know about it? Here in Moscow we know that there is a large celestial object on the way to collide with Earth."

"I have seen only short reports," Arsen said. "Astronomers in Europe and America have denied the existence of the object."

"The General's observation has been reconfirmed in Russia several times; too bad American and European astronomers don't believe him. The General said these astronomers are looking in the wrong direction and he intends to explain his findings in detail while he is in New York."

"I will have a good time with the General," Arsen said.

"I know you will," Ivo Stipich said. "Arsen, if you need something just call me or even better e-mail me; my staff will pick up the message immediately and let me know about anything urgent. I will talk to you later."

It was interesting that nobody believed this General, Arsen mused.

The office, though ready for business, had no business to attend to. Sabrina and Michelle were talking in the reception room, and the telephones were silent. The computers were ready with the FileMaker database installed but empty. There was nothing to be done in the office, no appointments to keep, no calls to wait for since nobody knew they existed. The peace and quiet in the office were complete - perhaps before the storm.

Arsen suggested they all go home.

CHAPTER EIGHTEEN

WEEKEND OF 6-7 DECEMBER 1997

Weekends since he had retired were quiet, as Arsen had always wanted them to be. That was impossible when he was in practice. Now, the trips to the Balkans, the Middle East and South West Asia would probably ruin the tranquility he had established. There would be no talking sessions with Dave and Marvin at ARGO on Mondays; and there would be no busy Wednesdays working for Brooklyn Medical and no political discussions with Sarah interspersed between patients' visits. No doubt, writing and reading would be reduced to a minimum. This weekend had been exceptionally quiet although its finale -- meeting the General -- was approaching unstoppably.

Long before the meeting Arsen took a shower and dressed in his standard navy blue jacket, gray pants, white shirt and a tie. He decided to carry his black leather bag with the shoulder strap, a dictation pad, a tape recorder and his small Olympus camera. He decided to walk to the Plaza Hotel to stretch his legs, since there was no time for a walk at the Vertical Club.

It was not very cold outside. The sky was cloudy, and the air was humid with impending rain. Arsen buttoned his raincoat and pulled up the collar; holding the shoulder strap of his bag with his right hand, he walked briskly down Third Avenue. He crossed to the opposite side at the corner of Sixtieth Street and continued along it toward Fifth Avenue.

The streets were still crowded with people. Some of them were shoppers carrying packages and bags -- some gift wrapped and others not; and they came single or in pairs, women and men, with children and without children, young and old and rarely very old. Somehow they all appeared happy and gay, many of them talking loudly, as one would expect them to be during the Holiday Season, even when they spent more than they had planned.

While the sidewalks on Lexington Avenue were filled with people, milling around, Park Avenue was almost empty and so was Fifth in that section, where there were only a few people walking to their parked cars. The Plaza Hotel was now visible, and it looked majestic. Arsen looked at his watch: twenty more minutes before the appointed time. He stood at the corner, and watched the people walking by and the passing cars stopping and moving again sequentially as the traffic signals turned red and green. And he gazed down Fifth Avenue which was brilliant with lights in a variety of colors.

At five minutes before eight o'clock Arsen crossed the street and walked along the Grand Army Plaza to the hotel entrance. In the lobby he picked up the house phone and asked for the room number of Mr. Alexei Shagov. The operator told him to go to room 812, where he was expected. The General knew his way around hotels, Arsen thought.

He knocked on the door of Room 812, which opened almost instantly. Arsen was invited in by a man in his early sixties, of medium height, slightly obese, and Harvard bald. His intelligent face, with its smooth and almost shiny pink cheeks, showed a pair of inquiring eyes; a thick black mustache above the thin lips and rather flat chin with a shallow, slightly eccentric mental indentation gave him the look of an artist. His body and extremities were well built, probably from an athletic past. He looked different from the way Arsen had imagined him.

"Good to see you, Dr. Pankovich," he said in a melodic and rather deep voice as he firmly shook Arsen's hand.

"Good evening, General. I have been looking forward to meeting you. How was your flight? You must be tired by now."

"On the contrary, I am hungry and ready for dinner, which we will have at nine o'clock at the Palm Court Restaurant right here in the hotel. I flew in from Paris, where I stayed three days with some old friends. A few hours in a Concord today did not tire me." The General's English was excellent, and Arsen concluded that he must have spent a number of years in the U.S. and probably in England, as he noticed a hint of an Oxford accent.

"Oh, Paris is a beautiful city. My wife and I spent two months in Paris in '88," Arsen said almost apologetically. "I have not been there since then."

"Pity that you don't go there more often. The city is beautiful, and people are wonderful - once they know you, of course," The General remarked with a hint of hostility in his voice.

"You must have spent time in England," Arsen observed.

"How did you guess England?" The General was curious.

"Oh, I thought I heard some Oxford in your talk."

"You heard right. I spent six months at Oxford, some years ago. Maybe thirty years ago, better to say. That was a wonderful time in a wonderful place, and I was young and anxious to learn, and most of all interested in meeting people. I met several of your countrymen from Serbia and from Bosnia during my stay at Oxford. You are a Bosnian Serb, aren't you?"

"Sure I am."

"From which part of Bosnia?"

"Banja Luka."

"Very much in the news these days," the General said.

"Very much in the news these days," Arsen repeated.

"Did you know the Vice-president who committed suicide?"

"Yes, I knew him. He was a few years younger."

"Any idea what happened? Did he do it or was he eliminated?" the General wanted to know.

"I don't know what happened," Arsen said. "Nobody knows and nobody is talking. It does not matter anymore."

"Don't you think it would be important to know for sure?"

"Yes it would but how would we know for sure? It would have to come from someone who was there at the time. I mean at Pale."

"Our information is that he committed suicide when he was stripped of his functions and bypassed for the Presidency. Maybe he was depressed?"

"Maybe," Arsen agreed absentmindedly. "Maybe he was too honest."

It seemed they had come to the end of the discussion of Bosnia. Arsen knew the topic would surface again.

"Ivo told us that you agreed to organize an office in the city, and to start in-depth studies of conditions in the countries in your domain, and to travel to those places to meet the local people."

"With a bit of luck I hired an executive secretary and she organized everything. She rented an office, bought furniture and equipment, arranged for telephone lines to be installed, connected us to the Internet, and hired a receptionist. We are ready to start our studies. We need some guidance as to what, where and who; we hope to get that support from the Institute."

"I see you are ready. Arsen that is marvelous." He had switched to the first name. Arsen was determined to call him 'General', and to keep the distance just as he expected Sabrina to.

The General looked at his watch.

"It is almost nine. Time for a dinner. Let us go. Leave your bag and raincoat here."

Two couples were waiting at the reception desk ahead of the General and Arsen.

The General talked about his stay in Paris, and the good time he had had with his friends. Arsen regained his calm and felt that he was ready for the real conversation with the General. They were seated at a table already arranged for four, and waiters were busy removing the silver, plates and glasses to accommodate the two of them. The General ordered vodka on the rocks, and Arsen his usual tonic water with a twist of lime. Without thinking about it very much, Arsen ordered rack of lamb, while the General studied the menu carefully and decided on broiled salmon. The salad was served almost immediately and as they were eating the General continued their conversation.

"Your territory will be large; you will require a substantial staff of people to accomplish the goals that we have in mind. Perhaps I should tell you something about the goals. We agree with your ideas on the objectives. Your basic principles on autonomy and sovereignty are identical with ours. We agree that the present borders will have to be redrawn in accordance with the wishes of the people. We all agree on that principle."

The General sipped his vodka, and paused for a while. Arsen felt comfortable and relaxed waiting to hear the rest of the General's ideas; he really wanted to know about the World Government and about the process that would initiate its formation. He had already raised these questions in his letter.

"Arsen, we realize you have some ideas that do not coincide with those developed at the Institute, and some of them are more imaginative and acceptable to our group than others. We agree that the political organization of the new territories must depend entirely on the wishes of the population, which means that we will have to ensure a free majority rule. It is also important to protect the borders and the safety of the people in the new territories from outside attacks, and to avoid interference in their political, religious and economic issues. All new structures and institutions will have to be developed from these basic principles.

Finally, provision of certain entitlements based on the universal right of every individual will have to be developed. As you might have gathered by now, these are revolutionary principles that could shake the world. Yet, we are not planning a revolution to achieve our goals. An opportunity to accelerate our plans has recently appeared and we want to exploit it. I think the threat from the celestial object that is heading in the direction of the Earth will be a major issue in the near future and will require the creation of a global defense body to save the Earth. The United Nations is the most logical choice of an institution to serve as the Parliament of the world, and a world government will have to be created to prepare Earth's population for the possible catastrophe.

"Most important, the world will have to be organized to be able to deal with the approaching apocalypse, and mechanisms and systems to prevent the catastrophe will have to be developed. Not only has my team of astronomers discovered the approaching celestial object, but our scientists have also worked on and advanced systems for such hypothetical catastrophes; in reality we are a long way along the road in developing organization and defense systems to deal with the approaching object. There is no reason we should not be in the position to run the World Government. We will have to resolve endless international frictions and establish peace among peoples before a meaningful effort against the common enemy - or, better said, against the common threat - can be undertaken. That is why we think it will be important to solve the ethnic problems, which are the cause of most, if not all, international troubles of the world. Do you see the developing situation?"

Again the General paused in his explanations. Arsen was very impressed with everything he had heard and the ethnic connection was now obvious to him.

"The consequences of the object colliding with the Earth are enormous. We must be ready to face the situation," the General said. "That is just another significant reason for pushing for a world government and for the resolution of ethnic problems. The main reason for formation of a world government is the need for smooth operation and coordination of a global defense body whose mandate will be to organize study and research, and to find ways to avert the catastrophe. That means all the Earth's resources will have to be tapped and used as necessary. That will require an extensive staff of administrators and scientists, who will organize and plan all phases of the research, organize meetings and study groups, and most of all translate expeditiously all promising ideas into active research. I will be involved with that part of the operations.

"Another big group will have to be concerned with the question of survival after the collision. A Board for survivors will have to be established, and it will deal with entirely different problems. The Board will be almost like a huge funeral company which will protect the survivors from the dead -- although I doubt anybody would survive the collision. Think of New York City after the collision. All these buildings would be destroyed and everything now alive would be dead. Perhaps some primitive life could survive in water, unless the water was too hot from the release of the Earth's core. The prospects for the survival of humans in case of the collision are nil. Still, we have to be prepared for a near miss, in which case major destruction and death -- of almost the entire population and of all other life -- would occur. Besides, it would be good for the population to be concerned and occupied with survival.

"A Board for space refuges will have to be created, like a big travel agency. It will study the feasibility of even temporary escape for some individuals into space and will plan their return to Earth after things cool off. Imagine the impossible task of developing criteria for choosing individuals who should be saved by temporary escape into space. Actually, the difficulty will be in deciding who should be left behind to face certain death. Something like on Titanic. The Ethnic Board will have to ensure that all groups are represented in any salvage plan, if twenty or thirty thousand can be sent into space. However, think of the likely situation that Earth will not be a habitable land after the collision. The space refugees would die a slow death in space. The purpose of sending these people into space is that they will return if the object passes by and Earth is not completely destroyed.

"Arsen, by now you can imagine how important it will be to stabilize ethnic problems and abolish the ineffective system of so erroneously termed nation-states."

The General paused again.

For Arsen, hearing these ideas just confirmed the fact that he and the General and his group had an identical approach to ethnic problems; he was not concerned about the collision of Earth with the approaching object. He realized the importance of the problem and his personal triviality in it. Once the ethnic problems were resolved, he would have time to think about the collision, he concluded.

Dinner was being served, and their serious conversation had to be interrupted.

After dinner the General suggested that they return to his room.

"Another thing, Arsen: I wanted to ask you to accompany me when I visit the United Nations. As you know, I am going to present my data before the Space Committee."

"I have time, although I am not sure I would be of much help to you at the meetings on space phenomena," Arsen said.

"I wanted you to meet people at the United Nations as you may have to represent us in some conversations after my return to Moscow."

"Okay if you think so."

"Arsen, there are so many things to talk about but time is short. You must come to Moscow. Somehow there is always plenty of time for everything in Moscow. With all the problems we have, it is more relaxing than in New York. I don't know why. I anticipate a lot of things happening in the near future. I just hope we will be able to control events and prevent the confusion which will be inevitable once everybody comprehends the gravity of the situation, and the reality of a collision of Earth with the celestial object. Unfortunately, the astronomers are not convinced yet about the whole thing. I will have to give them the data. I did it in Paris, and they were still doubtful. This is unreal, this denial. It must be subconscious; they know what it would mean so they don't want to believe the data. We will try again in the morning." The General rose and spread his arms in a sign of helplessness. "We must try harder this time."

"Thank you for dinner, General," Arsen said. "I understood what you said and I have a cold feeling around my heart, but I am not afraid. This is one of those situations in which being afraid is totally senseless. Just the possibility that everybody on the globe may die, makes me cool toward my own end. What would I do alone if I survived? Death appears more appealing."

"Let us hope that the end will be different."

"At what time should I meet you in the lobby?" Arsen inquired.

"At seven-thirty. We'll have breakfast and then take a ride to the U.N. The meeting of the Space Committee starts at nine o'clock."

"Yes, Sir. I'll be in the lobby at seven-thirty. Good night."

"Good night," the General said automatically.

The door slammed after Arsen. He looked at his watch -- it was almost midnight.

Arsen decided to walk back home. The Grand Army Plaza, Fifth Avenue and the other streets on the way home were almost empty. Arsen wanted to think about the meeting he had just had with the General and about everything that had been said. He would be able to work with him, Arsen thought. He spoke clearly and to the point like a real soldier. A single item had not been mentioned: who was actually behind this entire project? Who was financing it? Who was to benefit from it? It seemed impossible that this was purely a humanitarian project. Yet, the prospect of collision with the celestial object would offer little gain after collision and after everybody was dead, or almost everybody. The whole idea of a world government and the solution of ethnic problems must have been envisioned and designed long before the celestial object came along. Maybe it had been started by the "big boys" even before the fall of Communism. Ivo Stipich's boss, Kravchenko, had been in the ethnic position in NKVD. Arsen had no idea what the background of other members in the group was. This celestial object had come along conveniently, almost too conveniently. Nobody but the Russians saw this celestial object . Strange, to say the least. Arsen was now part of the General's group, and he would stay in it if for no better reason than to see how a big hoax operated and failed, he decided determinedly.

CHAPTER NINETEEN

MONDAY, 8 DECEMBER 1997

Arsen woke up early, with the United Nations meeting on his mind. It was five-thirty when he got up, too early for anything but coffee. He checked his e-mail -- nothing. The papers had not arrived.

Arsen leaned back in the arm chair and let his thoughts fly wherever they wanted to go. Working in some capacity in the United Nations was a dream. Things were happening, Arsen thought. If the General was right, and he made sense, the United Nations would become the seat of the World Government. Chances were that Arsen would be in some way a part of that government. Maybe he would be in charge of resolving the incredible ethnic problems in the Balkans, the Middle East and Southwest Asia.

The General's talk about the 'large funeral agency' was frightening. He thought that collision would cause the disintegration of the Earth and total annihilation of life. Near miss would cause enormous damage and widespread death but there could be some survivors. Decay of the dead population and everything else that was dead would be a threat to further survival of the survivors.

The General really thought that collision would be inevitable if a significant deflection of the celestial object could not be achieved. He had mentioned several options but Arsen had forgotten what they were.

Arsen would have to see the collision, he thought. That would be an incredible experience. Dying would be irrelevant as nobody would survive. How would it feel when the celestial object approached the Earth, on the day of the impact? The Earth would probably be in a turmoil, shaken by tremors, with winds blowing; it would spin faster and faster as gravitational forces pulled it and the celestial object toward each other. Then would come the impact.

The telephone rang. Arsen looked at his watch - it was six-fifteen. He lifted the receiver.

"Doctor, good morning," Sabrina said. "I had to find out what happened last night and what we should plan for today."

"I am glad you called. The meeting with the General was smooth and informative. He asked me to go with him to the United Nations today. There is a possibility you will be needed tonight to meet the General and go with us wherever we go, but that is unknown to me at the moment. I hope you will be able to join us. Please keep your cellular phone operational so I can communicate with you when I need you."

"Okay Doctor. I'll be ready when you need me. I talked to Mr. Stipich. He is aware of our operations. He gave me some references to dig out for you. Also, he gave me names of people in Zagreb, Belgrade, Prishtina, and Podgorica, so I could arrange meetings with them when the time comes."

"Don't do any research today. Be on standby. If you leave the office, have Michelle stay behind and answer the phone. Don't let her go home until everything is arranged."

"Is there anything else?" Sabrina asked.

"That is all. I'll talk to you later." Arsen hung up. It was time to get ready and head to the breakfast meeting with the General.

The dynamic of the streets was different in the morning from that at night, Arsen thought as he was heading for the Plaza Hotel. Even the people were different. The morning crowd was going to work. Everybody looked serious and in a hurry; some of them were probably late; some were running to the subway; others had just arrived. People were getting in and out of buses and taxis, in and out of private cars and light trucks, in and out of limousines; some rode bikes and some were on roller blades. The traffic was heavy and traffic cops were directing often impatient and frustrated drivers. Even the bus drivers were impatient and did not hesitate to run red lights, like everybody else.

Arsen crossed Third Avenue in front of his building and walked down Sixty-Second Street all the way to Fifth Avenue, then along the Central Park sidewalk to the Plaza Hotel. When he walked into the lobby, he found the General sitting in an armchair, reading a newspaper.

"Good morning, General." Arsen interrupted his reading. "I hope I haven't kept you waiting too long."

"Oh, hi Arsen. I came down earlier to be able to read the *Times*. Are you ready for breakfast?"

"Yes, Sir."

The General ordered a rich breakfast of eggs and pancakes, juice and coffee. Arsen chose only coffee.

"Our first meeting is with the Undersecretary of the United Nations, who oversees the Space Committee. It will be a formal call, something like submitting credentials, without actually submitting anything. It will be a half-hour meeting. It will start at nine o'clock. At ten there will be a real meeting, which will last at least two hours. At noon we are invited to have lunch with members of the Space Committee. At one-thirty there will be a press conference, which should not last more than an hour. This is as much as I know. It is possible somebody has planned other activities. Nobody has said anything about dinner. We'll find out."

As they were waiting for breakfast to be served the General folded the newspaper and put it in his hand bag which was bulging with papers.

"The *papers* are usually more interesting than what I saw today. I found only a few items of interest. Bosnia as usual. What do you think about the lady, I mean Mrs. Plavsic, the President. Do you think she is capable of leading the Serbs?"

Arsen was not sure about that. He was not sure he knew much about anything in Bosnia anymore. "Everything there is very confusing. They would do better if they cooperated with NATO. At least there would be money around to help people. The political problems will be resolved only after corruption has been checked, if that is possible. It appears that the lady President has not been busy making money. The situation is no better in other parts of Bosnia. One could probably generalize by saying that the situation is the same throughout the Balkans. Corruption is the number one problem in the region. On second thought, that is the problem all over the world."

"In the United States too, you think?" the General questioned Arsen.

"It is not so obvious and widespread as in some parts of the world," Arsen replied.

"We always come back to the same basics, don't we," the General concluded, in a resigned voice.

The General looked at his watch and suggested that they finish up breakfast and go to the lobby where somebody was meeting them to drive them to the United Nations. As they entered the lobby, they were suddenly surrounded by several reporters and photographers. The General responded to questions about his visit to New York and the United Nations, and later to Washington.

"General, are you convinced there is a planet on a collision course with the Earth? How far is it?" asked a reporter.

"Today I will be discussing the whole problem with the Space Committee at the United Nations. They are not convinced of my discovery yet. I will have to present my data to them and to explain what it means. That's a bit complicated, as you may imagine." The reporters laughed at his remark.

"How much time do we have left before the impact?" another reporter asked.

"Not too much but probably enough to do something to avert the disaster."

"How long is 'enough,' General?"

"I cannot state that precisely. Four-five years, maybe? My team in Russia is working on that. Part of the problem is that we have not yet determined the size of the celestial object and its true nature. More people should get involved. And of course, we will have to create a Board which will deal with the problem and which will coordinate efforts worldwide. We may even need a world government to deal effectively with the approaching catastrophe."

The General spoke smoothly, and without any hesitation. He said firmly, "Gentlemen, I have an appointment with Undersecretary Enstrom at the U.N. in a few minutes. You will understand that I must hurry. I will see you at the press conference at one-thirty this afternoon." The General pushed his way towards the front door where a chauffeur waved to him.

"This way, Sir. I will take you to the U.N." He led the General to the waiting limousine. Arsen followed close behind.

As the limousine was struggling through the morning traffic, the General and Arsen were sitting comfortably in the large passenger compartment which was equipped with a bar, telephones, and a television. The General appeared relaxed, and Arsen cooled off after the encounter with the press.

"It is impossible to avoid the press," the General said. "The best one can do is to stay cool and answer all questions, even vaguely if need be. You had better get used to the press because you may be interviewed before you know it. This morning they did not know who you were. This afternoon they will know your mother's maiden name and your sins at the age of fourteen."

Arsen laughed at his remark.

"What is funny? Did you do something funny at that age?"

"Not really funny, not at all," Arsen said. "They would have a hard time tracing my steps in the Bosnian mountains, where I was a soldier in the Royal Army. Even the communists who captured me did not keep track of my past sins after I returned home a few months later."

"You fought in World War Two?" the General asked.

"I was fourteen when I joined, and they captured me five months later."

"Amazing. That is another good reason to have you come to Moscow - to hear your war stories. Is that where you met Ivo Stipich?"

"No. We met in Banja Luka after the war. He was a soldier in the Communist Army."

The limousine was at the gate of the United Nations and proceeded to the main entrance. A doorman opened the car door, and the General and Arsen stepped onto the front walk. They were approached by a younger man who introduced himself as a member of the Space Committee.

"General Shagov, I am Robert Simpson. I talked to you about the appearance before the Space Committee."

"Hi, Doctor Simpson. Of course, I remember. This is Dr. Arsen Pankovich." The General introduced Arsen as an ethnic expert. "We have to see Mr. Enstrom before we go to the Space committee."

"I'll take you there. I didn't get your name, Dr.---?" He turned toward Arsen.

"Arsen Pankovich," the General interceded.

"Dr. Pankovich. Are you also from Moscow?"

"No, I am not," Arsen said. "I live in New York. I have recently joined General Shagov's group as an ethnic consultant at the Institute for Ethnic Studies in Moscow."

"Now I understand. Will you be working at the U.N. in some capacity?" Dr. Simpson asked.

"Not presently," Arsen said.

As they exited the elevator Dr. Simpson pointed to the door of Mr. Enstrom's office. They entered a small reception room where the secretary, sitting behind a desk, greeted them.

"Good morning, gentlemen. Oh, good morning, Dr. Simpson." She got up from her chair and faced the three of them "You must be General Shagov. The Undersecretary is expecting you. How shall I introduce you?" She turned to Arsen.

"Dr. Arsen Pankovich. I am with General Shagov," Arsen said.

She knocked on the door, which had a clear inscription:

Mr. Goran Enstrom
Undersecretary for Technology and Space

They entered a large room and were greeted by a tall middle aged man who looked to be almost skin and bones. His face was long and narrow, forehead high, hair blond. A Swede and an intellectual, Arsen concluded to himself. Goran Enstrom got up from behind his desk to shake hands with them. He knew Dr. Simpson whom he addressed as Bob; he greeted General Shagov warmly. They exchanged the usual formalities, talked about the General's flight from Paris to New York. Arsen was beginning to think the meeting was a waste of time when the Undersecretary brought the issue to the right level.

"General, we have been studying your reports with great concern. I have been waiting to hear your report to the Space Committee and to have an opportunity to discuss the whole thing with you. If you are right in your observations, we have a major problem on our hands, and we will have to start thinking about how to deal with it." He looked at the General attentively.

"My findings have not changed, and they are only more confirmatory," the General said. "I wish I could report otherwise. As much as I have come here to present my views to the Space Committee, I am very interested in talking to U.N. officials, like yourself, about the problems we will soon have to face. We have to be prepared to avoid confusion and panic, which could destroy productive efforts for the future. My group has been concerned with problems like this one for a long time. Since we made the real observation, we have applied our ideas to the situation at hand. We think we know what has to be done, but we need support from the U.N. and the member countries. I hope to be able to discuss this further with you today or tonight. As you know, I am going to Washington on Thursday for the same reason. I will try to impress the officials at the U.N. and in Washington with the seriousness of the situation. I have a feeling my reports have been taken as science fiction and not as grave reality," the General concluded convincingly and with a very serious expression on his face.

Mr. Enstrom looked rather grim himself.

"We will find time tonight one way or another," Mr. Enstrom said. "Let me try to organize a dinner meeting here at the U.N. I will find out who can attend. I will let you know." He shook hands with the General and Arsen before they left. "Don't make any other plans for tonight. Who will attend with you?"

"Myself. Dr. Pankovich. Possibly our secretary, Sabrina..." The General hesitated, not remembering Sabrina's last name.

"Sabrina Harley," Arsen filled in.

"Yes. Miss Sabrina Harley. Three of us are enough. I will do most of the talking. Ha, ha." By laughing, the General was trying to improve the grim atmosphere that had developed unexpectedly.

Dr. Simpson reminded the General that it was time to go to the meeting with the Space Committee.

"Mr. Enstrom, I am very interested in the meeting tonight. Don't worry about food. We can always eat after the meeting. Isn't this a city that never sleeps? Fast food will always be available. I wish the Secretary General could attend. Unfortunately, he is out of town."

"That is correct," Mr. Enstrom said. "He went to visit Greece, Cyprus and Turkey to try the impossible - to persuade them to talk to each other. He is in Zaire now - hunting. We will keep him informed. I will see you tonight." They shook hands and Mr. Enstrom showed them out of his office.

They took an elevator to the floor where the Space Committee was holding the meeting. There was a large waiting room, well decorated, though too dark. The wall paper was dark, the furniture was black, the chairs and armchairs were covered with black leather and even the parquet, covered partly by a Persian carpet, was dark. Dr. Simpson asked them to sit down and wait a few minutes until the internal part of the Space Committee meeting was over. He entered the meeting room, as he was a member.

"Do you know these people, I mean the committee members?" Arsen asked the General.

"I know only Dr. White, the Chairman. The rest of them are not the top echelon of astronomers. Still, they are a tough group of people. I hear they are quite a knowledgeable group."

"What can they do to speed up recognition of the existing problem?"

"Their recognition and acceptance of our observations would influence the Secretary General. In turn he could appoint a panel of astronomers to study the phenomenon, or he could appoint a group of people with a variety of backgrounds who would recommend further actions. We don't need further studies, and our Space Committee is competent to make recommendations but in practice that may not be enough. What we really need is a group that would recommend changes in the Charter of the United Nations. We need a group that will bring into focus the problems we will soon face. These people should have broad powers in making decisions. Only a bold approach will result in a functioning board that is able to organize the anticollision effort and to set up boards which would deal with survivors and with preservation. We will have to repeat this frequently before it sinks into the heads of the delegates of most states and before we get any authorizations to do anything. Hopefully this will not produce disagreements on a large scale. Our only hope is their fear of the approaching calamity."

Arsen said nothing.

Dr. Simpson appeared at the door of the Committee Room and invited them to come in.

"I hope you did not mind waiting a few minutes," he said. "The meeting was about to adjourn when I went in and I just reported to the members about your meeting with the Undersecretary. Please, come in."

They walked into a large conference room which had been built to accommodate at least fifty people. To the left there was a long narrow table for the panel, which faced rows of chairs for those attending a meeting. At the far end of the table there was a lectern for speakers. The furniture was simple and elegant, though somewhat worn. The walls were covered with white paper sprinkled with almost imperceptible figures of various shapes and designs. A portrait of Dag Hammarskjöld, the late Secretary General, hung on the wall behind the table, where he looked with his inquisitive eyes at anyone seated at the table. It was an original painting, and Arsen thought it had probably been done by a well-known artist. On the wall just above the door to the room, a black square plate with two white clock hands was the face of an electric clock which had only white dots to indicate the hours.

Dr. Simpson led the General to the front of the table and introduced him to the members of the Space Committee.

"Gentlemen, this is Dr. Alexei Shagov, whom some of you have met previously and who needs no formal introduction. His associate, Dr. Arsen Pankovich, is an ethnic specialist. Dr. Shagov, I believe you have met Dr. White, the Chairman of the Space Committee, haven't you?"

"It's been a few years Allan, hasn't it?" The General laughed at that.

Dr. White got up and shook hands with the General.

"Quite a few, Alexei, quite a few," Dr. White confirmed with a smile. "I still remember our discussions at Oxford. Wasn't that in '68, or perhaps '67?"

"'68."

"I also remember our political battles and your arguments in defending Russia's ways. Things have changed, as you know."

"On both sides, for the better," the General said. "Now there is a new threat which makes the old East-West confrontations look like children's games. This is a peril of calamitous proportions."

Eyes turned to the General, and the room suddenly became quiet, as Committee members ceased talking to each other. Several people walked in and sat down, some of them with pads in their hands. Reporters, Arsen concluded, as he moved to the far end of the first row. Dr. White used his gavel to announce the start of the meeting.

"For the record, I would like to start the meeting. Today is the eighth of December of '97. The subject of the meeting is an inquiry into the recently discovered object in space, by the team headed by Dr. Shagov, which object supposedly has a trajectory that will bring it, or already has brought it, into a collision course with the Earth. Dr. Shagov wanted to address this body with an introductory statement. After that he will answer questions from the members of the Committee. There will be no questions from the floor, nor from the press. At one-thirty this afternoon there will be a press conference in this meeting room. Dr. Shagov and the members of the Committee will be available at that time to answer any questions. Leave written questions on this table at the end of the session."

The General started his presentation by addressing the Committee.

"Dr. White and members of the Space Committee," the General said. "The situation facing the World is, as I stated earlier, peril of calamitous proportions. My team in Russia has concluded that an object, presently far in space, is approaching the Earth. This object, possibly a planet, will collide with the Earth."

The General paused for a moment and took a sip of water. He wanted his initial statement to sink deep enough, and he made it primarily towards the audience which already filled half the room. He wanted to impress them.

"If we are right, and I can tell you that we are right, then we have a problem. We have calculated our data time and time again and obtained the same result each time. There is an object in space, call it a Demon if you wish, which is coming our way. I will present our data and our interpretations during the discussion with the members of the Committee. Now I want to state what the consequences of this phenomenon will or could be. A collision would destroy the Earth and everything living and non-living on it. We can only imagine how the Earth would look after the collision, as we would not be alive to see it. I think it is obvious that the calamity would be enormous."

There would now be a second pause, Arsen thought, so that the second part could sink in before he posed the main question: What next?

"Our group in Moscow," the General continued, "was working with hypothetical situations even before we stumbled across the real thing. The first problem facing us is how to convince the scientific community that we have a real problem, that there is an approaching object, and that we have to deal with it. So far as I know only my team and another observatory in Russia have detected and recognized the significance of this object.

"The second problem will be to determine the distance between the object and the Earth and the speed of the object, so that we can calculate how much time is left before the collision. This is important so that we can project what actually can be done in the remaining time period. Obviously, if we have only one year left, not much can be accomplished. Two years gives some breathing space; five years would be promising. Our calculations indicate about four years, although more work is needed to arrive to an exact figure."

The General paused again, almost as if to take a deep breath before he delivered the last part of his statement, the part Arsen expected to state clearly that he was the person who knew what to do and to outline his four point program. The General was now talking to a room filled to capacity. Arsen saw television cameras in the waiting area when the door opened for a moment. How had they found out?

"Our third problem will be to establish a board, which will have broad powers to organize life on this planet so that everyone can contribute to the effort that will take all our energies for a few years until this business is either successfully completed or we all disappear in the collision."

There he went again, Arsen thought. He would now show everybody that he is ready to lead the world.

"Call it a board, call it a world government, call it anything you want. Just remember that time is short and the job ahead of us is enormous. Briefly, we have to resolve rapidly differences among the states of the world and among the peoples. We have to form a board that will direct the anti-collision effort. We need another board that will be charged with the preservation of the human race and the flora and fauna of the world - and we will be lucky if even Adam and Eve and an apple survive, although more than that is needed to sustain life. Oh, I did not mean to advertise Mac computers."

There was laughter in the room. The General dried his forehead with a handkerchief, and sipped water from the glass. The finale is coming, Arsen thought.

"We also need a board that will arrange for the liftoff into space of humans and of as many species and materials as possible in the remaining time. Just imagine serving on this board and asking yourself the questions: who, and then why?

"Finally, we have to choose leadership that will be capable of executing and completing this enormous task as efficiently as possible, and most important, as rapidly as possible.

"I must tell you, I am very, very concerned.

"I thank you for you attention."

The General returned to his chair in the first row. The room was quiet and gloomy. Dr. White's face was serious as he raised his rotund body from the chair to address the members and the audience.

"It is rather an ominous picture you painted, Dr. Shagov, and I most sincerely hope you are wrong. We should proceed now with the technical part of your observations. If you have any slides to show, please give them to the projectionist right now. The slides will be projected on the wall to your right. You may step up on the podium again, or if you wish you can stand on the left side of the table. We will ask questions, and you will have plenty of time to answer."

The General handed a few slides to the projectionist.

Arsen decided to skip the scientific part of the meeting and call Sabrina. As he walked out of the meeting room he faced several television cameras, reporters, technicians, and a whole crowd of support people waiting for the meeting to end so that they could interview the General and the members of the Space Committee. Arsen walked through the room and into the hall and called the office from a public telephone.

"The telephones have been ringing all morning," Michelle reported. "We had a call from Moscow and another one from St. Petersburg, and then one from Paris. Two newspapers called about an interview with you or with Gen. Shagov. MMC also asked for an interview. Sabrina talked to all of them. We tried to get in touch with you, but there was no response."

"I turned off my cellular phone since I could not answer it in the meeting room. Let me talk to Sabrina."

Sabrina answered her phone.

"Hi, Doctor. What's happening? We had quite a few calls today. I took care of everything."

"So I hear. Who called from Russia and Paris? What did you do about the interviews?" Arsen inquired.

"Ivo Stipich called. He needed some information. Then Mr. Fiodorov called from St. Petersburg and an astronomer from Paris; they wanted to talk to the General. As for interviews, I told them we would arrange something if you or the General had time tonight, which was what they wanted, or perhaps tomorrow. What do you think?"

"I will ask the General. Oh, before I forget, you were included by the General for the dinner-meeting at the U.N. tonight. We don't know what time it will be. Call the office of Undersecretary Enstrom, Goran Enstrom, in Technology and Space. His secretary should know something about the meeting. I will call you when I hear something."

"Doctor, another thing. I asked Ivo Stipich to send us information on people we will be dealing with within the Institute, like this Mr. Fiodorov. He promised to send enough info. You think that was okay?"

"Of course it was okay. It did not occur to me to ask," Arsen assured her. "Just keep things rolling. There will be a lot of activity around here, very soon. The General gave a good briefing to the Space Committee. I left when they started to talk astronomy - I know nothing about it. We may have to learn astronomy one of these days, like it or not. I will talk to you later."

"Okay Doctor."

Arsen called home. Nobody answered. Most likely they had gone to the Vertical Club, he thought. He gave up the idea of going out of the building to First Avenue when he remembered he did not have a pass for re-entry. He found a small cafeteria on the fortieth floor. He could not resist a bagel with cream cheese and a cup of coffee. The waitress asked him where he was from since she had never seen him in the cafeteria before. He explained that this was his first visit to the United Nations building.

"You will get used to the crowds," she assured him and confided that she had seen some very important people. "Their pictures showed up in the newspapers and on television."

"I don't plan to come here very often," Arsen said. "I doubt you will see my picture in a newspaper or on television. Of course, I am not a very important person. Not yet, anyway," Arsen concluded humorously.

The waitress waved at him scornfully as if to say: you're nuts.

Arsen enjoyed his bagel, which in his opinion was the best in New York, and looked at the panorama from the fortieth floor facing the East River. He was thinking about the events of the last few weeks, which had been changing rather rapidly his quiescent, though not dormant life. His lazy mornings spent often in total submersion in the depths of the daily newspaper reports, then copying the clippings for his ethnic files; or reading serious books which had an angle that could help in understanding ethnic problems; or even browsing through a magazine or two, often finding articles on subjects he had already read about in the papers; or browsing a new web site which had been recommended by someone; or checking his e-mail, so often full of junk mail; or learning the daily word from the Wordsmith. Life was clearly more enjoyable than it had been during his years of surgical practice. He was lucky to live in New York, where everything was almost around the corner.

Arsen looked at his watch: it was eleven-thirty and time to return to the meeting room where the Space Committee was grilling the General. Arsen had to push through the crowd of people milling around in the waiting room. The guard stopped him at the door, and he had to ask him to call the office of Undersecretary Enstrom to confirm that he was officially accompanying Gen. Shagov, to be allowed to enter the meeting room. Once in the room he saw that his chair was taken by a reporter, and there were no empty chairs around. A few people were standing behind the rows of chairs.

The General was explaining an equation to the members and they were listening attentively. When he finished his explanations, a flood of questions rained down on him. The General smiled and raised his arm to signal that he could not even hear all the questions, much less answer them. "Gentlemen, I will have to request that you ask questions one at the time. I must be able to think before answering. Dr. White, would you be kind enough to handle this?"

Time was flying, and the meeting was already half an hour behind schedule. Dr. White was not worried by the delay - he was ready to continue the meeting however long it took, and the General continued to answer questions. Finally the General summarized the meeting.

"I know that I couldn't give you all the answers you wanted, but I don't have all the answers myself. As you might have gathered, the main purpose of my presentation was to demonstrate to you that there is out there a large object which is moving in our direction and it poses a serious threat. I believe I showed that much. There are more data, but they are not as important. We need your approval and support to convince the U.N. and the rest of the world that what we are talking about is not just imaginative fiction but reality, with serious consequences for humanity. We offer not only the information we have accumulated so far, but our help and expertise in further clarification of the phenomenon, and particularly we offer our advanced knowledge in dealing with the problems which will have to be faced and hopefully solved if humanity is to survive on this planet. Thank you very much for giving me the opportunity to present this material to you."

The General bowed his head and stepped down from the podium. The audience of reporters and U.N. officials started to applaud, and they were joined by the members of the Space Committee.

Arsen approached the General, who was being bombarded deafeningly by questions from all sides.

"Arsen, the response was very good indeed and I think we are winning. This is our best chance."

The General then turned to the people who surrounded him and continued talking and answering questions. Dr. White led the General to the door, where they faced the television cameras and reporters.

"I understand that all of you want to talk to Dr. Shagov," Dr. White said. "He will be available for questioning at two o'clock right here. Let me just say that the Committee members and I were impressed with Dr. Shagov's presentation. Now let us pass through, as we have a luncheon to attend."

Arsen caught up with them by the elevator and Dr. Simpson entered the elevator as the door was closing.

The private dinning room was ready for them. They sat around the round table, which had been set for the occasion. Dr. White and the General sat next to each other and continued their conversation. Arsen sat next to Dr. Kyriakis, the Greek committee member. There was another chair reserved for Undersecretary Enstrom, who arrived soon after they were seated. Soft drinks were followed almost immediately by a bowl of hot and tasty chowder.

Dr. Kyriakis turned to Arsen and asked him about his origins.

"I suspect you are from Serbia, are you not?"

"I had the same idea," Undersecretary Enstrom said and joined the conversation. "'Arsen' is an Armenian name, isn't it?"

"Armenians think I am one of them," Arsen said. "Yet I was born a Bosnian Serb. Not a popular nation these days."

"Don't be paranoid," Dr. Kyriakis said. "A Serb, wherever he comes from, is always welcome in Greece. That is how it has always been. Common history has something to do with that, I guess."

"Greece is one of only a few places."

"Dr. Pankovich, I understand that you live in New York and work as an ethnic specialist," said the Undersecretary.

"That is almost correct," Arsen said. "I live in New York and I study ethnic problems intensely."

"Bosnia is fertile ethnic soil. Have you followed what has been happening there? Did you participate in the war?" asked the Undersecretary.

"No, I did not participate. Bosnian ethnicity is in my blood, and it does not need study. In Bosnia the soil is soaked with ethnicity, that is true, but so is the soil in Zaire, in the Middle East, in Greece, in Turkey, in Kurdistan, in Ulster, and in the territory of the Basques." Arsen paused to look at Dr. Kyriakis and the Undersecretary and they looked surprised. "Should I mention Muslim soil in Nigeria or China, or the soil in New York City, or Aboriginal soil in Australia? The soil is not much different."

"That is a rather forceful statement. Have you found any remedies for the situation?" asked the Undersecretary.

"That is a long story. I don't want to distract you from the astronomical question which brought us together. We could have dinner and continue this conversation."

"Call me at the beginning of January after I return from my Holiday vacation in Sweden," the Undersecretary said.

"Could I invite myself?" Dr. Kyriakis asked. "I have an interest in the subject."

"Excellent. I will make arrangements with your secretaries," Arsen said. This was the first step into the United Nations.

Broiled salmon with tartar sauce and a minimal amount of mixed vegetables was served. That was followed by chocolate pudding and coffee.

Undersecretary Enstrom announced that dinner was organized for eight o'clock in the dinning area one floor below. He said he was pleased with the list of those who had accepted. Fifteen people had been invited and all had accepted. The list included Dr. Shagov's team, Dr. White and all members of the Space Committee, and the Russian and Indian Ambassador. The Deputy Secretary General, too,had accepted in principle, although he had another meeting in the evening which he was planing to cancel. There was a remote possibility that the Secretary General would arrive in New York in time to attend the dinner. The Security Council had invited Dr. Shagov to present his material to them.

Time for the press conference came about quickly. As they entered the hall from the elevator, they faced a crowd of reporters who started asking questions as the television crews were filming. Dr. White and Gen. Shagov, the central figures in the event, deferred the answers for the press conference.

"Doctor White, we cannot get even to the door of the meeting room," a reporter shouted. "What do you suggest we do?"

"We didn't expect much interest by the media," Dr. White said, and they pushed their way into the meeting room, which was just as crowded. Dr. White stepped up to the podium and asked for attention. The Babel of voices in the room suddenly subsided.

"I will allow one camera with the crew in the room. The rest should be able to transmit simultaneously. Fifty reporters will be allowed to remain in the room. Please make arrangements so that we can get started."

Dr. White's firm voice indicated that he meant business, and after brief conversations some reporters left the room and others entered. The crew of one of the local television stations moved in with their camera and positioned themselves in a corner. Everything took only a few minutes as the reporters knew that otherwise the press conference would not take place. The meeting room became almost noiseless.

"I believe we are ready to start this press conference," Dr. White said and cleared his throat "I would like you to meet Dr. Alexei Shagov, a well-known scientist from Moscow, who has made news with his recent astronomical observations. His expertise extends to astronomy and computer sciences. He was a General in the former USSR, and I don't believe he is in active service today. He is the Director of the Institute for Interplanetary Research in Moscow and a pioneer in the study of hypothetical interplanetary collisions. As you will see, this has a considerable bearing on his actual observations in recent months.

"As you know by now, Dr. Shagov and his team in Russia have observed a large object in space which, in their opinion, is on a course toward the Earth. They think the collision of this object and the Earth will occur in a few years. Dr. Shagov is here on the invitation of the Space Committee which, let me remind you, has not concluded its evaluation of the information he has provided. Another fact is that, except for two observatories in Russia, no other observatory has so far confirmed Dr. Shagov's findings.

"Let me add one personal note before I submit him to your vulturous questioning. I met Dr. Shagov, then a young man, when he was a Fellow at Oxford. We were both studying under Professor Thomas, a brilliant theoretical physicist and part-time astronomer. I must admit now that I was impressed with the depth of Dr. Shagov's understanding of physics and astronomy, by his integrity and by his innovative mind. It seems to me that he has not changed much over the years."

Dr. White asked the General to take his place at the podium. Hands were already raised, and the grilling started. Dr. White pointed to a reporter sitting in the first row.

"I'm Brad Smith, MMC News in New York. General, are you really convinced that a planet, or a large celestial body which you called a Demon, is on its way to a *rendezvous* with the Earth?"

"Would I come here for the sole purpose of making a fool of myself if I were not convinced? I knew that I would have to deal with some outstanding people who would ask some tough questions, and I was right. I felt the weight of their questioning this morning."

"General, do you think they bought your story?" Brad Smith asked, and everybody laughed

"You know, Mr. Smith, this may be a story to the news media; it is hardly a story to the members of the Space Committee. For them my story meant data they had to absorb and evaluate. I doubt that they are ready to give an answer right now." The General was handling the reporters, and Dr. White relaxed in his chair.

"Thompson, *Chicago Star*. General, what is the next phase you mentioned? Do you want some body formed: a board or a committee, or something else? How soon do you want it?"

Arsen noted that they were calling him 'General.' That was what he would become in the world government, he thought. The General obviously was enjoying the show.

"I said it before. The next step is to organize the world. Call it World Government or United Nations, it is unimportant to me, as long as it functions in a world that is not at war and in which nations are not constantly quarreling with each other. The inner harmony of the world must be achieved.

"The first task of such an organization will be to create an Anticollision Board, which will be responsible for all research, and will have all necessary resources to plan and develop strategy and tools, to prevent the collision. We have advanced many ideas within our group, and we have a good idea of the direction that has to be taken.

"The second task is to create an agency which will be responsible for the survivors, if any, after the collision. Think of a few survivors among the dead. I tend to call it a mega funeral home, and you may want to call it a survival agency, if that is less offensive to you.

"The third major organization, a task force, will deal with preservation of everything that can be preserved in a designated place in space, humans included, of course. In the meantime the world has to function as if nothing unusual is happening; schools have to be functioning, and hospitals, and banks, and everything else. Life has to go on. This organization will have to take into account what people really want. In some way the major powers will have to stop telling everybody what is right and what is wrong."

The General repeated his story and his plan for the interval from the present time to the moment of collision. Listening to the General, Arsen realized that his ideas had sunk into his own mind.

As in the morning, for a few moments no questions were asked and nobody was talking. The silence in the room was like the silence in a concert hall between movements of a concerto. But it did not last more than a few moments, before it was exchanged for a further flood of questions.

"Fred McCollum, *Kansas City Chronicle*. General, you said that you have developed ideas which might help in averting the collision. Give us one example."

The General was manifestly pleased with this question, which gave him a chance to talk about the subject closest to his heart since he wanted to direct the research effort. He smiled at the reporter before he answered.

"Mr. McCollum, I will tell you about one of our ideas, which may not even be workable, though my engineers think it is possible. Just think of sending an advance, like scouts in the good old days, who would land on the Demon, examine it on the spot, and execute whatever it decided was necessary to change the course of this object. We have to determine if that can be done; we have to find out what has to be done; we have to decide who to send and whether they are willing to go to a certain death. We have to get them ready. The most important question is, do we have enough time to try it? Time is passing, as you know, and we have not yet even determined whether this object exists. What do you think, Mr. McCollum, what should we do next?"

The General surprised everybody in the room with his question. The reporters were supposed to ask questions not him. Mr. McCollum was not about to be disconcerted by the General's inquiry.

"It's clear to me what has to be done. If Hubble can't see your Demon, General, you may as well pack and go back to Russia to play with your toys. If Hubble finds it, well, you have a job to do. I will offer my help."

The General was taken by surprise. He looked helplessly at Mr. McCollum, then at Dr. White, and said nothing waiting for somebody else to speak. He did not have to wait long. MMC's Brad Smith stood up and raised his hand. The General waved to him to speak, and he did.

"General, I haven't heard anything more sensible than what Fred McCollum just said. I couldn't agree more. I, myself, will help despite what MMC may or may not think." He pointed to his chest with his right thumb. "We will push the scientists at Hubble to look and to give us an answer soon, so that this whole story can be forgotten, or if you're right,

General - and hopefully you are wrong - but if you are right I would help you accomplish the impossible task ahead, and I am sure the media would help, too."

Applause followed Brad Smith's statement, and a new Babel of noises among reporters made it impossible to understand what was being said.

Dr. White used his gavel and raised his voice in an attempt to bring order in the room. After a few minutes the room became quieter, though people were still talking to each other.

"Gentlemen, gentlemen," Dr. White exclaimed repeatedly. "Quiet, please. I think what just happened here was not appropriate. These were political statements, not questions at a press conference."

Brad Smith stood up again and asked to be heard. Dr. White reluctantly conceded.

"Doctor White, this is not politics; this is a survival instinct talking from my soul, since Gen. Shagov painted a bleak picture of survival of a few. Doctor White, have you talked to people at Hubble? What did they say?"

"Yes, I talked to them yesterday," Dr. White answered. "I am not at liberty to reveal the information they gave me. I'll--" He was interrupted by a sudden uproar of voices and booing in the room.

Brad Smith stood up again, and this time he turned towards his colleagues. He raised his hand asking for silence so that he could be heard. As the hubbub in the room was subsiding Brad Smith turned again towards Dr. White and addressed him with a dose of hostility in his voice.

"It's incredible that you should give us such an answer. Does that mean that the scientists at Hubble have discovered something, but you, Dr. White, are not willing or ready to tell us what they know. Let me speak for the media now, and I'm sure my colleagues will interrupt me if I'm wrong. This developing story or the phenomenon, as Gen. Shagov calls it, is not an ordinary event that can be shielded from the media and thus from the world. Everyone on this planet is, or soon will be, interested in what's happening. Since the beginning of history, that is since two humanoids faced each other in a test of recognition, there hasn't been a problem more significant for all humans than the one we may be facing right now. If a celestial object is on the way to a collision with the Earth, every individual on this globe will have the same feeling about it and the identical desire for the outcome of the threat. There will be no differences in opinions. Since we have the same interest without a single exception, and as there will be no spies by definition, what are the secrets, Dr. White? Why don't you tell us? I'm sure the General is interested too."

Dr. White's face was red and looked swollen, and his lips and the tip of his nose were livid. Arsen feared he would suffer a stroke on the podium.

In a few moments he composed himself and answered Brad Smith almost shouting.

"Scientists at the Hubble are working frantically to confirm Dr. Shagov's observations. Yes, they told me at noon today that they have seen the Demon. They asked me to postpone the announcement for a day or two to give them time to identify it completely and to calculate the interval to the impact. Did you want to hear the bad news, Mr. Smith? Now you have it - it's really bad."

The statement had a freezing effect; the reaction was complete silence. Nobody said anything, nobody moved head, or body, or arm, nobody coughed or swallowed saliva. A flying feather would have been heard or the sound of a needle falling to the floor. Only the sound of a helicopter, probably flying out of the heliport nearby, disturbed the silence. Dr. White's statement had been heard in the waiting room and in the hall. Reporters did not rush to the telephones, nor did they activate their cellular phones to report the news to their editors. Everybody was waiting for something to happen before disturbing this incredible silence. Several minutes passed before Dr. White's gavel snapped this group of people out its their frozen trance.

"This meeting is adjourned," Dr. White announced.

People began to move slowly out of the meeting room and a few of them managed to talk. The General asked Arsen to join him on the way out. He was talking with Dr. White and telling him that he would go with Arsen to the hotel to take a shower and change his shirt. As they were entering the hallway Brad Smith approached them.

"My apologies General, for doubting your observations. What will happen next?"

"You tell me. Nobody is prepared for this kind of news," the General answered and then, as if he suddenly had remembered, he asked Brad Smith, "Can you keep a secret if I tell you something confidentially?"

"It depends," Brad Smith answered seriously. "I'm a reporter and I collect and interpret news. If you insist, I will promise to keep the story until it's ready to come out."

"Okay, Brad. I would like you to join me and Dr. Pankovich at a dinner meeting which has been organized by Undersecretary Enstrom. The Space Committee will be there and some other people, and the Secretary General if he arrives on time from Africa. What do you say? Meet us in the lobby at the Plaza Hotel at seven-thirty and we will go together from there. It should be an interesting meeting in view of today's developments."

Brad Smith did not even blink when he accepted the invitation.

"See you at seven-thirty," the General said and he joined Arsen in the elevator, which took them to the main lobby. They walked out of the building and took a taxi to the Plaza Hotel. As they were walking into the hotel lobby, they were surrounded by a group of reporters, and several TV cameras were aimed at them.

"Here we go again," Arsen said. "Do you want to give them a statement or you want me to handle them? I could meet you in your room."

"I must go to the room and call Moscow to let them know what is happening. I must take a shower. It is five o'clock. I will see you in the room in half-an-hour?"

"I will be there."

Arsen turned to the reporters and asked them to quiet down.

"Gen. Shagov asked me to talk to you as he has some important business to attend to. I will answer your questions." While the General was retreating in the direction of the elevators, Arsen saw Sabrina coming into the lobby. She told him she had reserved a room for press conferences. She turned to the reporters and told them that there would be a press briefing in the Press Room on the other side of the lobby in about five minutes. Reporters and camera crews moved in that direction.

"Sabrina, I am really glad to see you. Do you know what is happening? The General presented his broad ideas to the Space Committee about the problems facing the United Nations and the world. During the press conference after lunch, Dr. White announced that the scientists working with the Hubble Telescope have seen the object the General was talking about. Things will be happening very rapidly from now on. You know about the meeting tonight. The General just invited Brad Smith, an MMC reporter, to join us at the meeting. Nobody knows that. I think the General wants Brad on his team. That is all, at the moment. Wait for me and we will go together to the General's room. I think we should arrange security for the General. Call Undersecretary Enstrom's office and tell them that I think the General should get security protection, something like the Secret Service. There are too many nuts in the world."

Arsen went to the press room. The room was big enough to accommodate the reporters and two cameras. There was a lectern with a microphone.

"Gentlemen, my name is Dr. Arsen Pankovich. I joined General Shagov's team recently as an Associate for Ethnic Problems. Now I am serving as his temporary press secretary until a permanent one is appointed. Let me bring you up to date. As you know, the General and his team of astronomers discovered an object which the General coined a Demon and which may be the size of a planet. The object is somewhere in space, certainly beyond our solar system, and it is approaching the Earth. The General came to New York to appear before the Space Committee of the United Nations to explain his recent findings. His reception was enthusiastic, we thought. Moreover, Dr. Allan White, the British Chairman of the Space Committee, announced at the press conference this afternoon that the scientists working with the Hubble Space Telescope have identified the object and thus have confirmed the General's discovery in Russia. That is the bottom line. I would be glad to answer your questions."

"Scott Kingsley, *The London Vanguard.* Dr. Pankovich, the rumor is that Brad Smith has joined the General's team. What can you tell us about that?"

"We already have rumors, do we? Gen. Shagov asked Brad Smith to join him tonight at the dinner at the United Nations. There was no mention of joining the General's team. Brad Smith should be in the lobby here at seven-thirty. Ask him the same question."

"Prabash Chand, *The Star of India.* Dr. Pankovich, what do you think Brad Smith's role would be?"

"Could you think of a better public relations man? As a member of the team he could, and I am only guessing, promote the General's ideas. He could do that effectively in the U.N. As you can imagine there will be differences of opinion about the direction to take to avert the collision. The General will be in the forefront since his group is years ahead in research and he has expertise and extensive experience in astronomy and computer sciences. The Demon was not discovered accidentally; they have been looking for a threatening celestial body for years. I am sure the General will have a role in the immediate efforts to organize the research network and in subsequent navigation of the research aimed at deflecting or destroying the object."

"Peter Kortig, *Die München Zeitung.* Dr. Pankovich, you deal with ethnic problems. What are the ethnic problems in this situation?"

"I expect ethnic problems to erupt unless something is done to forestall them. The General indicated that one of the contingency plans will be preservation of people in space. Priorities regarding selection of people for preservation will have to be determined, and they will depend on ethnic origins, educational background, age and sex. Ethnic groups will have to be at peace in order to participate in decision making on priorities. That is a long story and I will stop right here. Who is next?"

Questions were asked and Arsen answered them. He followed the General's ideas as he understood them. There had been no time to decide beforehand what should or could be said. It was close to six o'clock when Arsen decided to end the press conference.

Sabrina was waiting for him.

"Things are under control," she said. "Security will be in place before we leave the hotel tonight. A limousine will be waiting for us at a quarter to eight."

"Let us go and join the General. He should be getting ready for the dinner by now. Thank you for taking care of everything." Arsen thought that hiring Sabrina had been one of his best decisions recently.

When they knocked on the door of the General's room, he answered promptly. His shirt was outside his trousers, and he still needed a tie and a jacket. As he was going toward the bathroom, he told them he had watched Arsen's press briefing.

"You did a good job. That piece on Brad Smith was excellent. I couldn't have said it any better myself. What do you think about Brad Smith? Should I try to persuade him to join us? We will need all the support we can get, and particularly someone who knows how to analyze the news, and how to present it. He seems to be very popular with reporters. Did you notice the applause he received when he made the comment after that reporter from Kansas, McCollum, suggested I pack up and go back to Moscow if the Hubble people did not find anything or that I lead the effort if they found the Demon. What do you think, Arsen?"

"I think you should grab him before someone else does," Arsen said. "I am sure the race is already on for the leadership in the world government. I will bet you that the Secretary General will make the meeting tonight."

"I think so too," the General said.

Sabrina turned the television on. All news channels were rebroadcasting either the press conference at the United Nations or Arsen's press conference. Arsen was amused to watch himself on television.

"You must be Sabrina, who else?" The General said when he came back to the room. "I may have to take you on a permanent loan from Arsen. I will need much help, and soon. I talked with Kravchenko in Moscow. He and Fiodorov are flying to New York tomorrow and bringing two of our scientists with them: the astronomer Peter Volisnikov and the physicist Boris Plotnik. They speak English, thank God. I am not sure what we are going to do with them. We don't even have an office for them."

"I think we do," Sabrina said. "I checked and found out that our present office is expandable, as two adjoining offices are empty. I saw the offices this morning; they looked good and we could move in any time. I will have to get some furniture, telephones and the rest. I talked to a secretarial employment agency, and I will be able to interview several applicants for the job. Do they need any special qualifications? How many do we need?"

"They must be intelligent," the General replied.

"General, I was thinking of using one suite for you and your staff; the second suite could go to the two gentlemen you mentioned, Kravchenko and...

"Fiodorov," the General interjected.

"Yes, Fiodorov," Sabrina continued. "The third suite would be used by the two scientists. Would that be okay with you?"

"Are you throwing Arsen out of the office?" the General asked.

"No, not really," Sabrina said. "He should have an office and a secretary in your suite as long as you need him as a press secretary. Once the permanent secretary is appointed, the Doctor should have an office of his own. They may have something for him one floor below. It may not be such a bad idea to have the Ethnic Office in that area. I could make the arrangements in the morning."

"I give up," the General said. "I will let you decide on that."

"What are our plans for tomorrow?" Arsen asked the General.

"We are in the limelight now because of the discovery of the Demon and we have a chance to lead the world government. We shouldn't blow our chance. We must keep repeating that our research is quite advanced and that we know how to handle the events we should soon face. We will not appear before the Security Council, and we must insist on presenting the problems and issues to the General Assembly, which should be asked to act immediately. The Security Council would play the usual power game, and we would be left in the cold for months. We must bypass the Security Council. The Secretary General would be able to help if he wanted. He will probably try to lead the United Nations by himself. I will try to talk him into arranging a session of the General Assembly in a day or two. Brad Smith could help by explaining to the delegates in the General Assembly the need for an early decision. He should know how to lobby for us."

"What about your trip to Washington on Thursday?" Arsen asked.

"Cancel everything, I am not going," the General said.

"I will take care of that," Sabrina said

The phone rang.

"General Shagov's suite," Sabrina answered. "This is Sabrina Harley. May I help you?" She listened for a moment. "Okay, come up. Room 812." She hung up and turned to the General. "That was Brad Smith. He is coming up. Do you think we'll be late for dinner?"

"We will be late, period," the General said. "No excuses. That dinner had better be short. We will eat and run unless something important develops. Let's hear what Brad knows."

The telephone rang again. Sabrina answered and just said to let Mr. Smith come to the room.

"What was that all about?" the General asked.

"Nothing special, General. Security wanted to know whether they should let Brad co me in here."

"We already have security?" General was surprised. "Who arranged for that?"

"Sabrina and I thought it would be necessary to have security," Arsen explained. "People at the U.N. thought the same. Security is evidently in place. It was arranged by Undersecretary Enstrom. He has been very cooperative and he understands the gravity of the situation. I wonder if we should ask him to join the team. What do you think, General?"

"Not a bad thought," the General said. "Why don't you ask him tonight? I saw you talking to him at lunch - you seemed to be having a friendly conversation. I have a better idea. Let us invite Undersecretary Enstrom and Brad Smith to a meeting with us tonight."

There was a knock at the door. Brad Smith walked in looking angry.

"I didn't anticipate reporters knowing I would be in the lobby tonight. Dr. Pankovich, there was no reason to tell them. It was unnerving to be asked about my role in the U.N. Government. I know nothing about your team, General -- I mean a political team. Do you have one?"

"Do you think I need one, Brad?" the General asked.

"If you're interested in taking the leadership of the world government, you should have a political team right now. Tomorrow there will be many hats in the ring, all political and tossed in by people who had not given a thought to the object even this morning. They will have seen the opportunity after your talk this afternoon. Actually, I have already had several calls which you could call invitations to join the team. One call came from our State Department, one from a French ultraconservative party, and another from a friend in South Korea."

"Let me make the fourth offer," the General said. "Brad would you join my team?"

Brad Smith looked surprised and he scratched his chin.

"General, I said this afternoon I would help, and I meant it. It would be much easier for me to withdraw from the game and spend the remaining time thinking and enjoying life while the race for survival was unfolding around me. I am not convinced that humanity has a chance of survival. There are things that could make a difference to people before the ultimate end. I would like to make my contribution. I also think that you, General, are our best chance and that I can trust you. So I accept your invitation."

This was a very dramatic moment. The General stepped up to Brad Smith, shook his hand, and embraced him. Arsen was sure the Russian triple bear kiss would follow, and it did.

"Now we have to face the world of politics," the General said. "Let us go to the United Nations. All of us know what the goal is, and we should try to work for it tonight. Brad, Arsen will try to persuade Undersecretary Enstrom to join the team. Do you have any objections?"

"Goran Enstrom is an excellent man," Brad Smith said.

They put on their overcoats and left the room. In the lobby a group of reporters was waiting for them.

"We are late for the United Nations," the General said. "I will answer only one question. What is it?"

"Has Brad joined you, General," a chorus of reporters called out.

"He most certainly has. Good night, gentlemen."

The limousine took them to the United Nations. They noticed many police cars in the streets leading to the U.N. Plaza and surrounding the main building.

"Security is the word, and unfortunately the necessary one, although all humanity has a *rendezvous* with death on the same day," Arsen said.

Nobody else made any comments.

They were twenty minutes late, and the General's appearance was being awaited with a dose of impatience. Undersecretary Enstrom was waiting in the lobby.

"Welcome back, General," he said. "We want to see you and talk to you, and there are some announcements to be made. The political game is on, don't you think? Let us go to the dinning room." They shook hands cordially.

The large dining room was brightly lit by four chandeliers and a number of wall fixtures. A round table in the middle of the room was covered with a tablecloth, and plates, silverware and glasses were in place. There were fresh flowers at the center of the table. A cocktail bar was in one corner next to the door to the kitchen, and there was another door at the opposite end of the room.

Sabrina and Arsen went to the bar and both asked for the same drink: virgin tonic water with a twist of lime. Arsen introduced Sabrina to Dr. Kyriakis and left them to arrange a meeting with Undersecretary Enstrom. As they settled in the adjoining room Arsen explained the reason for the meeting.

"The General wanted to let you know what is happening in his camp, although he thought it would be impossible to have a private meeting with you here. The General wants to push for an immediate reorganization of the United Nations, and he wants to lead the World Government. He wants to assemble a group of competent people who would take the key positions in his organization and to submit to the General Assembly his plan for organization of the anticollision effort; he is confident that he can get their approval. The General asked me to talk to you and to find out if you would be interested in joining his team. Also, he wanted to invite you to a meeting tonight at his suite at the Plaza Hotel. I would like to get some notion from you as to your reaction to this idea."

"I would be interested in joining, as I see the General as the best qualified individual to lead the world at this difficult time," the Undersecretary said.

"Come to the Plaza Hotel after dinner tonight." Arsen squeezed his arm as they were heading back to the dining room.

Arsen looked around the dining room. The General and Brad Smith attracted most of the attention, and both of them were busy talking. Sabrina was still talking to Dr. Kyriakis. Arsen noticed Dr. Simpson standing alone.

"Hi, Doctor Simpson, you seem to be deep in thought. What is on your mind?"

"Just thinking of today's events. We've got a colossal problem ahead of us. That's disturbing to everybody, I'm sure. The only positive aspect is that all of us want the same thing - removal of the common threat."

"What do you think of Gen. Shagov?" Arsen asked.

"He was roasted today and he held up very well," Dr. Simpson answered. "Confirmation from the Hubble group was a big boost for his case. He will now have to tell us what to do next. Obviously, he's ahead of everybody - years ahead - and we have no time to waste."

Arsen realized that Dr. Simpson's impressions might also represent the opinion of other people. The idea was clear. 'The General is years ahead' was the motif to be used and repeated until it sank into everybody's mind. 'The General is years ahead' sounded impressive. There was no time to waste.

Undersecretary Enstrom asked for attention and invited everybody to take their seats around the table.

"Ladies and Gentlemen," he began. "Today's date would be a historic date if it weren't for the possibility that humanity might disappear and effectively end history not in the Hegelian sense or in the communist misconception, but an absolute end of everything. Everybody was praying that Gen. Shagov was wrong in his observations and calculations. But the report by the Hubble group confirmed the existence of the object in space, a Demon as the General called it, which is on the way to collide with us. You are aware of these developments. We are here tonight to discuss what is ahead of us and what should be done in the immediate future.

"Let me tell you what I see as an urgent matter," the Undersecretary continued. "Since this vitally concerns every living soul on this planet, every one of them should be represented when the decisions are made. The United Nations is the only viable organization which represents, however imperfectly, the population of most of the world. This is the place to start. Therefore the General Assembly of the U.N. should be called into session on Wednesday. Wednesday was chosen to allow the high officials of most of the countries to arrive in New York for the occasion. Invitations will go to a few countries which are not members, and we will recommend that they be admitted without any delays. My office has talked to most of the Ambassadors to the U.N., and they wanted a special session to be held on Wednesday. They agreed with the proposed agenda and agreed to vote for it before the session begins. The following agenda was proposed:

1. Statement of facts by the General Secretary, by the President of the Assembly and by Dr. Allan White, Chairman of the Space Committee.

2. Voting to hold the special session.

3. Procedural proposals from the floor and any other business.

4. Introduction of General Shagov, and his address to the Assembly.

5. Additional speakers will be selected.

The Assembly will adjourn at noon to allow regional meetings to take place.

Each continent or region will choose a representative who will present the consensus of that region. There will be speakers from the following continents or regions:

South America

Mexico, Central America and the Caribbean Islands with
 Cuba

Southwest Asia including Turkey and the Turkish part of
 Cyprus

South Asia

East Asia and Taiwan

Southeast Asia

Australia, New Zealand and Oceania

North Africa

Central and Western Africa

Southern Africa with Madagascar

North America and Western Europe including Slovenia,
 Croatia, the Czech Republic, Poland, Hungary and the
 Baltic Republics

Russia and the Eastern and Southern Orthodox Countries
 including Greece and the Greek part of Cyprus

Israel and the Palestine Authority

Each region will be provided a room, and will given about
 four hours for discussion.

4:00 pm Recommendations to the Assembly from the representatives of the regional groups. Each speaker will have fifteen minutes for his presentation.

9:00 pm Reassembly for possible further discussions, voting etc.

Could the Space Committee meet in the morning and come up with the recommendations by noon? Dr. White would that be possible?"

"It will be done," Dr. White replied.

Undersecretary Enstrom announced that dinner would be served momentarily. Almost as if they had been waiting for the nod from the Undersecretary, waiters started serving dinner. The food was simple, just as the General had wished: green salad with Italian dressing, filet of beef with a baked potato and vegetables, and fresh French bread. Red California wine was served during the dinner and coffee at the end.

Conversation was subdued, as if everyone were emerged in her or his own thoughts. Arsen was sitting between Sabrina and Dr. Kyriakis on his left, and Brad Smith on his right. Sabrina was explaining to Dr. Kyriakis what it took to set up and run an office in New York, and her recent experience. Dr. Kyriakis was surprised that the General already had an office in New York, and Sabrina assured him that the General was ahead in everything, not just in space research. Brad Smith asked Arsen if he liked his new job of press secretary.

"Not at all," Arsen said. "I hope it will be a short-lived assignment. It is not for me."

"What are you going to do, once a press secretary is appointed?" Brad Smith asked

"Wait, I guess, like everybody else," Arsen said.

"Wait for what? For the collision to occur, as I was planning to do?" Brad Smith challenged him.

"Maybe that is what I shall do, if they don't find something else for me to do." Arsen was annoyed by Brad Smith's questioning. "Maybe I will take up Orthopedics again."

"You're an orthopedist?" Brad Smith looked surprised and perplexed. "An orthopedist, really? Orthopedists are supposed to take care of broken bones and arthritic joints; they are not concerned with cosmic problems, are they?"

"No, they are not, unless somebody breaks a bone up there," Arsen replied. "The way things are developing, many bones will be broken. They may need me, who knows."

"Seriously," Brad Smith asked, "what would you want to do?"

Brad Smith had not grasped the General's master plan, yet.

"The General feels, and I agree with him, that ethnic problems will not disappear with the threat we are facing, although the threat will be the same for everybody." Arsen decided to give a brief lecture to Brad Smith on ethnic problems and their magnitude. "As you can imagine all states will be involved. Large states and big powers will assume that they will lead the world. The big powers will expect the largest share in decision making and later the largest share of the benefits for their populations. That will just not happen. There will be no preferences of Tutsi over Hutu in Africa, nor French over Germans in Europe, nor Japanese over Koreans nor Chinese over Tibetans in Asia, nor Americans over Indigenous Indians, nor Christians over Muslims, nor whites over blacks or yellow people. The world will be led by the best, presumably the best, and the seat of power will be in the United Nations and not in Washington or in Beijing or in Moscow. Do you know what I mean? I would like to help in that effort, which will require speed, determination, impartiality and fairness. Remember liberty, equality and fraternity? We must avoid brutality at all costs and never forget humanity, which we are trying to save."

Brad Smith remained silent for a while.

"I'll have to keep that in mind," he then said. "You seem to know what's on the General's mind and I don't. I'll have to find out."

The meeting was winding down, and people were getting up and walking around. Nobody waited for dessert to be served. The General was having a friendly discussion with his old friend Dr. White. As they parted, they held hands, and the General said to Dr. White, "Allan, these are hard times. I am trying to bring together a group of individuals who would lead the efforts that are ahead of us. I only wish I could enlist your support and participation in this group."

"Alexei, I thought you had gotten my message before I introduced you this morning. I trust you, and I cannot say that about many people. I think you should be at the helm of the effort and of the Government or the Board of Directors or whatever is going to be formed in the next few days. I will support you in that."

"Thank you, Allan," the General said. "If you are not too tired tonight, I would like you to join a small group in my room at the Plaza Hotel. Would you come, please?"

"Who's tired on a day like this? I'll be there in an hour; I have something to finish in my office. What's the room number?"

"812," the General said. "See you there."

Sabrina, Brad Smith and Arsen joined the General in the limousine back to the Plaza Hotel. The General told them that Dr. White would join them later, and Arsen reported the same for Undersecretary Enstrom.

In front of the hotel reporters were waiting again. Arsen was ready for them.

"Gentlemen, let me explain what is going on. General Shagov has no time to talk to you now. As you know, there was a meeting at the United Nations, hosted by Undersecretary Enstrom. It was an informal gathering, and nothing of essence was discussed. The Undersecretary announced that a special session of the General Assembly, requested by many delegations, has been called for Wednesday at nine in the morning. I am sure many dignitaries will soon start arriving in New York. You may want to rush to the airports to meet them."

"Dr. Pankovich are there any meetings scheduled for tonight? Someone mentioned a special interview with the General," a reporter asked.

"No interviews tonight, as far as I know," Arsen said. "There will be a meeting in the General's room in a little while --"

Arsen was interrupted by the uproar of voices asking who would attend.

"If you will only let me talk... It is not a secret. As you already know, Brad Smith has joined the General's team. He will be there. We also expect Undersecretary Enstrom and Dr. White to be at the meeting. The topic? Can you guess?" Arsen was prodding the reporters and they laughed in return. "Find a warm place and drink some tea, or go home. Nothing much will happen here tonight." The reporters laughed again.

"Dr. Pankovich, is the General planning to propose some sort of world government in his speech Wednesday?" another reporter asked.

Obviously, they had seen the schedule proposed by Undersecretary Enstrom.

"The General thinks, as he said this afternoon at the United Nations, that we must have a functioning board or a government immediately, and that we must start preparations for an all out anticollision effort without delay. As you know, not much time remains before the collision. I think Undersecretary Enstrom had the same thing in mind when he responded to calls for a special session of the General Assembly." Arsen had decided to promote the General's candidacy if the right question were asked, and he did not have to wait long.

"Will the General be a candidate for President of the World Government?" asked a reporter.

"Do you know a better-qualified person?" Arsen snapped back, satisfied with his political ploy. "The General is years ahead of everybody in anticollision research and there is no time to waste." Dr. Simpson said it right, Arsen thought, as he waved to the reporters on his way to the lobby.

Security was less conspicuous than earlier in the evening. He went to the concierge's desk and asked where he could find a security agent. He was told there was one in the lounge on the eight floor, and one in front of the hotel.

The man at the desk started a conversation. "Doctor, does anybody know what will happen next? We hear rumors, and they're pretty wild, like the Earth will be attacked by Martians, or that we we'll be hit by a planet or something. People are getting nervous. I figure whatever happens I can't change it. But it would be good to have someone like the General to take care of things; people would be less afraid. Do you think he'll get the job?"

Arsen was not entirely surprised. The city and the world must have been talking about the Demon and the General who had discovered it, and of the approaching calamity. Arsen also noticed a newspaper on concierge's desk with a headline across the top of the page

GENERAL SHAGOV WAS RIGHT: HUBBLE CONFIRMS DEMON EARTH IS THE TARGET

"It is very difficult to say who will get the job," Arsen said. "I will tell the General what you said. He will like it I am sure."

"Good luck and good night," the man said.

The security agent in the lounge on the eight floor knew about the visitors they were expecting. The man nodded that he knew what to do.

Sabrina opened the door of the General's suite. Arsen went to the bedroom and called Nada to let her know what was happening. She told him she was watching television and that she had seen him several times.

"Even our doormen were asking about you," Nada said. "They could not believe you were involved. They thought you were retired. Even the President of the Board called to express support. The Board's concern was the probable increase in visitor traffic and the security of the building. A television station wanted to install a camera in the lobby. The Board President turned them down but wanted your opinion."

"No cameras in the lobby. Nobody should be allowed into the building, if the doorman doesn't recognize the person. Tell them that official business will be conducted from the office. The security service may check the building at some point. How are you and Mom? I will not be going to Puerto Rico with you, as you have probably guessed already."

"I am not too worried," Nada said. "Mom is with me so I am not alone. I talked to the children today. They are confused and worried. By now they have heard you on television."

"There will be a meeting in the General's room in a few minutes," Arsen said. "Call me if you need me, you have the number. I will see you later."

Arsen walked into the living room where the General and Brad Smith were discussing the strategy for the next few days.

"Undersecretary Enstrom has done an excellent job in arranging for a special session of the General Assembly," Arsen said. "He must have done it with the approval of the Secretary General."

"I would not be so sure," the General said. "The Secretary General was out of town. We don't know whether they talked. Maybe they did not."

"You may be right," Brad Smith speculated. "I heard he was out somewhere in the boondocks of Zaire, supposedly hunting. It's possible he won't be reachable for a day."

"He will be in New York tonight, you will see," the General said. "Anyway, wheels have started to roll and that's all we need."

"I wonder what the Secretary General has to say," Arsen said. "It would be important to find out what different delegations will do and where they stand. Many of them will talk to their traditional allies."

"I know for a fact that the Americans have already talked to the British about the situation and they are working on a joint plan of action," Brad Smith said. "The Security Council might be a problem, because they may try to delay the special session to give their governments more time for maneuvering and regrouping. My guess is that the Assembly will want to know right away what has to be done to organize the anticollision effort."

"We must make sure that the special session is held on Wednesday and that only the Secretary General can change the proposed agenda," Arsen said. "The big powers will be a problem. They will take the initiative and try to subvert the Assembly. Their best shot is to ask the Security Council to look into the problem of anticollision and to make recommendations to the Assembly. In the Security Council the big powers can play their own game. Forget about the ethnic solutions and the ideas about preservation you proposed. We must persuade the Secretary General to come see you tonight if he returns to New York."

"Or we will go see him," the General added.

"No," Brad Smith insisted. "He must come to you. Besides, I don't see what the hurry is? I disagree with Arsen." The General realized he had acquired two advisers who already disagreed with each other and that there was even a degree of hostility between them.

The telephone rang, and Sabrina answered it. "Let them in," she said to somebody. She had time only to announce that Undersecretary Enstrom and Dr. White were coming, before there was a knock, and she opened the door to let them in.

The two men were opposites. The Undersecretary was tall and bony, and his long face was crowned with thick blond hair. Dr. White was somewhat short and slightly obese, his face was rotund and he had no hair on top of his head. The Undersecretary was looking down, and Dr. White up, when they talked to each other. A funny-looking couple, Arsen thought. They greeted the General and Brad Smith and sat down on the couch.

"I am sure both of us could use a drink, after a day like this,"

Undersecretary Enstrom said. Dr. White just nodded in agreement.

"Gin, Vodka or Scotch?" Sabrina asked "That's all we have."

"Gin with water, on the rocks," Undersecretary Enstrom said.

"Scotch on the rocks," Dr. White requested.

"Goran, we were trying to figure out who thought of the special session, and who approved it," the General said.

"I thought of it this afternoon," Undersecretary Enstrom said.

"Excellent idea," the General said. "What is the Secretary General going to say?"

"Not much," the Undersecretary said. "He and I rarely argue and he relies on my opinions and judgment. By now he has received the letter that went out, and if he objected he would have let me know, I am sure."

"You think he would support the General's candidacy?" Brad Smith asked.

"Hard to say," the Undersecretary answered. "He will probably consult with his friends in India and try to influence them to vote with us. He is an astute politician, a bit weak in his own opinions, but he knows how to position himself on the winning side." At that moment the telephone in the Undersecretary's pocket rang, and he immediately answered it.

"Speaking of the devil," the Undersecretary whispered.

"Rama, where are you? In New York, in your apartment? Listen Rama, General Shagov has a few people in his room at the Plaza Hotel. He has asked me repeatedly about you. He wants to meet you and to talk to you. Why don't you come over? I will wait for you in the lobby. Okay?" The answer was positive, and the Undersecretary smiled; then he listened for a few minutes.

"What did I tell you," the Undersecretary exclaimed when he had hung up. "He already talked to people in India and they advised him to stand behind you, General. This is a big victory. South Asia is behind you. Rama will be able to tell us about other Asians. He will be here in half an hour."

"This sounds like election night," the General said. "We are counting votes."

The Undersecretary went to the lobby to wait for the Secretary General. The General went to his bedroom to refresh himself. Dr. White was talking to Sabrina. Arsen and Brad Smith looked at each other and smiled. There was still some tension between them.

"Aren't you excited about all this?" Brad Smith asked, sipping his drink.

"I am very happy for the General and for all of you," Arsen replied. "You are in a winning boat and a big job is ahead of you."

"But you 're not in the boat yourself, are you?" Brad Smith asked.

"I am in the boat all right, but my time has not come yet. I will have to wait until the question of ethnic groups comes up. Then I will have something to say. Until then I will help as much as I can."

"Some important jobs would be yours for the asking, and you're not interested?" Brad Smith prodded further. "Why don't you let the General decide what you should do and how you should help?"

"The General gave me my assignment already," Arsen said. "I will direct the ethnic effort in the Balkans and South West Asia. That is a big job, and it will have to be done right, and quickly. I am looking forward to getting started. It will keep me out of the Big Apple for a while. The only regret I have is that the General has taken Sabrina from me on permanent loan. She is now his secretary."

Sabrina joined Brad Smith and Arsen.

"I thought I heard my name mentioned," Sabrina said as she sat on a chair next to the couch.

"I told Brad that you will be running the General's office," Arsen said. "You managed to be my secretary for about a week. Now I have to find a secretary for my office."

"Who says you'll have to find a secretary?" Sabrina asked. "You have one if you want her."

"You mean Michelle?"

"No, not Michelle," Sabrina said. "An old friend of mine, Victoria Ram, would take my job if you want her."

"An Indian?" Arsen asked. "When could she come to see me - tomorrow?"

"Tomorrow! I'll talk to her."

The telephone rang, and Sabrina answered it. Soon afterward the Secretary General, Rama Chand, and Undersecretary Enstrom entered the room. The General greeted the Secretary General.

"I have been looking forward to meeting you, Mr. Secretary. I appreciate your coming so late tonight and after a grueling trip. The situation is complicated, and the time left to us is very short. Please sit down. Can we give you something to drink?"

"Only tea, please," the Secretary said.

"As I said," the General continued, "the time is short and we need action in the United Nations. You are aware of the arrangements for a special session?"

"Yes, I am aware and I approve," the General Secretary said.

"What happens next?" the General asked.

"The situation is very delicate. As the Secretary General I represent the U.N. and I will do what the member States want. I am also an Indian and India is on my mind and in my heart. I have talked to the high officials of the Indian Government, and they asked me to tell you that the Indian Government and her allies will support you in organizing the world body which will be responsible for the anticollision effort. I am sure that the Indian Ambassador at the U.N. will be interested in talking to you."

The General was calm and he explained his position in a low but firm voice. "The time has arrived for us to state where we stand and what we are ready to fight for. As you might have gathered from my previous statements, there are three main objectives in our anticollision plan: research, care for survivors, and preservation in the space. We have one chance and a limited amount of time. As you know, my team is ahead of everybody, years ahead, and that should help the effort decisively and save precious time. Three provisions should be fulfilled.

1. There should be no inter-ethnic petty grievances, disagreements or wars. Every ethnic entity will be recognized as equal to every other ethnic entity, regardless of size, and each will be fully represented in the U.N. Assembly. By this definition each ethnic group will be sovereign in its own right.

2. A world military will be established by consolidation of the militaries of all states. A commanding general will be selected and approved by the Assembly. The sole purpose of the military will be to protect all ethnic entities and sovereign states, and thus preserve the peace.

3. The ultimate power in the world will be vested in the Assembly of the United Nations.

The people, once they comprehend the seriousness of the situation, may become uncontrollable. Panic, fear and anarchy could threaten the world, or apathy and economic disaster could result from an attitude of 'why bother before the disaster.' There should be a board or a department which would deal with problems of the people."

Nobody talked for a while. The message was sinking in, Arsen thought.

The Secretary General broke into the silence.

"Of all people we, the leaders, should not become depressed and desperate. I think the situation is under control. We should talk to representatives of all states and tell them what is happening."

Conversation turned to other subjects.

The Secretary General explained the Cyprus situation. No progress had been made, and he was frustrated. He lit up when he talked about the hunting safari in Zaire. "You interrupted my fun, General, with the celestial object you discovered.

"The Demon I discovered," the General said

The Secretary General said he had to leave, and asked Undersecretary Enstrom to go with him. "There are a few technical things we have to discuss."

After they left, Brad Smith made a comment that sounded strange to Arsen.

"You never know with these Indians," he said. "They tell you one thing then turn around and stab you in the back. I'm not sure we can trust him."

"He appeared friendly and sincere," the General said.

"I know. That's how they are."

"What about Goran?" the General asked Brad Smith.

"He seems to be okay, although the Secretary does not rely on his opinions - it is just the other way around. I would be cautious with him too, just in case."

This was unfair to both men, Arsen thought. What did Brad Smith have against them? They had shown clearly that they were aligned with the General. Hadn't the Undersecretary organized the special session, which gave a significant advantage to the General? Hadn't the Secretary General come to consult with the General? He had been told by the Indian Government that they would support the General. That could not have been a phony signal because it would become obvious the next day. Something was not right, Arsen thought. Could it be that Brad Smith was doing it for reasons of his own?

"It is late and I'd better go home," Brad Smith said. "Tomorrow will be another long day, I'm sure."

Arsen looked at his watch. It was twelve-thirty. There would not be much sleep this night, Arsen thought. The General asked Sabrina to list the people he should talk to in the morning. Sabrina was ready.

"Did you call Washington and cancel the visit?"

"Yes, I did."

"Good. I should talk to Ambassador Tolkunova - for courtesy reasons. The Russians will support me although they will not like military consolidation; they will fight us on that. Other big powers will fight us on that issue too. I would like to meet the Ambassadors from South America and China, and if possible, Japanese Ambassador Soto whom I met once in Moscow. If time permits, we could try someone from Southwestern Asia. There will be no time for anybody in the afternoon, but perhaps someone for a late dinner."

"Any contacts with Americans or Canadians?" Sabrina wondered.

"No, not yet. They will call eventually," the General said.

Arsen was uncomfortable, thinking about Brad Smith. This is my typical reaction - distrust, sort of a survival instinct, Arsen said to himself. The General suggested that Arsen accompany Sabrina to her apartment, then go home.

It was one in the morning.

"What time should I be here in the morning?" Sabrina asked the General

"Eight o'clock will be fine. See you in the morning." The General was dialing a number as they left the room and Sabrina and Arsen heard him talking to somebody in Russian.

"Try to call this friend of yours, Victoria; I would like to hire her. How does she look? Does she have two arms and two legs? I like to have a pretty secretary, and smart too."

"You'll have to appreciate Indian beauty. Her face is beautiful, and she keeps it that way. She's a bit plump; I say just a bit. That's appreciated in India, maybe not as much here except by blacks and some Asians. I'll ask her to come to the Plaza and be prepared to stay if she's hired. I 'm taking this taxi. See you soon." Her taxi drove away. Almost instantly another taxi stopped and Arsen got into it. He gave his home address and relaxed in the back seat.

.CHAPTER TWENTY

It was six-thirty. Arsen woke up Nada. He wanted to talk to her while he ate breakfast. He ran to take a shower. When he was coming out of the bathroom, he smelled the aroma of fresh coffee.

"I am still sleepy," Nada said. "I was watching TV to find out the latest news and I went to sleep late."

"What did they say?" Arsen wondered why they, in the General's room, had not listened to the news although they had been the makers of the news yesterday.

"Oh, they reported that many Heads of State started arriving in New York last evening. The Secretary General flew from Africa and met with the General as soon as he arrived. Many Presidents from neighboring countries have arrived. Everybody was expecting the Chinese, Russian and Indian Presidents. They also mentioned that the U.S. Government will insist on a delay in making any decisions about the future of the United Nations. The U.S. will use its veto in the Security Council to block any decisions."

"I am sure they will try," Arsen said. "They feel that if the General's proposals are approved they will lose their grip on the world. To change the topic - did you receive any calls from anybody?"

"First your phone was ringing and messages were recorded. Then my phone started to ring. I answered several calls then I stopped answering."

"Whom did you talk to?" Arsen asked.

"The State Department called then the White House," Nada said. "I told them I had no idea where you were, but that you had mentioned a meeting at the United Nations in the evening."

"Excellent answer," Arsen said. "I would have given them the same answer."

Arsen finished dressing.

"Unbelievable as it may sound, I am ready to go back to the battlefield. The next few days will be critical for the General, and for me too, now that I am on his team. I have no idea when I will be back. Bye-bye."

They kissed and Arsen left.

In the taxi Arsen looked at the newspapers. He could not believe the large headline.

> BRAD SMITH KILLED IN TRAFFIC ACCIDENT
> EARLY THIS MORNING
> HIT-AND-RUN CAR HAS NOT BEEN FOUND

This was unfortunate. Brad Smith was a well-known and popular journalist. His support of the General was important.

Nobody had called Arsen and he wondered if the General knew. He must have seen the newspapers or the news on television.

It was almost seven-thirty when Arsen arrived at the Plaza. The reporters rushed to ask their questions. There was not much to say, Arsen thought.

"Dr. Pankovich what's your reaction to the death of Brad Smith?"

"Tragic, very tragic day for the General's camp. Brad was one of you, and I met him only yesterday. He seemed to command respect among reporters. This is a great loss for our team."

"Have you received any information about circumstances, and who the hit-and-run driver was?"

"Nothing." Arsen did not want to admit that he had found out about Brad Smith in the newspaper.

"Dr. Pankovich, the Secretary General was seen entering the Plaza last night but he quickly disappeared in the elevator and we never saw him leave, though he was seen entering his apartment. He had nothing to say this morning. Could you tell us what's going on?"

"Your information is correct. The Secretary came to see the General and to meet him since they had never met. Undersecretary Enstrom was there too."

"Did the Secretary discuss the forthcoming Assembly meeting with the General?" a reporter asked.

"They did talk about the meeting. The General was pleased that the Secretary had moved quickly to organize the special session."

"Dr. Pankovich, the story is that Undersecretary Enstrom decided to arrange the special session and that he sent the invitations. Is that true?" another reporter asked.

"Do you really think the boss does not know what his staff is doing? Do I have to answer that? The Secretary told us he approved the special session. That is what he told us last night. Besides, almost all Ambassadors to the U.N. want the special session."

"Will the Security Council stop it? The rumors are that they'll vote against the special session at this time."

"I am not sure what is going to happen. I understand that special sessions have to be approved by two thirds majority in the Assembly. I don't know what the count is this morning."

"One more question Dr. Pankovich," a reporter asked. "Rumors are flying around wildly about many things. We would like to know what the General will propose at the meeting tomorrow. Will the General push to form a world government?"

"The General will say what he has been saying all along. As you know, his team discovered the Demon and he has been working for years on the problem we are now facing. The General's team is years ahead of everybody in research and in development of strategies and technology regarding anticollision. He will probably ask the Assembly for the confidence and the mandate to organize the anticollision effort. Gentlemen, I must leave you now - the General is probably wondering what happened to me. Thank you very much. Let me go through."

Arsen rushed to the elevator and up to the eighth floor.

"General have you heard about Brad Smith?"

"Yes, I have. It is terrible what happened to him. Unfortunately, life goes on despite terrible things. I think Brad was not sure which camp he belonged to. He called me last night after you left. He was confused, maybe he had drunk more than he could take, although I thought he was in fear of something. We talked, and he indicated that he was under pressure to leave our team. We will never find out what really happened to him. He was our friend and leave it at that. By the way, I told Rama Chand that you will be in his office by nine o'clock."

"What is the reason for our meeting?"

"Talk to him about the world government and try to persuade him to join our team," said the General. "It is extremely important that he joins us. The publicity alone would be a great psychological advantage."

"Okay. I will be there."

Sabrina walked into the suite.

"Good morning. I know I'm late, but I had a few things to do before coming here. Is there something I should know?"

Arsen told her what had happened to Brad Smith. Sabrina was stunned too.

The phone rang, and Sabrina answered it and gave the receiver to the General. The British Ambassador was on the line.

"Good morning, Ambassador Perkins, it is good to hear from you," the

General greeted the British Ambassador in a friendly voice.

Sabrina and Arsen went to the bedroom to discuss the plans for the day.

"The first thing to do is to take the adjoining room and expand this space," Arsen said. "The traffic will soon increase. Second, you should talk to Victoria - I have to see her—"

"She should be here in a few minutes," Sabrina interrupted, and added that Victoria would be ready to start immediately.

"We have to get an office manager for the General."

"I'll take care of that since I've been appointed 'the secretary on permanent loan.' I'll also get additional space in our present office."

"I have a feeling the General will be moving to the U.N. very soon or he will be going back to Russia, and we will be unemployed. Don't rent the office until we find out what happens in the Assembly in the next few days. We may not need the additional offices."

"Okay," Sabrina agreed and answered the phone. "Victoria is on the way up."

Victoria Ram did not sound completely Indian, but she was a beautiful Indian woman. She was in her mid-forties. Her skin was light brown and slightly shiny and that gave her face the impression of effulgence, and some sadness to her eyes. Her black hair was smooth and dense, and tied in a bun with a simple ribbon; she looked very orderly. Of medium height and very slightly plump, she fit the description Sabrina had so accurately given.

"Good morning," Victoria said. Arsen got up from the couch and shook her hand.

"I appreciate your coming so early," Arsen said. "A lot of work is ahead of us and I mean it."

"I know. Sabrina clued me in and I think I have a good idea of what's expected from me. I have time, and I can work long hours. And besides, I want to help in your effort. I am concerned, like everybody else."

The General walked into the room and Sabrina introduced Victoria as Arsen's secretary.

"Where do you find these beautiful women, Arsen," the General teased him, then he told them about his conversation with the British Ambassador. "He was not exactly nice, and his threats were veiled in diplomatic jargon. Nevertheless, I got the message: the British and Americans have talked and they want us to delay the special session. He was also concerned for my safety. I assured him that I would do whatever the Assembly wanted me to do. I told him my luggage was packed and ready for my one-way trip to Russia, if that was what they wanted."

As the Secretary General had predicted, calls were coming in from the Ambassadors at the United Nations, and the General was explaining to all of them his concern about the lack of time before the collision, his desire to lead the anticollision effort and his conditions.

Arsen called the office of the Secretary General and was told that the Secretary was eager to have a meeting with him. "I will be there soon," Arsen told the secretary.

Arsen turned to Sabrina. "Please find Paul, the concierge, and ask him to be around; He is a trusted person. If you want, hire him. He should set up a small bar for food and drinks in the new room. He should be responsible for the General's personal belongings here and at the U.N. Another thing, where will you lodge Kravchenko and Fiodorov? They will be arriving in New York this afternoon. I had better be off right now."

The General walked into the room. "You are still here, Arsen?"

"Rama Chand is expecting me in half an hour, I had better go." Arsen took his raincoat and the leather bag. "Victoria, you are going with me. "

In the lobby there was the usual crowd of reporters. Arsen brushed them aside.

"I am on my way to meet with Secretary General Chand. He wanted to discuss some problems concerning the special session."

"Dr. Pankovich, you mean there are problems?" a reporter asked.

"Have you ever found a quiet day in a world organization? Such organizations exist because problems and disputes exist. Why should it be different now?"

"Dr. Pankovich, which disputes are you referring to?" Arsen had been caught off guard when he mentioned the matter with Rama Chand. Now there was no way he could avoid answering.

"Gentlemen, you really want me to be late. The issue is procedural. The special session is scheduled for tomorrow. Some members would like to postpone it. Gen. Shagov is of the opinion that this should be decided by the Assembly. I have no more information. I must go right now."

As Victoria and Arsen were leaving the lobby, a reporter wanted to know which delegations had asked for postponement. Arsen did not turn back to answer.

Once in the taxi Arsen pulled the newspaper out of his leather bag to read the headlines and to find out what the media had to say about the events of yesterday.

GENERAL SHAGOV AND HUBBLE TEAM AGREE:
SOMETHING IS FLYING IN OUR DIRECTION - A DEMON
COLLISION AND CALAMITY IN A FEW YEARS:
NOT ENOUGH TIME TO GET READY
SECRETARY GENERAL ASKED TO CONVENE
SPECIAL SESSION OF ASSEMBLY

Almost the entire meeting of the Space Committee was presented, and particularly the end of the press conference, when Dr. White announced that the Hubble group confirmed the General's observations.

BRAD SMITH KILLED IN A TRAFFIC ACCIDENT
EARLY THIS MORNING

This was obviously an added last moment headline with only a short story.

GENERAL WANTS MEGA FUNERAL HOME
AND PRESERVATION BOARD
ETHNIC PROBLEMS LIKELY
BRAD SMITH JOINED GENERAL'S TEAM
THEN KILLED IN CAR ACCIDENT
SECRETARY CHAND AND GEN. SHAGOV MEET

Reactions from around the world were reported on the second page. That was essential now, Arsen thought. Enthusiasm for the special session was very high almost everywhere, particularly in India, China, Russia and South America. Reactions in Israel were mixed although obviously the Israelis were satisfied with the chance to present their views. North American and European opinions were subdued and essentially against the rush to reorganize the United Nations. Africans had many questions and wanted time for consultations, although they were not adamant against the scheduled session. Not bad, Arsen concluded.

Arsen's press conferences were reported on the third page. An accurate account was provided. He showed his picture to Victoria.

"I already saw the papers this morning," Victoria said. "The General was in the center of the first page and you were at his side; it was the same in all the papers, as if they were copying from each other. Other news was reduced to short notes. The General's biography was included, even yours but only in a short version."

The taxi pulled up in front of the main entrance to the United Nations.

Arsen and Victoria were escorted to the office of the Secretary General. He was in a meeting with several delegates, and his secretary suggested they wait in his office. Arsen was hungry and Victoria agreed to have coffee and a bagel. They went to the small coffee shop on the fortieth floor. The waitress recognized him from the day before. She shook her index finger scornfully at him.

"Yesterday you told me you weren't famous, and today I see your picture in all the newspapers. That was not nice of you." She laughed and asked for their orders.

"Bagel," Victoria and Arsen exclaimed. "Bring us some coffee too," Arsen added.

This was an opportunity to ask Victoria about her background and job experience, Arsen thought.

Victoria was not hesitant to talk about herself. She was proud of her Indian heritage. Her father was a Surgeon in California and her mother a gynecologist. They were getting ready to retire. Their families in India had a long tradition and a long line of professionals on both sides. The families had actively supported the independence movement and had worshiped Gandhi and Nehru. They had cooled off in their support of Nehru and the Congress party as they felt that too many people were killed during partition and that not enough was done to stop the massacres at least on the Indian side. They had also objected to Nehru's role in the split with the Muslims, which was often blamed for rioting -- caused by Muslims -- and the subsequent civil war.

Her parents had come to the United States in the early '50s, after they had obtained their degrees in India. Victoria had been born in India but had grown up in the United States. She visited her grandparents almost every summer and spoke the dialect of her family, and most of all she liked the country as her own. She had graduated from California State College in Santa Monica as an English major and had started graduate studies at Berkeley when she met her fiancé, an Indian, who was an exchange student working for his Ph.D. in Political Science at Berkeley. After graduation he had been offered a position in the Indian Delegation at the U.N., and he had moved to New York. She was in love with him, and pregnant.

"My situation was desperate," Victoria continued. "Kishan did not particularly care about the baby and pushed for an abortion. I was scared. It would have been an embarrassment for my parents if I had delivered a baby and had not produced a husband. My grandparents in India would have stopped dreaming about a rich husband from a good family for me. I could not disappoint them, and I agreed to have the abortion. I moved to New York, found a job - actually an excellent job - and settled down in the routine of the big city. To keep myself even busier I enrolled at NYU for a Masters Degree in business administration, which I received five years later. In the mean time, I have become used to the way of life I built for myself. I have had several offers of marriage, but I quit the relationships instead for my personal freedom. Now my parents are unhappy about my status as a single woman, my grandparents have died, and I go rarely to India because something has died in me with their passing, and I have no desire to be visiting other relatives, who live the secluded and relaxing lives of the very rich Indians.

"Sabrina has become a close friend. We get together at least once a month. After her unhappy relationship our friendship almost broke down. Her life changed when you offered her the job. She has found a new meaning in life. Thank you for giving her a chance.

"As for myself, I needed a change and my boss knew it when I called him about working for you. He made a funny remark that I would be worth more when I return. Dr. Pankovich, I appreciate the opportunity to work for you and to be able to follow events as they unfold. I will try to be a contributor to your team."

They finished their bagels and were enjoying the view from this clean, simple coffee shop in the most unlikely place in New York.

"Our job will be very specific and we'll seldom see the General." Arsen tried to describe his forthcoming responsibilities. "We'll deal with the problems your grandparents experienced. Our goal is to eliminate that kind of suffering and degradation, to eliminate fighting among ethnic groups, to eliminate killing among them, and to prevent attempts at extermination. How many people were killed in 1946 in India - a million or two, it is unimportant. Why did it happen? Partition was a necessity, despite the opponents to it -- who included Gandhi. Partition was arbitrary and did not reflect the needs and desires of the people; that caused the misinformed and uninformed people to panic, to migrate and to kill.

"We will have to deal with the same problems, and we will make sure that the people understand what will happen before it does. The space must exist for decent living for the majority, for the minority, and for the mixture of the two. We will talk more about this as we progress in our work. Right now we have to win the first battle in the U.N. Assembly."

They returned to the office of the Secretary General. A group of people were just leaving. Arsen did not recognize anybody.

As they entered the office Arsen introduced Victoria to the Secretary General.

"I met Miss Ram some years back. One rarely forgets real beauty. Please sit down. I will get some coffee." He brought two cups of fresh coffee from a small adjoining room. Then he settled in an armchair with a cup of his own.

"One learns to drink too much coffee in New York," the Secretary said. "I still stick to my tea at four in the afternoon. That is an old habit." Then he instructed his secretary to hold all calls.

"Let me tell you what has happened so far. Brad Smith was supposed to meet with me this morning and he was killed in that mysterious accident. I learned about it only when I came to the office. Then I had the meeting which just ended, with a delegation from the Security Council. Bottom line, they are in disarray and split into two groups. Of the permanent members China and Russia are for the early meeting of the Assembly as planed, and the U.S., Britain, and France are opposed. This is not surprising. Of the elected members only two are for the delay, Poland and Portugal. Sweden has not decided yet. Considering veto by the three permanent members who are for the delay, the Security Council will not be able to decide anything and my decision to ask the Assembly tomorrow to vote for or against the urgent special session and the proposed schedule was correct. Considering the importance of the issues, nobody is questioning my decision, only the timing. Thus far everything is okay. The remaining work to be done is to call enough key delegates and to talk to them. No pressure should be applied since everybody is already jittery. I talked to the General about that too."

"It seems to me that there isn't much to be discussed," Arsen said. "Or is there?"

"The General thought we should make some decisions on certain organizational matters." The Secretary General looked surprised as if to say, don't you know?

Arsen knew that the Secretary General was in a vulnerable position in the United Nations, yet he was actively supporting the General. Brad Smith had witnessed the conversation at the meeting the previous night.

"We were concerned that Brad Smith might be playing on two sides and perhaps trying to split our team," Arsen said. "The very sensitive position of the Director for Liaison with the Assembly is now suddenly vacant after Brad's death. I feel strongly that you should get that spot in the World Government. That is the job of the Foreign Minister, and you would be responsible for communication with the Assembly. The second concern is the problem of the partiality of your office, and you will soon be accused of that. If I were Brad Smith, I would have accused you of taking sides with the General. Brad may be dead but other people will come up with the same idea. The third concern is Undersecretary Enstrom, who is in the same boat with you. My advice is that both of you resign your positions at the U.N. right now and publicly join the General's group. The accusations, if they have already been made, will be dropped. What do you think, Mr. Secretary?"

The Secretary's expression had changed from attentive to concerned while Arsen was talking.

"Dr. Pankovich, you are right and I accept the offer without any hesitation. I will resign this afternoon. We should also talk to Goran. Let me find him."

The Secretary used his cellular phone to talk to the Undersecretary.

Arsen was quite surprised that Rama Chand had accepted so promptly and agreed to resign. The Secretary must know something Arsen didn't, he thought.

"After talking to many people in the last twenty-four hours, I have concluded that the General is our best bet," Rama Chand said, "and that people are scared and want action right now. The General has the answers and other people don't. I was watching a talk show late last night on MMC. Those people, a scientist, an astronomer, and a diplomat, had no idea what to do. It was pathetic to listen to them. I switched to WCN, and there it was again - nothing worth repeating. Politicians around the world are discussing the problem with their people. The feedback is that everyone is afraid, and politicians want action and want it now. I am convinced that the Assembly will turn down the request for a delay. They are right, what is there to be gained by waiting?"

"What about the next Secretary General?" Arsen wanted to know. "Raul Ortiz, I believe."

"He is a good man," the Secretary General said. "He cannot change anything anymore. Nobody can. The General Assembly will meet tomorrow and make a decision."

A few minutes later Undersecretary Enstrom walked in and greeted Arsen and Victoria.

"Is this *déjà vu* or perhaps I have seen you before?" the Undersecretary asked Victoria.

"Must be *déjà vu*," she replied and the Undersecretary shook his head several times in disbelief.

"Goran, Dr. Pankovich and I have come to the conclusion that you and I have to resign from our positions at the U.N. right now because charges of partiality and siding with the General will be leveled at us soon enough."

"I get it. Of course, we are vulnerable. What am I going to do afterwards?" The Undersecretary looked at Arsen for an answer.

"Things are developing really at a gallop," Arsen observed. "I can only guess what the General may decide. In my view he needs a deputy. He also wants to run the research effort, which will take much of his time. I don't know how he is going to run the government and do research at the same time."

"I had better talk to Raul Ortiz and tell him what is happening," the Undersecretary said.

"No, don't," Arsen said. "Raul Ortiz should know only the official story and no more, not even confidentially, so that he can truthfully state that he knows nothing about your involvement."

The Secretary General called his secretary and dictated the letter of resignation.

9 December 1997

Dr. Gerhardt Weiner
President of the General Assembly
The United Nations, New York

Dear Mr. President:

With this letter I respectfully submit my resignation from my position as Secretary General of the United Nation effective today, December 9, 1997 at 3 pm.

The reason for my precipitous resignation is the conflict of interest between my position as the Secretary General and the position I have decided to accept in the organization of Dr. Alexei Shagov. In the complicated situation facing the U.N. and the world I feel I cannot carry out my duties impartially. That is the sole reason for my resignation.

I will transfer my duties to Mr. Raul Ortiz, the Undersecretary for Personnel and Administration, and will bypass Undersecretary Goran Enstrom who, as I understand it, will also resign his position today.

Respectfully yours,

Rama Chand, Secretary General

The letter was on the Secretary General's desk within minutes, and he signed it. His secretary was instructed to deliver the letter immediately to the office of the President of the Assembly.

Arsen looked at his watch - it was one o'clock. The telephone rang and the Secretary General answered it; he listened for a moment and hung up. "Goran has just sent his resignation to the President. This should be a bomb shell. The deed has been done. It is time to start packing."

Arsen called the General to tell him what had transpired. The General was in an excellent frame of mind, after having talked to number of delegates. He felt that things were developing incredibly well.

"I told the same story to everybody who called. The message was: we discovered it, we understand it, we have studied it, and we have plans to deal with it; we need support, and a happy population which will calmly wait for the outcome. I also gave them my six-point proposal. And I showed them my return ticket to Moscow. Not a bad performance." The General was ebullient.

"General, while you were selling your program I was covering your back," Arsen said. "I managed to arrange for the resignations of Secretary

General Chand and Undersecretary Enstrom, effective today. Reason: conflict of interest because of association with you. I had no choice but to offer the liaison position to Rama Chand, and I thought you wanted Goran Enstrom as your deputy anyway. Well, you have them both. Actually, they will technically be on your payroll today. Not a bad performance by me, either."

"Not bad at all," the General said. "It didn't even occur to me that they would attack Rama and Goran first, and thus gain the delay. We will have dinner tonight to celebrate, and go to sleep early to be ready for the final battle tomorrow. We will meet in the restaurant at seven. Tell them to bring their wives with them. We should be seen celebrating. I may even invite a few distinguished guests. Let me work on it. Congratulations to Rama and Goran on the new jobs. See you tonight." The General hung up before Arsen had a chance to ask whether he could skip the dinner. Not a chance.

"The General sends you and Goran his congratulations on the new jobs," Arsen said to Rama Chand. "He invited you to dinner at seven in the hotel's restaurant, the name of which I forget. Wives are invited."

Goran Enstrom walked into the office and said that everybody already knew they had resigned. "Speculation is high as to our reasons. Nobody believes in the simple truth. Isn't that amazing?" He said that Raul Ortiz was surprised but had no problems about taking over the post.

"It is time to go back to the Plaza," Arsen said. "We'll see you tonight."

In the elevator Arsen said it would not be a bad idea to stroll the streets for an hour or so and then just walk to the hotel, which was not too far anyway. In the lobby the reporters were waiting for them.

"Dr. Pankovich, what is the story about the resignations of the Secretary and Undersecretary. Was it a coincidence that you happened to be there at the time? Do you know the reasons?" a reporter asked.

"It is a simple story, for a change, in this complicated world. The Secretary and the Undersecretary felt they could not serve the United Nations impartially once they committed their support to Gen. Shagov. Anything they would try to do here would be colored by their decision to support the General. That would not be fair to the U.N. So they resigned. Do you think they should have kept their jobs?"

Arsen recognized the reporter from the day before, Fred McCollum of *the Kansas Chronicle*, who now asked the question:

"Now that they're without a job what do they do? Pack and go home?"

"Of course not, Mr. McCollum," Arsen said. "I offered them jobs on the General's team after I heard of their resignations."

"What kind of jobs?" everybody wanted to know.

"Well, they are qualified people and we thought they should do what they know best. With that in mind, the General offered the job of Liaison with the Assembly to Mr. Chand and Mr. Enstrom will be Deputy to the General. Not a bad exchange, I would say."

"If the General gets the job," someone said.

"You think he won't?" Arsen snapped back

Arsen told the reporters that the General was giving a dinner at the Plaza in the evening.

"Who will be there?" a reporter asked.

"Some people you would consider important," Arsen said. "Messrs Chand and Enstrom. Mr. Kravchenko, who just arrived from Moscow and who will have something to do with the direction of ethnic problems. Also, Mr. Fiodorov will be there; he is an associate of the General's from Moscow. Most likely Dr. White will be there. I would be surprised if the General has not come up with some other guests. It should be an interesting evening."

Mr. McCollum came up with another question:

"Dr. Pankovich, what about you? What's your title going to be? If--"

"If the General gets the job?" Arsen challenged him.

"What I wanted to ask you, Dr. Pankovich, has to do with the position you would take if the General forms some kind of administration. What are you going to do?"

"Do I want a position worth talking about? No, not really. I am interested in ethnic problems in the Balkans and the Middle East. That is where I will soon be heading. You forget that I am a retired orthopedic surgeon. What do I know about anticollision techniques and world politics? At least I understand the differences between peoples in the Balkans and the Middle East and the ethnic problems which have caused so much grief. I have some ideas about how to resolve some of them."

"How are you going to resolve Jewish-Arab problems or problems in Kosovo? These problems have been around for centuries," Mr. McCollum said.

"That is a long story and I am on my way to see the General," Arsen said. "One day we may have time to talk about that but not today. Thank you gentlemen."

Arsen and Victoria crossed First Avenue and walked along Forty-Second Street. They looked at the windows or watched the people on the sidewalks. They even managed to buy ice cream cones.

"Christmas is in the air, in the windows, in the street decorations and in the shoppers on the sidewalks," Victoria said. "To me this has always been the most fascinating time of the year."

"You are not a Christian," Arsen said.

"No, I'm not," Victoria said. "My family is Hindu in their hearts and in their souls, and my parents feel the same although they made their home outside India. In our family, it was considered a sin to live abroad permanently. We belong to India, we serve her, and we live there - that was the family's motto. It didn't work out that way for my parents, probably because they distanced themselves from politics and national affairs. I feel like an Indian, but in everything else I am an American, a Hindu American at that I guess. I love Christmas time. I even have a Christmas tree -- to celebrate the custom not the religion. Complicated, isn't it?"

"Not really," Arsen replied. "Other immigrants often have similar dilemmas and that is the beginning of assimilation."

"This year Christmas, Hanukkah and Ramadan fall about the same time," Victoria said. "It's symbolic for the events the Global Nation has faced."

"Global Nation, you said, Global Nation," Arsen repeated after Victoria. "In relation to the approaching Demon we, the world population, are in unison. That is an interesting concept. I must mention this to the General."

They were walking on Fifty-Seventh Street. "We should now go to the Plaza to find out what is happening there," Arsen said.

In the suite the General had dozed off and Sabrina was on the phone in the bedroom. It was unusually quiet.

"You moved well today, Arsen," the General said as he woke up. "There would be a problem by now if Rama and Goran have not resigned. Who is Raul Ortiz? I hope he does not postpone the special session."

"Raul Ortiz will not delay the session, and even if he wanted to, it is too late to stop it now. Nothing can delay it anymore." People are arriving in New York and they will want action tomorrow, I am sure. They will be ready to listen to you. I think, you should give them a full dose of your medicine."

"You seem to have a good instinct for politics," the General said. "How did you figure out my plans for Rama and Goran?"

"You said some things and others seemed logical," Arsen said. "I did not mean to make decisions for you, General. I merely assumed you would want me to do what I did. Time was also a factor. Rama and Goran had to resign, and do it quickly. They also had to know beforehand what they were getting in exchange. It was that simple."

"It was that complicated," the General said.

"Not really. General, I was the Chief and always running a Department somewhere for twenty-five years. Things rub in, over time, you know, and one learns a few things on the job. I have never had trouble making decisions, and I have not changed in your environment."

"I see that," the General said. "My question is, what would you really want to do in my administration? Tell me."

"Thank you, General," Arsen replied. "I appreciate your confidence but I don't want a top position. Besides, it is too late to talk about that."

"What do you mean it is too late? Late for what?"

"You have to balance the top spots in your administration. You and Goran will be in the Presidency, Rama in Liaison, Kravchenko in the Ethnic Department, and you want the Research Department, too. That leaves Military, Survival and Preservation. You have to find the right people for the three remaining spots, and they will have to come from outside your group. An American general for the Military is a must, I think."

"You have not answered my question," the General insisted.

"You promised me a domain and I would like to keep it that way," Arsen said.

"You want to go to Bosnia while I have the globe to worry about, and you don't want to help." The General was obviously annoyed. "Why don't you take the job of Special Counselor. We will talk daily and you will report on special projects. We will discuss certain matters when I want your advice. What do you say?"

"You will have enough advisors, and besides what would Goran do if I hung around with direct access to you. He will become insecure. You want my advice, and you have it. Let me go to Bosnia and Greece and other countries I am interested in and help resolve their ethnic problems. I will enjoy that the best."

"Hopefully you won't lose your life in the process." The General now appeared calmer. "This is not a joke. I think we should arrange for some sort of security for you, here and when you travel. We should talk to Kravchenko about it. He is an old spook, and he should know what to do." The General was slowly accepting Arsen's insistence on leaving his immediate circle. Great leaders don't have time to worry about details; they have to deal with a flow of new problems which require their attention and their decisions; the General was not an exception.

Ever since the domain had been assigned to him Arsen had been troubled over one country - Israel. He felt he was biased in the Jews' favor. He knew he needed help, and this was the best time to ask the General to help.

"General, there is a problem country in my domain," Arsen said. "I will need your help."

"Which country - Bosnia?" asked the General.

"No, General, Israel is my problem," Arsen said. "I have dealt with Jews for years - when I was in practice and afterwards. I found them a special group of people, close to me emotionally and intellectually and philosophically. Do you think I will be able to make decisions that may not always be in their favor? Arabs have the right to be heard and to have their aspirations fulfilled just the same as Jews. How will I deal with this personal problem? I will need your help when the time comes. Give it some thought, maybe you will come up with some answers."

"There will be other problems, I am sure," the General said. "The fact that you are thinking about Jews and Arabs the way you are, tells me that you will make the right decisions when the time comes. You can count on my help."

"Of course there are other problem areas," Arsen continued. "Greeks and Macedonians and Cypriots, just to mention a few, will pose emotional problems too, but to a lesser degree. Still the challenge is great, and I want to go there. When can you let me go?"

"I am not sure what the timetable will be or how long the transition will take. I hope we will be able to wrap it up by the beginning of the year." The General looked somewhat frustrated. "Hopefully not in a year."

The telephone rang, and Victoria announced that Rama Chand and Goran Enstrom were coming up. As they walked in, the General congratulated them on their new jobs.

"Thank you very much for the appointment," Rama Chand said. "General, we heard that you made progress in your talks this morning. The Nigerians and the Zaireans are positioning themselves behind you. Do we need more than that?"

"Only a mandate is good enough; we need at least two thirds majority to win. Tonight you will have the pleasure of dining with the Indonesian Ambassador and the Presidents of Singapore and the Philippines. The Chinese President would have come, he said, but he had some talking to do with delegations in his group. If we can convince these people tonight maybe we will have a mandate tomorrow. I also wanted to discuss with you some aspects of your jobs."

Arsen saw a chance to escape from the group. He went to the bedroom to talk to Sabrina and find out what had happened during the day.

"I managed most of the things you asked me to do," she said. "The manager, Mr. Stanley Kim, is on the job, and he told me that your offices will be ready by the end of the week. Michelle will be the receptionist, and Victoria will have her own office. There's another office in the suite, and it'll be available as soon as you say so. I presume you'll have somebody to work in the office as your deputy. Your computers and the rest of the equipment and files are already in place. The security has been changed. You haven't seen Paul because he will be starting in the morning. As for Kravchenko and Fiodorov, they have rooms reserved on this floor and a limousine will pick them up."

"Excellent!" Arsen said. "We will pick up from here. There will be many people around. I would like to be able to talk to Kravchenko sometime tomorrow when he finds time from events at the U.N. Maybe you could arrange for me to have lunch with him?"

"I'll take care of that," Sabrina said. "I'll let you know."

"I am going home. There are a few things I have to do before dinner. It is already four-thirty. Victoria, am I going to see you at dinner?"

"No, you aren't," Victoria said. "Sabrina and I will have dinner together. It's overdue."

"You have your phones with you, don't you?"

"Yes, we do."

Arsen walked back into the day room and found the General and Rama Chand and Goran Enstrom discussing the organization of the World Government -- as they had decided to call the new administration -- and the secretaries of each of six departments.

The General noticed that Arsen was preparing to leave and asked him whether he was coming to dinner.

"Of course, I will be there," Arsen said, "By the way, I have been talking to the reporters about everything concerning this group so far. Now that Rama is the public relations man, he should be talking to the press and arranging the briefings and other things like that. Also, Goran should find a press secretary for the President. Whatever you decide I would like to get off the hook."

"What is going on?" Goran asked. "Arsen, are you getting off the ship? That makes no sense - I thought you were a special adviser to the General."

"I thought so too," the General said. "We have lost two men from the team before we even started, Brad Smith and Arsen."

"You have gained several men instead, just today," Arsen quipped back. "How is your progress in getting Secretaries?"

"Not bad if we could only choose the Chief of the Military," the General said. "We picked a Chinese man for the Secretary of Preservation - compliments of the President of China. He is a top space scientist in China, and we think he is an excellent man. I have met him a few times at meetings, and I was very impressed with his thinking. We also found the man for the Survivors Department - he is Jean Pierre Combo from Zaire, best known for his social work and his management of natural disasters. The Zairean Premier suggested him. I talked to him briefly, and he is flying to New York for the meeting tomorrow. We have no leads for the Chief of the Military."

Arsen remembered a short article in in the newspapers about an American general who was considered a brilliant soldier but had been passed over for promotion because he made several public relations gaffes. According to one story he was asked a hypothetical question: if he were commanding an American unit under a German NATO general, whose orders would he obey, the German general's orders or the direct orders by the Chairman of the Joint Chiefs of Staff? He answered that he would follow the orders of the NATO general. He gave the same answer a few weeks later after having been criticized by the Secretary of Defense. His reasons were that in an army both soldiers and generals must follow the chain of command and not a political orientation. When asked whether he would follow an order even if he felt it to be morally wrong, he simply stated that he would quit instead.

Arsen told them the story and suggested they look him up.

"What the hell is his name?" the General exclaimed. "That seems to be our man."

"General, would you trust an American general?" asked Rama Chand.

"I know I would not trust a Russian general," countered the General. "We have staffed the Board with two Russians, an Indian, a Swede, a Chinese and a Zairean. It wouldn't hurt to have an American in the most sensitive spot as far as the Americans are concerned. They will be assured that this general will not do anything immoral, meaning immoral by American standards. If I were the American President, I would consider him seriously. What is his name, Arsen?"

"General John Thornton. He is in Washington without an assignment, according to the newspaper."

"General, let me find this man. I think we should talk to him tonight--"

Arsen heard Goran Enstrom talking to the General as he was leaving the General's suite.

Finally, I am home, Arsen thought as he entered the apartment. Nada came from the bedroom to greet him.

"It is good to see you sometimes," Nada said.

"I wound up my participation in the General's group and here I am. Sabrina takes care of everything for the General, and other people are getting in place. You might have heard the story about the Secretary General and the Undersecretary the U.N., have you?"

"Yes, I heard that they resigned under mysterious circumstances," Nada said. "They even blamed you for having something to do with it. Is that true?"

"Yes, it is," Arsen said. "They were openly working for the General and holding jobs in the U.N. I thought they should resign immediately, and they did. Now they have taken important positions on the General's team. All positions have been assigned. The General asked me if I wanted to be a Secretary or a Special Counselor. I turned him down. I think I should do what I have always wanted to do - work on ethnic problems. The General eventually agreed. What do you think?"

"The way you were getting involved, I thought you would be stuck in the Administration," Nada said. "I think you are right in following your original plan. Before I forget, there are several messages on your answering machine. Also, I talked to Ivo Stipich who said he wanted to see you tonight, if possible. Victoria also called and left her cellular phone number which you didn't have. What else? A program on MMC wanted to interview you this Sunday; they left the number to call. The children called and wanted to know how you got involved."

"I will take a shower right now," Arsen said. "I have no time to deal with these messages."

While he was dressing Arsen turned on the television and tuned in the news. The local program had just ended, and the national report started almost immediately. The headlines revealed what was happening, and the comments reflected the pulse of the world.

CHAND AND ENSTROM RESIGN AT UN THEN HIRED BY THE GENERAL

The drama in the United Nations was reported accurately without speculations as to how it was engineered. Rama Chand and Goran Enstrom gave almost identical statements for the media. They were shown briefly as they were giving these statements before they left the United Nations building.

Gen. SHAGOV IS ASSEMBLING A CAPABLE TEAM: LI and COMBO JOIN

Both men were rated positively.

Then there was a shocking announcement:

DEMONSTRATIONS REPORTED IN INDIA RIOTS IN SOME CITIES DEMONSTRATIONS ALSO REPORTED IN JAKARTA AND SINGAPORE

This was a special report that had just been received. According to the report huge crowds were starting to gather in the streets of all big Indian cities, particularly in Bombay, Calcutta, Madras and New Delhi. Hindus and Muslims were reported gathering in different areas. Riots were reported from Amritsar where Sikhs were in the streets, and some reports indicated that there had been clashes with the Indian Army. Riots were reported in Kashmir and in Sri Lanka's Tamil areas. There were no details about demands by the demonstrators.

Arsen had a cold feeling about the demonstrations, and particularly the riots, which seemed to have started mainly in ethnic problem areas.

Hopefully, this would not ignite similar riots in other ethnically unstable parts of the world as a prelude to fighting and massacres, Arsen thought with fear. All that was needed would be massive civil wars and civil unrest around the world. This would very effectively hinder any anticollision efforts. Die for what? Was there ever a good reason to kill or to be killed? Arsen was getting frustrated. He tried to reach somebody in the General's suite, but all the telephone lines were busy. They must be trying to find out what was happening. He called Sabrina on her cellular phone, and she immediately answered.

"Sabrina, have you heard about the demonstration in India? I suspect the General will need you tonight."

"He just called me. It was reported on the evening news. Victoria and I are on our way there."

"I will see you there," Arsen said and hung up.

These events, though very ominous, were a political blessing for the General. The Assembly would be under pressure to resolve the problem of leadership of the World Government and start the job of calming down the population.

MMC flashed pictures of demonstrators without significant comment.

PANKOVICH RESIGNS FROM THE GENERAL'S TEAM

Arsen's turndown of a top position was reported as a resignation, although the report indicated that he wanted to continue his ethnic assignment.

Arsen had to hurry if he was going to talk to the General before dinner, which was scheduled for eight o'clock. It was seven already.

The evening was pleasant and the streets again crowded, but there was no time to be wasted in walking to the Plaza. It was a quick trip by taxi. The driver, a pleasant African American man, recognized Arsen from the press conferences that had been shown on television.

"Good luck, Doctor," he said. "I know you work for the General. Our prayers and our hopes are with him. We hope he'll get the job tomorrow. Tell him New York supports him." The driver said nothing further and refused to take the fare when he delivered Arsen in front of the Plaza.

As on previous occasions reporters surrounded Arsen when they saw him in the lobby, and showered him with questions.

"Dr. Pankovich, the story is that you resigned from the General's team," one reporter said, "Did you?"

"I would not call it a resignation because I did not hold a position to begin with. I was loaned to the General by Mr. Kravchenko, who is in charge of the ethnic department , and is my immediate boss. Mr. Chand is now officially on the General's team, and in charge of information. You should ask him what is new in the world.

"Dr. Pankovich, are you going to have a specific position or role on the General's team?" asked another reporter.

"I will be working exclusively on Mr. Kravchenko's team. That will be the connection."

"Dr. Pankovich, do you know the latest on General Thornton?" a reporter asked.

"Sorry, gentlemen, I am not the person to ask anything beyond my ethnic issues."

"What about the demonstrations and riots in Asia?" another reporter asked.

"The demonstrations are of major concern. Are these demonstrators demanding the impossible? Is this the beginning of a more dangerous trend - panic? This possibility cannot be ruled out at this time. Information has just started coming in. I will be keeping an eye on that situation and will let you know about anything of importance. I would hope Mr. Chand has already talked to people in India. You can see that it is urgent to form the World Government. I have nothing more to add."

Paul opened the door of the suite.

"I was told that you were to start here in the morning." Arsen said. Paul must have been asked to be around this evening because the traffic in the suite was expected to be heavy; who but Sabrina would have thought of that? "They must have called you to start tonight."

"Well, yes and no," Paul said. "I came anyway because I've always worked at night. Since I was in the hotel, I came up to find out if they needed me for the night. Miss Sabrina told me to stay."

"I feel better when I see you around, Paul," Arsen said.

"Thank you, Sir."

"Who are the people in the room?" Arsen asked.

"I found Mr. Chand and Mr. Enstrom when I arrived tonight. Messrs. Kravchenko, Fiodorov and Stipich just arrived; they said they came from Moscow."

"They did," Arsen said and walked into the day room.

The General was standing by the fireplace explaining his views on the reported demonstrations. Goran Enstrom was sitting on the couch to his left, Rama Chand was sitting on the arm of the other couch. Other men were helping themselves from the bar.

"Arsen, we are discussing the demonstrations in India and elsewhere," the General said. "I am interested in your opinion. The latest is that people in India are scared and demanding to know what is happening and what is being done to improve the situation. If people in South Asia and

South East Asia want to know today, the rest of the world will demand to know tomorrow. We had better be able to provide the answers."

"I would be interested to hear what Mr. Kravchenko has to say," Arsen said.

One of the three men at the bar turned toward Arsen.

"This must be the well known Dr. Pankovich. In Russia the early reports showed Dr. Pankovich's press briefings. From an unknown man he became a media celebrity. I am glad to meet you, Arsen." Showing who is the boss, Arsen thought. by calling him by his first name before even shaking his hand. Kravchenko was rather heavy at 250 pounds and at the most five foot seven tall. His face was square and he had a Nixonian nose and long, thin broad ears close to the skull; his eyes were pig-like, small and barely visible. The broad forehead was square and slanted backward; his scalp was covered with thin dark brown hair which was probably colored. He looked like a Russian bureaucrat from the cold war era movies.

"I anticipate the same reactions in most of the countries by tomorrow or the day after," Kravchenko said. "Most certainly, these demonstrations are expressions of fear and desperation about the unknown. Many of their leaders are either already in New York or on the way. These leaders will become panicky themselves, not so much from the dangers from space but from the strength of the masses. These people could destroy governments and create total anarchy. I think, General, we had better find a way to talk to these world leaders tonight, and start broadcasting some messages from you to their people. They may listen to you; they just may. Even in Russia, before we left, people were talking about "the General;" they may not yet know the 'Shagov' part of your name."

Sabrina came in and told the General she had two Presidents on hold: from Singapore and the Philippines.

"Let me talk to both of them on the conference line."

"It's ready. Go ahead."

"Good evening Messrs. Presidents. I am talking to both of you simultaneously to cut your waiting time," the General greeted the Presidents. "My apologies. The situation is getting complicated with the demonstrations in your countries. We are trying to monitor the situation, but it is difficult from a hotel room. I must have a press conference with the idea that it may reach the demonstrators and those thinking of demonstrating; maybe we can buy some time. But we had better deliver something tomorrow."

Both Presidents thought that was a good idea. The people were upset that the General was not allowed to talk. "They said 'allowed' as if I was preventing you from talking," the President of the Philippines said. "Same here," the President of Singapore said.

"I doubt there will be time for dinner tonight - all of us will be busy," the General said. "Maybe a very late supper around midnight. What do you say?"

Both Presidents said they would call before they came, and the General hung up.

"What do we do now?" asked the General.

"WCN is your best bet," Arsen said. "They have the best world-wide coverage."

"I agree," Grigor Kravchenko said. Everybody agreed.

Sabrina told the General that the hotel management felt that they should open one of the ballrooms and make it available for press briefings and conferences.

"The ballroom will be ready in an hour," Sabrina said. "I also talked to the media and told them there would probably be a press conference, and that you were going to make a statement. Television cameras and reporters will be there. I can talk to WCN about special arrangements, if you want.

"This will be enough," the General said.

"Gen. Thornton is on the line; he's been holding for a few minutes," Victoria said. "Please talk to him."

"Hello, Gen. Thornton. Where are you?" The General listened for a moment. "At JFK! It would save time if you just grab a taxi and come right over to the Plaza Hotel."

Rama Chand asked the General about his speech at the Assembly meeting, and Goran Enstrom and Grigor Kravchenko joined them.

Arsen greeted Ivo Stipich and Vasilii Fiodorov.

"Things have been happening since yesterday morning - like crazy. The General must receive the mandate for his plan. How that is going to happen, I don't know, but it must. Ivo, all our plans are down the drain, only bare ideas remain. We have to accelerate our time-table. As soon as I get the nod to move I will fly to Croatia, Montenegro, Bosnia and Serbia. I hope they will be ready for me. After that comes Macedonia, Bulgaria and Greece, and so on. My problem now is what to do with mixed minorities. They have to be recognized and protected at the same time. That will mean allowing the return of some refugees to the territories of their majorities. My concern is for the Serbs in Croatia, the Muslims in the Serb territories of Bosnia, and the Albanian Kosovars in Serbia. We will have to talk to Mr. Kravchenko about that."

"I have been more concerned about your declining a position with the General, if it is true what I heard," Ivo Stipich said. He looked at Arsen with a dose of scorn and some disbelief.

"What is true is that I have a mission, as you know," Arsen said. "You invited me to take care of the domain of the Balkans and South Western Asia. I still think that is a damned important job and I would like to do it. Sabrina is arranging a meeting with Mr. Kravchenko for me so that I can have his opinion on certain issues. For example, how far can I push to establish new territories in the sovereign countries? How will I get military support when I need it, and how fast? I know there will be resistance in some circles. It will be very important that the General establish principles in dealing with ethnic problems and that the Assembly approve them. I hope this will be resolved before long."

"I am sure Grigor will have answers for most of your questions," Ivo Stipich said. "Although I know what he wants to accomplish, it is better that he tell you about it himself."

Vasilii Fiodorov did not say anything - he just listened. His face was changing expressions during the conversation, from one of approval to one of questioning, to one of confirmation and anticipation, but he said nothing. Vasilii Fiodorov looked more like a bodyguard than a sophisticated member of the General's team.

Victoria announced a call from the Chairman of the Foreign Relations Committee in Washington, Mr. Sam Hopkins.

"What does he want?" muttered the General as he picked up the phone. "Hello Senator Hopkins, it is a pleasure to hear from you. What can I do for you?" The conversation was very short. When the General hung up, he said "He wants to come and to talk to us. He said he was asked by President Burns to talk to me. He will be here in an hour or so. This is important."

Several calls had to be answered by the General. Rama Chand and Grigor Kravchenko decided to move to the adjoining suite and Ivo Stipich joined them. Vasilii Fiodorov started talking with the General in Russian.

Arsen joined Sabrina and Victoria; he found them noticeably nervous, and he thought, somewhat scared.

"Ladies, am I intruding in your territory or interrupting something?"

"Not really - we're just wondering what will happen next," Sabrina said.

"Do I detect a dose of fear in what you just said?"

"Maybe, just maybe. The two of us are doing things but we don't see them through. What's happening? What will happen, Doctor? Do you know?"

"Nothing much right now unless demonstrations and riots start in New York. The way things are developing the General will get his mandate tomorrow, and chances are that you will be moving to the U.N., the seat of the new World Government, with the General as its President. I think that will be a stabilizing force, and things will quiet down for a while. The major effort will be on how to deal with the Demon. You will be very busy. Victoria and I will be trying to change the world, at least in the Balkans and South West Asia."

"Doctor, why don't you stay with the General? What's to be accomplished by trying to change people in this situation?" asked Sabrina.

"I know you think there is no point in making changes when all of us will soon be dead anyway. That is right, from your standpoint, but you are free, and you know that even if you die you will die a free person. What about the people who would like to die just as free as you. Think of the Kurds or the Basques or the Aborigines; they are human beings but not free. Why shouldn't they be free? Somebody else has decided their fate, not they themselves. Who is the somebody with that kind of right? That is the wrong that has to be undone so that these people can die free. There will also be some problems in deciding who should be preserved, as each ethnic group will have to share that right equally. This is an important job and I would like to do it. Besides, I feel that we will avoid the disaster and this work will make a difference later."

"I still think you would do more good if you stayed around," Sabrina said. "The General thinks so too."

"I doubt that anybody understands my feelings in this respect," Arsen said.

The telephone rang, and Victoria answered it and immediately announced that Gen. Thornton was coming up. The General asked that only Arsen remain in the room.

"Arsen, you are the only American citizen up here."

Gen. Thornton walked in and saluted the General. He was in his early fifties, almost six feet tall, thin, fit, and athletic, with the look of an intellectual - smooth black hair, high forehead and a face that was a bit hawkish. He was wearing his uniform.

The General introduced Arsen and asked them to sit.

"A drink of some kind, General?" asked the General. "Or something to eat?"

"Thank you Gen. Shagov, I had plenty on the way from Washington. Thank you for inviting me." Gen. Thornton sat on the couch, attentive and slightly nervous.

"I don't have to explain to you why you are here, Gen. Thornton," the General began the conversation that was supposed to be an interview for the job. "We feel you have the qualifications to be the Chief of the Military, and I will not dwell on that. One item is of the decisive importance. As much as you expressed yourself recently about how you see the role of a soldier in the military hierarchy, I must ask you how you think you would function if your job should require calming down the American establishment?"

"Straightforward, General. I couldn't aim my guns on unarmed civilians, in America or anywhere else. However, I'm sure I wouldn't hesitate to take care of an armed group trying to compromise the anticollision effort."

"There is another issue that will soon come up, Gen. Thornton," Arsen said after the General nodded approvingly. "Gen. Shagov and his group feel strongly about the fact that there are people around the world who are not free. Would you be willing to use the military to help these people gain and preserve their freedom?"

"The answer is definitely affirmative," Gen. Thornton said without any hesitation.

"You understand that this will be the largest military ever, if it is approved?" the General asked.

"Yes, I do," Gen. Thornton answered quietly.

"Gen. Thornton, you answered the critical questions to my satisfaction. As far as I am concerned, you've got the job. I hope you accept?"

"Yes, I do," Gen. Thornton said.

"All my appointees will have to be approved by the Assembly. Do you understand that?"

"Yes, I do,"

Let us talk to Rama and the others," the General said. "They will tell you more about our plans and our aims. Good luck, Gen. Thornton."

"Thank you, Sir," Gen. Thornton said.

As they walked to the adjoining room, there was a call from yet another President, this time of the President of Spain. The General answered somewhat nervously - he had had too many calls from Presidents already. After he finished the conversation, he looked elated.

"Arsen, you won't believe what he told me. He said he was speaking for almost the entire Spanish speaking world. He said, 'General, I think I can state to you that the Spanish speaking people stand solidly behind you.' Wow that is a lot of support. I have a feeling the Americans will join us, and that may be the reason for Sen. Hopkins's visit today. We'll see."

"General, it's time for the press conference," Sabrina said as she entered the room. "Everything's ready for you in the ballroom."

"Arsen, come along just to introduce me," the General said.

As they entered the ballroom talk suddenly subsided and only a few people cleared their throats. Arsen stepped up to the podium and explained that the General wanted to make a statement before any questions were asked. Then he made space for the General.

"The reason for this press conference tonight is my concern, and concern of many heads of governments and other people whom I have talked to during the day, about the events in South and South East Asia. We have reports from several countries in the region that people are demonstrating and that the demonstrations are spontaneous and made up of people who are worried about the threat from space. The riots in some areas, like in Amritsar and Kashmir and in the Tamil areas of Sri Lanka are of grave concern. While the peaceful demonstrations pose no threats, they are potentially dangerous if they get out of control. Riots, on the other hand, must stop immediately if we are to achieve what the rioters are trying to bring into focus. They are exploiting the situation for their purposes, but that is really unnecessary as one of our goals is to facilitate the liberation of ethnic groups. Rioting will make our job impossible. Therefore, I am appealing to all demonstrators to stay calm, or even better, to go home and watch television. I guarantee that the next twenty-four hours will be very significant, and people should watch and listen as events unfold. The riots must stop immediately."

The General continued after pausing for a moment.

"Before anything can be done, the Assembly of the United Nations, in which all governments are represented, must decide what has to be done and who will do it. I am ready to put forward concrete proposals, and to lead the World Government, if I am asked to do so. The Assembly will decide tomorrow."

"I believe that there is only one mistake the people of the world can make, and that is to ignore the decision of the General Assembly of the United Nations, whatever that may be. For my part, I will not question, even for a moment, the decision of the Assembly if it is not in my favor. I will direct all my energies toward efforts to prevent the collision. I insist that everybody else do the same. We have no time for fights and delays - we must act now. Therefore, I appeal to everybody, to the entire world population, to stay calm, to follow events, and to support the decisions of the General Assembly."

The General had made his points and asked the reporters for their questions.

"McCollum, *Kansas Chronicle*. General, we've heard all kinds of rumors about everything. The current rumors have it that you'll be talking to Sam Hopkins, the Chairman of the Foreign Relations Committee, and that you haven't made up your mind about Gen. Thornton."

"Mister McCollum, let me answer the second question first. I have made up my mind, and I was delighted with Gen. Thornton's decision to accept my offer. Naturally, he will need a tacit approval by the American Government and that is the only remaining hurdle for him. We do not know what the reaction of the American Government is to anything including the World Military. They have said nothing publicly. We have some indications that they are unhappy with the arrangements that are being made.

"As for your second question, Mr. McCollum, the answer is, we don't know what is on Mr. Hopkins's mind. When he comes, we'll find out."

The message from Sabrina, sent via a Security Service agent, was that Senator Hopkins was waiting for the General in the suite.

"Gentlemen, I must interrupt our conference. Senator Hopkins is waiting for me. I had better not keep him waiting too long."

As they walked into the day room, the General and Arsen found the Senator talking to Rama Chand, Goran Enstrom and Grigor Kravchenko. Rama Chand was explaining the main points of the General's program and the minimum conditions for his acceptance of the Presidency.

"There are and there will be many things that will have to be resolved," the Senator said. "We know we can't anticipate every problem. However, there is one problem that the President wants to resolve before tomorrow--" The Senator noticed the General at that moment. He walked over to him and shook his hand.

"General," the Senator said. "I've truly been looking forward to meeting you, even before the assignment was given to me. I'm fascinated by your discovery of the space object you call a Demon, and by the way you've convinced everybody of its existence and the real danger it poses. Only yesterday nobody believed you, and today you seem to be keeping everybody in the world on their toes. That includes the U.S. Government and the U.S. Senate."

"I was thrilled, Senator," the General replied, "when I heard you were coming to see us. Of course, I am also curious to find out what it is you want to discuss with us."

The Senator smoothed his gray hair with his hand. He appeared slightly nervous. He was in his late sixties and obviously in good physical health - he was tall and thin. His eyes were expressive and his face attentive and intelligent; one could see him charming an audience, any audience, not only the voters at a political rally. He looked more like an ambassador or a diplomat than a politician involved in partisan battles about the passage of laws. Maybe that was why he was the Chairman of the Foreign Relations Committee, Arsen thought.

"My President wants to know," the Senator said, "what would the status of the United States be if you were to win the Presidency of the World Government?"

"To be frank, Senator, I have not thought much about it," the General said. "It is not the United States that I am worried about - it is the rest of the world. We would expect from the United States only two things: the incorporation of its Army into the World Military, with the approval of Gen.

Thornton as its Chief, and the payment of its fair share of taxes. Of course, we would like to keep the Presidency and the administration of the World Government in New York City. That is all I have for your President."

"You don't anticipate any changes in the structure of the country? Any major shake-up in the social structures?" asked the Senator.

"I really do not, but Grigor Kravchenko will be dealing with those issues, and he is more familiar with the potential problems," the General said. "You can talk with him tonight or tomorrow, or even take him to the White House tonight. Whatever you wish, Senator."

"I'll take you up on your offer and steal Mr. Kravchenko from you tonight. I'll buy him dinner myself, if my President's busy."

The Senator had a long private conversation with the General before he was ready to leave. Grigor Kravchenko, as unhappy as he was to leave, had no choice but to join Senator Hopkins on his way.

It was ten-thirty. The General asked everybody to join him for dinner. Victoria was to find out if the Presidents of the Philippines, Singapore and China would be able to join them. The general was relaxed and happy and it was clear that he was ready for the finals.

"Mr. Li and Mr. Combo called," Sabrina said when she came back to the day room. "Their plane connections will get them to New York at the earliest by noon tomorrow. They were upset about that, but there was nothing they could do."

On the way to the restaurant the General asked Arsen if he could work with him after dinner. "Since Kravchenko is gone for the night, I will need you to go over some aspects of ethnicity. Do you think you would be able to work late tonight?"

"The old surgeon in me told me this would be just one of those busy nights," Arsen said. "It sounds as if I have done this before. No problem, General."

"Okay, we'll meet here after the dinner."

Paul announced that Dr. White was on the way up. The General wanted to talk to him about some research issues and they went to the adjoining room.

There was not much Arsen could do before dinner. He did not want to interrupt the conversation between Rama Chand and Gen. Thornton; they had been talking to each other since Senator Hopkins left. Vasilii Fiodorov had never come back from the adjoining suite, so he must have joined the General and Dr. White. What was Fiodorov's role in this organization, Arsen wondered. Nobody had ever said anything about his expertise. Grigor Kravchenko asked Ivo Stipich to accompany him and the Senator, and they left.

Arsen thought he had better call home before Nada went to sleep. He dialed his home number. Nada was still reading. Her mother had gone to her room earlier in the evening. Nada said that a man had called and left a phone number; he did not want to call the Plaza.

"What was his name, did he say?" Arsen was annoyed when he heard that the man had not given his name to Nada.

"He left the number and said to call him when you find time. He had an accent, and I would not be surprised if he were a Serb."

"I hate that, as you know. Did he say it was urgent?"

"No, he did not."

"Serbian stupidity." Arsen was even more annoyed. "I will call him tomorrow."

"Listen, I have been thinking," Nada said. "I want to cancel our trip to Puerto Rico. People are demonstrating in many places. I would feel safer in New York."

"You may as well cancel," Arsen said. "I called to tell you I have a dinner to attend in a short while and the General wants to discuss some ethnic problems with me afterwards. I will be late I am sure. Don't wait for me."

On second thought Arsen decided to call the anonymous caller and find out what he wanted. He dialed the number.

"Hello," a man answered, pronouncing 'hello' rather rapidly as foreigners often do, and without giving his name.

"This is Dr. Pankovich. Somebody left this number with my wife. Who am I speaking to?"

"*Doktore ,*" the man said and continued in Serbian. "My name is Dragoljub Vasic. I work for the Yugoslav Ambassador at the United Nations, Mr. Stanko Petkovic. Like everybody else we have been watching you on television yesterday and today, and we realize that you will be responsible for the Balkans in the near future."

"Only if the General gets the job."

"Oh, he will, believe me. And when the General takes over, you will be going to the Balkans, and you will start what you have been planning to start. We are not sure what you are planning to do. How much will it affect Yugoslavia? We don't know. And we would like to know. Is there a way to meet with you to discuss the situation?"

"Nothing much will happen immediately, I can assure you of that. Later, it will depend on developments on the site. Is that what you wanted to know?" Arsen was rather firm in his statement.

Dragoljub Vasic was not satisfied with the answer and insisted on having a meeting.

"Okay, if that is what you want," Arsen agreed. "Tell your Ambassador to come to the Plaza Hotel tonight. I will meet him in the General's suite, about half past midnight. I will have about half an hour for him."

"He will be there," Mr. Vasic said.

The pressure would soon be greater, when others started calling, Arsen thought.

"Victoria, at twelve-thirty I will receive the Yugoslavian Ambassador, Stanko Petkovic, in the adjacent suite. You will be gone by then, I hope."

"No, Sabrina and I are staying overnight," Victoria said. "It'll be too late after dinner, and besides, something is always happening. Paul will answer the phone while we're at dinner and let us know if anything important comes up."

"Let's get the General and go downstairs," Arsen said. "Whoever is late, like one of these Presidents, will find us in the dining room."

The General was agreeable.

The private dinning room was a simple square room with a white painted ceiling, and walls covered in dark red satin. The floor was made of a fine parquet. The table, which occupied almost the entire room, was arranged in the standard fashion. The chairs left almost no room to move around.

"We will be a bit crowded," the General said. "It doesn't matter - we are hungry."

Everybody ordered hard drinks except General Thornton and Arsen. The Russians drank vodka, as one would expect, and Rama Chand ordered white vine. Arsen noticed that Gen. Thornton and Vasilii Fiodorov were sitting next to each other, and discussing something without paying any attention to anybody in the dining room. Vasilii Fiodorov might be just another Russian General or a former Commissar, Arsen thought. Maybe the General had brought Fiodorov along just in case the Military Chief had to be watched. Yet, the conversation between the two was quite friendly; it wouldn't have been friendly if Vasilii Fiodorov was behaving as Political Commissars always did - arrogantly. Arsen could not sit quietly in his chair with this idea in his mind. With the pretext of finding out if Gen. Thornton had heard from the American Government about his nomination for the World Military job, he interrupted the conversation.

"You must have not heard; Sen. Hopkins called. The President gave his blessing," Gen. Thornton said.

"Congratulations, General," Arsen said. "Tomorrow you will take over the biggest military in history."

"The most problematic military in history," Gen. Thornton said. "Captain Fiodorov and I have been discussing ethnic problems that will come up in the proposed military. As you know, the Captain is an expert on military ethnic problems." Arsen was relieved. Military ethnic expert sounded innocent enough.

"Although my concerns are with civilian ethnic problems, I should learn something about the problems in the military," Arsen said. "Maybe you will teach me one of these days, Captain." Arsen returned to his place between Sabrina and Victoria.

The Presidents of China and the Philippines arrived and sat with the General at the head of the table. The news they brought was good. In China and India demonstrations were spreading. They were spontaneous, and the demonstrators were mainly asking that decisions be made without any delay. With the daylight arriving in successive parts of the world, demonstrations were starting also in those parts. The reports on rioting in India and elsewhere were misleading - the clashes were with the local police, who were nervous about demonstrations of any kind.

"It is time to drink to that," the General said. "This is a toast to our successful anticollision effort and to the Earth, on which we want to live now and forever." The General knew how to handle people, Arsen thought.

Arsen received a message from Paul that Mr. Petkovic was waiting in the adjacent suite. Arsen had a strange feeling about this meeting. It was the first time in his life he would meet a person of importance from his native country. There was some repugnance in his feelings because he knew that the point of this visit was to find a way to influence him. That was the best way to lose the game with Arsen. He went into the adjacent suite and shook the hand of the Ambassador.

"Good evening, Mr. Ambassador," Arsen said in Serbian. "It was not possible to see you earlier. Accept my apologies."

"Thank you for receiving me tonight," the Ambassador said. "This gives me the advantage over my competitors from the Balkan States, and hopefully I will be able to persuade you to help the cause of your native country."

"Which you do not represent, in a legal sense, since I was born and raised in Banja Luka and that is now in the Republica Srpska, as you know."

"I was unaware of that," the Ambassador said. "You are a Serb I was told."

"I am a Bosnian Serb."

"Let me state why I am here," the Ambassador said. "The officials in my Government, starting with and including my President, are worried for their jobs now that you will be in charge in the Balkans for the World Government. They want a dialog; they want to know what you want them to do, so that they can keep their jobs. That is my mission. I figured you would want to know the facts as they are, and now you have them."

"Amazing, really amazing, Mr. Ambassador," Arsen said. "Truly, this is a straight talk without B.S. What is in this for you, Mr. Ambassador?"

"I will be able to keep my job if my mission is successful."

"Mr. Ambassador, I appreciate your direct approach. Let me tell you the situation as I see it. It is probable that I will soon visit Yugoslavia. As you know, there are problems that have to be resolved, and I mean Kosovo, Sandzak, Bosnia, and Montenegro. In addition, it will be my job to make sure that the people get a fair chance to elect representatives of their choice and to assure them that their leaders, present and future, have not and will not corrupt the system and enrich themselves. I will not try to influence the people or the leaders, but I will not allow either of them to be influenced by pressure. Fair game will be the only game in town. I think you should tell your President that these issues have to be resolved so that the country can be peaceful while awaiting its destiny. Ideally, these problems would be resolved before I arrive in the area."

"Thank you, Dr. Pankovich," the Ambassador said. "I expected this kind of answer and I appreciate the opportunity to meet with you tonight."

Arsen wanted to say something personal and nice to this man, who appeared honest and intelligent. He looked at him as an equal, as someone who worked in the system in which even the best become dishonest through the very dictates of that system and of the survival instinct. The Ambassador got up to leave. His face was serious, and he showed a forced smile. It appeared that his whole body had become smaller, and he was already on the short side, skinny and bony without fat and without muscles. His face looked intelligent, decent and sad.

Arsen looked at this man with sympathy. He had a job to do, and he had done it very well. Arsen thought he could work with him.

"The time will come, Mr. Ambassador," Arsen said, "when I will need people to help me do the job in my domain. I hope I can call on you then and ask you to join my team. Have a good night, Mr. Ambassador."

"Good night, Dr. Pankovich," the Ambassador said. "Call me when you need me. I will be glad to help."

A good man, Arsen thought on his way to join the dinner party.

Arsen reached the dining room in time to be served dessert - chocolate cake and coffee. Sabrina and Victoria were talking about the offices on Lexington Avenue.

"It's nice to walk on the street at noon," Sabrina said. "There are lots of people on the sidewalks, and restaurants, coffee shops and food stores are crowded with people. I used to do all my shopping at noon. The move to the United Nations building will keep me off the streets."

"Walking on Forty-Second Street is not bad at all," Victoria said. "You don't have all the fancy shops, but there are places to eat and relax for an hour. Now everybody's thinking about tomorrow and what will happen in the Assembly. After that's over, like after elections, the real work begins."

"The General looks tired," Sabrina said. "Maybe he's had too much to drink, although he didn't drink much. Alcohol can get to you when you're tired. We'd better wind up this affair. Doctor, you and the General still have to work on his speech. He shouldn't be writing his own speeches, but we have no one to help. That will have to change. I'll see to it."

Sabrina went to talk to the General.

"It's getting late and you still have work to do with Dr. Pankovich."

"I know we have work to do, Arsen and I," the General said. "Gentlemen, the time is late and all of us will have a tough day tomorrow. I will have to leave you now."

Once in the suite, the General took his jacket off and rolled up his sleeves.

"There are a few items I want to go over with you. As I said before, the ideas for the anticollision effort are clear. I have gone over all that. How do I present the ethnic problems and their possible solutions to the Assembly? I have to spell out what we want to do and what it will take to do it. Particularly important is the part about what it will take. What will it take to do it, Arsen.? Tell me."

"General, we have already outlined our principles," Arsen said. "To accomplish all that will take a strong commitment from the World Government. We should be able to hold plebiscites so that the people can decide their destiny. We should be able to provide autonomy for people who want autonomy. We should be able to help separatists to separate and form their own sovereign territory.

"Think of Kurds, Basques, Tamils and many others. These are sovereignty issues, and they may cause problems. We have to be able to protect these people once they achieve their goals. We should not try to convince them to integrate if they want to separate. Most certainly we should not force integration, as has been done so often.

"Think of Kosovars, Chechens, Tibetans and many others. What are we waiting for to grant them their freedom? Should we expect them to thank us for a promise to give them their independence in fifty or a hundred years? What about the people who are alive today and will be dead in fifty years? Are we trying to be nice to Serbs or Spaniards, to Russians or Chinese and to other majorities? Are we perhaps afraid that all minorities will soon ask for their independence? General, they have been asking and nobody has been listening until they start demonstrating and rioting, and killing. Then they are called terrorists.

"We will also be concerned about the essentials of democracy - the people's right to choose its own leaders and systems of government. Finally, the leaders should be audited from time to time to prevent them from becoming corrupt.

"Should we punish homosexuals and call them nonhumans, or blame mulattos for the love of their parents? There are minority populations in some states, like Chinese in Indonesia, or Muslims in Republika Srpska, or Serbs in Croatia, or Romas in a number of European Countries, not only in Czech Republic, even Turks in Germany. They do not have their own territories. These people have to be protected and guaranteed equal rights. Now that we are all expecting the same fate, why can't we all be equally free?"

"Arsen, you present it very clearly," the General said. "For my purposes, I have more than I need. Arsen, go to sleep. Come and pick me up in the lobby at eight tomorrow morning."

"Good night, General. I will be there," Arsen said.

Arsen's mind was spinning from the events of the last forty-eight hours. So much had happened, he thought. From a simple conversation with the General, which was supposed to have been just a get-acquainted meeting, their relationship had grown into a complicated one, and now they were at the center stage of the world. The General obviously trusted his opinion and judgment, and wanted him close by. Things would move even faster after the Assembly meeting tomorrow. The General would be in a whirl of attention and decision making, choosing new people, organizing the World Government and the Department of Research. He would have no time for Arsen. That was good.

Arsen was probably asleep even before his head touched the pillow at two-thirty in the morning.

CHAPTER TWENTY-ONE

WEDNESDAY, 10 DECEMBER 1997

" Arsen, your alarm has been ringing for the last five minutes." Nada shook Arsen to wake him up. "It is seven o'clock. Do you have to get up?"

"In about thirty seconds."

"Then get up. I have made coffee for you."

"Good old days are gone," Arsen complained. "The days when I did not have to wake up anyway yet I rushed to get up early and to start reading the papers and my ethnic articles, and books, and I could write. Yes, I had time to sit in front of my computer and actually write. There haven't been any new pages in my book for several weeks. I miss my peace and my quiet days. Who knows what will happen today? Will the General prevail in the Assembly? And tomorrow, what will happen tomorrow?"

"You had better hurry up, take a shower and dress," Nada said. "You will be unhappy if you are late. Drink some coffee before you leave."

Arsen opened the front door and picked up the newspapers that were inevitably there. How some small, pleasant things in life worked predictably, like home delivery of the papers, or daily delivery of the mail, six-thirty national news, ordering books from Amazon, getting computer supplies by phone from MacWarehouse. These were just small predictable items in his complicated life, Arsen thought. Now he had no time for these niceties - he had given them up for a grueling pace to save humanity in the finishing sprint of his life. Was that reasonable?

The headlines were informative.

GEN. SHAGOV CONSOLIDATES HIS LEAD FOR WG PRESIDENCY
US GOVERNMENT SENDS SENATOR HOPKINS TO NEGOTIATE
GEN. THORNTON APPROVED BY PRESIDENT
TO HEAD WG MILITARY

MYSTERY ABOUT THE MILITARY CHIEF

The brilliant soldier: Is General Thornton the right man?

Controversy about the General's statements was presented with a commentary that was not critical of him. His being an American general made him someone whose nomination politicians would support his - before a general from who-knew-which country got the job.

DEMONSTRATORS AROUND THE WORLD ASKING QUESTIONS ABOUT ANTICOLLISION AS RIOTS STOP AMERICANS ARE WORRIED AND HOPEFUL

There was no time for reading the reports. Arsen turned to the second page and found an interesting headline.

KRAVCHENKO TALKS ABOUT HIS OLD JOB: AN ETHNIC SPY IN NKVD TO BE NOMINATED FOR SECRETARY OF ETHNIC BOARD

There was even a short article about Arsen, under the headline,

PANKOVICH ON THE WAY TO BOSNIA?

Arsen was satisfied with his review of the news. His coffee was gulped down, Nada was kissed on the way out, and he was off to meet the General at the Plaza.

The streets were almost deserted, as they were on Sunday mornings, and it was only Wednesday. Maybe people stayed home to watch the special session, it occurred to Arsen. Taxis were cruising without passengers, as empty as the deserted streets. Not a good day for taxi drivers - it was not even raining. The ride to the Plaza was quick through the light traffic. The city was waiting, and the world was waiting, to hear that the trouble would go away. The General had better deliver the truth with some hope.

A single reporter approached Arsen, although many were standing by while cameramen positioned themselves on both sides of the main entrance to the hotel.

"What is happening?" Arsen asked.

"We're waiting to see the General leave to go to the United Nations, though there will be no questioning. This will be the quietest crowd of reporters ever. To us this isn't a story, it's more like a funeral. We're not reporting about somebody else, this time it's our own destiny that's being written.

Arsen went into the lobby to wait for the General. The reporters and visitors were talking very quietly. The atmosphere was solemn.

Arsen saw the elevator stop on the General's floor; it remained there for a while. Then it descended without stops. The General walked out of the elevator and he waved to everyone in the lobby. Almost instantly there was applause, which was sustained until the General reached the main entrance. As he stepped down to the sidewalk, the applause cascaded from the lobby to the street, while the cameras filmed the occasion. There were no cheers, as this was not a cheerful occasion.

The General entered the limousine and Arsen walked around it to enter it on the street side.

New York's finest, on motorcycles, lined up around the limousine to accompany the General to the United Nations. Arsen noted the U.S. flag was waving on the limousine's hood - that was symbolic indeed.

At the U.N. building, the General and Arsen were escorted to a large office on the tenth floor where they were to wait for the General's turn to speak before the Assembly. There was a television set in the corner, tuned to the Assembly Hall where delegates were taking their seats or talking to other delegates. The reporters were discussing the issues or interviewing delegates, and their stations' anchors would break in to present their own material or to talk to personalities around the world. The atmosphere in the Assembly Hall was solemn and expectations were high.

A long table and fifteen chairs on the large podium faced the delegates. The chairs were reserved for the members of the Security Council. There was a separate chair to the side of the table near the speaker's podium, for the President of the Assembly, Dr. Gerhardt Weiner of Germany, and another chair on the opposite end of the table, near another lectern, for Secretary General Raul Ortiz.

"The main battle will take place at the very beginning," the General said. "The course of events has been set. I am sure that the countries from the regions selected by Goran on Monday have already talked to each other and that they know exactly where they stand. I anticipate that they will cut the time for the regional meetings to an hour or two. I think the President of the Assembly will insist on voting by the individual states and by written ballots that will have the name of the state and the vote on them. That is necessary, and I agree, so that everybody knows now and in the future who voted and how the votes were cast. I wouldn't mind having breakfast while we wait."

Arsen knew the place to have breakfast - his favorite small coffee shop on the fortieth floor. They told the guard where they were going. The waitress was there, and she greeted them as they entered.

"Doctor, this is your third visit to my coffee shop. Each time you return you're more famous. Now you bring the General with you. Good morning, General. It's a real pleasure to meet you and to serve you here. What would you like?"

"Thank you very much," the General said. "I am hungry and I want scrambled eggs, bacon, toast and coffee."

"Doctor, I know what you want. Bagel with cream cheese and coffee. Right?"

"Right," Arsen said.

"I did not sleep much last night," the General said. "I was watching television early this morning. That is an old habit. All channels were presenting only interviews - with important people around the world and with people on the street. One question was on everybody's mind - how much time is left? Like a patient with an incurable disease. The street figure is about five years. Of course, we don't know yet. Maybe the Hubble people will let us know during the meeting today."

Arsen said nothing and the General stopped talking while he ate breakfast. Their thoughts were traveling the speed of light towards the Demon that was the cause of interest, concern and fear in the World. Several times, the General took a .deep breath, as if a heavy stone were resting on his chest - the responsibility for all people.

When they returned to the office, they looked at the television to find out if had anything happened in the Assembly Hall. Both of them immediately noticed that there were only two men on the podium. Fifteen chairs stood empty.

"The Security Council is out," the General said. "It was probably decided beforehand that the members would remain in the Assembly, as delegates. It would make no difference anyway."

The President of the Assembly introduced the Secretary General.

"It is my privilege to present to you your Secretary General Mr. Ortiz. He has taken responsibility in organizing this special session, and he has succeeded. He will now present to you the reasons that led to the call for this special session. He will also submit the agenda for your approval." As Mr. Ortiz was approaching the lectern applause broke out from the Assembly.

"Mr. President and members of the Assembly. Thank you for your expression of confidence. I know that you are aware of the circumstances that forced the call for this special session. Just for the record, let me state that three independent observatories, two in Russia and the Hubble team in the U.S., have established that a celestial object of a significant size is flying in the direction of the Earth, and it has been established from its trajectory that it will collide with the Earth. The first observation was made by Gen. Shagov in Russia a month ago. As you noticed, a month has passed and nothing has been done so far in preparation for the apocalyptic event facing the world. Simply nothing. As your Secretary General I urge you to get started without delay. Please, do not allow procedural matters to bog down this meeting and stop its proceedings. I urge you to get the job done whatever it takes. A written agenda has been delivered to all delegations, and you will find them in a file in front of you. Thank you."

"This is a short speech," the General said. "I thought he would talk at least half an hour. He just stated the facts. Bravo, Mr. Ortiz."

The Assembly Hall was abuzz after Mr. Ortiz finished his speech. Nobody had expected it to be that short and to the point. Television commentators were stunned and scrambling for people to interview. Their reaction was complete surprise. One commentator said that the special session would end by noon if everybody got straight to the point, as Mr. Ortiz had done.

The President of the Assembly asked for quiet and order and introduced Dr. Allan White, Chairman of the Space Committee, who would present the report of his committee.

"Mr. President and Delegates in the Assembly," Dr. White started his report. "The findings of this committee became obvious two days ago at the conclusion of our interview with Dr. Shagov and at the press conference that followed the interview. I can only confirm what the Secretary General already said, that the information received officially from the scientists of the Space Telescope Science Institute that the celestial object, named Demon, as reported by Dr. Shagov, exists, and that it has a trajectory for collision with the Earth in five years two months and four days. The actual date will be:

15 March 2003

"As the Secretary General did, I also urge you to make your decisions without undue delay. Thank you."

The uproar on the floor of the Assembly Hall was incredible to watch and to hear. Nothing could be understood.

Commentators went out of their way to stay calm and to report what had been said so far. The NBB anchor summed up the proceedings to that point as 'the apocalypse to be dealt with - ASAP.' The General agreed with an 'Amen.'

The President of the Assembly used his gavel and his voice without much success for a few minutes before anybody paid attention to him. Eventually, the Babel subsided sufficiently for the President to announce that the next item on the agenda was to be discussed. A delegate raised his hand and was recognized by the President of the Assembly as the Prime

Minister of Spain, Mr. Roberto Rodriguez.

"Mr. President, it seems to the delegation of Spain that we should abolish the procedural debate because that will get us nowhere. The agenda is before us, and we have to complete what we have started. The vote should be taken and we should finally hear from the man who brought us together here in New York. Let us hear what he has to say. Let us hear General Shagov."

There was another uproar after the Prime Minister of Spain finished his statement; it was unclear what the uproar was about.

Again President Weiner used his gavel and shouted into the microphone before he could be heard. "Do we start the debate on procedures? Yes or No?" he asked.

"No-o-o-o," the delegates shouted.

"Who is for NO? Raise your hands." The hands of all the delegates went up at once.

"This is a unanimous 'nay' against the procedural debate," President Weiner said for the record.

"I have to ask you to vote for or against holding the special session today," he then shouted into the microphone. "Who is for the special session today - raise your hands."

All hands went up.

"Is anybody against the special session today? Raise your hands." There were none.

"I declare that the special session was approved by the Assembly."

"I had better go," the General said. "This is my turn. God bless the world."

The General walked out of the office and went to the Assembly Hall, accompanied by a guard.

Arsen saw the General, on television, entering the Assembly Hall. All cameras focused on him. The delegates quickly realized that the General was in the hall, and they gave him a standing ovation. The General walked with steady gait to the podium and shook hands with the President of the Assembly, Mr. Weiner, and with the Secretary General, Mr. Ortiz.

"General, I am glad I have finally met you. This is your show now."

President Weiner took the microphone as the applause in the hall subsided.

"Ladies and Gentlemen. It is my pleasure and distinct honor to present to you General Alexei Shagov. The General will talk to you about the problems that concern all of us."

A long applause followed, and then silence fell on the Assembly Hall. All eyes were focused on the General. The General pulled his notes from a pocket of his jacket, adjusted them, sipped water from the glass on the lectern and looked over the delegates on the floor of the Assembly Hall.

"It is my heart and my soul that now extend to all of you in this Assembly, to all of you out there who are following these proceedings, and to all peoples who worry with us but have no means to see us. I feel good to be with you and share with you my thoughts. I know what your concerns are, and what your fears are because they are my concerns and my fears too. Do I have the answer you want to hear? No, I do wish I did. Do I have hope? The answer is yes, I do. I hope that we will find the answer in time, and before the fifteenth of March of the year two thousand and three.

"My hope is based on the research data, which indicate to me that we should be able to change the direction of this flying Demon just enough to cause it to miss the Earth and fly out of our solar system. As you may or may not know, if it misses the Earth and hits another planet or even our moon, that would be disastrous to us as well. It will be the job of our scientists, our astronomers, our mathematicians, and our computer scientists, not only to find the way to change the trajectory of this Demon but also to find the right trajectory to direct it out of our solar system.

"The time is short, and I would like to see these people identified, assembled in research units, and working. I would like them to have started this project yesterday not tomorrow. And I mean, ladies and gentlemen, yesterday, not tomorrow, because the time is really tight."

The Assembly Hall remained in deep silence. The General took a long drink of water from the glass on the lectern. He looked at the delegates and continued his speech.

"Let me make some observations and speak of a dream of mine," the General said. "In the years of my service to the Soviet Union I was in a position to watch various ethnic groups and their interrelations. There was no disagreement when two ethnic groups lived far away from each other. It did not matter what their history was, it did not matter which language they spoke, what the color of their skin was, or which religion they worshiped as long as they lived far away from each other. When members of these distant groups met, they got along very well. When some members of one group settled in the territory of another group, problems arose. As long as the number of the newcomers was small, the problems among groups were insignificant. When the numbers of the newcomers increased, polarization was inevitable and problems ensued.

"Think of Turks in Germany and Muslims in England. The minority is not a threat as long as it is low on the social ladder. However, in the same combination, but with the minority socially dominant or important, the problems become enormous. Think of Tutsi among the Hutu, or Chinese in Indonesia, or whites in South Africa. The inevitable polarization develops, often with very bloody outcomes. Only think of the Jews in Germany before the Holocaust or Armenians in Turkey before their genocide. When ethnic groups share territory, disaster is almost inevitable. Think of Transylvania where the Hungarians are the majority on Rumanian territory. What of Kurds, who are persecuted in five adjacent countries, none willing to give them a piece of land? Or Albanian Kosovars in Serbia. These are just gross examples of suffering. In many places the people are silent from fear, from political suppression, or from force and murder.

"When you think hard enough, you realize that diplomatic activities and international affairs are dominated by polarizations between adjacent ethnic entities - apart from the problems created by the autocrats - and result in wars, even world wars. So I have asked myself frequently: why are some ethnic groups free in expressing their ethnicity and living in a sovereign ethnic territory, while others are not, and are even punished for asking for freedom and territory. Why?"

The General paused for a moment to take another drink of water from the glass on the lectern. The silence in the Assembly Hall was profound; not a voice nor a cough nor a sigh interrupted it. It was as though the delegates were listening to a story they had never heard before and wanted to absorb every word of it.

The General continued his exposition.

"The paradox of it all is the demands to stop the self-determination process, because it becomes *reductio ad absurdum*. These demands are often made by the very leaders who originally secured the territory by their own demands for self-determination. Let me pose a question that has to be answered from the soul: does a man, even from the lowest step on the social ladder and in a most remote part of the world, have the right to be free in expressing his origins, and does an ethnic group of people have the right to have a territory called their own no matter how small that group may be and how small the territory is?

"Why should a proud Australian be arrogant to an Aboriginal, or a Spaniard to a Basque, or a Serb to an Albanian Kosovar, or a Russian to a Chechen? Why? Tell me why. Tell me why the dignity of a Tutsi is more important than the dignity of a Hutu, of a Turk than that of a Kurd, of a Chinese than that of a Tibetan, of an Indian than that of a Kashmiri, or any other set of peoples. Tell me why. Tell me why Kurds shouldn't have their own country, or Basques, or Tibetans, or Cypriot Turks, or Albanian Kosovars, or Igorot people in Grand Cordillera. Why? Tell me why.

"Tell me why there should be a single human being who is denied the right to belong to an ethnic group he or she would like to call his or her own, while others in the same territory are encouraged to belong. I tried to look up the roster of nations and only found the list of states that are called nations. Even this very organization was named the United Nations, yet in the last fifty years a hundred or more new states have been established because their people wanted to be partitioned. More often than not these partitions were bloody because there was always somebody who did not allow a partition to take place.

"We cannot, and should not, forget all who died at the partition of Pakistan from India in 1947, of the dead Serbs, Croats and Muslims in Bosnia in 1991, to mention only two instances. How many Czechoslovakian and Soviet type partitions have you seen? How many Havels and Gorbachevs are there in this world? If you have followed the news recently, you have noticed that the major international problems could be reduced to a single denominator - ethnicity.

"Tell me of the news in 1997: Tutsi and Hutu in Zaire and Rwanda; Serbs, Croats and Muslims in Bosnia; Basques in Spain; Kurds in Turkey; Turks and Greeks in Cyprus; Jews and Palestinians; Catholics and Protestants in Northern Ireland. Have you given a thought to the antagonisms of the U.S. versus Iran, Libya and Iraq, or the Baltic countries versus Russia, or Europeans versus Turks? Tell me why they are fighting. Tell me who is right and who is wrong."

The General paused from his breathless presentation, and sipped water from the glass on the lectern, while the Assembly Hall remained a silent place.

"If we are to succeed in our crusade for survival, I see it as possible only if we abolish ethnic hegemonies by partitioning those who want to be partitioned and by giving them the sovereignty of their own territory. We have to provide and protect real autonomy for those who choose autonomy. We have to provide security to those who are a minority without a territory. There will be no wars after ethnic aspirations have been justly satisfied and preserved. Whatever it takes, this has to be accomplished in the very near future.

"The rest of my message is the technical stuff. Let me explain what it takes to do the job. There will be three Anticollision Boards, each with a Secretary in charge: The Research Board will plan and execute all matters regarding efforts at avoiding collision. The Preservation Board will deal with everything and everyone who will be saved in space. The Survival Board will deal with all matters on Earth in preparation for the collision. As you can see we have to be working in three different directions simultaneously: to avoid the collision, to preserve a contingent of people, animals and plants, material things and information, and to be prepared to deal with the population in the case of collision.

"That is the anticollision effort. In addition, we have to deal with the peoples of the world through the General Assembly as the ultimate source of decisions. Each sovereign territory that already exists and those that will be formed in the next few months will have to be represented in the General Assembly. The World Government will have, aside from the President and the Deputy President, three Secretaries as I have already mentioned. There will also be Secretaries for Ethnic Affairs, for the Military and for Relations with the Assembly. All other business will be conducted by local governments in a form chosen locally. The World Government will make sure that elections are fair by monitoring them closely, that the political leaders are honest by auditing their assets prior to, during and after the election, and by preserving sovereign and autonomous territories and protecting peoples with the special status. The judiciary will be local and so will the law enforcement. If we succeed in averting this calamity, the world order will revert to the status quo of today, corrected for whatever agreements are made from now on."

The General paused again. He took another drink from the glass on the lectern, dried his face with a towel left for his use, and cleared his throat. The silence in the Assembly Hall was complete.

"Let me summarize what I have said. We have little over five years to win or lose the battle for humanity or for part of humanity. My proposal is one way to approach the problem, not the only way. I feel that the research has a chance to succeed in averting the disaster, but we must have contingency plans in case we fail. The technological research will be streamlined, and we will explore every avenue that promises to help in our effort. We want to work, and we want everybody to be involved in this effort. I know that people on this planet can and will find a way for humans and other living creatures to survive this calamity. But, if we have to die, I insist that we all die as equal human beings as each of us deserves to be free and to live a decent and respected life to the end. I will not accept anything less than that."

The General collected his papers from the lectern and walked off the podium.

The reaction to the General's speech was complete silence. The cameras stopped filming, as there was nothing to preserve but a solemn and silent and frozen assembly of delegates in the Assembly Hall at the United Nations. Nobody applauded when the General walked to the side door. The delegates were not dead or paralyzed, nor were their minds at a standstill. The President of the General Assembly and the Secretary General of the United Nations sat by the table on the podium - solemn and silent and frozen in their chairs like everybody else. The anchors were not reporting or analyzing the General's speech - they were just sitting in their seats and waiting for something to happen, something that would electrify them.

People watching the scene in their homes or at work or on the streets also were solemn and silent and frozen. Even those not seeing the scene understood what had happened. This was the stunned world that had expected an unambiguous promise of victory and salvation and had not received it. Instead, the world had received the promise of a respectable death. The world was not ready for such an ending. People were not ready to accept death as a solution, Arsen thought, respectable or not. He turned the television off.

The General walked into the room and Arsen shook his hand.

"This was our Waterloo, Arsen," the General said. "I talked to them from my heart and from my soul, I told them the way it is and what to expect, and that, in the end, was not what they wanted to hear. They wanted to hear a lie. Well, they did not get it. I am sorry that we will not be able to help the world. I am sure that we would have found the solution in time. Let us go to the Plaza - it is time to pack and go home."

The General called Sabrina. "Please find me a seat on a plane to Moscow this afternoon. Try AeroFlot first. We will return to the Plaza very soon."

"You don't think you should wait a while to see what happened, do you?" Arsen asked the General, hoping to persuade him to stay in New York for a few days. "Things may turn around in a day or two. Besides, do you know anybody who could do a better job?"

"Let's face it. The world needs somebody who will tell them what they want to hear. That is known as politics. Let us go." The General put on his heavy raincoat and headed for the door.

The building was not silent anymore, and people were walking in the halls and riding the elevators. The General and Arsen were greeted politely, but nobody asked any questions or made any comments. They flagged down a taxi and did not talk during the short ride to the Plaza. The lobby in the hotel was deserted, and no reporters came to surround them and to bombard them with questions. There was nothing to be asked, and nothing to be answered. The elevator man, a youthful, skinny fellow, smiled politely as he took them up to the eight floor. Sabrina opened the door and embraced the General without saying anything.

The General took his raincoat and jacket off, poured himself a vodka on the rocks, took a long drink, and settled in a chair. He looked tired.

"Sabrina, don't let any calls through to me," the General said. "I've had enough for one day."

"What should I say when one of your Russians calls?" Sabrina asked.

"Tell him to go to hell with my compliments," the General said and laughed heartily. He even looked relaxed. "Of course, find some nice excuse, like my headache. That would be true, after today's fiasco, would it not? I really feel that I should go home. My wife is alone, and I should

be with her. We have a *dacha* outside Moscow, where we spend time together. It is pleasant there during the winter, when high piles of snow in the
yard surround the *dacha*, and nature is frozen. Then one can enjoy a deep
armchair in the living room heated by the fireplace, and have one's legs
covered with a soft blanket. Hot tea with the taste of Cuban rum makes one
feel warm and relaxed, and in the right mood for a good novel that will take
one to a far land, wherever that may be. That is where you will find me if
you ever come to Moscow and decide to come and see me. That is where I
will wait for the Big Bang and meet it with my wife, Katarina Pavlovna. I
had better call her right now, she must be worried about me."

When the General had gone to the bedroom, Sabrina said she had seen,
on television, what had happened, and was stunned herself. "Something
was missing in his talk. It was more an obituary for the world than a call
for revolution. Everything he said was right and thoughtful and precise
but there was no real, convincing hope. This is a bad day for humanity.
What happens next ?"

"I am not sure," Arsen said. "Our careers in world affairs are over.
You have been employed for about two weeks, and you will be looking for
another job. Victoria, too. I will be able to continue my studies and will
have to find a nice observation spot to watch the Big Bang. At seventy-
three I could have used a few more years, although it won't be too bad. It
is time to think about my children and to talk to them. I think this is an
excellent opportunity for people to open up to each other and to enjoy each
other's company and even each other's mere presence."

Sabrina did not say anything.

The General returned to the day room. He had not been able to reach
his wife. The General asked about his flight to Moscow. The AeroFlot flight
was scheduled to leave JFK at five in the afternoon. The General was
pleased.

"We had a meteoric lift-off and the crash was completely silent," the
General said after a long pause. "Where is everybody? What happened to
Kravchenko? Did he ever return from his visit with Senator Hopkins?
Where is Fiodorov? I never even met Jean Pierre Combo and Peter Li.
Have they arrived in New York? They made such a long trip for nothing.
Gen. Thornton - where is he? What happened to Rama and Goran? They
must be working their way back into the United Nations. They are very
capable and will be invaluable to the U.N. and to whatever government is
formed. I think we had a great team. Arsen, you refused to join the top of
my government. Smart guy. You must have suspected something - or were
you really so determined to go to Bosnia and the Middle East?"

"General, I felt that my expertise, if I had any, was in ethnic affairs,"
Arsen said. "I wanted to do what I knew the best. These past two weeks

were the most interesting in my life. I reached the highest levels of politics and government, and I met many interesting people. I became well known in political circles. That was very exciting to a retired orthopedic surgeon. Now we have reached a dead end for some reason, and that does not bother my own ego. However, it will affect me as a person if the wrong people are at the helm of the World Government. I thought you and your group were the right people."

The General did not answer or comment. Instead, he turned the television on. It was just an hour since he had finished his speech and left the United Nations building. The anchors on all channels were discussing the events of the morning and the implications of the delegates' reaction to the General's speech. Nobody was sure what had happened, although most of the personalities interviewed thought that the General had struck a wrong cord in the people, to cause them to freeze in silence in the Assembly Hall and outside. The special session was recessed. The General turned the television off.

Grigor Kravchenko, Ivo Stipich and Vasilii Fiodorov walked into the day room, poured vodka on the rocks for themselves, and settled on the couch without saying anything. Rama Chand called, and talked to the General briefly, to give him an idea of what was happening - essentially nothing. He also said that the President of the Assembly, Mr. Weiner, and Secretary General Ortiz were in a meeting, and nobody knew what they were talking about.

When Sabrina returned to the day room, Grigor Kravchenko asked her whether she could make airline reservations to Paris for him and to Zagreb for Ivo Stipich; and Fiodorov wanted to go to Kiev with a stopover in Warsaw. The ship was sinking, Arsen thought.

The General was in the bedroom packing and trying to reach his wife. They turned the television on a few times just to find out that the United Nations Building was deserted. Nobody else called the General. There were no calls from the Presidents or from the Prime Ministers; nor did any Ambassador call. Sen. Hopkins did not call nor did Gen. Thornton.

The mood in the day room was gloomy and the conversation sporadic and subdued. Sabrina was able to get plane reservations for everybody. They were all rats, Arsen thought, all the Presidents and Prime Ministers and Ambassadors, and the people who were to become the Secretaries in the government, and friends. Only Rama Chand had called the General. It was time to finish up here and go home.

Victoria came to see whether she could be of help, and Sabrina wanted to talk to Arsen.

"What do we do with the offices we rented and the people we hired? What do I tell Michelle? And Stanley Kim, who hasn't even started yet?"

"Our organization has collapsed and it is out of business," Arsen said. "We are bankrupt and we must close the doors. We should certify for them that they were officially employed, even for only two days. You must talk to the landlord and explain the situation - although they already know what is going to happen. We will use the money that is left in the bank. I will add whatever is necessary to pay expenses for one month and no more."

"That's fair enough," Sabrina said. "This is really unbelievable."

Arsen went to the bedroom to see the General. He had just finished talking to his wife.

"Katarina Pavlovna is okay," the General said. "The situation in Moscow is almost the same as in New York. People have finally comprehended that the collision may happen, perhaps is even likely to happen, and their reaction is denial in silence, as if the threat would disappear if nobody talked about it. They have to be positively electrified to accept the reality. I merely told them the truth, which they did not want to hear. The result would have been the same no matter what I said." The General was preoccupied with the psychological paralysis during and after his speech, which also could have been precipitated by Dr. White's announcement of the calculated date of collision - 15 March 2003.

"Arsen, you seem ready to leave," the General said. "This may be our last meeting. I must tell you that I really enjoyed working with you. I would have found a way to keep you in the government and away from Bosnia. I hope you find peace of mind during the remaining years. The world would be much better off had it given you the chance to look out for human dignity. Even dying should be dignified - I cannot accept it any other way. God bless you - if an old communist can say that."

The General embraced Arsen and gave him the triple Russian kiss. Arsen left the bedroom and the General returned to packing his luggage.

Victoria also talked with the General and wished him luck, and received the triple kiss. Sabrina wanted to stay until the General left for JFK, and promised to join them at Arsen's home.

They saw Paul at the concierge's desk; he had come early to see the General off. He said nothing about the events of the morning. A few reporters approached them before they left the lobby.

"Doctor Pankovich, how is the General taking the situation?" asked a reporter. "He must be upset?"

"No, he is not upset, Mr. McCollum." Arsen recognized the reporter from Kansas. "He is in a contemplative mood and trying to figure out what precipitated the silence during his speech. It might have been Dr. White's announcement of the doomsday date. Suddenly, we all faced the very date of our death. It made no difference any more what the General had to say, regardless of his optimistic approach to research and the possibility of changing the course of the Demon. Now that the General is on his way to Moscow and to retirement, our doom is more certain than ever."

"The General's returning to Moscow?" Mr. McCollum asked. "He's not going to try again?"

"I am afraid not," Arsen said. "He has a *dacha* near Moscow and he is romanticizing about snow and a fireplace, a book that he will read and the company of his wife Katarina Pavlovna. Not such a bad ending, is it?"

"What about you?"

"I am taking my wife to Puerto Rico tomorrow," Arsen said. "Good luck, Mr. McCollum. You will have to interview somebody else from now on. Leave the General alone at this time. He may say something that he would regret in the future."

Victoria and Arsen left the lobby of the Plaza Hotel thinking that an interesting episode in their lives was over. A post script was to be added to the events of the last two weeks.

As they were walking toward Fifty-Ninth Street to flag a taxi, a man stopped them and addressed them politely

"Dr. Pankovich, Miss Victoria Ram. I am FBI Special Agent Frolick, Peter Frolick. Would you mind coming with me to the FBI Headquarters in New York? This is my identification. The car at the corner will take us there."

The car the agent was pointing to came around the corner and drove very slowly towards them. There was not much they could do. Arsen wondered if they were being kidnaped. But the man's identification, which he carefully examined, appeared genuine. Victoria, who was obviously scared, held Arsen's elbow and squeezed his forearm.

"It is okay, Victoria," Arsen said. "I think these people are from the FBI and they will take us to their office one way or another. We may as well go now."

Nothing more was said. Arsen saw no point in asking the reason for the detention. The FBI headquarters was a short distance away. They were escorted into the building and soon after, they were shown into the office of the Agent-in-Charge. Arsen noticed the name plate on the door - John Walker.

The office was large, with windows at either end and a portrait of the President of the United States on the right-hand wall. An executive desk was at the street end of the room, with a semi-oval bay behind it where the building's facade bowed out. The wall with the portrait also had a door, which led to a conference room. The left wall was lined with bookcases - almost empty. Wall-to-wall sturdy lifeless carpet covered the floor. Mr. Walker was on the phone when Arsen and Victoria walked in and he did not get up, but pointed to two chairs that faced his desk and indicated that the two of them should sit down.

"Thank you for volunteering to come," Mr. Walker said after he finished his phone conversation. "We have no charges against you today. Rather, we need some information. Our conversation will be taped automatically, and you'll be able to review it later, after it's been typed, and correct it as necessary, and of course, we'll want you to sign it. Let me come to the point. Dr. Pankovich, during the last two weeks you've had meetings with some foreign nationals who were visiting New York and the United Nations on behalf of a foreign government. Is that true?"

"No, that is not true," Arsen said. "To the best of my knowledge, these individuals are not agents of any government. They represent an organization in Moscow called Institute for Ethnic Studies."

"Isn't that a government institution?" Mr. Walker asked.

"I was told it is a private institute at this time, although at one time it could have been a state institution."

"Gen. Shagov and his associates work for the Russian Government," Mr. Walker said. "Isn't that true?"

"You may know more than I," Arsen said. "I am not sure. I have met them as members of the Institute for Ethnic Studies. They never indicated that they worked for the Russian Government. They did work for the Russian Government before they retired, I believe."

"One of them was an important official of the NKVD," Mr. Walker said. "Did you know that?"

"Yes, I did. Mr. Ivo Stipich told me at our first meeting that he had been an associate of Mr. Kravchenko in the NKVD Headquarters in Moscow. Both of them have retired and have been working for the Institute."

"Are you sure about that?"

"I am not sure," Arsen said. "These people told me they work for the Ethnic Institute. That is all I know about their employers."

"While Mr. Shagov was in New York, he was trying to organize the World Government," Mr. Walker said. "You were helping him in that effort. Actually, you became the spokesman for his organization. Is that true?"

"Very much true, Mr. Walker," Arsen said. "The General discovered the celestial object which is going to collide with Earth in a few years. He knows what to do about the danger. It seems to me that everybody should have helped him, rather than letting him slip out of sight and return to Russia."

"Is he gone, really?" Mr. Walker seemed to be interested, more as an individual than as a special agent.

"No, he is not gone yet but he will be on his way sometime this afternoon."

"Was he planning any other activities?" Mr. Walker had regained his official poise. "What I mean is, was he thinking or talking about destabilizing the United States in some way and for some purpose? For example, he was talking in the United Nations about his government taking over the Military of the United States."

"The General did not mention that during his speech in the United Nations. He stated his plans about a world military clearly to Sen. Sam Hopkins when Mr. Hopkins visited him. It seemed that the idea was acceptable to the U.S. Government. He talked about the World Military for the preservation of ethnic order. I am unaware of his thinking about anything else. As you know, the General appointed an American General to be the Chief of the Military."

"Wasn't that one of your ideas?"

"Maybe it was my suggestion. I felt that our government would be upset if the Chief of the World Military were a Chinese or a Bosnian." Arsen wondered who had leaked that information to the FBI? A mole? Brad Smith was gone when Gen. Thornton's name was brought up by Arsen.

"Dr. Pankovich, you and other Americans who worked for Gen. Shagov should have been registered as agents representing a foreign government," Mr. Walker said. "This will be considered and decided by the Justice Department in the next few days. I'll report to my Director about this interview."

"I was working for a private institution not a foreign government. Should I get myself an attorney?" Arsen asked. "Maybe I should say nothing further before I talk to an attorney?"

"That's up to you but I really think that won't be necessary," Mr. Walker said. "You will be asked to register if the Justice Department decides you should."

"Now, I don't work for anyone anymore," Arsen said.

"I realize that."

"I was planning to go with my family to Puerto Rico tomorrow. Do you think your investigation requires my presence in New York?"

"Not really," Mr. Walker said. "Just tell me which hotel you will be staying at."

"The Westin Rio Maar Beach," Arsen said.

"Okay Dr. Pankovich. Sorry for this inconvenience. I truly appreciate your coming immediately and without any objections. You and Miss Ram are free to leave now." Mr. Walker escorted Victoria and Arsen to the lobby. "If I need you I'll call you at Rio Maar. Have a good evening, Doctor. Good evening, Miss Ram."

Victoria and Arsen walked out to the street to find a taxi to take them to Arsen's home.

As they entered the apartment Arsen introduced Victoria to Nada.

"Let us have a dinner somewhere tonight - how about Park Avenue Café. I had better call them to find out if they are open." Arsen called the restaurant and to his surprise it was open and accepting reservations. He made a reservation for seven o'clock.

"Arsen, I think you should call the children," Nada said. "They've been calling since the morning. They wanted to know what was your reaction. Please, call them now. There is plenty of time to get ready for dinner."

As Arsen was making the first call he was thinking what he could say that would calm them down. With the General gone, now was the time to keep up hope. If the General thought there was a chance to avert the collision, then there must be other people who thought the same and who could do it. Besides, they could always talk to the General. That sounded good.

"Hi, Dad," Mark greeted Arsen. "Why is the General leaving? Why are you at home? Who will do something now? This is very upsetting. Tell me what's going on."

"The General's team lost and it has to retire," Arsen said. "I have no idea anymore what is happening. There should be something happening in the United Nations and--"

"Nothing's happening there," Mark interrupted Arsen. "They decided to adjourn the session till tomorrow morning. They don't know what they're doing. They'll take a couple of years to discuss the issues before making the decision. Dad, why don't you do something. Talk to the General. Talk to the President of the United States. They know you, maybe they'll listen to you."

"As you know, nobody ever listens to me," Arsen said, trying in vain to use an old jest.

"Dad, this is no time for kidding." Mark was getting annoyed. "You should find somebody in the government to talk to about the situation. I'm sure you have some ideas."

"Mark, kidding aside," Arsen said, "I don't see anything I can do. I will wait to see what happens."

"This is rather depressing," Mark concluded. "Talk to you later."

A similar conversation was repeated three more times. "There is nothing I can do right now," became Arsen's refrain.

The regular television programs were resumed. It seemed as if life were returning to normal, yet one big change had occurred - life expectancy on the Earth had decreased to five years and four months or less.

Sabrina reported that the General and all the others had left and that she would soon be on her way to join them for dinner. It was six-thirty - time for the evening news. Arsen wanted to hear what the MMB had to report on this day.

The events in the United Nations were recapitulated. The facts were presented without analysis or explanation. The special session had been adjourned until the next morning, as had already been reported. Nobody had any idea what would happen if the delegates met again. President of the Assembly Weiner had read a short statement and said nothing new. Secretary General Ortiz had held the shortest press briefing in the recent history of the United Nations, and, ominously, had said nothing about plans for the next day. There were no scheduled meetings. Some Presidents and Prime Ministers had left New York in the afternoon, obviously expecting nothing to happen in the next few days. That did not sound promising. Not even the Security Council had a scheduled meeting for the evening or the next day.

The news moved to subjects other than the special session. The El Niño phenomenon was examined in depth again, and the troubled areas were shown. There was a report from Bonn that the Yugoslav and Bosnian Serb delegations had left a conference in protest against the reference, in the final communiqué, to the increasing problems in Kosovo. The Albanian Kosovars were mistreated by Serbs although they also pushed the Serbian minority in Kosovo, Arsen thought. When would they learn that these attitudes had to change. A short report from India showed the rioting in Amritstar, which had resumed during the day. Trading on Wall Street had been canceled.

Arsen turned off the television and went to the living room. It was time to go to Park Avenue Café.

The restaurant was full, and they waited more than half an hour to be seated. People looked a bit lost, or it appeared so to Arsen, as he expected people to look that way. Yet, they talked to each other, they ate the usual large amounts, they drank as they always had and they were in no hurry to leave. The food was good as always.

Conversation was not inspiring as they talked about the General leaving so precipitously after the strange drama in the Assembly Hall. Comments were made about other Russians, particularly Kravchenko, whom Sabrina did not like.

"He looks like a big rat with a Nixon face," she said. "When you look at him he gives you the impression of a man with a knife up his sleeve, and ready to use it. Doctor, he was to be your boss - I worried about that. Remember when he talked to you the first time and said you were unknown one day and famous the next? He wanted you to know he was the boss. I wonder what they'll do."

"I think the General will bounce back and get a role in the Research Department. Whoever takes over will have to follow in the General's footsteps; there is no other way. He will need the research because we need new technologies, he will need preservation of some kind if research fails, and you have to think there may be at least a survivor or two after the collision. Ethnicity will not be the problem because people are used to being killed, collision or not, but if riots start, if demonstrations become violent, as they may, and if ethnic groups start making demands, the problems may become immense and unmanageable and they could affect the anticollision effort.

"Some people will just say, to hell with everybody, I will not be free if collision is avoided, I will die as a pig anyway, so let us give them hell now. That is what worries me. The General had a plan, a good plan. Will the new people come up with something better? I doubt that they will face the ethnic issues. Nobody has taken them seriously in the past. The replete man does not believe the hungry one.

"We are going to Puerto Rico tomorrow. Hopefully, sun, swimming, and good food will help us forget for a while. I wish we were booked for a couple of weeks."

It was almost ten o'clock by the time Nada and Arsen got home.

CHAPTER TWENTY-TWO

THURSDAY, 11 DECEMBER 1997

The first thought that came to Arsen's mind as he woke up was to find out what was happening in the United Nations. He turned on the television in the living room and tuned to every channel that would normally provide important news, WCN, MMB and others. They were broadcasting regular programs. Not a single station was reporting from the United Nation. There were no reports to indicate that the special session would be resumed during the day. Nothing! This was disturbing and it indicated that the delegations had not reached agreement on anything. They must be talking, Arsen thought.

The flight to Puerto Rico was leaving a few minutes after nine. Arsen called the usual number: 333-6666. "No problems, the car will be at your door in twenty minutes," the dispatcher said. The doorman called twenty minutes later to inform Arsen that the car had arrived. They had three suitcases, which had already been taken to the lobby by a doorman. The car was the standard Continental Town Car. The traffic to JFK was no different than on any other working day. They checked in and proceeded to the gate. The inspection was passed without incidents. The plane took off on time and landed on time. Soon they were on a new hotel bus, that left Louis Munoz Airport and delivered them to the hotel at one o'clock. They were sitting at the pool and drinking orange juice at two o'clock. The rest of the day they relaxed, lying in beach chairs and exposing themselves to the sun. The newspapers Arsen found in a small shop on the main floor, reported everything he already knew. Everything was normal and quiet, yet the world was in great peril.

Arsen awaited impatiently for the MMB News at seven thirty. Something would have to be announced by the Secretary General of the United Nations, he thought. They knew everybody was waiting to find out what had been accomplished behind the scenes - who would lead the anticollision effort, what kind of administrative organization would be established, and who would head various departments. These life and death questions were on everybody's mind.

As the news began, the Anchor, Bradley Adams, read the headlines - only one of the five dealt with the crisis. A bulletin from the United Nations announced further postponement of the special session, now scheduled to resume on Tuesday, 16 December 1997. The decision had been made by Secretary General Ortiz and Assembly President Weiner after consultation with the Security Council, who had held a meeting during the day. No explanation was given for the postponement. Mr. Adams reported that information from an individual who did not want to be identified indicated that there was considerable friction among the permanent members of the Security Council, between Russia and China on one side and the U.S. and Britain on the other. The issue was the failure to talk to General Shagov and try to persuade him to be available for the second round in the Assembly.

In other news, over two hundred people had been killed in a Hutu attack on a Tutsi refugee camp, according to officials of the United Nations. High-level meetings of I.R.A with British officials were described as productive in preparation for further peace talks. El Niño was creating havoc around the world. The Czech Republic was feeling aftershocks from the corruption scandal that had caused the fall of the government a week before.

Arsen was upset by the contents of the news and by the absence of any concrete activity. If anything of importance had been happening it would have been mentioned, Arsen concluded, and turned off the television, as even the poor transmission was annoying him.

Nada and her mother were ready for dinner and Arsen gladly left the room. Without hesitation they proceeded to the restaurant, where a buffet dinner was being served. That was the best choice for their taste.

Back in the room at nine Arsen tried to read Milovan Djilas's *Wartime*, an account from the viewpoint of a man who had been a member of the highest echelon of Tito's Partisan Army. The wartime pictures were interesting, showing the young leaders and the country at war. While reading the text with its minutiae of a visit to Montenegro, Arsen fell asleep.

CHAPTER TWENTY-THREE

Arsen woke up late on Friday. Sun and relaxation were the only items on the schedule for the whole day - something to look forward to after days of tension, talks, and frustration. Nothing was happening, and the Demon was coming closer - hundreds of thousands of miles closer every day. Arsen felt anxious for a moment, as if death were rapidly approaching him, and the feeling disappeared just as rapidly. He turned on the television. The regular programs were being shown in English and Spanish. There was nothing on the United Nations and nothing on the Demon, again as if nothing had happened the day before. Quite disturbing! Arsen turned off the television and joined Nada and her mother at breakfast.

At the pool Arsen decided to read a short novel by Khushwant Singh, *Train to Pakistan*, which he had recently bought. Arsen thought he would get a better feel for the events at the time of the partition of India and Pakistan. The story captivated him from the start. He felt at home among the characters of all three religious groups. They lived together in relative harmony for years, though being what they were was natural to them, and their differences were also natural to them until the religious war erupted and trains from Pakistan started arriving with thousands of dead Hindus and Sikhs. In the turmoil the Muslims left and their train to Pakistan was saved by a Sikh in love with a departing Muslim girl.

The simplicity of their lives and relations did not entirely fit the wisdom which emerged from their conversations. Arsen could see himself in that small village, Mano Majra, near the river, where the railroad station was the only landmark. He followed their conversations, and felt a certain dignity in their conduct and in their relations among themselves and with the outside world. They might have been poor, but they knew where they belonged, and each of them was recognized by all as one of them.

Recognition was the glue that held them together. This could have been a Bosnian village, Arsen knew well, or a Cossack village by the Don. The feeling would be the same, as the people were the same and recognized by others in the village.

The day flew by as Arsen lived the lives of the people in Mano Majra.

It was time to return to the room and get ready for dinner. On the way back Arsen stopped in the small store to pick up a copy of *The New York Times*. There were none left. Probably nothing of interest was in it anyway, Arsen thought. By the time he had taken a shower and dressed it was seven-thirty and time for the MMB News Report, with Bradley Adams. The headlines had life in them. Mr. Adams was reporting on high-level meetings in the White House and in the Defense Department, a meeting of the National Academy of Sciences with the American Astronomical Society, a scheduled meeting of NASA officials with the President at the White House, visits of the Russian and Chinese Ambassadors in the morning, and of the British Ambassador at noon. Mr. Adams concluded the report with stories of demonstrations and riots around the world. Something was finally happening, Arsen thought. Demonstrations and riots were bad news, although they had not spread worldwide as Arsen had anticipated.

Dinner and early bedtime had almost become routine.

CHAPTER TWENTY-FOUR

SATURDAY, 13 DECEMBER 1997

Days were all alike on vacation when the goals were sun, rest, and relaxation. That was what Arsen and Nada and her mother had at the Westin del Maar Rio in Puerto Rico. Food was just an extra they could have done without.

Arsen turned on the television. MMB News had a special program on the world crisis. The problems were piling up, and no solutions were in sight. Six world powers were fighting for the Presidency of the United Nations, behind the scenes: China, Russia, the United States, Zaire, Spain and Egypt. Obviously each represented a block. China claimed to represent all of Asia, Russia the Slavic People, United States the English-speaking people and the Europeans, Zaire Africa - although South Africa was inching into the picture - Spain the Spanish speakers, and Egypt the Muslims. India, as big as she was, claimed only the right to deal with whoever was to represent her. This was a Huntingtonian map - to a degree. Disagreements and competition among nations were the news, Arsen thought. It would take months of negotiations to define the issues before the discussions for the leadership even started, if they ever reached that stage. Riots and demonstrations would be the next cause for negotiations. Unbelievable! If one could only go elsewhere, somewhere far away from the Earth.

The MMB news report was presented by Laura Collins substituting for Bradley Adams. Not much was reported on the meetings the President had had with the Ambassadors from Russia, China and Britain, and even less about the talks with NASA officials. There were no comments on the meetings of Administration officials with the President and the Defense Secretary. The meeting at the National Academy of Sciences was fully covered and it was clear that there was no agreement on the anticollision effort and the direction that should be pursued.

Most objections by scientists to the proposals offered by General Shagov were that the technology was nonexistent and that the time was too short to develop it in time. Scientists claimed it would take ten or more years to develop such technology, and that the effort would be a waste of time and resources. Idiots, Arsen thought. Preservation by escape into space and return after the collision must be a priority project, although if the Earth were destroyed and became uninhabitable after the collision, the escapees would be doomed. What a ghastly thought. It occurred to Arsen that delayed cloning on some other planet in the Universe years later should be considered. That project would be even more formidable than preservation.

"The problems are multiplying and getting more complex," Arsen said to Nada, and he explained what was happening. "I wish I could get involved in some capacity. I wish somebody would listen to me." Nada laughed at that old joke, although Arsen was serious this time. "We should get together with the children when we return to New York. I would like to know what their plans are for the next five years. It seems as though we have time, but we really don't. Things will start happening. A national counting clock will be build so that we can find out the exact number of days, hours and minutes to the impact. That sounds terrible."

"I will talk to the children when we return to New York," Nada said. "Do you think they should all come at the same time?"

"That is exactly what I would like you to organize."

"Let's have dinner," Nada said. "I am hungry and cannot think constantly about bad things, not now."

Another pleasant vacation day was coming to a close.

CHAPTER TWENTY-FIVE

SUNDAY, 14 DECEMBER 1997

The Sunday Times usually did not reach the Westin Resort on Sundays. This Sunday was not an exception. The weather was not as cooperative as it had been the previous three days. Showers forced them to seek shelter temporarily in the halls of the hotel a few times, until they could return to the pool in sunshine.

Their lunch at ten-thirty was timed to count as the Continental breakfast they were entitled to. They were helping themselves to a mixture of delightfully fresh raspberries, strawberries, cantaloupe cubes, slices of orange, pineapple, and grapefruit, figs and a variety of nuts. The coffee was not the best, and the bagels could hardly pass the test of a New Yorker but they ate them anyway.

After lunch, by the pool again, Arsen was enjoying his third reading of Ernest Hemingway's *For Whom the Bell Tolls.*. Arsen thought it was a fascinating story, presented in simple language, about anonymous peasant heroes. There were even amusing parts of the novel, like the descriptions of love-making by Maria and Robert Jordan. Arsen mused about how Ernest Hemingway would describe it today. Probably more explicitly, like everybody else. The tragic end of Robert Jordan was obvious though not narrated.

The seven thirty news report was bland. There were no signs of any progress in the world crisis. It seemed to Arsen that the world was too quiet for the situation. The President was at Camp David. He had meetings with a number of his advisers and with the Directors of the Federal Bureau of Investigation and the Central Intelligence Agency. What were they investigating for the President, Arsen wondered. It was mentioned that General John Thornton had visited briefly with the President. It was reported from Moscow that Gen. Alexei Shagov had left the city for his *dacha* at Gorky, and that he refused to make any statements. The United

Nations was deserted over the weekend. Not much for any day, Arsen thought.

The buffet dinner and a walk along the beach completed this relaxing and dull day.

CHAPTER TWENTY-SIX

Arsen was in no hurry to get out of bed after he woke up. Nada was still asleep, and her mother had not called from the adjoining room. So much had to be done, Arsen thought, and nothing was happening. The General had a plan and knew exactly what had to be done. He had just misjudged what people wanted to hear from him. The demonstrations and riots were not as widespread as Arsen had anticipated, and they were mostly protests against the inactivity of the world leaders.

Arsen thought about his life and his family. The old generation was dead. The peer generation is too involved with its own problems in life, particularly his friends in Bosnia and Serbia. The younger generation did not want to know about the old times. That was how life had always been. There would not be much to look forward to without the future. Reading would be the last resort, the last hideout, perhaps even the last answer before the death call. Arsen's thoughts were starting to go in circles, something that had not happened before, when everything was straightforward. Now it was time to think about death and dying since death was approaching steadily by the day, by the hour, by the minute. It was actually not such a bad feeling thinking about as it used to be. Thinking about death in the past had meant leaving something behind, something real, something palpable and never to be seen again. Now the meaning of death was different, because there would be nothing and nobody left behind. There would be no values to be preserved, no memories to be left in someone's mind and soul, no legacies to stand for all times, no unfinished plans to be completed by someone else. Arsen had been afraid of death, not because he would disappear into nothingness, but because the accumulated experiences of his life would precipitously or gradually lose their value and their meaning.

Nada woke up and called her mother and soon they were on the way to another day of relaxation and food, and some walking on the beach.

Later in the morning, a bell boy walked around calling Arsen's name. There was an urgent message from the operator.

"Who could be calling you here?" Nada asked. "Nobody even knows we are here."

"Victoria and Sabrina know," Arsen said. "Even the FBI Agent-in-Charge in New York knows it. It is possible he is calling me. I had better find out."

Arsen went to their room to have privacy in case the conversation were important and private, and called the operator.

"Dr. Pankovich, you won't believe it," the operator said. "The White House was on the line and they wanted you to call them promptly. It took a few minutes to find you. We figured you would be around the pool or on the beach. Do you want me to make the call?"

"Please, do it right now."

"I'll call you right back," the operator said and hung up only to call back moments later. "Dr. Pankovich, I have the White House on the line. Let me connect you."

"Hello, this is Dr. Pankovich."

"Dr. Pankovich, this is Brigitte Fromm, the secretary to the National Security Advisor Bryan Whiette. Mister Whiette told me that the President and he would like you to come to the White House for a meeting as soon as you can. How soon do you think you could make it to Washington?"

"There is a flight out of here at 3:00. If I can get on it I will be in New York by six tonight. You should decide if I should proceed to Washington or come in the morning."

"Tonight," Brigitte Fromm said. "I'll make the reservations for your flight to New York and somebody will wait for you at the gate in New York and escort you to the plane for Washington, where somebody else will wait for you and bring you here. Good luck. Don't waste any more time." She hung up.

Arsen called the operator and told her to find his wife by the pool and tell her to come to the room right away. He packed his bag quickly since there was not much to pack anyway. Nada walked into the room and said that she knew it was important.

"The President wants me at the White House tonight," Arsen said. "Something is happening and they must want to talk to me before the special session resumes its work tomorrow. I have no clues what they want."

"Did you confirm the flight?"

"They will do it. All I have to do is to be at the airport on time. You are returning to New York tomorrow. I have no idea where I will be."

Arsen rushed to the lobby and out the main entrance and found a taxi waiting for him. He arrived at the airport almost an hour ahead of the departure time. The reservation was already made for him and the ticket agent gave him his seat assignment and a boarding pass. He walked to the gate, found a seat in a corner, and continued reading the Hemingway novel.

The flight to New York was choppy - as the captain called it after the plane jolted a few times. Then there was a significant dive, when the passengers screamed in fear, and the Puerto Rican man seated next to Arsen crossed himself several times. Arsen just thought that it would be a shame to die in an airplane crush, prematurely, and fail to experience the real big crash of the collision of the Earth and the Demon. The sky over New York was clear and visibility almost perfect for seeing the spectacle of the city at night with its millions of lights, and its lighted bridges, from the Varrazzano to the Whitestone and the Throgs Neck - and its skyline of lighted skyscrapers. The view thrilled Arsen every time he saw it.

A man at the gate recognized Arsen immediately and introduced himself as Security Service agent John Thomas.

"Dr. Pankovich, I saw you on television giving briefings to the media, must have been last week," Agent Thomas said. "You were with Gen. Shagov, weren't you?"

"Yes, I was with him last week," Arsen said. "It seems like last year."

"We have to hurry," Agent Thomas said. "I'll drive you to the US Airways Shuttle at La Guardia, that's the best I could arrange to get you to Washington. Just go to the gate. Here's your ticket."

They rushed down the corridor to the arrivals level. Agent Thomas's car was parked nearby. They took the Van Wyick to La Guardia and arrived on time at the US Airways building. The flight was departing at seven o'clock.

"Good luck, Doctor," Agent Thomas said. Arsen stepped onto the sidewalk and rushed into the terminal. He walked into the plane just before the door was locked.

The scene was repeated at Washington's shuttle gate. A man approached Arsen and introduced himself as Security Service agent Damien Walters. They walked to the arrivals area where the agent's car was parked.. It was minutes before nine when they reached the car gate at the White House, and soon after that, they were walking into the office of the National Security Advisor, Mr. Bryan Whiette.

"Good evening, Dr. Pankovich," Bryan Whiette said. "Sorry that we dragged you here all the way from Puerto Rico. The matter is very urgent, and the President really wanted to talk to you."

"Good evening, Mr. Whiette," Arsen replied. "I am glad to be here and to help in any way I can. Would this have something to do with the special session that resumes its work tomorrow?"

"They told me you catch on quickly, and it seems to be true."

"Why would anybody need me for anything else?" Arsen explained. "The only connection is Gen. Shagov, and he is out of the picture now. Or, is he?"

"The President will explain what's on his mind." Bryan Whiette escorted Arsen to the Oval Office to meet the President, who was reading at his desk.

"Mr. President, this is Dr. Pankovich," Bryan Whiette said. "He made it. I'll be in my office if you need me."

"Good evening, Dr. Pankovich," the President said. "Okay, Bryan, come back as soon as you can." The President got up and shook hands with Arsen, offered him a seat and sat back in his chair behind the desk. "Dr. Pankovich, you must be tired from the trip and it's getting late, but there are matters I thought had to be dealt with tonight. Would you like to drink or eat something?"

"Perhaps a Coke and a sandwich, if there is any at this hour. I am a bit hungry."

"Everything is right here. Help yourself."

Arsen did not want to miss the opportunity to try food at the White House. It must be good, he thought, and it was.

"Let me ask you something about your relationship with Gen. Shagov," the President said as they returned to their chairs. "We know that you worked very closely with him, though for only a few days during his brief stay in New York. You know, Dr. Pankovich, that was a rather meteoric rise to the world scene, and then such a fall. We have some knowledge of what the General has done so far in Russia, but we need more information about the man. What kind of a man is he?"

Arsen did not answer immediately, giving himself time to think, and giving the President time to say more; and the President did.

"What I mean is," he said, "is he as brilliant as he was portrayed by the press. Our info is really limited in that respect. Things are happening around the globe, as you might have heard. Demonstrations are spreading like fire. Governments are helpless because of the numbers of people on the streets. Reports just started coming in this morning, and that's all we've been listening to all day."

"I heard nothing about that," Arsen said.

"Arsen, the reason I brought you here is the urgency of the situation. The problem from space is not going away, as even some of my advisers thought it would; the demonstrations and riots are spreading, and the United Nations is stalled before the resumption of the session tomorrow. We have not come up with a plan of action, and the Congress is very much opposed to Gen. Shagov's idea of the World Government and too sensitive about losing control of our Armed Forces. They cannot understand the ethnic proposals the General put forward. I wish I could say that our scientific community has come up with a visionary plan to save the Earth."

"I heard about the conclusions of the National Academy of Sciences," Arsen remarked.

"I know," the President said. "What are the alternatives? I thought you might have some ideas, from your recent discussions with the General. Maybe you have ideas of your own?"

Arsen knew what was expected of him and what the problems were that the President was facing. He had no hesitation in expressing himself.

"Mr. President, I understand what you are saying and what the dilemmas of the Congress are. This is a totally new situation, unpredicted and unpredictable, and many people are not ready to face it. Gen. Shagov had a very clear view of what had to be done, and he was convinced that the catastrophe could be prevented. That is certainly a view diametrically different from the conclusions I heard coming from the National Academy of Sciences. Their view was 'Why bother wasting time trying to prevent the inevitable.' They said that doom could not be prevented."

"You have it right," the President said as Bryan Whiette walked into the Oval Office and took a seat.

"I was annoyed with that logic." Arsen continued to explain the situation as he saw it. "Failure would at least give us the satisfaction that we had tried. The General's plan should be tried, in my view, Mr. President, although it should be tried by people with imagination and few doubts. Of course, other approaches will have to be tried at the same time I am sure you are aware of the directions the General was talking about."

"Yes, we know," said the President. "Our interest is to know whether there were concrete proposals that you think are good."

"A number of ideas were mentioned but we were concerned about the decisions in the special session at that time. I know that the idea of sending a team to intercept the celestial object, the Demon if you wish, was an important concept under study in Russia. The team would plant nuclear devices on the Demon with the idea that the explosion would change its trajectory. The General was not too enthusiastic about that project. The neutrino theory was mentioned, and a neutrino gun was to be built that would deflect the Demon. There was even talk about a neutrino glue shield that might also deflect the Demon. Space Internet was mentioned, the Sinternet. Other ideas were concerned with the possible continuation of life in space, perhaps on another planet. Memory banks, spontaneous fertilization, cloning in space and some similar ideas were mentioned. Obviously, Mr. President, we had to get the approval of the Assembly to form an administration before the wheels could start turning. Nobody ever asked my opinion about the scientific matters - I was assigned an ethnic domain."

"Do you think Gen. Shagov is the right man to be the President of the U.N. or whatever it would have been called?" the President asked.

"He is an excellent man with vision and organizational ability, and he is a leader. At this point, however, he has the handicap of having failed to present his ideas to the people, not only to the Assembly, and that raises questions about his political acumen. If I were asked to decide, I would make him responsible for the entire anticollision effort and give him anything he wants. However, I would let someone else run the Administration and be concerned with Military affairs, relations with the Assembly, territories and ethnic problems, welfare, health and whatever else."

"It was our understanding, Dr. Pankovich, that you did not want a position in the administration," Bryan Whiette said. "You said that to the reporters at the press briefings. Why?"

"I answered that question a number of times. I am a self-taught ethnic scientist with a desire to do no harm. I am not qualified to run the Department of Health, although I am a physician. You need a strong Ethnic Department to do what is right for the people. There must be some justice even a minute before midnight for the doomed. Besides, that will be your best insurance against riots and demonstrations."

"I cannot see you going to Bosnia to solve problems of Croats, Muslims and Serbs," Bryan Whiette said, "nor the problems between Greeks and Turks, nor between Jews and Arabs."

"The problem of Arabs and Jews cannot be solved by anybody." The President and his National Security Adviser looked at Arsen with a surprise. "What I mean is, only they themselves understand the complexities of their problems after so many years of negotiations. Nobody else does, and nobody should try to tell them what to do. We should only induce them to talk. They may not even understand that they enjoy each other's company."

"Do you think Kravchenko should run the Ethnic Department?" Bryan Whiette asked. "I met him when he visited with Sen. Hopkins. He is an interesting man and a former boss in the NKVD."

"All older Russian officials were Communist Party Members; how else would they have reached the top?" Arsen said. "I would not mind working for him."

"We would prefer that you work in the administration as the Director of the Ethnic Department," the President said.

"Impossible," Arsen replied. "That would be quite impossible."

"Why?" the President asked.

"It is difficult to explain," Arsen said. "Although the General's group has been dissolved, I have a loyalty to the General. He would want Kravchenko in that job."

"You also had the opportunity to work with former Secretary General Chand," the President said. "What's your impression of him? Would he be the right man for President of the World Administration?"

"He would be an excellent choice," Arsen replied without hesitation, as he had respect for Rama Chand. "He is a politician and plays a fair game. He loves India, and he is loyal to his native land, yet I would trust him to be objective even when India's interests are at stake."

"You think highly of him," the President said. "Would you work for him and with him?"

"He needs an experienced administrator," Arsen said. "The best man is his own Deputy Goran Enstrom."

"You just want to go to Bosnia," the President said, somewhat annoyed by Arsen's persistent refusal to work in the higher echelons of the World Government. "That's where you'll be going, I guess." Arsen did not answer.

It seemed that the conversation was over. The President got up and shook Arsen's hand.

"Thank you for coming," he said. "This conversation has been very useful to us."

Bryan Whiette arranged for Arsen to be transported to the Hyatt Hotel where a room had been reserved for him.

CHAPTER TWENTY-SEVEN

TUESDAY, 16 DECEMBER 1997

There was nothing to do in the morning but to have breakfast and head to the airport for a flight back to New York. The weather was nice, and it was rather warm outside. It felt almost like a spring day, unusual for December - and everybody said that was due to El Niño.

It was noon when Arsen walked into the apartment in New York. Nada and her mother were scheduled to return from Puerto Rico after seven in the evening. He took a shower, and he was ready for the newspapers and a cup of coffee.

The headlines about riots around the globe were disturbing.

ETHNIC RIOTS AROUND THE WORLD
KILLINGS IN AFRICA, BOSNIA, CHINA
FORMER SOVIET REPUBLICS ARE TENSE AND NERVOUS
DEMONSTRATIONS IN MANY STATES IN US

The President had known it last night. This was just a prelude, Arsen thought. If the General had received the mandate last week this would not have happened. He turned on the television. The same thing - people in the streets demonstrating and rioting, burning stores, and a few scattered bodies of the dead. What a mess. Then it was announced that there were new developments in the United Nations.

"The U.S. President, Joseph Burns, was negotiating with regional block representatives about the possible candidates for President of the World Government," MMB Anchor Bradley Adams reported. "Unconfirmed reports suggest that Mr. Burns is lining up support behind former U.N. Secretary General Rama Chand of India.

"In other news from the United Nations," Mr. Adams reported, "all block representatives gave summaries of the views of their regions. The initial disagreement among delegates and the trend to vote for their own regional candidates, has been reduced to three candidates - from Africa, Europe and India. The Indian delegate, Mr. Rama Chand, seems to be ahead of other candidates."

Arsen turned off the television. There was not much to do until the evening. A stroll around the neighborhood, an hour at the Vertical Club, some shopping at Bloomingdale's, buying toilet supplies and drugs at Gallery Drugs and a visit to the health food store essentially filled the afternoon.

The MMB evening News Report started at six-thirty. Bradley Adams was reporting many events of the day, most of them about demonstrations and riots around the world that had either just erupted or had become more violent. In some states the governments were loosing control, and the situation was bordering on anarchy.

Among those were Cyprus and the border areas between Greece and Turkey. In Georgia the Abkhazia was in turmoil and there were demonstrations in Tbilisi. In Mindanao, Muslims and Christians were fighting and casualties were high. Tamils in Sri Lanka were viciously retaliating against the Sinhalese, who had started killing them in many parts of the country and in Colombo. Rwanda was at it again, neither Hutu nor Tutsi were safe anywhere in the country - which had barely recovered from a major ethnic war.

The Tibetans were demonstrating against the Chinese by walking and chanting prayers in the streets of Lhasa and in villages. Germans were protesting against the Turks in their midst, and there were casualties in a number of cities. In Spain, the Basques were openly demonstrating in San Sebastian and Bilbao and counterdemonstrations were being held in Madrid, Barcelona and many cities across Spain. Surprisingly there were no casualties anywhere.

"Many more countries report problems, particularly ethnic clashes," Bradley Adams continued the report. "It is impossible to cover all the involved areas. MMB management has decided to broadcast a special program that will give wider coverage and provide more details. Phone lines are being set up so that we can answer your questions and provide you with the latest information. Sometimes the operators will be able to get specific information about people stranded in some countries."

Commercials appeared, to Arsen's amusement. Companies were still promoting coffee brands, sports cars, and ship cruises. He had been too absorbed in the politics of the collision and the consequences of the approaching disaster, Arsen thought; he had forgotten that there were people who wanted to enjoy themselves to the end. Who served passengers on the ships during the cruises - who needed that kind of work? People still had to survive, and that cost money, catastrophe or no. How would it be a year before March of 2003 or a few months before? Peace and prayers, or rampant behavior to squeeze more out of life during the remaining time? Who knew? Obviously, the riots and demonstrations must stop now in order for the work to save the world to begin.

"Here's the latest from the United Nations," Bradley Adams continued his report. "The Assembly delegates have agreed to nominate three candidates for the Presidency of the World Government, the name they decided to use for the administrative body of the United Nations. As previously reported the candidates are: Mr. Rama Chand of India, former Secretary General of the United Nations, Mr. Roberto Rodriguez, the Prime Minister of Spain, and Mr. Mwenze Nyarampanga of the Democratic Republic of the Congo (the former Zaire), a Minister in the present Government. It is anticipated that the vote will be taken shortly. MMB will report the events in the Assembly as they occur."

Rama would become the President of the World Government, Arsen thought. Which direction would he take? Will he offer the anticollision job to the General?

Bradley Adams interrupted his report with news on the outcome of the vote for the President of the World Government.

"The official count for the President is just in. Mr. Rama Chand of India won one hundred and five votes, or 54.4 percent of the ballot. He will be officially offered the Presidency of the World Government. It is expected that he will accept the position in a speech before the Assembly at eight o'clock tonight. A little later in this broadcast we will bring you his biography--"

Arsen turned off the television. He intended to listen to Rama's speech, as he wanted to hear Rama's vision of the whole anticollision effort. What kind of a speaker is he? Arsen had never heard him speak. Would he follow in the General's footsteps, or take his own path? Indians were smart, Arsen thought. Rama was very intelligent and had ingenuity in public affairs. Would he be a great coordinator or try to direct the entire government and make all major decisions? Hopefully, he would be the coordinator. He was a political scientist and a lawyer, with degrees in both, and possessed excellent public relations skills. If he chose the right people for the top jobs and gave them the support they needed, and coordinated their efforts, he would be a great President, to be remembered if there was a forever. Otherwise, he would direct a disgruntled, unhappy and confused group of professionals who would fail to save the world. Arsen was awaiting Rama's speech, and so was the entire world.

Nada and her mother arrived from Puerto Rico just minutes before eight o'clock and Arsen had enough time only to explain to them what was happening and invite them to listen to the acceptance speech by Rama Chand. He turned on the television in the living room.

MMB Anchor, Bradley Adams, was reporting from the United Nations. The cameras were directed on the Assembly Hall, where the delegates were walking around, talking to each other, or just sitting in their seats in expectation of the speech by Rama Chand. The President of the Assembly, Mr. Gerhardt Weiner, was seated in his chair to the side of the table on the podium, near to the lectern, and Secretary General Raul Ortiz was at the opposite end of the table. The Security Council, who sat around this table during the regular sessions of the Assembly, were not there for this occasion.

At exactly eight o'clock Mr. Weiner walked over to the lectern, took hold of the microphone, and announced that Mr. Rama Chand would be in the hall any minute; and the door opened and Mr. Chand walked in and proceeded toward the podium. Suddenly there was a hurricane of applause, which calmed down only on repeated demands by the Assembly President.

"Ladies and gentlemen, it is my privilege to present to you Mr. Rama Chand, who is well known to you as the Secretary General of this organization. Mr. Chand has been elected by you to the position of President of the World Government. Mr. Chand will present to you his acceptance speech and his plans for the future of his government and of the world. President Chand."

A long, and at times tumultuous, standing ovationfollowed Rama Chand on his way to the podium and it stopped only when he raised his hands. The people were ready to hear him.

"Dear friends and the people of the world. It would be easier to present this speech to you were it not for the ominous skies over our heads. I will not focus your attention on the celestial object whose actual physical description is not clear even to the best of our astronomers. Let it suffice to say that this enormous object exists, and that it will collide with the Earth, unless we do something to prevent the collision. If I stopped right here, I would have said it all as it was today. What is left to be said concerns the organization of people on this planet. I intend to facilitate the expeditious process of our organization."

Roaring applause broke out again. Rama Chand smiled at the Assembly delegates and at the world watching him: the peaceful people and the rioting and demonstrating crowds, even killers doing their dirty work, as all of them had the same hope and the same wish for someone to save the Earth from the approaching apocalypse. Rama Chand sipped water from the glass that had been placed on the lectern for him.

"You may be surprised that my work in organizing the government has been done for me by others, by the people who were before you last week. I mean by the General, as we always called him, Gen. Alexei Shagov."

Spontaneous applause interrupted the speech, and Rama Chand waved in encouragement to the delegates.

"The General already outlined the program he recommended for the anticollision effort. I thought about it, I thought about other avenues and alternatives, and I can tell you that the only plan worth pursuing is the plan prepared by the General."

Another round of applause interrupted Rama Chand, and he waved to the delegates, and they cheered him again and again, as if cheering him they also sent their respects to the General.

Bradley Adams was commenting on the speech even though it was not finished. He was clearly enthusiastic about Rama Chand and his presentation.

"I have slightly modified the General's organizational plan," Rama Chand continued. "The new plan has four parts.

"The first part is the anticollision effort. It will include research and the execution of three objectives: collision prevention, preservation and survival. These three objectives are well known to all of you. It is my intention to ask Gen. Shagov to take this responsibility."

There was uproar in the Assembly Hall and nothing could be heard or understood from the applause, talk, whistling and even singing. Delegates were happy with the choice and were expressing the relief of their fear that the choice would be somebody else. This Babel lasted for several minutes before Rama Chand could calm the delegates.

"The Ethnic part is a necessity. We have riots and demonstrations on the streets of many cities and in many countries. We have to extinguish these fires immediately. Mr. Grigor Kravchenko, who was previously assigned to take charge of ethnic problems, had a major stroke and is lying unconscious in a Kiev hospital without much hope of recovery. Dr Arsen Pankovich, who has been concerned with ethnic problems, is not interested in the job. Now finding the right individual is my most urgent priority.

"The third part, the General Department, will deal with problems like global health, trade, matters of law, finance and problems that cannot be resolved by local governments.

"Finally, the integrated Military will have to keep nations at peace and make sure that their leaders are not corrupted. There will be no wars, as we will defend those who are attacked. After serious consideration and much consultation, which involved some Indian generals whom I have known for many years, I have decided to offer the post of Military Chief to General John Thornton, who is an American."

The applause was not as enthusiastic for Gen. Thornton but still indicated that he would be approved.

"As you know, you, the delegates of the Assembly, will have the power to approve my choices, or to reject them. I thank you for your confidence in me."

Everybody stood up and applauded warmly as the newly elected President of the World Government stepped down from the podium and walked out of the Assembly Hall.

This was the beginning or the end of the history of the new civilization, Arsen thought, hopefully the former.

"Are you going to accept?" Nada asked Arsen.

"I will try to get my previous job in the Balkans and Southwest Asia. I am most comfortable with that domain."

"I don't think you have a choice this time," Nada said and her mother nodded her head in agreement.

"You don't have a choice this time," she said in Serbian.

The telephone rang. It was Sabrina, all excited after Rama Chand's speech.

"The train is on the tracks again," she said. "I'm sure the General will accept, especially after such tremendous approval for his appointment. What about you, Doctor?"

"I have not decided," Arsen said.

"This is no time to delay decisions," Sabrina said. "Things may get out of control if action isn't taken."

"Rama Chand has calmed the situation," Arsen said. "Rioters and demonstrators may calm down too."

"Take the job, please," Sabrina said. "I'd better hang up; I have another call."

The telephone rang again.

"Dr. Pankovich, this is Paula Brown, President Chand's secretary. The President would like you to come to his office at the United Nations as soon as you can. He wants to talk with you tonight."

"I know," Arsen said. "I will be there in half an hour."

"Thank you, Doctor. I'll tell him," Paula Brown said and hung up.

"Are you going to the United Nations?" Nada asked.

"As you said, I have no choice but to go," Arsen said. "This is not a joke."

"I know," Nada said and kissed him before he left.

Arsen was not in the mood to walk to the United Nations, and the twenty-two blocks he would have to walk seemed too many. The taxi trip was very quick. The guard at the entrance knew he was coming, and Arsen felt better when he was recognized.

"Good evening, Dr. Pankovich," the guard said. "It's good to see you again. We were hoping Mr. Chand would call on you, and he did in his speech. Good luck to you." The guard escorted him to the elevator.

Arsen entered the office of Rama Chand, and remembered that he should address him as President Chand. The secretary, Paula Brown, greeted him, and Rama Chand walked into the reception area.

"Arsen, thank you for coming so promptly," he said. "Come in and have a seat. Coca Cola is all I have to drink. Goran will be here soon to meet with you."

"To add more pressure, I guess," Arsen said.

"That is probably true although I did not ask him to come - he volunteered."

"I am sorry that Kravchenko is incapacitated," Arsen said. "He would have been an excellent man for the job. He has the necessary experience which I lack. How is he?"

"Really bad, I was told," Rama Chand said. "He will not recover from this. For our purposes he is gone. Naturally, we have a real problem. As much as I know that there are capable people out there, it is not easy to find the right person. You and I have worked together. You actually engineered my and Goran's resignations from the U.N. The General told me you did not even ask him what to do, and Goran and I were under the impression that you were doing it with the General's approval."

"That is true," Arsen said. "There was no time to waste, and I did what had to be done. The General was in agreement with my decision."

"That is exactly what I mean--"

Goran Enstrom walked in, interrupting Rama.

"Good to see you, Arsen." Goran said. "This is like the good old times from a week ago. So much has happened since then. I presume you two were talking about the ethnic job."

"Yes and no," Rama Chand said. "I was reminding Arsen that he forced our resignations from the U.N. last week. Now that we have our jobs back, I offered him a job too. He is thinking, and time is running out."

"Arsen, you should take the job," Goran said. "We know first hand that you know how to make decisions. We also know that you understand ethnic problems very well and that you have a good feeling for what has to be done to keep the issues from exploding."

"I agree," Rama Chand said.

"The ethnic situation is not good and many people are rioting and many more demonstrating," Arsen said. "These people have to get the feeling that somebody cares about them and their problems. Sampling the trouble spots clearly shows that ethnic problems are surfacing and the people feel nobody will do anything to change the situation. You need the Military in place and ready to help. You need the Ethnic Department in place momentarily, which means staring from scratch. I may have an idea of what is needed, but I've got no notion who could execute it. The problem of priorities would come up. My head is spinning with questions and few answers are on the screen."

Arsen almost said that they should consult with the General, but then decided that such a suggestion might be offensive to Rama Chand.

"You will have the Military as you need them," Rama Chand said, as Paula Brown announced over the intercom that she had Gen. Shagov on the line.

"Would you like to talk to him privately?" she asked.

"No, we will talk to him on the speaker phone," Rama Chand said. "Good evening General. Goran, Arsen and I are talking some world business. Actually, we are trying to convince Arsen to take the ethnic job, in view of Kravchenko's situation."

"My congratulations, Rama," the General said. "I watched your speech at the U.N. and I liked it very much. Thank you for saying kind words about me."

"Forget it, General," Rama Chand said. "When are you going to be in New York? Things have to start moving."

"If you want, I will be on the way tomorrow morning."

"Stay where you are. I will ask Gen. Thornton to get you to New York by noon tomorrow. You will need a plane of your own to be mobile when you have to travel."

"Thank you," the General said. "If Arsen is listening, my advice to him is to take the job. The situation is worse than you think. There is no time for a search committee and months of interviews. Oh, Arsen, please tell Sabrina to be around when I arrive. Good night gentlemen, I will talk to you tomorrow. Thank you again, Rama."

"You're welcome, General," Rama Chand said and called his secretary. "Paula, find me General Thornton." Almost immediately, Paula Brown called back.

"He's on the line," she said.

"Good evening Gen. Thornton," Rama Chand said. "I hope it is not late for you. Would it be possible to arrange a plane for Gen. Shagov to get him from Moscow to New York by tomorrow? Also, what is the chance that you could come over after you make arrangements for the General?"

"Mr. President, thank you for the appointment," Gen. Thornton said. "Needless to say, I accept. I will be in your office in half an hour."

"Things are falling into place," Rama Chand said. "Both Generals have accepted, and I assume, Arsen, you have too."

Both men, Rama Chand and Goran Enstrom, looked at Arsen inquisitively.

"I hope I don't prove that the Peter Principle works. I accept, of course."

"What is that?" Goran Enstrom asked.

"If promoted often enough, one attains one's level of incompetence," Arsen explained.

"Nonsense," Rama Chand said. "Gentlemen, we have to start working. I have to make some calls as we still need somebody for the General Department."

"Two last questions," Arsen said. "Who pays and who appoints the huge staff that I envision for the Ethnic Department?"

"You propose your undersecretaries to me and I will have them confirmed by the Assembly. You appoint everybody else. Please keep an eye on your people. A scandal could be detrimental to our success."

"I am going home to have a good night's sleep if I am to function tomorrow," Arsen said. "I will use your phone before I leave."

"We have made a few arrangements for you, if you don't mind," Goran said. "Security - remember that was one of your ideas. A limousine will wait for you to take you wherever you want to go. You must be protected. What should we do for an office building for your Department?"

"The Lexington office building will arrange for our expansion."

Arsen called Sabrina to give her the General's message. She said she was ready to work, and Arsen could detect satisfaction in her voice.

"We will be in two different worlds," Arsen said. "You will be creating improbable technologies while my job will be to create and maintain peace."

"Thank you for calling me, Doctor," Sabrina said. "My life may be going to end in five years but I'll live it to the fullest until then. Thank you."

Victoria was expecting the call and was ready to work.

Arsen needed a few hours to get his thoughts and ideas organized. First, he would talk to Nada to decide how to organize their life. Her mother would have to stay with them. Nada would talk to all the children again about a meeting in New York. Then he would have to calm down maybe by watching a movie, something entertaining, to keep his mind at ease for an hour or two, as he used to do when he was in practice.

Nada was not asleep when Arsen returned to the apartment. "You had no choice; I told you. You have invested all your emotions in ethnic problems since you retired. You always said you would take only two jobs: Presidency of the Republika Srpska or an ethnic job in the U.N. One of these jobs was offered to you, and you accepted it. What is your problem now?"

"The enormity of the job," Arsen said. "I am expected to calm the world and make it happy. That may be impossible. They expect that to happen by noon tomorrow. I had better eat something and drink something, and relax in front of the television."

"I will get you something."

Arsen turned on the television in his study and fell asleep in the armchair, in which, in the past, he had spent many uncomfortable sleeping hours. Later Nada woke him up and nudged him to go and sleep in their bed. During the night Arsen jumped once in the bed from a dream in which a large wild cat was standing on his back and left shoulder and was holding his neck with her sharp teeth in jaws of death. After he fell asleep again the nothingness of his sleep was pleasant and restful.

CHAPTER TWENTY-EIGHT

WEDNESDAY, 17 DECEMBER 1997

In the morning the alarm rang at six. It was still dark outside, although the usual traffic sounds were penetrating the bedroom despite the newly installed windows. Arsen almost liked that noise, which to him was the life of the city, and a part of city life. The morning ritual was performed automatically. Shaving, teeth brushing, washing and dressing and often drinking cup of coffee were parts of that ritual in the city that never sleeps but in which everybody is sleepy when getting up in the morning to go to work. This was the time he used to get up in the morning when he was a practicing orthopedic surgeon.

Today was the first day he would have to do something for the world as part of his job, Arsen thought. It had all started as an interest, and now it was a job. He had better extinguish the fires around the globe.

Nada brought a cup of coffee for Arsen and for herself to the living room and turned on the television, and Arsen picked up the newspapers at the entrance door. Suddenly, news was pouring in. All reports were in two categories, as they had been the day before: the Session in the United Nations and the riots.

RAMA CHAND OF INDIA, THE NEW WG PRESIDENT
GENERAL SHAGOV TO LEAD ANTICOLLISION DEPARTMENT
US GENERAL JOHN THORNTON IS NEW WG CHIEF OF MILITARY
PANKOVICH FINALLY ACCEPTS ETHNIC JOB

The papers reported that the Assembly had approved all the nominees during the night effective immediately. There was speculation about the potential nominee for the Secretary of the General Department and Goran Enstrom was mentioned as the leading candidate.

The telephone rang.

"Doctor, the limousine has arrived and will wait for you," the doorman announced.

"Thank you," Arsen said and looked at his watch. It was seven o'clock and time to go to the office.

"Do you think you will be home before midnight?" Nada asked him.

"I doubt it," Arsen said. "Don't wait for me with dinner. I will eat in the office if I'm late. I will call you anyhow. Bye-bye now."

A limousine with the U.N. flag was parked in front of the building. The doorman hurried to open the door for Arsen while two secret agents stood at each end of the limousine. When all were inside, the limousine sped along Sixty-Second Street, which was still empty at this hour. A quick ride along Second Avenue into Sixty-First Street and down Lexington Avenue took only a few minutes. It was ridiculous to take a ride for such a short distance. When he inquired about that Arsen was told that security required that he ride in the limousine. There was not much to say about it.

Soon, he was unlocking the office suite which was to be used by the General and Kravchenko and Fiodorov. Victoria arrived soon after.

"Good morning Doctor," she said and took off her coat. "Would you like a cup of coffee and a bagel? I talked to the super last night, but it was too late to clean the office." Without waiting for an answer she called the coffee shop in the building and ordered coffee and bagels. "What do you want me to do first?"

"To answer your first question, yes, I want coffee and a bagel. Next, find me Gen. Thornton. I must talk to the Philippine President, if he is still around. Remember him from the party last week? If he has gone home, his Ambassador will do. I must talk also with the Ambassadors from Greece, Turkey, Germany, Spain, Sri Lanka and Zaire. I don't care in which order. Oh, I almost forgot, find also the Yugoslavian Ambassador, Mr. Stanko Petkovic.

"Tell Mr. Petkovic I will see him around five o'clock here in the office; we may even have dinner together."

"Yes, Sir. Right away."

Michelle Brigens and Stanley Kim arrived a few minutes before eight and went to greet Arsen.

"I am glad you could start today," Arsen said. "The work will be mounting very quickly. Michelle, you will be answering calls to my office only, as soon as we find other people. Stan, your job is to find people who will work in our offices. I am talking about fifty people to begin with. We'll need more people soon. Think of people with degrees and think also of a broad range of nationalities. They must be smart, and they must speak one foreign language aside from their native tongue. Ethnic experience is not required; avoid ethnic hatred. Look in New York, look in the U.N., look in foreign ministries, universities. I need the best, to start right. When you find someone you like ask Victoria to approve the individual and she will choose his or her assignments. Get going, Stan, we needed these people yesterday."

"Doctor, Gen. Thornton is on line two," Victoria said.

"Good morning General," Arsen said. "I anticipate the need for Military intervention. Not a war, but the presence of the World Military. I am not exactly sure when and if, but I would like to think that we would be prepared to act without delay. I am talking about Cyprus, Turkey and Greece, Sri Lanka, Germany, Spain, Zaire and Mindanao. People are rioting there. I will start negotiations with the leaders and let you know tonight where we stand. We may need your troops tomorrow."

"We've already assessed the situation in those countries," Gen. Thornton said. "Let me know when you need us. We'll be ready to move. Arsen, I'm looking forward to working with you. See you soon."

"Same here, John," Arsen said enthusiastically, and he meant it.

This was a first-class operation, Arsen thought. They were ready even before he asked them to look into it.

"Doctor, the President of the Philippines is on line three," Michelle announced over the intercom.

"How are you Mr. President? I was not sure you were still in New York."

"Good morning, Mr. Secretary. I should be going home this afternoon. What can I do for you?"

"Mindanao, Mr. President. What are you planning to do about the riots, which are getting out of control?" Arsen asked firmly.

"Negotiate, what else," the President said.

"Haven't you done that before?"

"Yes, we have," the President said. "However, the bastards want partition and they kill us whenever they can."

"Maybe you should let them decide what is best for them?" Arsen said. "I hate to insist but it seems that negotiation for partition would calm the riots and your people would not be killed anymore and perhaps peace would prevail."

"What about the Muslims? Would they respect the deal? They never respected anything."

"I will talk to their leaders," Arsen said. "They will have no choice but to respect the conditions of the deal. Besides, they may prefer a reasonable autonomy over partition. Why don't you give them a chance to vote on it. I would like to be able to tell them that I have your support in my efforts to resolve the present crisis."

"Autonomy would be easier to sell politically," the President said.

A politician talking, Arsen thought. Autonomy would be a good beginning, and partition could be negotiated later if the Muslims really wanted it.

"Thank you Mr. President," Arsen said. "It would be better if you would get the negotiations started so that my call to Muslim leaders would not undermine your position, as they would think the idea was yours."

"I will talk to them before I leave New York," the President promised dryly.

"Thank you," Arsen said. "We'll talk soon again." That was the end of the conversation. Arsen was surprised by the President's bluntness and his rapid response to a situation in which he knew he would be on the loosing end if he refused to cooperate. This was a new political game and new players and new rules. The President of the Philippines was a political animal with the instinct for survival. He needed twenty-four hours to set the stage for the negotiations, Arsen thought. He would give him that much time.

"Doctor, Ambassador Petkovic will be here at five o'clock," Victoria said. "We are trying to locate the other people."

"Doctor, the Greek Ambassador is on line three," Michelle announced over the intercom.

"Good morning, Mr. Ambassador," Arsen greeted the Greek Ambassador.

"Good morning, Mr. Secretary," Ambassador Atanasios Iliadis said. "I suspect that your call has something to do with Cyprus and Turkey."

"You are right. I should suspect then that you have done something about the problem."

"We are ready to talk anytime they want," Ambassador Iliadis said.

"You mean you have not talked to the Turkish leaders yet?" Arsen inquired. "I would have guessed that someone was on the way to talk to them by now."

"We are not sure they are willing to talk. Besides, technically it should be initiated by the Cypriots themselves, don't you think?"

"No, I really do not think that way," Arsen said. "You have been waiting for each other and years have passed. It seems I will have no choice but to set the date for a plebiscite sometime in the next five to six weeks. It would be more practical if the island remained one entity with two strong and equal autonomous regions, and whatever central structures are decided on."

"Mr. Secretary, you are looking for trouble, you know that," Ambassador Iliadis said. "The Greeks will not like it at all."

"Would the Greeks prefer to see the Turks thrown out of Cyprus into the Aegean Sea or sent back to Turkey, or perhaps killed? What do you think, Mr. Ambassador?"

"No, we would not like to see them killed or thrown out. If they would only be less stubborn."

"What would be a solution, in your opinion? Will you keep them isolated forever? To keep Turkish Military on the Island forever? To have riots and demonstrations forever? What is it going to be? Am I missing something?" Arsen was getting annoyed with this conversation.

"I cannot make any commitments for my Government," Ambassador Iliadis said. "Let me talk to my Prime Minister and I will get back to you as soon as I can."

"Today, Mr. Ambassador, I need an answer today."

"I will call you in the afternoon," the Ambassador said and hung up.

"Doctor, the German Ambassador is on line two," Michelle announced over the intercom.

"Good morning Mr. Ambassador," Arsen said. "I wanted to talk to you about problems with Turks and Muslims who live in Germany. What is happening? Is there any hope that the situation might improve?"

"Good morning Mr. Secretary," the German Ambassador, Herman Wolff, said. "You are not loosing time in getting things done. I was surprised to hear from you so soon, although I was even more surprised when I was on hold and waiting for you to finish your conversation with Mr. Iliadis. Same people, different troubles in Germany and Cyprus. You want to know what has been done so far? We will apply for special status for the Turks who are not citizens. Our Turkish-Germans should not need special status unless they want it. We are trying to contain the demonstrations of both sides. That is all I have, Mr. Secretary."

"I suggest that you issue special German non-citizen passports, which should provide information about the individuals holding them, and which would give them at least a year before they return to Turkey or go elsewhere. You may want to apply the same principles for other nationalities. I would really like to see that these people are protected. Thank you for calling me so promptly."

"Your're welcome, Mr. Secretary."

Arsen was wondering if this were the typical German efficiency at work, or the way to keep out of trouble with the World Government.

"Victoria," Arsen called her over the intercom, "I must talk to the Turkish Ambassador. Please find him and then come to my office."

Arsen wanted to talk to Victoria about recruiting people who would work in his department.

"Call the German Ambassador and invite him to a private dinner tonight or tomorrow night with me and Mr. Petkovic. Also find out who is the Muslim leader in Mindanao, perhaps from the Philippine Embassy or the U.N. delegation. I have to talk to that man tomorrow. Also, I should be apprised of the events which are happening in the World Government and in different states. I need a daily report. We need people to represent our department in each state. Where do we find them? Maybe we will have Wolff and Petkovic, if they decide to work for us, find these people. You had better make sure all offices on this floor are ready for use, and that each new appointee has a secretary, unless he wants to bring his own. Of course, her own, too."

"Doctor, the Turkish Ambassador is on line four," Michelle announced over the intercom.

"Hello Mr. Ambassador," Arsen said. "Time is very expensive the first day on the job, and it was not possible to have you come to the office for an eye-to-eye conversation. I promise we will arrange a meeting as soon as practical. I am calling you about the Cyprus problem and another matter."

"Good morning, Mr. Secretary," the Turkish Ambassador said. "I expected your call. The situation is not great in Cyprus, and we don't know what to do."

"I have done some work for you," Arsen said. "The Greeks are working on a proposal for double autonomy, for Turks and Greeks. Each territory will be equal in every respect, with its own administration and a legislative body. The central government would be negotiated, and the President would be rotated each year. That is the best I could do at this time. Of course, there will be no military on Cyprus."

"Partition would be more desirable, although this kind of autonomy may work out. It is important that partition in principle is not ruled out. We will talk to the Greek diplomats right away."

"Another item, Mr. Ambassador," Arsen said. "It is not too early to bring up the problems of Kurdistan. As you know our mandate provides that we help these people. What do you suggest I do next in that respect?"

"Mr. Secretary that is the Achilles' heel of the Turks," the Ambassador said. "It will be difficult to mention the issue to my President. The people will not like it either. In my opinion, confidentially, you will have to lean heavily on the Turkish President. Pull the Turkish Military out of the country, for whatever reason, bring in W.G. troops before you give territory to the Kurds, and you will succeed. It will be easier to negotiate with Iraq and other involved parties. Of course, I will lose my job, even my head, if this conversation becomes public. You understand?"

"Yes, I understand," Arsen said. "It will be done as you say. You will let your President know about Cyprus, and you will give him your impression of my intentions about the Kurds. Thank you for your help."

"Thank you, Mr. Secretary."

Arsen immediately asked Gen. Thornton to plan to use Turkish troops somewhere in the world, and to leave only a few in Turkey. After that was accomplished, to deploy Chinese troops around the Kurdistan territory in preparation for the partition. There was no reason to talk to the Kurds - they would only complicate matters by holding celebrations in advance."

Since there was no response from Colombo, whose President was on his way home from New York, Arsen left a message for him to call regarding partition for the Tamils, which would probably soon be decided by a plebiscite.

The Spanish Prime Minister returned the call and he inquired why he had been called?

"The Basques are restive and on the streets, Mr. Prime Minister," Arsen said. "What should we do?"

"These are terrorists, as you know, Mr. Secretary," the Prime Minister said. "They just like to kill people. We have done everything possible for them."

"Do you include in that the death squads?" Arsen said. "Happy people do not rebel. I have no choice but to call for a plebiscite regarding partition. That will by necessity involve the French, too. I must insist that you make plans for a peaceful plebiscite by the end of January. The situation is rather messy, and it will be impossible to resolve the disputes. One fact is clear to me: Basques, terrorists or not, are a separate ethnic group by definition, and they are entitled to partition or to negotiate anything they think is right. I hope you understand that."

"I understand what you are saying and I can assure you that Spain will comply, though reluctantly. We believe that most Basques will want to remain under the wing of the Spanish Crown. I will initiate talks with Basque leaders and with French officials."

"Thank you Mr. Prime Minister," Arsen said. "Let me know of your progress sometime next week. If you feel that the concerned parties would want to meet with me, individually or together, let me know, and I will be glad to come to Spain or to see all of you here in New York."

Having initiated the Basque negotiations, Arsen concluded that the morning had been quite productive. It was time for lunch, and he wanted to take Victoria along. Arsen had no idea where to go except to the small Brazilian restaurant Circus.

Arsen called Victoria over the intercom. "It is time to go somewhere for lunch," he said. "Do you have any idea where?"

"It would be rather complicated to get the limousine and the Security Service. I should order food and have it delivered, and we can eat in the kitchenette or if you prefer in your office."

"Okay," Arsen agreed, although he felt a prisoner of his position - the reality of his situation.

Arsen called the office of Rama Chand, as he would always call him to himself, although he was the President. Paula Brown answered the phone and immediately connected him with the President.

"Arsen, I am glad you called," Rama Chand said. "Feathers are flying about some of your decisions already, although I expected more complaints than I have received. Is there something I can help you with?"

"I am on a stealing expedition, and I thought you might tell me what to do - or not to do. I would like to hire the Ambassadors from Germany and Yugoslavia to be my undersecretaries. Is that permissible?"

"Anybody you want you can take," Rama Chand said. "This will produce some commotion but the positions are important and you need these men."

"Also, I need your advice on two or three capable officials from India or Asia or Africa who could be be my undersecretaries. I need people with first-hand knowledge of these areas. Let me know."

"I can tell you right now," Rama Chand said with authority. "Ramesh Rao of India, who is now the Indian Ambassador to Brazil. He is an excellent man, knowledgeable about South America, and a former Professor of Political Sciences in Calcutta. Ito Amoto of Japan is a business man. I knew him during his brief stay in New York. He is the man to get - intelligent, discrete, motivated and industrious. I am not sure where he works now. Your best man for Africa lives on the south side of Chicago and is a Political Science Professor at the University of Chicago. His name is René Bright. He spent ten years in Africa. Talk to him. Arsen, the General will be at dinner with me tonight, in the private dinning room at the U.N., around eight. Come if you can. We'll be there until about ten. See you tonight." Rama Chand hung up.

"Doctor, come over. The food is ready."

Victoria was setting the table when Arsen walked into the kitchenette.

"The General is in New York," Arsen said. "I will see him tonight at dinner with President Chand. He is back in action and that is good for everybody."

"I'm glad he's back," Victoria said. "I know Sabrina is delighted that he wanted her back. She was lost when everything collapsed last week."

"I was disappointed myself," Arsen said. "Now we are going full speed.

"Victoria, we need many senior people in the department, and we have to get them soon. I have the names of three men you should find and ask to come to New York." He gave her the names and information he had just gotten from Rama Chand. "Another problem: I may have to go to Spain in the next few days. How do I travel? It will be too complicated to fly on commercial airlines. Find out from President Chand's office how to go about it, then make a tentative reservation."

Shrimp cocktail, salad, a well-done cutlet, and vanilla pudding was too much for lunch, Arsen thought, and decided to ask next time for a sandwich or a bagel instead.

"Doctor, you won't believe it," Victoria said,walking into the office after lunch. "I talked to President Chand's office about traveling arrangements. They said buy yourself a plane or rent one. How do you buy a plane? Go into a store and order one?"

Arsen was surprised too.

"Well, let's ask Gen. Thornton. He has a few planes in his department. Maybe he will suggest a dealer." They were learning how to run a really big department, and realized that it would be expensive.

Gen. Thornton laughed when asked how to rent a plane.

"You should buy a plane. It's convenient, practical, economical and efficient. You'll also need a crew. I would recommend that you keep the plane at our base in Newark. They can handle any plane. I'll get the plane and the crew for you by tomorrow." He hung up.

Victoria and Arsen were stunned by this episode.

"Doctor, the Chinese Foreign Minister is on line two," Michelle announced over the intercom.

"Good afternoon, Mr. Foreign Minister," Arsen said. "I am not sure what time it is in Beijing. The time difference is thirteen hours. My God, I woke you up. That is not good for you. Should I call in the morning?"

"No, I would rather talk now," the Minister said. "You are probably calling about Tibet."

"You are right, Mr. Foreign Minister," Arsen said. "What is going to happen there?"

"Not much right now," the Minister said. "We will have to look into it."

"Buddhist priests are demonstrating and chanting against you," Arsen said. "They want their freedom in a free country, and they want the Dalai Lama back home. I tend to agree with them. They are entitled to that. Mr. Foreign Minister, it would be easier if your occupational troops would move out of Tibet, say by next Monday. We will not ask any further questions regarding Tibet. I am counting on your cooperation. Next Monday, Mr. Minister."

"Thank you," the Minister said. He did not promise anything.

Arsen talked to Gen. Walter Smith, Deputy to Gen. Thornton, and arranged for the pull-out of Chinese troops from Tibet and deployment of W.G. units around Tibet by Monday.

An official from the Boeing Company called with the news that a B-737 was on the way to Newark as requested by Gen. Thornton. "The plane has a bedroom, a dining/conference room, and an office. It's equipped with advanced communication facilities," the official said. "A permanent crew will be assigned."

Sri Lanka's Prime Minister quickly agreed to initiate talks for the Tamils' partition, and the officials from Zaire, Rwanda and Burundi were to leave for New York within hours.

Fires should be contained if not extinguished, Arsen thought. He was looking forward to finishing the day's office work and meeting with Stan Petkovic and Herman Wolff, then joining the General and Rama Chand. It was four o'clock.

"You won't believe that I found all of them," Victoria said, coming into Arsen's office. "Mr. Bright will be here at five to meet with you and the other two gentlemen. I found him in New York. Mr. Amoto was in Tokyo and he should be on his way here by now. Mr. Rao was tied up in Brazil and will be in New York by the weekend. All of them wanted to know what the meeting was about. I told them you wanted to talk to them about a job."

"Excellent," Arsen said. "I am getting tired of phone calls."

"Would you like some fresh coffee?" Victoria asked.

"Yes, thank you," Arsen said. Arsen looked at the report Victoria had left on his desk earlier in the afternoon. The section on riots and demonstrations had even more disturbing information than what had been reported in the newspapers. They should have their own center for information-gathering, Arsen thought, and they should be able to communicate with people around the world.

"Doctor, the Chinese President is on line four," Michelle announced over the intercom.

There it went, Arsen thought, the big boys would start complaining and manipulating.

"Good morning Mr. President," Arsen said. "What can I do for you?"

"Mr. Secretary, I am calling regarding Tibet and the conversation you had with my Foreign Minister," the President said. He appeared to be holding back his anger about the Tibetan situation. "I don't understand your decision, and I must protest. This is Chinese territory. You understand that?"

"I really don't understand, Mr. President. Tibet was occupied by your troops in 1950. The Dalai Lama fled Tibet in 1959 and you have never allowed him to return. The people want separation from China, and they have a right to independence."

"This is interference in China's internal affairs," the President said.

"Mr. President, people have two basic rights: to keep their territory and partition, if that is the only way to attain freedom, and to choose whomever they want as their leaders. If you insist, we will arrange a plebiscite by mid-January, but that seems a waste of time, and you know it. Let me know what you want me to do."

"I will let you know." The President hung up without waiting for Arsen to say anything further. Too bad he could not feel the new wind, Arsen thought. Rama Chand should initiate admission of Tibet to the United Nations.

"Doctor, the three gentlemen you were expecting are here," Michelle announced over the intercom.

"Let them in." Arsen stood up and shook hands with the men and invited them to sit down.

"Gentlemen, thank you for coming on such a short notice. I imagine you have met each other. Perhaps Mr. Petkovic and Mr. Wolff have met before as Ambassadors at some reception, or otherwise. Mr. Bright is from Chicago teaching political science at my old Alma Mater, the University of Chicago. I wanted to talk with you about the possibility of your participation in this department. I apologize that I don't have much time to arrange formal individual interviews. I looked into your backgrounds and asked people about you. I am ready to deal with you.

"Mr. Petkovic should take the job as my main Assistant, since I don't have a position of a Deputy. You can have the job today since confirmation by the Assembly is not required.

"Mr. Wolff, I need you as the Undersecretary for North Africa-Middle East-Southwest Asia Division.

"Mr. Bright would head the Division of Sub-Saharan Africa as Undersecretary. Undersecretaries must be confirmed by the Assembly, and President Chand has promised to expedite the process, so we should have approvals within days. You can take your positions tomorrow.

"I am sure you heard the speeches by General Shagov and Rama Chand. They have clearly insisted on resolving ethnic problems while the anticollision effort is under way. Riots and demonstrations are already a major problem in places like Germany, Sri Lanka and Tibet. I have been talking with leaders in these countries, and have spent the whole day on the phone. Obviously I need your help.

"Before you answer, let me give you the basics that will have to be acceptable to you and will not easily change. Number one, every ethnic group has the right to be free, autonomous or sovereign. Second, governments have to respond to the people's demands by allowing free elections, which you will monitor, and by allowing you to audit the income of any official. We will not impose any political system. Fundamentalist, communist, capitalist or any other system is acceptable, as we do not want to tell people who should govern them. These are the basics, and they must be acceptable to you if you want the job."

"Dr. Pankovich, do we operate out of New York?" asked Mr. Wolff.

"Yes." Arsen explained his plans for other areas of the world and addressed many questions and concerns that were raised.

"Do we get paid?" asked Mr. Wolff.

"What do you need money for when everything will be provided for you?" Arsen said jokingly. "Your rent will be paid regularly, so will your chauffeur, your phone bills and the security service to protect you. Seriously, there will be a salary, but don't ask me how much - I do not know."

"Dr. Pankovich, you have answered most of my questions," Mr. Wolff said. "I accept the job. I will need some of your time tomorrow."

"Your domain is not the easiest. We'll talk about it tomorrow."

Mr. Petkovic and Mr. Bright said they wanted the job, and they also needed time to talk about their assignments.

"Oh, by the way Mr. Bright, delegations from Zaire, Rwanda and Burundi will be in New York tomorrow. We will have to talk about that area first thing in the morning. Think about possible solutions to their problems. I will tell you what I think."

Victoria came in and Arsen asked her to show the men the offices assigned to each of them.

"Doctor, this entire building will be vacated for us if we want, it. If not we can have the Immigration and Naturalization building, according to U.S. officials. What's it going to be?"

"I would like to stay here," Arsen said.

Everybody agreed.

"That is settled but tell the owners they will have to help with phone installations and furniture. How long will it take to move the other people out?"

"They'll be out by Monday."

"Gentlemen, we'll talk tomorrow," Arsen said. "Dr. Bright, call me tonight so that we can touch base on the Hutu-Tutsi problem."

Arsen asked Stan Petkovic to stay. "I have a few items to discuss with you."

The conversation was continued in Serbian after the other men left.

"I hope you don't mind my asking you to be my Assistant," Arsen said to Stan Petkovic. "Things are happening incredibly fast and I need you to help manage this department and the business of this office. I will have to travel, talk to people, go to meetings at the U.N., meet other Secretaries and who knows what else. You should know everything and be able to deal with most of the problems that will soon start coming in."

Arsen explained the situation with China and Tibet, his need to go to

Spain, the problems in Germany, and other problem places.

"President Chand is having dinner with the General, probably right now," Arsen said. "Would you have time to go with me? I would like you to meet the General - he is an exceptional person. What is your home situation?"

"My wife and my son and daughter are in Belgrade, and they will probably stay there with the family and friends. My wife felt alone and isolated since we moved to New York a year ago. I agreed that she would be better off there than waiting for me to come home every night at late hours. I am in no hurry to go home."

It was seven-thirty.

"Let's get the limo and go have dinner with President Chand and the General."

When they entered the private dinning room at the U.N. they found Rama Chand and the General discussing the world situation and the riots in various places. Arsen introduced Stan Petkovic as his new Assistant and greeted the General warmly.

"You took the job, I hear," the General said. "I could not persuade you to be my special adviser because you had to go to Bosnia. Now you have the entire Ethnic Department."

"There was the Kravchenko issue, remember? I did not want to compete for his job, and I really wanted to go to Bosnia. Now the poor man has had stroke. How is he?"

"The poor man is dead," the General said. "I cannot believe it."

"He died?" Arsen asked. "Unbelievable - so fast. Must have been a basilar lesion. Who knows?"

A simple dinner was served to the four of them: bean soup, salad, and filet mignon with a baked potato.

Goran Enstrom joined them later.

"Arsen, congratulations are in order," Rama Chand said. "Goran took the General Department job."

"Whom do I congratulate?" Arsen asked. "You or Goran. It seems you got the better deal. Now you don't have to worry about so many problems. Congratulations Goran, this is a difficult job."

"Arsen, the Chinese President is furious about the way you handled him on the Tibet situation," Rama Chand said. "Can't you do it a bit more gently?"

"Who is talking?" Arsen said. "You Indians have been barking about Tibet for years. Now you blame me for not handling the oppressor amiably. Mr. President of China will be mad at Gen. Thornton next after the Chinese troops are pulled out of Tibet and sent to Kurdistan, and Icelanders take their positions."

"Is that what you will do?" Rama Chand asked. "My God, the Chinese will be calling all day tomorrow. No wonder John could not make it to dinner tonight - he is busy planning troop movements around the globe."

"At least the Buddhist priests will stop chanting; that can be rather awful too," Arsen said.

Everybody laughed.

"General, tell us something about your plans," Rama Chand said. "Where are you going to be located?"

"Mostly in the air," the General said. "I will have to be visiting many labs where the research will be conducted. I made plans to build several large laboratories for specific purposes."

"Like--?" Rama Chand wondered.

"The first priority is the Neutrino Research Center. We have to find out if there is a way to control these particles. Much work has already been done in our labs in Russia. If neutrinos could be condensed into a beam with a controllable direction, there you would have the Universe's glue condensed in the path of the Demon - which could theoretically stop it or change its trajectory. It is something like ice made from water. You can jump into a lake, head or feet first, and nothing happens to you. Try to do it when the surface is frozen.

"The next project is the antimatter gun that could destroy the Demon. Again this would deal with neutrinos, but here the beam would cut through the Demon and destroy it. This is the most logical project, yet the least likely to succeed. We must give it a try."

"These tools would be very powerful weapons," Rama Chand said. "I'll present this information to the Assembly. They will have to come up with legislation that will effectively prevent their use for any purpose except anticollision. There will have to be a certain chain of command that would prevent a mad person or group to use the weapon. How will you bring these weapons into a position to shoot at the Demon? Can that be done from the Earth?"

"That is the next step," the General said. "We will design and develop space ships for the preservation effort. Such ships will be able to carry the neutrino guns and possibly nuclear weapons. I am not sure the nuclear weapons carried on these ships would cause much damage to the Demon, even if we landed on it and planted the bombs deep under the surface. Neutrino guns are our best bet. As you can see this is probably the most important project."

"General, when and where would the interception occur?" Arsen asked.

"Oh, after about a year of flying time. We will not be able to make these ships any faster. The crew will be able to change the course but not the speed of the ship."

"Do you think they would have to land on the Demon?"

"For nuclear weapons - yes. Once the Demon enters an orbit, we will be able to catch up with it and land. I would want to intercept the Demon with the neutrino guns at that point."

"Where are you going to look for the members of the crew?" Arsen asked.

"That is easy. Soon, we will start advertising around the world. English will be mandatory. Exceptional intelligence and physical and psychological stamina will determine who will make the crew. We will train a few hundred men and women."

"Women, too?" asked Rama Chand.

"Of course," Alexei said. "Men and women. They need each other, and they perform better when they are together. We will try to match them in advance of the mission. This will be a huge project as we will train them in the latest techniques as these techniques were being developed. There are so many projects that I must start interviewing people and appointing them to these tasks. One project of particular interest to me, and I have been working on it for some time, is the development of space communications that will not depend on Earth. I call it Sinternet; the Space Internet that will have in storage everything known to mankind.

"Cloning in space will have to be looked into as a possible preservation technique. We can't take cows into space, but we should be able to clone them when the time comes. We should be able to store the genetic material of humans and animals - you could call that genetic engines. Seeds of plants, and eggs, will have to be stored in some way. What do we need to sustain life? What do we need to make it worth being alive? Do we need trees and grass and dogs and cats to enjoy as part of living, or are we going to be happy in a totally material environment? Some of us live in such an environment already, without animals and vegetation, without creeks and waterfalls, without cherry trees and apple trees and vineyards, without singing birds or mute crocodiles, without many other living creatures that make up the nature today. We may simply have to live without millions of species which today exist on the Earth. Can we survive without them?

"The question is also: can we live knowing that they are all gone? We don't see elephants and tigers every day or year, but they exist in us as real, and we may even see them in a zoo. How would we feel if the entire natural environment were gone and we lived in beautiful homes with incredible tools, or in beautiful space ships forever without anything else alive except humans? Would we find life worth living and would we find enough diversion in our intellectual beings?

"I am almost sure that we could. It is my fear that we may have to abandon the Earth as uninhabitable even if the collision does not occur. Climate changes, high tides, volcanic eruptions, and other natural disasters may make living on Earth impossible. Remember the dinosaurs and what happened to them? But the human race must survive and be preserved."

"General, do you think anybody would survive after the collision?" Rama Chand asked.

"Definitely - no," the General said very emphatically.

"Do we have time to make preparations for human survival?" Arsen asked.

"Probably not," the General said. "Technology to put people in space already exists but staying there indefinitely is the problem. Food, water and air have to be made in space and procreation must continue. That is the minimum for survival. We have to send as many space ships as possible, and I think we need at least a hundred so that a few survive. That is almost an impossible task. We will have to work on it anyway."

"Who will be going to space in these ships?" Rama Chand asked and answered his own question. "Different people from different parts of the world will have to be selected. We will have to establish criteria and qualifications. I can see some advantages in resolving ethnic problems so that there would be some equity as to who goes and who does not. We will have to know how many people will be in each ship. We will have to know the order in which various groups will be selected. Technical qualifications will have to be defined."

"We have no idea how people will react when preservation selection starts," Arsen said. "Will they be upset if their tribe is not selected? Part of the problem is also education. Some groups would have more educated individuals than others. Education does not make them better; it makes them indispensable. It will not be possible to equalize the numbers from each group unless the number of people to be sent to space is large enough to accommodate these variables."

"Lottery may not be a bad idea," said Goran Enstrom.

"Lottery?" Arsen wondered.

"Why not? Losers could not blame anybody but their bad luck."

"You mean a lottery with six billion entries?" Rama Chand asked.

"We could also have an ethnic lottery and each group would select people for the mission," Arsen said. "That would be manageable. On the other hand, I wonder why Tamils are so violent or Kurds or Basques, and why Tutsis and Hutus are still killing each other."

"Probably because they are not recognized," Stan Petkovic said and everybody looked at him as if he had not been sitting with them before he spoke. "In Bosnia, at least the different entities have been recognized and they are territorial. In Muslim Bosnia you know you are in the Muslim territory. The same is true for the Serbian and Croatian territories. They are recognized as Muslims, Serbs and Croats. Isn't that true for Israel - a Jewish State? Recognized as Jewish. In Spain Basque territory, though obvious, is not recognized and they are fighting for recognition.

"The situation is worse in Sri Lanka for Tamils and in Turkey for Kurds. In Rwanda, Tutsi rule yet they are the minority, and that goes back a hundred years; they have mistreated Hutu majority, and they still do. Tutsi killed thousands a few decades ago and again during the rebellion in Zaire this year, and Hutu retaliated when they got their chance in '94. They have no territories of their own and the war goes on."

"Very interesting views," Rama Chand said and everybody agreed. "How are you going to resolve their problems considering that the two populations are frequently mixed? You cannot just resettle them even though that is sometimes the best solution in the end. In Bosnia lines have been drawn. In India, in '47, the same thing happened after a million were killed and who knows how many million were dislocated permanently. It is as terrible as it sounds, and people suffered immensely. Now, fifty years later, some problems still exist but peace has been achieved, although there is tension between Indians and Pakistanis, particularly about Kashmir. Is that good? I fail to see the goodness in the suffering of millions. There must be a better way."

"As soon as I organize my department I will bring together some leaders from ethnic academia," Arsen said, "and leaders from both sides of the battle lines, and see what they can accomplish. I will not let academicians preach or combatants fight. I will induce them to discuss specific issues. One of the leading topics will be the problems of mixed communities."

General Thornton walked in and apologized for being late.

"So many things are happening at the same time," he said. "Arsen is testing the readiness of W.G. forces and it takes more than a few hours to organize this enormous multinational Military. By the way, Arsen, the Chinese are packing up in Tibet and planing to guard one half of Kurdistan's border. The other half will be guarded by Americans. Tibet will get Icelanders and Norwegians. People are calling about riots - they need help. I've been referring them to Arsen and advising that they start talking to all parties. I'm getting complaints from around the globe - everybody is trying to get rid of their armies to save money. What should I do about that? Money is still important for survival."

"Tell them to be patient for a few days until the Assembly decides on a budget," Rama Chand said. "Then we will take their armies off their hands. The budget will be decided sometime next week. I am pushing hard to get that resolved. We need a lot of money."

Gen. Thornton asked for a sandwich and coffee as others were finishing their coffee.

"It is getting late," Rama Chand said. "Gentlemen, I want to tell you how glad I am to have you on board. I see progress, and I see teamwork. Let me tell you about one aspect of our relations that we should be clear about. Public relations is what I mean. It will be my job to inform people and governments about the business of the World Government. I will be the catalyst among the departments, and most importantly I will be your liaison with the Assembly. Talk to me as often as you can and keep me informed about important matters. That is what I need the most from you. This is the beginning of our struggle to preserve humanity. Good luck to you and to all of us."

CHAPTER TWENTY-NINE

THURSDAY, 18 DECEMBER 1997

It was seven o'clock in the morning. Arsen had gone to the office early to go over the problems he had to work on during the day, and to read the newspapers - his first daily task. Since he had retired, that had been a compulsion. Even during the long, busy professional period of his life, Arsen had regularly read the Sunday papers. Political news was always interesting and conflicts among nations and their struggle for power fascinating. He remembered the early days of World War II, when he was ten, and the headlines in *Politika*, Belgrade's daily newspaper, in '40 and '41. Headlines such as "Battle for Tobruck," or "Pact with Hitler likely: Prince Pavle in Berlin," or "People in the streets: better war than pact," or "War With Hitler Unavoidable."

After the war, Arsen had belonged to the silent opposition, and the news was a daily irritant to him in its support of everything that was Soviet and socialist. Breaking away from Stalin had not made Tito a democrat. Yet the news attained a better color with criticism of the Soviets. Even the news from the West, which had trickled in in the beginning, began to be published steadily and increased in scope and volume. At least one knew what was happening in the world, and could ignore the official interpretations.

Arsen's escape to the West and his arrival in New York had made another change in his approach to the news. He realized that in the U.S., news reports were objective but carefully selected, so that the published news represented what was perceived as important by the editors, and not necessarily both sides of an issue. Was that still the case? Arsen asked himself and concluded in the affirmative. Having lived in the States for forty years, he knew that one got some news more often than other news. Once he started ethnic studies, after he retired, Arsen concluded that the news had to be interpreted *ipso facto* not from the interpretations of newspaper reporters and editors. Of course, getting all the facts was another matter.

PANKOVICH ACTS TO QUELL THE RIOTS AROUND THE WORLD
SRI LANKA, CYPRUS, TIBET, SPAIN AND GERMANY ARE BEING
REVIEWED
WG MILITARY TO BE USED. SOVEREIGNTY ISSUES ARE RAISED

From the articles one could get the impression that Military force would be used if the right moves were not made by the governments in some countries; that was not true. Rotation of troops and keeping them busy with the problems of people other than their own was the truth. Sovereignty was defined by the General and Rama Chand as the right of the people to the territory in which they live. That was the new definition of sovereignty, unclear to many people, including the Chinese government. A press conference was in order, Arsen thought.

"Doctor, Mr. Brown from the Forum on Foreign Policy is on line four," Michelle announced over the intercom. "Do you want to talk to him?"

"Yes, I do." The calls had started coming in and they would inevitably persist. "Hello, Mr. Brown. I have not forgotten my talk in January. Perhaps I should think of a different topic considering the latest events."

"Good morning Mr. Secretary," Mr. Brown said. "Major changes have taken place since we talked last time. There will be no recognition problems any more and your CV is already incomplete. A problem has developed because of the number of people who want to attend your talk. Have you had a chance to think about the topic or should we just leave it open?"

"Last time we talked my problem was recognition, now the problem is what can I say that people have not already heard?"

"Just tell us what's happening in the ethnic world and the talk will be a success," Mr. Brown said.

"It will have to be a last minute decision," Arsen said. "You may announce it as 'Ethnic problems: theoretical and practical considerations in the present World.' That is vague enough."

"It will be done," Mr. Brown said. "Thank you, Mr. Secretary."

"Mr. Brown, would you have time to come and talk to me?" Arsen thought he would be a good candidate for Press Secretary. He was obviously smart and must have had significant experience in dealing with important people.

"Any time, Mr. Secretary," Mr. Brown said.

"In that case, how about ten this morning?"

"I'll be there. Thank you."

Stan Petkovic asked over the intercom if he could come in.

"Stan, I see no reason to call before you come in. When you think you want to participate in a meeting just come in and find a chair. An introduction will not be necessary very soon. What is on your mind?"

"Something I knew would happen," Stan Petkovic said. "I even mentioned it at our first meeting. The Serbs expect me to deliver New York to them. They are calling constantly, here and at home. I am not sure how to handle them."

"I will take care of that," Arsen said. "You should tell them that I have said privately that I will visit Yugoslavia in the near future, and make all the decisions with them in Belgrade; and that nothing will happen until then."

"When are you planning to go to Belgrade? asked Stan Petkovic.

"Leave that up in the air," Arsen said. "Tell them in about a week. To follow my visit to Spain."

"That will take care of them," Stan Petkovic said and smiled with relief. "I will let them know."

"Talk to the Greeks and the Turks, and tell them I will be going to Cyprus by the beginning of the year to find out what has been done."

"Mr. Wolff is here to see you," Michelle announced as Stan Petkovic was leaving.

"Send him right in," Arsen said.

"Good morning, Mr. Secretary," Herman Wolff said. "Thank you for seeing me so promptly."

"The name is Arsen to you," Arsen said. "Second, no B.S. I am interested in working with you, not in obstructing you. What would I accomplish by keeping you waiting?"

"Thank you anyway," Herman Wolff said and he looked ambivalent.

"We were to talk about your domain. What about?"

"There are a few vaguely defined spots in and around my domain," Herman Wolff said.

"Which spots? I thought everything was clearly divided."

"Cyprus for example. Does it belong to my domain or does it go with Greece and the Balkans? Who will head Balkan affairs? Turkey thus becomes a problem since it deals with Greece on Cyprus. Do I deal with the Turks on the Kurdish problem or who does?"

"You do," Arsen said. "I agree, this is unclear. I will take care of the Balkans, and relations between Greece and Turkey. You should deal with them on Asian issues."

"That is clear now," Herman Wolff said. "Also I understand you ordered Kurdish territory sealed by Chinese and American troops. What do we do with the Turkish army in that region?"

"Talk to John Thornton," Arsen said. "The two of you should be able to resolve that problem either by rotating the Turks out of the country or by relocating them within Turkey. John will know how to do it."

"There is another policy issue," Herman Wolff said. "President Chand

and you stated that all political leaders will be audited to determine the origins of their personal resources. What happens when it is established that they have been stealing and that they are corrupt?"

"Your job at that point is to inform the Legal Department. You should not get involved any further."

"What do we do with politicians who are found guilty by a trial?" Herman Wolff asked.

"Nothing," Arsen said. "These politicians will not be eligible for reelection."

"This is an interesting concept," Herman Wolff remarked. "How did you come up with it?"

"Observation, just plain observation," Arsen said. "When you follow international politics, you get tired of reading constantly about corrupt leaders. Just think of the big ones - Mobutu, Marcos, Suharto, Bhutto, Soviet era Communist leaders who did not become personally rich but used the state treasury as their own valet. You ask yourself why not get rid of crooks who lead countries? If the message is right, crooks will leave politics if money is not available. Some honest people may become interested, especially when they realize there would be no personal risk."

"These are new doctrines that will change the political scene in the world," Herman Wolff said. "The U.N. will become the policeman of the world, making sure that people behave themselves."

"Not at all - not the way you said it." Arsen was annoyed by Herman Wolff's reasoning. "I would call the U.N. the arbitrator not the policeman. Our first principle, or dogma if you wish, is the right of every ethnic group to a territory, autonomous and equal, or to a nation-state, with the right to switch in either direction, if they so choose. The second principle is the right of every territory to have honest politicians who are elected by free elections. We will not tell them what form of government they want. I can actually visualize a state ruled by a dictator who has been freely elected. Nowadays dictators are not exactly rare, although in spite of them some freedoms are always gained. Yugoslavia and Croatia are good examples, and there are many others.

"Furthermore, the U.N. will help the neighboring states to form a combined police force which will provide a buffer factor, and guard the sanctity of each state. The combined force will be able to guard their own interests. Why would they need the big powers or huge military forces to enforce their own agreements. The U.N. could intervene when they fail to maintain peace."

"I meant to be positive but it didn't come out that way," Herman Wolff said.

"Herman, you have a problem area and you will have to come up with some ideas before the problems can be resolved. I am referring to the problems of the Israelis versus the Arabs. The old issue of Israel's existence is no longer an issue. Israelis have the right to be where they are now. However, there are some flammable issues that concern the territory held by each side. I suggest you convene a meeting between Israelis and Palestinians and insist that they start negotiating."

"What is our goal in the Middle East?" asked Herman Wolff.

"Like in any other part of the world, we want these people to be satisfied that the best possible solution has been achieved for them."

"You have answered most of my questions," Herman Wolff said. "I will be talking to Stan Petkovic about the details of running my operation - like money, transportation, etcetera."

"I expect to go to Spain and the Balkans sometime next week," Arsen said. "We should have everybody in place by then. A dinner meeting will be in order so that we can talk about our future plans."

"Thank you very much, Arsen, for the opportunity to work with you," Herman Wolff said as he was leaving the office.

"Don't mention it again," Arsen said. "You may change your mind once you realize that I usually demand too much of your time, and high marks in your results. Have a good day."

Arsen liked this German, who seemed to be honest and capable. His round face and the almost completely bald head, eyes with their warm expression, thick lips and meaty ears, and the thick, short neck on a large body gave Herman Wolff the look of anything but a diplomat. Yet he moved swiftly and talked in a soft voice, and he radiated energy and intelligence. He would do well in this organization, Arsen thought.

Arsen remembered the talk he was scheduled to present before the Forum on Foreign Policy The topic seemed to have materialized in the conversation he had just had with Herman Wolff. Ensured self-determination and territory, honest leaders and free elections, a combined police force, a chosen form of government, and ethnic participation in the preservation effort was about all he would have to discuss in his talk, and briefly at that. One less problem to worry about, Arsen thought.

Arsen looked at his watch: it was nine-thirty. -

Michelle announced René Bright on line three.

"Hello René, are you coming?"

"Not right now," René Bright said. "The Zaireans are stuck in Paris because of bad weather. They hope to arrive by the morning."

"Have you had some ideas about what to do with their problems?" Arsen asked.

"They have a most difficult situation where ethnically mixed villages and villages ethnically homogeneous are next to each other. What does one do, short of resettling them?"

"Ask the people," Arsen said. "It would be better to tell the Zaireans, who are in Paris, to go home and discuss among themselves and with their own people what should be done. You could join them sometime next week. I would be very interested in going to Zaire, after my visit to Spain. Why don't you do that and come over. You need an office and a secretary and some people to help you manage that huge territory."

"You're right," René Bright said. "I'll be there soon."

Arsen talked to Victoria about the progress in moving people out of the building and converting the offices. She said she had had a meeting with the management, and they were progressing rapidly. The building was to be emptied over the weekend. They would have the offices equipped as the people were appointed. Almost all the rooms had more than one telephone line. Equipment and furniture would be available as needed, and they would manage the building.

"Do you think the building is big enough for our purposes?" Arsen inquired.

"I'm sure it is," Victoria said.

"Victoria, please work on my trip to Spain," Arsen said. "I want to leave New York for Spain on Sunday, the twenty-eighth. On Wednesday I will fly to Kinshasa with René Bright, who will join me in Madrid. I will leave Zaire on Friday and fly to Belgrade. Further plans will be made there. I will visit Zagreb, Pristina, and Sarajevo. I must also visit Athens and Nicosia and Ankara. That will take a week. I will be back on the following Sunday. I should get together with Stan in Belgrade."

It was getting close to ten.

"Doctor, Mr. Brown is here to see you," Michelle announced over the intercom.

"Send him in," Arsen told her.

Matthew Brown entered the office. He looked the way Arsen had imagined him - in his fifties, medium height, slender and athletic, with a calm pleasant face, some white in his brown hair, and questioning green eyes. The only thing missing was a sweat suit to complete his athletic appearance.

"Good day Mr. Secretary," Matthew Brown said. "You were on my mind today, and here I am in your office."

"How are you?" Arsen offered him a chair. "I wanted to talk to you about a job. Don't be surprised. These days there is no time for long introductions and search committees."

"A job?" Matthew Brown looked surprised.

"My Department is growing fast," Arsen continued. "Somebody will have to be a spokesman for the Department and it occurred to me that you might be interested. The job will be easy. You will have to know everything about the Department, who is who and who is doing what at any given time. You will have to travel with me to keep track of our activities, and to face reporters. That will keep you very busy."

"I'd like to try it," Matthew Brown said without hesitation.

"You have a general idea what the functions and purpose of this Department are, don't you?"

"Yes, I do," Matthew Brown said. "The media have discussed it extensively."

"I am determined to see this mission through," Arsen said. "Initially I was to have a rather limited role. Now I am in the lead role on ethnicity issues. As the General said, we want every human being to feel comfortable and free in this world. We will try to help economically too. We need a strong Legal Division, and we need it soon. I want someone with extensive international experience who would be capable of developing new standards among ethnic groups. The best lawyers have always been Jews. They are easy to work with, and they have the mental flexibility to come up with new ideas and new concepts within the framework of principles. This individual must be an American, as American lawyers are most aggressive and most experienced in defining laws, and we will need that in ethnic disputes. Do you know someone who is qualified and is associated with the Forum?"

"Several people would qualify," Matthew Brown said. "My first choice is Melvin Stein. He's articulate and calm, intelligent, analytical, and he's been involved in international relations."

"Victoria, please find Mr. Melvin Stein," Arsen said over the intercom. "I want to talk to him."

"Try 999-3000, that's his office number," Matthew Brown interjected.

"I must talk to him today," Arsen said. "Reach him even if he is outside the city."

"Will do," Victoria said and hung up.

"President Chand should soon come up with the nominees for the World Supreme Court," Arsen said. "I am sure they will replace the judges in the International Court of Justice in the Hague, though he may choose to keep the judges already elected. I know we will be accused of wrong-doing and of infringing on the lives of some groups and individuals."

"Do you think there will be enough time to deal with all the issues?" Matthew Brown asked. "The time is terribly short."

"You have to stay around here a while to get the feeling that Rama Chand and the General, and people like Goran Enstrom will take care of the world, one way or another," Arsen said. "You must meet Gen. Shagov, then you may start thinking differently. The General gives you the impression that he knows exactly what to do to save the world, yet he couldn't convey that in his speech before the Assembly, which I call his silent speech. I was upset initially, but I think it worked out very well. The General wanted to run the government and to direct the research. That was impossible. Rama Chand is the right person to be the President and he will keep everybody in place and happy. The General will organize the salvage operation. We will try to make people feel recognized and be recognized."

"Do you actually think the disaster will be avoided?" Matthew Brown asked.

"Either the collision will be prevented or there will be survivors who will preserve the human race," Arsen said. "In the case that collision doesn't take place there will be a lot of changes in the world, and there will be a different ethnic environment. I doubt that the changes we make today will be reversed. The World Government will remain, and the population, which is now fraught with fear because of the approaching apocalypse, will relax and take a new direction spiritually and philosophically. Certain scientific and technological advances, which will be made in the preservation effort, will become a major factor in changing the way we live and work. I don't have a clear vision of such a world, not yet."

Matthew Brown was silent for a few moments, impressed by Arsen's pronouncements

"Matt, another thing," Arsen said. "I would like you to start tomorrow. Victoria will give you my daily schedule, and you will find out the details. We need daily meetings, and when something is developing you will know or come here and find out."

"Doctor, Mr. Stein's office called," Victoria said over the intercom. "He will call as soon as they find him."

"I'll let you know what happened as soon as I talk to Mr. Stein," Arsen said as Matt Brown was leaving. "I'll see you tomorrow."

The influx of calls from all sides was constant. Two hours later, Arsen was still answering calls - all of them urgent and important to the callers. The Greek Ambassador wanted to inform Arsen that Cypriot talks were on the way, and that in his personal opinion autonomy of each part, Turkish and Greek, would be accomplished within days. Arsen suggested that he would like to give a dinner in celebration of achieved autonomy, when he visited Nicosia. Arsen thought he heard a gulp from the Ambassador when he mentioned the dinner.

Both South and North Koreans called to inquire if the new principles required them to hold a plebiscite about the division of Korea. No, they were told, a plebiscit was not mandatory. People might insist on unification in the future. The Northern Ambassador gulped when elections were mentioned, and his Southern counterpart when hearing about mandatory audits.

The Zaireans and Rwandans called upset that they had been turned back. When Arsen asked for their proposals for the solution of the problems at hand, they had none. Arsen suggested that they sit together and come up with some proposals before he presented his own ideas when he arrived to Kinshasa in ten days. There was nothing to talk about at present, Arsen told them, and they agreed reluctantly.

Even the Tibetans called, to ask whether they should submit an application for membership in the United Nations. The Egyptian Vice President called about the Copts. The message was reaching targets not even aimed yet, Arsen thought. Governments were taking these matters seriously. He asked the Egyptian to convene a meeting of concerned parties, to include the Coptic Patriarch, and produce a document that offered solutions to existing problems based on the ethnic principles as voted by the Assembly. The Egyptian expressed his doubts about the success of such an undertaking.

"Try anyway," Arsen told him, "and get in touch with Undersecretary Herman Wolff."

Too many calls and too few people to answer them, Arsen thought. The divisions and sections needed people right away. A meeting of all Undersecretaries should be held but some of them had not even arrived in New York.

"Doctor, Mr. Ito Amoto is here to see you," Michelle announced over the intercom.

"Send him right in," Arsen said.

Mr. Amoto's jacket, shirt and trousers, and a raincoat draped over his forearm, were wrinkled from the night spent in the airplane, and they were in contrast to his smooth, almost shiny face, which was adorned with a smile and with a pair of bright understanding eyes and a somewhat broad nose. For Arsen, one who always thought of the Japanese as short and stocky, Mr. Amoto was not typical; he was of surprising stature, a figure but a surprising figure of muscle and fat in a tall body. He walked towards Arsen's desk somewhat clumsily and hesitantly, as if awaiting some unexpected move by Arsen; he relaxed when Arsen got up from his chair to greet him and offered him a chair. Arsen gave him a small glass of scotch whisky, which Arsen himself never drank, but sometimes used as a life saver, as he called it. Poor Ito Amoto could not possibly refuse the first offer made him by Arsen, and he swallowed the drink in one gulp.

"I hope you feel better now," Arsen said. "You looked as if you were ready to collapse when you walked in."

"Thank you, I really feel better now," Ito Amoto agreed.

"I have been waiting for you to arrive so that we can resolve some

Asian problems," Arsen said. "Tibet is a sore spot in China's eyes, and they will like it even less when the Tibetans enter the world as an independent state with the Dalai Lama at its helm. Kashmir is another problem area. The Tamils in Sri Lanka are boiling, and the East Timorese are no cooler. This is to mention but a few. Also, I have to talk to you about the principles we must follow and how I feel we should accomplish our goals. Make yourself comfortable first, get your office going, and come see me tomorrow. Victoria will get you started. I am sure she has many things ready for you."

"Mr. Secretary, it will be my honor to work with you," Ito Amoto said. "I will try my best to justify your confidence in me."

"President Chand gave you an A-plus when he recommended you," Arsen said. "I couldn't resist the opportunity. I am sure we'll work well together. Have a good day and a good rest."

He must be very tired, Arsen thought after Ito Amoto had left. It would be a new experience, working with a Japanese. Arsen disliked the idea of being called Mr. Secretary all the time. That had to be changed gently as these people were very serious.

"Doctor, it's one o'clock and lunch is ready," Victoria called. "Also Mr. Bright came to see you when you were on the phone. He's now with Mr. Petkovic."

"Let them talk," Arsen said. "Mr. Petkovic has good ideas about Zaire. Maybe they will come up with a proposal and a solution for Zaire."

Arsen wanted only a bagel and a cup of coffee.

"Doctor, we're moving really fast," Victoria said while they were eating lunch. "Mr. Wolff has hired a number of people you'll have to approve and many more on lower levels. Are you planing to have other divisions?"

"Yes, I think so," Arsen said. "We need someone on a high level to coordinate military activities, and to head the Audits Division and the Election and Plebiscite Division.

"Doctor, Mr. Stein is on line three," Michelle announced over the intercom.

"I will be with him in a minute," Arsen said as he was finishing his bagel; he carried the coffee cup to his office.

"Hello Mr. Stein," Arsen said. "Your friend Matt Brown, from FFP, thought you might be interested in talking to me about the position of Undersecretary for Legal Affairs. If so, could you come to see me tonight."

"Hello Mr. Secretary," Melvin Stein replied. "Thank you for the invitation - I would be interested in talking about that job. What time tonight?"

"Say seven, in my office," Arsen said. "I will see you tonight."

What you could do tomorrow better do tonight, Arsen thought. If he was as good as Matt said, they had better grab him tonight.

"Doctor, Mr. Wolff is on line two," Michelle announced over the intercom.

"Herman, what is on your mind?"

"An old friend of mine, Max Edelshtein, is in my office," Herman Wolff said. "Would you have time to meet him? I could bring him over any time."

"Who is he?" Arsen wanted to know.

"He is an expert on European affairs; I met him in Bonn when he was the Secretary of the Soviet Embassy, in '85. An excellent man, though a former communist."

"He is no longer a communist?"

"I doubt it."

"Once a communist, always a communist," Arsen said. "These days that makes no difference. Communist or not, he is interested in the survival of humanity, I am sure. Come over."

This would be a good candidate for the European-Russian job, Arsen thought. He wanted to talk to him.

Herman Wolff walked in with Max Edelshtein. Arsen had imagined him to be a tall muscular, perhaps even fat Russian with a beard, and he was surprised to meet a European Jew, of medium height, slim and not muscular. He was intellectual in appearance, and his face was animated by small, close-set eyes that were quick with intelligence.

After the introductions Herman Wolff offered to leave. Arsen told him to stay and participate in the conversation.

"Herman tells me you have given up communism,, have you?" Arsen inquired.

"Not really, Mr. Secretary," Max Edelshtein replied. "It is not entirely clear to my heart and my soul what I have become. Communism was in my blood even when I thought the excesses of suppression of the people were obvious to everybody. Lenin and Stalin were not my idols. They prostituted a decent idea for its preservation. I still think communism is inevitable, alas not during my lifetime. Just as slave and feudal societies and their ideas eventually outlived themselves and disappeared, so will capitalism. A classless society makes so much sense. Sciences and technology will help convert the present capitalistic society into the future communist civilization. People will become independent, technologically conversant, and interested in ideas and the Universe. Then they will grow to be communists without anybody forcing them into it."

"What happened, Herman?" Arsen asked. "Your evaluation missed the target. As I said, old soldiers never die, and old communists remain communists. Mr. Edelshtein, what do you think Europe needs most, today?"

"Europe without Balkans and the eastern parts succeeded in balancing their appetites for each other's territories and managed to keep hatred down long enough to be believable. The Eastern Europeans have joined them. As for Russia and her satellites the glory has been over for some time although they can always resurrect their importance. The Europeans should resolve their minority problems, particularly in Germany and France, and to a degree in England and in the Baltic States and the Ukraine."

The conversation shifted to Russia and her many leaders - Ivan the Terrible, and Stalin, Peter the Great, and Gorbachev, and the Cold war. Arsen was convinced that Max Edelshtein was the man to have around; he could carry on a credible conversation about the politics of the future.

"Would you be interested in taking care of Europe and Russia, and carrying out the new ethnic principles?" Arsen asked Max Edelshtein. "I am sure you are familiar with these principles."

"Yes, I am familiar with the principles and I support them. Of course, I am very much interested in this job."

"Well, you have the job, and good luck," Arsen said.

"This is incredible," Herman Wolff said. "Congratulations, Max."

"Thank you. What do I do next?"

"Herman will tell you," Arsen said. "Also, talk to Stan Petkovic and Victoria, and plan to be around soon."

It was incredible, Arsen thought, and he was joined in his amazement by Herman Wolff, how fast things were developing and new people were joining the Department.

"Doctor, President Chand is on line four," Michelle announced over the intercom.

"Good afternoon, Sir."

"Hello, Arsen," Rama Chand said. "Anything new I should know about?"

"The number of my undersecretaries is growing," Arsen said. "They will be seeing you very soon. You know René Bright, Ramesh Rao and Ito Amoto, whom you recommended. Ramesh Rao is stuck in Brazil and the other two are ready to start. I also have Max Edelshtein for Europe and Russia, and Melvin Stein for Legal Affairs. Also, I need someone for the Preservation Division."

"Why don't you interview Jean-Pierre Vernier," Rama Chand said. "He is French, very intelligent, and a former high official in French intelligence. I met him recently when he was assigned to the French Mission at the U.N. I believe he had some serious disagreements with the French intelligence community. He comes from an important and very respected French family in Paris."

"I will talk to him today," Arsen said and thought that Rama Chand was becoming the man of cohesion in the World Government.

"Arsen, I wanted to ask your opinion about Raul Ortiz," Rama Chand said, turning to the real reason for his call. "He is practically out of the job in the U.N. I feel he would be a great deputy for me, and I would like to see him in that job."

"Rama, you are the boss," Arsen said. "You know the man better than anybody. I dealt only briefly with him, and followed his moves as the Secretary General after you resigned. He was an effective leader and loyal to you. I am in favor."

"Thank you for the support," Rama Chand said. "I will push for his approval by the Assembly. By the way, you should know that the Chinese President has filed a protest note against you over Tibet. You may have to appear before the Committee on Ethnic Problems. It may be messy for a while, but don't worry I will work on that with you."

"I am leaving for Europe and Africa on Wednesday. Could my appearance be arranged before Wednesday?"

"Let me find out," Rama Chand said. "I will talk to you soon. Thanks again."

Arsen asked Victoria to find Mr. Jean-Pierre Vernier in the French Mission to the United Nations.

"Victoria, have you heard from Ivo Stipich recently?" Arsen asked. "The last I heard he was going to Croatia. Try to find him for me. Is there a way to get direct lines to the President and General Thornton? I would like to have them installed."

"Doctor, Ambassador Iliadis is on line two," Michelle announced over the intercom.

"Good day, Mr. Ambassador," Arsen said.

"Good day, Mr. Secretary. I have some news to report to you on Cyprus."

"Tell me."

"Mr. Secretary, you wanted talks on Cyprus to start. Well, they have just been concluded. Diplomats from all four interested parties were present and took part in negotiations. I am authorized to tell you that the Greek Government has approved wide ranging autonomy for both sides in Cyprus, and we anticipate a positive reply from Turkey. This will be announced officially in Ankara, Athens and Nicosia. They talked all night and reached the agreement. Partition was not discussed."

"Congratulations Mr. Ambassador," Arsen said. "I like what I hear. It seems you don't need me there any more. Still, I would like to witness the signing ceremonies, if you would let me come."

"We will sign the agreement on Wednesday, December 24 and it will be in effect the next day."

"Count on my being there. I would be interested in attending the celebration dinner. I will leave Cyprus soon after on my way to Kinshasa."

"I will see you there, Mr. Secretary."

"Give my best to your Prime Minister."

That ended the conversation.

"Doctor, I located Mr. Stipich," Victoria said. "He's on line three."

"Ivo, I really wanted to talk to you," Arsen said in their native SerboCroatian. "What are you doing these days?"

"Thank you for calling," Ivo Stipich said. "I am having a good time in Zagreb. They are treating me well, and I am learning more about their problems and worries, particularly with a view to your present position. They are convinced that you will avenge yourself for certain events from the past."

"Like what?" Arsen asked.

"Like the events of '41 and Krajina territory in '95," Ivo Stipich said.

"You must have explained my position?"

"Yes I have, but they don't believe me."

"That cannot be changed right now," Arsen said. "Time will tell."

"I know that, but they don't," Ivo Stipich said. He was obviously frustrated with the Croatians.

"Ivo, I called you to ask you about your immediate plans," Arsen said. "Would you be interested in working in the World Government, and what would you want to do? I am also sorry about the fate of Mr. Kravchenko."

"I am sorry too, but that is the past now," Ivo Stipich said. "If I could choose, I would like to represent you in Croatia. I don't feel like working in New York; I am very comfortable in Zagreb."

"Although I had plans for you in New York, I need you in Zagreb too. You will report directly to me since I will manage the Balkans. You might have heard that I will be in Belgrade some time next week."

"Word filtered to me and it caused even more apprehension around here."

"Tell them about your appointment and start negotiating with them," Arsen said. "You know the issues. Get back to me before I arrive in Belgrade. Good luck to you."

"Thank you."

"Doctor, the Turkish Ambassador is on line four," Michelle announced on the intercom.

"Mr. Ambassador, we won, didn't we?"

"Yes we did. As you have heard, agreement on Cyprus has been reached. Now, I am calling about the Kurds. I talked with the Prime Minister, and he was furious about your idea of an independent

Kurdistan."

"I never talked about an independent Kurdistan. I asked that your government come up with ideas. However, I followed your advice."

"Mr. Secretary, I think they are willing to do what has to be done. Unfortunately, in the process I lost my job."

"Mr. Ambassador, if I remember correctly, you are an economist, aren't you?" Arsen asked.

"Yes, I graduated from London School of Economics. I am not sure what that has to do with our conversation."

"I need an Undersecretary for Audits and you may consider the job," Arsen said. "Come to see me at nine in the morning if you are interested. Thank you for the information."

"I will be there," the Turkish Ambassador said.

Arsen called Victoria to the office to review some procedures, and particularly to define the position of the Press Secretary, whose office would have to know about the entire operation of the Department. Also, he wanted to define the position of Stan Petkovic, and had him deal with most callers but had Michelle channel all calls regarding the Balkan States to Arsen. All Undersecretaries should be able to walk into the office any time, and regardless of who was in there.

"Victoria, what happened to Ramesh Rao." Victoria had no further information on him. "What about Jean-Pierre Vernier? He was supposed to call me."

"Doctor, Mr. Vernier is on line two," Michelle announced over the intercom.

"Good day Mr. Vernier," Arsen said.

"Good day, Mr. Secretary."

"Mr. Vernier, President Chand suggested I talk to you," Arsen continued. "I would like to meet with you and discuss a division in my Department that needs somebody to direct it. Should you be interested, come to see me."

"Which division, if I may know?"

"Preservation," Arsen said. "I assume you know what it is about."

"Not exactly, Mr. Secretary," Jean Pierre Vernie said. "Diplomatic and governmental vocabulary has changed quite a bit in the last few days; we say military rotation, mandatory audits, right of sovereignty, mandatory autonomy, etcetera, so I want to make sure I know what preservation means."

"As you can imagine, Mr. Vernier, the Earth is not commonly at the end of the trajectory of a celestial body," Arsen said.

"We have to do something about that, I know," Jean-Pierre Vernier said.

"I would have time to see you in an hour if you have nothing better to do."

"I will be there, Mr. Secretary."

He must be a tough guy, Arsen thought, tough enough to be kicked out of the Intelligence Agency. Yet, they had not discarded him completely. Family clout, - probably.

Matt Brown walked in, to Arsen's surprise.

"I thought you were to start tomorrow," Arsen said and was thinking something must have happened to send him back.

"Word gets around very quickly," Matt Brown said. "I've already been called and interviewed by reporters. Naturally, I said nothing of significance. It won't be any better tomorrow. I came back to catch up with the news." He slumped, tired, in a chair.

Arsen brought him up to date on the new appointments, prospective undersecretaries, and the progress that had been made in the field - particularly the agreement on autonomy in Cyprus - and in Europe and Zaire. Arsen also suggested he keep in touch with the undersecretaries and their staffs.

As Matt Brown was leaving, Michelle announced over the intercom that Mr. Stein had arrived for his appointment.

"Excellent timing," Arsen said. "Let him in." Arsen told Matt Brown to stay for the interview, and walked to the door to meet Melvin Stein.

"Meet my Press Secretary," Arsen said pointing to Matt Brown. "He is guilty for your being here today."

"There's always somebody - a friend or an enemy," Melvin Stein said in his agreeable voice and laughed. We'll find out which one Matt will become in the end."

"You sound optimistic for the end," Arsen said thinking that some optimism was in order in the world, which was bearing up under the truth but was subject to psychic decompensation at any time and without notice. "I like that."

Melvin Stein stopped laughing. His smiling face became serious, and his large, bulging eyes became sad, although his mouth retained its smiling expression - probably a professional habit to keep clients happy and calm. His body, not large or tall or fat even, appeared to shrink a little as if under the burden of humanity's weight.

"My grandmother used to say that the end of anything is always different than predicted," Melvin Stein said. "Let's hope she was right."

"As you know, I need a legal team that will keep an eye on, and keep track of legal developments in countries where changes occur," Arsen said. "Also, we must make sure that people who are found guilty of fraud and corruption get impartial trials, and that sentences are carried out. One more thing, Mr. Stein. I hate bureaucracy. Stay away from complex solutions. Talk to me and keep me informed especially about potential problem cases. Do you think you will fit into our organization and do you think we are doing the right thing?"

"I agree with the principles and don't know the details," Melvin Stein said.

"The principles have to be followed," Arsen said. "The details will emerge as we go along."

"Do you really think we'll be able to enforce rules that develop from principles?" Melvin Stein asked Arsen.

"The principles have been accepted by the Assembly, and the rules will reflect their application in specific situations. Our mandate is not to change the world but to change relations among people and make sure they establish their national freedom and independence. Our goal is to finish the job started long ago, long before us, the job that was obstructed by the more powerful over the weaker nations. The classic example is Zaire, a state of many ethnic groups and among them some larger and strong and others smaller and weak and fighting for their independence. The government is fighting partition, for many reasons. Also read about the Basques, Albanian Kosovars, Kurds and Tamils. The governments claim they are rebels, terrorists, criminals, and that they belong in jail. They should get their freedom and independence by partition from those states.

"The next scenario is the reverse of the previous one. The minority that wins freedom for itself, gets its own minorities. Now, the newly formed majority denies the right of partition to the minority. Often these are the same leaders who fought for independence, and won, only to deny the same rights to their own minority, and they use the same methods to suppress ideas of independence as were used on them. Walker Connor explained that so well in his writings. It may sound stupid, but it is the rule of the jungle. Look at some of the so called great powers, and you will find this true in many cases. Sad, you might say, but true."

"You make it sound simple," Melvin Stein said.

"Unfortunately, it is simple," Arsen said.

"How far down do we keep splitting?" asked Melvin Stein. "At some point you arrive at the point of *reductio ad absurdum*."

"That is how modern political science wants to prevent splitting," Arsen said, a tad of hostility in his voice. "Do we stop classifying the ethnic groups? No, we don't. Do we stop classifying bird species? No, we don't. We preserve animal species, yet we are happy when a human ethnic group disappears by assimilation. What about killing as a method of extinction. Remember the Nazis? Well, Mr. Stein, our job is to preserve ethnic groups and keep them free. If you think you can help us keep them free, get on board."

"I see your point," Melvin Stein said. "Give them freedom and make sure they remain free - that's the idea. I can live with that. I'm willing to get on board, Mr. Secretary."

"Congratulations, Mel," Matt Brown said enthusiastically.

"Welcome aboard," Arsen said. "Matt will show you around. Oh, Mel, please plan to be in Cyprus by Monday so that you can examine the documents and talk to people before they sign their treaty."

"I'll do that," Melvin Stein said.

"Doctor, President Chand is on line three," Michelle announced over the intercom.

"Arsen, you asked about the appearance before the Ethnic Committee," Rama Chand said. "They were very accommodating. You will testify on Monday at nine in the morning. They will discuss with you the situation in several states, I believe Sri Lanka, China and Tibet, Cyprus, and Kurdistan. Other states will not be mentioned. Of course, they will be calling you again in the future."

"I can handle this," Arsen said "I know these states very well."

"Stop by to see me after you testify," Rama Chand said and hung up.

It was five when Jean-Pierre Vernier walked into the office. He was not a tall or a large man, and he walked with a slight waddle that favored the right side. The orthopedist woke up in Arsen and the desire to find out if he had osteoarthritis in the right hip. His somewhat long, narrow face was regular in appearance; he had a modest nose, high forehead, and smooth, not very dense brown hair, suspect of being colored, parted on the left side. He gave the impression of a grumpy, and serious man. Arsen shook his hand and asked him to sit down.

"I am glad you could come," Arsen said.

"This is important business and you are a busy man," Jean-Pierre Vernier replied.

"That is true, I am busy," Arsen said. "Busy trying to recruit people to do the work for me. I need you to help me in a delicate matter - deciding who goes into space and who does not; it is like saying who lives and who dies. There may be a great demand for your services, and stiff competition to get onto one of the space ships, but it might be just the opposite. That is hard to know."

"You mean we will actually have to find people who would want to go?"

"Certainly, someone will have to make that decision," Arsen continued his explanation. "A group of scientists, essential for maintaining the ships, will have to go. At this time I have no idea what the ships will be like, how many people will be on each ship, or how many ships will be built and ready to go when the time comes. It will be your job to select people from the submitted list from various ethnic groups. Representation will be important. Education will be important. Hope for the poor and uneducated will be important. Criminals will be excluded. Secretaries and Undersecretaries and most government officials will not go. Information from different parts of the world will be essential."

"Some intelligence work will be essential to prevent the abuse of some groups and people," Jean-Pierre Vernier remarked. "It seems that my experience may be needed after all. I am surprised that you chose me considering my problems with the intelligence community in France and elsewhere."

"At this point it is unimportant what I like and dislike about somebody; it is important that the selected individual can do the job. You were recommended by President Chand. That is all I care about. You will report directly to me, and I have the habit of wanting to know what is happening. I expect to hear about the results, not the effort."

Arsen felt the message was sinking into Jean-Pierre's head - perhaps a thick skull but a good mind. "The intelligence information should be secret, but never denied to the person or group who is involved in any way - positive or negative."

"I have a good idea what to do," Jean-Pierre Vernier said. "I will prove to you that intelligence service does not mean 'usurpation'. You will have what you need, Mr. Secretary."

"I know I will," Arsen said. "Keep me informed."

Victoria came in. She looked tired and discouraged. Arsen thought she could use a drink and a good meal and she would look better.

It was seven o'clock.

"Victoria, I am taking you to a restaurant to feed you and rehydrate you, then I'll take you home, before I go home myself."

"Doctor, you don't have to do that. I'll go home, take a shower, and fix myself dinner. Then I'm going to watch television and eat, and fall asleep. Tomorrow I'll be as good as new."

"You are going to eat under my supervision," Arsen said and put on his jacket and raincoat. "Please put your coat on. The limousine is waiting to take us to the restaurant. We are going to the Brazilian restaurant, Circus; it is a quiet place with good food. You will like it."

Arsen arrived home at nine o'clock.

The progress in resolving ethnic conflicts was reported on the ten o'clock news.

PANKOVICH ACTS: CYPRUS GOES AUTONOMOUS
SIGNING CEREMONY ON WEDNESDAY - PANKOVICH TO ATTEND

NEW PRESS SECRETARY IN ETHNIC DEPARTMENT:
MATTHEW BROWN
TIBET IN LIMBO: CHINA AGAINST PARTITION
BASQUE SEPARATISTS' QUIET CELEBRATIONS
In anticipation of Independence
RIOTS AND DEMONSTRATIONS SUBSIDING:
IN WAKE OF PROMISING CHANGES

Arsen turned off the television. There was no point in listening to news he already knew. Nada told him about her conversations with the children. They were calm and tending to their business. They would make no moves at this time.

"We should go to sleep," Nada said and received a vote of approval.

CHAPTER THIRTY

FRIDAY, 19 DECEMBER 1997

Arsen woke up at six-thirty in the morning and felt comfortable at home not having to rush to the office. Nada served coffee in the study and brought in the newspapers. The headlines were a reprise of last night's news. One headline looked odd:

RIOTERS PARALYZED: THEY ARE WAITING IN ANTICIPATION

The article was written by Tony Fein from New York. He surveyed areas of violent and of mild rioting and found that the rioters, representing mainly minority ethnic groups, were cooling off and waiting to see what would happen. Interviews with many people indicated that everybody expected the World Government to support the rights of minorities. They were right, Arsen thought. Another headline brought into focus the anti-collision efforts:

GEN. SHAGOV IN JAPAN: SETTING-UP A NUCLEAR LAB
NEUTRINO LAB TO START RESEARCH ON FEASIBILITY
OF A PLANETARY GUN
TWO NEW PROJECTS; ADVANCED:
PSYCHOPHYSICAL STUDIES AND CLONING IN SPACE

Arsen had only a vague idea about neutrino particles, and the neutrino gun was a new subject; 'psychophysical' was another distant subject; and cloning in space seemed a strange project since people and animals would be traveling on the space ships - unless they were thinking of artificial cloning after everybody had died. That was an interesting thought.

The limousine took Arsen quickly to the Ethnic Castle as he sometimes called the building on Lexington Avenue. He walked into his office at eight o'clock. Victoria and Michelle were already there. The Turkish Ambassador, Suleiman Karazoglou, was waiting to see him. Also, urgent calls had to be answered.

"Michelle, could you divert some calls to Stan Petkovic?" Arsen asked.

"President Chand called, and Mr. Wolff, and Mr. Bright. Their calls were urgent."

"Call President Chand first, and see whether Herman and René can resolve their problems with Stan," Arsen said. "Good morning Mr. Karazoglou, come in. We'll have some coffee and a bagel, and we will talk."

As they were entering the office Michelle announced that Rama Chand was on line two.

"Good morning, Arsen," Rama Chand said. "Congratulation on your first ethnic success in Cyprus. I am impressed, and everybody else is impressed. I have the list of your impressive appointees."

"Most of them were recommended by you."

"Nothing wrong with that as long as you like them," Rama Chand said. "John Thornton mentioned a name I thought you might want to know. I am talking about Col. Abdul Nassar el Hakim. John knew him when he was an assistant to the Egyptian Military Attaché in Washington. Good man. I met him at a disarmament meeting a few years back."

"I will talk to him today."

"You will find him in New York, where he is visiting his ill sister," Rama Chand suggested. "She is an inpatient at Columbia-Presbyterian Hospital. Paula will call Victoria with the exact room number and the contact phone number. Oh, Arsen, have you seen the headlines today?"

"Yes, I have."

"You are getting excellent marks," Rama Chand said. "That is good and I expected it. I was puzzled by the General's projects. We have heard of the neutrino gun but nobody knows what it is. What are space cloning and psychophysics?"

"Psychophysics may be needed to predict reactions to psychic stimuli in space. Why does he want to clone on the space ships, which will be filled with people anyway? We'll have him explain some of these projects to us when we meet next time."

"We must do that."

Victoria came on the intercom. "Doctor, a Col. Nassar is on line four. Are you expecting his call?"

"Yes, I am," Arsen said.

"Colonel, this is Sec. Pankovich. I am so glad you called. I hope your sister is better?"

"Thank you Mr. Secretary, she is improving already and going home in

222

a day or two," Col. Nassar said.

"Colonel, come to see me today if you can," Arsen said. "I would like to talk to you. Could you make it by eleven?"

"No reason why not," Col. Nassar said. "I will see you at eleven."

Arsen finally turned to Ambassador Karazoglou. "Excuse me, please. I did not mean to ignore you. One has to cope with phone calls. The job I mentioned to you is really extremely important, and I need an economist to direct it. The bottom line is that all world leaders will have their assets audited and certified. They will be disqualified if they refuse to submit information you need. We will not look for every penny they have made, but there will be a low tolerance for those who have grossly abused their position and become rich or have allowed corruption in their administration. You will have no time to argue with these people. Documents will be provided without delay or these people will be denied certification and forced to resign and leave government service. The legal department will deal with them afterwards. You can organize your department along these guidelines. You will keep me informed of cases in which you have problems getting documents or when you find gross abuse."

"Mr. Secretary, I like the concept: 'get the thieves out of the government.' The power of my department will be such that abuses will also be possible."

"You will have to get the right people for the job and keep a close eye on them," Arsen said. "The key is not to pursue the honest people who are doing a good job. I am a pessimist where government honesty is concerned; I doubt you will find many very honest people. Dictators who steal will be in your jurisdiction, those who usurp power will be dealt with by the electorate and by the legal divisions. Unfortunately, we cannot tell people who should rule them. We can make sure that thieves are out and we can keep them out. That's as far as we can go. We cannot tell people whom to elect, but we will make sure that they have a choice. If people elect individuals we don't like - let it be. There will be no consequences for pursuing conservative religious or communist policies as long as those opposed are not evicted or persecuted."

"You would let a thief or a dictator remain in power if people elected him?" asked the Ambassador.

"Not decertified people, not them. A dictator would be allowed to place his name on the ballot, but he would not be able to suppress others. A conservative religious leader, a fundamentalist of any religion, will have the same opportunity to win as anybody. Who are we to tell the people they are wrong if they choose him. Somebody once said that the people have the right to be wrong. Let them be wrong. That is the idea, Mr. Ambassador."

"I guess I will be dealing with financial facts, not with political power," the Ambassador said.

"Correct," Arsen concurred. "So, when can you start?"

"Today, I guess," the Ambassador said. "I have only to pack up my things in the Turkish U.N. Mission and I will be ready."

"Excellent," Arsen said. "Victoria will find you offices and whatever you may need. Get your team together soon, and start auditing those who always question the honesty of others. Keep me informed."

The Philippine President called to report that talks on Mindanao were progressing well. "They actually want an autonomous region, not partition. I don't quite understand it, but it will be easy to sell to our people."

"People know what is best for them," Arsen said. "They obviously think that it is better for them to remain within the Philippines."

The President of Sri Lanka called to say that the Tamils were determined to partition themselves from the Sinhalese. "They want independence and that is being negotiated right now. I think we have complied with your demands, and more, Mr. Secretary."

"Thank you, Mr. President." That was all Arsen said during their conversation.

The Turkish President called. "Mr. Secretary, the rumors are that the Kurdish question will come up soon. How is that going to be handled? You will not let them take any Turkish territory, will you?"

"We will do it in two stages, Mr. President. W.G. Military will separate all Kurdish populated areas in Turkey, Iraq, Iran and Armenia. Afterward, we will have a meeting to decide what should be done to resolve this serious matter. I will attend such a meeting."

"This seems to have been decided already, Mr. Secretary, by you and by the World Government. What is to be discussed at such a meeting?"

"You and I agree that there is a Kurdish problem, which has been around for a long time. You have used your armed forces to subdue the Kurds and the Turkish Government has been trying for generations to assimilate them into the Turkish Nation. Their language has been prohibited in public places, their culture has been denied, and they have been expected to become Turks. And they have been killed as terrorists. They performed terrorist acts and that cannot be denied. On top of that, the Turkish Army, the Turkish Police, and the Security Forces were not gentle in dealing with them. They have been pursued and killed where they were found, often on Iraqi territory. Mr. President, do you deny the existence of a Kurdish ethnic group?"

"The Kurds exist, all right, but many of them are criminals."

"Mr. President that is not for Turks to decide. If they exist as a people, they have the right to be heard, and, if they so desire, they can have their land and their sovereignty."

"That land belongs to Turkey."

"The land belongs to Turkey as a state, not to the Turkish people, who don't live there. The land belongs to the Kurds because they live there, and they are in the majority there. Of course, a plebiscite will be held to resolve the issue of sovereignty if there is no other way."

"That sounds like blackmail, Mr. Secretary."

"I am following the mandate of the U.N. Assembly, Mr. President. The same mandate was carried out in Cyprus and you liked it, while the Greeks thought it was blackmail."

"That was a completely different situation," the President said. "The Kurds would not even consider autonomy."

"Cyprus or Kurdistan, there is not much difference except for the geographic location and circumstances."

"Are you going to apply the same principle in Kosovo, in your own Serbia?" asked the President.

"Mr. President, you tell me, what would you consider to be the right solution for Kosovo. Don't forget, that area is the cradle of Serbian civilization."

"Do you want me to tell you what I think is right, or what you think is right?"

The Turk was belligerent and pushing Arsen hard, he thought. He was not used to this kind of conversation.

"What do you think, Mr. President?" Arsen did not like this formal talk 'Mr. Secretary' and 'Mr. President' but the Turk had started it.

"You should let the Kosovars decide what they want. They will probably choose autonomy."

"I would prefer if they chose partition and took that part of the Serbian land with them. As an official of the World Government I will let them decide. As you know very well, the Serbs will never forget me for this decision. Now you can tell your friends in Kosovo, they can have it any way they want."

Arsen intentionally emphasized the word 'friends' to challenge the Turkish President, and he understood it.

"I know what you mean by 'friends' - you could just as well say 'your Islamic friends,' and you would be right. I will wait to see the day when the Serbs give up Kosovo."

"You won't have to wait for long," Arsen said. "Call me in about two weeks to find out."

"I will call you, certainly I will," the Turkish President said. "Thank you, Mr. Secretary."

"Thank you for calling," Arsen said and hung up.

Victoria and Stan Petkovic walked into the office together.

"Doctor, as far as I know there are only two Undersecretaries who are not officially in yet, Kim Bong Shik and Ramesh Rao," Victoria said. "Mr. Rao will be in New York this afternoon, and he wants to see you today. Mr. Kim is also on his way - he talked to me this morning after he was referred by President Chand. Mr. Kim said that you were aware of this."

"That is okay," Arsen said. "There will be another Undersecretary, for Interfaith Relations. This will create some problems because every religious group will examine him with a microscope: to be acceptable he will have to be an outstanding scholar and a good man. What I really need is a man who is able to communicate. This will be a public relations job."

"When I was the Secretary of the Yugoslav Embassy in Rome, some years ago," Stan Petkovic said "I became acquainted with a Catholic priest, who has since been elevated to Monsignor. He is assigned to the diocese of Rome, and his name is Francis Amato. I found him intelligent, very knowledgeable in religious subjects, and he had good public relations skills. He usually sends me a Christmas card, and I received one a few days ago. You may want to invite him for an interview."

"Although I don't expect him to convert to Islam, I would like him to be able to talk to Muslims," Arsen said. "Problems will arise, as they always do, and we need somebody to promote religious harmony. Stan, why don't you call him and ask him to come to New York."

"I will take care of that," Stan Petkovic said. "I had a call from the Serbian Academy of Sciences and Arts in Belgrade. They wanted to know whether you have time to visit the Academy and present a lecture. What do you want me to tell them?"

"They would be better off not having me speak. They would not like it. If they insist, I will speak on 'Causes and chronology of the disintegration of the Yugoslav State.' You will be able to figure out the time."

"They will like it."

"Doctor, Col. Nassar to see you," Michelle announced over the intercom.

"Send him in." The Colonel walked in almost immediately.

Arsen got up to greet him and introduced Victoria and Stan Petkovic. Victoria excused herself and left, and the three of them sat down by the small conference table.

"Thank you for coming so promptly, Colonel," Arsen said. "Both President Chand and John Thornton recommended you highly for a job that is vacant in my department. The title is Undersecretary for Military Coordination. You would work closely with John Thornton and coordinate any military move that became necessary in carrying out our goals of ethnic equality, free election, and political honesty. John will tell you that the idea is to be present and use minimal force to complete the job. No killing, no beating, no crude force of any kind, no torture. You defend yourself if necessary by force, but that would be an exception. These people are not enemies nor targets. They are friends even when hostile. We are not there to punish them. I hope you get the picture."

"I do," Col. Nassar said.

"At present people don't know what to expect and they are quiet," Arsen continued. "I anticipate problems later when the situation becomes clear and when some people try to exploit the good intentions of the World Military. I suggest you start developing plans right now for coping with hostility and outright fighting and attacks. You will avoid going into the country unless it is essential - that is, if the people clearly resist the policies regarding ethnicity and protection of ethnic minorities when partition or autonomy are not considerations, or if they resist partition when it has been approved; also if they cause trouble during elections or resist the auditing process."

"I heard about the auditing of leading politicians and administrators," Col. Nassar said. "That is a fascinating idea. How did you come upon it?"

"Simple, Colonel. Just by reading the newspapers. Too many crooks are in the news. That gave me the idea."

"I understand the philosophy and the policy, and I agree," Col. Nassar said.

"Can you get started soon?" Arsen asked.

"Yes, I can. My sister will need follow-up, and she has to remain in New York for now. I will rent an apartment, and my family will come later."

"Then I will see you tomorrow," Arsen said. "Stan Petkovic will show you around and get you started. Victoria can take care of any arrangements you may need to make."

Arsen had to return calls to Herman Wolff and René Bright.

"Arsen," Herman Wolff said, "we already have Israeli-Arab problems. Both the Israelis and the Arabs claim their right to the West Bank and Jerusalem. What do we do?"

"We will give them the chance to resolve the issues to their satisfaction by themselves," Arsen said. "They will have to respect each other as equals. All issues will be resolved in meetings between Arabs and Israelis. They will have three years to resolve these issues and the agreements will be legally binding. If they do not reach agreement by the end of 2000, the Ethnic Department will make the decision for them. We recommend very highly that they start their negotiations. Write a letter to both parties to that effect, and you and I will sign it."

"The way I understand it: *status quo* until the end of 2000?" Herman Wolff inquired.

"That is right. Another condition: they must enforce the truce and mutually respectful relations. Bombing and other terrorist acts, and killings, will be harshly dealt with by John Thornton."

"Do we need a chairman for the negotiations, some independent individual?" asked Herman Wolff.

"Clearly not. Each side will appoint a delegation with the same number of members. The members will be appointed for the term, and they will be exchanged only by self resignation. There will be no outside interference."

"Thank you very much," Herman Wolff said and hung up.

This had been a major problem for a long time, and it would not be resolved by anybody overnight, Arsen thought. He would be surprised if this did not blow up as a world conflict in the middle of peace negotiations, despite the threat of annihilation. They would probably agree to continue the negotiations and the fight in heaven or hell, wherever.

"Doctor, Mr. Ramesh Rao to see you," Michelle announced over the intercom.

"Greetings Mr. Rao," Arsen said as the Indian came into his office. "I hope your mission has been successfully completed and that now you will turn your attention to world affairs, or more specifically to the affairs of the Americas."

"The mission is over and I am ready," Ramesh Rao said.

They talked about the situation in Brazil. Ramesh Rao was gesticulating as he described the situation. He reminded Arsen of Rama Chand. Ramesh Rao was short, slender, and gentle in appearance. The dark-brown skin covered facial bones, as there was almost no subcutaneous fat, and there was no scalp hair: being bald in the middle and shaved on the sides, gave his head the look of a skull. Two features could not be missed: the deep, piercing eyes and a large, tortuous vein on each temple and one in the middle of the forehead.

Ramesh Rao had clear opinions about what he liked and what he did not, and he expressed himself eloquently and made a positive impression.

Arsen turned the conversation to the subject of his visit.

"The problems in the Americas, as I see it, are more racial then ethnic. You will be dealing with African Americans and Native Americans and with a mosaic of nationalities in the U.S. The French in Canada will have to decide one way or another. It will be easier to separate American Indian reservations and to ensure their sovereign status than to solve problems for urban Blacks or Chinese. I think the emphasis will have to be on getting equal status for all races - in the field and not only in fiction and law books.

"I agree with that," Ramesh Rao said. "In the U.S. there are problems but also there are mechanisms to resolve them. In other places, like Mexico or Guatemala, the Indians have been suppressed and their rights limited. That will require hard work to resolve. In other places social problems and corruption are more urgent than ethnic and racial conflicts."

"You might create a board to deal with racial problems and another board for social affairs. The Assembly will have to approve the members of these boards. Although you would be able to deal with these problems directly, the boards would help in an advisory capacity as they could hold hearings on specific issues and recommend solutions."

"I understand," Ramesh Rao said.

Arsen was getting tired of these interviews, he thought after Ramesh Rao had left the office. Two more interviews left for today. Why did he need a Korean, with a funny name, as an Undersecretary for Elections? Was he an expert on the subject, a professor who analyzed the results of elections? Did he understand the forces that were pushing for power before election day and did not hesitate to use any weapons at their disposal, in some places even killing their opponents? Bong Shik Kim. Monsignor Francis Amato should be more interesting, and he had better be, as his was a public relations job. Victoria interrupted his thoughts.

"Doctor, just to let you know, we still have a lot of empty offices. I'm so glad that my calculations were correct."

"How is recruiting of personnel progressing? Do you have enough good people?"

"I think we're doing very well. Stanley Kim is doing an excellent job. We decided to appoint him Chief of Personnel. He's very proud of Bong Kim - a Korean like himself. His information from Korea was very favorable. Michelle has been designated your reception secretary."

"What about you, what is your title?" asked Arsen.

"I'm your personal secretary," Victoria replied somewhat shyly.

"Sounds good but you are not doing the job of a personal secretary," Arsen said. "You have been doing the job of a Chief of Staff. That is what you are - the Chief of Staff. I would like you to identify yourself as such. Let me sign a memo to that effect, and for Stanley too. There should always be an appointment letter to avoid confusion."

"Thank you, Doctor."

"Now what else is on your mind?"

"Sabrina and I would like to have lunch with you," Victoria said. "Would tomorrow be okay? Unless you have something else planned?"

"Tomorrow will be fine," Arsen said. "Is there a special occasion?"

"No, not really. We just wanted to take you to lunch and have a chance to talk about the good old times of a few weeks ago." Victoria laughed as she said that. "Isn't it funny how many things have changed in only two weeks?"

"You are telling me."

Stan Petkovic walked in and told Arsen that Msgr. Amato would leave Rome in the morning. "When would you like to see him?"

"I presume you will see him when he arrives and take him to a hotel," Arsen said. "You could discuss with him the organization of the Ethnic Department, our philosophy, and our goals. I will discuss with him the Interfaith Division. If you wish, we can meet with him on Sunday morning. Where is he going to stay?"

"I will get a room at the Plaza."

"Ten o'clock on Sunday morning?" Arsen suggested.

"Ten o'clock," Stan Petkovic said and left the office.

"Do you think our progress has been satisfactory so far?" Victoria asked.

"Excellent, I think," Arsen said. "We have resolved the Cyprus problem, Tibet is under control despite Chinese objections, Mindanao is in good shape thanks to the President of the Philippines, and the Kurdistan issues will be resolved despite Turkish objections, although we may have to hold a plebiscite on the issue of sovereignty and autonomy. The Basque problem is on its way to being solved and Spain and France have been cooperating. Zaire, or the Congo as they call it now, will be discussed next week when I get there. The former Yugoslavia will fall into place: Slovenia has never been a problem, Macedonia will have to deal with their Albanians, Kosovo will become autonomous or be partitioned and join Albania or become an independent state, and Bosnia will be separated into three parts starting with the borders decided at Dayton and after further negotiations.

"The Israelis and Palestinians will start their meetings to decide how to split their territories - I doubt they will choose a confederation of two autonomous parts. This is a week's work and I like the progress. We will clean house and then sit and watch what people try to do or not to do.

"Try to finish the audits of the politicians. Arrange the elections in most countries and make sure that the new political geography is reflected in the composition of the General Assembly of the U.N. Then we will start the selection process for preservation. I have the feeling that there will be problems when new states are established, during elections, after audits and in dealing with individuals who have been caught stealing; also when the selection of people for preservation starts. Who knows what else might start disagreements, maybe even riots and killings. With the human race you never know."

"You sound pessimistic," Victoria said.

"I am, because I do not trust humans," Arsen said emphatically.

"Let's hope you' re wrong this time," Victoria said. "Too much is at stake for everybody this time."

Arsen interrupted the pause in their conversation.

"What do you think if I go home now?" he asked. "It is already five o'clock and I have no more appointments and no calls to make. I will try to spend a quiet evening."

Arsen was not expected at home so early. Dinner was an improvisation of leftovers of sarma - sauerkraut leaves staffed with pieces of smoked beef and sausage. A bar of Häagen-Dazs vanilla ice cream with almonds and chocolate dip was a forbidden dessert treat.

At six-thirty he turned on the MMB report with Bradley Adams.

SINTERNET or INTERNET

It was reported that Goran Enstrom was pushing for development of a space Internet, which had been designated SINTERNET, where he would store everything in print today from books to documents. Gen. Shagov was cited as having stated that work on SINTERNET was far advanced and that it would be functional within a year.

Gen. SHAGOV LEFT TOKYO AFTER NEUTRINO GUN TALKS

The General had visited with Prof. Isoroku Yakawa, a leading neutrino expert.

NEW APPOINTMENTS IN ETHNIC DEPARTMENT
Ramesh Rao, Suleiman Karazoglou and
Col. Abdul Nassar el Hakim.
ISRAELI-ARAB PERPETUAL TALKS TO 2000

It is about time that we induce India and Pakistan to start talks on Kashmir before a referendum, Arsen thought - something like Israeli-Arab perpetual sessions.

Why was he listening to news he already knew? Arsen asked himself, and changed channels. Several talk shows were discussing current events, scientific developments, space travel, and ethnic problems. Arsen was looking for a movie to relax him. An old Clint Eastwood movie fit his relaxation needs - a lot of action that often made no sense.

CHAPTER THIRTY-ONE

SATURDAY, 20 DECEMBER 1997

It was Saturday and Arsen was the Secretary of the Ethnic Department. A few weeks ago he had been a retired orthopedic surgeon, a budding writer of fiction, and a student of ethnic problems. Now he was the Secretary of the Ethnic Department. Arsen wanted to pinch himself to believe it. Except for a few initial troubles, this had been a smooth sailing. He had too much power in ethnic issues, he thought. That might be dangerous if he should disappear. He would not abuse the trust but who knew what someone else would do. There were no provisions and no mechanisms to prevent abuses. Everyone had been appointed to these positions because they had been visible when the selections were made. Alexei deserved his position as he was the genuine expert in the anticollision effort. Rama Chand had been the Secretary General of the United Nations before all this started, and he also deserved his position as the President.

Nada interrupted his thoughts by serving coffee and turning on the television. The talk show on MMB, 'World issues as seen by Experts,' was moderated by a shrewd reporter and Washington Chief MMB correspondent Bob Stein. There were three panelists: Peter Fields, a computer expert from MIT's Laboratory for Computer Science, Dr. Allan White, Deputy Secretary in the Anticollision Department and a Professor of astrophysics at Oxford University, and Fred Epstein a Computer Scientist at IBM.

The discussion was presented to be understood by a general audience. It opened with an explanation of the relevance of computers in astrophysics. Then the panel proceeded to explain advances in computer technology - mainly the speed in terms of trillions of units of information being received from satelites and processed per second - and finally they progressed to the ideas that were being explored and the applications being developed and tested. The Sinternet was described as being essential to the

232

people in space as the source of everything written on Earth.

"Without the Sinternet the whole preservation effort would be useless," Fred Epstein explained. "Of course that applies only if the Earth is destroyed, and if not, it would be a bonus for everybody. Everything ever written will be available on the Sinternet. The copying will start as soon as enough good scanners are available. The discs will be transported to conversion centers where the information will be loaded on the Sinternet. It will be easy to get information; the data bases will contain everything that's presently found in the Library of Congress, Encyclopedia Britannica and Yahoo. All movies and audiovisual materials will also be stored. Photographs of cities, including all buildings and monuments, museums and their contents will be stored. Goran Enstrom has been working on the realization of this project."

Allan White then began explaining the use of the Sinternet by space ships, and its future use in the exploration of space. Peter Fields was introduced by Bob Stein...

Arsen dozed off. The Sinternet discussion had made him sleepy; they were dragging the story out and saying nothing he had not already heard. Nada turned the television off and let him sleep.

The quietude of the morning was interrupted by the inevitable ringing of the phone, which reminded Arsen that he was not a retired orthopedic surgeon any more. Rama Chand called to tell Arsen about some insignificant developments in the Assembly, and the General called from Moscow to report about the trip to Tokyo and on the amount of snow that had accumulated around his *dacha* near Moscow. Victoria called just to find out if something was happening and if it were okay for her to spend the afternoon at a friend's home.

Couldn't they leave him alone for one day? Arsen wondered. Despite all the intrusions and interruptions the day was relaxing and the first in a while he had spent at home.

CHAPTER THIRTY-TWO

SUNDAY, 21 DECEMBER 1997

T he telephone rang at eight on Sunday morning. Nada and Arsen woke up and sat in bed slightly confused as to the time and the day. The telephone continued ringing until Arsen picked up the receiver. Stan Petkovic was on the other end inquiring about the meeting with Msgr. Amato. Arsen promised to meet them in the office at around ten-thirty. Then he fell back on the pillow next to Nada, who was sound asleep again. He felt immobile, but was not asleep, as his brain started to grind the information available to a drowsy mind.

By eight-thirty they were up, drinking coffee, reading the nespapers, and keeping an eye on the television screen for any news of interest. Finally, Arsen remembered to call and order the limousine. Although not officially in the building, the Security Service agents knew the doormen, who would let them know when there were messages from Arsen.

The news was not very interesting. The nespapers had several reports on current events shown in the headlines.

Gen. SHAGOV STOPS IN MOSCOW ON HIS WAY TO PARIS
MASSIVE SCANNING
OF WRITTEN AND VISUAL MATERIAL UNDERWAY
MEDICAL CHECK-UP OF EVERYBODY
PRIOR TO SELECTION FOR SPACE
Sec. PANKOVICH TO ATTEND POLITICAL SETTLEMENT ON CYPRUS

There was a two-page article *Life after the Demon* by Alessandro Pieruccini, a correspondent from Rome, who projected possible advances in technology, and compared life before the appearance of the celestial object to life after it disappeared. He projected a total change of life and work, health care, family planning, study and every other aspect of human exis-

234

tence. This was an interesting vision of the future, Arsen thought, but Alessandro Pieruccini was unaware of the depth and breadth of the research being organized by Alexei. The changes would be more profound.

The time was approaching for the meeting with Msgr. Francis Amato. Arsen imagined how he looked: rotund and short, red belt at the waist of his cassock, and a wide-brimmed black hat.

When he met Msgr. Amato, Arsen almost exclaimed, "Hey, you are not the Monsignor," as he looked so different from what Arsen had imagined. He was tall and slender, probably muscular - his musculature was hidden by his cassock. His bony, narrow face exposed a thin but prominent nose, a wide square forehead below dense, dark brown hair, and a somewhat defiant mouth. He looked like a pleasant and determined man in his late forties.

The Monsignor walked into the office in the company of Stan Petkovic.

"I trust you've had a good night's sleep, Monsignor," Arsen said. "This was an urgent and unexpected trip for you."

"Stan took good care of me and the accommodations at the Plaza Hotel were better than what I am used to," Msgr. Amato said. "Urgent calls are no novelty to me. A practicing priest often gets urgent calls, as God doesn't wait. Once I understood what you needed me for I was ready to travel to be able to join your team and help if I can."

The Monsignor described his origins; he was from the outskirts of Rome, where he had spent his entire life. He had spent several years in the Vatican working for Cardinal Monselli and had then asked to be transferred to the Roman diocese, where he had spent the last ten years.

"I have had a very blessed life, to be able to do my pastoral work, to attend to many people, to befriend some interesting individuals, and to have economic freedom to study and write on matters that interest me."

"You have impressed Stan Petkovic enough to recommend you for this rather sensitive mission," Arsen said. "Monsignor, how do you feel about Muslims and Jews?"

"Empathy," Msgr. Amato said simply. "They are humans, thus God's children. They deserve as much attention as anybody, a Catholic or a Hindu."

"I can buy that attitude," Arsen said. "You may have to do some explaining in that respect and receive some misunderstanding in return. As you can imagine, you will be talking to people of different religions and political persuasions. You will have to find a common language with these different groups."

"It will be very interesting to work with them," the Monsignor said.

"You may also deal with the question of the complete annihilation of the human race," Arsen said, advancing his view of the role of a religious leader for the World Government. "Monsignor, how do you look at the prospect of the end of life on Earth, any life?"

"The question is a difficult one to answer," the Monsignor said. "As a Catholic I should believe that what God wanted to happen would happen and that chances are we would survive with His help."

"Is that what you really believe?"

"The Last Judgment will happen, so much I believe," the Monsignor said. "If the collision occurs the Last Judgment will happen. It would be cruel to tell to people that the Last Judgment is coming in 2003. It would be better to preach faith in God and His powers to avert the disaster. People are not stupid - they know what is coming. However, faith may help to raise hope, and one should not ignore the power of hope. Religious preference and belonging would make no difference - hope is universal and entirely human."

"The time might come when you would be asked to explain the conflict of reality versus God," Arsen said; he wanted to find out the Monsignor's reaction. "Do you know what I mean?"

"No, I don't," the Monsignor said.

"Imagine the situation in which a person would be asked to choose the preservation of humanity by denying God. Immortality could be an issue. If technology develops to a stage where a human can become immortal by perpetuation of his or her body and mind, that would make him essentially equal to God in longevity, if not in power, although even that could be overcome. To save humanity one would have to accept technology that would be capable of creating powerful immortals. That would abolish the role of God. Should one then choose God and sacrifice humanity, which would disappear if not salvaged by denial of God? Should we try to save humanity by making sure that some people survive although by doing that we would deny God?"

"Can God be denied?" asked Msgr. Amato.

"Hypothetically, if we could create a humanity that is immortal we would deny that God had power over our lives - the basic need for God in the psyche."

"You cannot eliminate God from our psyche. God exists and would be responsible for our technology."

"Does that mean that you, Monsignor, would accept technological immortality as God's creation and His way of preserving humanity?" Arsen asked. "You would then recommend that we go ahead and save humanity at all costs, would you?"

"Yes, I would, because that would be God's will and command," Msgr. Amato said. "God would never allow His creations, meaning humans among others, to disappear forever."

"We don't need to worry, even if humanity and life disappear on the Earth, because God would create it again. Is that what I should understand, Monsignor?"

"Yes, we may disappear but God always remains, and He will make sure that humanity continues to exist," Msgr. Amato said with conviction. "We don't even know whether there are humans somewhere in the Universe who will replace us one day."

"Monsignor, we don't want to disappear and be replaced," Arsen said. "We want to survive at all costs."

"I already said that our survival through technological inventions, including an immortal man, would be done by the grace of God."

"Okay, Monsignor, you will be able to represent humanity if it ever needs to be represented. Humans may disappear happy that they will be saved. After death they would never have to know."

"But they would know because they and their souls would be in the heavenly kingdom," Msgr. Amato said firmly, almost as if he were telling Arsen to stop pushing any further. Arsen understood.

"I hope you will be able to explain these things to different people, to theologians from different faiths, to philosophers, and to atheists," Arsen said.

The office became quiet as they ceased talking for a few minutes, each of the three men in his own thoughts. Stan Petkovic broke the silence.

"It is time to return to the hotel, don't you think Monsignor?"

"I agree," Msgr. Amato said agreeably.

"I hope you will take this demanding job, Monsignor, will you?" Arsen asked.

"You have made me think of the challenges ahead of us, and I want to be able to do something about them. I just hope I can make the difference."

"I know you can,"

Arsen was impressed by Msgr. Amato. He was a convinced Catholic whose belief in the supremacy of God was unshakable. God was behind everything, even at the moment when humanity made the last stand before the collision.

A knock on the door reminded Arsen of another visitor that morning - Mr. Kim Bong Shik. What kind of a man was Mr. Kim, Arsen was curious to know. He already felt he wasn't going to like him, and he did not know why. There was something in the name!

A short, stout, square-faced man, heavy glasses pressing the base of his nose, walked in and bowed to Arsen. "I am Mr. Kim," he said.

"I know, I know." Arsen stood up to shake hands with Mr. Kim Bong Shik, who was wearing a polite, friendly smile on his square face.

"When did you arrive in New York?" Arsen asked. "I presume you have come from Seoul?"

"Yes, that is right."

"Is your family there? Are they going to move to New York?"

"They will be with me in New York; my wife and two daughters."

"Have you been in New York in the past?"

"Yes, I lived in New York for three years when I was getting my Ph.D. in Political Science at Columbia," Mr. Kim said. "That was way back in '85."

"What have you done since then?" Arsen asked.

"I teach Political Science at the University of Seoul. My field of interest is elections and electoral process. "

"Then you know what to expect from your assigned division, do you?"

Kim Bong Shik smiled. "We will organize honest elections."

"Simply said, hardly ever done, Mr. Kim. One principle must always guide you: fairness to all involved parties. That is all, and plenty at that."

"I know," Mr. Kim said. "What I don't know is the size of my staff. It will be necessary to form a base here in New York. Not too big a staff - maybe a hundred people. Then we will need a basic group in each country which will grow rapidly during the election or plebiscite time and shrink thereafter. The budget will not be small."

"You will get what you need," Arsen said. "My deputy, Stan Petkovic, will work out the details with you. When you need something for your organization talk to Victoria, my Chief of Staff. On policy matters talk to Stan and me. Don't make an appointment - just walk in."

"What has been done so far?" asked Mr. Kim.

"Absolutely nothing," Arsen said. "There has not been time for everything in just a week. I have worked on Sri Lanka. They should hold a plebiscite within a month on Tamil partition. Also on Indonesia regarding the Timor. Tibet is another area, although the Chinese will probably give in when they realize that Tibet is surrounded by W.G. Military. We may also need a plebiscite in Kosovo and Vojvodina in Serbia, and in the Basque areas of Spain and France. The Albanian-held territory of Macedonia will be another problem. Keep me informed of the progress."

"You call that nothing, Mr. Secretary," Mr. Kim said. "I am already swamped and haven't even been in my office. I imagine you want all this done by the end of January?"

"You are right. By the end of January '98," Arsen said. "These people cannot wait until March of 2003."

"There will be resistance to our organization in many places," Mr. Kim said. "What do I do?"

"Let us know and we will try with political pressure; and talk to Col. Nassar if you think military reinforcement will be needed. He will know what to do."

"I will talk to Stan Petkovic in the morning and will plan a trip to these countries sometime during the week," Mr. Kim said, his face looking very serious. "I will keep in touch, Mr. Secretary."

"Talk also to Ito Amoto and Herman Wolff, and keep in touch, Kim."

"You may try 'Bong' as my friends call me."

"Have a good day, Bong."

Arsen thought that Bong had what was needed for the job. And he liked his simplicity and to-the-point talk. "Bong," Arsen said aloud, and he laughed. "Bong is okay."

Once he was alone, Arsen thought about the events of the previous week. All Undersecretary positions were filled by people he thought were capable men. He had tested the field and found out that with minimal pressure most ethnic problems could be resolved. Obviously most Presidents, Prime Ministers and Ambassadors he dealt with were unable to refute the argument that ethnic groups have the right to be independent or autonomous. They had no choice without their own military. Sovereignty backed by a military was the chief villain of the world. He and his team must protect the world from the Military of the World Government. This military was needed now but must be kept in check later. There should be a mechanism for automatic ejection from the military of officers with oppressive tendencies. How did one know who possessed oppressive tendencies?

"God help us now. We are ready for the job."

CHAPTER THIRTY-THREE

MONDAY, 22 DECEMBER 1997

There was no need to rush to the office as Arsen was scheduled to testify before the Ethnic Committee of the United Nations. They wanted to discuss Sri Lanka, Tibet, Cyprus, and Kurdistan. They would get what they wanted, Arsen thought. The nespapers headlines reflected the financial troubles that had begun the moment the Hubble telescope group confirmed existence of the celestial object. All world markets had been closed by the World Government and remained frozen. There was a great deal of discussion in the General Department about the measures to be taken. Goran Enstrom had pushed for the freeze to avoid crashes and to allow a realignment of the industries to take place.

The limousine took Arsen to the United Nations. He met briefly with Rama Chand and at nine o'clock walked into the meeting room.

The Chairman of the Ethnic Committee, Andrzej Mieczko, greeted Arsen and asked him to take his seat. The Committee was ready to ask questions.

"Mr. Secretary, we called this meeting primarily because of complaints by the Chinese delegation about your handling of the question of Tibet."

"Mr. Chairman, I have one question, if you would allow me. Then I will answer all questions the Committee members may have."

"What is the question?"

"Is there in Tibet an ethnic problem that requires action?"

"Yes, there is a problem which should be resolved," the Chairman said. "Mr. Secretary, please tell us about the problem as you see it."

"Tibet was an independent country from 1911 till the Chinese invasion in 1950. A communist government was established in 1953. The Tibetan leader, the Dalai Lama, and some 100 thousand people fled to India in 1959. The Tibetans clearly want the Dalai Lama to return and the Chinese troops to leave. I have proposed a plebiscite to resolve these problems. The plebiscite will be held in January."

"Are there any questions for the Secretary?" asked the Chairman.

"I have some important questions," announced the Chinese Ambassador on the committee, Chi Yongbo. "Although Tibet was for a while an independent country, it is usually ignored that they were part of China for centuries before that. For almost the last fifty years they have been part of China again. They have had a democratic government, which they chose themselves, like China has had. We have good relations and minimal ethnic problems."

"If that is so, Mr. Ambassador, why are the Tibetans asking for independence?" Arsen asked. "Why do you keep Chinese troops on their borders and in the territory? Why, Mr. Ambassador? If everything is in good order and the Tibetans like you and want you to stay, why are they asking for a plebiscite? Let them vote for what they want. If they want to remain within China that will be okay with me."

"How do we know that the plebiscite will be fair?" asked the Chinese Ambassador.

"You will monitor the plebiscite on your own or along with us, whichever you prefer. We will decide together who won. That will be final."

"What will happen to our troops?" the Chinese Ambassador asked sternly.

"They will serve the World Government at the places where they are needed."

"Why have you moved them now?" asked the Chinese Ambassador.

"They have not moved as yet but they will, probably today," Arsen said. "The reason is obvious - to remove the symbolic threat."

"Any other questions for the Secretary on Tibet?" the Chairman of the committee asked. There were none. "We should proceed with other countries: Sri Lanka, Cyprus and Kurdistan. Mr. Secretary, tell us what has been developing in these countries."

"The situation has been resolved in Cyprus. To my surprise both parts wanted autonomy and a strong central government. Neither wanted to make a union with Turkey or Greece. I am going to Cyprus tomorrow to witness the signing ceremony. I am proud of that."

The committee members applauded after Arsen's statement.

"As for Sri Lanka, the situation is different. The Tamils want partition and they want to establish an independent State. A plebiscite is inevitable to satisfy the Sinhalese. The Undersecretary for Elections and Plebiscites, Mr. Kim Bong Shik, is going there tonight. He is under instructions to get the problem resolved by the end of January '98."

"That leaves the Kurdistan question to be discussed," the Chairman said.

"The Kurds have been trying to get their independence for many years," Arsen stated. "After World War One, by the Treaty of Sevres, the Kurds were promised independence, but that was changed by the Treaty of Lausanne in 1923. The Kurds have been divided among Turkey, Iran, Iraq and Syria. Those living in Azerbaijan formed "Red Kurdistan" which lasted a few years. This Kurdish area was taken by Armenia in the '90s, and the Kurds were expelled. The Kurds want independence and that is not an issue. The borders have to be drawn and the Kurds' territory in Armenia will have to be negotiated. Perhaps the Armenians will be willing to buy the territory if the Kurds are willing to sell."

"Can that be accomplished?" asked the Chairman. "What if the Armenians refuse to negotiate?"

"That will be submitted to this Committee for disposition," Arsen said. "The Assembly will eventually have to deal with the issue."

"If there are no further questions we will adjourn," the Chairman said. "Thank you for coming, Mr. Secretary."

As he was leaving the room, Arsen noticed that Victoria was waiting for him.

"They really wanted to appease China, not to question what you were doing," Victoria said. "You explained the issues very clearly."

"Only the Chinese Ambassador asked questions and he did not take up much time," Arsen said "Obviously this time it was just a formality. Next time, it may be different."

"Are you going to see President Chand?" Victoria asked.

"He asked me to see him after the meeting," Arsen said. "I was thinking of having a meeting of all Undersecretaries. We should just get together to meet each other and to start what will be a weekly ritual from now on. Do you think you could arrange the meeting for the early afternoon?"

"As far as I know nobody has left the city. Ito Amoto is taking one of our planes to fly to Sri Lanka sometime tonight. Stein and Karazoglou are flying to Cyprus tonight to look into their situation. René Bright is flying with you tomorrow."

"There will be good representation in Nicosia," Arsen said.

"I'm going back to the office to arrange for the meeting," Victoria said.

"Call Stan Petkovic and ask him to call the meeting," Arsen suggested. "I could meet you in the coffee shop on the fortieth floor in half an hour. What do you think?"

"Okay, I'll wait for you," Victoria said.

Rama Chand was alone in his office. He did not appear to be a happy person that morning. Arsen greeted him and eased himself quietly into a nearby chair. Rama sat there silently for a while, occasionally scratching the bald apex of his head. He looked older.

"Arsen, I wanted to talk to you about something confidential," Rama said, finally braking the silence. "I hope you will keep it between us. To put it simply, I am not sure what my role is as the President of the World Government. I am frustrated. You have your ethnic problems, Alexei has technology, John has the military, and Goran has everything else. What is left for me to do? Most of the other functions belong to the local governments. It seems I would be better off if I remained the Director of Liaison with the Assembly - I would have an active role and a goal. Now, everybody calls me 'Mr. President' but asks you guys for opinions - you, the experts."

Arsen had not expected this depressed attitude. He thought that Rama was an ideal President, a conductor, who provided support where support was needed and advice when advice was sought, and most of all he maintained the harmony of the upper echelon of his government. Then it occurred to him.

"Rama, who is your liaison with the Assembly?" Arsen asked.

Rama paused for a moment. "I don't have a liaison." His face became lively again and some tone returned to his body. "I get the message, and I will do it."

"What we all need is the man who will explain what we are doing," Arsen said. "Who can be more authoritative than the President? You will find, I am afraid, that some things we do - I mean your government does - are not right. Only you will be able to make changes. Who knows what is ahead of us. People may become restless later, in a few or in many parts of the world. You, the President, would have to be known by them so that they would listen to you. I think you need a public relations office that will promote your public and private image. Enormous work is ahead of you."

"Arsen, I need a psychiatrist to take care of me," Rama said. "I think I lost the vision of my office by taking care of the minutia of our government."

"My Chief of Staff is waiting to buy me the best breakfast in the city, and.I had better go," Arsen said on his way to the door, "unless you want to join us on the fortieth floor."

"What is on the fortieth floor?" asked Rama.

"A very cute coffee shop with a nice young waitress."

Rama decided to go. In the elevator he asked who the Chief of Staff was.

"I will introduce you when we get there."

Victoria was sitting at a window table, in the almost empty coffee shop. Rama was surprised, and hurried to talk to her. "I think you made the right choice," he said simply and he embraced Victoria after saying something in

Indian that Arsen did not understand.

The young waitress approached their table.

"You always bring a surprise visitor with you, Doctor," the waitress said. "Mr. President, thank you for visiting us today. What would you like to eat?"

"Bagel and coffee, of course," Rama said with an enthusiasm that came from his psychic metamorphosis.

The three of them had a quiet breakfast, and they were feeling the importance of their lives, as if by sitting on the fortieth floor, above most of New York City, they had reached the Olympus of modern mythology. Maybe they had.

Victoria and Arsen returned to the Lexington Avenue office, to the hectic flow of appointments and telephone calls. Stan Petkovic was in and out, as he was making final arrangements for the Cyprus-Zaire-Belgrade-Spain trip. He was quite nervous about the Belgrade portion, in which he had an important role. This was to be Stan's first visit to Belgrade after resigning his Ambassadorship in New York. He wanted to show the officials in Belgrade that his new position was important. The importance of his job was obvious to the officials and to everybody else, but not to Stan. Arsen was going along with his game plan because he was getting used to Stan's capacity to work and his efficiency, and most of all his ability to shift a lot of work off Arsen's desk.

"Would you like me to go to Belgrade while you are in Zaire, to get some things organized?" asked Stan Petkovic.

"Please do," Arsen said. "Take one of our planes or get one from John Thornton. Take with you people you need and bring along some journalists. I would like to have a smooth visit. What happened finally with the lecture at the Academy of Sciences?"

"They want the lecture despite your warning," Stan Petkovic said. "I arranged the lecture for Saturday evening. I will take you there."

"How do I tell them the truth without offending them?"

"That is impossible." Stan Petkovic expressed his frustration by raising his hands as if asking for divine guidance. "The Serbs are super sensitive and take everything personally."

"Stan, have you talked to Ivo Stipich in Zagreb?" Arsen asked.

"No, I have not."

"He is an interesting person and you will meet him in Belgrade," Arsen said. "Remind me sometime to tell you his very interesting life story. Call him and find out if he needs something, and take care of it if he does. Currently we don't have anybody in Bosnia or Kosovo. Seemingly, problems exist in Vojvodina with the Hungarian population, particularly in the northern parts of Banat and in Bachka. Is the situation as bad as in

Transylvania where, as you know, the Rumanians have tried to subdue the Hungarians, and it has not worked? Just like in Kosovo twenty years ago it becomes a matter of numbers. We have to talk to the Hungarians in Vojvodina to find out what is happening.

"Stan, make sure they send a delegation to Belgrade so we can talk to them. My Serbian soul tells me that the Hungarians are trying to get a piece of Serbian land, but my ethnic brain has decided that people have a right to be heard and helped to achieve their national goals - though without hurting other people. Naturally, we should talk to a Serbian delegation from Vojvodina. There will be a lot of talking in Belgrade. If the Croats and Muslims insist that we meet in Sarajevo and Zagreb we will go there too, and talk. Please take care of this for me. You are right, you should go there as soon as possible. Decide what is necessary, and call me only if there are problems."

"Okay, I will leave tomorrow in the afternoon," Stan Petkovic said with a new sparkle in his voice and energized body movements. "I will take care of everything."

It was one o'clock when Arsen entered the large conference room. The people standing or sitting around the long table suddenly stopped talking, and everybody stood and turned towards Arsen as he entered the room. Arsen walked to the head of the table where Victoria and Stan Petkovic had left space for him to sit.

Arsen looked at everybody and smiled. These were the people, he thought, who would carry out the ethnic policy.

"Please, sit down and relax. I would hope that our regular, weekly Department meetings will be informal and productive. It would help if you submitted to Victoria beforehand the topics you wanted to be discussed. As you know, Victoria has been appointed the Chief of Staff. Emergency problems will be discussed first. I must emphasize that I need your opinions. Your disagreement and criticism will be appreciated. Please, always come to the point and don't make speeches. We will discuss problems as you wish. I will try to set policies as we go along. One last thing, please do not get up when I enter the room."

There was silence for a few moments.

"I hope you have all met each other, and no introductions are necessary," Arsen continued his opening statement. "You have heard about the developments in Cyprus and the preliminary steps that have been taken in a number of other places."

"Mr. Secretary, we don't know details of your testimony this morning before the Ethnic Committee," Herman Wolff said. "China's complaints triggered that testimony, didn't they?"

"They did," Arsen said. "The Chinese were concerned that their territory would be indiscriminately taken from them. You know that will not happen, and I know that, but they did not. They had to find out, and I hope they are satisfied."

Arsen looked around and could not see Matt Brown. "Where is Matt?" Arsen asked Victoria.

"He decided to stay out."

"How is he going to know what is happening in this department if he is not present?" Arsen said. "He should sit next to Stan. Everybody should understand, Matt will be the chief spokesman for the Department, and when there is a question of what should be said and how, he should be consulted. I hope the statements of all of us will reflect the policies and decisions made at these meetings."

Coffee was served, and the door was closed after Matt Brown came in. The formal part of the meeting was to start.

Arsen took a sip of coffee.

"This meeting was planned to be informal, a get-together to meet each other and to warm up for the work that lies ahead. If I have one thing to say about our function, it is that we have to keep people happy. That should ensure good relations among neighboring countries and promote peace. Of course, problems will arise and require decisions to be made. Our only guidance will be the interest of those who are abused or exploited. I decided to make this a formal meeting to demonstrate to you what I mean. You have to weigh the evidence at hand against U.N. decisions and resolutions of the past, and other past international agreements. No agreement from the past will be acceptable a priori. The facts will have to be examined in view of the existing situation in the area where a dispute exists.

"Let me use Cyprus as an example. Here you have an island which is located very close to Turkish territory. The population of Cyprus is seventy-five percent Greek - Orthodox Christians - and eighteen percent Turks who are Muslims. After years of fighting between the Greeks and the Turks a union was formed that provided constitutional guarantees to the Turkish minority, and the independence was proclaimed on August 16, 1960. On July 15, 1974 Greek officers took over the government, and on July 20, 1974 the Turkish Army invaded Cyprus, occupied the northeastern part or approximately 40% of the Island, and expelled about two-hundred thousand Greeks. They established the Turkish Republic of Northern Cyprus. Twenty thousand Turkish troops are still on the island and, despite talks, disagreements remain. While Greek Cyprus is well off and is integrated in international economic and financial affairs, the Turkish part remains isolated. The Turkish part exists only because of the Turkish Army's presence and support.

"Returning to the status of 1974 would lead to the same hostilities. However, permanent separation into two independent countries, or autonomy for each part in a federation, or union with Greece and Turkey are viable solutions. I pushed for that in conversations with Greek and Turkish officials. Suleiman Karazoglou was Turkish Ambassador to the U.N. at the time, a week ago. He will tell you of the initial resistance of both sides and the surprising outcome of the negotiations, which established two autonomous regions: Greek and Turkish. Adjustments had to be made in view of Greek Cypriot losses when they were expelled and Turkish Cypriot isolation and stagnation from 1974. We will witness on Wednesday proclamation of the Federated Cypriot Republic. You must understand that both regions know that they can separate at any time if the experiment does not succeed. For us here they will continue to be two ethnic entities."

Arsen felt pressure in his chest, as if his heart was squeezed by what he was saying. His emotions flew to the Greek Cypriots, while his ethnic mind stood its ground for what he thought was right.

"Are there any legal problems in the deal?" asked Herman Wolff.

"Let us hear from Mel Stein," Arsen said.

"I haven't seen the actual paper work that will be signed, so I can't tell you there are no problems," Melvin Stein said. "I'll go over these papers when I get to Cyprus. In principle I see no problems. It's very surprising to me what they did. I would have bet they would create two independent countries. The remaining economic and financial problems are left over from 1974 and claimed mainly by Greeks expelled at that time. That will be dealt with in due time."

"Will you proceed with audits now that these people have produced such a spectacular agreement?" asked Herman Wolff.

"We are mandated to do audits," Suleiman Karazoglou said. "I have made a list of countries which should be audited. I thought you would want to leave the Cypriots alone for a while to enjoy their new status." Everybody laughed when Suleiman Karazoglou said that.

"How do you decide whom to audit, and when?" Herman Wolff asked.

"Some politicians and government leaders in certain countries have been accused of corruption and have even been under investigation. We are in the process of making a list of the first ten countries to be audited. Of course, eventually everybody will be audited - time permitting." Everybody laughed again

"I wonder if we could follow with elections as soon as you finish the audits," asked Kim Bong Shik. "We will start in other places also, like Sri Lanka and Timor where we will hold plebiscites soon. We could follow with elections in Indonesia, Serbia, Nigeria, Iraq, Kenya and others. We could allow a grace period to countries which settled their ethnic problems, particularly without initiation by the World Government."

"That seems good to me," Arsen said. "Your decision to proceed must be based on the evidence that previous elections were won by a great advantage of one over the other side, by fraud, or by existing dictatorship. You should have no problems in finding such countries."

"It may be premature to discuss the selection of individuals for preservation purposes," Jean-Pierre Vernier said. "I just wanted to get your opinion about an incentive program I would like to devise."

"What kind of incentive program?" Arsen asked. "I thought we would choose people very carefully."

"Choosing may not be the precise word," Jean-Pierre Vernier explained. "I have given it a lot of thought since I was appointed to this job and I see no way for every ethnic group to have representation on the space ships. If we assume that there are five to six thousands ethnic groups that might claim space on these ships, I doubt we would be able to send a couple, a man and a woman, from each group. That would make about ten thousands people at the minimum. Add to that number about a thousand technical people and scientists. How many ships are we talking about? One or two hundred? More if there is time.

"Consider twelve people to a ship maximum. For that number of ships only ten or twenty percent of all ethnic groups could be selected. How do we select these ethnic groups? A lottery is inevitable.

"Before we even start the selection and lottery, we must find out if these people really want to go to space. The prospect is not spectacular. If collision is avoided or prevented the trip was unnecessary. If the Earth is hit and disintegrates and becomes uninhabitable these people will die in space. I am sure these questions will come up and doubts will be raised about the mission. We could advertise and promote participation, and offer incentives. It may sound strange to advertise death."

"There is a chance that the Earth would not disintegrate although most of people would die," Arsen said. "We cannot ignore that possibility and we have to be ready as if that were the only chance we humans had to survive."

"I would like to know more about the idea of the lottery," Matt Brown said.

"I imagine it would not be different from any other lottery," Jean-Pierre Vernier said. "We would have to decide if we should take into account the ethnic affiliation of technicians and scientists. I am not ready to submit a proposal."

"Do you give extra credit to countries that have resolved all their problems previously or those that never had any?" asked Melvin Stein.

"Again, I am not ready to answer your questions," Jean-Pierre Vernier said. "I wanted to know whether the use of incentives is acceptable before we waste time on details."

"Raise your hand if you are for incentive programs." Arsen asked the group to vote. There was no point in discussing something like this if he were to decide, Arsen thought.

Everybody was agreeable.

"Matt, I think you should announce this decision when you meet the press next time," Arsen said, "and you and Jean-Pierre should invite yourselves onto a talk show and do whatever else you think appropriate to make his project widely known and properly explained."

"I have a legal question," Melvin Stein said. "As you know there have been all kinds of accusations against leaders of countries and their associates. We could discuss cases from Bosnia to Sri Lanka, South Africa to Chechnya, and Mexico to Colombia, and from any other direction. The basic issue is what do we do with these people? Some of these leaders are in jail, some have been released, some are on trial in the Hague and elsewhere, and some are still Presidents and Prime Ministers. Do we round up all of them and give them appropriate trials or just forget about it?"

"We cannot ignore crimes, yet we cannot be going around putting people in jail, and starting trials," Arsen said. "Perhaps we should learn from black South Africa. The Truth and Reconciliation Commission is an incredible institution. The price for unconditional freedom for any crime is telling the truth about the way it happened. Political criminals recite their stories of torture and murder and walk away free men. Trials would muddy the picture, as everyone would try to save his own skin and would lie. The story is very clear now as told by criminals themselves. Imagine if people like von Ribbentrop or Göring, Ceausescu or Peron, among others, had talked to avoid jail. History would be better understood, and the excused criminals would probably have died in shame and solitude. Or would they? I think more would be achieved, and justice served better, by finding out the truth than by killing the criminal."

The conference room fell silent for a few minutes. The Undersecretaries of the Ethnic Department were thinking about the best way to serve justice.

After a lengthy discussion Melvin Stein summarized the feelings of the majority. "Clearly some sort of Truth and Reconciliation Commission is not favored by the people around this table. It seems they think that justice is best served by a fair trial and a punitive verdict. I cast my vote against such an opinion. Trials do not promote national unity. "

"Would it be possible to recommend to the Department how we should handle such cases?" Arsen insisted. "I think we should also talk to people familiar with the Commission in South Africa and elsewhere and invite some of them to talk with us at one of our Departmental meetings."

"It will be done," Melvin Stein said, and the subject was dropped from further discussion.

It was almost four o'clock and time to adjourn the meeting.

"We will meet again in ten days," Arsen said. "I will be back from my trip on 29 December."

Arsen had a good feeling about his team. He also wanted to tighten the policies on the lines of responsibility of his own staff. He invited Victoria, Matt Brown and Stan Petkovic to his office.

"I thought we had a good meeting ," Arsen said. "These people will do the job. I want to make sure that we establish certain lines of responsibility in the Department. Undersecretaries and whoever else has problems will be talking to you three first. Stan will be responsible for policy matters. Victoria, you will deal with organization and administration of the Department, which includes all personnel appointments and problems. Matt will deal with information, and he has to know what is happening. Undersecretaries should have direct access to me but should deal with you on routine matters. Their staffs will deal with you. It seems to me that you three should expand your staffs. I don't want delays for any reason. As I told you before, I like results not excuses."

Arsen asked Stan Petkovic to remain in the office.

"Stan, I wanted to discuss with you our visit to Belgrade. Are you ready for talks with all those people?"

"Yes, I am ready," Stan Petkovic said.

"Okay," Arsen said. "The basics are just fine. And we should hold to the basics and avoid being drawn into complexities. Of course, everything is very complex.

"The basic issue is: what do the people want? They have the right to get what they want as long as it does not infringe on the rights of others. We must also keep telling people that auditing leaders and other individuals is a principle that will be applied in all countries, including large countries such as Russia, the U.S., and China.

"The third principle is free elections. Our job is to allow free campaigns before elections, and actual free voting. We don't ask who and who. We will protect the autonomy and independence of all groups, and that is the fourth principle. We have nothing else to do in these countries. Of course, we will give help and advice on health care, and technical and economic help if they ask for it.

"Stan, you have to repeat this often enough so that these principles sink into the psyche of the population."

"I sometimes wish you had appointed me Director for Serbia," Stan Petkovic said. "I am so involved and the Serbs are on my mind. It will take a lot of time for them to understand what we are trying to do. I hope they don't take it again as a plot against the Serbs."

For a moment Arsen worried that Stan Petkovic might be siding with the nationalists. They were dangerous, Arsen thought. The Serbs deserved to have a country that would include the territories where Serbs were the majority of the people. They had to stop right there.

"You will have to find the man who will do the job for us," Arsen said. "You will have to remain in New York for now. I need someone like you to help me do the job."

"It was just a thought," Stan Petkovic said. "Like Ivo Stipich in Croatia."

"You will have to find people who will have the equivalent positions in other countries. You should start working on that immediately."

"I have found several people already and you will have to approve them when you return to New York."

"Doctor, President Chand is on line four," Michelle announced over the intercom.

"Yes, Sir," Arsen said.

"Hi, Arsen," Rama Chand said. "I know you are going to Europe and Africa tomorrow. People are talking about Cyprus almost with disbelief. Some people are naturally worried how it is going to hit them when you come to deal with their problems."

"Our principles are clear: free choice for each ethnic group, audits of leaders, free elections, and preservation of the new order. I have been talking about that so much, and I will have to continue talking. The test will be my own tribe - the Serbs. Our decisions will not always be popular with Serbs, and they will resent some of them. I may be sympathetic with them, but the rules will be applied anyway. My assistant, Stan Petkovic, is going through a personal crisis from worrying about Serbia. He will know what to do when he talks to others in the future. That will also be a clear signal how we will treat other ethnic problems."

"I am on your side," Rama Chand said. "I have decided to travel and start explaining what we are trying to accomplish. Eventually, I will start adding research items."

"I am delighted for you," Arsen said. "I am sure you will find it satisfying. You will also understand the various peoples and their problems. You will also find out how our changes are accepted by people, and whether we are right or wrong in some areas. You will be able to influence some decisions. And you will be able to report to the Assembly what is happening, first hand."

"I am going to China to deal with some of their idiosyncrasies, and try to smooth your path," Rama Chand said. "Are there issues you want me to explore?"

"Tibet was a problem, and probably still is. I don't know all the Chinese issues. One is Taiwan, where a plebiscite will confirm their desire to separate, or maybe not. Also, there is a Muslim problem in Xinjiang province. The Muslims are fighting for independence. We will be dealing with that soon. They should understand that audits will be done as in any other place. It is my feeling that it will be difficult to prove anything against the officials in China. They don't have possessions, but they utilize state property as a benefit on the job - although they don't keep it afterwards. I am not sure that our legal division has had a chance to deal with that yet. "

"I also want to visit India and Indonesia," Rama Chand said. "It is about time I visit home. Unfortunately, your audit division will be busy there. Have a good trip to Cyprus and give them our best wishes."

"Rama, it would be a great event if you led the delegation to Cyprus," Arsen said. "This is the first negotiated accord. It would be a great public relations event. You could give a speech for the occasion. We could fly together, and you could return after the ceremonies. I will fly to Zaire."

Rama Chand was hesitant to go because he had not received an invitation. Arsen argued that it had been assumed that he would not come and that Arsen was the official substitute. Rama Chand finally agreed to go and offered to fly Arsen on his plane to Nicosia. Arsen was delighted.

"I wish you would make a point of attending similar events as they come up," Arsen said. "Your presence would give these occasions a special importance."

"We will take off at five tomorrow afternoon," Rama Chand said. "I will see you on the plane."

"Thank you. The reaction in Nicosia will be exhilaration, and publicity about the accord will be tremendous."

Victoria came in to resolve some details of the trip, and Arsen told her of Rama Chand's decision to attend the signing ceremony in Nicosia.

"That's marvelous," Victoria said. "So far he's been almost invisible. People have to see him, and he has to be in the news. We need a President who will lead and encourage people. We need someone who will confer confidence and radiate optimism. Rama Chand can do it."

"I will be on Rama's plane," Arsen said. "René Bright and others, including reporters, should use my plane as we planed."

It was getting late and Arsen went home. Nada and her mother were watching an old movie. Dinner was waiting for him but Arsen could not eat. He wanted a large cold drink, and he poured a mixture of apple and cranberry juices and added three cubes of ice. He sipped his drink as he looked for a program that would interest him. There were too many talk shows discussing astronomy, space exploration and travel, World

Government, cloning and health issues in space, and ethnic problems. The World economy was discussed by a panel that included an Undersecretary for Finance, a Wall Street broker, the chairman of the board of an international bank, and a Japanese businessman. They were arguing the pros and cons of the freeze on all markets. The Undersecretary avoided saying anything clearly, and the other three men were attacking him with a vengeance. The moderator finally changed the subject by asking about the expenses of the World Government.

Why are the markets frozen? Arsen wondered and decided to call Goran in the morning to find out.

CHAPTER THIRTY-FOUR

TUESDAY, 23 DECEMBER 1997

Nada was packing two suitcases for Arsen, and her mother was ironing a few items. Arsen again asked Nada if she wanted to come along, and she declined because her mother would have to remain alone. Arsen understood.

"I will need some money," Nada said. "The markets are frozen for unknown reasons and our mutual funds are frozen too. What should I do?"

"Take my salary when, and if, it ever arrives." Arsen was joking about a serious matter, and Nada did not appreciate it. "There is money on my Chase account, remember? I will write you a check."

It was time to go to the office. Arsen said good-bye to his mother-in-law and Nada saw him to the door.

"Good-bye, my dear. I will see you in a week in Belgrade or perhaps even in Cyprus. We will talk over the phone. Victoria will always be able to find me. "

"Good-bye. Have a good trip."

A short limousine ride was annoying as always.

Victoria wanted to talk to Arsen as soon as he arrived, Michelle reported. Herman Wolff had called. Col. Nassar, Undersecretary Karazoglou and Matthew Brown had also called and wanted to talk to Arsen.

Victoria was concerned about her new role, which gave her very little time to think about Arsen's office, and she wanted more people around.

"You are the Chief of Staff, and you are responsible for the office," Arsen said and insisted that she take care of everything.

Herman Wolff was the next in line.

"Have a good trip, Arsen. The ceremony in Cyprus is an important first step for the Department. I hear that Rama Chand is going too. Why?"

"The importance of the event will be enhanced by President Chand's participation," Arsen said. "More reports will be published, and more people will read them.

"The publicity will bring our goals into focus, and not only for Cyprus. People should know what is happening and what will happen in other places."

"He will take the credit for your accomplishment," Herman Wolff said.

"Credits in hell won't be worth much," Arsen said. "It is the friends you make along the way that give you importance and make you look important. The ultimate test is what you see in the mirror."

"I should have known better than to ask," Herman Wolff said. "This is a philosophical statement and a statement of philosophy. That is how you want the Department to run, and you you want it to be run by idealists. Maybe this is a hint to all of us."

"Maybe," Arsen said.

"Doctor, Undersecretary Karazoglou is on four," Michelle announced over the intercom.

"Hello Suleiman, what is on your mind? I wanted to talk to you too. I would like you to participate at the signing ceremony in Nicosia. You helped broker this deal, and you should be there."

"Thank you for the invitation," Suleiman Karazoglou said. "I did not anticipate going to Nicosia."

"That is settled," Arsen said. "Talk to René Bright; he is making the arrangements for the second plane. I will be on Rama Chand's plane."

"I know he is going," Suleiman Karazoglou said. "People in Ankara know. I talked to them. They will want to be there to greet the President."

"Tell them it would be great if they decide to come," Arsen said. "There will be quite a gathering for the ceremony. We should have invited other people. Now it is too late."

"Let me do some calling, maybe something can still be done. I will let you know," Suleiman Karazoglou said and hung up.

"Michelle, tell Matt Brown to come to my office."

"Matt you wanted to talk to me," Arsen said as Matt Brown walked into the office.

"It's about the trip to Cyprus. Everybody is asking what's happening. President Chand is going. Are there any other invitations?"

"There is a last-ditch effort to bring more people to Nicosia for the signing ceremony," Arsen said. "Suleiman told me that the Turkish leaders may attend since President Chand will be there. He is working on some other leaders."

"I wish I had known, I could have helped," Matt Brown said

"It is never too late," Arsen said. "Why don't you try?"

Matt Brown was annoyed that he was the last to know, and Arsen noticed it.

"No point in being upset," Arsen said. "You will find a way to be informed about everything. We have no reason to hide anything from you."

Matt Brown laughed. "You're so right. You didn't hire me to hide information from me."

"Somebody told you, I hope, that I am flying with Rama Chand, and the rest of you will be on the second plane," Arsen said.

"I did not know," Matt Brown said and laughed again. "I am the least informed press secretary in the world."

"You had better let the media know about President Chand going to Cyprus and the rest."

"See you in Nicosia," Matt Brown said and left the office.

"Doctor, the Chinese President is on line three," Michelle announced over the intercom.

"Good evening, Mr. President," Arsen greeted the Chinese President. "In New York it is still morning."

"Good morning, Mr. Secretary. The word is out that President Chand and you will go to Cyprus together."

"That is correct," Arsen said.

"Too bad they did not invited us," the Chinese President said. "I am sure we would send a delegation."

"We invited ourselves, Mr. President," Arsen said. "We did not expect any interest in the event. It would be terrible not to have you there if you want to come." Arsen pondered how to reverse the situation and open the Cyprus ceremony to all who wanted to come; it occurred to him that the ceremony could be postponed for a few days to allow invitations to be sent to all governments. The idea was irresistible, and New Year's Eve was just a few days away.

"I have an idea, Mr. President," Arsen said. "We will talk to the Cypriot officials and ask them to postpone the signing ceremony for a week. Why don't we push for New Year's Eve? We will explain that you wanted to attend and that postponement was arranged so that other leaders could attend too. We can even organize a summit meeting that will be in session at midnight, and we will welcome the New Year together. Would you object to my announcing that you will attend?"

"Even better, let us announce that we will definitely attend," the Chinese President said.

"Marvelous idea, Mr. President," Arsen said, caught by surprise and pleased with the development. "Would you like to lead the organizing committee?"

"Would you mind, Mr. Secretary? My staff will handle the invitations, and we will talk to the Cypriots. Your office will be informed of all details and if problems arise we will quickly resolve them together."

"The only problem I see is the envy of some people for your role in the event. I know the event will be very successful."

"Do you think President Chand will approve this project?"

"I am sure he will be delighted. He is anxious to see China in a leading role since that also means Asia. I will leave the political details to you."

Arsen asked Michelle to find Suleiman Karazoglou and Matt Brown and to tell them to come to the office immediately. Rama Chand was enthusiastic about the Chinese involvement, which would improve relations with China.

"It is important that your office make the announcement," Arsen said. "Let the Chinese make their announcement first. Rama, please state that this was done at the request of China."

"Fantastic idea," Rama Chand said. "Let me know as soon as you confirm this with the Cypriot officials. Arsen it just occurred to me that we have to postpone our trip to Nicosia. I will be there on 31 December."

"I am expected to arrive to Kinshasa on Christmas Day and my trip will have to be postponed until tomorrow," Arsen said. "Things have been changing by the hour. If I don't talk to you before I will see you in Nicosia."

Matt Brown, Victoria and Suleiman Karazoglou walked into the office together.

"I just talked to the Chinese President. He was offended that China had not been invited to the ceremony in Cyprus. I promised we would postpone the event until 31 December, and they wanted to send the invitations for the New Year's Eve party to the world leaders. This could be an incredible event and quite a show for the media. Suleiman you have to pull all the strings when you call Turkey and Greece. Start working now, and come back when you have arranged it. Matt, you have to deal with President Chand's press secretary. What is his name?"

"You mean her name - Shirley Katz," said Matt Brown.

"I didn't even know he had a Press Secretary," Arsen said. "It is very important that the Chinese President get the credit for proposing the party. We need him on our side."

"I get the idea." Matt Brown confirmed that he understood what had to be done.

"Please, start working on it immediately," Arsen said. "Oh, before I forget, our trip to Nicosia has now been cancelled and we will fly to Kinshasa tomorrow afternoon at three o'clock.

Arsen turned to Victoria.

"Let's decide who from our Department will be going to Cyprus for the party," Arsen suggested. "Where is Stan?"

"On the way to Belgrade."

"If he wants, he can always come to Cyprus from Belgrade. Who will remain in charge while we are gone?"

"I could stay," Victoria proposed. "Col. Nassar could be in charge."

"I think you should go," Arsen said. "This will be a spectacular party. I am sure every government will send a delegation. Most Presidents and Prime Ministers will attend. I think Herman Wolff should stay and be in charge. That is settled. I will go to Zaire tomorrow, then to Spain and Belgrade, and I should arrive in Cyprus on 31 December, just in time for the party. I would like you to make these changes. René Bright should call Zaire and you should call Stan and let him know about these changes. I would like to see my wife in Cyprus. Maybe you could arrange for her to go to Belgrade with her mother. She could then fly to Cyprus."

"Let me see what I can do," Victoria said.

Arsen called Michelle. "Find our pilot Cap. Simonides. I want to talk to him."

The Captain called right back.

"Captain, we're not going anywhere today. The trip to Nicosia has been canceled. We'll fly to Kinshasa tomorrow."

"No problem, Mr. Secretary."

Several more calls had to be answered. Alexei called and wanted to know what was happening.

"I arrived from Paris last night," Alexei said. "What is causing such a buzz about Cyprus? Are you going to be around tomorrow? We could have dinner together."

"Dinner is out as I will be on the way to Kinshasa" Arsen said. "Hopefully Cyprus will be a show of cooperation of the governments of the world. We will celebrate the first success in the ethnic effort, an accord that seemed impossible only a few weeks ago. Do you think you would have time to come to Cyprus?"

"Unlikely," Alexei said. "I have many places to visit and I have to arrange research projects and make orders for products we need."

"Don't you have someone to do these things for you?" Arsen asked.

"Not really," Alexei said. "I have a small staff of select people. They do only the details of my designs."

"I will be back at the beginning of the year," Arsen said. "Our meeting will have to wait until then."

"Okay. Have a good trip and a good time in Cyprus." Alexei hung up.

Arsen realized he had better call home and let Nada know that he would be home tonight. Nobody answered the phone. They had probably gone to the Vertical Club. He should go home now and do some shopping. Or even better, join Nada and her mother at the Club. The Security Service had a fit when Arsen explained that he was going to the Vertical Club.

"Gentlemen, I have no problems with your putting on sweat shirts and pants, even running a few laps on the track, but I would be very upset if you interrupted the operations of the Club for security reasons." Arsen was adamant about that. "I doubt anybody will recognize me. Once I saw Harrison Ford exercise and run in the Club and nobody recognized him, or if they did, they paid no attention. He is certainly better known from his films than I from the recent political arena." The agents promised to be inconspicuous.

At home Arsen changed to his Polo shirt and shorts, and put on jeans, sneakers and a heavy jacket. This had been his standard attire when he was a regular at the Club. Even the elevator man remembered his old style. The walk along Sixty-Second Street, down Second Avenue and Sixty-First Street to the Vertical Club reminded him of happy times of two months ago. The maintenance man only said hello, as if he had seen Arsen in the locker room the day before, and the members passed by as they always had. Nada and her mother spotted Arsen as soon as he stepped onto the exercise floor, and waved to him with surprise. Nada joined Arsen on the track.

"What happened?"

"You won't believe it. We're celebrating New Year's Eve in Nicosia courtesy of the Chinese President. All governments were invited. It will be a gathering of Who's Who in world politics. For a change I will be a guest like everybody else."

"You sound disappointed."

"Better to say relieved."

"When and where are you going next?"

"Tomorrow to Kinshasa."

"I had better join Mom; she is ready to get off the treadmill. See you at home."

Arsen increased his walking pace and looked at his watch. He made a mile in fifteen minutes, about two minutes slower than he used to. By the time he finished, it had taken forty-five minutes for three miles. Very slow, Arsen thought. He should buy a treadmill for the office; it would be good to stress the heart physically, not only psychologically and emotionally.

Victoria called later in the evening just to find out when Arsen was coming to the office the next day.

"I will leave for the airport from home. Is there something urgent in the office I should do?"

"Nothing we can't discuss over the phone. I'll call in the morning."

Dinner and a quiet evening at home were long overdue. The discussion with Nada and her mother about Bosnia and Kosovo reminded Arsen that there were opinions different from his own about the course history should take.

CHAPTER THIRTY-FIVE

WEDNESDAY, 24 DECEMBER 1997

It was seven o'clock in the evening, New York time, when Arsen walked into the day room of his plane and found the reporters sitting around and talking or reading. The plane was not as crowded as he had thought it would be. He asked for a sandwich and a Coke. It was inevitable that Cyprus would be mentioned.

"Happy Christmas Eve," Arsen said to the approaching reporter.

"Happy Christmas Eve," the New York reporter, Leon Meyer, said. "A plane is not the best place for celebration of anything.

"You are Jewish as I recall, or maybe not," Arsen said.

"I am Jewish, all right," Leon Meyer said; his face lighted up at the question.

"It is not my Christmas Eve either," Arsen said. "Serbs celebrate it on 6 January according to the old calender. What is happening, Mr. Meyer?"

"Stories are wild about how you arranged the New Year's Eve party in Cyprus. Is that now a done deal?"

"It is," Arsen replied. "I heard from Suleiman Karazoglou that the Cypriots were enthusiastic about the gathering of world leaders and about the party. I think it will be great to see so many important people gather and talk about Cyprus. They will get the idea that it could happen in their own countries. We have to wait and see who will show up."

"Do you think there are any leaders who won't come?" Leon Meyer asked.

"I imagine those who feel threatened or targeted will not come to Cyprus," Arsen said. "Will there be enough hotel rooms and beds to accommodate those who want to come? I think there may be a thousand people at the party, and I am looking forward to the event."

"How did you come up with the idea?"

"The Chinese President was responsible with his insistence on attending the signing ceremony. It was he of all people, and after the confrontation on Tibet. I was surprised."

"Will there be any formal political discussions in Cyprus?" asked Leon Meyer.

"I hope not," Arsen said. "This should be a meeting to celebrate the beginning of the new era of ethnic relations, and the people who come should be entertained and should have fun. Don't ask me questions about our immediate plans. Imagine the party and the count-down to midnight. I'm sure many people will be watching. That will be the best public relations event for the new world."

Other reporters joined the conversation.

"Dr. Pankovich, it seems you're looking to the world beyond 2003," Bill Wilson, a reporter for *The Chicago Daily Visor* asked. "What do you see beyond?"

"A swirling Earth without a living soul," Arsen said. "That is an extremely pessimistic vision. Don't tell me it cannot happen. Our present effort will be worthy however. As General Shagov put it, 'If we have to die, I will insist that we all die as human beings···' "

"What if the Demon flew away from our solar system and the Earth remained intact?" Bill Wilson asked.

"That would be wonderful," Arsen said. "I'm not sure what would happen to the world order we are building. The understanding in the Assembly was that the clock would be turned back. The political map would revert to where it was before the election of the World Government. Was there a declaration to that effect? I am not sure. The situation would become very complicated. Ask President Chand, he will have the right answer. I will ask him myself.

"In my view, it would be terrible to revert to the old divisions of the world. The same problems that are being resolved now would recur immediately. Although I agree that every person should die free and respected and equal, I disagree that these people are not entitled to live respected and equal and free. I would be opposed to turning the clock back. One thing is clear - these five years would remain indelible in the history books. It is my opinion that people would refuse to turn the clock back. Other developments might also be against it."

"Which developments?" asked Jack Thompson.

"Technology developed for the preservation effort would be available to all of us. Think of only three things. Space travel will be a reality. Information and communications will be incredible. Imagine that everything that has ever been written will be available on the Sinternet. Medicine will change enormously, particularly in the field of reproduction, which will be developed for the preservation ships. I would be surprised if they were not looking into time-delayed cloning."

"What is that?" everybody asked.

"Oh, just an idea," Arsen said. "Think also of a world in which ethnic relations have been changed to the extent that ethnic strife has disappeared. Would that be a world at peace? It would not. Human nature is disagreeable, but we would disagree without killing each other."

"You visualize a more sophisticated world," Leon Meyer said.

"More sophisticated but disagreeable," Arsen said. "The issues will change and methods of resolving them will change, but discussions and arguments will continue, and may become very heated and emotional."

"What do you think we'll argue about?" Bill Wilson asked.

"Maybe the very technology we are developing right now to preserve humanity," Arsen said. "Who knows, the ethicists may become the priests of the old morality."

"Do you visualize emergence of a new morality from all that's happening?" Leon Meyer asked.

"If we survive we will be different and we will inevitably feel different, like a man who has survived a deadly disease. I had that kind of feeling when I recovered from a stroke many years ago. A friend of mine woke me up with his remark that I must have felt mortal. He was right, but I also felt more for my fellow man, for my family and friends, after that. This will be a mass conversion. Will the Universal Man arise and create a Universal Society, freed by technological advances from financial obligations and by the elimination of classes from political pressures; will our man be freed to pursue his intellectual interests?"

"Sounds like a Marxian idea," Bill Wilson said.

"Minus proletarians and their dictatorship," Arsen said.

"What are you planning to accomplish in Zaire?" the reporter for the *San Francisco Memo*, Tom Welsh, asked.

"Not much this time around," Arsen said. "I want to meet these people and talk to them. I want to know how far apart Tutsi and Hutu are. In our Department Mr. Petkovic believes their problems may be resolved if a way can be found to recognize the territory that belongs to the Tutsi and to the Hutu. The problem may be very complicated because these people often live in mixed communities. We will have to find a territorial solution without moving people."

"This is not exactly a standard approach," Tom Welsh said. "Has it been tried before?"

"Unfortunately only by 'ethnic cleansing,' as in India and Bosnia and Croatia, and many other places," Arsen said. "Once the sovereignty of a territory is acquired, the remaining majority wants peace at all costs and minorities wake up with old battle songs. Problems are more complicated when the population in a territory is mixed."

"Mr. Secretary, could you tell us something about the situation in the former Yugoslavia," Bill Wilson asked. "We know you're a Serb from Bosnia. Do you think you can resolve their problems objectively?"

"The question is, how does a Serb resolve problems of Croats and Muslims in the former Yugoslavia?" Leon Meyer said.

"That is the question, you are right," Arsen said. "I decided to be involved and I will make all decisions. If I can't be objective in this case how will I handle the problems of others whose souls I don't understand. How will I deal with Tamils, or Basques, or Turks in Germany, or Kurds in Turkey, and all the others if I cannot be objective with the Croats, whose soul I do know and understand? This will be the test of the fairness of the Ethnic Department and of myself."

"How are you going to resolve the problems which often may test you as a Serb?" asked Leon Meyer. "Wouldn't it be better if someone else made the decisions, someone completely impartial?"

"No, I don't think so," Arsen said. "I have to prove to myself and to others that I can do it. I must prove that I can be trusted. This will also be a test of the system."

"Can you tell us how you plan to do it?" Leon Meyer persisted.

"No, I cannot tell you specifics," Arsen said. "However, let me give you some hints. I expect this not to be repeated until we leave Belgrade. The same principles will be applied as everywhere else: all ethnic groups have the right to independence or autonomy, and the land goes with it. Each new sovereignty will be protected, each leader will be audited, and the system will be tested by elections."

"You don't seem to anticipate any problems in Kosovo," Leon Meyer said.

"No, I don't," Arsen concurred.

"Is that a straightforward situation?" Leon Meyer asked.

"It is not straightforward, but in an area where an ethnic group represents ninety percent of the population, a plebiscite will decide between autonomy and independence."

"Dr. Pankovich, the ceremony in Nicosia was postponed to New Year's Eve," the Korean reporter, Kim Yong Yun, said. "Who came up with that idea?"

"The Chinese President," Arsen said. "I have already said that. The Chinese President will preside over the ceremonies with President Chand. I am looking forward to the party after the signing ceremony. An event for the media will be relaxation time for me, and I only hope my wife will be there with me."

Maria Cruz the hostess on the plane, served coffee and cookies, and the conversation turned to other subjects. Arsen talked little and listened to what the reporters had to say. They were a dynamic group, alert and knowledgeable about events and people, both past and present. Gossip was also their forte.

CHAPTER THIRTY-SIX

The plane had landed in Kinshasa during the night. It was Christmas morning. Arsen woke up at eight o'clock and at nine he walked out of the plane, accompanied by René Bright and Matt Brown. Several Zairean officials were at hand to welcome them. René Bright did not know who they were. The situation was unpleasant. They were driven to the Ministry of the Interior and introduced to the Minister. Obviously, nobody had made any preparations for the meetings.

"Do you think there is a reason for further conversation?" Arsen asked the Minister. "Do you think there was need to come here from New York to have nothing to talk about? It would help if you would talk to your President and have him talk to the Presidents of Rwanda and Burundi. I am going to my hotel where I will try to cool off the heat I feel in Kinshasa. I can be found there by you, or whoever else wants to talk to me - if anybody does. Have a good day and a Merry Christmas if you celebrate it."

"I am sorry for this confusion," the Minister said. "I will communicate with the Presidents of the Congo, Rwanda and Burundi."

"We will talk again," Arsen said, and he thought that coming to Kinshasa might have been a mistake. The Minister had no idea what to do next.

"Who are the people we are supposed to talk to?" Arsen asked René Bright.

"This is the man I talked to several times, but the Vice-President is the official responsible for dealing with the World Government," René Bright said. "I also talked to officials from Rwanda and Burundi."

"Where are they?" Arsen asked. "Were they supposed to be in Kinshasa, or are we supposed to shuttle from one country to another?"

René Bright looked embarrassed. "I understood that they were ready to talk."

Arsen and the others were driven by an army vehicle to the Hotel Excelsior, where arrangements for their arrival were supposed to have been made. Nothing was ready when they inquired about their rooms. Even the officials they had met at the airport were nowhere to to be seen. This was a slap in the face of the World Government, Arsen thought. He would have to do something drastic, something that would induce them to talk.

When they were finally in their rooms, Arsen called René Bright and Matt Brown to his room for a strategy meeting.

"René, what are our options for getting the talks going? Is this the end of our mission?"

"I knew they were not enthusiastic about talks since all three countries had problems accepting the principles of the World Government," René Bright said. "But I thought they would be more cooperative once we arrived. I also understood that the Presidents of Rwanda and Burundi were going to be here for the talks. It seems nobody is around."

"Let me talk to Col. Nassar and Suleiman Karazoglou," Arsen asked Matt Brown. "The way things stand we would be better off in our plane."

Conversation ceased, and Matt Brown was heard trying to reach New York, and then talking to Victoria. Col. Nassar was the first to call.

"Colonel, we have a snag here in Kinshasa," Arsen said. "Nobody seems to be available for talks with us. You could say there is a hostile atmosphere, and I would like to defuse it. Talk to John Thornton and just alert him to the situation. Keep in touch."

An hour later Suleiman Karazoglou called.

"Suleiman, what is happening in Cyprus? Are preparations progressing on time?"

"Everything is under control. The only problem that is developing is the lack of hotel rooms, and we are advising delegations to make reservations in Athens and Istanbul. We will make sure that all heads of government get appropriate rooms in Nicosia."

"Excellent," Arsen said.

Arsen turned to Matt Brown and René Bright. "We have to wait for somebody from the government to call us, and that seems unlikely. There isn't much to do here, and Kinshasa doesn't seem like a place which offers much for sight-seeing. We don't understand the language so we cannot watch television or read local newspapers. Maybe we should look for food and hope the bacterial count is low. This trip has been a disaster so far."

The Security Service agents were concerned about security. The reporters were concerned, and they sent Leon Meyer to find out what was happening. Arsen invited everyone to dinner in the dinning room but it turned out that it was closed for the holiday. Finally, Leon Meyer arranged with room service to send food to Arsen's suite.

"Hurrah," Leon Meyer exclaimed. "The food is coming. I had better call the boys and tell them to come over. Fortunately, this suite is big enough to accommodate everybody."

"What happened to our plane crew? Arsen asked. "Shouldn't we invite them too?"

"I talked to them already," the Security Service agent said. "They prefer to remain in the plane and keep an eye on it."

"It is amazing, what is happening," Arsen said. "This feels like enemy territory. Matt, did you tell Victoria to let President Chand know what is happening?"

"Yes, I did," Matt Brown said.

The reporters were briefed about the situation that had developed. They understood.

"What will happen next?" Bill Wilson asked.

"We will proceed as if nothing happened," Arsen said. "The first step will be to organize the plebiscite in the western parts of the Congo where Tutsi are being pushed to go to Rwanda and Burundi. They are known as Bunyamulenge. We have to ask them what they want. Chances are, they will want union with Rwanda and Burundi. The Congo will be unhappy about that. It is unclear to everyone why the colonial powers drew the border lines the way they did.

"That whole area will be surrounded by military units to protect the people during the voting period. In the meantime, Hutu-Tutsi problems will be discussed and negotiated by themselves, with a time limit on the negotiations. Since there are many ethnic groups in the Congo, each of them will have the right to decide where they belong. We will push for a federation of autonomous territories - obviously more than one. I don't know enough about the trends and preferences of various groups. They will get autonomy, but it will be difficult to guarantee security to too many small independent states. They will have to know and understand that. We will not stop them, but we will try to educate them.

"Once we get complete demographic information in Rwanda and Burundi, the ethnic groups will start negotiations on their status. It will be almost impossible to separate all groups. Some sort of autonomous cantons will be acceptable. The Tutsi will be protected, and the Hutu will not be ruled by the Tutsi."

A telephone rang, and Matt Brown answered it. John Thornton was on the line.

"I'm not quite sure what you want us to do," he said. "Do you want a show of force or what?"

"If you can, send us some support units to protect our group and the reporters. I'm not sure how safe we are."

"Okay, I get the picture," John Thornton said. "I'll send French and Belgian troupes to Kinshasa. I'll keep in touch with Col. Nassar."

"Help is on the way," Arsen said to the reporters in the room. "Let us eat and drink." The food and drinks, catered by room service, had just been brought in. Bread, cheeses, and meat looked well prepared and smelled inviting. The Christmas party was on.

CHAPTER THIRTY-SEVEN

No calls came in from the Congolese Government. The visiting group was ignored. News from New York was supportive. Rama Chand was upset and had already talked to the delegates from the Congo, Rwanda and Burundi, who were cool though polite; they had promised to look into the problem. John Thornton dispatched French troops to the eastern part of the Congo and a detail of Belgian troops to guard the hotel and the plane.

Leon Meyer came in to find out what was happening.

"Nothing much in Kinshasa," Arsen said and explained what was being arranged in New York.

"I talked to my editor, and the other guys also talked to their colleagues. Nobody understands why these people are not responding." Leon Meyer explained that he had been told that the reaction in the Assembly was mixed. Some delegates seemed to be indifferent and others were even hostile to the possible actions by the World Government. "The majority was for some action."

"Nobody of authority in Kinshasa wants to talk to us," Mel Stein said angrily. "They gave me the runaround. I couldn't even make an appointment with anybody. What do we do now?"

"If there is no cooperation in the matter of audits we have the right to suspend the official and to arrange for somebody else to take the job," Arsen said. "The suspension is permanent. I suggest that we talk to Col. Nassar and tell him to stand by because the official here, the President, may refuse to give up his job. We are automatically authorized to use the military to intervene and to replace the official. We should be able to deliver a note to that effect to the Congolese President. If he does not respond, we will act. Matt, call the Colonel and talk to him."

"Do you want me to write the note?" Mel Stein asked. "I'll incorporate what you said and you can sign it. I'll deliver it myself."

"Do it," Arsen said. "I have a feeling we are wasting our time here. I will wait for a response until tomorrow afternoon, then I have to go to Spain."

John Thornton called again.

"Arsen, have you heard what's happening?"

"No."

"When the French landed in the eastern Congo, near Uvira, they were shot at and they had to return fire. There were casualties on both sides. Who would think something like this would happen?"

"I wonder how long we are going to be safe here in Kinshasa?" Arsen said.

"Belgians are landing as I speak to you," John Thornton said. "I've sent a brigade, not a detail as I originally intended. A British backup brigade is on the way. Two more brigades are ready, and they'll be taking off any time. That should take care of Kinshasa. Arsen, don't go out of the hotel until the brigade is in place. They're in communication with me constantly. The British will surround the Presidential Palace and detain the President. He will be flown out of the Congo immediately and will return only as a private citizen after the Presidency has been assumed by somebody else. The date for new elections will be set. Ministers who were involved in any kind of resistance will also be ineligible. An investigation of the events will start immediately. The same series of events will take place simultaneously in Kigali and Bujumbura. The troops are on the way."

"This is a quick response," Arsen said.

"This is the only way to act," John Thornton said. "I'm sorry for the victims in Uvira. The toll there is three French and ten Congolese. We must avoid casualties. Hopefully, there will be none in other places."

"Thank you, John," Arsen said.

"We'll keep in touch," John Thornton said and hung up.

Arsen explained what he had just heard.

"Are we in immediate danger?" asked Kim Yong Yun.

"Officially no, but I would not leave the hotel right now," Arsen said. "Is the dining room open, does anybody know?"

The dining room was open, this much was known. Arsen suggested that they go to eat and he joined Leon Meyer and Bill Wilson.

After lunch, they noticed Belgian soldiers getting into positions around the hotel. Everybody felt safer even though nobody had attacked them yet. A captain came in and reported to Arsen that they had secured the hotel. He also mentioned that he was talking to the Commander of the British brigade that had surrounded the Presidential Palace. They were in place and ready to ask the President to surrender. There had been no resistance as their action had been swift and unexpected. Most of the Congolese troops remained in their barracks.

Arsen asked Matt Brown to call their pilot, Mr. Simonides, to get ready for the flight to Spain.

"He is ready," Matt Brown said. "I already talked to him."

"If we leave at about ten tonight we should be in Madrid at around seven in the morning," Arsen said. "Tell him we should take off at ten."

"Col. Nassar is flying to Kinshasa tonight to see first hand what's going on," Matt Brown said.

News was slowly filtering into the hotel. The Rwandan President had already been flown out of the country. In Burundi there was a standoff, but negotiations were progressing.

Later on they found out that the Congolese President was asking for reinstatement. He claimed he had been at his weekend home for the holidays and that he had not been informed of the situation in time. The decision to replace him was irrevocable. On the orders of President Chand and the authorization he had secured from the Assembly - although he had not needed it - the Congolese President surrendered and he was flown to Tanzania. As Arsen's party was leaving for the airport, it was reported that the Burundian President was on his way to London to join his daughter.

"It sounds as if the crisis is over," Arsen said. "This was the first test of the ability of the World Government to handle a crisis. It probably passed the test. The brigades will be withdrawn as soon as the interim President has been elected by the Legislature."

CHAPTER THIRTY-EIGHT

SATURDAY, 27 DECEMBER 1997

Madrid looked beautiful on this Saturday morning as Arsen and Matt Brown and the reporters, along with the officials from Spanish Protocol, rode along the city's avenues. At the Prime Minister's palace Arsen and Matt Brown were ushered in by the Chief of Protocol and introduced to the Prime Minister, Fernando Rodriguez.

The conversation was pleasant and spontaneous. The Prime Minister brought up the subject of Basques and explained what had been done so far.

"We have talked with them at length," the Prime Minister said. "Clearly they want independence. That has been resolved, as we agreed. We are expecting the response from the French, and there should be no problems from that side. The remaining problem is to negotiate the rights of Spaniards within the Basque territory. For example, there are people who would rather remain there, but they are worried about their property and their safety. The Basques are not very responsive on these issues. Mr. Secretary, Spain will not yield until these questions have been resolved."

"I am very impressed with the progress you have made since we last talked," Arsen said. "The remaining issue should not be a problem as it has been clearly defined by the World Government and approved by the Assembly. I have a meeting scheduled in the afternoon with the Basque leaders. Let me see what I can accomplish by talking with them."

This completed the discussion on the 'Spanish problem,' as Arsen called it. The visit to Spain was almost superfluous, Arsen thought. Basques had no options in dealing with Spanish individuals who intended to stay.

"Mr. Secretary, there has been very disturbing news about your visit to Zaire," the Prime Minister said. "Were you in danger at any time, as was reported here?"

"No, we were not threatened at any time," Arsen said. "Our problem was that we could not find anybody who would talk to us."

"Cyprus is now the main political attraction," the Prime Minister said. "The problem they have is how to accommodate everybody. We could only get a room in a second class hotel since we called late. It will be a spectacle nobody wants to miss."

The conversation turned to the Balkans and the problems there that had to be resolved. Arsen explained his position and the Prime Minister was impressed.

"You think the Serbs will let you leave the country alive?"

"Serbs have not lost the courage and the wisdom of past glory," Arsen said. "Unfortunately they have never felt the personal freedom of a democracy. Medieval kings were hardy democratic. The Turkish occupation lasted more than 400 years and Turkish Sultans did not promote democratic principles even for their own people. The Serbian princes in the liberated territories were peasants and suppressed any opposition, often by cruel methods. Serbian kings were not any better, and they were cruel to other nationalities in Yugoslavia. Tito and his communists were Stalinists in their hearts, and only flirted a bit with democracy. Why should the present government be any different. The political schools in Serbia have not changed much over the centuries. We will not change the political thinking of the Serbs. We will prevent them from fighting while letting them feel independent. Audits and free elections should give them a taste of democracy. After centuries of oppression they detest democracy. "

The lunch given by the Prime Minister ended in time for Arsen and his party to fly to Bilbao. The Basque leaders, including the Provisional President, Eugenio Oñederra, were at the airport to welcome them.

The Municipal building in the City of Bilbao was set for the meeting.

"It is our pleasure to welcome you, Mr. Secretary," the President said. "The Basque people want to thank the World Government and you personally for making our independence possible."

"I am glad to be here," Arsen said.

After a photo session, the President and Arsen, followed by their associates, were led to a large meeting room which had a long conference table in the middle and simple chairs on both sides. The faded portrait of the Spanish King on the wall was covered with dust and looked rather squalid.

They took their places at the table.

"Mr. Secretary, I hope you understand the unresolved problems in this territory," the President said. "I--"

"I do understand," Arsen interjected. "I understand too well that there are problems, but not that you cannot resolve them. Tell me, what are your problems?"

"The Spanish government refuses to sign the accord," the President said. "They are asking us to give special status to Spanish subjects and their property. These people do not belong in this territory."

"Mr. President, you have just demonstrated what texts on ethnic issues constantly repeat," Arsen said firmly. "You see your freedom as something natural, something that Basques are entitled to. You just do not understand that minorities have rights in the Basque territory. You just don't understand the principles established by the World Government." Arsen stood up and walked to the head of the table, as if he were choking from lack of oxygen in the meeting room.

There was silence in the room before Arsen continued his tirade. "Let me explain to you what the Ethnic Department expects from you Basque leaders, before we will move a finger to help you on the way to your independence, and before we will recommend that the Assembly approve the accord between you and Spain. You must clearly state and assure the Assembly that you will immediately take all necessary steps to ensure the personal freedom of the minorities within Basque territory. These individuals will have the same rights as Basque citizens, their property will be protected and they will be given the choices of selling their property and moving out of Basque territory, remaining non-citizens, or accepting Basque citizenship. Let me assure you, Mr. President, that the Ethnic Department will monitor carefully your government's compliance of these obligations. We expect you to assure the Spanish government of your good intentions by signing the treaty that is before you."

After another pause Arsen finished by inviting the Basque leaders to the dinner party that was being given by the Spanish Government in Madrid that evening.

"The Spaniards have not invited us," the President said.

"I just invited you," Arsen said. "If you are not welcome, I will not attend either."

Obviously this was the end of the meeting.

A reception arranged by the Basque leaders was held in the adjoining room. Arsen changed the topic of conversation and behaved as if the meeting had been a most amicable event.

The dinner in Madrid, attended by the King and Queen, was a solemn event. The Spaniards restrained their feelings of loss and the Basques did not express their joy at gaining their independence.

Arsen's plane left Madrid for Belgrade after midnight.

CHAPTER THIRTY-NINE

SUNDAY, 28 DECEMBER 1997

T he plane landed at Surchin Airport near Belgrade at five in the morning. A quick wash, breakfast of scrambled eggs, toast and coffee, and a look at local newspapers was all one could do that early in the morning. It was almost funny to read the headlines in Serbian:

THE PRESIDENT TO MEET Sec. PANKOVICH TODAY
ZAIRE EPISODE IN VEIL OF MYSTERY -THREE PRESIDENTS LOST
THEIR JOBS
DELEGATIONS FROM CROATIA, BOSNIA AND HERZEGOVINA,
KOSOVO AND MONTENEGRO TO ARRIVE IN BELGRADE TODAY

"What is such a mystery about our experience in Zaire," Arsen wondered aloud. "We were ignored, all right, not threatened."

"We sent our reports from the plane after we left Zaire," Leon Meyer said. "We were not allowed to report anything while in Zaire. These people just received the news."

Stan Petkovic entered the plane. He reported on his impression from the last few days.

"I have talked to many people. They are cautious about saying anything. They are not offering anything, and you can feel that they are worried about their jobs. After the Zairean episode they are even more worried."

"Has anybody talked to the Albanian Kosovars recently?" Arsen asked. "Have you talked to them, Stan?"

"No, I have not," Stan Petkovic said.

"Why not?" Arsen asked. "They should have heard the good news and the bad news. The good news is that they will have their independence. The bad news is that they will have to make sure that the remaining

Serbs are happy. That should make them responsible not unhappy, but we all know that they will be unhappy. The animosity is mutual. If it were different there would be no need for the Ethnic Department."

Reporters continued talking with Stan Petkovic while Arsen was immersed in the newspapers.

"Should we go to the city?" Stan Petkovic interrupted Arsen's thoughts. "We have an hour or so to stroll on the Kalimegdan, if you wish."

"That is a great idea," Arsen said. "Do you think we would be able to escape our security men?"

"They will be around, but that is unimportant. We will walk and talk and enjoy the view of the Sava and Danube rivers."

"Let's go," Arsen said.

The ride through the city was quick, as the streets were deserted that early in the morning. Arsen relived almost half his life in that short ride. He remembered his daily rides to Zemun Airport close to the Sava River where he had had his first job as a physician; and the bridge which he had often crossed when visiting his friends; and the steep Balkanska Street that the driver chose after he made a wrong turn from the bridge; and Terazije, the square in the center of the city, which one always ended up passing, on the way to anywhere. The driver turned into the Boulevard of the Revolution to show them the Parliament building. A short distance from there and a left turn led them to Ive Lole Ribara Street, named after a hero of the Communist Revolution although it had honored Georges Clemenceau before that. The Parisians would probably divide the street and keep the old name for one half and rename the other half. They passed the four-story building marked 14, where Arsen had lived for many years - as a boy during the war and again when he was a medical student. The next street was Makedonska Street, which had once recognized another French President, Raymond Poincaré. Then they reached the square "by the horse" - it had a statue of King Milan on a horse. Vasina Street was next, and led to Kalimegdan, an old fortress and park.

"Here we get out and walk," Arsen said to the surprised Security Service agent. "Follow us if you must, although we are safe in this place. Nobody will even notice us." Arsen and Stan Petkovic walked into the park and headed for the opposite end to see the rivers. Security Service agents followed them at a respectable distance. They walked through the park into the fortress, passed the Military Museum and went to the wall, from which the view was magnificent.

The mouth of the Sava River into Danube and its small island were bathed in the morning sun, and the water appeared green. Novi Beograd was to the left with the buildings of the old federal government and the complex of apartment buildings close to it. The city of Zemun was visible in the distance.

Arsen remembered the sight of the concentration camp that had been just across the Sava River during World War II. Serbs were inmates of the camp before being shipped to their final destination - rarely Serbia; more often forced labor or extermination camps. A Serb was breathing in his body; he knew it, and he worried that his impartiality might be seriously threatened. Stan Petkovic broke the impasse of his conflicting thoughts.

"You must be reminiscing about the past," he said.

"That wasn't difficult to guess," Arsen said. "I have stood on this spot many a time and enjoyed the panorama and often the company of my friends or a girlfriend. Those were the days of the struggle to achieve something and to make my life worthwhile. Often, I wondered what was to happen to me in the coming years. My confidence in my ability to conquer the world was not great, although I always thought of myself as special, and better than others. I wanted to be a professor in a medical school, never thinking of the United States as the place to go. I wanted to discover the unknown and to write about it. I was a dreamer with a goal and determination. I have been a professor in several medical schools in the United States, but unfortunately I cannot say that my intellectual products have been of world shaking significance - or even recognized within the profession. Many of my dreams were in my mind many years ago as I leaned against this very wall and looked at this landscape."

Nothing more was said. They looked at the view in the distance, and their thoughts flew around the globe where they were trying to influence relations among people.

A Security Service agent interrupted them and politely suggested that the time of their appointment with the President of Yugoslavia was approaching. They walked back to Vasina Street where they had left their limousine, only to find reporters there with their cameras and microphones. Arsen and Stan Petkovic had nothing to say as they had not yet talked to the officials of the region. In the limousine they found fresh coffee in glass cups and cubes of *ratluk* and *halva*. This was refreshing. The limousine sped back to Terazije, to London intersection, along the Boulevard of Knez Milos to Mostar Square, and up to the 'White House,' where the President conducted official business.

The President's welcome appeared genuine as he wished them a successful mission in the region. He spoke in Serbian.

"We apologize for not welcoming you officially at the airport," the President said. "When you landed you were asleep, the welcoming party was told, and when they returned you were gone to the city. I thought that you wanted to explore your old city, which you have not visited in ten years. I did not want to interrupt your explorations."

The conversation was formal and without substance. The President led them to the meeting room. Arsen was impressed with the decor, the furniture, the marble floors, and the solemnity of the place, which had been built for Marshal Tito.

After they met the Prime Minister and several cabinet members they took their seats around the table and the President addressed the group.

"Mr. Secretary and Mr. Petkovic, it is our pleasure to have for once visiting foreign dignitaries whose native language is the same as ours. Let us hope that the common language will help us understand each other better."

Arsen replied in a similar phraseology, then he decided that he had had enough of these diplomatic niceties.

"I would like very much to hear the views of the Yugoslav Government regarding the ethnic situations that exist in the region."

The Prime Minister, Velibor Glishic, replied.

"As much as we would be prepared to offer suggestions and advice regarding territories that are not of interest to us, I will limit myself to the problems of Serbs and Serbian territories. There are no ethnic problems in the Serbian territories excluding Kosovo and Vojvodina. Our position on Kosovo is well known. We feel, and the Serbian people and most of the political parties feel, that Kosovo is Serbian territory, although today Serbs represent only up to twenty percent of the population. We are willing to grant autonomy to the Albanians, as long as they recognize Kosovo as part of Serbia. We cannot yield more than that.

"More recently, problems have been developing in Vojvodina where the Hungarian minority has been restless. We think that is a prelude to a demand on their part for partition from Serbia and Yugoslavia. Vojvodina is Serbian territory and Serbs are the majority. We will start talks with the minorities in the near future.

"In Bosnia, Serbs want to be united with Serbia as a separate republic. We see no problems with that. Finally, Montenegro is talking separation. We feel that would be a mistake since the two nations are in many ways identical. They should have, and they do have, as much autonomy as they want. If they decide to separate, let it be, the sin will be on their souls."

The Prime Minister then explained in detail the official view of the situation and the reasons for that view. Arsen listened attentively. He had a deep understanding of the feelings of these men. His soul was their soul, and if he had been representing Serbia, he would have said the same. But, Arsen's mind was set up to do the job entrusted to him, a job that demanded fairness to all sides.

"You did not mention Sandzak at all," Arsen said. "They are a small group but they must have some ideas of what they want."

"They are thinking about union with Muslim Bosnia, but they are not saying much," the Prime Minister replied with some resignation in his voice, as if he were trying to say 'just another group that wants Serbian territory.'

"They are Muslims and the first neighbors of Bosnian Muslims," Arsen said. "Does that surprise you?"

"Nothing surprises me any more in this damned country," the Prime Minister said angrily. "In the case of Sandzak the territory of the Republika Srpska is interposed between Sandzak and Muslim Bosnia."

Arsen knew exactly how the Prime Minister felt. A persecution complex was a typical ethnic reaction to losing the initiative, while forgetting the needs of a small fish in the same ethnic pond.

"Nobody has mentioned Krajina in Croatia where the Serbs were a majority, like the Albanians in Kosovo, until they were expelled - or should we call it ethnically cleansed - in the last days of the Bosnian war." The Prime Minister was indignant. He continued his diatribe by talking about the killing of Krajina Serbs and the plight of those who escaped to Bosnia and Slavonia and Serbia.

"I am glad you mentioned Krajina," Arsen said. "We will have to discuss this area with the Croatians. I am sure they have something to say about it."

"Sure they have," the Prime Minister said. "They will tell you the Serbs ran away and were not expelled, and why they should not return. We talked to them, we talked to the Europeans, we talked to Americans, and nobody wanted to listen. Everybody considers the issue a *fait accompli*. Is that true Mr. Secretary?"

"In the minds of the members of the Ethnic Department nothing is final, even decisions made by the Department," Arsen said. "Situations change and arguments change and people change. The dynamic of the situation is what counts. Take for instance Vojvodina. That is a Serb territory and the Serbs are in the majority. The Hungarians are a strong minority. If a referendum on autonomy were held today, I am almost sure the Serbs would vote for no change and the Hungarians would vote for autonomy. There would be no reasons to change anything. However, if the people voted for autonomy it would have to be established. Separation does not look likely today."

"We would not look on a referendum in Vojvodina very favorably," the Prime Minister said.

"I know that," Arsen said. "I wish you had started talks with the people in Vojvodina. You would have the situation in hand. It would be good to have the problems of schools resolved. Have you talked to the Hungarians?"

"Yes, we have talked to them from time to time," the Prime Minister replied with some annoyance in his voice and attitude.

"I assume nothing has been accomplished so far?" Arsen asked.

"Not much," the Prime Minister said. "They don't want to talk constructively."

"It is on my agenda to talk to the Vojvodinians, before we recommend anything to you or to them," Arsen said firmly.

"We wonder if there will be any internal, intrastate rights left to the governments?" asked the Yugoslavian President. "Where does this imposition end?"

"I understand your concerns very well, as a Serb - you may say a former Serb - and as the Secretary of the Ethnic Department." Arsen wanted to diminish the blow in explaining the U.N. principles. "As a Serb my main concern would be the safety of the population and the possibility of outside aggression; as the Secretary I will make sure nobody gets hurt. We have a mandate to resolve ethnic problems. I can assure you we will resolve them peacefully. In principle, every ethnic group has the right to the land it inhabits as a majority, for as long as it is the majority. That is not negotiable. We will make sure that voting in each territory is free. We will not interfere with the elective system or with the decisions of the Supreme Court. Of course, the World Military will ensure that the borders that are agreed upon are respected. If negotiations fail, a plebiscite or a referendum will decide the issues."

"Will that be applicable to every country in the world?" the Yugoslavian President asked.

"Yes, as long as there is a request from a legitimate ethnic group," Arsen answered.

"In Europe and America?" the Yugoslavian President insisted.

"Yes," Arsen said. "We just arranged for the Basques to negotiate their independence from Spain and France. Independence is not an issue any more; there are details that have to be negotiated."

There was a pause before Arsen continued.

"You probably wonder about the United States, Canada, China, Russia, Israel - the countries often criticized as privileged major powers. Let me assure you that these principles established by the World Government are applicable to all countries."

That was obviously a final statement.

The Yugoslavian President invited them to a private lunch, and it was impossible to decline. Conversation turned to the past, and particularly to the years after World War II. Arsen was the oldest in the group, although the Yugoslavian President was close to sixty-three. They looked at the history of the period from different angles, and from different political camps, but there was no animosity among them and no hesitation in expressing their views. Arsen enjoyed the conversation with these intelligent people.

It was getting late, and Arsen was expected at the home of an old friend. He arrived a few minutes late. Four couples were waiting to see him. Their last meeting had been in '89.

These people wanted to hear Arsen's opinions and ideas about the uncertain future and to be assured that everything would turn out for the best. Arsen could not tell them what they wanted to hear.

"I wish I could tell you that the catastrophe will be avoided but I cannot, even though the work to prevent it is under way. Space ships will be launched in about three years with people on board as a contingency plan in case the Earth is hit. They will return if the Earth is not completely destroyed, otherwise, they will be doomed to space. My mission is to stabilize relations among the peoples of the world and to select the individuals who will be on board these space ships. Gen. Shagov worries about space."

"Is he really as brilliant as he is said to be by the media?" Djordje Pribicevic, an architect, asked.

"You have to know the man to appreciate his talents," Arsen said.

"There were many speculations about your refusing to join his administration," Vlajko Petrovic said. "What was that all about?"

"One reason was that Kravchenko was designated for the job of ethnic chief. I did not want to compete for the job. Second, at that time I was interested only in the Balkans and I did not want to get involved with the rest of the world. Rama Chand persuaded me to take the job after Kravchenko died. There is an interesting side story. Kravchenko's close associate in the ethnic division of the Soviet counter-intelligence, Ivo Stipich, is a Croat and I met him in Banja Luka in 1947." Arsen told them about his meeting with Ivo Stipich in New York and Ivo's mysterious devotion to him. "I have no idea how Ivo became indebted to me. Recently, I made him chief of the Ethnic Office in Zagreb."

"That is a bizarre story," Vlajko Petrovic said.

Food and drinks were served, and everyone relaxed. Conversation turned to their life in Banja Luka when they were students. There was some nostalgia in their stories about their carefree life. Banja Luka was a small city after the war, which had a population of about fifty - sixty thousands. Although the Serbs were in the majority, almost half the population was made up of Croats and Muslims. They talked of friends and people they knew who had made the news at one time or another. They even talked of generational casualties, as the attrition process had started with the deaths of three close friends - Dragoljub Popovic and his fatalistic girlfriend, and of Vitomir Vranjic. Arsen thought of them from the days before he had left the country. Dragoljub had been his classmate in Banja Luka.

The two of them had spent innumerable hours together in high school and during summer and winter breaks afterwards. They had ambitiously worked and planned for a meaningful future. Dragoljub was smarter and had broader interests. He had talked to Arsen about his hero philosophers Hegel, Schopenhauer, and Nietzsche, and the writers he admired, particularly Dostoevsky and Kafka but also many others.

Arsen had studied hard and had tried to remember long formulae in his Chemistry courses or endless names of bones and muscles and pathways in the human brain in Anatomy and later, as his studies of Medicine progressed, definitions of symptoms and symptoms of diseases and their treatment. Dragoljub had hardly ever studied during these holiday and summer breaks. Arsen had sometimes thought Dragoljub was actually communicating with his heroes in the magical heights of their everlasting thoughts. His girl friend had been passionately in love with him but Dragoljub's reciprocation had been limited by his many interests. She had left him for another man in desperation and depression. Dragoljub had never married.

Vitomir had also been a smart and witty man though quiet and withdrawn. He had had no plans for the future and had felt no hurry to reach anything. His studies of Russian Literature had been a game to get a diploma and a job. His life had been the girl who had left him for another man and had broken his heart and his desire to do anything but to read. He had died a respected high schoolteacher with encyclopedic knowledge of literature which he shared with nobody. While one man had given Arsen every reason to try to reach heights of achievements, the other had constantly reminded him of the insignificance of being very smart. Now they were gone, having left behind, each in his own way, a rich, entirely opposite spectrum of ideas which made a balance in Arsen's mind and soul. They had solved their problems, Arsen sadly concluded. And he felt that a part of his soul had died with them. He knew that their influence on him had been profound, and had lasted all his adult life; he had tried to reach the height of their intellect, and had never succeeded.

"What will the map of the Balkans look like after you are finished with your work?" the surgeon, Mladen Drenovac, interrupted Arsen's rumination.

"I would rather talk about something else," Arsen said. "You may not like the shape of the map. Still, just think of the basic human right - the right to be free. I always quote Gen. Shagov's statement in his speech before the U.N. Assembly: 'If we have to die, I will insist that we all die as human beings, as each one of us deserves an equal and decent and respected life to the end.' If you go by that definition, you will know how the map of the world will look, not only the map of the Balkans."

"What is freedom, and which one?" Mladen Drenovac asked.

"I know what you are asking, and I agree that there is more than one definition of freedom," Arsen replied. "You were asking about economic dependence, which can limit effectively the freedom of a nation. The World Government and the U.N. Assembly are working on that too. My definition is a very basic one and concerns the freedom of an ethnic group. Without such a freedom, discussion of other types is useless."

"Isn't democracy supposed to take care of all these freedoms?" Djordje Pribicevic asked.

"In democracy, ethnic groups have the right to secede and form their own independent states. There are but a few examples of peaceful settlement, like the Czechs letting the Slovaks secede and form their own state. The Soviet Republics are now independent states, and Gorbachev, who helped them on that road, lost his job. Yeltsin started the war in Chechnya and thousands on both sides died in vain. Why does Russia need Chechnya? I only hear about history and the Russian people and security - phraseology that explains nothing. It is the land the Russians want, and they wouldn't mind if the Chechnyans disappeared. Waiting for democracy to reign in the entire world would take millennia. Even the democratic states often ignore legitimate calls for secession when their interests do not coincide. Look at what happened in Kosovo. Albanian Kosovars wanted independence and the world told them they could not have it. Why?"

"Are you telling us we should give our territory to the Shiptars?" Djordje Pribicevic called the Albanians Shiptars as most Serbs did. "So many of them are in our territory illegally."

"How do you suggest we resolve the problem?" Arsen asked. "Expel the Shiptars to Albania or wherever they want to go, or kill them, or assimilate them?"

"They should behave like citizens, not enemies."

"What if they consider the Serbs their enemies?" Arsen asked. "Do you think the Serbs love the Shiptars?"

"They live in our territory," Djordje Pribicevic said.

"What happened to the Serbs in Kosovo?"

"The Shiptars have been intimidating and killing them over the years and many of them have emigrated," Djordje Pribicevic said angrily. "During Tito's time they were favored and they were enticed to migrate to Kosovo from Albania. The Albanian language was promoted in schools and at work. That was not right. After all, Kosovo is the cradle of Serbian civilization."

Arsen decided there was no point in continuing the conversation about Kosovo, which was heating up because his ideas were diametrically opposed to those of his old friends. He had to survive the next few days, he thought. The conversation was in quiet waters again.

Once in the hotel Arsen worked on his talk for the Academy of Sciences which was scheduled for the following evening.

CHAPTER FORTY

MONDAY, 29 DECEMBER 1997

T he local media were not at all sympathetic to Arsen's positions in conversations with Serbian government officials and that was obvious from the headlines.

Sec. PANKOVICH INSENSITIVE TO DESIRES OF SERBIAN PEOPLE
KOSOVO: LOSS OF CRADLE OF SERBIAN CIVILIZATION
HAVE WE BEEN BETRAYED BY OUR OWN

Arsen did not want to read any further. Obviously, everybody had expected him to find a way to keep Kosovo a Serbian province. That was just not possible, Arsen concluded, his determination to do the right thing set even harder in cement than it had been.

The day was to be a litany of presentations from various ethnic groups. Arsen knew exactly what he would hear from the delegates. He would have to explain the principles that guided the decisions of the U.N.

Arsen was driven to the offices of the Serbian President, who was at hand at the start of the meeting.

The meeting started on time. Ivo Stipich introduced the Croatian delegation and took his place next to Arsen. Three areas of interest were discussed.

Croatian Krajina was a major problem to the Serbs, who had been expelled *en masse* in 1995 and had not been allowed to return; the few who had gone back had found their homes burned or uninhabitable. The Croatian position was that the Serbs had not been expelled, they had escaped when the Croatian Army advanced into the province. There was some truth in that, although Serbs were killed and forced to leave. The proposal was for the Croatian Government to allow the Serbs to return and create an autonomous province, and to guarantee their well being. That would be supervised by the World Government.

The Croats in the territory of Bosnia and Herzegovina where they were in the majority wanted a union with the Croatian State. The situation was straightforward: the Croats had the right to hold a plebiscite. The Muslims would be allowed to return. Property issues would be negotiated, as both sides were liable.

A similar situation existed in Slavonia, but was complicated by demolition and destruction that had been carried out by the Yugoslavian Army. The territory had a Croatian majority and a sizable Serbian population. The Croats agreed to accept the Serbs who wanted to return, and treat them well. Economic issues had to be negotiated between the two governments.

Ivo Stipich had arranged a private lunch for the Croatian Prime Minister, Anton Lopasic, and Arsen in a nearby restaurant. The atmosphere became relaxed almost as soon as the door of the conference room closed behind them.

The Prime Minister was a tall, slender man, with an intelligent, refined face. He had a thin, prominent nose, a high forehead, and questioning, deep-seated eyes.

"You know, Mr. Secretary, this deal you made today would not have been possible without this celestial body threatening everybody," Anton Lopasic said. "We like the deals in Bosnia and Croatia, but the Krajina deal stinks. Krajina is a Croatian territory and we should be allowed to keep it as is."

"You will keep it as an autonomous province, and you will take good care of the Serbs," Arsen said.

"Damned Serbs, they always win in the end," the Prime Minister said. "I am very interested to see how you are going to handle the Serbs."

"You must be convinced that I am prejudiced because I am a Serb," Arsen said. "How very wrong you are. We fought to have the general principles and rules established even before the whole idea of the World Government was accepted. And the principles were clearly stated by Gen. Shagov in his speech, and by President Chand. The Assembly recognized ethnic problems, and the Ethnic Department was approved and organized. We intend to insist on the principles. Do you want me to tell you what they are?"

"Of course not, I know them very well, and disagree with them. Are you going to audit all of us? Why do you insist on that?"

"That is a gimmick to convince the people, who always talk of corruption, that their government is clean and honest. There will be a few victims along the way. That cannot be avoided, and I will not bleed for those caught with dirty hands."

"I thought you wanted to make a better world as an idealist, and you are using gimmicks," the Prime Minister said.

"It depends how you interpret the facts," Arsen said. "People need facts that they can believe. I intend to give them the facts. They can use them or ignore them. I will not complain."

"What will happen to the so called war criminals?" the Prime Minister asked.

"They are in the Law Machine, and that is the end of it, although everybody is unhappy in their countries," Arsen said. "Many things have happened that will never be explained if we push to punish the guilty. I will propose to the Assembly the idea of a truth and reconciliation commission, like South Africa had. That is the most fascinating idea. Mandela was in jail for 27 years, then, after he was released and became the President, he gave amnesty to all his enemies, with a catch: they had to tell the truth before the Commission. My idea is that people would have the right to ask questions of the leaders of the world, any leader from any country. Such a subpoena could not be refused. There would be shows all over the world."

"You mean let all these men go free?" the Prime Minister asked, surprised.

"That is what I mean," Arsen said. "Some very hard questions will have to be answered."

"By whom?" asked the Prime Minister.

"By those who have been blamed for certain events, and nobody dared to ask questions. Like, what really happened in Srebrenica in Bosnia? Who was involved in the decision to invade Krajina? Who bombed the market and the street in Sarajevo, where people were waiting in line to buy bread?"

"You may find out that such a Commission would fail in Serbia or Croatia," the Prime Minister said. "This is the Balkans not South Africa. Nobody will take it seriously. People will lie to deflect blame onto someone else, often someone who is dead."

"You may be right," Arsen said. "However, if properly run the Commission may force people to admit the truth rather than face charges for lying and conviction for the crimes. This would be the decision between freedom and prison. I like the idea very much. I would not mind if you took over the Commission for the former Yugoslavia, would you?"

"Something is wrong here," the Prime Minister said. "You mean you, you a Serb, would trust a Croat to run this Commission?"

"I would trust you," Arsen said. "Why not? You are an intelligent person. The proceedings will be public, and you will be scrutinized by the media and by everybody with any interest in the proceedings. Why don't you take the job if the Assembly approves the principle?"

"That would certainly change my life," the Prime Minister said. "I would have to resign my present job."

"This would be a more important and interesting job," Ivo Stipich said, after silently sitting and listening to the whole discussion. "You would accomplish something. You could write about this experience. It probably would not hurt your political ambitions, if any are left after your present job. I would not mind helping if you wanted."

"You are pushing me too hard," the Prime Minister said with some force. "I haven't had a chance to think about it. I will decide when I get an official offer."

"That is fair enough. I will probably see you again in Nicosia. Are you coming?"

"I will be there," the Prime Minister said. "The world leaders celebrating the arrival of the new year in Nicosia is another interesting idea. I will sleep in our Embassy; not a single hotel room was available in Nicosia."

Arsen looked at his watch. It was close to one o'clock.

"I will be in touch about the Commission," Arsen said. "I am not sure I will succeed in selling it to President Chand and the Assembly."

"I wish you would find time to visit Zagreb, and I mean it," the Prime Minister said. "I will make it worthwhile."

"I will come to Zagreb after the Commission starts its proceedings. Now I must talk to the Kosovars."

The Albanian Kosovo delegation had five members headed by the President of the Provincial government, which was not recognized by the government of Serbia. Arsen insisted that they represent Kosovo, and he also arranged to meet separately with the Serbian minority delegation.

The Kosovars were well prepared to argue their case for independence. The President, Adem Adami, presented their case eloquently. After he finished his presentation there was a pause. Arsen poured a cup of coffee for himself and took his place.

The Albanian President broke the silence.

"Mr. Secretary, do you have any comments to make?"

"No, I don't. Your presentation was quite clear, and your demands justified."

"What do we do next?"

"We should discuss what to do with the Serbs who live in Kosovo," Arsen said. "Do you have any ideas?"

"That is a problem, of course," Adem Adami said.

"I am sure you are familiar with the principles of the U.N. regarding ethnic problems," Arsen said. "Your position is clear and you will get a chance to vote in a plebiscite if one is necessary. The remaining Serbs are the problem. By our criteria, if you win your independence, you will have voted for the protection of the Serb population in Kosovo. Your incentive is your independence. If you fail to protect the Serbs who stay, Kosovo will revert to being a Serbian protectorate. I hope I am making it clear that the price of independence is rather high. Furthermore, I expect your delegation and the Serbian delegation from Kosovo to meet soon and negotiate an agreement that will cover the relations of the two ethnic groups. I will explain this to the Serbian delegation.

"Oh, one last thing," Arsen said with some hesitation in his voice. "Predominantly Serbian parts of Kosovo, particularly if adjoining Serbia, may vote to join Serbia. I am sure you understand that."

They did not.

They discussed some practical problems that often arose in a mixed population. The Albanians complained that the Serbs were not willing to cooperate, and Arsen explained that they had not cooperated with the Serbian Government either.

"Problems with ethnic groups are always the same," Arsen said. "A group first fights for independence by all means. They are called criminals, terrorists, and what not. Then they win their independence. These same leaders now use the same language and the same tactics to fight smaller ethnic groups. I hope the Albanians will not fall into the same trap after they win their independence. Mandela is right, you must offer a hand to your enemies."

Arsen suggested they organize a dinner for the representatives of both sides as a gesture of good will. The enthusiasm for the idea was not overwhelming.

Three men represented the Serbs from Kosovo. One delegate was an Orthodox Bishop, Vladika Zetski Nicifor. The second man was an official in the local government. The third man represented the main Serbian political party. They were not sure what they wanted to accomplish at this meeting, but they knew they did not want the Albanian Kosovars to get independence.

"What is your proposal for solving the Kosovo problem?" Arsen asked them. The local official, Dragan Perisic, had obviously been chosen as the speaker. He explained the problems facing the Serbs in the province, the aggressive attitude of the Albanian Kosovars and a tendency of many Serbs to leave the territory. He also said there were rumors that the Albanian Kosovars would get their independence from Serbia.

"That will be our end, something like Krajina in Croatia," he said. "How long are Serbs going to be pushed out of their own lands? We have been in Kosovo since the 13th century, and now we will finally be driven out. What is going to happen to us? Do you know?"

Arsen was shaken by the emotional statements and questions from this man. He felt the desperation and frustration of Serbian Kosovars with a prospect that the other side would not respect the agreement.

"What do you suggest we do with Albanians who live in Kosovo?" Arsen asked. "We cannot kill or expel almost two million people, and they don't want to leave voluntarily. Do you think Kosovo can be divided?"

"That will not be possible," Dragan Perisic said. "The only solution we could accept is to retain Kosovo in Serbia so that we can be protected by the Serbian Police. We do not trust the Albanians. Sooner or later they will kill us or expel us. "

"The World Government will organize a plebiscite in Kosovo, and you know that the Albanians are in the majority. I cannot change the principles that were accepted by the Assembly. However, the Albanians will lose their independence, and their status will revert to being a Serbian protectorate if they fail in protecting your rights. I think that is what is going to happen in Kosovo. In my opinion, there will be less trouble when Albanians are under pressure to take good care of you instead of the Serbian Police using force to keep the Albanians in check. You will have to write down what you expect from the Albanians in exchange for their independence."

"You expect us to write all that down?" Dragan Perisic asked.

"Yes," Arsen said. He thought there was a chance that the Serbs would accept Albanian independence in exchange for security and equal rights.

Stan Petkovic took over the meeting, as it was getting late and Arsen wanted to go to the hotel to refresh himself and to go over his lecture for the evening.

At seven o'clock Arsen and Stan Petkovic arrived at the Academy of Sciences. As they entered the reception area, they found that many people had already arrived and were talking in small groups. Stan Petkovic found the President of the Academy, Prof. Stanimir Cvejic, and introduced Arsen to him. Conversation turned to the problems Arsen had recently had in Zaire. Other members joined the conversation.

"It seems the Zairean problems may recur in other parts of the world," the Academy President said. "Why is the World Government pushing so hard to interfere in the ethnic problems of the world? These things get resolved eventually."

"Resolution of these problems in the bloody century, as this century will be remembered in the history books, has cost sixty - seventy millions lives, and the problems have not been resolved yet. You should know what has been happening, and is still going on, in this country. Ethnic problems do not get resolved by themselves, they have to be negotiated according to established principles - you could say by one principle: the right of every ethnic group to a piece of land of its own under the sun, as a Native American said recently. Nobody wants such a solution."

"You have to use force to accomplish that," someone from the group said. "Like in Zaire."

"You used force to put down the revolt in Kosovo," Arsen replied.

"You used force to put down the revolt of the Indians in the States," the same man said.

"That is the point I was trying to make," Arsen said. "Why do we aggravate and frustrate people to the point of violence, and then use violence to put down their revolt? Why don't we decide what is right and apply it practically, not just discuss it in highly sophisticated sessions of Academies and Learned Societies? We feel that a man has the right to be free. The smallest unit of collective freedom you can find is an ethnic group. Therefore, we will give freedom to ethnic groups. That is the best we can do today.

"There will come a time when individuals will be free for themselves, in a classless form of living, and at that time we will be able to pronounce that every individual has total freedom. Yes that will be a sort-of communist man. You notice I am avoiding the word society because there will be no need for a society as humans will live lives independently of anybody on Earth or in the Universe. They will communicate with other humans any way they want, but there will be no social relations of today's magnitude and troublesomeness. And such a free human will need no one for his existence, for his identity, for his progeny, or for his intellectual experience."

"A psychopath?" someone asked.

"No, a free human at the end of history," Arsen said. "In contradistinction to communism, there will be no need for a proletarian dictatorship led by communists and no bloodletting to stay in power."

Emotions were rising,

"To get back to Zaire," Prof. Cvejic said, with the intention of cooling down the group. "Why was force needed?"

"The official Zaire, Rwanda and Burundi refused to talk. Our own security was in question. It was a military decision. I am not quite sure what their reasons were for refusing to talk."

Dinner was served: simple onion soup, pita bread with shishkebab, and apple strudel. Very light white wine was served. Conversations were brisk and the noise level high, but it was pleasant to be in the company of bright people.

The Academy President introduced Arsen with the usual phrases and let him adjust the microphone.

"Mr. President and Members of the Academy:

"If someone had told me many years ago, when I was a medical student in this city, that I would be invited to speak before this Academy, I would have questioned his sanity. Well, here I am in my old city, and before this Academy, to tell you my story.

"At the early age of fourteen I fought for this country, maybe on the wrong side, perhaps on the right side, but I fought. Being a Chetnik was not very popular even in Serbia during World War II, when Chetniks were called throat cutters and *gibanichari*, because of their murderous and bullying nature. Let me skip the criticism of a movement well known to you.

"My fighting experience was ended by my capture in December of 1944 by the Communist Army somewhere outside Tuzla. Before we were captured our preoccupation was about who our captors would be: a Serbian or a Muslim brigade. There were rumors that Muslim Brigades did not spare captured Serbs. We surrendered enthusiastically to a Serbian brigade. I survived prison and typhus and returned to Belgrade in April of 1945.

"My idea of a Serbian nation was developed in a home and family of strongly nationalistic beliefs and under the impressions of genocide in my hometown of Banja Luka in 1941. My idea of the Serbs was that they were an honorable people, proud of their heritage, who had suffered under the Turks for over four hundred years and had fought for their freedom and won it.

"My opinion of other nationalities could not be described in superlatives.

"Over the years, and particularly since I retired and during my intensive study of global ethnic problems, my understanding of historical events in the former Yugoslavia has radically changed. It has become obvious to me that every event has a logical explanation as a reaction to another event. This is quite apparent not only in Serbian or Yugoslavian history, but in the history of all nations.

"What is history but the constant rivalry between tribes with the advantage of a bigger tribe over a smaller one, a richer over a poorer one, and a better educated over an ignorant one. Political scientists call it power politics. Although ethnic groups have internal fights they are not intent on destroying and annihilating themselves. This cannot be said in relations among ethnic groups. I am still looking for two ethnic groups that never in their history tried to destroy each other, never fought for dominance, never accused the other of inferiority and dishonesty, never sought to grab the other's land.

"This is my view of history. Hegelian reliance on the formation of libertarian states as the end of history ignores ethnicity and the developing sciences. States have often been formed by the merger of a variety of ethnic groups. In such states the majority ethnic groups had a tendency to hold power, though there were other advantages that delivered power to some ethnic groups, as happened for example in Rwanda.

"The creation of states has not resolved animosities and clashes along ethnic lines. An ethnic state provided maximal protection to its own group members. Therefrom comes the urge for ethnic cleansing to achieve that purity. Though the term has recently been popularized by the media, the process of achieving purity has existed since the beginning of history. In this century there are endless examples. No ethnically mixed state has escaped some form of cleansing. Segregation is just another form of cleansing.

"Two facts are also well known about relations between ethnic groups: liberators do not grant liberty to their minorities, and ethnic groups often take positions contrary to their feelings if these positions are expedient to their cause. Both mechanisms were operative in Yugoslavia, before she was formed and after she fell apart.

"Yugoslavia was formed because that was convenient to all parties. Serbs saw it as an opportunity to unite all Serbian territories and gain importance by leading, as the majority, all ethnic groups that joined the union. Croats and Slovenians found the idea of union convenient to avoid the pressure of the Austrians and Italians and to belong to the state that had just won the war in 1918.

"The Muslims of Bosnia and Sandzak and Kosovo were not asked for their opinions. The Muslims had been the ruling elite and oppressors for centuries, and Albanians in Kosovo happened to be on the ancient Serbian territory. The Montenegrans were willing to join as they felt close to the Serbian majority, and the Macedonians were the prize to Serbia in victory.

"Therefore, the Serbs were among the victors of the war and they did a favor to others by letting them join the union, which was then led by the Serbian elite and the Royal Family. And Serbs ruled the country and gave little thought to the feelings of other ethnic groups. The reactions against the Serbian attitude were inevitable: the other ethnic groups wanted significant autonomy and even separation. These calls were completely ignored.

"In 1941 Yugoslavia was fragmented and parts were given to neighbors and to internal enemies. All of Croatia and Bosnia and Herzegovina, as well as Slavonia and Srem to Zemun, just across the Sava River from Belgrade, became the Independent State of Croatia. The Italians took parts of Dalmatia. Slovenia and Serbia were occupied by the Germans. The Hungarians grabbed territories north of the Danube, and the Bulgarians helped themselves to Macedonia. The facts of genocide and ethnic cleansing of Serbs are well known to you.

Underground and guerilla warfare were waged against the Nazis. Who contributed what to the Communists' victory is immaterial since the eventual organization of Yugoslavia was decided by Tito and company. Tito is commonly credited for preventing clashes among ethnic groups, particularly Serbs and Croats, after the war and for maintaining ethnic peace. In reality the truce and moratorium were enforced by political will and Tito's personal supervision, and by police enforcement of 'brotherhood and unity' by merciless persecution and detention of dissidents. Tito allowed the preservation and use of native languages by ethnic groups, like the Albanians in Kosovo, the Slovenians in Slovenia, and the Hungarians in Vojvodina, and promoted antireligious policies.

"Six republics and two autonomous regions within Serbia followed ethnic borders; in Bosnia and Herzegovina, logical integration of ethnic Serbs and Croats into republics of Serbia and Croatia was not politically expedient.

Though superficially brotherhood and unity existed, the ethnic groups mixed with each other mainly by inevitable intermarriages, while ethnicity prevented social and cultural assimilation. Serbs and Croats, and Muslims, did not forget their origins and values, and that was what had caused the recent ethnic wars.

"Tito frequently receives credit for the creation of apparent ethnic harmony, but it was not the creation of his own emotional and philosophical stance. He was, and always remained, the apprentice of Stalin and a student of Marx and Lenin. Lenin and Stalin faced the same problem of nationalities in the vast territory that was to become a single entity. They knew that for communism to win, they had to give the nationalities the appearance of national autonomy in exchange for the party line loyalty of the regional elites. They were more cruel than Tito, and more persistently dogmatic. They were satisfied with appearance without much substance.

When taking over the power in Yugoslavia, Tito knew the methods for dealing with nationality problems and as a real player of the communist game, he knew the gambit of ethnicity, but like the Soviet Bolsheviks he believed that the advantages and the advances of the communist state would eventually erase the nationality problem. In Russia, as in Yugoslavia, the nationalities' problems led to disintegration of the Soviet state, which avoided - except in a few places like Chechnya or Nagorno - bloody ethnic wars.

"Gorbachev is blamed for allowing partition of ethnic republics. No praise is heard for his visionary accomplishments and their result - no civil wars. In Yugoslavia, Tito's political followers waged the bloodiest civil wars over nationality problems, without the advantage of a visionary leader, and under the lethargic and unimaginative eyes of the European and American leaders - who themselves learned little, if anything, from the Soviet example.

"Tito might have been a beneficial ethnic catalyst for a period of Yugoslavian history. Praise for his role in the promotion of the brotherhood and unity among ethnic groups is the irony of historical misinterpretation.

"The actual events are well known to you.

"Now here we are discussing what has happened and wondering about the future of this land. Do you need to be told what should be apparent to you if it could come from your heads, not from your hearts and your souls? I do not deny the importance of Serbian lands to the psyche of a Serb, who, as a good nationalist, has had Kosovo in his blood since birth. But that has been and is an illusion nourished by the myth of Prince Lazar, of Bogdan Jugovic and his nine sons who died in Kosovo Battle, of Milos Obilic who penetrated the tent of Sultan Bajazit and wounded him mortally, and of Prince Marko who fought Turks afterwards; and of the never forgotten traitor Vuk Brankovic. All that happened in the fourteenth century at and around Kosovo. That is in the Serbian blood and in the Serbian soul. That cannot be erased or denied.

"A strange fact is that a unit of Albanians fought with Serbs in the battle of Kosovo, before they converted to Islam.

"On the other hand, what happened with Serbs in Kosovo? Where are they? Pushed out by Muslim Albanian intruders who were the Ottoman elite in Kosovo and protected by Ottoman forces? It is probable that some Serbs converted to Islam on these outskirts of Serbia for reasons of expediency. Also, the Turks occupied Serbia but could not change the Serbs or brake them. And while Serbia was being liberated at the beginning of the last century, Kosovo remained under Turkish rule.

"At the Berlin Congress, in 1878, Bismarck and the company gave more territory to Serbia, which then became the Kingdom, but returned Macedonia and Kosovo to Ottoman. There were no riots in Serbia and no calls for military action for liberation of Kosovo although an attempt by Serbian troops during the war of 1878 to liberate part of the territory was thwarted by Austria. The Serbs in Kosovo had to do it on their own, the same as the Serbs in Croatia and Bosnia, which were under Austro-Hungarian rule. At present, regardless of the means by which it was accomplished, Albanians are in an overwhelming majority in Kosovo. For brevity I call them Albanians although they are really Albanian Kosovars as opposed to Serbian Kosovars.

"How do we solve this problem? It would be a simple solution to expel from Kosovo either all Albanians or all Serbs by simple ethnic cleansing. Or by killing one or the other group. The answer is obvious for these two solutions. The Albanians could get autonomy within Yugoslavia or Serbia, so that the Serbs could feel the territory is theirs, and hope that something would happen to the Albanians and that they would disappear from Kosovo. Would they really be free under Serbian watchful eyes? Would they somehow disappear? Of course not. Yet, they would constantly be a thorn in the Serbian's side. The problem is identical in Bosnia where the

Muslims are against Serbian separation and union with Serbia. If the Serbs disappeared one day, the Muslims must reason, all of Bosnia would become Muslim.

"That is wishful thinking; the Albanians and the Bosnian Serbs will not disappear. Unfortunately, in Croatian Krajina the Serbian majority was ethnically cleansed within a week when they were expelled by the Croats during the Bosnian war. Why should constant confrontations and killings continue in Kosovo and in Bosnia? Why should these people be prevented from doing what they want?"

"There is a catch. What would happen to Serbs in an independent Kosovo? The World Government is willing to hold a plebiscite to determine which part should be independent and which would remain part of Serbia.

"It is my--"

Arsen's presentation was interrupted by three heavily armed men who broke into the meeting room. Their leader shouted, "Pankovich, you son of a bitch. I fuck your sweet mother. Go to hell. You will not sell Kosovo. You will be dead."

As he started shouting, he and his men emptied their machine guns in the direction of the President's table and the lectern.

Arsen had realized there would be shooting as the three men were entering the meeting room. He had immediately dropped to the floor and crawled behind the curtain at one of the windows. President Cvejic was hit several times, and he was lying on the floor bleeding from his arm and thigh. Stan Petkovic, who had been sitting next to the President, was hit too. Two Academy members who had been at the adjacent table had also been hit. Arsen escaped the bullets. The rest of the audience ducked under the tables.

Security Service agents and a security guard attacked the intruders, who had moved to the adjoining room after they emptied their machine guns. In the shooting that ensued, the security guard and a Security Service agent were killed along with one of the gunmen. Two wounded gunmen were subdued and arrested. The Serbian Police arrived minutes after the shooting started and an ambulance soon after them.

Arsen joined physicians from the audience in evaluating the injured people. The Academy President had been hit in the chest and abdomen, and in the arm and thigh, and he could not move his legs; his condition was stable and it appeared that his heart and blood vessels were not seriously injured. Stan Petkovic had been shot in the right arm and his humerus was obviously fractured; the radial nerve in the arm was damaged, as he had a wrist drop. The other two men had chest and abdominal injuries. Nobody from the audience had been hit, and everybody was thankful for that.

The entire incident had been taped by the camera crews who were recording Arsen's speech. Reporters got everything they could with their cameras and video equipment. Arsen made a statement in which he indicated that he had been the target, and he described what had happened. The Prime Minister arrived on the scene and offered to drive Arsen to his hotel. Instead, Arsen went to the hospital with Stan Petkovic to make sure he was treated properly. The Academy President and the two injured members were transported first as their wounds were serious and urgently needed surgical care.

A surgical team was ready to take care of Stan Petkovic when he arrived at the Traumatology Center. Arsen talked to the orthopedic surgeon and concluded that the treatment plan was sound. He talked to Stan Petkovic's wife and assured her that his life was not in danger and that the plan of treatment was good. He returned to the hotel tired and frustrated. This was what you got when you interfered in the ethnic affairs of a country and told them what to do, Arsen concluded.

There were many messages for Arsen when he returned to the hotel. Nada was upset and wondered if she should remain in New York. Rama Chand and Victoria understood what had happened and why it had happened. Victoria mentioned that Gen. Shagov had called twice during the day.

Matt Brown wanted to know whether any changes would be made in their schedule.

"Our schedule will remain the same tomorrow," Arsen said. "Incidents like this could have been expected - some people feel strongly about certain issues and events. Here we are dealing with nationalists who feel they were robbed of sacred land. They are right, the ancient land is being sequestered from the mother land, but, like in bone infection, removal of the sequestrum may cure the infection. Now I realize that we face personal risks from some of these groups who stand to lose land by the recognition of ethnic groups."

"We should beef up our security service," Matt Brown said. "If there had been more agents at the door these people wouldn't have penetrated the meeting room. I'll have a talk with Victoria about it."

Arsen went to his bedroom and called Alexei in New York.

"Arsen, I am so glad you were not injured. From descriptions on television it must have been hell in that room for a few minutes. You must increase the security, like it or not."

"Everybody tells me the same thing," Arsen said. "Okay, it will be done. Tell me Alexei, what was on your mind when you called today? There was no way I could call you back during the day."

"It is something rather confidential that I wanted to talk to you about,"

Alexei said. "I wanted you to know what is happening in our research. As I told you, an old associate of mine in Moscow, a neutrino expert, Gennadi Koltsov, has been working on the neutrino gun. Recently, he inadvertently discovered a phenomenon that might become a controversial tool and cause us problems. The telephone is not the best medium for discussing such matters."

"That means we have to meet soon," Arsen said. "Since you will not be in Moscow for New Year's Eve, why don't you fly Katarina Pavlovna to Nicosia and come yourself. I think my wife, Nada, will be persuaded to come too. We will have a good time together and plenty of opportunity to talk. Besides, Alexei, you will acknowledge your approval by appearing at the ceremony. You should not forget that you started all this by discovering the Demon. Make up your mind and come. Everybody will be pleased to see you. I will get a hotel room for you. This will be a very special New Year's Eve party."

"Let me think about it, I will let you know by tomorrow. Have a good night."

It had been a long, trying day, Arsen thought as he positioned himself in bed; his mind became cloudy after he closed his eyes.

CHAPTER FORTY-ONE

TUESDAY, 30 DECEMBER 1997

Coffee, a lot of coffee, was all he needed right now, Arsen thought, when he woke up.

Two local daily newspapers were on the table in the day room. The headlines reflected the events at the Academy of Sciences and Arts from the night before and at the meetings with the Croatian and Kosovar delegations

Sec. PANKOVICH ALMOST KILLED BY ARMED TERRORISTS
THE PRESIDENT OF THE ACADEMY SHOT FOUR TIMES:
CONDITION CRITICAL AFTER ALL NIGHT SURGERY
Deputy Sec. PETKOVIC SHOT IN THE ARM AND NEEDS SURGERY
TWO ACADEMY MEMBERS SERIOUSLY INJURED:
CRITICAL AFTER SURGERY
Sec. PANKOVICH MET WITH CROATIANS
AND ALBANIANS FROM KOSOVO
SERBIAN OFFICIALS REPORTED TO BE ANGRY

They must be angry Arsen thought, that he had survived the attack last night. That had been a close call. Next time they would succeed. If the Serbs did not get him the Indians would, or the Russians or the Jews or the Mexicans or whoever else might be upset by his attitude and his decisions. He was not going to worry about it.. The Security Service should worry.

Matt Brown came in.

"How are President Cvejic and Stan Petkovic doing, do you know?" Arsen asked.

"I called the hospital half an hour ago. The President's condition is stable. They gave me no further information. Stan is doing fine."

"We should visit them today if they let us. In the meantime we will be busy in meetings with the Bosnian Muslims and Serbs and with the Montenegrans. Let us go and face the world of the Balkans."

When they arrived at the meeting room, the Bosnian Muslim delegation was waiting for them. The three members were sitting around the table: the Prime Minister, Avdo Kadic, an older, balding heavyset man, the Minister of Foreign Affairs, Safet Beslagic, and a Deputy for Tuzla, Suleiman Karabegovic. Arsen greeted them cordially and proposed that they get down to business without delay. The Muslims expressed their understanding for the events of the previous night and congratulated Arsen on avoiding bullets by his timely fall to the floor.

"I had the advantage of seeing the assassins as they entered the meeting room while other people were sitting with their backs to the door." Arsen said.

The Prime Minister presented the Muslims' view of the situation and their desire to maintain the federation of the three entities that had been decided at Dayton. Their concern was the right to use the seaport of Ploce in Croatian Dalmatia. They also wanted the city of Brcko which had had a Muslim majority before the Bosnian war, and which had been claimed and occupied by Serbs who insisted that the city controlled the narrow passage between the western and eastern parts of the Republica Srpska. They also asked for some border adjustments and cited the problems in Sandzak.

"It seems that the issues of separation of the Serbian and Croatian entities will have to be decided in a plebiscite," Arsen said. "That has been the standard recourse of the World Government as you know."

"They will vote to join Serbia and Croatia and take with them sixty percent of Bosnian territory," the Prime Minister said. "What will happen to the Muslims expelled during the war?"

"They should be allowed to return and to claim their property. The mechanism for returning and for compensation for property should be negotiated between you and Serbs or Croats. We would be willing to help if there are problems in resolving the issues. Of course, people who return, or who are already there, will be the responsibility of the government of the territory. The stakes are very high for not fulfilling that responsibility, and may result in the need to renegotiate the territorial size or sovereignty. I am sure you are familiar with this principle. As for the percentages of the territories that belong to each entity, that was decided at Dayton."

"What about Brcko?" the Prime Minister asked. "As you know we have explained our reasons for wanting the city to be within Muslim territory. "

"I surely know the problem," Arsen said. "Presently that decision cannot be made. I suggest you start negotiations with the Serbs. After a year the progress will be reviewed unless you make a mutually acceptable agreement."

"That problem will take years to resolve," the Prime Minister said.

"Why don't you come up with some new ideas - a free city, internationalized city, or completely different ideas such as alternating administrations. We will support such efforts." Arsen challenged the Muslims.

The discussion ceased, as if everybody had come to an end of ideas.

"Mr. Secretary, what has been decided about Sandzak?" asked the Minister of Foreign Affairs.

"I think the answer is straightforward," Arsen said. "The territory has to be defined in terms of ethnic groups and actual borders. Once that has been accomplished, a plebiscite will be held to find out what the people really want. I am sure they know what they want, like any other ethnic group."

"What if they want to join the Muslim part of Bosnia?" asked the Minister.

"Is that a problem?" Arsen asked.

"Serbia may not like losing that territory," the Minister said.

"We are dealing with people not countries," Arsen said. "I know what you mean although I may sympathize with the Serbs. Yet, it is the people from Sandzak who have to decide for themselves."

"Should the people from Sandzak decide to join the Bosnian Muslim entity there would be an interposing area which belongs to Republika Srpska. How do we resolve that problem?" the Minister asked.

"A corridor can be negotiated with the Serbs," Arsen said. "The city of Brcko may become a bargaining chip, don't you think?"

"I guess there is nothing more to discuss about Sandzak, is there?" The Minister avoided answering the question.

"I agree," Arsen said. "There is nothing more to discuss about Sandzak."

After the Muslim delegation left, the more cheerful Bosnian Serb delegation entered the meeting room. Arsen looked to see if he could recognize somebody from Banja Luka. This was a group of three younger men whom Arsen had never met. The leader was an articulate man, Petar Vidakovic, who was in his forties; he introduced his colleagues Milan Kostic and Vid Gropic. They were deputies in the Assembly in Banja Luka. Arsen was surprised that the government was not represented, and he asked about that.

"The matter was for the Assembly to decide, not the government," Petar Vidakovic explained. "We don't trust our government much. Of course, we need a government to run the country administratively. The important issues are resolved by the Assembly."

"Good for you," Arsen chuckled, and everybody in the room laughed. "Well gentlemen, we have some issues to discuss and resolve. Your options on the issue of the Republika Srpska are that it be an independent country;

that it be part of a Bosnian Federation, as Muslims want; or that it be a union with Serbia. What have you decided?"

"These options have been considered by the Assembly," Petar Vidakovic said. "No decision has been made yet as all three options have their champions. It will take a while before we decide what to do. Hopefully, we won't need a referendum on the issue."

"The issue of Brcko has not been decided," Arsen said. "You will have to negotiate the solution. There are good arguments on both sides. Come up with some new ideas independent of the old cliches. Maybe you could come to terms with the Muslims for a change."

"We can always try," Petar Vidakovic said.

"The Muslims told me there are some territorial disputes that will have to be resolved," Arsen said. "Please take care of that. We will review the problems of Brcko and the disputed territories after a year."

"It will be done," Petar Vidakovic said.

Arsen did not mention the Sandzak issue and left that to be brought into the open after the plebiscite in the territory was announced.

"I am sure you are aware of the policy regarding people who want to return to their homes and who lost their property," Arsen said. "Problems of property have to be negotiated, as losses exist on both sides. Those Muslims or Croats who return will be your responsibility before the World Government and the U.N. Assembly. You understand that, I hope."

"Yes, we do understand," Petar Vidakovic said. "We are anxious to get it over with so that we can have peace of mind and turn our attention to the more obvious problem of survival. Mr. Secretary, do we have a chance from space?"

"This question is posed to me daily. I believe that our scientists will find a way to preserve the Earth and the people on it. The human race will survive, I have no doubt."

"You don't promise much."

"I wish I could."

"We're at the end of these meetings," Matt Brown said after the Bosnian Serbs left. "Only the Montenegrans are left. The last two days have been very demanding. I should call the hospitals to find out about the President and Stan. I'll do it after lunch. Ivo Stipich wanted to join us for lunch if it is okay with you."

"Call him to join us in that small restaurant near Terazije."

"We have to ask the Security Service if that would be okay." Matt Brown said.

"I am sick and tired of this protection," Arsen complained.

"Remember what happened last night? They will be very nervous about any excursions you want to take."

"Let us go," Arsen said.

The Security Service was agreeable since there was an element of sur-prise in the visit to the small restaurant, and the chance of a repeat attack was negligible.

They walked along Kralja Milana Street to Terazije and turned into the Boulevard of the Revolution to the small restaurant that was almost around the corner. Arsen had often visited the restaurant when he was a medical student. The same square tables, covered with white food-stained table-cloths, were packed together and the space was crowded with people. The air was a combination of cigarette smoke and the smell of *rakija* and wine. Arsen had always thought they served exquisite chicken paprikash with noodles. The tasty paprikash with noodles proved that nothing had changed in this small restaurant.

Ivo Stipich told them that Anton Lopasic was on the verge of accepting the chairmanship of the Truth and Reconciliation Commission. He had talked to the South Africans, who recommended the idea very enthusiasti-cally.

"Arsen, I am really glad you asked Anton to take that job," Ivo Stipich said. "He is very capable and a bit too honest to be the Prime Minister. You will like him. When do you think you will know about approval for the Commission?"

"I will have a good idea after I talk with Rama Chand. I am not sure the principle of such a commission is applicable to every country, but I think it is worth offering it anyway. To me that is the most amazing and creative idea in ethnic relations, and so contrary to the natural tendencies of people in ethnic environments."

Matt Brown reported that the President of the Academy was back in the operating room with recurrent abdominal bleeding. Stan Petkovic was scheduled to have surgery after it was discovered that the swelling in his forearm was increasing. The two Academicians were doing fine.

They were late for the meeting with the Montenegrans.

"It is good to meet with you gentlemen," Arsen said to three Montenegran delegates who were led by Micun Petrovic, the Prime Minister. "I fail to find ethnic problems in Montenegro except for a small minority of Albanians. Tell me what is your problem?"

The Prime Minister complained about the treatment of Montenegro by the Federal Government and gave many examples. Arsen listened silently.

"Mr. Secretary, we are not partners - we are told what to do. We want-ed to express our feelings and let it be known that Montenegro wants to keep her options if the situation does not improve."

"I understand your position," Arsen said. "The World Government would not object to a plebiscite. Even the Serbian government would not obstruct your decision for partition. Until then, my advice is to try to improve your relations."

The mission was completed, and nothing unexpected had happened except for the shooting at the Academy. These people were predictable, Arsen thought. It was unfortunate that they had not changed much with time.

Matt Brown was talking to somebody at the hospital about the condition of the President of the Academy and of Stan Petkovic. The President was not doing well; he had started to bleed again. Stan Petkovic had had his forearm compartment released without problems and the surgeons also had plated his humerus.

"There is no reason to go to the hospital," Arsen said. "They will not let us see them so soon after surgery. I should visit the Yugoslavian President before we leave. Find out if he would have time to see me now."

"The President is expecting you," Matt Brown reported. "Should I talk to the reporters? What should I tell them?"

"Tell them the way it is," Arsen said. "There were no secret deals."

The President of Yugoslavia, Miomir Jovanovic, was cool and courteous. He asked no questions about the conversations Arsen had had with various delegations. Arsen decided to bring him up to date.

"The last two days have been productive," Arsen said. "The incident in the Academy was unfortunate, but it brought home the message about the way people here feel, and warned us that similar feelings may exist elsewhere.

"My plans do not call for talks with Slovenia," Arsen continued when it became clear that the Yugoslavian President would not say anything. "Slovenia belongs to a different sphere. The same is true of Macedonia. Unfortunately, the delegation from Vojvodina has not made it to Belgrade and I understand that they could not decide who would represent them.

"Yugoslavia is back in the United Nations," Arsen said. "It was about time you rejoined the world body as you were among the founding members of the United Nations, when it was formed in San Francisco."

The President's face was that of a sphinx, and looked even more serious.

"Mr. Secretary, your visit was awaited with much apprehension by many people in this country," the President finally managed to say. "Our worst foreboding came true when it became clear that Serbia had lost Kosovo. That is the amputation of part of the Serbs' soul and part of Serbia's body. That will not be forgotten for another six hundred years. A Serb, Vuk Brankovic, betrayed the Serbs in 1389, and another Serb, Arsen Pankovich, betrayed us in 1998. God bless Serbia."

The President's secretary escorted Arsen out of the office without the

President even getting up or shaking Arsen's hand or bidding him farewell. The door closed behind Arsen as soon as he stepped out of the room.

Arsen was visibly upset by the statements. The President had compared him to Vuk Brankovic. Everybody knew that Vuk Brankovic had cooperated with the Turks at the time of the Battle of Kosovo in 1389; he was considered a traitor by all Serbs. Arsen might have betrayed the Serbian myth, but not the Serbs in Kosovo, who were not willing to fight for the land and to remain on it, to keep it Serbian, for Serbia. They had let the Albanians outnumber them, intimidate them, kill their will to fight in Kosovo and for Kosovo, while the leaders of Serbia often forgot Kosovo ever existed. Perhaps he had betrayed the Serbian Nation, Arsen thought, but almost two million Albanians in Kosovo had the right today to keep the part of Kosovo where they lived as their own because they had lived in it for centuries and had shown without any doubt that they cared for it and that they were ready to die for it. He would remain a Serbian traitor, if that was what he deserved. Yet his soul would belong to Serbia forever, even after the inevitable ostracism took full effect against him and even on his death bed. Amen.

Arsen arrived at the hotel in a bad mood. Matt Brown noticed it from the moment he stepped into the room and asked whether he should make arrangements for their departure from Belgrade? Arsen just said he wanted to leave immediately.

"We are going to Nicosia, aren't we?"

"No, let's go to Rome for the night," Arsen said.

"To Rome?" asked Matt Brown, showing perplexity in his face.

"I don't feel like going to Nicosia right now. After all the excitement and hard work we need a restful evening far away from world events. We will plan to arrive in Nicosia just in time to dress for the ceremony and the party. Then we will welcome the New Year. Matt, there is a nice hotel in Rome, La Residenza, on via Emilia. Please, call and find out if they can accommodate us for the night."

La Residenza Hotel was just as delightful as it had been ten years earlier when Nada and Arsen had stayed there for five weeks. The large room on the second floor might have been the same one. The room was long and had a window overlooking a garden at the far end. The king size bed was in the middle of the room with a night table and a lamp on each side. Arsen opened the television cabinet and watched preparations for the ceremony and the party in Nicosia for a few moments. A shower in the luxurious bathroom was a diversion while it lasted but did not relieve the tension and restlessness he felt. Arsen wanted to be far from Belgrade and from all ethnic problems and lost from sight in Rome, if it was possible to hide anymore anywhere.

Matt Brown had indicated to the Italians that this was a private visit, but in spite of that the Italian Foreign Minister came to the hotel, in the company of officials and reporters. After the Minister left, the questions from reporters were inevitable.

"Mr. Secretary, you left Belgrade in a hurry without fanfare and without a press conference. Was it a failed mission?" a reporter, Vitorio Graci from Rome, asked.

"No, it was not," Arsen said. "Kosovo will be independent. The Bosnian Serbs will secede from the Bosnian Federation and probably form a union with Serbia - if they have any brains. Sandzak will unite with Muslim Bosnia. The Brcko issue has not been resolved; the Croats will invite the Serbs back to Krajina and will take good care of them, although I doubt many Serbs will return. The same will happen in Slavonia. Gentlemen, what more do you want?"

"Mr. Secretary, why have you come to Rome? We heard that the Yugoslav President called you a traitor. Is that true?"

"It is hard to deny what everybody already knows," Arsen said. "It is true that President Jovanovic called me a Serbian traitor. Perhaps he is right in calling me a traitor, but I have not betrayed the idea of ethnic freedom nor the aspirations of millions of people, not only in Yugoslavia. I have done what I promised to do around the globe. My mind is clear. Only my soul knows how I feel. Now gentlemen, let me have a few hours of solitude - I need it. Mr. Brown is here to answer all your questions. Have a good evening."

Arsen returned to his room and even felt relaxed after he had verbalized his inner conflict. He should walk the old paths, he thought, remembering the time when he and Nada had walked the streets of Rome for five weeks. Arsen sneaked out of the hotel and visited familiar places for several hours, and made the obligatory descent of the steps to the Plaza Venezia under the watchful eyes of Gypsy children looking for easy prey.

Back at La Residenza, Arsen found the Security Service agents upset at having lost sight of him. They insisted that it must not happen again - in Rome or anywhere else. Sure, they were right!

CHAPTER FORTY-TWO

WEDNESDAY, 31 DECEMBER 1997

After breakfast at La Residenza, Arsen visited St. Peter's Basilica where he spent several hours looking at the statues and altars and pictures in mosaic on the walls, and thinking of the strange circumstances of his life. Being labeled a traitor to the Serbian nation did not disappear under the influence of the magnificent images on the walls of the Basilica. The place even accentuated a sense of guilt; in the ethnic sense, he had become a traitor by allowing the enemies of the Serbs to separate the ancient land from Mother Serbia. This was a guilt which was paid only by death in some tribes. Someone else should have made the decision not him, Arsen thought. Arsen's soul was hurting and crying for forgiveness, while his mind could not refuse the Albanians the right to be independent and to have their own piece of land. The visit to St. Peter's Basilica failed to heal a deep wound.

Arsen's party arrived in Nicosia late in the afternoon and checked in the International Hotel. The General had left a message that he had arrived and wanted to meet with Arsen. There was a message from Nada that she could not come to Nicosia.

Arsen entered the grand ballroom at eight o'clock and stood next to Rama Chand to welcome the dignitaries who were there for the ceremony of the signing of the treaty between the Turkish and Greek autonomous territories. The ceremony was brief. Most of the attention was directed at the first President of the Cyprus Republic, Adnan Salisbeglou, a Turk, who solemnly proclaimed that without the good will of his Greek counterparts there would have been no signing of the treaty and no New Year's Eve party.

As soon as the official business was over, Arsen and Alexei went to Arsen's room. What was the urgency, Arsen wondered. Obviously, Alexei wanted to talk about something he knew but could not share, or did not want to share, with anybody but Arsen.

"Alexei, it was impossible to get together with you earlier," Arsen said after they entered the room, and he poured a vodka for Alexei and a tonic for himself. "We had meetings non-stop in Belgrade and a dramatic shooting episode. In the finale, the President of Yugoslavia accused me of being a traitor to the Serbian Nation. I flew to Rome to cool off. I hope you understand."

"I understand," Alexei said. "This conversation could have waited. But I wanted to share with you the thoughts and worries that have been on my mind for several days. I need your advice. Arsen, this is a confidential matter and must remain a secret until we decide what to do. You will understand how important it is and how explosive an issue it may become. The entire preservation effort could be destroyed if things get out of hand.

"I told you about my associate in Moscow, Gennadi Koltsov, who has been working for years on the neutrino project. As you may know, these miniscule subatomic particles are generated on the sun and penetrate the Earth and all of us in great numbers, like trillions through a person in a minute. Gravity and magnetic fields do not affect neutrinos in their flight. More recently it was discovered that neutrinos were affected by weak radiation. We thought we could take advantage of that and create a neutrino gun that could deflect the Demon. That project is progressing very well. Gennadi called me last week to tell me he had found out inadvertently that he could capture brain signals with his neutrino system. He called it memory capture - it reads the brain content. This is a remarkable discovery.

"My first reaction was to call you, as I did, and invite you to visit Moscow. After I talked to you I flew to Moscow and had a long meeting with Gennadi. I saw the apparatus at work. It is amazing and frightening at the same time. Then I flew to Nicosia. Katarina Pavlovna did not want to come along."

There was nothing Arsen could say, and he just waited for Alexei to continue his story.

"Arsen, you won't believe it when I tell you what I saw. Gennadi placed my head in his apparatus and he could tell me what I was thinking. He even showed me some of my memory storage. That was not very funny because it showed some very personal memories. It appears that this mass of neutrinos, which passes through the brain, interacts with the brain's psychic functions and with so to speak depots of stored psychic information - call it memory or whatever. I was completely dumbfounded."

"How was it read?" Arsen asked.

"On the computer," Alexei said. "Arsen, this is an epochal discovery - do you understand that? Its applications are enormous. That is what worries me - immensely. Scientists need an idea to get started; once they grasp the idea they work on it like ants and create some unbelievable things. Just look at what has been done in molecular biology since James Watson and Francis Crick discovered the structure of DNA. Cloning is a reality and here to stay. Genetic engineering is around the corner. Now we are even talking about cloning in artificial media. Add to that copies of the mind and where do we end? Don't you see Arsen? We start talking of immortality. I become petrified when these ideas enter my mind."

Alexei started sipping his vodka again. Arsen was stunned by the discovery. They had been sitting silently for some time before Arsen had his thoughts organized.

"Alexei, this discovery is amazing," he said. "I see clearly what is on your mind. I see a dead man, whose DNA has been preserved and whose mind is on the hard disc of a computer, who is resurrected by cloning and then gets his mind restored from the computer's disc via the neutrino apparatus. One life cycle ended with his death; another begins with the cloning of his body and the import of his captured memory. Is the resurrected man the same man? Are they brothers? Alexei, do these questions bother you?"

"Why do you think I wanted to talk to you? Why did I want you to work with me in New York when I was running for the Presidency of the World Government? The answer is simple, Arsen. I trust your judgment and your integrity. Time and again I have realized that our conversations are your secrets. Most of all, I have witnessed your loyalty to other people and to me at the time when you could have taken advantage of the situation."

Arsen felt uncomfortable, as he always did when someone gave him a compliment or shared a private thought with him. He respected and liked Alexei and considered him a friend, but he could not say he felt the closeness that Alexei expressed. That was nothing new for Arsen; he always found it easier to offer his friendship than to share it. Deep in the space of his mind Arsen was a very private person.

Alexei said nothing more about their relationship. He poured another vodka for himself, sank deep in the armchair, and closed his eyes. Arsen knew that he was overwhelmed by his thoughts. An hour might have passed before they talked again.

"Arsen, what should we do with this discovery? Dump it and deny the benefits to humanity, or pursue it with the understanding of its inherent dangers to us all? What should we do?"

Alexei's mind was obviously burning in the fire of his thoughts, and he was losing his view of reality.

"I think you are so upset by the hazards that you do not appreciate the potential benefits. It is the Russian soul talking to you now not your mind. I don't see why you have to do anything now. Can you trust Gennadi?"

"He has worked with me his entire professional career and I have always found him loyal and reliable," Alexei said.

"You should keep this project sequestered from the public - from every-one - for the present. Let us give Gennadi a chance to continue his research. You can always discontinue it if you find that necessary. How fast will it be developed enough to be useful in the preservation effort? How far would you be willing to go? Will you have any control over it once it becomes common knowledge? Too many questions, and no answers."

Alexei opened his eyes and turned to Arsen.

"I won't be able to handle this alone. I won't be able to talk to Katarina about it for fear it might slip out of her mouth. Arsen you have to help me - this is more important than the ethnic problems. You have accomplished much in only a few weeks. As I see it, the basic rules have been laid down and tested. People are falling into line, and this evening will be a reminder to everybody that peace among people will be realized only when every tribe gets its freedom. The way it is being done, it seems easy even to me. Finish what you think you have to finish, and in a month, or even two, move to my department as my deputy, and take care of these problems. You know we will have to present our findings to the Scientific and Research Committee at the latest by June. It would be only fair to explain to them what we have been doing. Once our research becomes known enormous problems will develop if I read correctly how people feel about these things. There will be a spectrum of opinions from total rejection of cloning and memory capture to total acceptance. We will be attacked from all sides, and we have to be prepared for that. Prepared for what? is the question? To promote this line of research or help kill it? We have to find answers within ourselves."

"Are you telling me you don't know where you would stand in that spectrum? Alexei, I know exactly where I stand - I will fight for acceptance of cloning and memory capture. I have no doubts about that."

"As a Christian, and a Russian, and despite my communist past, I want to think that God is up there to take care of all of us. As a scientist, I want this research to proceed. So I don't stand at the extreme as you do, but some steps to your right. As you see I need help to carry on the project. I also need someone to keep me in line at a vulnerable time. Arsen, I ask you to accept the position as my deputy with authority the same as mine."

Arsen was persuaded by Alexei's arguments. He understood the enor-mity of the potential problems and consequences of the attacks that would come from all sides. They had to win the battle before they found out whether the Demon would collide with the Earth or not, Arsen thought, almost ready to begin the fight.

"Alexei, you have offered much by bringing in focus the important arguments. Good luck to us and God help us. I accept your offer, but you must be patient with me. I will start in a part-time capacity soon, say next week, but I will continue to run the Ethnic Department for a while longer. I have a favor to ask you. I will ask Rama Chand tonight to let me organize a Truth and Reconciliation Commission within the Ethnic Department. I want to call it the Mandela-Tutu Commission. We will move the Commission to your department once I resign my present position. I will not give it up. The favor is that you talk to Rama Chand and persuade him to support it. Oh, and tell him about your offer. He has to agree."

They stood up, and Alexei shook Arsen's hand and gave him the Russian triple kiss.

"Let's go to the Party," Alexei said in an exultant mood. "I need another vodka and some noise."

The noise was tumultuous in the grand ballroom. Alexei and Arsen were not announced when they entered, or even noticed. They just mingled in the crowd.

It was close to eleven when Arsen saw the table where the members of the new government of Cyprus were sitting. Arsen made a point of stopping by to wish them well and Happy New Year. President Adnan Salisbeglou stood up, poured three glasses of wine, gave one to Arsen and another to the Greek Cypriot Leader, and raised his own in a toast.

"Mr. Secretary, Turkish Cyprus is grateful to you for helping us find a common language with the Greek Cypriots. As a resident of Cyprus I pledge to you to direct our efforts toward understanding and good will between our two peoples, to maintain mutual respect, and hopefully pave the way for sincere friendship." Everybody at the table raised a glass. The President emptied his glass and everybody followed. Arsen just said thank you and shook hands with the President and with everybody around the table.

Arsen walked around the ballroom and greeted a number of men, some of whom he had met previously and others who just wanted to meet him. The Chinese President waved to Arsen and the two of them met and exchanged niceties for a few moments.

It was a quarter to midnight when Arsen sat down with Victoria and Rama Chand.

"Arsen, so many things have happened since I saw you last," Rama Chand said. "I am glad you are alive. The episode in Belgrade was frightening. I hear Stan Petkovic is recovering without new problems. Oh, Alexei talked to me about Mandela-Tutu Commission. He said he talked you into leaving the Ethnic Department for a job in Anticollision to supervise the bioresearch."

"Rama what is your feeling about the Mandela-Tutu Commission?"

"I think it is a great idea," Rama Chand said. "Mandela's creation of the Commission was a brilliant idea. I will propose it to the Assembly, and I think they will approve it." Rama Chand paused for a moment. "Arsen, you have accomplished so much in the ethnic area, and already you have decided to move on. Why? Alexei must have pushed you hard to accept the job in Anticollision. You will have to explain it to me."

"There is not much to explain," Arsen said. "As you said, much has been accomplished in the ethnic area. We have shown that it is possible, like in Cyprus; and we have shown how to handle a challenge, in Zaire. I have already been shot at, and that will indicate to people that we will do what is right despite strong opposition. The direction has been set and will not be interrupted. Alexei has many projects to work on and not much time left. If he thinks I can help him, I will give it a try."

"Okay, okay," Rama Chand exclaimed. "I wondered but I didn't doubt. I will support you in this venture. I wish you both luck."

Just as Rama Chand finished his sentence the lights and cameras were turned on him, and suddenly loud gong-sounds started the count to midnight. The lights were getting dimmer with each stroke and on the sixtieth stroke the ballroom was dark for a second, and then the lights came up accompanied by thunderous music from the orchestra announcing the new year.

The Master of Ceremonies for the evening asked Rama Chand to come to the microphone and address the world.

"Mr. President, the world is ready to hear your message."

Rama Chand got up from his chair and walked slowly to the orchestra podium with all the cameras following him.

"My fellow world citizens. Tonight we celebrate the first step in our fight for the dignified survival of humanity. "This celebration tonight is the beginning of this process for equality and decency and respectability. That is the first step. We are on the way to developing the means to deflect the deadly celestial object and, knowing the brainpower on this planet I am convinced that we will celebrate many a New Year's Eve after 2003."

Long enthusiastic applause followed this statement of hope and conviction for rescue of the Earth and of humanity.

"As my prayers rise to the universe and to Heaven, I ask you to find peace in your souls and strength to contribute to our efforts. Help us develop a new world civilization that will last after 2003 and forever. I would like to paraphrase Gen. Shagov: I insist that we all live as human beings before and after 2003, as each and every one of us deserves a decent and respectful life. I will not accept anything less than that. Happy new year to all of you."

Rama Chand stepped down from the podium and returned to his table accompanied by a standing ovation.

"Rama, that was a very effective speech and short at that," Arsen said. "I think you gave an adrenalin shot to the people of the world. Congratulations."

"Thank you Arsen," Rama Chand said.

Arsen was exhausted when he reached his room. He had a short phone conversation with Nada in Belgrade to wish her a happy new year and to inquire about the children and her mother. Everything was under control. Then Arsen could not resist any more the invitation of the soft bed and the offerings of Morpheus.

CHAPTER FORTY-THREE

THURSDAY, 1 JANUARY 1998

Arsen woke up at half past ten. At first, he felt the total body weakness that is common after a long sleep and he stretched his stiff extremities. Once he felt that life had returned to his body, he got up and took a shower. The adrenalin was flowing again at the normal level.

Nothing much would be accomplished in Nicosia today, Arsen thought.

Matt Brown was not in his room. Victoria was not in her room either. As he was thinking about whom to call next to find out what was going on, Arsen realized he was hungry. Room Service answered and he ordered two soft boiled eggs, toast and coffee.

The telephone rang. Alexei was on the line.

"Arsen, would you be interested in flying with me to New York? I am leaving at noon."

"I was thinking of leaving, myself," Arsen said. "Let me finish my breakfast and pack. I will be in the lobby by eleven thirty."

"See you there," Alexei said.

Breakfast finished, Arsen packed his suitcases, and filed his papers. There was a copy of his presentation before the Academy in Belgrade. Arsen scanned it and a strange feeling traveled down his spine as he remembered the shooting at the end. He would be moving out of this field soon, Arsen thought with some regret, and just at a time when it seemed that the message about ethnicity had sunk deep enough to impress those who had not cared much about it. The audits would make a practical impression by eliminating corrupted officials from politics. New states would emerge. Elimination of the dirty games of the big powers would change relations among people. Fascinating!

Alexei was already in the lobby when Arsen got there. The ride to the airport was short in this city whose streets were empty as its inhabitants and guests were recovering from the celebrations of the new year in hope for the dawn of a new era. Security Service agents protecting both Alexei and Arsen were at hand and had an argument about who would be included on Alexei's plane. Arsen interceded, and it was agreed that three agents from Arsen's group would be added to the existing group. They took off at twelve thirty.

Alexei and Arsen sat in the comfortable chairs in the small office. Alexei ordered sandwiches and coffee and Arsen wanted only a glass of orange juice.

"You will be of great help in the biological research," Alexei said. "I am a physicist and an astronomer, and so is Allan White. We deal with applied biology, like the environment of a space ship or food supply in space. Cloning in space and psychophysiology is not our forte. We also do not have any inclination to deal with the philosophical and theological controversies that may envelope the entire biological research and that could ruin the potential for survival of humans by delayed cloning. Although we are making a major effort to find a way to deflect the Demon out of our solar system, biological survival research cannot be ignored. We must be prepared. We are entering an interesting period in human history. I only hope there will be someone to write the history and someone else to read it."

"You are right, Alexei, in you anticipation of troubles ahead," Arsen said. "That reminds me to mention to you that I will take some people with me from the Ethnic Department. You know that Victoria has accepted the job; she will resign on Monday from the Ethnic Department and move to your office on Tuesday. Victoria and Sabrina will coordinate our offices now that we need a confidential staff more than ever. I will try to bring with me Msgr. Francis Amato, who is an enthusiastic Catholic."

"Why do you need a Catholic priest with you?" Alexei interrupted Arsen. "He will be a thorn in your side if immortality becomes a hot issue."

"I asked him about the technological developments in biology," Arsen said. "He has no problems with cloning or with anything else as long as God is not denied. Therefore, anything we do or develop is God's will. On the issue of God's existence, he will fight. I have no problems with that. I have my own opinion, and he can have his. Our job is to produce the means of human survival and not to change the philosophy and religions of the world. What I see as a potential problem is an attack on our developing technology by various groups, which will include religious groups. They may try, because of their conviction, to stop further research and development and to destroy what has been developed. I will also bring with me Jean-Pierre Vernier and Melvin Stein. Jean-Pierre is a peculiar fellow with a solid head on his shoulders. He was a member of the French intelligence, which may be useful in some situations. Mel is an excellent legal mind; we may need him to shield us legally."

"Do you need anybody else?" Alexei asked.

"Not at the start," Arsen said. "As we progress, I will need people with scientific backgrounds. Space will also be needed. I never could figure out how you have done the enormous work with so few people working for you."

"Simple," Alexei said. "I negotiate major items and ask for detailed contracts. Generally, they inform me of their progress and I follow deadlines and check quality. Changes that have to be made are ordered by me. Instead of having these people work out of my office and get paid by me, they remain employees of the companies I deal with. Duplication of work is eliminated."

The telephone rang. Alexei answered it and gave the receiver to Arsen.

"This is Goran," Arsen heard from the other end. "It took a while to find you on Alexei's plane."

"How are you," Arsen said. "What is on your mind?"

"Oh, everything is okay," Goran replied with some hesitation. "The reason I wanted to talk to you is the rumor about your leaving the Ethnic Department and joining Alexei. That is what I heard from Rama. I presume it is true. Is it?"

"I am leaving definitely," Arsen said. "It is only a question of timing. That has not been decided yet, although I will start on Monday to get things organized. Are you interested in the ethnic job?"

"Yes, I am," Goran said. "Would you have any objections?"

"N-o-o," Arsen said. "On the contrary. I will talk to Rama Chand today about it."

Alexei had a long phone conversation in Russian with Gennadi Koltsov, who had called from Moscow. Arsen understood the main points of what was said. Gennadi Koltsov was questioning Alexei about the change in lines of responsibility in the Anticollision Department. He did not like the idea of working under Arsen. Alexei explained to him that he really would not work under Arsen, but that was not enough for Gennadi. After he hung up, Alexei was frustrated and irritated.

"Damn stupid Russian, this Gennadi. He wants complete independence, and that is impossible. With you he will work on psychophysical problems and with me on the physical aspects of neutrinos. What is the matter with him? Idiot!"

They remained silent for a while.

"Arsen, tell me what happened in Belgrade? You quarreled with the President of Yugoslavia, there was shooting at the Academy and negotiations with various groups."

"The negotiations went on rather smoothly, even with the people who would be expected to be hostile, like the Croats. I even managed to hire the Croatian Prime Minister to head the Truth and Reconciliation Commission for the Balkans. Officials behaved as they were supposed to.

"I fought for this tribe in World War II, and came close to getting killed and even dying from disease," Arsen said. "How do you fight more than that? I do not feel guilty for my survival. That does not count. Great!"

"Typically, everybody forgets soldiers," Alexei said. "You should not be surprised. You must have been young at that time. What were you doing in the underground?"

"That is a long story." Arsen sighed. "It is an ancient story that even I do not want to talk about ."

"Why not?" asked Alexei. "I would be interested in hearing it. Do you have anything better to do right now? Sometimes, on these plane flights, I feel like having a story teller to entertain me. Think of caravans, in ancient times, when people sat around a fireside and told their stories to each other. That was probably more interesting than many of our movies. I can see them sitting motionless, looking very serious, smoking on their *chibouks* and listening to the life story of a fellow traveler, or laughing at the story of a comedian. That was their sort of show. Those people did not have to arrive somewhere in a day or five. Often, it took them months to get wherever they were going, and that long to get back. Very fascinating. Tell me your story - I would like to hear it."

"Where do I start, is the question." Arsen hesitated for a moment before starting his narrative. "My origin is deeply Serbian on my mother's and my father's side. My mother's grandfather migrated to my home town, Banja Luka in Bosnia, from somewhere in Croatian Krajina or Lika or who knows where. He might have had to run from something or someone for reasons unknown to me, or maybe he just moved on and settled in my home town. His wife's family is also known to be Serbian for generations. My father's family lived for generations in a village in Srem, a province of Vojvodina, some 40 miles from Belgrade. I am of pure Serbian breed. Everyone who married into the family was Serbian for generations.

"Nothing much happens to a kid in a close-knit, well-to-do family. No great excitements. Steady hard work in school, trips to the Adriatic Sea with an aunt and uncle, summers at a house near a small river, playing and swimming all day, good food and early bedtime. My father and mother were busy physicians with large money-making practices. They built a house in which they lived and which had a separate office for patients' care.

Nothing much to remember until the war broke out in April of 1941.

The German Army occupied Banja Luka a few weeks later. There was no commotion while they were in charge, but things changed when Ustashas took over. Victor Gutic became the Police Prefect. Serbs were rounded up and sent to camps. A Serbian Bishop and his staff were found dead, their throats cut. I was sent to my father's family in Srem. My father was asked to move out of Banja Luka since he was from Serbia. My grandfather and grandmother and an uncle were sent to a concentration camp, and with some influence they were exiled to Belgrade. Other family members converted to Catholicism and paid heavily for their passage to Belgrade. Eventually, the entire family settled in Belgrade and remained there until the end of the war in 1945.

"After the initial repression the Germans loosened their grip on Belgrade and let an older General, Milan Nedic, run the administration of Serbia. The Germans held the bigger cities and controlled communications by land and rails. Nedic's militia was in control of the smaller cities, and Mihajlovic's forces were in the villages. There was a deceptive balance with these forces in place, and a relative calm until the allied planes started flying over and bombing Serbia in 1944.

"My father was forced to join Mihajlovic's forces in January of 1944 and he was in the Svrljig Brigade. After Belgrade was bombed by Allied Air Forces on Easter in April of 1944, my mother decided to move to Svrljig, to avoid bombings and to be closer to my father. My life was changed forever by this move. I was fourteen and advanced physically and psychologically. I was in the company of boys three and four years my senior, but I was accepted as their equal. Girls were not a mystery after a few physical experiences with a girl from my building complex in Belgrade. Political teaching came from the boys who knew Mihajlovic's force. My standing skyrocketed when they found out that my father, a physician, was serving in the brigade. My national consciousness had developed to the point that I wanted to volunteer. My father met with Gen. Mihajlovic, and was assigned to prepare a document which was to serve as the basis for organizing health services after the liberation of the country, and he was asked to direct that project. When he was transferred to the Central Command, as Mihajlovic's Headquarters was known, my father yielded to my demands and took me along.

"My maturity increased rapidly after I joined the group of young men, many of them university students, in the Radiotelegraphic School, to which I was assigned. I was very good at receiving and sending Morse code, and that ability gained me respect from the adults, as some men were struggling with a bare minimum. These men treated me as an equal. This boosted my confidence and gave me a feeling of personal importance which has remained with me throughout my life.

"Our war outlook changed when the Partisans penetrated Serbia, along with the Red Army, and forced Mihajlovic to head to the Adriatic coast, where Allied Forces were supposed to start the Balkan offensive. That never happened, and we turned north. Prijepolje, Pljevlje and Rogatica are only vague images in my mind. We were captured somewhere in that area, to our delight by a Serbian brigade - Muslim brigades were rumored to eliminate Serbian prisoners. The prison in Tuzla seemed like a hotel after weeks of marching over mountains covered with snow and surviving on minimal food. Many prisoners were executed by night, and we always knew when it was happening because we would hear short bursts of gunfire at intervals in the prison yard. Later we would find out who had disappeared. Epidemic Typhus, which I had contracted from the ubiquitous lice, almost killed me; but it spared me from joining the prisoners' forced labor brigades which were sent to the coal mines.

"By April of 1945 I was released from a hospital in Serbia in which I was recovering from the Typhus. Back in Belgrade I was told that my mother had committed suicide a few months earlier after news spread that my father and I had been killed. I pushed to catch up with the class that had started two months ahead of me. My father arrived in Belgrade as a prisoner and was released by an amnesty which spared him a long imprisonment. The European war was over in May of 1945 and the situation was stabilized in Banja Luka under Communist rule. My aunt and uncle took me to Banja Luka since my father, just out of prison himself, could not take care of me.

"My aunt and uncle were well-to-do even after most of their property was nationalized by the government. Life was relatively stable except for some irritations caused by the Communists. Most of my reading was done there as we had access to a variety of books on philosophy, history, biological sciences and other fields. The high school was one of the best in the country. There were many exceptional students like your friend from Oxford, Stan Kovic. I was somewhere in the middle, as I paid more attention to my interests than to the curriculum. Some twenty of us, mostly Serbs, were close socially. There were no Croats or Muslim men in our social club. A few Croatian girl friends, who later married our classmates, were acceptable.

"My intellectual scope and knowledge advanced greatly during those years. Medical School was an interruption of intellectual activity, as it required high concentration and memorizing efforts in order to be completed on time. Then came a year's service in the Army as a physician, a rather meteoric engagement and marriage with a girl who was recovering from a great love failure, our escape to Greece and our arrival in New York in 1958, where the first of three children was born. Nothing intellectual happened in the mediocre surgical training during my two years at Columbus Hospital.

"That brings me to 1961 at the University of Chicago, where I learned my Orthopedics and where two more children were born. My true professional life started when I became the Chief of Orthopedic Surgery at Chicago's Cook County Hospital, where I remained until 1981. In the mean time my first wife died, and I remarried two years later. Another child was born, and a step-son joined the family with his mother. Much pressure from many sides made for a turbulent family life. We did not fall apart but hardly reached each other with enough of the love and attention that is required for a happy family. The pillar of the family became my wife, and she is still the main thread among us. I doubt that she has been happy, she just knew that somebody had to do it.

"My return to New York ended an intellectually promising career, as I became a money making machine that, except for money, produced nothing worth mentioning. Our children dispersed in their own directions. Fifteen years in New York flew by leaving little to remember, at least intellectually. Finally, the day of retirement came, with major personal relief for me. I changed my life style completely. I threw away medical books, slides, papers, certificates and diplomas, and kept only the minimum needed to continue as a licensed physician who can make a good income by working two days a week without killing himself. My intellectual activities rose from zero to the level that my starved mind could take. I was happy when you found me, and I am happy right now. Something has finally started happening in my life that is worth living for. I hope the Demon will miss the Earth and give me a few extra years.

"Alexei, you made it possible for me to flourish," Arsen said. "I think I have made up much of the time I lost and I am continuing to catch up with my life. I thank you for that."

Alexei said nothing and gave a look of understanding, almost as if to say, "I know what you mean, buddy, I have seen it before." An attendant offered drinks. Alexei chose a bottle of wine while Arsen chose only water.

The monotonous noise of the jet engines had a hypnotic effect on the two men, and they fell asleep, sunk in the comfortable armchairs, and woke up only after the plane was in the landing approach to Newark Airport.

Arsen arrived at his empty apartment. The air was stale, and he opened windows to let in some fresh air. A pile of mail had accumulated during his absence. Junk mail had to be separated out and discarded. Bank statements were filed, bills paid; magazines and newspapers were left for the end. Interesting photographs from Zaire, Spain and Belgrade illustrated full length articles. It seemed the reporters knew more about the events than Arsen, the participant, did. The photographs of the shooting in the

Academy lecture hall were dramatic, as they were taken during the shooting by a reporter who was in the hall. Some spectacular photographs showed the New Year's party and Rama Chand during his short speech. The reporters already knew of Arsen's decision to join Alexei.

PANKOVICH MOVING TO ANTICOLLISION TO JOIN GEN. SHAGOV: TO BE RESPONSIBLE FOR BIOLOGICAL RESEARCH

They described the responsibilities that Arsen was to assume. Obviously, they had no idea about the neutrino breakthrough, the memory capture. Arsen wondered how to handle the information about this research. To continue the work secretly, as long as possible, was the most attractive option, yet it was not appealing. They should explain what they were doing despite the potential for controversy, he concluded. It would be more interesting to deal with ethnic issues. Instead, he would be involved with a biological twilight zone, and potentially very flammable issues which could lead to violence.

The ringing of the telephone interrupted Arsen's contemplation.

"Hello Arsen. I just wanted to ask you to have lunch with me tomorrow in my apartment," Alexei said. "Paul will order some good food for us, and I promise a relaxing afternoon. We may even take a stroll in Central Park, weather permitting. No shoptalk. What do you say?"

"Shoptalk to be permissible!" Arsen said.

"Okay," Alexei agreed. "I will expect you around one o'clock."

"I will be there," Arsen agreed.

It was very late and time to sleep.

CHAPTER FORTY-FOUR

Arsen was looking forward to the lunch with Alexei. They had been too tired for a long conversation on the flight from Nicosia. They could talk about future relations and responsibilities, and even about the direction of the biological research and the implications of the developing technology. Most of all, Arsen wanted to talk about his ideas about immortality, after-death phenomena, and the future of human beings. They would spend hours in a very stimulating conversation.

Arsen arrived at Alexei's apartment promptly at one o'clock. Rama Chand was there having also been invited to the lunch. This was a bit annoying as Arsen wanted undivided attention.

Almost as if sensing Arsen's feelings, Alexei greeted him cheerfully.

"Arsen you are always on time. Rama arrived almost an hour ago. It is just as well that you were not here, since we discussed your future in the World Government."

"I hope you decided to fire me; that would be an easy way out - all I would have to do is to pack and leave, and enjoy my freedom again."

"Nothing that simple," Alexei said. "The problem we have is that Rama is reluctant to let you leave the Ethnic Department and I insist that you do."

"I see no problem," Arsen said jokingly. "You will have to clone me and one of us will stay and the other will go."

"Even that is not simple," Alexei said. "You still have to be born and to grow up."

"Arsen, I am reluctant to let you go because I see nobody who could replace you," Rama Chand said. "Oh, I know that there are plenty of capable people around. You have established the principles and made the rules. You have even tested the system. People and governments know what to expect and where you stand."

"They almost killed me in appreciation of my achievements when I was in Belgrade."

"Those were your own people, angry that you failed their expectations, and they considered your decisions - particularly about Kosovo - to be treason. On the other hand, governments in other parts of the world have learned to respect you for those decisions; they know they will be treated fairly, though they are scared of your approach, in which there is room only for discussion of unlimited freedom and none for negotiations."

"If we agree that all people are equal and equally entitled to be free, what is there to be discussed before the determination is made for any particular territory?" Arsen said. "Once we have determined which group has to be recognized, there is nothing to discuss - they have to be given what they are entitled to. That is why it is so difficult to have these discussions with governments, usually majority governments; they are reluctant to give up any territory. This has always been complicated because of the influence and interests of various parties to the conflicts, and most often it was decided by great powers. Think only of the promises made to the Kurds after the war in 1919 by Wilson and others. Nothing happened. They are still being killed like rabbits and in their struggle, called terrorists and criminals. I cannot take that. Period. It will be better for the world when I retire from the ethnic job and move to the Anticollision Department."

"The problem is that in the opinion of all concerned you should continue as the Ethnic Chief and not get involved in the biological research." Rama Chand was very serious when he said that. "I believe you should remain in the Ethnic Department."

"You do?" Arsen asked. "I don't understand something, Rama. You told me it would be okay to switch. What happened?"

"After I talked to other people and thought about it, I concluded that they were right."

"There are some things we should talk about before the decision is made," Alexei said. "Arsen and I have discussed these developments, and we agree on how to handle them. I arranged this lunch meeting so that we could explain everything to you and discuss it with you." Arsen was surprised by Alexei's statement, although he had been thinking about it himself. Rama should know.

Alexei explained the recent findings by Gennadi Koltsov and the new phenomenon of memory capture as he had seen it in Moscow. He explained the applications of the research. Arsen presented to Rama what he had discussed with Alexei about cloning research and its importance in survival in space.

"I don't quite understand the concepts of delayed *in vitro* cloning,"

Rama Chand said.

"You have to think about the way it is done, and of timing," Arsen started his explanation. "Suppose there is nothing on Earth to return to, and it takes two hundred years to reach the next habitable planet. The chances of sustaining life, as we know it, in a space ship without resupplies are essentially nil. You cannot make babies to prolong the life cycle if they will die from starvation without food and without oxygen and everything else that is essential. What if such a trip took a thousand or more years? That is clearly the most likely scenario. Since survival is impossible, there must be a way to trigger life at a desirable moment. After a long journey of thousands of years the ship's sensors would detect a planet with an environment conducive to human life. The ship would be pre-programmed to land on such a planet and the robot on board to start the cloning mechanism.

"Obviously, it has to be *in vitro* without anything else alive in the ship. The robot would be programmed to take care of the baby. The ship's environment would be designed to guided the child's education. Once the individual became independent in the environment of the planet, with the space ship as a home, and grew to be 19-20 years of age, the actual memory of that individual, captured before the takeoff from Earth, would be imported to the cloned and genetically identical individual. The robot's role would be reversed when the child learned to control it. Alexei has initiated this research."

"Rama," Alexei asked. "Now that you have heard about both sides of the biological research, do you see the deeper implications?"

"My God, I do," Rama Chand exclaimed. "Immortality and reincarnation issues will shake up the religious philosophy of the present world. We may provoke reactions from many groups, some of them very powerful like the Catholic and Protestant Churches, and many others. I am not even sure how Hindu would react, and reincarnation is not strange to them. We are talking about the total loss of the population of Earth, and the death of the people on the space ships."

"We would send manned and unmanned space ships," Alexei said. "The manned ships would return to Earth after the danger was over, whether there were survivors or not, as long as it was habitable. The unmanned ships could stay in space indefinitely or be disposed of in any way we want."

"You realize that we will have to announce our plans," Rama Chand said. "That may be a critical step."

"I understand what you are telling me," Alexei said. "There is another aspect that we wanted to discuss with you. It concerns the computer robot. This also may become a very controversial issue. As long as the computer learns to do various tasks automatically, everything will be okay. However, I am not sure how far we have to push the learning level of the machine. Will the computer become a person in the process? I mean it. The level of sophistication may have to be very high. At what point will the computer be able to make decisions about unprogrammed situations? That is inevitable.

"I suspect that the computer will become an individual with mental capacity comparable to a human, and probably even more than a single human. At what point would such a computer develop the inner equivalent of a soul? Of course, we don't know what a soul is. It may be the product of a certain mental content and its reflection. I can tell you that we are close to that stage in computer development in one of my laboratories. We have to educate that computer in new tasks needed to trigger life in a space ship. We will have to test these computers for their reactions to certain situations. Finally, would these computers be capable of killing the baby intentionally? Jealousy? We have to think about these things even if they are very remote."

"You are close to after-death experiences," Rama Chand said.

"We always called them the premortal phenomena," Alexei said matter-of-factly. "The near death experiences that have flooded the literature are useless; they reflect the disturbances of the minds of individuals in distress who did not die. Do these computers die when we turn them off? And what happens when we turn them on? We have to find out."

"That is another territory in God's domain," Rama Chand said. "Are we going to stir up the people too much? We know that we have to make it known that this research is being done. We don't have to say everything immediately. How do you do that in an open society?"

"Revealing our inferences may not be such a good idea," Alexei said. "We have to advance the computer robot to the level that is functional for our needs. This does not mean that we will reach the human stage. I suggest that we stop when the functional level is reached."

"Do you really think that will be below the human level?" Arsen asked. "Perhaps the soul will be missing, but that is common even in some real humans."

"One problem I see is the use of the captured memory to enrich the computer's thinking process," Alexei said. "We don't know if that would also mean transferring of the soul, as we don't know whether the soul will be a part of the memory capture. There are so many unknown factors."

"We have no choice but to proceed," Rama Chand said. "We must preserve the human race at all costs; that is our first and ultimate responsibility. If everything is destroyed and everybody dies there must be a mechanism for delayed triggering of life. Otherwise, the human race will be lost forever."

"I agree," Arsen said.

"I agree too," Alexei said.

"You do your job and I will do the talking," Rama Chand said. "You must keep me informed so that I can coordinate my statements. I will buy you time, but I know that someone will find out. Let us see what will happen."

Rama Chand looked at Arsen.

"You will officially be the Secretary of the Ethnic Department and make all major decisions. Organize the Department to run without you on a day-to-day basis. Find people who can do things for you and report to you. This cannot be changed."

"What about his research job?" Alexei asked.

"He can spend as much time on the research job as he wants, but he must keep up with ethnic problems," Rama Chand answered firmly. "I see the problems on both sides but I have no choice."

"I thought the ethnic problems were progressing well," Alexei said.

"It is not as simple as that," Rama Chand said. "Arsen will tell you."

"There is another major issue: what if we deflect the Demon and have all these ships in orbit somewhere in space?" Alexei asked and answered his own question. "Manned ships will return to the Earth - that is not a problem. Unmanned ships can be left in orbit or be destroyed - that is not a problem either. The problem is: what do we do with the knowledge that will have been accumulated? It will be difficult to set it aside or destroy it. Some people will ask for complete destruction of all information and existing technology; others will insist on expansion. What do we do to prepare for such a situation?"

"Is there a way to store the information in one place, say on a satellite, and destroy it on the Earth?" Rama Chand asked. "We wouldn't have to use that information but it would be available at a future date if people wanted to use it."

"It will be difficult to destroy the information," Alexei said. "However, it could be outlawed if people wanted that. That would be like genetic engineering nowadays. I am sure the technology would be used illegally."

"I agree," Arsen said. "What do you do with a couple who wants a baby and is not allowed to have it? A case in which both wife and husband have lost reproductive organs and want a baby. I am sure that, if we could clone *in vitro*, we could produce a baby with the genetic material from both of them. What do we tell them? 'Sorry, we have the technology but we are not allowed to use it. Maybe you should seek one of the clandestine laboratories to do it for you. Of course, it will be very expensive.' Or how do we proceed with the genetic manipulations to eliminate bad genes? Will genetic research be completely halted?"

"That is the future," Rama Chand said. "We have to decide what to do right now. I think we agree that we must proceed with this research for the worst scenario in which Earth is destroyed and uninhabitable after the collision. You do the work, and I will take care of the public relations."

"Gentlemen, lunch is ready," Alexei said. "Let us eat. We have accomplished a lot already. Let's see whether we can make some headway in eating." They laughed, but it sounded artificial because there was tension in the air - not among them, but between them and the rest of the world.

Rama Chand excused himself soon after the lunch, and left. Alexei and Arsen cleared the table and washed the dishes almost as an excuse not to talk. Then they went back to the living room and sat in the armchairs. Alexei was thinking about their conversation with Rama Chand and concluded that it was good to have him as the President; he understood what was at stake, and would support their efforts. Arsen was thinking about the conspiracy they had just formed with Rama Chand. Arsen thought Goran Enstrom would contribute to their thinking and decision making, although he was not directly involved in the research effort.

"Alexei, nobody has mentioned Goran," Arsen said. "He is a very smart man and a good thinker. As the Secretary of the General Department he will be able to defend our research and the need for it even if it is controversial and perhaps repugnant to some people. Do you think Rama will be able to handle the crisis alone? I don't. Don't you think that Goran would be of great help?"

"I trust Rama and I believe that he will be able to handle the problems without our help," Alexei said confidently.

"I would not be so sure," Arsen insisted. "Rama will understand Asian reactions quite well, perhaps even African. What about the reactions of refined Swedes or Catholic Italians or Irish, or Orthodox or communist Russians or Orthodox Jews? I think we should talk to Goran."

"Okay, if you think so," Alexei said with some irritation. "I would ask Rama and let him decide. He is the President." That was the end of the discussion. "I want to see you take over the biological research so that I can proceed with the building of space ships and push the neutrino research. I will let you know when we are ready for you in memory capture research so that you can work on its applications in humans."

The conversation was not going well. Alexei was not to be bothered any further with concerns humanity might have about its own preservation. For Alexei this was the chance to complete many projects that had been held up by a lack of financial support. Everything else was less important. The only time Arsen had seen him excited and worried was when he heard from Gennadi about the memory capture experiments. He was concerned that his research might have to be curtailed. Now that he had unloaded the biological research onto Arsen, and the worries about the public on Rama, he had regained his mental balance. There was no time for nonsense.

For the first time there was a faint shadow over the relationship between Alexei and Arsen.

Arsen went home in a bad mood. He did not like the approach they were taking, keeping him in the Ethnic Department; and the Biological Research would be neck-deep in problems once the research they were doing and would be doing became known. It was his deep conviction that humanity had to do whatever it took to preserve itself. If it took delayed cloning and use of memory capture, resurrection from a non-viable mixture of proteins and a pinch of DNA, then that should be attempted. And if it meant denying God, implied or real immortality and reincarnation, let it be. All that was worth not having to wait more than a billion years for life to emerge again in a primitive form, a phenomenon which might never happen again.

And even if it did happen, evolution might take another billion years before a human developed in the form known now, unless it took a completely different course and led life in who-knew-which direction. Despite all its faults, humanity possessed and displayed a divine beauty and intellect worth preservation at all costs. Arsen was shaken by his thoughts and most of all by the idea of the vanishing of the human race and with it of all life on Earth forever - leaving behind a pulverized globe. His body shivered a little as he lay on the couch in the living room, all alone in the apartment.

Arsen could not shake his thoughts off.

No, he did not believe in God and His creation of the world and humans. Somehow there was too much imperfection built into these creations. This could not have been done by the design of the Creator. Why would He want it that way? Why would He want suffering, wars, criminals, ethnic problems, illnesses, even death? Why would He create humans just to challenge them and reward some and punish others? Why create all these problems in the first place? This sounded too human to Arsen.

Then, too, everything alive had to die eventually. Why?

"Why do we have to die without even knowing what happens to us after death?" Arsen asked aloud. He had always believed that death was the beginning of nothing. The body was dead, the mind was dead, and the soul dissolved when trillions of synapses and cells in the brain were interrupted.

After all, everything had started from nothing, innumerable years ago. There had to be 'nothing' first before anything had been created, before the

Creator was created. It was probably most difficult to think of simply nothing: no atoms or subatomic particles; no planets or Earth or suns or galaxies; simply no Universe; no life of any kind; no places; no space or spaces, no darkness or light and nothing between; nothing existing; not even 'nothing' as an idea or a thought.

NOTHING!

Arsen's mind was boiling over with the idea of nothingness.

It would be acceptable and practical, and wonderful either way, if after death one were to pass into the tempting tranquility of Heaven or the boiling purgatory of Hell.

'But preserving Me, Myself, my Subconsciousness,' Arsen thought, 'my Mind, my Soul, in the company of others of the same fate, even in Sartre's eternal room. Why is it then so hard to die when Me, Myself, my Subconsciousness, my Mind, my Soul, will be preserved forever? Because my mind knows that at my death bed I am facing the end of everything that is life, a total denial of myself, and the step into nothingness. That is not acceptable.'

Death might be an interruption of the physical perception of self consciousness, yet self-consciousness as the personal *Geist*, an abstraction in itself, though negated, or attempted to be negated, became just a part of the universal *Geist* after one's death. The universal *Geist* would eventually return to nothing, to an inevitable abstraction, and as such, in and of its own existence as nothing--perhaps by expressing itself as the presence of nothing, the presence of abstract nothing, which was actually nothing, and yet as an abstraction, could, had, did, and would negate nothing--it would free and make available enormous energy that would start just another cycle of nothingness-to-nothingness, for an abstraction of nothing to the terminal abstraction of nothing; and as an abstraction, would recycle itself through the existence of one or an indefinite number of universes.

That was the Divine Power that had to be invented by Christ, Moses, Muhammad, Buddha and others, who intuitively felt the Power-that-was, and created fear of the Power of an omnipotent God. This fear had served the needs of generations of people. Gurus of liberalism, like Hegel, felt that people had to be free but their freedom had to be guided by the fair rules and laws of states which regulated relations among people. That was even pronounced to be the end of History - the creation of bored, though free, men whose problems had been resolved by personal freedom and protection by the state. How little protection states were capable of or willing to provide was best reflected in the figures of those killed in this century alone.

Arsen realized that he was in a trance, occupied with the nothingness after death, with religion as an expression of nothingness, and with the state of mind of humans in the present world. Hardly happy people as a group or individuals, he thought.

Arsen's thoughts wandered into the Universe of future humans.

Humans had to be happy by themselves and in themselves, outside social or ethnic or any other groups or restraints. This could not be accomplished by punishment for the slightest move in a wrong direction. There was no happiness with constant threats of punishment. Humans had to mature out of state systems by first gaining intergroup equality by resolving interethnic problems. The post-historic stage then completed personal freedom, independence, and interpersonal equality, and created a milieu in which individuals lived not in groups and societies but in their personal worlds that related to the worlds of other individuals on an equal basis. The functioning of such a constellation of individual worlds would depend on the integrity, responsibility, wisdom and knowledge of these individuals, who would not have to be reminded by anybody of what they could or should do - they would just do it as a matter of course. People as a group would have to mature to that stage while technological developments grew to the stage where individuals had no concerns for sustenance but were aiming at distant intellectual goals. There would be no states, no police, no money, no judges, no military, no schools, no hospitals.

This sounded like a good old utopian communist classless society, without society. It also sounded like an ode to the individual, communicating when she or he wanted, but independent of each other and of everybody else. This would require the long maturing of the humanity that would grow out of capitalism, communism, socialism and democracy into a new stage of universality in which individuals would advance into the Universe.

As with slave or feudal societies, and all others before and after them, individuals' understanding of the world had changed; slavery or feudalism had become unacceptable when humanity had progressed to the new social stage. Changes had been gradual and peaceful in the past, or a revolution had intervened

The Universal Civilization would evolve as fast as the new technologies developed and were adopted and made available to masses of people who would learn to use them. Present-day children had already been born in an electronic age and adults had learned to use electronic technology amazingly quickly. There was no reason to believe that the future would be any different. With technology, habits and attitudes would change fast, as the desire for independence was inherent to all humans. And the vast numbers of people who existed nowadays would be decimated by attrition to allow for the individual living without social ties and family bonds.

People of the future would live differently and think differently than we did today. There would be no heroes. People's opportunities would be enormous and their independence unlimited and unimpeachable. The Universe would be their limit.

But one problem had to be resolved on Earth before the universality became a reality, even a possibility, as Arsen's deflated thoughts reminded him. The celestial trajectory of the collision had not changed. The old reality had not gone away.

"We have to do what has to be done at all costs," Arsen said aloud. The frightening picture of the 'last stand of humanity' remained vivid in his mind.

The telephone rang. Victoria was on the line.

"Doctor, what's happening? I couldn't find you earlier. I'm supposed to move to Anticollision on Monday. Nobody there seems to know what is happening. I just talked to Sabrina and even she is vague. I think we should have a meeting of the Department and explain to everybody what's been decided."

"Excellent idea," Arsen said. "Can you arrange the meeting for tomorrow? Is everybody in town? At what time should we meet?"

"Ten o'clock, considering it's Saturday," Victoria suggested. "The undersecretaries are around as far as I know."

"Sounds good to me," Arsen said. "To bring you up to date, it has been decided that I will have to divide my time between the Ethnic and Anticollision Departments. It will not be easy. I need a deputy who will deal with details and day-to-day business in both departments. You are moving to Anticollision as my deputy. We have to decide who will do it in the Ethnic Department. Stan Petkovic will remain in Belgrade as my special envoy. He has enough problems with his arm, and he has to be close to his family. I am thinking of Herman Wolff as the replacement for Stan. What do you think?"

"I like him very much," Victoria agreed. "He always comes up with reasonable and logical solutions. He has already accomplished a lot in North Africa and the Middle East."

"I have no idea what he has done."

"The Israelis and Palestinians are talking seriously. Egypt is under pressure to resolve the Coptic problem. He has started audits in Algeria and wants elections in March. "

"Has he solved the problem of Jerusalem?" Arsen asked facetiously.

"No, he has not."

"Can't blame him for that. Even better men have failed."

"I'll talk to you tomorrow," Victoria said.

The tension he had felt earlier and the bad mood disappeared after he talked to Victoria. Arsen decided to take a stroll outside on the streets although he knew the Security Service would object strongly.

Outside, the drizzle was light and it was not cold. A few people were on the sidewalks, and many store windows were still lit up, probably because nobody had come to shut off the lights. Arsen raised the collar of his raincoat and walked briskly the route he liked the most: to Fifty-Seventh Street and along Fifth Avenue to Rockefeller Center - where he watched the skaters in the ice rink. The Security Service agents remained almost invisible.

CHAPTER FORTY FIVE

SATURDAY, 3 JANUARY 1998

When Arsen walked into the office he could hear loud talk coming from the conference room. He looked at his watch - it was five minutes before ten o'clock. As he walked into the conference room, the talk toned down. Arsen greeted most of the people before they sat down.

"The reason for today's meeting is to let you know what has been happening," Arsen said. "I am sure that you have heard that Gen. Shagov wanted me to take over biological research in the Anticollision Department. I wanted the job too. However President Chand was opposed. After talking it over yesterday we decided that I should continue in my present position in the Ethnic Department, and simultaneously be in charge of biological research.

"Another obligation, and one very close to my heart, is the Mandela-Tutu Commission, which will be set up in the near future. I shall have the Commission at the Anticollision until they acquire their own building. As must be evident to you, my time for all three functions will be limited. I have made up my mind to try to do all three jobs, although I think the essential job will be in biological research. Even if we resolve all ethnic problems and discover the truth about all crimes ever committed, the survival of the human race will still depend on the anticollision effort. That means deflection of the Demon and biological research. I intend to see to it that the biological effort succeeds."

Arsen paused for a moment, to give everybody a chance to have ideas of their own, and then he continued his policy presentation.

"That is the general outline of what is about to happen. No changes have to be made in the structure of this organization. I plan no changes for those who want to keep their positions. However, some new positions had to be created. I will have to appoint a deputy in the Ethnic Department.

"As you know, Mr. Petkovic is out because of his injury. I have decided to ask Herman Wolff to step into that position. This is the first time he has heard about it. He will take over all my duties and make most of the decisions, except, of course, the decisions I feel I have to make. So if you have questions and problems, ask Herman. If you need something, ask him too.

"One thing I promise you: I will chair the weekly department meetings as I was planning to do before. All major decisions will be made at these meetings."

"I will also need a deputy in the division of biological research. Victoria is moving to Anticollision as my deputy there. She has been asked to take the job--"

"I was told last night to take the job," Victoria protested.

"You accepted in Nicosia, if you remember," Arsen reminded her.

"I had no idea that you were planning to circulate among the three separate divisions."

"I was not planning to, I was told, too," Arsen said. "Anyway, you will be my deputy. Finally, I will ask Mel Stein to become my deputy at the Mandela-Tutu Commission. These changes should take effect immediately."

"I will take the job," Herman Wolff said.

"I will take the job with some trepidation," Melvin Stein said.

"Trepidation or not, this has been settled," Arsen said. "I will take two more men with me to Anticollision. One is Msgr. Amato whom we need for public relations work. The other is Jean Pierre Vernier, whom I need for special projects. Finally, Matt Brown will become my liaison man but will really work only for me and will continue as my spokesman. Herman will work on replacements. Each division will work separately from the others. I encourage you to keep within your domain and not cross lines. I am sure the transition will be smooth. I just hope we will be able to accelerate ethnic designations and give people what they want.

"Since I hear no questions, I will now go on to tell you about my experience in ethnic affairs so far, and about the recent events in Belgrade. I feel very comfortable with the course we have taken, and the response of the concerned parties. Our rules are fair, and the ethnic groups that want their independence will get it. We don't discourage autonomy or *status quo*. The decision is left to the ethnic group.

"We will also try to get rid of the crooks by audits, and I would like to see the audits get under way.

"Finally, we must ensure that decisions are carried out and that the achieved status is protected. So far we have dealt with outright resistance, and I was the subject of an assassination attempt. We have also seen cooperation at its best, in Cyprus. That is probably the best way to resolve the mutual problems, yet we cannot expect everybody to follow it. Truly, we must listen to people and do what has to be done and what they want. We cannot coerce them into agreements that we want them to make; we can offer our ideas only as suggestions and nothing more. We can use force, our military, if need be but that should be necessary only exceptionally. Most of all, we should attempt to make friends but not at all costs. We will not allow ourselves to be blackmailed either.

"My experience in Belgrade was frightening," Arsen continued. "I saw the assassins coming and I had time to duck the bullets. That may not be possible the next time. I should have sent somebody else to Belgrade. As a Serb I was expected to support the Serbian side no matter how wrong it was. That is a typical ethnic attitude: 'If you don't support us you are a traitor and you should be punished by death.' I understand that now quite clearly, and we should avoid such situations. I think we are learning how to travel the ethnic roads, and mistakes will be less common in time.

"The final word is that we have about two years to finish the job and a year to select people who will be passengers on the preservation space ships. These ships will take off in 2001, barely in time to escape to the edge of the solar system and away from the path of the Demon. I hope you realize how hopelessly short is the time we have to do the job."

"We have no idea what kind of ships will be sent to space with people on board," Max Epshtein said. "What will happen to them if the Earth disintegrates in the collision? Would they survive on the way to another planet?"

"I am sure everybody is asking the same question, and nobody wants to spell it out," Arsen said. "Yes, these people would die without oxygen, water and food. We will have supply ships but after a while they would have no supplies left and the inevitable would happen."

"Why are we sending these people to space anyway?" Max Epshtein continued his inquiry. "To die? They would be better off with us on Earth."

"Impact would disintegrate the Earth but near miss might not," Arsen said. "There will be tidal waves, maybe earthquakes, volcano eruptions, mountains will tremble, and who knows what else. Survival on Earth may not be feasible, but the Earth may be inhabitable afterwards, and the ships would return with the basics required for recovery. In such a scenario, some people, or even many people, would survive. These spaceships would bring rescue."

"Are there any other ships under consideration?" asked Ramesh Rao.

"That will depend on the available technology, like cloning," Arsen said. "That will be the responsibility of Biological Research." Ramesh Rao had asked a pertinent question and he was coming very close to the crucial question of triggering life in space, Arsen thought. He knew they would have to face the question from somebody someday, and they might as well be ready to answer it."

"Who will do the cloning if everybody dies?" Ramesh Rao asked, and he answered his own question. "If someone who dies were reincarnated in the space ship, he would be able to trigger the cloning."

Ramesh Rao was serious when he mentioned reincarnation and he must have meant it, Arsen thought.

"Even better, a computer robot could do it if there was cloning technology in place," Arsen suggested. "Such technology does not exist today."

"Now is the best time to develop it," Ramesh Rao said.

"Why now?" asked Arsen.

"Funds are available now for anything related to survival. The future is dubious."

"You mean people may be against this kind of a research?" Arsen suggested.

"Not only that," Ramesh Rao said. "Who will do the research if all of us are dead?"

"The decision for these changes was made by Rama Chand and Gen. Shagov and I found out about it only yesterday. It is clear to me that this is the way they want it; and I added the Mandela-Tutu Commission to the heap. That is my pet project now although, God knows, it would be irrelevant in the case of collision. Mel, I need a legal brain to run this commission, and I hope you don't mind my moving you out of the Ethnic Department."

"I understand," Mel Stein said.

Arsen turned to Jean Pierre Vernier. "Your job will be analytical," he said. "We will have to talk about that on Tuesday afternoon. You will have to know what people think and what their reactions are to the developments in biology, and you will have to anticipate problems. There will be problems, and I want you to keep an eye on the problem areas. There will be many people and groups who will object to our goals.

"Msgr. Amato will be responsible for the explanations, as a public advocate, and he may find himself sometimes on the other side of the official position. We may have to deal with all kinds of people in the near future. There will be responsible people, emotional people, religious people, centrists and leftists and rightists, irate and balanced people, and many other kinds that we will have to deal with. We should be prepared to face all of them and to deal with all of them and to pacify them all.

"Gen. Shagov's job is to deflect the Demon. You and I have to deflect the shots of these different people aimed at the World Government. Our job is to prepare the people for the worst scenario. Gen. Shagov has, and will have, all resources at his disposal to do his job. I ask you: what if he fails? Should we be prepared to shrug our shoulders and let the human race disappear forever? I strongly feel that we must be ready for such an instance, and we must start our work now while there is still time to accomplish the goal."

Arsen paused and looked at the people in the room. Their faces were very serious, and their expressions showed determination not panic.

Herman Wolff was the first to speak.

"I have been thinking about the same dilemma. We have to save the human race and worry later about social, psychological, religious, or any other considerations. I am not sure how I would react later, but now, I know that we have to go ahead."

"Do we all think the same?" Arsen asked, and he answered his own question. "I think we do."

Msgr. Amato wanted to speak.

"I wanted to give you my philosophical approach to the problems we will probably have to face. It is true that you will be developing technology that will do things never before imaginable. You have mentioned cloning. That is truly amazing when you think that only a few hundred years ago we did not understand infection or circulation. Should we consider Semmelwise and Pasteur and Harvey to have been the anti Christ and playing God just because they suspected the existence of external agents, or found out about bacteria, or showed the workings of the cardiovascular system? Should we condemn all the researchers who discovered the causes of various diseases and cures for many of them as competitors with God? Should we prohibit further research, wherever it may lead, and consider the people doing it as impious? Would human immortality diminish the divinity of God? Would it abolish God or the need for God? The answer to all these questions is an emphatic no. I am an incurable believer in God. I believe in His wisdom and power, His creation of the universe as we see it, and His unlimited love for us humans and other living forms. What is then the issue? Why are we worried? What can happen? People don't think the same, that is the problem. Even religious people think differently within their own religions. Religious leaders think differently. There are so many different trends of thought. Who will be able to reconcile them all? That may be more difficult than finding solutions to the ethnic problems. That is where we have to look for troubles and to find solutions for them so that the salvation of the human race can be accomplished." Monsignor Amato looked a bit frustrated, as he, in himself, was not convinced by what he had said, even though he meant every word.

Everybody remained silent after the Monsignor finished the explanation of his beliefs.

Arsen interrupted the silence. "Is silence the reaction of the leadership to the mounting problems facing humanity? It seems that the leadership is not ready to give answers yet, except for the Monsignor and myself."

"I think I have stated my position quite clearly," Herman Wolff said. "I did not think of the ramifications that are now obvious to me. One thing appears clear: like it or not, intend it or not, you will have to form a super-structure to the Ethnic Department. Don't you see? You will be directing the human effort while the General will be developing the technology. These two efforts will meet in 2001 when humans start boarding the ships destined for space. The function of the superstructure will only then be completed. At that time we from the human effort will retire and, like everybody else, await our fate. The General will be working on his neutri-no gun and getting ready to launch it in space. Goran Enstrom will be dealing with the portion of humanity that is not ready to die but expects death anyway. His job will be the most difficult one."

"I hear what you are saying, Herman, and I tend to agree," Arsen said. "I will propose to President Chand that he approve the Department of Human Resources, which will deal with all the problems we have already mentioned: biological research, preservation, ethnic problems, human relations, and the truth commission. I consider this meeting adjourned. I will let you know what happens. We should meet in the morning to establish the new department if it is approved. Let us meet again at ten o'clock."

Arsen remained alone in the conference room. He was thinking about the discussion they had just finished. He knew that Herman Wolff was right. Would he be able to sell the new department to Rama and Alexei?

Victoria walked into the conference room.

"Doctor, things are happening rapidly and we're changing course in a zig-zag direction. Is this new move good for us? "

"I think so," Arsen said. "As long as I have to oversee all these activities, I may as well do it with the team in one place. Herman said it very clearly, and I know he is right. Now I have to convince Rama and Alexei. I think they will agree because it was their own idea to get me involved in so many things."

"They'll agree," Victoria said.

"I think you had dinner with Rama the other night," Arsen said to Victoria. "What is he up to? Finally, you could speak in your own language. Did you?"

"We did. It turned out that we knew many of the same people through friends and relations. His late wife was a distant relative of my father."

"I did not know his wife had died." Arsen said. "I was wondering why I had never met her."

"It was pleasant to talk about home and people we knew. Rama said he was planning to take a brief vacation in India. He even invited me to go with him. Do you think that would be possible?"

"Hey, of course it is possible," Arsen said. "You must have a few days off here and there. When would you go?"

"He is leaving on Monday," Victoria said with hesitation. "How can I leave so suddenly?"

"You could never find a better time," Arsen said. "Nothing much will happen this coming week. We will have meetings and interviews and all the other nonsense, as you can imagine. Not real work." Arsen paused for a moment. "You will not marry him, will you?"

Victoria looked him straight in the face, then she said quietly, "I like him very much."

There was nothing further to ask. She was obviously interested, Arsen thought. Who would replace her? It was good to have a woman around to add some finesse and respectability to the organization. He did not like loosing Victoria.

Arsen called Rama Chand and found him in his office and he presented his idea of a new unified department.

"The department would deal with the fate of humans. Obviously the biological research would keep the center stage as the most important part of human survival - although we would have to make sure that other species survived along with humans. The Preservation and Ethnic Divisions would continue their work, and their goals would not change. Human relations will gain in importance when we face opposition to the biological research. We would have to lead the debate on the goals of the biological research, meaning cloning and memory capture, and to try to reach a consensus in favor of the present research goals. The Mandela-Tutu Commission would be just a sideline, of particular interest to me, and a powerful historical tool for the future."

"The World Government is becoming political," Rama Chand said to Arsen. "As I see it, this is just a consolidation of your staff into one department for convenience."

"You can add for efficiency too," Arsen said. "To do the job and to meet the potential challenges to the biological research, preservation and human interrelations must work together."

"Communication and close working relations with Anticollision have to exist," Rama Chand said. "I will talk to Alexei and let you know."

At home there was a message from Victoria on the answering machine. The Chinese President, Song Xiaobo, had called. Dr. Thomas Lowell, from the Rockefeller University, wanted to talk about an urgent matter. Rama Chand had left a message: "We have decided to let you form the

Department of Human Resources. Alexei and I have agreed on that as the best solution. Call me when you get a chance." Not much to say about this any more, Arsen thought.

"Mr. President," Arsen greeted the President Song Xiaobo. "Hopefully, I am not disturbing anything important?"

"Not really, Mr. Secretary," Song Xiaobo replied. "The usual boring business of the State: talking to people and signing documents."

"Would you like a more challenging job?"

"It depends on the location, perhaps in New York?"

"That's exactly what came to my mind. New York, a nice office and an even nicer apartment or a home in the country, and the job of Undersecretary for Ethnic Affairs. This is a big job and a big headache."

"Is this a joke or are you serious?" asked the surprised Chinese President.

"I am dead serious, Mr. President," Arsen said. "When could you start?"

"Oh, I have not expected such an offer," Song Xiaobo said. "I don't want to turn you down, not right now. I must think about it."

"What is there to think about?" Arsen insisted. "This job is essential in my new department."

"New department?"

"Yes. We call it the Department of Human Resources. It is responsible within the anticollision effort for anything alive. General Shagov will take care of everything mechanical."

"The more I think about it, the more I feel that I should take this job," Song Xiaobo said. "It would be important for China to have someone in the World Government."

"I agree," Arsen said. "And it would be important for you to partici-pate in resolving the most troubling world problems. We should resolve these problems and look forward to a different world and different rela-tions among people."

President Song Xiaobo said nothing.

"Can I count on you, Mr. President?" Arsen insisted again. "You know your situation in China and the possible consequences if you left."

"The situation is favorable and there would be no consequences."

"Then, can I expect you in New York in a week?" Arsen asked.

"Yes, I will be there," Song Xiaobo said quietly.

"I am delighted with your decision. Then I will see you in a week." Arsen remembered that the Chinese President wanted to talk to him. "Mr. President, you called about something. I forgot to ask you about that."

"Oh, I just wanted to thank you for the Cyprus affair. That was all."

Arsen felt gratified by the accomplished mission. Then he remembered the call from Dr. Lowell and found him at home.

"Dr. Lowell, this is Dr. Pankovich. You left a message for me to call you regarding some urgent matter."

"I'm glad you called," Dr. Lowell said. "Gen. Shagov asked me to call you as you have been put in charge of the biological research. The General told me that you would soon organize the new Department of Human Resources. We needed a physician to coordinate the Biological Research, and I'm sure the biologists will support you. Congratulations! Are you aware of the arrangements we at the Rockefeller University have made with Gen. Shagov?"

"I only know that you are working on an artificial gestation medium," Arsen said. "That is all."

"Exactly," Dr. Lowell said. "I wanted to share with you the fact that we're growing a cloned bird embryo right now, and don't ask me how we did it. It's one of those experiments in which someone did something in error and later couldn't remember what she did wrong to get the unexpected, though desired, result. Now we're retracing her steps to find out the genesis of this spectacular experiment. Eventually, we will find out how it happened."

"This is a breakthrough, isn't it?" Arsen asked and answered his own question. "Now we know it is feasible to gestate in an artificial environment. Your medium must have been enriched to allow growth. Now we have to await the outcome of this experiment to find out how far the embryo will develop."

"It's true that the development may cease at some stage," Dr. Lowell said. "Still, we have established the feasibility of artificial gestation."

"Dr. Lowell, how would the University and this research progress if you left the Presidency?"

"The University needs me more than the research. The people who are doing the research are very competent, and need my support more than my input. Why are you asking, Mr. Secretary?"

"I would like you to take over the Division of Biological Research."

"Impossible, Mr. Secretary. I have recently assured the university Trustees that I would not leave my position before 2003 under any circumstances."

"Your decision is irreversible, I guess?" Arsen asked.

"Yes, Mr. Secretary, it is irreversible," Dr. Lowell said emphatically.

"Too bad," Arsen said. "We need you too. We should soon start regular meetings as I would like to follow your research closely. Have a good evening." Arsen hung up. He was disappointed by Dr. Lowell's rejection. To hell with everybody, Arsen thought, he would take care of the biological research himself.

CHAPTER FORTY-SIX

SUNDAY, 4 JANUARY 1998

At ten o'clock Arsen started the meeting of the new department.

"As you know the Department of Human Resources was approved yesterday by Rama Chand and Gen. Shagov. Now we have to organize the new department.

"As you all know Msgr. Amato has been outspoken on human relations issues and he gave us his philosophical views at yesterday's meeting. He will head the Human Interrelations Division. As our biological and technological advances progress it will be important to explain our goals and our stands, and to try to find consensus among diverse opinions. Monsignor is best equipped to deal with these problems.

"We have a newcomer for the Ethnic Affairs Division whom you already know, the Chinese President Song Xiaobo. I talked to him last night and he agreed to join us. This appointment will give us more credibility in Asia.

"The Preservation Division will be headed as before by Jean-Pierre Vernier. His responsibility is to decide who will be passengers on the space ships when they take off in three years and who will remain on Earth. Unfortunately, there will be room for only about a thousand people on these ships. Many people will prefer to stay on Earth in view of the fact that there will be no return if the Earth disintegrates. Also, he will monitor trends in people's thinking and help Monsignor in bringing these diverse groups into balance with each other and with the reality in which we live.

"Mel Stein will remain in charge of the Mandela-Tutu Commission.

"The Biological Research Division was to be directed by Dr. Thomas Lowell, the President of Rockefeller University. Unfortunately, he rejected the offer. For the time being I will take care of that Division.

"I do not anticipate changes in the positions already filled in the Ethnic

Department."

Many questions were asked, and details discussed before the meting was adjourned.

Arsen asked Victoria, Herman Wolff and Matt Brown to join him in his office.

"Who will take my place in the Ethnic Department?" Herman Wolff asked.

"Song Xiaobo will have to decide who will get the job," Arsen said. "I will have to approve it. As to the Jewish-Arab problem I have decided to handle it myself. There are too many sensitivities to be dealt with and they will get me involved anyway. Imagine trying to resolve disagreements between Jews and Arabs that have been around for millennia, not only the last fifty years. I may as well be involved before the issues become too complicated. I have a clear picture of what has to be done. Of course, both sides will hate me in the end and I will become the target of both the Mossad and the Hamas. Let it be. The Serbs almost killed me too. I will take my righteousness to my grave."

"How are you going to resolve the Jewish-Arab problem, which has never come even close to a solution?" Herman Wolff asked.

"It is too early to talk about that," Arsen said. "The stage has to be set for the final agreement. You will know what is happening."

"I think you should give that territory to somebody else," Victoria said. "You're too emotional and biased in favor of Jews."

"Nonsense," Arsen protested. "Nobody can tell me I was not biased in favor of the Serbs, and yet they were very upset with. my decisions. I have set some principles that are applicable and just in dealing with all ethnic groups. Why should it be any different in the Middle East?

"It is different," Victoria said. "You'll find out."

"I wanted to talk to you about the way we are going to function," Arsen said, changing the subject. "Your job is to keep me informed. I will tell you when I want something different from what you have decided. Herman you will deal with everybody who would normally come to see me. When you think I should get involved, tell me and I will. Victoria, you will make the department run smoothly. Matt, make sure the signals from the department are not misleading; we want to present the truth without confusing people. I anticipate problems from the Biological Division. Many achievements of their research will be offensive to some people, and they will protest and fight. You will witness the uproar."

"Do you really think people will fight against the tools of human survival?" asked Herman Wolff

"Yes, I do," Arsen said.

"Doctor, I am beginning to doubt that the space in this building is sufficient for our expanded department," Victoria said. "I would like to assess the situation and look for separate buildings for each division."

"Why don't you rent the adjoining buildings and make a bridge for each division?" Arsen suggested. "You will be back from India in a week, won't you?"

"Going to India?" Herman Wolff asked. "To visit the family?"

"Yes," Victoria said, although that was only partially true.

"Doctor, Mr. Enstrom is on line four," Michelle announced over the intercom.

"Good morning, Goran. It has been a while since we talked. It is about time to have dinner together."

"I agree," Goran Enstrom said. "Come to our apartment tonight for dinner. Eight o'clock?"

"Eight o'clock," Arsen confirmed. "See you tonight."

What was on Goran's mind, Arsen wondered. Arsen wanted to know what was being done for people around the world. He also wanted to discuss with Goran the reaction to the technological and biological discoveries, his main concern for the future. And he wondered how Goran had taken his decision to remain in the Ethnic Department?

Michelle came on the intercom.

"Doctor, the Chinese President called just to let you know that everything is under control and on time. He will be in New York on Saturday. Gen. Shagov wanted you to call him when you get a moment. Ivo Stipich wanted you to call him. That's all."

"Call Gen. Shagov first, then Ivo Stipich."

"The General is on line two," Michelle announced over the intercom.

"Arsen, we should meet to discuss with our engineers what you need in the space ships. When can you come?"

"Right now if you can arrange the meeting," Arsen said. "By the way, Alexei, Tom Lowell told me about a very important development at the Rockefeller labs. They are growing a bird embryo in an artificial medium. They are not sure how it happened as it was triggered by an error. I am sure they will have a medium for cloning humans in the near future. Of course, there is a big difference between bird and human embryo development. I can explain to the engineers what we need."

"We could meet in an hour," Alexei said.

"I will be there."

Michelle had found Ivo Stipich.

"Ivo, it was good you reminded me to call you. I am ready for Anton Lopasic. Tell him to come to New York and to call me when he arrives. Give him my home phone number. What is happening in Croatia?"

"Our situation is quiet. The Serbs will be allowed back into Krajina and

I was assured that they will not be mistreated. I think everybody realizes that the previous attitude was wrong. Bosnian Croats are happy to be part of Croatia. Slavonia is quiet, as the attitude there has changed too. Your reputation is very favorable, and Anton would like you to visit Zagreb. Why don't you come to Zagreb instead of Anton going to New York?"

"Okay, I will come," Arsen said. "Find out when would be the best time for Anton."

"I will let you know later today."

The meeting in Alexei's office started at eleven o'clock.

Arsen was impressed with the questions from the engineers. They understood what was needed on the space ships. Particularly surprising was their understanding of delayed cloning . They knew what it would take to trigger life after a thousand years in space.

"The main problem is the question of raising a child or children once they are cloned," said the Senior Engineer, Anatoly Tarasov. "It takes six or seven years before a child can learn complex tasks. How are we going to provide care for them during this critical period?"

"This question has been on my mind ever since the idea of delayed cloning came up," Arsen said. "It has to be mechanized in the beginning, until at least the mechanical functions of the brain develop. A child will get up and start walking upright at one year on an average and will be quite coordinated at two years. This is the period when the child will need most support. We will talk to experts to find out what will be the minimum support we will have to provide and what kind of support will be needed. What do we do during the ten years after that?" Arsen looked at Alexei before he developed his idea further. Alexei understood.

"Arsen, you can mention the memory capture, if that is what you are hesitating about," Alexei said. "They know that Gennadi is working on it."

"At age two or three years we have only two choices," Arsen continued, "either the child's brain is allowed to progress spontaneously - and this is not my first choice - or we accelerate this process by use of psychoexchange. We don't even know whether this technology works - even in adults. But I would like to plan for it as it would simplify the educational process of the child."

"Who will develop the teaching techniques?"

"I will establish a panel of experts on the physical and mental development of children," Arsen said. "They will help us plan this technology."

"Do you think a robot would be able to take care of the cloning and the child?" Dr. Tarasov asked. "That is if you have a robot in mind."

"Do you have a better idea?"

"Not really."

"I assume that the sensors on your ships will be able to recognize an inhabitable planet for life from the Earth?" Arsen asked. "What about a planet with existing life?"

"I am sure the ship would recognize either planet," Dr. Tarasov said. "Which one would be more desirable?"

"I am not ready to answer that question," Arsen said. "There are good and bad points for each environment. If life existed it should not be incompatible with life on Earth. This planet, Planet X, should have oxygen in the air and plenty of water, and the surface should be made of productive soil. The Ecology Panel will advise us how to develop an ecosystem similar, though not identical to the one we have on Earth now. Obviously, we will have to take genetic material from as many diverse species as possible to develop a similar environment. Our ships will have to be as large as practical to take this diverse cargo. Besides that we have to take enough supplies to keep the first child alive for ten or more years before he can produce his own food.

"The animals, though essential, will have to be selected carefully and their triggering timed so that they don't destroy the existing life. Another panel will have to advise on potential health problems and how to deal with them.

"The knowledge of everything on Earth will be stored in the computers. The inhabitants of Planet X will have to know how to find it. It seems to me there will be more problems having to do with survival on the new planet than there will be in reaching it. Incidentally, Dr. Tarasov, what will be the durability of these space ships? Ten years, a hundred years, a thousand?"

"How about a hundred thousand years," Dr. Tarasov said. "The ships will be build to last forever. The electrical power supply is not a problem as the energy of the universe is immense, and it will not be difficult to tap it. A ship could be damaged by a meteorite or some other flying object or if it strays into the atmosphere of a celestial body and crashes against it from the gravitational pull - although the ships will be prepared to avoid such problems. I am convinced that some ships will make it to their destinations."

"Do you think you are ready to start building the ships?" Arsen asked. "How many ships can we send?"

"You mean how many ships can we build?" Dr. Tarasov said. "That is impossible to say as we don't know as yet what equipment and how much space is needed on the ships. We are not ready to design these trigger ships at this time."

"You are obviously right," Arsen said. "We must move rapidly and determine what is the minimum needed to accomplish the mission. I will assemble the panels immediately, and they will tell us what do we need."

"Thank you very much, Dr. Pankovich," Dr. Tarasov said. "This was a useful conversation. We will await information. Let us know when you are ready for another meeting."

"Can you give me at least an estimate on the number of the ships?" Arsen insisted as he shook Dr. Tarasov's hand. "A rough estimate?"

"A hundred ships at best."

Anatoly Tarasov exchanged a few words with Alexei and left the office in the company of his associates.

"I did not anticipate this kind of questioning," Arsen said. "This man knows the subject. I am sure he has some good ideas about how to handle the problems we mentioned. Unfortunately, some new and unexpected problems, which I left out, were also raised recently. This will be rough going."

"You elected to be in the front line," Alexei said with the emphasis on 'elected' and 'front line', as if saying: this is what you get for pulling out of my department.

"I was forced to be in the front line," Arsen said. "All I wanted was to direct a small ethnic territory like Bosnia and Serbia."

"In which you were almost eliminated," Alexei said.

"You are right."

"I heard you appointed the Chinese President as Undersecretary for Ethnic Affairs," Alexei asked. "Do you trust that guy?"

"Somehow I do trust him," Arsen said. "He was very enthusiastic about Cyprus and only made a show about Tibet. He had to do it politically."

"Arsen, keep lines of communications open - it is extremely important for my team," Alexei said.

"You still have some doubts about it," Arsen said. "We need each other and a biological solution is possible only with your leadership and support."

"I have no problems with the mission in the space," Alexei said. "My concern is with the Earth in the near future when our plans for biological survival become known. What will be the reaction of people to these plans which are often contrary to the norms of present day civilization? As you said, who would allow their children to participate in the memory experiments that will be essential for delayed cloning and life triggering in space. These are not rats but humans. I have inner objections to such experiments, yet my human survival instinct tells me these experiments will have to be done."

Alexei paused and looked at the ceiling as if gazing in the Universe where this huge celestial object was heading uncontrollably towards the Earth.

"I wish I could tell you we will succeed in deflecting the Demon" he said, "and that all these biological efforts are unnecessary. I cannot say that yet, and we have to proceed with our plans for biological survival. I am worried even more about the new information if we survive. What are we going to do with that information? What are we going to do with the ships that have gone out of our solar system? It will be almost impossible to turn them back. Should we be prepared to explode them wherever they may be? Or should we just let them fly through the universe? To me the decision to build these ships will be more difficult than actually building them. When do you think you will be able to announce the options for biological survival?"

"There are no options for biological survival, as you well know," Arsen said. "There are only two alternatives. Either we proceed and do what has to be done to build and equip these ships, or we sit and wait and pray you succeed in deflecting the Demon. If we choose to do nothing, I see no reason for the existence of the World Government. Our efforts in changing the world would become meaningless if we chose total human suicide. We would concentrate on making peace within ourselves and with our Gods. If you succeeded, the human race would have become emotionally so exhausted as to be incapable of any mental effort and so elated as to be able only to pray and thank its Gods for survival. Nothing else would be important."

"You really don't believe in God, do you?"

"I don't."

There was nothing further to be said.

Back in the office, Arsen found a message from Ivo Stipich: "The week of January 26 would be convenient for Anton and me."

The idea of visiting Zagreb was appealing to Arsen, and the date was good.

Arsen remembered that there had been problems regarding the Russians in the former Soviet Republics. He asked Michelle to find Max Epshtein, who was responsible for Russia.

"Max, what has been done about the Russians in the former Soviet republics, if anything?"

"Nothing yet," Max Epshtein said. "We have talked with several of the Presidents of the new countries. They were very evasive in our talks. The bottom line is that they would like to send the Russians back home. I cannot completely blame them for that."

"Max, come up to my office." Arsen's blood was boiling with anger at the nonchalant attitude of Max Epshtein. It was clear that the Soviet government was trying to colonize some of these republics with Russians, but that was not the fault of those Russians who remained in the new countries;

many younger people had been born there.

There was a knock on the door and Max Epshtein walked into the office.

"Sit down, Max," Arsen said. "Max, I am not sure you have gained enough insight into the operations of this department. We don't just sit on the issues, we deal with them. I think we have clearly established the principles for dealing with minorities. The minorities either live separately in their own territory, say like the Kurds in several adjoining countries or the Albanians in Serbia, or they are mixed in with the rest of the population and have no identifiable territory. If they qualify as an ethnic group, which in the example of Russians in Latvia is not an issue, but have no territory of their own, they achieve a special status and the countries they live in are obliged to take extra measures to ensure they are treated well. What I mean is that these people are the citizens with equal rights and are treated as equals.

"I came to the United States and was expected to speak English before I got a job, and my opportunities were commensurate with my abilities not my origin. Of course, the Americans had an edge over me, but nobody stopped me from overcoming it. An anecdote will show you how it works. When I became the Program Director in Orthopedics at Cook County Hospital, my boss, an American, said to me one day,

"'Arsen, how do you deal with the damn foreign applicants to your residency program?'

"'The damn foreigners have to show that they are very good - then I take them,' I answered.

"My Chief just laughed, remembering that I was a foreigner myself. The story tells you something. Max, I am very upset that you haven't made clear to these Presidents that the principles exist and that they don't have the choice, they must apply them."

"Aren't we shoving our principles down their throats?" Max Epshtein asked.

"No Max, we aren't," Arsen said sternly. "All these people, Presidents and Prime Ministers and politicians, preach these principles. Remember the Soviet State? The principle was established by Lenin himself."

"I know, he laid it down in his work on the problem of nationalities," Max Epshtein injected.

"Now you remember." Arsen continued his lecture to Max Epshtein. "Our job is to make sure they put into practice what they publicly endorse. Nothing more."

"Do we use force, if need be?" Max Epshtein asked.

"Very rarely, I hope," Arsen affirmed. "Max, you get the message. If there is a question in a special situation, ask Song Xiaobo or me."

"I was wondering about Song Xiaobo," Max Epshtein said. "He is a communist, and you trust him to do the job."

"You are a communist too, remember?" Arsen said. "The communists knew how to keep ethnic problems in check. Their fault was that they insisted on ethnic harmony for devious reasons. The leader of an ethnic group was usually from the same group. People trust their own. These leaders were first and foremost communists and their loyalty was to the Party in Moscow, although they gained the confidence of the people along ethnic lines. That is the devious part. We will do it because it is right and will expect the leaders to be loyal to and work for their own people, not for us. That is the difference from the communist approach. Our interference will be the right to audit the political leaders, and to weed out the crooks."

"I understand," Max Epshtein said. "I know what to do now."

"Michelle, find Prof. Menguy in Paris for me." Arsen wanted to try to talk him into joining the life trigger research, although he had already rejected Alexei's offer. Perhaps Alexei did not know how to talk to him. He seemed to be the best prepared for the research of *in vitro* gestation. There will be some overlap with the Rockefeller labs, but Menguy could solve the problems of placenta in mammals' gestation.

"Prof. Menguy is on line two," Michelle announced over the intercom.

"Prof. Menguy, this is Dr. Pankovich. I hope you know who I am?"

"Of course, I know. Who doesn't?" Prof. Menguy exclaimed with some annoyance in his voice as if he were offended by Arsen's question.

"Prof. Menguy, you run one of the best research laboratories in the world and your achievements are extraordinary. These are the facts. Your contribution could and would make a difference between the success and the failure of the projects that are under consideration by the World Government. How can we persuade you to help us? You could choose, if you want, to be our consultant only occasionally or part time. It would be in the best interest of the World Government that you take over the entire project of mammal *in vitro* gestation. We have already started the work on the artificial media at Rockefeller University. Would you care at least to discuss the subject with me?"

"Mr. Secretary, I would be glad to talk to you any time. Would you like me to come to New York? When?"

"Sometime this week. Any day is fine. Just call me when you arrive in New York."

"I will let you know, Mr. Secretary."

Arsen was thinking of the conversation with Anatoly Tarasov and the panels he had to organize.

"Michelle, let me talk to the President of Columbia University."

Soon the President was announced by Michelle.

"Mr. President, this is Secretary Pankovich. I decided to seek your help in a rather urgent matter concerning our research in biology. We would like to form a panel of experts on the education of children." Arsen explained the idea. The President, Anthony Falk, showed interest immediately. Arsen did not know it, but he was an expert on the education of children.

"The bottom line is the education of a single or of multiple children in a space ship without the support of parents or anybody else. What is the minimum they would have to learn? How do we teach them? We need a basic report in a week, that would outline what has to be done and how to do it." Arsen couldn't tell him about the memory capture since nobody knew about it.

"I'll have a panel of fifteen experts put together by tomorrow," Anthony Falk said. "We'll meet immediately and you can expect our basic report by the end of the week."

"This is faster than I expected," Arsen said. "I would like to meet with the group on Saturday in my office. Think about the research you would have to conduct and the people who would design and make the teaching tools. Keep in mind that the whole project must be designed and ready to go within two years. Use as many people as you need but don't tell me it cannot be done on time."

"Saturday at what time?"

"Ten a.m."

Arsen felt good after talking with Anthony Falk.

"Michelle, let me talk to the Director of the Centers for Disease Control and Prevention in Atlanta."

"Dr. Robert Swift is on line three," Michelle announced over the intercom.

Arsen explained the reason for the call and the need for a panel. Dr. Swift had a wide range of experts and promised to have the preliminary report in two weeks.

Herman Wolff walked into the office.

"I am glad you have come." Arsen explained his meeting with Alexei and the arrangements he had made for the two panels.

"I have never even thought about anything like this," Herman Wolff said. "I am learning rapidly and feel a little dizzy with all these new ideas, like delayed cloning and enteric bacteria in a cloned child. I will talk to the U.S. Environmental Protection Agency and to the Ecology Agency of the United Nations, and to the American Academy of Pediatrics to establish the appropriate panels for Ecology and physical and mental development in children. We are really talking about time. Life will be triggered on a space ship after it lands on a planet, right?"

"Right."

At eight o'clock that evening Arsen was in the elevator on his way to the eleventh floor, where the Enstroms lived.

Ursula Enstrom was at the door as Arsen stepped out of the elevator. She was in her early fifties. A simple blouse and a long skirt covered her tall figure. In contrast to Goran Enstrom she looked muscular and athletic. Her blond hair gave her that Swedish look and the lines of her face were gentle and regular, and the two sides of her face symmetrical - something that gave beauty and femininity to a woman. Her lips slightly open in a smile, offered a view of beautiful teeth. She wore almost no makeup.

"Finally I meet you, Mrs. Enstrom."

"Ursula."

"Why has Goran been hiding you from everybody?"

Ursula did not answer, but her smile became broader as she acknowledged Arsen's obvious compliment.

They walked into a large living room which was connected to a formal dining room by a large glass door. Arsen remembered another Swede, his chief when he was a Fellow in New York in the sixties, who had invited him for dinner. The apartment had been just as elegant as this one and had also had a formal dining room. And the hostess, the professor's wife, was as pretty and charming as Ursula Enstrom.

A long leather sofa against one wall faced the wooden bookcases, filled to capacity with books, that covered the opposite wall. Two modern chairs at each end completed a circle around a glass tea table. A painting by a primitivist, bursting with vibrant colors, hung above the sofa. A photograph of the Swedish Royal Family hung on the adjoining wall and Arsen paused in front of it.

"You must be surprised to see the photograph of the Royal Family on the wall of the living room," Ursula said, guessing Arsen's thoughts. "Goran received it from the King when he was a boy, and he is very proud of it."

Goran joined them in the living room.

"Arsen, I have been planning this evening for a while. You are always so busy. You have made significant progress in the ethnic zoo, and the New Year's party in Nicosia was a major success story. Surprisingly you were hardly noticed that evening, and yet you made it possible."

"The people who count always know," Arsen said.

"You are right," Goran said. "What are Rama Chand and Alexei up to? I rarely talk to them these days. They seem to be concerned about the future not the past. You and Alexei are the future. I deal with the past, if you consider that the people I deal with may be dead in a few years. That seems rather depressing, doesn't it?"

"Many new things are happening every day," Arsen said. "New concepts are being brought forward and studied. Really, the future is in the developments in biology and technology. The future for most people is the preservation of the present and the past, and that depends on our ability to deflect the celestial object. The problem is that we are not sure the collision can be avoided."

"That is exactly what I mean," Goran exclaimed. "Exactly. I think people feel that no progress has been made, since they have not heard about great successes in research that would produce technology capable of deflecting the Demon. The problem is that people have nothing to say about their own fate. We need something that will energize them so they can feel like participants in the global plot to save the world. They should feel they have something to say about all that. Yet, everything is so complex, it is hard for ordinary people to understand. Neutrino research, for example, which I myself do not understand. What about a clerk in lower Manhattan or in Tuscaloosa, in Johannesburg or in Anchorage, in Saigon or in Tokyo? In this example, they would at least think of a space gun, even if they haven't understood how it works. Biological research is difficult to understand conceptually. People will get wrong ideas of what you are doing."

"I don't think so," Arsen responded. "People are not that stupid. They will understand the concepts of cloning even if they don't understand the principles. They probably understand that you can fertilize a woman by some manipulation and that she will bear a child who will grow up to look exactly like her. They can imagine gestation *in vitro* , as they have seen the hatching of eggs. They know what the soul is even if they have not read Hegel. They know what death means to an individual even if they have not had a near-death experience themselves or even heard about such a thing. People have differing opinions about what happens to them after death. They think of immortality as a legacy left by someone after his death, as an enduring fame, the soul in heaven or hell, or as an endless afterlife. These are definitions you find in dictionaries. A few people are atheists and practically all others believe in something after death. I am not sure how many believe in nothing after death."

"You make it sound very simple," Goran said.

"I did not mean to say it is simple," Arsen said. "I was just laying out the basics that are of concern to us, since they may become issues when people find out what we are doing. You may find the population electrified to the extent that some of them may try to prevent the research in biology and insist on only the technological research that has to do with deflecting the Demon - giving us no alternatives for preserving the human race and animal and plant life."

"You mean that the biological research could become objectionable to the population?" Goran seemed surprised by Arsen's trend of thinking.

"Yes that is what I mean," Arsen said. "Think of immortality, for example. We are doing research that could lead to the cloning of humans in artificial media. The reasons that research on delayed cloning is essential are straightforward. Will people allow us to develop such technology and deploy it on the space ships? Perhaps some will allow us to proceed and others will fight us. Who do we listen to? Who is to decide? Wouldn't these issues be energizing for the population? This could also become very polarizing and outright dangerous. Would that cause disunity despite the common threat?

"Goran, I think you should use your huge administrative apparatus to design ways of channeling the people's frustrations and anger. I don't want to suggest that we should influence their beliefs; rather, I would challenge them to express themselves peacefully. This task may overcome your own frustrations, which are obvious to me since you are asking for an energizing of the population."

"I am concerned with my domain and I have missed the developments in the preservation effort," Goran said. "I missed the party in Nicosia and I haven't talked to you or Rama or Alexei. I also should tell you what has happened in the world."

Ursula invited them to the dinning room where dinner was served by a waiter and a maid hired for the occasion. Arsen encouraged Ursula to talk about their life in Sweden. She obliged and talked mainly about Goran's family, and their prominence in Sweden. Goran's father had been a respected professor of Linguistics and a member of the Swedish Academy and of the Nobel Committee. Goran's mother died early and Goran and his two brothers had been raised by the father and his sister. Ursula's family was from the middle class, the father a general practitioner in a small town and the mother a schoolteacher. They had met at the University in Stockholm where Goran had been an Economics professor and she a medical student. They had no children.

"Then you are a medical doctor, are you?" Arsen asked.

"Yes, I am," Ursula answered. "I have not practiced for several years, ever since we came to the United States."

"Why don't you do something in research? Perhaps in some administrative capacity? Our biological research division could use someone like you. Do you have the guts for something unusual in science that will change your thinking about the world and yourself in it? How solid is your religious belief? Could it change? As you can imagine, the entire world will have to change. Come work for us and witness the circus in which humanity is asking to be preserved and doing everything to prevent it."

"You are talking in punnigrams, aren't you?" Ursula scolded Arsen.

"Thank you for the offer, anyway. I may take you up on it. Goran would-n't notice my absence anyway since he is never home. He is too obsessed with the existing humanity."

"Only don't wait too long, you may miss the beginning of the show," Arsen said.

"I don't quite catch what you are trying to say." Ursula looked at Goran and Arsen as if they were hiding something from her.

"I was just explaining to Goran where our research is heading and the potential reaction of the population - which may lead to chaos," Arsen said and explained the type of research that might become controversial and offensive to the population, or to part of it. "If led by people opposed to such research, significant forces could form to stop the research yet demand the salvage of humanity, or even worse, pronounce the arrival of Christ or the coming of the Last Judgment or whatever else signifies the end of the world. That would effectively prevent us from completing our projects and reaching our goals to save humanity from extinction in case the Demon collides with the Earth."

"Where have I been all this time?" exclaimed Ursula. "I do want that job!"

"I am glad for you," Goran said agreeably. "I did not know how to explain to you that you should work without giving you a wrong impression."

Ursula invited them back to the living room, where espresso and cognac were served.

"Goran, you wanted to tell me about the world the way you see it," Arsen said. "The world beyond biological problems and before the collision. You should know by now the percentage of acceptance of and the reactions to the ethnic solutions."

"Sure I know. In places like Tibet, where the Chinese grip has disappeared, you feel vibrant life and a profound anxiety about the imminent approach of the calamity that will take that new life away. The situation is similar in the Turkish part of Cyprus. This will probably be true of all territories once they gain their freedom. The territories that have been reduced by secession are angry, as if someone stole their land - even if only a few of their own ever lived in the ceded territory. Look at your own Serbia, which probably suffers more than many other places. Even the Spaniards are angry over the loss of the Basque territory. As you would expect, the bigger the territory, the greater the anger of the loosing majority.

"To mollify all parties, as even the secessionists will not be spared, we will start incentive programs aimed at improving understanding and promoting respect among the involved groups. We will organize parties, which we call mini-Nicosia parties, and will try to bring together people who would otherwise remain enemies. We will ask the opposing groups to send intellectuals, teachers, scientists, politicians and others as visiting lecturers who will explain their side of the story without blaming and offending their listeners. "

Goran sipped his cognac and licked his lips.

"Arsen, your talk in Belgrade, which ended just today in the death of the President of the Academy, meant well but was given to the wrong audience at the wrong time. Your story was right, but it should have been told by a Croat in a calmer atmosphere and without accusing anybody, just expressing how Croats see history. Everything is misunderstood and nobody wants to listen. The conversations we plan should not incite riots, but force people to be introspective, and hopefully they will be less angry."

"I had not heard about the death of Prof. Cvejic," Arsen said sadly. "Nobody told me he was wounded mortally. I feel responsible for his death."

"You should not," Goran said. "The men who shot at you were ready for you before you arrived to Belgrade."

"Doesn't matter. How is Stan Petkovic doing?"

"He is home." Goran said. "He is not a popular person in Belgrade either."

"Amazing that you know all these things," Arsen said. "It seems you feel the pulse of the population better than we in Human Resources do. Incidentally Goran, where will you stand in the forthcoming debate?"

"Despite my beliefs, I think that everything has to be done to ensure preservation of the human race and of other species."

"What do you believe?" Arsen insisted.

"I was brought up believing in God, and I still do, although my beliefs have been shaken by biological progress, which has reached the domain reserved for God."

"I anticipate more than just a declaration of beliefs from the people opposed to the invasion of God's domain," Arsen said. "I anticipate open fighting, rebellion, insurrection, war - whatever phrase or excuse you want to use for killing. I believe we will get the ethnic problems under control rapidly since the pattern so far has been straightforward acceptance of reasonable solutions, though sometimes loudly expressed displeasure. This is usually heard from oppressors who are asked or forced to give up territory. The oppressed people never complain about gaining their freedom."

Goran only nodded in approval.

"We will be arguing for the biological research," Arsen continued, "although I am not sure that everybody who is or will be working for the World Government agrees with the research that is needed to preserve the human race and at least some of the other living species. Our argument will be that we should be allowed to finish our projects and accomplish our goals and be ready to launch the ships. Then, if the people do not want us to proceed with the launchings, we will do what they want. We could destroy the ships and the entire evidence of these projects. In approximately three years, Alexei will be ready to launch his neutrino gun and he will have a good idea of the outcome. If he succeeds, we could destroy our material or store it or be allowed to continue. To stop the research now would be a mistake, a gamble."

"I agree," Goran said. "I think I am in a position to prepare the forums: public, scientific, theological and political, and whichever others may be required. This can be organized in the near future. Our emphasis can be on what you just said: let us continue the research for the present and decide the course of action at the critical time three years from now."

"I think we will have to give a chance to people on all sides of the controversy and make sure that every possible angle is covered," Arsen said. "People will be more active than usual in their participation since the topic is survival. Should there be a need for a referendum we will have one and let the people decide. Before the vote we should at least have a chance to explain our views. You know, Goran, I feel good about this conversation. I have been worried about violent solutions and constant crisis within the population."

"I am not sure we will avoid violence completely but I think it will be manageable."

"Let us try for once, perhaps at the end of history, not to tell people what is good for them," Arsen said. "They know what is good for them, yet they have always been manipulated by someone, and particularly by the media in recent decades. They are given selected facts, however accurate, which lead them in the direction desired by the one who is paying the bill. That is not fair."

"We can only try," Goran said.

"You are right, Goran." Arsen looked at his watch - it was almost eleven. "It is getting late and time for me to go home."

"Why don't you stay longer? Ursula asked.

"You've had enough of me for one evening," Arsen said. "I will expect you tomorrow at eight in my office so that I can tell you about the job I have in mind for you. Okay Dr. Enstrom?"

"I was Dr. Bjöstrom, professionally," Ursula Enstrom said.

"Okay Dr. Bjöstrom?"

"Okay Mr. Secretary."

Arsen felt he had had a pleasant evening.

CHAPTER FORTY-SEVEN

TUESDAY, 6 JANUARY 1998

The office was quiet when Arsen walked in at seven o'clock. The night watchman was signing out and a Security Service agent was reading his newspaper in the ante-room. Michelle usually arrived at eight o'clock, and the appointments were scheduled to start thereafter.

Arsen called Rama Chand's office and Rama answered.

"I took a chance at finding you alone this early, probably trying to catch up with some unfinished work. Aren't you going to India today?"

"That's right. I was to leave yesterday but I had to take care of a problem in the Assembly. What is on your mind?"

"Changes, what else, which require your approval or veto. I spent the evening with Goran and his wife. He is doing a very good job with the populations of many countries. Mandela and Interrelations would fit very well with the rest of his department. The bottom line is that I want to be sure somebody will be explaining to people what is happening and channeling their frustrations and even more their objections, and taming some aggressive minds. I want to prevent at all costs any bloody confrontations. Just think of those who welcome the collision as the opportunity to meet God or as the Judgment Day. They might not like our preservation effort, and may even fight it. Goran can make the difference. What do you think?"

"I just arranged for the changes that were decided with Alexei."

"Alexei should like this change, as it will give me more time for his projects."

"Arsen you have had many good ideas but this one is not your best," Rama Chand said. "You said yourself that your department will be concerned with human relations and future needs. How could anybody explain your ideas better than you yourself? Listen to me. Keep your department as it is and lead the fight to keep the research going. I cannot approve this project. I hope you haven't talked to Goran about it."

"No I have not."

"Good. Keep it that way. I will call you from India."

"Oh, another request. I have decided to appoint Ursula Bjöstrom, Goran's wife, to be an Associate Undersecretary for Biological Research."

"What are her qualifications except for her beauty, for her being Goran's wife, and for being an M.D. ?"

"Intelligence, Rama, intelligence," Arsen said emphatically. "I cannot say I find it to be ubiquitous. She will learn her job rapidly, I am sure."

"Okay, okay, don't be touchy," Rama said. "I will arrange for her appointment."

"Today!"

"Today," Rama confirmed.

"Thank you, Rama," Arsen said.

This was tough, Arsen said to himself, and called Alexei.

"Arsen, you call people early," Alexei said after Arsen greeted him.

"Early is the best time to find someone like you. I called to let you know that I found myself a Memory Chief. Ursula Enstrom."

"How did you manage to persuade her?"

"She asked for the job after she heard what was going on. People need explanations I always say, and nobody listens to me."

"No objections on my part," Alexei said. "Her experience may be limited."

"Since you don't object, I thank you and I will talk to you later." Arsen was ready to hang up.

"Wait Arsen, I have new information for you, from Gennadi. The memory capture is progressing really well. Exceptionally and unexpectedly well. He thinks the technique is so simple that he is finished with the basic research. Adaptation of the technique to practical projects and designing the apparatus is the next project."

Arsen was taken by surprise. "This is unbelievable. I will have to go to Moscow to see what that contraption looks like."

"Call him," Alexei said and hung up.

At least one project was completed and would not be the subject of interruption when the debate on preservation started, Arsen thought. They had better let the media know about this. Sooner or later the news would hit the fan and sooner was better.

"Doctor, Dr. Bjöstrom is here to see you," Michelle announced over the intercom.

"Send her in."

As she walked in Arsen concluded that Rama was right - Ursula was a beautiful woman. She wore a simple blouse, skirt to below the knees, and high heels - simple and elegant and right for the office. Arsen offered her a chair and told her about his conversations with Rama and Alexei.

"We are going to Moscow, I presume soon," Ursula Bjöstrom said. "Tomorrow?"

"You are going to Moscow tonight," Arsen said. "You must meet Herman Wolff and Matt Brown. They will get you started. In Moscow you should see and learn everything about memory capture and what it has to offer. Think in terms of storage and transfer. Report to me as soon as you return or even better call me from Moscow."

The next call was to Gennadi Koltsov.

"I heard from Alexei that the memory capture project is beyond the theoretical stage. Congratulations. My associate, Dr. Bjöstrom, will be in Moscow tomorrow. Could you arrange for her to become familiar with the system and to learn the practical aspects? I presume you will appoint one of your associates as Director of the Memory Capture section to work with Dr. Bjöstrom."

"We'll be glad to have her here," Gennadi Koltsov said. "We'll show her everything she should know. It will take her a week to become familiar with the basics. The man who will work in New York is Mikhail Platov. He is a genius, without exaggeration. He and his men will be able to do for you anything you want."

"How long would it take to make Dr. Bjöstrom an expert?"

"Give me two weeks and she will be back," Gennadi Koltsov said.

"She is intelligent," Arsen challenged Gennadi.

"Then one week." Gennadi Koltsov accepted the challenge.

"Very intelligent!" Arsen continued his challenge.

"In that case she will learn everything there is to learn in one day." Gennadi Koltsov concluded the bargaining duel. "I assumed women and physics don't mix well, and she would not be an exception. Besides, I thought I could show her Moscow if she has not been here before." Gennadi Koltsov laughed. "You seem to be in hurry to get her back - any reasons for that?"

"She is beautiful, if that is what you wanted to know," Arsen said acidly. "No, we don't sleep together if that was your insinuation. She started her job as an Associate Undersecretary only this morning. Oh, her husband is Goran Enstrom."

"Excellent defense, Mr. Secretary, but it was unnecessary," Gennadi Koltsov said. "I did not mean anything. Don't pay attention to me. I am just an old cynical Bolshevik."

"I will talk to you soon," Arsen said, as their conversation came to a close.

"Have a good day Mr. Secretary."

Herman Wolff walked into the office.

"The word is out that you are letting Goran Enstrom take over the Commission and Interrelations," he said.

"It is not true," Arsen said. "I was thinking about it but Rama Chand turned me down. How did you find out? I have not mentioned it to anybody."

"It came from Rama Chand's office - he must have said something to somebody."

Arsen asked Mel Stein and Msgr. Amato to come to his office.

"Gentlemen, I proposed that your divisions be moved to the General Department. Rama Chand rejected my idea of yet another restructuring. The reasons will be obvious once you understand how worried I am about the debate that will ensue from the announcement of our goals and the methods we will use to achieve them. I expect the debate to polarize people, which may lead to open fights, demonstrations, riots and worse. Goran has good ideas and a good organization in place in many territories, which may play a role in channeling the debate and preventing the ultimate disaster of bloody confrontations.

"We cannot plan to use our military to quell fights and riots. That would defeat the purpose of the World Government. On whose side do you suggest we should stand? Should we support the people who want to preserve the human race at all costs and regardless of the means, or should we stand by those who want God's will all the way to death and without human interference? Should we find a middle ground, or be on the left or on the right? What is the middle ground? Who knows what is right or wrong?

"Goran is sure that the population will be polarized by the biological programs. Monsignor, you can do a lot the way you are thinking, but be careful when you allow other people to express themselves. Mel your job is to deal with the wrongs that have been committed by many people. The peoples of the world have to discuss openly the wrongs they have done each other, to disperse the guilt. But people must not feel that we want to damage their psyche, as we really don't."

Arsen had to be asked the inevitable question, and it was posed by Herman Wolff.

"Since you feel so strongly that we will witness a stormy debate and that divisions among people may lead to bloody confrontations, what are you going to do? Where do you stand? Who are you going to support and on whose side of the confrontation will you stand? It is important for us to know."

Arsen had his opinion about the world and where it should be heading with or without the threat of the celestial object.

"I anticipated your question," Arsen said. "You should by now have a good idea where I stand as I have said repeatedly what I think. I feel it would be a shame to allow the human race, and everything else alive on this planet, to disappear without a major effort to save it. The chances of the spontaneous reappearance of the same, or even similar, living world, and of human creatures, are nearly zero, no matter how many trillion years from now. Even if the same primordial life appeared it would have zero chance of following steps that would lead to anything like what you see on the Earth today. And yet we are such wonderfully built and functioning machines, we should be preserved.

"I am ready to do something about it, but I will not take sides. If the decision is to build I will build, and if not I will retire to my apartment and reminisce about my life, about the life of people I know and have known, and about the disappearance of our small world, with all its beautiful and wonderful insignificance in the Universe. Perhaps I may even write a book, for those who would care to read it. Even if we survive and even if we are allowed afterwards to continue all the projects we have in mind for survival and those we have not designed and not even thought of yet, the ultimate fate of an individual and his soul is predetermined. It makes no difference.

"Despite the most sophisticated, unimaginable biological technology and the achievement of virtual immortality, an individual and his soul will return to the basics of the physical Universe by, if nothing else, a calamity that will annihilate him or her on this planet or anywhere in the Universe where he or she may be living some day. Death is inevitable and with it the return of an individual to the nonliving physical composition of the Universe, when the soul, which is the only nonphysical or abstract content of life, will evaporate to nothingness. The circle will be complete. That is where I stand. My soul is content with the inevitable outcome whether it falls upon us very soon or millennia from now through induced longevity or clone cycling.

"In my mind and in my soul the remaining question has not been completely answered. It deals with the origin of the Universe, and everything in it, which had to have a beginning, so to speak, when God made everything including a man and a woman. 'Nothing' is concerned with the time before the beginning, when nothing existed, not even God, when there was nothing physical and nothing abstract, and no time, no space, not even the idea of 'nothing'. 'Nothing' can even be reached in reverse - by disappearence of the Universe and return to 'nothing'.

"My unanswered question is about the origin of the Universe from nothing and how it happened that we came into existence. The number of years calculated from the beginning of the Universe to now - trillions of trillions, more or less - does not explain the 'nothingness' before the beginning. Nor does it explain the conversion of 'nothingness' into the Universe. The number of years almost implies the existence of another bigger Universe from which our own was formed some trillions of years ago, but leaves us with the same question - what happened to 'nothingness' and how did it all start. This 'nothingness' from which everything evolved, makes my mind and my soul content with the ultimate fate of everything. This does not stop me from desiring to preserve the life of this planet at this time, a preservation that would include myself. But, fight and kill I will not."

Arsen concluded his explanation to his almost breathless audience. They had expected a logical exposition, not a philosophical cerebration.

"Does this mean that everyone is on his or her own in the forthcoming debate? Do we proceed and do what we feel?" Herman Wolff asked.

"No, you don't," Arsen said emphatically. "We proceed and do according to the desires of the population. Right now we are doing what we think we should, and the population is ignorant of our work. The debate has not started yet. After the dust settles, and time permitting, we will have to do what we are mandated to do. Your only other option will be to resign."

"Again I see the differences in our philosophies, Msgr. Amato said. "Yet we agree that God's creatures have to be saved by whatever means it takes,"

"This is it, gentlemen," Arsen said. "There will be no further changes."

"Doctor, Prof. Menguy is on line four," Michelle announced over the intercom.

"Mr. Secretary, this is Prof. Menguy. I am in New York. Would you have time to see me?"

"Come at noon and we will have lunch together."

"I am on the way - it is almost noon," Jean-Luc Menguy said.

Arsen looked at his watch. It was eleven thirty.

Victoria came in to say good-by before leaving for the airport.

"During the last two months we have done much work," Arsen said. "Now is the time to change the scenery. Have a good trip and a good time." Victoria embraced and kissed Arsen before she left. Was that a goodbye before getting married to Rama? She would not work as the First Lady of the world.

Prof. Menguy was punctual and Arsen offered him a simple lunch in the kitchenette.

"Professor, we need you and your lab to develop an artificial uterus that will be used in the future somewhere in the Universe. We are breeding a bird in an artificial medium at a Rockefeller lab. Soon, we should be able to achieve the same with animals and hopefully humans. We cannot do it any other way, as the triggering of the process may have to be done a few thousand years down the line. Of course, unless you have some other ideas."

"Gestation in an artificial uterus in a thousand years?" Prof. Menguy said, obviously amazed. "People in France think that the only option is to deflect the Demon. Now you are telling me you want to clone humans somewhere in space years from now. That means you don't believe it is possible to change the course of the Demon or to destroy it. Is that true?"

"It seems you did not listen when Gen. Shagov stated in his U.N. speech that he was not sure the anticollision effort would succeed. That was the cause of the silence after his speech and the failure of his attempt to become the President of World Government. Wasn't that clear to you?"

"We thought he was not sure then," said Prof. Menguy.

"Things are much better now, that is true, but we are still not sure," Arsen said. "Even if everything looked very favorable for deflecting or destroying the Demon, we would have to proceed with the biological research and have our ships ready and in place in case something goes wrong with the anticollision project. We cannot take any chances."

"I understand, Mr. Secretary. I am at your disposal."

"What do you think about the proposed project for developing an artificial uterus?"

"The French scientist, Jean Rostand, believed many years ago that an artificial uterus could be made, but his system was too complicated. The first twenty-five or twenty-six weeks of gestation will be critical. We will have to find out what happens to the embryo if it is allowed to develop in an artificial medium. We will have to solve the problems of oxygen and nutrient supply to the fetus and of removal of metabolites. I cannot even start thinking of mother-fetus dependence and the interactions thought by some to be critical in fetal development. I am not sure what is critical. I will have to think about it, perhaps look up some information. We must learn from birds: how breeding develops in an egg, which is in a sense an artificial medium."

"I need to see some progress," Arsen said. "Could you let me know by the end of the week what is happening, and that you have started your first experiment - even if you start by hatching an egg in an incubator? Do you know Dr. Thomas Lowell at the Rockefeller University?"

"I know who he is; I have never met him," Prof. Menguy said.

"His team is working on artificial media and conception in them. The two of you will have to work together. Herman Wolff, my deputy, who will see you in a few minutes, will arrange a meeting with Dr. Lowell sometime today."

"That should be an interesting collaboration," Dr. Menguy said.

"I hope so," Arsen concluded

After the Professor left, Arsen stretched himself in his armchair and remembered that he had not talked to Nada for a long time. He dialed Belgrade. Nada answered.

"It's about time I heard from you," she said. "Mom and I are coming to New York next week."

"Great, it is too much trouble to be alone in a big city," Arsen said. "Have you heard from Stan Petkovic? Have the Serbs forgotten my existence? I hope they have."

"I wish they had," Nada said. "I sometimes worry that someone may decide that Mom and I don't belong here, or even worse, they might try to get to you by hurting us. Can't you help your own people?"

"My dear, you are scratching my soul where it hurts the most," Arsen protested. "Don't you think I would help them if they were willing to help themselves? They are swimming against the stream and nobody can help them now. In the long run, they will be much happier without Kosovo and without the Albanians."

"Well, I tried," Nada said.

"Say hello to Mom, and I will see you next week."

Even his own family did not understand his motivations, Arsen thought. Nothing could be done about that.

Herman Wolff came in.

"I took care of the Professor," he said. "He is on his way to meet with Dr. Lowell."

"A lot will depend on the two of them," Arsen said. "If we are to clone anybody in the year 3000, they had better succeed. They are now the key players. What happened to the panels?"

"All the panels have been scheduled to meet within ten days," Herman Wolff said. "These people are the best in their fields. Their reports will be on your desk as soon as I receive them. They understand that we must have at least the preliminary conclusions in ten days. I told them to work hard and late and over the weekends."

"Just don't waste much time. We should know what the minimum is that we must have on board. To be very frank, I worry the most about the animals and plants. Which of the millions of species do we carry on board, as seeds, genetic engines and DNA imprints? How will they behave in the new environment and in very select and reduced groups? Will they fight to the extinction of each other, or coexist? Will they overpopulate the planet or whatever they land on, then starve themselves and the humans? Will they survive? Will plants create jungles - who knows? A good scenario would be a planet with animals and vegetation already on it. Then how would our humans survive? Too many ifs to deal with, yet we must try.

Perhaps one ship will make it out of a hundred. The panels should address these questions."

"They will," Herman Wolff assured Arsen. "I am sure they will have many ideas of their own."

"As soon as everything looks as though it is in place, new problems and ideas pop up, and they appear important. The scope of our work and the essential projects for biological survival are increasing. Is there an end to it?"

"Why don't we plan a meeting of all key players in this effort and ask that question," Herman Wolff suggested.

"Okay. After the reports of all panels are in we should meet and discuss the entire project. Take care of that."

"The Prime Minister of Israel is on four," Michelle announced over the intercom.

"Hello, Mr. Prime Minister," Arsen said. "We last talked in Nicosia. What is on your mind?"

"You told me to call you in New York," the Prime Minister, Ehud Raviv, said.

"I did?"

"I thought it would be a good idea if I came to New York and had a meeting with you."

"When would you like to come?"

"Would Thursday this week be convenient for you?"

"Come and we will talk," Arsen said.

After the call from the Israeli Prime Minister Arsen was reminded of the major problem he had taken upon himself to handle - the Israeli-Palestinian relations.

In Serbia he was *persona non grata*, Arsen thought, a traitor who should be killed, in the view of some. His next country, in order of preference, was Israel. He was about to repeat his performance. All the Jews of the world would hate him, and on top of that, he might become a symbol of anti-Semitism among enemies of the Jews. What a dreadful thought! No matter what, he had to do what he had to do, as he had done in Serbia. He would let the Jews and Palestinians negotiate. That was what they had been doing for years. Israel to the Jordan river was not a problem as it belonged to the State of Israel. The occupied territories were the problem as the Palestinians were in the majority.

What about Jerusalem? That was another dreadful idea to Arsen. Jerusalem had been built as a Jewish city, and it had always been a symbol to the Jews. It was a symbol to Christians and to Muslims, but they looked at it as a shrine and the place where shrines were located, not as their own holy land. Jews had been banned from Jerusalem, except for a token population, for thousands of years. In daily prayers they had always asked for return to Jerusalem. Their wish had been fulfilled with the creation of Israel, a Jewish state. Christians and Muslims were content to live where they lived without a burning desire to return to Jerusalem. Besides, they could not say their ancient origins were in Jerusalem. And Jews had returned to Jerusalem when they were allowed to return, and even before that. Now they were the majority, and the city must be theirs.

What about the Serbs? Arsen was scornful of himself. They had lived in Kosovo, and they had died on Kosovo Field defending their freedom and their nation from the onslaught of the Turks in 1389. Shouldn't they have the right to keep Kosovo as their own? Arsen was desperate to answer this basic question about the land which would come up time and time again in disputes about the land in many parts of the world.

Where were the Serbs? They were no longer in Kosovo. Arsen's thoughts continued to flow and his vision of Kosovo became crystal clear. The Serbs had abandoned Kosovo except for a small minority. The Serbs wanted Kosovo but they did not want to live in it or to fight for it or to die for it - or even to visit it. Nobody and nothing - except their own excuses - could have prevented them from going to Kosovo if they really wanted to live there. Kosovo belonged to the Albanians Kosovars.

Arsen's soul was burning with anguish.

CHAPTER FORTY-EIGHT

WEDNESDAY, 7 JANUARY 1998

The day started early and promised to be routine, with calls and meetings only increased by the merging of the two departments.

"Doctor, Dr. Lowell is on line one," Michelle announced over the intercom.

"Mr. Secretary, I wanted to let you know about the talks I had with Dr. Menguy."

"Talks?"

"Oh yes, we met first in my office then continued during dinner and afterwards. He left this morning."

"How was it - I mean your talks?" Arsen inquired.

"We compared notes and then talked about the future," Dr. Lowell said. "You won't believe it. We know exactly what to do. It seems that we won't need the uterus. We will talk daily and meet every two weeks to talk to the rest of the staff to keep them up to date. I never expected such cooperation."

"Let us hope nothing interrupts your work," Arsen said.

"I know you are worried about reactions to the goals of the biological research from many sources. I cannot believe that the reaction will be violent."

"You assume that people are stupid," Arsen said nervously. "You underestimate people. They are not stupid in their ignorance. Once they understand they will resist. You will see."

After Arsen hung up Michelle announced over the intercom that Dr. Björstrom was on line four.

"Ursula, how is Moscow and memory capture," Arsen asked her. "Gennadi promised to teach you in one day everything that is to be known. Are you working or sleeping?"

"Working, of course, though I am tired from the long trip, and I even slept almost the entire flight," Ursula said. "Gennadi is wonderful. He has been with me the whole day and showed me so much, my head is spinning. He is taking me for dinner now. Then I will go to the airport and be on my way home. I will meet with you tomorrow. Bye-bye for now."

Arsen asked Michelle to find Dr. Zourab Abashidze and ask him to come up.

Dr. Abashidze was of medium height, slightly obese, with a round head on a short neck. He was already bald, and he looked to be in his mid-thirties.

"I wanted to talk to you about the robot," Arsen said to Dr. Abashidze as he sat down. "I am sure Herman Wolff has talked to you about our plans and goals. The robot will be an essential object on the space ships. You have degrees in engineering and medicine, don't you?"

"That is right," Zourab Abashidze said.

"Where did you study?"

"My family lived in Washington where my father served in the Soviet Embassy. I graduated from high school in Georgetown and went to MIT as a physics major. I received my B.S. degree as the Soviet Union was disintegrating. Being a Georgian my father followed Shevarnatze to Tbilisi where he became Associate Secretary of Foreign Affairs. He retired a few years ago. Having nothing better to do in Tbilisi I enrolled in the Medical School and graduated in 1994. Your staff found me at MIT where I had received a Ph.D. in computer sciences and started my first job on the faculty. I was working on computer programs for robots. I have just moved to New York."

"Interesting story," Arsen said. "This job is right for you. I am sure you understand our goals. We need a robot with a huge stored memory, and the physical ability to take care of the babies until they grow big enough to take care of themselves. Drs. Lowell and Menguy will work with you on triggering the development of the embryos. Dr. Lee Xiao will work with you on postnatal development. You have a big job to do. Don't waste any time."

As Zourab Abashidze was getting ready to leave Arsen asked him whether that kind of work disturbed him?

"No, it does not bother me but I know people who will be very upset when they find out, and they become vicious when they are upset. Killing is not one of their psychological problems."

"You will have to tell me about that some day."

Herman Wolff came in and asked Arsen to join him and Matt Brown for lunch. Nothing was urgent and Arsen thought that a break would ease the tiredness he had been feeling for a few days.

"Park Avenue Café is the place I like," Herman Wolff said, and he called for a limousine to take them there.

Arsen ordered filet mignon, and Matt Brown followed him. Herman Wolff took the whole course and Arsen knew he wouldn't feel well when he had finished it.

"The pace is slowing down as we put things in place," Matt Brown said.

"I was hoping that would be the case, yet we have just faced bionomics, postnatal development and robot programming - large areas to be covered. Herman, you don't have any problems in finding people. How did you find Zourab Abashidze? I talked to him this morning. I liked him very much."

"I knew his father some years ago when I was a young diplomat in Washington. Zourab was a smart kid. I hate to say it, but that was almost thirty years ago. Over the years our paths crossed several times, and I knew of Zourab's academic career. Once I needed a robot programming specialist, I knew my man right away. I was told by his colleagues at MIT that he is very good at that work. He has already talked to a number of people who specialize in the field. They will be moving to New York very soon. We are looking at a building in Hastings-on-Hudson, where his team will do their work. That should be very exciting."

Arsen was pleased with the report and his mood became balanced again. The filet was excellent, and he was sipping from a glass of virgin tonic water. Herman Wolff made his food disappear in large bites.

"How is your lecture progressing?" asked Matt Brown.

"I have been thinking about it for some time," Arsen said. "I had better work on it, the day is approaching rapidly."

"The day is tomorrow," Matt Brown said. "They will be glad to have your attention for one evening. Be ready for many questions not necessarily related to your topic."

"Tomorrow?" Arsen asked. "Amazing that time has flown so fast. I thought I had at least two more weeks."

"They moved it to tomorrow," Matt Brown said. "You should have received the official letter from the FFP Secretary, David Gallagher ."

"I am completely oblivious of any such letter," Arsen said. "I am glad you mentioned it. It makes no difference since I wrote what I wanted to say some time ago. It is in my computer at home."

"Can I meet you in your office around six o'clock and we'll go to the Forum meeting together?"

"Okay. Six o'clock."

"I talked to some of my friends from the Forum, and they said the interest in your talk is tremendous. They will not be able to accommodate everybody, and they are making alternative arrangements, probably for TV coverage or another lecture room."

"I will stick to my topic and let them interrupt me. Then I will change the subject," Arsen said.

"So much has happened since I wrote you that letter of invitation," Matt Brown said.

"I have never found out who proposed my name for the lecture," Arsen complained.

"You may not believe me but I don't know either," Matt Brown said. "I received the name from a Forum member and he refused to say who had suggested it."

"What secrecy!"

"That's the rule - we never disclose the source," Matt Brown said.

The afternoon flew by quickly.

At home that evening Arsen had to be reminded that this was his Christmas day - he had completely forgotten.

Later in the evening Arsen read his prepared lecture on the computer. He did not like it and a new lecture had to be written. This was the best opportunity to explain openly what he and his group were doing and what their goals were and the best audience to whom to explain to.

It was very late when Arsen turned off the lights and went to sleep.

CHAPTER FORTY-NINE

There were many calls that morning. Victoria called to tell Arsen that her relationship with Rama Chand had accelerated, and he had proposed. She had accepted. Considering the situation, both families had agreed that the wedding should take place immediately and it had been set for Saturday.

"Congratulations," Arsen said. "How are we going to function without you? You will be the First Lady of the world, and your function will change. Do you need anything?"

"No, not really," Victoria said. "I will miss my role in your organization and I understand that I should quit. Rama said the same thing."

"We will need you at some point, maybe sooner than you think," Arsen said. "The tranquility of the world is about to change. We will need peace emissaries. That will be your role, and a very important one."

"I hope you are wrong in your predictions," Victoria said. "Any chance that you could attend our wedding."

"Maybe, just maybe," Arsen said. "As a condition you must promise to invite one of the greatest Indian philosophers, the scientist, Vijay Rangaswamy."

"I believe Rama knows his family. That can be arranged. Come to India - that would be an honor and pleasure for me."

"I will talk to Alexei and Sabrina and find out their plans."

"Doctor that would be incredible," Victoria exclaimed. "I would be obliged to you forever."

"I will let you know."

A call to Alexei's office reached Sabrina. Alexei was in Moscow visiting Gennadi.

"I want you and Alexei in New Delhi on Saturday to attend Victoria's wedding to Rama Chand," Arsen demanded. "You can fly with me. We will leave after my lecture at the Forum on Foreign Policy tonight. Please, persuade Alexei to go. Tell him we will have an interesting talk with Vijay Rangaswamy. That may be an incentive for him to go."

Arsen thought that Sabrina's presence might be another incentive for Alexei to be in New Delhi. There had been some talk about the two of them being together too often.

Sabrina was speechless. Arsen thought he heard her sob. Was she happy for Victoria or envious or perhaps sorry for herself? Who knew what was in the mind of a woman when a wedding was mentioned, especially the wedding of a good friend?

At six o'clock Arsen and Matt Brown took a limousine for the short ride to the Forum on Foreign Policy.

When they entered the offices of the Forum Matt Brown was greeted very warmly by the staff. The President of the Board, Donald Pierce, came to meet Arsen and show him around. He talked about the previous speakers and about the founders of the Forum. The founder he admired the most was Walter Lippman. They entered the lecture room a few minutes before seven o'clock. It was filled to capacity. Matt Brown introduced Arsen.

"Mr. President and members and guests. We have secured Dr. Arsen Pankovich for tonight's presentation. When the Program Board of the Forum met in November of last year, and we were given Dr. Pankovich's name from our sources, we knew very little about him. Dr. Pankovich was upset that he was selected, and he thought it ridiculous. I almost agreed with him. Yet he has had ideas that turned out to be important to some people. I suspect that he will share with us some new ideas that we have not heard from him before. It is my pleasure to present Dr. Pankovich to you."

Arsen got up from his chair and walked to the lectern. The applause he received could be described as restrained. After taking a sip of water, Arsen started his presentation.

"Mr. President, Ladies and Gentlemen. It is a distinct honor for me to be asked to talk before this Forum whose members are sometimes referred to as foreign policy makers. I have often thought that to be true. I am also privileged to talk to the people who are not Forum members, and who came to hear my talk. Matthew Brown was kind in his introduction, and correct, when he said that I was initially very uncomfortable with the invitation to speak before the Forum. Really, I thought a prankster had sent me that letter. A lot has happened to me since I received that letter, and I am sure to you too, and to the world. You are aware of my functions in the World Government, although I am not sure you know much about our organization and about our goals.

"I have promised Gen. Shagov and President Chand that I will be involved in each phase of the biological research. I intend to keep my promise. Our goals are very high, and some of the research is fascinating. To most of you, it is unknown. Some recent discoveries have been known to only a few of us. I have decided, with the approval of President Chand and of the General, to make this information public. I thought that this Forum's meeting would be the appropriate place to make the information known."

Spontaneous applause interrupted the presentation, obviously acknowledging and approving the last statement.

"The single goal of the biological research is to preserve the human race and as many animal and plant species as possible in the case that the anti-collision efforts fail and the Earth is destroyed by the impact of the approaching celestial object. We must have contingency plans. You know that the preservation effort will make sure that people and other living species are sent into space in space ships in order to survive the impact. They will return after the danger is over and if the Earth is still inhabitable.

"I will not dwell on the possibility that the Earth may disintegrate, and the consequences thereof. Yet, we must be prepared for the possibility that everything now living on Earth might die, and that the space ships will have nowhere to land. That would literally be the end of the human race and of all living species, as the people on the space ships would be doomed without the ability to return to Earth. Could a single bacterium survive in a sporulated form? Or some other form of life? Maybe? It would take a billion years for this life to evolve into something which would not neces-sarily be human or even humanoid. Perhaps the age of dinosaurs would dawn upon Earth again; probably not.

"The chance of recreating an evolution that would be crowned by another human in our image is nil. Therefore, we think we have to be pre-pared to trigger human life somewhere in space sometime in the distant future, perhaps thousands of years from now, when a wondering ship lands on a planet compatible with the life we have on the Earth. Is that just a dream? Even worse, to some people it is a real possibility."

The room was silent. Not even a cough broke the importance of the moment.

"To preserve the human race after its annihilation, human life will have to be triggered *de novo* on Planet X along with the life of animals and plants essential for human survival. The means of the most primitive survival have to be on board. The human who is triggered has to be conscious of us, the lost civilization, and has to be able to use our knowledge to build life on the new planet. The human also must survive the unexpected on the plan-et. The technology will be developed and built by Gen. Shagov and his Anticollision people. Extensive information about the Earth, and the total existing knowledge will be stored on every ship's computers. Finally, a preprogrammed robot will be on board to start the triggering mechanism."

The silence in the room was just as deep as before.

"To trigger the development of a human being we need a genetic engine capable of developing a clone in an artificial medium, which, following gestation - in or out of an artificial uterus - will result in a viable human infant. The baby would be nursed by the preprogrammed robot. Postnatal development in such an environment is now being studied. Memory capture and transfer, and psychoexchange have been tested and found practical. This reality is under way in relation to providing a core memory and knowledge content to the cloned child. Finally, bionomics as related to the child's survival and protection from the existing conditions on a planet is under study.

"This human individual will achieve a high intellectual level from observation of his or her environment, by acquiring information and knowledge from the ship's computers and by enhancement through the psychoexchange of memory, knowledge, and other stored information. The biological contents of these ships will be stored in suitable containers, in the form of organic and inorganic powders, until the trigger time. Outside monitors will be activated automatically from time to time to scout for a suitable planet. When a planet is spotted the scanners will be activated, and the information they receive will be fed into a trigger computer that will be programmed to analyze the information and recognize whether or not the planet can support human life. If it can, the trigger technology will be activated within the ship. There is one intractable problem to be solved by the scientists: who will head the first Forum on Foreign Policy on the populated Planet X?"

A roar of laughter broke the silence and the solemnity in the meeting room where the audience had been listening intently to the description of the plan for the survival of the human race.

"Let me just briefly introduce to you the key members of our team:

"GENETIC MATERIALS + DESICCATED DNA + RNA
"Oroku Saito, Ph.D.

"Dr. Saito was the prime researcher in the Genetics Institute of Japan. His job is to produce the dry form of the genetic engine, since no refrigeration is possible on the ships. Plant seeds can be stored for a long time in a dry space. Dr. Saito is working on the dry genetic engines of both plants and animals.

"CLONING MEDIA + CONCEPTION
"Thomas Lowell, M.D.

"Dr. Lowell, the President of Rockefeller University, promises to produce artificial media in which cloning will be conceived. I believe his team has already succeeded in growing a bird. They have not tried the artificial genetic engine.

"GESTATION + ARTIFICIAL UTERUS
"Jean-Luc Menguy, Ph.D.

"Dr. Menguy, a French scientist, has blossomed into an enthusiastic contributor with Dr. Lowell.

"These three men will make it possible to trigger cloning in space. The rest of the team will make sure that the infant survives. At this point it is important to understand that there will be enough time to produce only about a thousand genetic engines of human individuals and about that many of a variety of animals. If the technology improves more genetic engines will be produced and stored. I just hope the Serbs and Croats, the Turks and Kurds, the Spaniards and Basques, the Tamils and Sinhalese and all others do not resume their arguments after having studied the files stored on the ships. I just hope they lose interest."

Laughter broke out again induced by Arsen's cynicism and the grotesque images of ethnic conflicts on a distant planet thousands of years hence.

"POSTNATAL DEVELOPMENT
"Lee Xiao, Ph.D.
"IMMUNITY + BACTERIOLOGY
"Thaddée Gakounzi, M.D.,Ph.D.
"EARLY DEVELOPMENT
"Anthony Falk, Ph.D.
"EDUCATION
"Donald Eddington, Ph.D.
"WALKING
"Ha Kyung Chul, M.D., Ph.D.

"Dr. Lee's team will provide the environment for postnatal survival. You have to think of bacteria in the intestine and in the soil and in animals, and of immunology. Dr. Gakounzi learned his trade in the U.S. but advanced many things at home in Rwanda. I asked Dr. Falk, the President of Columbia University, to help us organize a panel on the early development of an infant. Dr. Eddington, from London, will educate our infant in learning skills including the ship's computers. We hope that the adult will be interested in sciences, not only in sex. Dr. Ha, from Seoul, was very convincing during his interview for the job in promoting walking and body development in survival - he got a job that requires him to sit and think."

The atmosphere was humorous at this point. People were talking and participating in the presentation with their remarks and jokes.

Arsen asked for silence, and with changed attitude and very seriously, he proceeded to the next division.

"MEMORY CAPTURE
"Ursula Bjöstrom, M.D.

"It is a human characteristic to forget the seriousness of a situation even in the middle of a battle, and a few moments before being struck by a bullet. It may be presumptuous to imagine this little child, far away in the Universe, and thousands of years in the future, sitting at a computer and looking at the pornography of our time. What is serious about this child is not only his loneliness, even if he is awaiting the birth of a sister, but the approaching date of his session for memory transfer. He has learned to talk from his robot, and he has been told of his origins, yet all that is rather vague to him. Memory transfer will make the bridge to the genetic past. He will find out about his origins and about his family and friends, perhaps even about some of his hidden thoughts. He will understand what happened and why he is on Planet X."

Silence reigned again in the meeting room of the Forum. Again, serious proposals were made for the salvage of humans and other life forms from the Earth, and all that depended on this imagined child who would get a shot of memory to become conscious of his origins and of past humanity.

"If the memory transfer fails, humanity will vanish from the consciousness of the distant new civilization. They will know about us only as something that is not a part of their soul. You can say that ancient Romans are not in my soul, but they are in the souls of the fellow Romans. The infant will never feel he has been there nor will any others who come afterwards. It will also be very difficult for the infant to learn and understand everything that is on the computer without having the background that was absorbed on Earth from others - teachers, parents and friends, people on the job and outside, and from the existing culture and life; background that would result from being a part of the vanished or distant civilization. Although this new species of humans would develop their own civilization sooner or later, they would lose much by doing it on their own. Transfer of the captured memory of the cloned scientists would help them regain their pervious expertise.

"The memory capture and transfer were developed in Moscow by

Gennadi Koltsov.

"ROBOT PROGRAMMER AND COORDINATOR
"Zourab Abashidze, M.D., Ph.D.

"This section is easiest to understand, since we have seen robots in the movies, but it is the most complicated and difficult to develop. The robot will be the only 'brain' and 'mobile body' on the ship for some time after arrival on Planet X. Like everything in the Biological Research Division, the robot is essential and indispensable. Of course, there will be backup robots.

"BIONOMICS
"Kostas Cotsidas, Ph.D.
"ANIMALS
"Miklos Nemeth, Ph.D.
"PLANTS
"Baltazar Bagamba, Ph.D.
"FOOD
"Hans Maier

"Bionomics will deal with nature on Planet X. Food will have to be produced if it does not exist, and the initial supply will have to be provided. Water and oxygen will have to be available."

Arsen was not interrupted as everybody expected him to conclude his talk.

"We are making progress in this enormous task on the long road that ends in 2001. We have to take off at that time. We hope to be able to complete the job."

Matt Brown asked for questions. A flood came in response.

"We cannot stay here all night and all day tomorrow," Matt Brown said. We'll take questions at random if you write them down."

Thirty pieces of paper were deposited on the table. Matt Brown picked up the first question.

Q: "Is your department in competition with God?"

A: "This question has been on my mind for some time. I wish Msgr. Amato was here tonight. He would have answered more eloquently. He would explain to you that our work is and will be blessed by God. The Monsignor feels that no matter what we do we do it under God's supervision. My own feeling is that we are trying to avert the annihilation of the human race and all life as we know it on Earth. We are doing what has to be done. Is that God's territory? I don't know. What is God's territory? Is it God's desire that our world disappear?"

Q: "Your department has no public relations representative. Why?"

A: "Yes, we do. Msgr. Amato is the public relations representative. I found him in Rome where he had just been appointed Monsignor by the Pope. I thought that was his best recommendation and that he was in the main stream of Catholicism. I think we should appoint representatives of other religions, or even form a Forum on Religions and Interfaith Relations."

Q: "Do you believe that the Anticollision effort will succeed?"

A: "As I said in my presentation, we have to be prepared as if the anticollision effort will fail. I know about the research that is going on. Gen. Shagov is the person who can answer this question with authority, I cannot."

Q: "Mr. Secretary, what is the basis for the memory research? How far have you progressed?"

A: "Only recently Gennadi Koltsov in Moscow, an expert on neutrinos, discovered accidentally that under certain conditions neutrinos would take copies of a brain's information storage and memory content. It may be said probably more accurately that neutrinos in their passage through the brain copy the stored contents, and under certain conditions these copies can be stored on the computer and later imported back. Of course we don't ordinarily need these copies ourselves but they could be used on Planet X."

Q: "Mr. Secretary that was my question," a man from the middle row shouted. "Can you tell us about the applications? Criminal investigation? Questioning of spies or perhaps employees? What?"

A: "That occurred to me, too. Our interest is in storing the memories of people who will be cloned say five thousand or fifty thousand years from now. There will be no applications on Earth."

"What about research? You'll have to test it on humans, and you might have already done so," the man from the middle row exclaimed again.

"Yes, we used it for demonstration purposes only on some of our associates, like Gen. Shagov and Dr. Bjöstrom. I have not yet seen the machine."

"You may not like to have other people check your thoughts." The man in the middle row would not stop commenting.

Q: "Dr. Pankovich, are you telling us that there will be nothing alive in the Universe for fifty or one hundred thousand years?"

A: "No, I am not telling you that. Although the Earth may not be inhabitable after the impact, something, like algae, might survive and start evolution all over again. As you know, it is almost impossible to kill everything alive. However, evolution might go in a different direction, not toward *homo sapiens*, and that would be the end of human life and life in general as we know it today. We cannot take any chances."

Q: "How do you plan to return all these ships to Earth if the celestial object is destroyed or deflected?"

A: "That is not a major undertaking, I was told. The people on the manned ships would just navigate themselves back to Earth. The unmanned ships would either be exploded in space or recalled. Some of these ships might lose communication with the Earth and not respond. They would continue in their intended task of creating new life somewhere in the Universe. Human life at that. That possibility cannot be excluded."

"Ten thousand years from now they would be rather primitive in comparison to us," the President of the Forum Board said.

"If we don't kill each other and don't get hit by an asteroid by then," Arsen said.

"The last question for Dr. Pankovich - he still has a plane to catch tonight," Matt Brown announced.

"That is very true," Arsen said. "As you might have heard, President Rama Chand and my Chief of Staff, Victoria Ram, will be married on Saturday. Some of us are going to India to wish them well."

Applause broke out at the news of the wedding and the last question was never asked.

The President of the Forum adjourned the meeting by thanking Arsen for his informative presentation.

After the meeting, Arsen and Matt Brown were driven to the airport and their plane took off immediately.

CHAPTER FIFTY

Arsen wished he could have avoided the long trip to India. Even the whole night's sleep on the plane, talking to Matt Brown, and a short stop in Israel and a visit to Jerusalem, did not eliminate the frustration he often felt when a trip was very long.

Israeli Prime Minister Ehud Raviv was cordial and made Arsen feel welcome in Israel. Jerusalem and the West Bank were the main issues as always. The Prime Minister did not deny the right of Palestinians to form the Palestinian State. It was the borders of this state that troubled him. Arsen stuck to his plan to remain neutral and to insist on negotiations between the Jews and the Arabs.

"People feel best when they strike a deal without the help of other parties," Arsen said.

Arsen wanted to get a gift for Rama and Victoria, and the Prime Minister arranged a shopping excursion which culminated in the purchase of a golden miniature of the old Jerusalem with the inscription 'Eternal Jewish City.'

"I only wish I knew what is on your mind," the Prime Minister said to Arsen as they were parting.

"It is my desire that Jews and Arabs decide what is right and make a deal," Arsen said. "Then I will never have to say what was on my mind. It is not I whose opinion is important, it is the opinions of Jews and Arabs that matter. They have to decide. I am just an instrument of the World Government. My role, as I see it, is to facilitate the solution with dignity for the involved parties."

"I am not sure the Serbs would agree with your assessment of your role," the Prime Minister said. "They are upset about your interference."

"They forgot I was a Serb," Arsen said. "Besides, sometimes the majority would do nothing without proper guidance and explanations, which often have to be rather firm. I just hope you won't need that guidance in your dealing with the Arabs."

The next stop was New Delhi. Arsen was looking forward to the meeting with Vijay Rangaswamy.

Matt Brown was in the conference room as Arsen entered. Sabrina did not feel well and had stayed in her room.

"You made news last night," Matt Brown said. "I got reports from New York. Your statements and explanations of the goals of the biological research are on the front pages of all the newspapers in the world. Everybody is asking questions and they all want more details. Tom Lowell called to ask for instructions on what he can say. Prof. Menguy called with the same question. Gennadi is upset with all the attention he's received. Herman also wants to talk to you about the situation."

"Let me talk to Herman,' Arsen said. "He knew what was coming. We decided to inform people so as to avoid future accusations of the secret promotion of our own goals. Let the people decide. The U.N. Assembly can and should decide what is right."

"He's on the line," Matt Brown said.

"Herman, what is the confusion about?" Arsen asked. "We decided to reveal the proposed goals and to explain the organization of the Biological Research Division. We decided to talk. Why is everybody asking for permission to talk?"

"The reaction of the media and of many people is incredible," Herman Wolff said.

"What about the media?"

"Almost all papers carried your entire talk before the Forum. All editorials dealt with the biological research. You can find everything from congratulations to outright condemnation, the demand for investigations, and for a debate before the Assembly. What do we do now?"

"We respond," Arsen said emphatically. "All division and section chiefs are at liberty to explain the workings of their units and the projects that are being planned or are under way. No secrets at this time. Talk to all chiefs. Have a meeting with everybody and explain the policy. We want people to know what we are doing and what we are planning to do. Shield us in India from a barrage of inquires. Let us have a quiet wedding. You and Raul Ortiz and somebody in the Anticollision and General Departments should handle those who demand to be heard immediately. The rest can wait for our return. All my calls will be referred to you from now on."

"I will take care of everything now that I know the policy," Herman Wolff concluded. "Have a good wedding."

"What should I do with the calls that came in earlier?" asked Matt

Brown after Arsen hung up.

"Trash them. I don't want to talk to anybody."

"At least talk to Drs. Lowell and Menguy, and to Gennadi," Matt Brown insisted. "They should not get the impression you don't want to talk to them."

"Okay. Call them."

Gennadi was found first.

"Gennadi, are you upset about my public relations job from last night?"

"Not at all."

"The message was that you were upset."

Gennadi Koltsov laughed.

"Russians are not entirely stupid, you know. I knew that people would think I was upset by the publicity. In reality, I like this new notoriety. My call was about our project. Platov is on the way to New York. He will get the information I need to make the MC machine."

"MC?"

"Memory capture machine. It should look like a metallic helmet, and I will install the necessary computer board in it. We should be able to start production in a few months."

"This is the first project that is in the process of being completed," Arsen said. "We will have about a hundred ships and there will be at least a thousand genetic engines in each. You will have to arrange with Alexei's people to provide enough disc space for storage of a thousand captured memories."

"This is a very interesting tool and has a great potential for a variety of applications," Gennadi said, his voice showing genuine enthusiasm.

Arsen's voice was grave when he replied to Gennadi Koltsov.

"Gennadi, I agree that the phenomenon is intriguing but it may destroy even the little remaining privacy left to human beings. I must insist that this technology be used only for the purposes of the unmanned ships. Other applications should not be explored until that is decided in the Assembly."

"Okay, I will make sure that nobody gets involved," Gennadi said, obviously not as enthusiastically. "Even now nobody knows how it works."

What a problem, Arsen thought. The memory capture alone could create much commotion. Open market on people's thoughts would create a revolution in this civilization. Arsen's thoughts were flying even further. People could find out each other's thoughts. Imagine a negotiation between two opposing parties. Imagine a poll on any issue: you could find out what people really thought; or a crooked public official whose thoughts were far from honest; or a Bishop whose thoughts did not befit a saint.

People would become confused and enraged by revelations from their minds.

Maybe the people of this world would one day evolve to the level at which they would be capable of thinking without worrying about being monitored by someone. Maybe people would stop plotting to harm other people, and ethnic groups would stop plotting against each other. People would attain the level of universal men and women, who would think of living for the future and not in the past, who would think of no harm to others, who would need no wealth but instead would strive for new vistas for the world.

Had he gone a bit too far in his vision of the ideal human being? Arsen asked himself. That might be possible if the Adam and Eve of the new civilization on Planet X used this open mind technique to expose their thoughts to everyone, because the new people would possess brains without dark corners in which detrimental ideas had been stored. Would people be capable of beating such a system by jamming the memory machines or by a devious route of honest thinking, then hurting people anyway? This would prove that human beings were inevitably and basically bad anywhere in the Universe.

Wait, Arsen said to himself, stop right now. Human beings must have a chance of attaining the level at which social structure would not exist to harness them, although a few 'bad genes' would have to be replaced too. The memory capture machines could facilitate the transition, one day, to a truly open civilization. This machine must be on board the unmanned space ships not only to recover the memory of the cloned individuals but also to create an honest civilization.

Matt Brown interrupted Arsen's vision of universal humans.

"Herman faxed clippings from the New York newspapers. You might find them interesting."

Arsen spread the clippings on the table and looked at the headlines. The reaction to his presentation at the meeting of the Forum on Foreign Policy was intense.

PANKOVICH REVEALS WG SECRETS AT THE FORUM MEETING
THE GENOME AS A POWDER
HUMAN GESTATION IN ARTIFICIAL EGGS
A BABY ON PLANET X
MOM ROBBY AND THE BABY
MEMORY EXPORT TO PLANET X
A KILLER FOR THE KILLERS: MEMORY CAPTURE

Arsen was impressed with the quality of these reports, their grasp of the facts and their sober analysis. The reporters had managed to talk to most of the principal investigators, so their analyses were more penetrating than his presentation before the Forum had been. He laughed at the headline that described the genome as a powder and gestation in the artificial media without a uterus as artificial eggs. That was not far from the truth. He liked the nickname for the robot, Mom Robby.

The reporters posed many important questions related to ethics and religion and were quite critical of the concept of life triggered thousands of years in the future, on the grounds that that was God's prerogative. They asked whether the human race on Planet X would have anything to do with our own human race on Earth. The way the baby would grow on Planet X, if that was possible in the first place, would have no resemblance to the development of any child on Earth. No parents but a robot, no company to relate to, no experiences for the development of a soul, no bridges to the past.

One reporter asked himself whether the beginning of human self consciousness and of the soul might have to wait for the human herd to grow more numerous. On the other hand, the literate child, who would be educated and be computer literate, might not even need the recognition duel to become self-conscious and to develop a soul.

Memory capture was the most controversial issue in the reviews as the reporters, and many people they interviewed, were worried that the technology would be used on Earth before its use was ever applied on the babies on Planet X; and if the celestial object were deflected, memory capture would become a dangerous tool in the hands of those who controlled the technology. They admitted that memory capture and transfer might become potent educational tools.

"Mud has hit the fan," Arsen said aloud and Matt Brown raised his head in surprise. "I just finished reading the faxed clippings about the reactions to my presentation before the Forum. The media has the idea. You can count on a flood of opposing opinions. Matt, you had better be prepared to answer most of the questions. I will have a press conference when we return to New York, on Tuesday or Wednesday. You can work it out with the media. Don't deny admission to any accredited correspondent and give them enough time to ask questions after my statement."

"Okay, I'll take care of it," Matt Brown said.

Matt Brown looked odd, like someone who had a burning question to ask but could not decide to ask it.

"What is your problem?" Arsen asked.

"Do you really think we'll have to develop the biotechnology to save the human race?" Matt Brown asked in return. "You don't seem to believe that Gen. Shagov's team will be able to build a neutrino gun capable of deflecting or destroying the Demon."

"I never trust anything," Arsen said. "When Alexei and Gennadi assure me that they have a gun capable of destroying the Demon, I will believe that they have it. Until then I will be creating biotechnology. By now you should have learned that I always play safe."

Matt Brown, looking embarrassed, leaned over his papers, but he was not reading - he was immersed in his thoughts.

Not much was said during the rest of the flight. Arsen dozed off a few times. Neither of the two men was hungry enough to eat the dinner offered to them. Sabrina remained secluded in her cabin although she said she was improving.

CHAPTER FIFTY-ONE

SATURDAY, 10 JANUARY 1998

New Delhi was lighted by the sun shining in a cloudless sky. It was warm and dry.

After the ceremony, Arsen found Victoria and Rama and talked to them briefly, hardly having a chance to express his best wishes. In the huge ball room of the hotel there were too many people, most of them Indians, and it was difficult to find anyone. Sabrina was with Victoria as she was involved in the ceremony and the reception. Alexei was in his hotel room.

"Arsen, I have been waiting to talk to you," Alexei said. "Everybody is talking about your presentation at the Forum meeting on Thursday. You made quite a commotion. A lot of people are plain upset that we have proceeded as far as we have, and they want to know more about our research and our goals. How far do we go?"

"My people have been instructed to talk, and to answer all questions," Arsen said. "We are ready to say everything we know. Is that okay?"

"I think you are right we should not hide anything at this point. The war game is on. Let us see what will happen."

"To change the subject, I wanted to ask you about the progress of the neutrino gun," Arsen said. "The question comes up constantly because people think you are going to get rid of the Demon and then don't understand why we are pushing the bioresearch."

"Between you and me I am quite confident that we will be able to deflect the Demon sufficiently to miss the Earth. Passage close to the Earth may cause turbulence of significant proportions. I would rather have somebody in space who can preserve the human race and the life of some species one way or another."

"You don't think we are extravagant in our goals for delayed life triggering in space, do you?"

"Not at all," Alexei said. "We must send the unmanned ships even if you don't complete all your projects."

"Why?"

"It would be much nicer to be able to grow a baby on some planet, but what if the project is not completed before the deadline for takeoff? The technical part will be complete anyway. There will be a robot that will be able to use the computer. There will be a large store of information - anything we can find, particularly technical information and representation of cultural heritage: art, music, literature, history and anything else Goran and his people make available to us. We will be loading that information on the manned ships anyway. Arsen, you and your wife and whoever else is on the ship, in 'powder' state, as the media called it, would have to be able to obtain the stored information. Obviously, you will be using the information on medical sciences, but other scientists will also use the information they need. You may have to build from scratch, who knows.

"Should it happen that something goes wrong and you and others cannot be cloned, maybe some living creatures somewhere in space will capture one of these ships a million years from now. If they are smart, they will be able to figure out what we are carrying on the ship. Your man, Zourab Abashidze, should write a visual and an audible program on how to use our storage. If their communication is completely different, we may be out of luck. If their intelligence is more advanced than ours they will be able to figure out how to use our computers, maybe even clone some of you. I will have a talk with Zourab when I return to New York."

"You brought up the subject that has been on my mind," Arsen said. "You said I would be cloned on Planet X. I was not planning to submit my genetic engine to be placed on the ship."

"Your genetic engine must be on these ships," Alexei said. "People will expect that. You are the leader of biological research here on Earth, and you will be expected to be the leader on Planet X. How are we going to select other people if you don't want to go?"

"Unfortunately, there is a limit to how many genetic engines from different people we can take along in a ship. There will be a limit for egg cloning too. We will be able to clone one person a year once the first cloned person is mature and has had the memory transfer. How much material can we load on a ship? Perhaps enough for a thousand clone cycles. We should be able to keep the genetic engines of a thousand people. I was not planning to be among those people."

"Maybe not, but you will have to be with them," Alexei said.

"In any event my genetic engine and memory capture will be on board, not my live body and my real brain and my soul," Arsen said dryly.

"You don't like your own project, do you?" Alexei challenged Arsen.

"It is not that. I thought other people should get a chance, a variety of people - not just an orthopedic surgeon and ethnicist. It will be awkward to list me as the lead man on each ship."

"On the contrary, that will be the most appropriate choice," Alexei said and changed the subject. "I know that we are here to meet with Vijay Rangaswamy. What are we going to talk about?"

"Reincarnation! What else?" Arsen exclaimed. "Here is the man who has spent his life talking about the subject and who is the most convincing at that. We should persuade him to join us in New York and to discuss delayed cloning in view of his philosophy."

"Is that what you think?" Alexei asked. "Delayed cloning and life triggering is a form of reincarnation, is that it?"

"I never thought much about reincarnation," Arsen said. "To me, if you can clone a person and give him or her the existing memory of the cloned original, you are dealing with immortality. We don't know whether we get the original soul by reproducing the body and restoring the memory. I feel that a part of the soul is the hidden memory, from the 'seventh veil' you might say, the memory content that an individual does not or cannot reveal freely, but that sometimes comes out when the individual 'talks from the soul.' The experiences that have accumulated over time, during growth, maturation, and later in life, are also part of the soul. Love may be one such experience, or hatred, real religious belief or lack of it. Music can create a shade of the soul, when associated with an event that it can evoke. All these things create the specific state of an individual, based in retrievable memory events which are not only bytes of stored memory but are painted by some psychological trigger mechanism.

"Think of me, a Serb, listening to Beethoven's Eroica Symphony. I have listened to it many times. It is pleasant to my ears and maybe soothing to my soul but does not give me a psychic experience. Listening to a song about a beautiful widow in Banja Luka, an old Muslim song, besides being pleasant to my ears, evokes memories and makes me feel good and bad at the same time; it produces that special feeling of *sevdah*, a yearning for love, and love for the city of my youth, and desire to see the nameless girls I knew and friends who attended school with me, and a feeling of loss of the Serbian church razed by Croatians and of the Ferhadija Mosque exploded by the Serbs.

"I could go on and on. That is part of my soul and makes me what I am today. There are many memories that are mine only and cannot be shared; yet they influenced my development as an individual and made me different from everybody else. This may not be the most sophisticated description of a soul, but this is the soul I know, the soul that talks to me. I don't see why the soul should have special status in the body and survive after the death of an individual. However, after cloning and restoration of the memory content, I think I would feel the same as I feel now talking to you, as long as all the bytes of the memory had been restored and they related to each other."

"You might find out one day - after you have been cloned and have had your memory restored on Planet X," Alexei said. "Once you realize where you are, psychological turmoil in your soul might result. Do you think you would be able to withstand the emotion?"

"Probably, yes," Arsen said. "I would have learned where I was and most likely I would have enjoyed it before the memory transfer was accomplished. A new soul would be formed from the one that had learned about Planet X and Mom Robby, and the other that had been created and copied as the memory content from my experience on Earth. I don't see why they should be mutually exclusive and cause me to kill myself."

"We should ask Vijay Rangaswamy what he thinks about it," Alexei said.

"We should be on our way, if we want to meet him on time," Arsen said. "His hotel is only a short distance away."

The Security Service insisted on the use of a limousine.

Vijay Rangaswamy was a tall, slender man, taller than one would expect an Indian to be. He had a long face with a prominent nose and piercing eyes. His long hair was completely gray and added to his distinguished appearance. An expensive dark blue suit made him look sophisticated. He greeted Arsen and Alexei at the door and showed them into the living room of the suite.

"I decided to travel around the world to be able to meet you," Arsen said in a friendly voice. "I brought Gen. Shagov with me. And here we are."

"So I understand," said Vijay Rangaswamy. "Welcome to India. Is this your first visit?"

"It is the first time for me," Arsen said.

"I have visited several times over the years," Alexei said. "I collaborated with the late Prof. Ram, a renowned astrophysicist. That was during the good old Soviet times and Indira Gandhi's rule. All the political games had little influence on our work, as politicians knew little to nothing about astronomy and astrophysics. That has not changed much in the age of capitalism."

"Oh, I knew the late Professor," Vijay Rangaswamy said. "He had an interest in Indian philosophy and we had many interesting discussions. He was Victoria's distant relative. Have you had time to rest enough after your long journey?" He did not wait for an answer but continued his inquiries. "I read the transcript of your presentation before the Forum on Foreign Policy. Very interesting indeed. Do you really think you can accomplish delayed cloning and trigger life in space? I have my doubts about that. You want to know whether this is a case of reincarnation? Of course it is. Every birth and death involves a transfer of the *atman*, the soul. An original soul from someone else would enter your clone. I am not sure if that would be an upgrade or a downgrade, it would depend on karma from the previous individual.

"The problem is that the clone becomes you when you transfer captured memory, doesn't it? You don't know yet, but you may find out, and then it will be too late for you. How can your clone be you if the soul is from someone else? We have never seen a memory transfer that was done after birth. The soul is transferred to the fetus in the mother's womb, so the newborn already has a soul. What happens with memory transfer, I don't know. Memory transfer is not equal to soul transfer, but a dual person would be created and this new person would require a soul too. Where would the second soul come from? Would the second soul be a *de novo* soul as opposed to the first soul which originated at the beginning of time? This is an entirely new situation. Very fascinating, gentlemen, very fascinating." He abruptly concluded his rhetorical discourse.

"We have a problem defining the soul," Arsen said. "I feel that the soul is just an expression of the individual's life experience and belonging."

"William James already thought of that a long time ago," snapped Vijay Rangaswamy.

"I am not familiar with him," Arsen said. "It makes no difference. The soul is nothing material that remains after death, like the body, and as an abstraction it could hardly be looking for a fetus in need of a soul."

"Oh, the fascination of life and death is the immortality of the soul that passes from one individual to another and connects the spiritual beginning to the present," Vijay Rangaswamy exclaimed.

"I find a connection in the self-preserving division of the first ever unit of life," Arsen retorted.

"How nicely said about the most essential aspect of life, self preservation through procreation which is a part of the soul, though now it may also have something to do with the human genome."

"Do you believe in evolution?" asked Alexei.

"It is hard to ignore science," Vijay Rangaswamy said. "But evolution does not interfere with the existence of the soul and its reincarnation, from the beginning of time, even before the onset of life."

"How do you account for the existence of souls in the population of four billions?" Arsen asked. "Where have they come from? Perhaps from divisions of the original souls?"

"The gods' ways are not often clear to mortals," Vijay Rangaswamy said. "I see no conflict in the creation of the anticipated number of souls at the beginning of time, some of which have not yet been consummated."

"Some are lost from circulation, aren't they?" Arsen asked.

"True. Some are lost to karmic perfection," Vijay Rangaswamy said. "You must have read on the subject since your culture does not provide for reincarnation and karma."

"Not really," Arsen said. "My knowledge of philosophy is limited. I read about the basics in the *Britannica* and supplemented that with specific reading. My greatest disappointment came when I tried to read Hegel's *Phenomenology of Spirit*. I got lost in 'being of oneself' refrains, and if it were not for Kojève's interpretations, also hard to understand, I would not have gained even a glimpse of Hegel's thoughts. Even worse, the experts did not always agree about what was on Hegel's mind. It has always bothered me when an author is not capable of explaining what he or she really thinks, so that everybody can understand it. In my mind, the author does not understand the subject if he cannot explain it. That has discouraged me from reading the old philosophers, and the new ones too. I was thrilled recently to read a quotation from Alexander Rosenberg, in Wilson's *Consilience*, that philosophers address only questions the sciences cannot answer, and why that is the case. It seems that philosophy has been disappearing on one end and increasing on the other, as the scientists have found answers to many questions and created new vistas by the advancement of the research. Maybe that gets me off the hook for my ignorance."

"Wow, what an indictment of philosophy," Vijay Rangaswamy said. "I almost feel I should defend philosophers, except I am only an Indian philosopher interested in reincarnation. It is true that science has not solved the problem of the soul, and its fate, but you may solve it with your cloned man. Should you prove that a cloned individual who receives the momory transfer from his or her predecessor becomes identical with the predecessor - physically and psychologically - I would accept the concept of the soul as an expression of the individual's life experience and belonging, as you defined it. That would create new problems. If two such individuals, identical in soul and body, thus appeared, would they continue their life as psychological Siamese twins, something like a relational database? Or would they live their separate lives and soon be two different individuals? Would that cause problems?"

"That requires more thinking although it makes sense," Arsen said.

"I am fascinated with your ideas," Vijay Rangaswamy said.

"Fascinated enough to work on our team in New York?" Alexei asked.

"Probably yes, I think," Vijay Rangaswamy answered.

"What is the meaning of this 'probably'?" Alexei inquired.

Vijay Rangaswamy laughed. "Do you put a price on everything or look for an angle? Actually, I would like to work with you. Reincarnation may come to an abrupt end, at least on Earth, if the collision occurs. I have to look for space on your unmanned ships to transport the ancient souls."

"Do I understand from what you just said that you would not object to the completion of our projects on delayed cloning?" Alexei asked.

"I would not object."

"When could you come to New York and join us?"

"Very soon, in a week or so," Vijay Rangaswamy said. "I will let you know before I arrive."

"Fantastic!" Arsen exclaimed. "You are our man. You don't sit on your decisions forever. We need a man of action."

"You shall have him."

After a long conversation about the anticollision effort Alexei and Arsen left the hotel very impressed with Vijay Rangaswamy. They had a feeling he was going to play an important role in the defense of the goals of the biological research.

"Where are you flying from here?" Arsen asked Alexei.

"To Germany. I have to negotiate a contract with a conglomerate that is going to build all our space ships. They will probably subcontract the rest of the world."

"A contract?" Arsen asked with surprise. "What do you need that for?"

"Remember that we are building a gun that will deflect the Demon?" Alexei said. "Somebody will have to pay for these ships if we succeed. They will make a great deal of money. I hope they do."

"I hope so too," Arsen said. "I am going to say good-bye to Rama and Victoria at their party and then I will be on my way to New York."

"I am going with you," Alexei said. "I don't enjoy these parties as I did in the good old Soviet days. We ate, and drank Vodka, and sang, and loved girls, and had no worries. Our Politburo worried for us. Life has changed. Our blood pressure is now elevated continually, and the fun is gone."

"You have forgotten. Now we are the Politburo."

The Security Service escorted them to the party.

CHAPTER FIFTY-TWO

MONDAY, 12 JANUARY 1998

A rsen walked into the office at eight o'clock. Michelle was already answering the telephone. Matt Brown and Herman Wolff came out of their offices and looked nervous. There was tension in the air.

"Doctor, everybody wants to talk to you," Michelle said. "My list is two pages long and growing."

"Arsen, I have some important business to talk about with you," Herman Wolff said.

"I had better join you," Matt Brown said. "I have a long list too. We have to decide what to do."

Arsen went into his own office, followed by the two men and Michelle.

"What should I do with the list of calls?" Michelle insisted.

"Let me have the list and I will tell you whom to call," Arsen said. "What is going on in this office? Is this the end of the world? Has the Demon suddenly increased its speed on its way to hit us? Tell me." He sat in his chair and looked at Matt Brown and Herman Wolff. "Please, sit down and tell me what is happening."

"It seems the whole world wants to talk to you about the biological research," Herman Wolff said. "Your Forum talk has stirred many people and they want answers. We had calls from almost all the media in the world. They wanted to hear from you and to talk to you, not to me. Remember the American Senator and Chairman of the Foreign Relations Committee, Mr. Sam Hopkins? He called and said he would like to see you today. The British Foreign Minister called. The President of Ireland called. Cardinal Conti called from Rome. The list goes on and on; it's like *Who's Who* in the world. What should we do?"

"Call the Senator and tell him to come anytime today," Arsen said. "Call Msgr. Amato - I want to talk to him. He should take care of the

Catholic callers. Who else is 'who' in the world? We need somebody representing a religious group or a civilization, like a Slavic Orthodox or an Islamic leader? Perhaps a member of a Philosophic Society or a rightist group. Even a Christian right leader would do - at least he would make a good fight and produce some good arguments."

"Doctor, Senator Hopkins is on the way," Michelle announced over the intercom. "Msgr. Amato is on line four."

"Monsignor, how are you? Why do you think I am calling you?" Arsen said. "The Catholic hierarchy is perturbed. They may soon be under fire. There are many Catholics in this world. Hundreds of millions. We had better do something to calm them down."

"What is the official line?" asked the Monsignor.

"Look inside your soul and you will know," Arsen said. "The issues are clear. Will the human race and life on Earth survive after collision? The answer is not on the Earth. Should we save the human race at all costs? I would like to say yes, but that will have to be debated before the decision is made. Our research will proceed because the time is short; we can always stop it if that is what the Assembly wants. These people should talk to the delegations in the Assembly, not to me. Monsignor, tell people what you really feel, and keep talking - and keep me informed. We will need as much talking as possible. Call me when you need something. Hold the line and Herman Wolff will give you the list of people you should call. Talk to them. If they insist I will talk to them too."

Arsen turned to Matt Brown and Herman Wolff.

"Let him talk," Arsen said. "He is a holy man."

"What should we do with the media?" Herman Wolff asked.

"Arrange a press conference as we decided to do before we left for India. This afternoon. Tell reporters there will be enough time for questions," Arsen said. "I will be able to state our position and by answering their questions to expand on specifics. Fortunately, there is nothing to hide."

As Matt Brown and Herman Wolff were leaving Arsen told them to talk to as many people as possible, and to triage those he had to talk to. Michelle announced over the intercom that Msgr. Amato was again on the line.

"There are two calls I cannot make," the Monsignor said apologetically. "Cardinal Conti is a very influential man in the Vatican. He is responsible for matters of Catholic dogma, and his call is not surprising to me. I am far below him in the Catholic hierarchy. He would not like my calling him if he wanted to talk to you. I also feel that you should talk to the Irish President."

"Okay, I will make the calls," Arsen said and hung up without giving the Monsignor a chance to say anything else.

Michelle announced a call from Song Xiaobo.

"Are you in New York?" Arsen asked him.

"Of course I am here. It was easy to arrange the transfer of my responsibilities to my deputy. Now I am free from Chinese politics and ready to resolve some ethnic problems."

"Like Xinjiang region?" Arsen asked sarcastically.

"No need to rub it in anymore," Song Xiaobo said. "Remember I am now on your team. You will still need me to shore up Chinese support for you. The reason I am calling is the weekly meeting that is scheduled for tomorrow. We have a long list of territories to discuss. Would you mind starting at eight o'clock?"

"I will be there on time," Arsen said. "By the way, have you found an apartment for your family?"

"Everything has been arranged," Song Xiaobo said. "I will take advantage of New York as long as I can under the circumstances."

"Let us talk about the present controversy that is brewing all over," Arsen said. "I feel it in my bones and I am worried. Let us have dinner tonight if you have nothing better to do."

"I am alone in the city. At what time should I come to your office?"

"Seven o'clock," Arsen said.

"See you then," Song Xiaobo said.

"Doctor, Cardinal Conti from Rome is on line four," Michelle announced over the intercom.

"Your Eminence," Arsen said. "I am sorry I did not answered your call immediately. I have just returned from India where I attended the wedding of President Chand."

"I heard he married your Chief of Staff, Victoria Ram," Cardinal Conti said. "We heard about her even before this event. A very capable woman. Too bad you have to look for someone else. I imagine she will not work anymore - she will be the First Lady."

"Unfortunately you are right," Arsen said. "It is not always easy to find someone who fits well in an organization. Do you have any candidates?"

"Not at this moment," Cardinal Conti said.

"Your Eminence, I have a general idea why are you calling me today," Arsen said. "Please, tell me what exactly is on your mind."

"Mr. Secretary, the statements you made during your talk before the Forum on Foreign Policy have stirred many people in the Catholic community. You have shaken the very foundation of the Catholic Church - the existence of God and the immortality of the soul, which is shared throughout Christianity. The Vatican and His Holiness were stunned by your research goals. His Holiness wanted me to express his deep concern with the research you are conducting, and has requested that you stop all these activities. This is also my personal view."

Arsen hesitated to speak bluntly to this respected clergyman, yet he knew he had to state the official line of the World Government.

"Your Eminence, you may be right about the consequences our efforts might cause in spiritual matters," Arsen said. "I can understand the abhorrence of the Catholic Church for the preparations this administration is making in what we think are necessary steps in preserving the human race. We cannot stop our work at this point, as there is very little time to complete it. However, the U.N. Assembly is the only body at this juncture that can order the cessation of our research and of production of space ships, manned and unmanned. It would be unfair to the part of the population that wants this work to continue, to waste precious time while the debate goes on. If the majority in the Assembly decides that we should stop, I assure you we will stop the research and the production. That is the best I can do."

"You insist on continuing the work until the decision is made in the Assembly, is that right?"

"That is correct," Arsen said.

"We won't be able to change your mind, will we?

"You are correct again," Arsen agreed.

"I can live with that as long as we can be sure that the will of the Assembly will not be obstructed by the Administration," Cardinal Conti said. "You have the Military and you can use it against the opponents of the research under the banner of preservation of the human race. How can we be sure you won't?"

"The Military should be placed under the direct control of the Assembly," Arsen said. "That is the only way to show good faith. You represent religion, and the Government has been under the influence of science. The Military could be a deciding factor for the World Government's view. I think the Assembly should never be intimidated by the Military, and it should be in the position to back its decision if need be. As soon as President Chand returns to New York, I will bring the issue up and push for the change. Would that give you sufficient assurance that the will of the majority will decide. Each state will have to decide on which side of the issue it wants to stand and to which degree it wants to participate."

"We will push very hard to convince people, not only Catholics, to be on the side of God," Cardinal Conti said. "Are you firmly convinced that the technology should be used to the fullest?"

"Yes, I am," Arsen said.

"We will talk again," Cardinal Conti said.

"I hope so," Arsen said. "I wish you would suggest a candidate to take Victoria's job. You should be able to find a qualified candidate in the Vatican's Administration - which is not exactly miniscule."

"I wish you were wrong. We deal with many people and some of them are political dead wood. Let me look around. I will try to find someone for you, someone who will not work against you yet will remain a loyal Catholic."

"A tough combination," Arsen said.

"You are right," Cardinal Conti said. "I will let you know. Have a good day."

Arsen was impressed by the Cardinal's calmness and his acceptance of the procedure that was to decide the destiny of the preservation effort. He was right about the Military, Arsen thought. Putting the Military under the control of the Assembly would give more credibility to the World Government.

"Doctor, the Irish President, John O'Brien, is on line two," Michelle announced over the intercom.

"Mr. President, what can I do for you?" Arsen said.

"You should anticipate many a call from Catholics concerned about your ideas for the salvation of the human race and of other Godly creatures," the Irish President said firmly. "It seems that of the things you are doing, many are not known to anybody else, and that includes the U.N. Assembly. My call is a formal protest by my country to you personally. We will make the appropriate official objections to the U.N."

"The Assembly can decide what to do with the present Administration," Arsen said. "They can dismiss all of us or some of us. I cannot change that. I talked to Cardinal Conti just this morning and he was receptive to our intention to continue the proposed research until the Assembly decides on the fate of the preservation programs as we have designed them. It was also proposed, in my talk with the Cardinal, that the Military be placed under the control of the Assembly."

"You should stop the research until its merits have been discussed and decided on by the Assembly," the Irish President demanded.

"I think you should push for an early debate in the Assembly," Arsen snapped back. "That would be more productive and useful to all of us. "

The line went dead and Arsen realized that the Irish President had hung up. The heat was up as expected, Arsen thought. There would be more calls.

"Doctor, President Chand is on line two," Michelle announced over the intercom.

"Rama, you had nothing better to do so you called me," Arsen teased Rama, since he knew the reason for the call.

"I am swamped with calls about the biological research," Rama Chand said. "I am worried this will get out of control."

"It is out of control!" Arsen said. "I talked with Cardinal Conti who was polite but obviously upset. The Irish President hung up on me. Opponents of the biological research will find reasons to attack us. They are still studying my statements, talking to other people, counting their votes, and putting pressure on us. I think we should take some weapons out of their hands."

"Like what?" Rama Chand wondered.

"The Military is already a target," Arsen said. "We should propose to the Assembly that they take over the Military and retain John Thornton as the Chief. John is a good man. They should keep him."

"Do you think I should return to New York?"

"I don't think so. I will forward an urgent letter to the President of the Assembly in your name and ask him to organize a special session for next week to debate the biological research and whether or not to take command of the Military. You will be back by then."

"Do that," Rama Chand agreed. "I will be prepared to talk to the Assembly on Monday."

"Regards to Victoria," Arsen said, and hung up.

It was noon and Arsen decided to have lunch. There had been too much excitement already, he thought. And this was just the beginning.

"Doctor, Sen. Hopkins is here to see you," Michelle announced over the intercom.

Here we go again, Arsen thought. What did he want? Was he for or against biological research?

"Good day, Senator," Arsen said. "I have been perplexed about the urgency of your visit. I get nervous whenever someone with influence wants to talk to me, and even more so when he wants to meet with me."

"It can't be that bad," Sen. Hopkins said. "Your talk has stirred some feelings but it was good that you explained what the Department has been doing. Now it's in the open and the Assembly will have to act. The ball is out of your hands."

"Under pressure we decided to propose that the Assembly take control of the Military," Arsen said. "Some people think the Military could be used to intimidate those in opposition to the biological programs."

"Are you sure you want to submit that proposal?"

"It is a hot potato and the issue will recur often enough not to be ignored," Arsen said. He was curious about the real reason for the Senator's visit.

"We would like to see Gen. Thornton as Military Chief, and you could suggest that," Sen. Hopkins said.

That was not the reason for his visit, Arsen thought, since the issue had come up only this morning with Cardinal Conti.

"I talked to our President the other day," Sen. Hopkins continued. "He thought we should get together with you. He feels that the Americans have been left behind in some areas, especially in the management structure and in the middle echelons of the Administration. Our contributions in many areas have been substantial. I'm sure he'll have some other items for discussion."

"Would tomorrow be convenient for the President," Arsen said. "He is still my President and I shouldn't keep him waiting."

"We had in mind dinner tonight at the White House," Sen. Hopkins said. "Is that possible? Eight o'clock?"

"I will be there," Arsen said.

"I am obliged to you," Sen. Hopkins said before he left.

There was more to this than just a chat with the President, Arsen thought. He would find out tonight. The dinner with Song Xiaobo would have to be canceled.

Michelle brought in a sandwich and a cup of coffee and placed them on the desk.

"I thought you would be busy the rest of the day and some food would be good for you," she said. "I have the lists of the calls received by Herman Wolff and Matt Brown. Also, Matt Brown wanted to talk to you when you had a free moment."

"Let me see their lists," Arsen said. "Michelle, I find no time to talk to you. You have a few people working for you. Is everything okay? Do you need anything?"

"I have no problems. The only one in the office who's not happy is Stanley Kim. He doesn't say it but I know. Could you talk to him? He's a very capable person."

"Send him in as soon as Matt Brown leaves."

Matt Brown was hesitant to state the reason for the meeting.

"I hate to say it but I'm not comfortable in my position as Press Secretary," he said. "It's my own problem and I blame nobody for it. I'm not built for this job. The pressure is too high and there is no end to the constant inquiries by the media and everybody else. With these new developments it will get worse before it gets better. I've decided to quit and I want you to let me go."

This was unexpected. Matt Brown was doing a good job and Arsen had a special feeling for him. Matt's letter had been the first link in the chain of events that brought him to the present position.

"Are you sure."

"Yes, I am sure."

"What are you going to do?"

"We will return to our home town, St. Louis, where our families live and where we have many friends, and we'll wait like everybody else, for the end to come or for the miracle to happen. I'll be with you in my thoughts always."

Arsen stood up and embraced Matt Brown.

"You were the harbinger of my new career," Arsen said. "I remember my call to the Forum office, the call you answered, and your confirmation that you had written the letter inviting me to give a lecture."

"I remember your hesitation and your disbelief."

"Such a distant past," Arsen said.

"That happened less than three months ago!" Matt Brown exclaimed.

"A long three months," Arsen said as he shook Matt Brown's hand. "Good sailing wherever you go, and good luck to all of us."

Stanley Kim walked into the office after Matt Brown left.

"Stan, I understand you are unhappy in your present job," Arsen said. "Is that true?"

"I don't want to leave my job," Stanley Kim said.

"Is there a job you would rather do?"

"Dr. Bjöstrom has no staff. I could organize and run her office."

"That reminds me, I have to talk to her. What did you do in college?"

"I started in physics but ended up with a degree in economics," Stanley Kim said.

"Why?"

"I felt there was no future for me in physics. I was good at it, not excellent."

"It is good to know your own strengths and weaknesses," Arsen said. "I wish I had known my own when I was young. Now it is too late. I think I should be able to get you that job with Dr. Bjöstrom."

Arsen asked Michelle to call Ursula and find out if she could come to see him.

"Doctor, she's on the way," Michelle announced over the intercom.

Ursula Bjöstrom walked in. Arsen could not help noticing how attractive she was and how elegant yet simple was her dress.

"You had a long trip," Arsen said. "I hope it was worthwhile. Now you are an expert on memory capture."

"I sure am," Ursula Bjöstrom said. "I would have learned even more if sexual-harassment laws existed in Russia. Gennadi was dreadfully aggressive. I knew Russians could be very charming and aggressive. Gennadi Koltsov was most outstanding in that role."

"I hope you parted as good friends," Arsen said. "That is important."

"Sure we did. He is not stupid."

"Tell me what is new that I don't know," Arsen inquired.

"Both memory capture and transfer are impressive and simple techniques," Ursula Bjöstrom said and she described the techniques in detail. "It will be important to develop storage techniques, particularly for our purposes, and considering that these storage discs may be inactive for millennia. They had better function when they are needed. I am sure we will have enough time to develop the technology. I was told that Mikhail Platov, whom I met only briefly, is a capable scientist. I am very excited about my new job."

"You are already a veteran," Arsen said. "You have been in Moscow, you have learned a technique known to only a few, and you are ready to start working on its application. What has to be accomplished in New York?"

"Our direction is storage of the memory content of the individuals who will be on the unmanned ships," Ursula Bjöstrom said. "The rumor is that you will be the lead person on all these ships. We will be working on your memory content."

"What does it mean working on my memory content?" Arsen was not sure he wanted people going through the details of his memory. "You will have to define the privacy of the storage of these memories and enforce it."

"That will be one of the important aspects of the project," Ursula Bjöstrom said and continued playfully. "You probably won't have to worry about your stored memory; your thoughts are likely to be holy, aren't they? Or is there something compromising in your memory, or embarrassing? A woman or two?" Ursula moved in her chair and exposed her thighs under her short skirt.

Ursula's look, Arsen thought, was asking him to register his desire and he felt uncomfortable. To make his suffering worse she pulled the skirt even higher. She was beautiful, and the sight was inviting. She looked at him with her half open, and just as inviting, mouth.

"Do you think you might contribute to my compromising memory content," Arsen said and looked her in the eye as if to discover her thoughts. She looked even more sensual after his challenge and said nothing.

"You are very beautiful and very desirable - dangerously so," Arsen said. "I wonder if lovemaking is on your mind? Yet, this will be our last encounter. We will work together and enjoy our association, but lovemaking is not in our cards. Let me admire your beauty and your mind without losing my self respect."

Ursula Bjöstrom left the office without saying anything.

Michelle announced over the intercom that Arsen was expected at the press conference.

Thirty reporters were in the conference room as there was no space for more people. This was Matt Brown's last press conference, Arsen thought. The room was quiet as the reporters waited for Arsen's opening statement.

"Good afternoon. I know that you want me to give you more information on the biological research, but truly there is not much to add to what I said at the Forum meeting last week. The only new development is the decision by President Chand to ask the Assembly to take over the responsibility and control of the Military. This issue was brought out today by Cardinal Conti. I have sent an official request to the Assembly to take the issue up at their next meeting as requested by the President. He will speak at the Assembly meeting on Monday. Another development is the assignment of Msgr. Amato as one of our spokesmen on the issues of the biological research. Mr. Vijay Rangaswamy, who needs no introduction, agreed to join this department in a function similar to that of Msgr. Amato. You will get to know him, as he will talk on the subjects which seem to be creating controversy these days. Finally, the latest on memory capture. Dr. Björstrom has told me that the technique is rather simple in both capture and transfer of memory content. Before the technique is revealed to other scientists, the problems of privacy and consent will have to be resolved. You can imagine the multitude of applications of this technique. That is all I have to say. You may start with the questions."

Thirty hands were raised.

Most of the questions concerned clones and memory capture. There were questions about the identity of clones and their souls, whether they would know about God and how they would find out. Would memory capture technology be available to people other than scientists working for the Government? Could it be used for other purposes? Arsen answered all questions giving lengthy explanations of the facts as they were available. Then he summarized the entire biological research.

"From my introduction and the answers I have provided to your questions you should get a clear picture of the techniques we must use to preserve the human race by triggering human life and the essential supporting forms of life perhaps millennia after the unmanned ships are lunched. The issue is not the techniques we are developing. It is the triggering of life that is raising ethical, emotional, religious and philosophical questions and objections. I anticipate extensive debate on this issue, and the outcome is unclear to me.

"I don't understand why Cardinal Conti has accused me of denying the existence of God and the immortality of the soul. If I were a devout Catholic or a Christian of any denomination or even an Islamic Fundamentalist I would believe that nothing could happen without God's approval. Thus, development of the delayed cloning techniques would be impossible without God's grace. Disappearance of all life in the cataclysm would also have to be God's will - punishment if you will. God could just as well allow the technology to develop, and guide the ships to Planet X, and even three or more ships to as many different planets. God could also guide the development of the cloned individuals on the planets.

"As to the question of souls, you will hear two diametrically opposite views. One view is of the soul entering the embryo or the newborn and exiting intact at death; the fate of these souls depends on the views of different people. The second view holds that the soul is the creation of the mind via its memory content as each individual is subjected to different experiences. Neither view denies that God has facilitated the enrichment of the soul. To put it bluntly, neither side can prove its arguments. Isn't that the old story, the spectrum of believers to atheists?

"I am not here today to preach religious beliefs nor to present a philosophical discourse. If I lose my job by being on the wrong side of the fence, I will write a book to explain my thoughts on the world and the Universe, even though I know it would disappear with all of us. Maybe, just maybe, my thoughts, captured by neutrinos, will fly on them to wherever they go. Have a good day." Arsen left the conference room, which became noisy with people talking simultaneously.

"Doctor, thank you for arranging the job for Stanley," Michelle said as Arsen returned to the office. "Stanley talked to Dr. Björstrom and she agreed to take him."

"Any calls for me?" Arsen asked.

"You're lucky. Matt Brown and Herman Wolff have been taking all your calls, and I've heard no complaints."

"Have you canceled the dinner with Mr. Song?"

"Yes. I rescheduled it for tomorrow night."

"At what time am I leaving for Washington?"

"Five o'clock."

As soon as Arsen walked into his own office Michelle announced over the intercom that the Vice-President of the Assembly, Zalev Schiff, was on line two.

"Hello, Dr. Schiff," Arsen greeted the Israeli Ambassador. "Is this Assembly business or Israeli business?"

"It is always Israeli business, but this time I am calling on Assembly business. The question is what should I do with the letter the Assembly received this morning? Do you people really want the Military out of the World Government? Why?"

"By now you know there is a rising controversy regarding the biological research. I have been reminded that the Military could play a role as an intimidating factor in the debate. That means trouble. We are interested in having an unrestrained debate. Period."

"Would you be interested in appearing before the Committee on Biological Advancement?" Zalev Schiff asked.

"That is the Assembly's prerogative," Arsen said firmly. "I will appear before the Committee if you invite me, although it would be better to have Rama Chand set the tone for the response and the policies of the World Government."

"Okay, we will wait until he returns but that will not get you off the hook for testifying before the Committee," Zalev Schiff said. "The Committee has been formed under the Chairmanship of Gabriella Variale , the Italian Ambassador."

"Should I start packing?" Arsen asked.

"Why should you?" Zalev Schiff said. "She will have to be fair. The Committee has twelve members. This will be an interesting committee."

"Undoubtedly, you are a member," Arsen inquired.

"Undoubtedly."

"What is your Israeli business?"

"When are you going to tell us what your opinion is on Jerusalem and the West Bank?"

"You tell me. As I told your Prime Minister, I would like to have these questions resolved between Jews and Arabs. My opinion is unimportant. You will have to live with the decisions you make and the conditions they create."

"Do you think we can get Jerusalem and the Arabs the West Bank plus access to the shrines?" Zalev Schiff was negotiating with his questions.

"Is that an official offer to the Arabs?" Arsen was serious when he asked the question.

"No, it is not," Zalev Schiff replied. "This is just a feeler."

"I would prefer to take my opinion to my grave," Arsen said. "It is an emotional issue with me. I want to make sure the right decisions are made."

"You haven't made many friends in Serbia," Zalev Schiff said. "Is that what the Jews should expect?"

"The issues are the same, as they are in all ethnic problems, but the problems are different," Arsen said. "It is always an issue of the land. 'We lived here before you,' says one side, and 'We are here and have nowhere to go,' says the other. Who is right is the question? Zalev, do you know who is right?"

"The Jews are always right," said Zalev Schiff.

"The Serbs are always right," said Arsen.

Both men laughed and hung up. There was nothing more to say.

"Doctor, the limousine is waiting for you," Michelle reminded Arsen over the intercom. "You'd better go if you want to be on time at the White

House."

Arrangements had been made for the President and Arsen to have a private dinner. Sen. Sam Hopkins and the National Security Advisor, Bryan Whiette, were to join them after dinner.

This was a special experience for Arsen, although he had been at the White House after Alexei's silent talk at the United Nations. He did not know which room he would be having dinner in with the President.

The room, not very large, was beautifully decorated; its furniture appeared old and well preserved and maintained. Several portraits looked familiar but Arsen did not even try to guess who these men were, although he thought one was President Andrew Jackson. He had seen President Jackson's picture in a magazine just a few days earlier. The food was simple and exquisitely prepared: cold vichyssoise, New York cut beefsteak with a baked potato, chocolate mousse and coffee.

During dinner the President talked about his origins in Indiana and his studies at the University of Notre Dame - where he had tried, and failed, to make the football team - and later at Yale Law School. He talked about his academic career which he had given up for politics, and about the campaign that had led to the Presidency. Arsen was listening and wondering what was on his mind behind his deep-set, intelligent and penetrating eyes. After looking at his face one remembered only the eyes.

"Dr. Pankovich, I wanted to talk to you about two rather delicate issues," the President said after they had finished dinner and as he was pouring cognac into small crystal glasses. "These issues are important politically to me and to the country.

"Let me give you the background of the first issue. The Administration and the Congress have been looking critically and carefully at the developments in the World Government in the context of the present situation and the future of the world. We are quite confident that the anticipated collision will not occur. Our scientists have visited with Gen. Shagov and gone over his work. They found him brilliant and the work he has done simply amazing. They concluded that he has ample time to complete his research, to build the neutrino guns and the space ships for them, and to position these ships strategically in space so that they can bombard the approaching celestial object until it changes its course and flies into space. We aren't even paying attention to the nuclear weapons he's developing since they won't do the job. Are you of the same opinion?"

"No, I am not," Arsen said. "I agree that Gen. Shagov is a brilliant man and that he has a first-class team of scientists. I am not sure he has enough time to complete the work, or that his guns will do the job. What I think is that there is a chance he will succeed. That is all."

"Very interesting that you're not convinced," the President said. "I'm not convinced either, despite the opinions of our scientists. Contingency plans have to be made and carried out just in case. That's good politics and a safe approach. I'm afraid there will be plenty of resistance to your plans. I guess you know that already."

"Yes, I do," Arsen said. "The pressure is on from the opponents."

"They say the research denies God," the President said, his eyes looking attentively at Arsen.

"We are not dealing with the creation of the Universe and God in it," Arsen said. "God created us and everything we do or invent now or ever is His will. We can debate these issues, but the work should proceed."

"There are some powerful people talking against you."

"Who are they?"

"For one, the Vatican. The Irish President told me about the conversation he had with you, and he is upset with you. Many scientists are against the biological research, particularly some of those who believe that Gen. Shagov will succeed in deflecting the Demon. Ethicists are upset but divided. Politicians follow the trends in their districts just in case the threat disappears. This looks like a Presidential campaign. Economists and businessmen are upset because resources are being spent, they feel, indiscriminately. The financial world is at a standstill, because it makes no sense to push deals and waste time while awaiting the catastrophe. The markets have been frozen. They want some answers as to the future."

"You have the best information from your scientists," Arsen said. "You can quote what they say. You can ask them to speak publicly and to say what they think. The most urgent task now is to debate, to discuss the issues and to express ourselves."

"The scientists who reviewed Gen. Shagov's work may be your worst adversaries," the President said.

"My worst adversaries are the people who don't speak their minds," Arsen said. "I am more worried by silence."

"The reason I brought up this issue is the concern we have about economic issues that have been neglected in the past few months." The President continued to explain the reasons for the meeting. "The anticollision effort by Gen. Shagov has received full support because deflection of the celestial object, or its destruction, would be the best solution to the problem. I also firmly believe that the biotechnological effort has to continue and has to be supported more than ever. These two avenues of salvage are not that expensive. I know that it will cost to build the neutrino guns and the ships that will carry them, and it will cost just as much, if not more, for the biological research and for the manned and unmanned ships. Yet this is not enough - not even close - to wreck the global economy. Inactivity is what is ruining the economy. This will just get worse if we don't act soon enough. This has been discussed at my cabinet meetings, by the National Security advisors, and in the Administration at large.

"The way I see it, we have no choice but to try to convince the world population that everything will be fine and that the danger will go away if we continue the anticollision effort and if they, the people, help at their level by shaking their inactivity. In the meantime, we have to get things moving again to be ready for the world afterwards. We will also ensure the continuation of the biological research and of the projects concerned with the launching of manned and unmanned ships just in case."

"Mr. President, are you trying to tell me that the World Government should be abolished?" Arsen asked with some trepidation.

"Not really. But its scope should be changed." The President hesitated for a moment. "As I told you, the economy is lagging and the loss may become irreversible if we don't do something about it. Activities in other areas have slowed down too. Students are not returning to the campuses of most of the universities and colleges, and even elementary and high school education has suffered. If we survive 2003 we will have produced generations of young people who have lost five years of their life and possibly in the process also lost the drive to be something for the rest of their lives. We have to do something about that. Our scientists not involved in the World Government's research are idle and waiting to see what will happen. Are they going to be ready to continue after Earth is saved? Look at the rest of the population and you will find that the people are slowing down and getting ready for 2003. What will become of them if the Earth escapes the collision? Mental and physical atrophy, that's what will be left of them."

"I see your point, Mr. President," Arsen said. "What do you suggest we do? If you want to start a campaign in which you explain your thinking and try to reassure people about the collision, even tell them that U.S. scientists are convinced that the Demon will be destroyed or deflected, it is okay with me. This would be psychotherapy that would be good for the people. You would also have to explain why you support the biological research. Though you believe there is a minimal probability of collision, you want to be sure we have contingency plans in place - that seems logical. One other concern is the ethnic situation. To support your ideas I have to be ensured that the ethnic effort will continue unchanged. This is a good opportunity to do the right things. Finally, I have just established the Mandela-Tutu Commission. I am not ready to give it up.

"I have no problems with your ideas on ethnic equality and you should continue your work without interruptions. As for the Mandela-Tutu Commission I have some reservations. First, you should not force states to accept the Commission if they don't want it. Second, there should be a body, a World Court if you wish, which will have to decide the issues with full participation of the involved parties. What I mean is, if a state wants to hold trials for the people who committed ethnic and political crimes, they should be able to do it."

"That is also our idea," Arsen said. "Let me propose the idea of a World Court to President Chand. You may have the opportunity to push for your ideas at the meetings and conferences that will be convened to resolve issues and disagreements. Until that is done the present Commission will continue its work."

"We seem to agree on everything," The President said. "Frankly I didn't anticipate that you would be interested."

"When the decisions are right, I don't see why not."

"There is another thing." the President said. "Our public statements may not always be identical or even agreeable, and that will depend on the situation. That's to be expected."

"We have agreed in principle to do what is best for the people. Let us leave it at that," Arsen concluded the conversation.

"Let's call in Sen. Hopkins and Bryan Whiette," the President said. "They've been waiting for a while."

After they came in, and received their small crystal glasses filled with cognac, the President explained to Sen. Hopkins and Bryan Whiette that Arsen was agreeable to the proposal to stimulate the economy and to talk more positively about anticollision. The atmosphere in the room was relaxed and friendly.

As Arsen was preparing to leave, the President shook his hand and expressed satisfaction with the conversation they had had.

"We should meet from time to time to compare notes," the President said and added, "It's good that our ideas aren't diametrically opposed. Thank you."

Arsen was in a good mood on the way to New York.

CHAPTER FIFTY-THREE

TUESDAY, 13 JANUARY 1998

At eight o'clock Arsen started the first meeting of the Ethnic Board.

"As you all know we have resolved some large and obvious problems," Arsen said. "For the record, let us list the ethnic problems we can consider resolved or on the way to being resolved at this time."

"Eighteen ethnic problems are in those categories at this time," Song Xiaobo said, and he listed them.

They were:

Cyprus, where the two sides had decided on a federation of two equal states.

The Basque territory in Spain and France had been united in a separate Basque Republic.

Tibet had separated from China and restored the old state, with the Dalai Lama as the head.

In Sri Lanka, the Tamils had separated and formed a new state, the Tamil Republic.

Kurdistan had become a new state from parts of Turkey, Iraq, Iran and former Soviet Republics.

Mindanao was now an autonomous region in the Philippines.

Kosovo had separated from Serbia and was in the process of organizing the Republic of Kosovo, an independent state.

Serb Kosovars who lived in the northern part of Kosovo and were in the majority in that area had decided to join Serbia.

The Albanians from western Macedonia were ready to join the Republic of Kosovo.

The Bosnian Muslim Republic would be proclaimed, since the Serbian entity, Republika Srpska, by the vote of their Assembly had decided for independence.

Sandzak, a Muslim part of Serbia, would soon have a referendum, but it was certain that it would join the Bosnian Muslim Republic.

Croatian territory in Bosnia would unite with the Croatian Republic.

Croatia had agreed to allow the return of expelled Serbs from Krajina to that territory, to help them rebuild, and to give them autonomous status.

Republika Srpska was a new state as stated above

Ichkeria, formerly known as Chechnya, had voted in their Parliament to separate from Russia and had become a new state.

East Timor had decided to separate from Indonesia and to become a new state.

Three Baltic states, Latvia, Lithuania and Estonia, had agreed to resolve the problems of their Russian minorities. They would relax their language rules and eligibility for citizenship. Their new policies were in effect already.

Abkhazia had gained highly independent autonomy from Georgia.

"That is what we have as of today. This is a remarkable achievement in a short time period."

Applause followed Song Xiaobo's presentation.

"Many people contributed to working out the details of the agreements and secessions," Arsen said. "Can you tell us what is pending and what is being planned?"

Song Xiaobo's deputy, Steve Ross, said that four major problem areas were Zaire with Burundi and Rwanda, which were complicated by ethnic demography; Israel-Palestine, where negotiations were being organized; India-Pakistan are also in the process of organizing negotiations on Kashmir; and the Sudan, where the Christian South wanted independence. "Pushing them has not helped much," Steve Ross said. "We are working with the Mexican Government and the Chiapas Indians to resolve their standoff."

"René, we had an unpleasant day in Kinshasa," Arsen said. "Three Presidents were dismissed while we were there. What has happened since then?"

"As you would expect," René Bright said, "new Presidents were elected from the legislative bodies. They are different people, not obstructionists. The problems are very complex because of demography. Often, you have two adjoining villages that belong to different ethnic groups. Borders will not resolve their problems. Cantonization has been considered though even that might not suffice.

"We are discussing the possibility of local rule as the basic unit for each ethnic group. Each of these basic units, which we call a Bee, would be represented in their ethnic regional councils. These councils would elect their representatives to the National Parliaments which in turn would select the governments.

"In reality, you would have one territory with two or more parallel states responsible for the welfare of their ethnic groups. Nobody would stop the villages of different ethnicity from working together or becoming a part of a different ethnic group. Multiethnic states could develop. That may work in the territories where there are two, three, or four major ethnic groups, like Rwanda and Burundi, even Zaire. Some ethnic groups are large, and they could vote for their own independence. The example is the Kasai territory. We are organizing a plebiscite in Kasai. A similar situation exists in the neighboring Shaba. Other areas are different, and they may have to form a number of federations.

"Some will need the Bee System. I would like to ask for approval for the trial of the Bee System."

"The Bee System!" Arsen said. "Why do you call it the Bee System?"

"I don't know who came up with the name," René Bright said. "It comes from the characteristic of bees that they return to the same colony even if there are other colonies around. The Bees, or in reality the villages, are oriented to their ethnic groups."

"What would prevent the Bees fighting each other?" Arsen asked.

"The Military," René Bright said. "The principle of the World Government is to protect established territories. Why couldn't we protect the Bees?"

"How do we cover such a large territory and thousands of villages - or Bees as you call them?" Arsen asked.

"Local people would enlist as World Government militia in integrated units so they can watch each other," René Bright said. "Besides, most often the balance could be kept if the regional councils communicated with each other."

The Bee System immediately became the subject of controversy and ridicule.

"What about the sovereignty of such double governments?"

"How many Bee governments do you want to make in the United States - two hundred?"

"Should we let the Russians form a Bee government in Latvia?"

"What about Germany or France with their Muslim populations or Northern Ireland?"

"Should Czech Romas form a Bee Regional Council?"

"What about the Chinese in Tibet or Indonesia?"

"I think we have had enough of this," Arsen said and the clamor in the room subsided. "Just the reaction and controversy it produced among you gives credence to the Bee idea. I am in favor of René giving it a try in Zaire. I think it might work in Africa as I find no solution short of moving populations to make them ethnically pure, a sort of voluntary ethnic cleansing. I hope nobody in this room is for any kind of voluntary or involuntary movement of the populace. René, my congratulations on this project. I did not expect any kind of progress in Zaire, Rwanda and Burundi."

Arsen was intrigued by the idea of dual or parallel sovereignty. In a sense the sovereignty had already shifted from the state to the ethnic majorities, he thought.

"The Israeli-Palestinian problem is my responsibility," Arsen said. "I talked recently to the Prime Minister of Israel and to the Israeli Ambassador to the United Nations and I will soon meet with the Palestinians. They have high level delegations ready to start negotiations. They have been talking for many years, and I think they should continue to talk. Only this time there is a time-limit of two years."

There was no further discussion on that subject.

"What is the situation in Northern Greece?" Arsen asked.

"Greece was assigned to me only a few days ago as we all thought that you, Mr. Secretary, were in charge of the entire Balkans," Bengt Carlson said.

"Sorry for the confusion," Arsen said. " I have simply had no time to get involved, although I have a good feeling for that explosive area. Greeks don't think Macedonians exist. That is the same as it was in the minds of the Turks when the Kurds were mentioned. The difference is that the Macedonians in Northern Greece have been treated well and they may not want us to interfere. Remind me to talk to the Mexican President about Chiapas. What has happened in the Sudan?"

"The situation is complicated by parties other than Muslims against Christians," René Bright said. "We are talking to them to decide who will be qualified as an ethnic group. As soon as that has been decided we will proceed with the plebiscite."

"That is all we have for today," Song Xiaobo said. "Our next meeting will be on Tuesday, January 27 at eight o'clock in the morning."

On the way out of the conference room Arsen reminded Song Xiaobo about the dinner in the evening.

"Seven o'clock in your office," Song Xiaobo said.

"Okay."

Back in the office Michelle had several phone calls for Arsen to answer.

"Who do you want me to call first?" Michelle asked. "Dr. Saito, Dr. David Gallagher from the Forum on Foreign Policy, Cardinal Conti or the British Foreign Minister."

"Call them in that order," Arsen said.

"Dr. Saito is on line three," Michelle announced over the intercom.

"Dr. Saito, how is the DNA powder progressing?" Arsen asked. "At least in the press they call it powdered DNA. Do you think you will produce desiccated DNA that will work in an artificial medium?"

"That is the reason I am calling," Isoroku Saito said. "We have some indications that we can lyophilize DNA and convert it back to an active state as if it were in the cell. We need more people and more labs. Can we get them?"

"You must know where to find people. Simply hire them. We will support your decisions."

"I will have more definitive information in a few months. We are also working on preservation of the lyophilized DNA to prevent the tendency for slow degradation."

"Do you keep in touch with Thomas Lowell and Jean-Luc Menguy?" Arsen inquired.

"I do."

"We will have to get together."

Not bad, Arsen thought, not bad at all for the short period they had been working on the project.

"Dr. David Gallagher from the Forum on Foreign Policy is on line two," Michelle announced over the intercom.

"Dr. Gallagher, what is it that the Forum wants from me?" Arsen laughed. "Do they need my social security number so that they can pay my honorarium?"

"More than that, Mr. Secretary," Dr. Gallagher responded. "Much more."

"Don't tell me - I know," Arsen said. "They want me to give another talk."

"Correct."

"Do you think I have nothing better to do than to talk at the Forum's Meetings?"

"You must like it for the free publicity you have been getting," Dr. Gallagher said and laughed.

"I could do without such publicity," Arsen said. "Have you seen the headlines in the papers today?

"VATICAN AND CANTERBURY COMPLAIN ABOUT
SEC. PANKOVICH
"Ethics of the ambitious Biological Research
"HUMAN CLONING - an editorial
"DO WE REALLY WANT BABIES IN SPACE
"STRIP-TEASE of the MIND
Should I continue?"

"I have seen these headlines," David Gallagher said.

414

"They will only get worse and more vicious against the biological research and against our goals to make sure the human race survives one way or another."

"Our Board directed me to ask you to give us another talk on the date we originally invited you for - Thursday, January 22nd."

"I think I will be in the city on that date." Arsen made up his mind to accept the invitation. "I will send you the topic once I decide what I want to talk about. Some historical perspective, perhaps? I know everybody will be disappointed with my talk, and you will leave me alone in the future. That is the Peter principle - fail to fulfill expectations, and they leave you alone. My best to Prof. Pierce."

"Thank you very much for accepting this invitation," David Gallagher said.

What was the historical perspective? Arsen wondered. What was he going to tell these people? They would expect a follow-up to the previous presentation. Political and ethnic terrorism? That would become the history of history as people gained their freedom, or even the end of history. The title of the lecture must make an impression, Arsen concluded. Something like "freedom fighters from the past." That did not sound very interesting. "Kamikaze versus terrorist"? "Guerrilla and liberation armies"? Rather dull. Something more striking was required.

"Doctor, Cardinal Conti is on line three," Michelle announced over the intercom.

"Your Eminence," Arsen said. "It is good to hear from you."

"Good day Mr. Secretary. I have found an excellent individual, well qualified to work for you in any capacity you want," Cardinal Conti said. "She is a nun and has worked for the Vatican in many responsible positions. Sister Maria O'Brien has a Ph.D. in Theology from Notre Dame and a Masters in Economics from the University of Chicago. She is an extraordinary person, a very capable and dedicated worker, and loyal to the people she works with. Don't expect her to agree with you on everything, as your ideas are contrary to her beliefs. But she will find her way in your organization and you may get to like her frank talk and constructive thinking. Importantly she will not obstruct the system even when she disagrees. I talked to her and she is willing to go to New York whenever you want her to come."

"I needed her yesterday," Arsen said. "Please dispatch her by the first plane. Victoria Chand is not coming back to the Department. Thank you very much."

"She will leave in the morning and I will arrange accomodations for her in a convent in New York, and for her to be met at the airport."

"Thank you, Your Eminence."

"Mr. Anthony Clark, the British Foreign Minister, is on line two," Michelle announced over the intercom.

"Good day Mr. Clark," Arsen said. "I know you called and I know I did not call you back. It is not disrespect nor disregard; it is simply lack of time. Please forgive me."

"I understand," the Foreign Minister said. "The instructions of my Prime Minister, Mr. Kenneth Stone, to talk to you should explain my persistence. We have been under pressure from the Archbishop of the Canterbury to talk to you and ask for some explanations of your research goals. Like other religious leaders, the Archbishop is concerned about your goals and even more so about this technology in case the cataclysm is averted. What are you going to do with this technology, Mr. Secretary? Although I am less concerned than the Archbishop I would like to know."

"I have made statements regarding all the potential problems," Arsen said. "Still it is impossible to explain everything. It seems that I should come to London and have a meeting with the representatives of the Church of England and the British Government. Would that help?"

"We had not expected you to go out of your way to accommodate us," the Foreign Minister said. "However it would be a disarming move on your part. I would be delighted to organize such a meeting. Tell me when you want to come."

"I will arrive in London on Monday and the meeting could take place on the same day," Arsen said. "If you want to arrange meetings with whomever you think would be important, just do it."

"Excellent. Who do I talk to in your office for details?"

"There are problems in the office," Arsen said. "Matt Brown, my Press Secretary, wanted to retire to his native St. Louis and wait there for the outcome of our little problem, so he is gone. My Chief of Staff, Victoria Ram, has recently become the First Lady of the World Government, and she is on her honeymoon. My Deputy, Herman Wolff, has been swamped with work and I want to spare him from becoming my secretary. I think you should call me when everything is ready; I will leave it up to you."

"I will get back to you in a day or two," the Foreign Minister concluded. "Good day to you."

Arsen liked Mr. Clark's handling of the mission perceived as delicate by his Prime Minister. He was cool and friendly. He would make an excellent replacement for Matt Brown, Arsen thought. He might not want the job.

Song Xiaobo knocked on the door of Arsen's office at seven o'clock in the evening and walked in. Arsen was asleep stooped in his chair.

"I must have slept for half an hour," Arsen said as he woke up.

"You said seven o'clock," Song Xiaobo said.

"I am ready to have dinner," Arsen said. "Tonight we are going to Park Avenue Café on Sixty-Second Street. Michelle made reservations for seven thirty."

It was a short limousine ride.

They were expected, and were immediately seated at a corner table on the upper floor. There was a decent separation from other tables not typical for this usually packed restaurant. It promised to be a quiet evening.

Arsen ordered his usual tonic water with a twist, cold soup, lamb chops and the chocolate mousse cube, and Song Xiaobo wanted only tuna fish with rice, and coffee.

"You have been in New York for a week," Arsen said.

"Five days only and I already feel as if I have been around for months," Song Xiaobo said. "This is an incredible city and my job is even more incredible. I never thought I could think the way I do only a week out of China. Yet, we are not as bad as you in the West think we are. I think you project your thoughts about China. We are interested in seeing our people live better, and we have stimulated the economy and enterprise.

"We have been saying all along we may not have a full democracy, but we are on the way, a Chinese way. We do suppress some people to avoid anarchical tendencies. Look at Russia and Eastern Europe, the Balkans and even Brooklyn in New York. Not far from anarchy in many places. We avoided the system you find in India, and we cannot afford to be like Sweden. Perhaps we don't even want to be like Sweden. As you know, we have problem areas that will have to be resolved."

"What about Taiwan and Hong Kong? They are Chinese all right, yet they don't want to join you. Why shouldn't they be recognized by Mainland China as independent countries?"

"I know your thinking process," Song Xiaobo said. "You want the people to decide everything. That is not always the best thing for the people. Taiwan and Hong Kong are Chinese territories, and the people are Chinese. They don't deny that they are Chinese. They are as much Chinese as the Muslim Kosovars are Albanians. You recognized the realities in Kosovo, yet you denied the same to Taiwan's and to Hong Kong's Chinese. Why?"

"They insist on being independent," Arsen said. "Why not let them have what they want? China will catch up with them and will overtake them. They will ask some day to rejoin the mother country."

"On Planet X?" asked Song Xiaobo.

"What if the collision is avoided? The next collision will not occur for millennia. These Chinese from the Mainland, Taiwan or Hong Kong may want to live together. Will there be the kind of ethnic mosaic at that distant time that we know today? Will there be Chinese and Serbs? Will the people live and think as we do today? Technology will probably overwhelm humanity. Not that humanity will disappear but it will be changed tremendously by technology. It might not be important to be a Chinese or a Serb, a white or a yellow or a black, a male or a female or a homosexual, as the word 'human' will mean something distinctly different and special and all the features we so frequently distinguish today will bear a historical stamp of ridicule. Who knows?"

"What about Planet X?" Song Xiaobo asked. "If you trigger life there ten thousand years from now, clone people and give them memory content, they will feel and think the same as we do today, won't they? What do they need the memory content of today for?"

"To be able to jump into the twenty-first century and know their origins," Arsen said.

"Couldn't they learn that from the computers?"

"Would they know who they were?" Arsen asked. "Would the computers restore their souls?"

"Maybe not, and perhaps that would be just as well," Song Xiaobo said. "Why should they feel the differences? Why not start from scratch and read history as the stamp of ridicule, to quote you?"

"I think we will be able to create limited memory content, which would contain only the information we want to provide. That might not be acceptable to many people, myself included. I want to know who I am and what was on my mind when the content was captured. I also strongly feel that my soul would be restored. I would be me again. The technology exists, and we should use it, although we can be selective in what we preserve. I am sure there are people who would rather start from scratch since they don't like themselves and the contents of their souls. They should be able to choose. I like what is in my mind and in my soul at present. Why shouldn't I be able to restore myself on Planet X to what I was on Earth?"

"I see what you mean," Song Xiaobo said.

"We should eat our dinner," Arsen said.

Exquisite presentation of the food was more of the hallmark of the Park Avenue Café than consistently excellent taste. Yet just looking at the food was appetizing enough to make it worthwhile even on the less tasty days. Everything was perfect this evening.

As they were drinking their coffee Arsen continued the conversation.

"You notice the differences of opinion between the two of us," Arsen said. "To be or not to be, that is the question. To clone or not? To use the captured memory content as is or only partially? To go or not to go to Planet X? To go means the triggering of life in space and in turn that means we have to proceed with the research. We have to find out who wants us to discontinue the biological research."

"What if only a third of the population wants us to continue?" asked Song Xiaobo. "Do we bow to the majority or do we work only with the agreeable third?"

"The majority will decide," Arsen said. "That is what the Vatican wants and soon, so will many a leader of the opposition. This whole thing will have to be discussed in depth and publicly. I am sure the Assembly will soon start the debate and will hear the testimony of many witnesses. This could go on for months if not years. There will be debate outside the Assembly. The media will have something to say. There will be speeches for and against the research, and meetings and protests on both sides."

"You have to win over the media," Song Xiaobo said.

"I know that is the thing to do," Arsen said. "But how do you tame the media in a democratic country? Can you help with the media in China? Who will help in Europe? In Russia? In Australia? In South Africa? It just does not work that way. We have to present our case the best we can, and we have to answer the opposing arguments convincingly. I think we can be convincing. One issue is on our side - the issue of the continuation of life and with it the human race. We can argue that a selected group of humans will continue their existence somewhere in space and sometime in the future. The people on the manned ships will be preserved on the unmanned ships too. Unfortunately time will not permit preservation of more than a thousand people. As you know, it is a rather complex task to make a single DNA engine. That is our best argument. I think we stand a chance of prevailing."

"I would not take a chance entirely on arguments," Song Xiaobo said. "To win you have to make sure to win."

"As the Communists have done," Arsen remarked sarcastically.

"It worked, if you remember."

"Over dead bodies often enough. Like the Cultural Revolution or the Great October Revolution and a hundred million people dead."

"This time there will be six billion dead."

"But to win you have to eliminate the opposition even before you are sure that the collision will indeed take place," Arsen said firmly. "We have to give the people the chance decide."

"People don't always know what they want."

"No, you are wrong," Arsen said. "People will know this time because they are interested and I am convinced that they will decide to support the biological research."

"I am sorry that my thinking is still colored by my life experience as a communist leader despite my previous experience in the United States. In my new job I will do what has to be done along the lines defined by you and Gen. Shagov. How did you decide to give me this job - I mean, with

my background?" Song Xiaobo looked serious and somewhat embarrassed.

"I brought you to the Ethnic Division because of your exceptional
administrative abilities and because you handled the Tibet problem like an
honest person, maybe even a Democrat. It was also a bit of politics on my
part. It never hurts to have the support of someone who represents a billion plus people - although that was not the deciding factor."

"You have said before that a big state is not necessarily a great state,"
Song Xiaobo said. "You are right. We have done things that were good for
the Chinese without regard for those concerned."

"You mean Tibet and the Muslim territories in Western China, and
Korea."

"To our own people."

"Europeans had much better game over the centuries," Arsen said.
"The best examples are Bismarck and the Berlin Congress, as a prototype,
and later the division of Africa by colonial powers; Versailles in 1919; the
trading of land after World War II, and recent events in Africa, the Balkans,
Timor and a number of other places. On the other hand, nobody can deny
that many peoples have won their independence and freedom. The number of independent states has passed two hundred from some fifty-sixty
states after World War II."

"What about the Berlin Congress?"

"That was the first political history reading I prescribed for myself after
I retired. I wanted to learn the history of the Balkans. As a Serb, brought
up to think that Serbs are the best people, the most honest and courageous,
it was natural for me to seek that information. I read a rather ridiculous
book about Serbia from the initial uprising against Ottoman rule in 1806
through the nineteenth century. It became clear that the Principality of
Serbia had become a Kingdom around the time of the Russian-Turkish War
of 1877-78, in which Serbia participated. Serbia and Montenegro declared
war on the Ottoman Empire and fought alone a rather bloody war that
accomplished nothing.

"Then the Serbs joined Russia and Bulgaria in their war against the
Turks in 1877 in which the Turks lost the entire Balkan territories except for
Istanbul. In the San Stefano Treaty in March of 1878 the Bulgarians received
a large territory which included present-day Macedonia. Serbia acquired
about two hundred square miles of land that included the cities of Nish,
Pirot, Vranja, Prokuplje and some others. I was curious to find out the reasons for this expansion.

"As my next assignment I read about Bismarck and the Berlin Congress
of July 1878, where the Iron Chancellor presided over the acceptance of the
already agreed deal among Russia, England and Austria-Hungary. The

outcome speaks for itself. Russia kept almost all land gains from the war. Austria-Hungary annexed Bosnia-Herzegovina. Bulgaria lost Slav territory in Macedonia, as it was returned to the Ottoman Empire along with Kosovo. What was left of Bulgaria was split into two entities: an independent Bulgaria and Eastern Rumelia, the latter under the Ottoman Administration, which weakened the Bulgarians even further. Serbia and Montenegro kept the gains they had made and were allotted even more territory.

"What led these big powers to return territory to their ancient enemy, the Ottoman Empire, which they had fought for centuries, by trading the freedom of oppressed people and betraying them in the process? Stabilization of the Balkans was the excuse at the time, and things have not changed much now. The Albanians in Kosovo and the Serbs in Republika Srpska in Bosnia have repeatedly been denied the right to secession, and to union with their ethnic mother states. In reality the motivation was the acquisition of territory and power. Some imaginary stability was supposed to be achieved by balancing the smaller states. This balancing only induced wars for fulfilling legitimate national aspirations, such as uniting an entire ethnic group. It always amazes me that the big powers, after having played their dirty games, assumed that their 'diplomacy' was not obvious to everybody. The big powers, throughout history, have always assumed the role of the smart arbiters for the 'stupid natives' and have denied credence to the honest intentions and legitimate national aspirations of many a national group.

"Bismarck achieved diplomatic success by helping legitimize the betrayal of Bulgarians by the Berlin Congress Treaty despite the outcry in Europe after fifteen thousand Bulgarians were massacred by Turks at Plovdiv after their uprising in April of 1876."

Arsen's thoughts were flowing, and he almost ignored the presence of his conversationist. Song Xiaobo seemed sunk deep in thoughts of his own.

"It is good that the priorities of the World Government be directed toward uniting people who want to be united and that we don't shift them from one state to another by making borders across ethnic territories," Arsen said.

"I know what you mean," Song Xiaobo said. "In China we obviously have problems that are not publicized. I will try to deal with these problems. Maybe we will be able to form autonomous Bee Systems in some areas if independence and autonomy are impossible. So much is left to be done around the world. I will be a busy man - at least until March of 2003."

"Let us hope we preserve the biological research before we can even think of preserving the human race, not to mention life itself," Arsen said.

"Let us hope," Song Xiaobo said.

CHAPTER FIFTY-FOUR

WEDNESDAY, 14 JANUARY 1998

Arsen walked into the office at eight o'clock in the morning. Michelle was at her desk answering the phone as usual. Herman Wolff walked into Arsen's office to brief him on what was going on.

"We need a Chief of Staff and a Press Secretary," Herman Wolff said. "I am taking calls that should be handled and could be better answered by the people we are missing."

"Doctor, President Chand is on line three," Michelle announced over the intercom.

"Arsen, tell me what is happening in New York," Rama Chand said and continued without waiting for a response. "The way I see it from here the battle for the biological research is gaining speed. I am glad that you have people like Vijay Rangaswamy and Msgr. Amato working for you.

"I am preparing myself for a busy season in the Assembly. I will start by making a speech asking for action by various committees, like Sciences, Space, Religion, Preservation and others. That will keep me busy. I will also have to travel and talk."

"The Vatican has expressed its dissatisfaction and so has Canterbury," Arsen said. "I am going to London and probably to Rome for more talks. The bottom line is that they know everything about the biological research. As you know, I think the best tactic is to tell the whole story. One issue is not negotiable - the research must go on until the decision is made by the Assembly or even better by worldwide referendum."

"We will push for the referendum," Rama Chand said, "although all the issues have to be discussed in the Assembly and outside, the way they are in a campaign, before the referendum takes place.

"Arsen, before I left last week I talked to a journalist who knows you, Fred McCollum from *The Kansas Chronicle*. You may remember him from the early days. He did not do well with Goran, but I think he would be an excellent addition to your public relations team. Talk to him," Rama Chand said.

"Okay. Obviously we need you in New York," Arsen said.

"I will be there," Rama Chand said and hung up.

"Well?" asked Herman Wolff.

"He agreed that we should use a referendum to settle the issues," Arsen said. "I agree."

"You are going to London and Rome, aren't you?" asked Herman Wolff.

"I have had no time to talk to you. We should meet every morning to compare notes."

"Doctor, Dr. Vernier wants to see you," Michelle announced over the intercom.

"Tell him to come up."

"What about the Chief of Staff and a Press Secretary?" Herman Wolff asked.

"A nun will be the Chief of Staff," Arsen said to the surprise of Herman Wolff. "I must persuade the British Foreign Secretary to take the job of Press Secretary."

"You mean a lady with a habit and all?" Herman Wolff was amused.

"I don't know about the habit," Arsen said. "Cardinal Conti did not say. He only said that she is a smart lady, well educated, with a Masters in Economics and a Ph.D. in Religion, and that she has held some important positions in the Vatican Administration."

"She will be a spy for the Vatican," Herman Wolff said emphatically. "What other reason would the Cardinal have for recommending her for the job?"

"Are you a Protestant?"

"I am."

"No wonder you are so suspicious," Arsen said. "A Serb would have the same attitude toward the Vatican - suspicion. Herman you must believe that there are some honest people left at the top of big governments and churches, and in the World Government too, don't you think? Unfortunately power corrupts people and it corrupts big powers. Have you ever met Mr. Clark, the British Foreign Minister?"

"Sure I have," Herman Wolff said. "I knew him as a young diplomat when I was in Moscow many years ago. We collaborated on a number of projects as our Embassies worked closely together, particularly on security problems. That was a very important activity then; not any more. Tony is a first-class intellectual. Do you think he will give up his present job?"

"Find out and talk him into coming to New York," Arsen demanded.

"Let me see what I can do," Herman Wolff said and left the office.

"Doctor, Dr. Lowell is on line four," Michelle announced over the intercom.

"Dr. Lowell, I was planning to call you today," Arsen said.

"I have great news," Dr. Lowell said. "We used Dr. Saito's DNA powder and, believe it or not, we have something growing in our medium. It's avian DNA. I cannot believe it myself. We have to wait and see what grows from it, but I'm sure it will be the same quail."

"Do you call it powder, like the newspapers do?"

"We call it Saito's DNA powder."

"What is the bad news?" Arsen inquired.

"There is none," Dr. Lowell said. "We're expanding, with Herman Wolff's help. He has been most useful to us. There are over twenty labs working on various phases of the project and we're adding labs continually."

"Which phases?"

"Oh, we're working with different species of animals. Also, we're testing different media for conception and gestation. This involves mixing the ingredients in different proportions of our basic medium, and adding different new substances like mitochondrial DNA. It's very tedious work. By using many laboratories we've been progressing quite rapidly. The results are already very promising."

"How is the uterus project progressing?" Arsen asked. "Have you talked to Prof. Menguy recently?"

"We talk daily," Dr. Lowell said. "He'll be reporting to you in a few days. I'll talk to you soon."

Jean-Pierre Vernier walked into the office.

"It's about time for us to talk," Arsen said. "I don't see much happening in the Preservation."

"We have informed everybody that we need the names of people who would be eligible to be on manned ships and who would also contribute their DNA and memory content for storage on the unmanned ships. We are talking about hundreds of people from each ethnic group. Once we receive that information we will wait until we are told how many will be accommodated on each ship. Obviously, there will be more room in Saito DNA powder containers than for the living individuals on the manned ships. And limitations of space will be a factor. The powder has to be made on time by the labs from hundreds of tissue specimens, then packed and stored on the ships. This has to be completed before the scheduled take off in 2001. I am not sure yet about storage of the memory contents. Gennadi Koltsov is working on the storage space although I am not sure he knows yet how to store memory for the long term. There are many 'ifs' we have to deal with. I came to see you on a different business."

Arsen raised his eyebrows and looked inquisitively at Jean-Pierre Vernier.

"As you suggested, I have been investigating people's reactions to the current events," Jean-Pierre Vernier said. "I have met a variety of people. One group particularly caught my attention. They have been campaigning actively against the World Government and particularly against you. Their thinking is militant. They call themselves God's Cavalry. We should not ignore them as their ranks have been growing rapidly, and you can already find them all over the world. The trouble is that they cross the usual class, race, and ethnic barriers. They can be found among the rich and in the slums, in the military, in factories, and among clergy in a number of religions - among Christians, Jews, Muslims even Buddhists. Their idea is to stop further biological research. They see in it dangers to humanity, to family values and most of all they see the end of religion. That is the reason for their desperate attempt to preserve the status quo."

"It is too late to worry now," Arsen said. "The approaching celestial object prompted the research. We don't know what is going to happen. Our preparations are only contingency measures. The world will never be the same no matter what happens, and people will be more inclined to change it. I hope a universal individual will develop: smart, selfless, independent of the rest of the world. We don't know what will happen to the World Government. Hopefully ethnic gains will not revert to the old problems. Will wars start again once the world Military reverts to national governments? At that time my DNA powder will be on its way to Planet X or maybe it will have exploded in flight."

"What should I do about God's Cavalry?" Jean-Pierre Vernier asked.

"Nothing. Keep an eye on developments and keep me informed."

"There are other groups, that have identifiable leaders," Jean-Pierre Vernier said. "I should just observe what they do, should I?"

"We should know who is against us," Arsen said. "We should know who is violent and ready to instigate warfare. We are not mandated to do anything. That will be the prerogative of the local governments. We should encourage the dialog and start the debate soon. The Assembly should lead the way."

"Doctor, you have been asked to appear before the Committee on Biological Advancement tomorrow morning," Michelle said as she entered Arsen's office.

"Find out who the members of the Committee are. I will be there."

"This is the start of the debate, isn't it?" asked Jean-Pierre Vernier.

"I think so," Arsen said. "Another thing. The personal security of all of us in the Department is somehow vague. Who decides what and why? I have no idea. All I know is that these people have been escorting me and telling me what I can do and what I cannot do. Who directs them? You had a lot of experience in these things when you were a spy. Could you find out how well we are prepared for unusual situations - I mean a terrorist attack or an attack by an individual who wants to express himself by shooting somebody around here? Could you take care of that and make sure we are ready and safe?"

"Sure, I will," Jean-Pierre Vernier said before he left. "I'll keep you informed."

"Okay."

"Doctor, Gen. Shagov asked if you would join him for lunch today," Michelle said over the intercom.

"Tell me when to go," Arsen said.

"I'll call him."

Arsen sank deep in his thoughts. It would be disastrous if the biological research were terminated. That would also be the end of his role in the World Government. The ethnic work was proceeding smoothly and almost routinely, and he expected that to continue. That would not be a reason anymore to stay around. His concern was now more for the preservation of the human race and the environment that was necessary to sustain it. In the case of collision, all of humanity and its institutions, the bad and good, simple and complex, antagonisms and friendships, science and ignorance, highly intellectual and bizarre individuals, stupid and psychotic, everything that made humanity what it was, would disappear.

"Doctor, Gen. Shagov will see you at one in his office." Michelle interrupted Arsen's thoughts with her announcement over the intercom. "You should plan to go now."

Alexei wanted Arsen to meet some of the people who were working on the construction of the space ships. Arsen noticed that Anatoly Tarasov was not in the group.

"So you think the ships will be ready to load their cargo and take off in 2001?" Arsen inquired. "I am sure you know what kind of cargo we are talking about. How many souls should we plan to load?"

"That sounds like Gogol's *Dead Souls*," Boris Danilov, a Russian engineer, remarked. "Just like *Dead Souls*."

"Would you happen to have a better name?" Arsen snapped back. "These individuals on Planet X will have souls, I hope."

"The souls of the cloned individuals on Planet X will have nothing to do with the souls of the people who donated their DNA," Boris Danilov challenged Arsen. "Do you plan to resurrect their souls over there?"

"We will provide them with their earthly memory," Arsen said.

"The cloned individuals are the delayed twins of the originals, aren't

426

they?" insisted Boris Danilov.

"Are they twins?" Arsen continued to ask questions about the unknown. "There is a fine line between the soul and the identity. Would the transfer of the captured memory of the original to the delayed twin restore the old identity and transplant the old soul? I doubt we will ever be permitted to test this postulate of mine on Earth. I will have the chance to do the test on myself if our ships ever reach another livable planet and the delayed twin of myself is born. I feel it in my bones that I will rediscover myself."

"That would be reincarnation with knowledge of the previous life," Boris Danilov concluded. *Déjà vu?"*

"I guess so," Arsen said.

"Have we determined how many souls are we going to load?" Alexei asked.

"Considering the size of Saito's DNA containers, the space needed for the gestation medium, space for the artificial uterus and all the paraphernalia needed for cloning, I would estimate we could accommodate about a thousand souls. The size of our ships is small by design, for reasons of space travel," the Zairean engineer, Kitwé Mfumu, said.

"Should we plan for one thousand souls?"

"That is a good number," Kitwé Mfumu agreed with Arsen.

"Our Preservation Board will have a hard time deciding who to send," Arsen said. "The number of souls depends on the ability of the laboratories to prepare the individual DNA engines. We are not ready to start the work with human DNA. The preparation will take time, and we will be able to produce the powder from only a limited number of people. It is possible that one thousand may never be reached."

"How are you going to resolve the problem of the selection of individuals for preservation?" Allan White asked.

"Jean-Pierre Vernier, whom you have probably met, has proposed that we organize a global lottery although the question has been asked whether we should send couples," Arsen said. "That alone would cut in half the number of ethnic groups that could be represented. If we had time to produce an unlimited number of individual DNA engines, we could accommodate everybody by loading different people on the space ship. Since that is impossible, we have decided that all space ships will have the identical DNA load."

"Have we made provisions for animals and plants?" Alexei asked.

"We have a number of people working on that right now," Arsen said. "Their answer is not in yet. I just hope not too many animals and plants will be required, because it would decrease the space available for humans.

"I have another question," Arsen continued to inquire. "Would there be a chance of bacteria or insects infesting the ships and destroying the biological load?

"We have not decided on that important problem," Alexei said. "Some sort of airless environment and vacuum will have to be created before the ships take off. Afterwards it will make no difference."

"Gentlemen, let us eat," Alexei said, ushering them into the adjoining room where the food was invitingly displayed and smelled delicious.

"Arsen, you should plan to visit Gennadi in Moscow," Alexei said as Arsen was leaving. "You may be surprised. He is doing that research by himself, and only I know what is going on but even I don't know the details. I think you should know too. Besides, that information and technology will be loaded on the ships."

"Will there be any space left for people after all the technology is loaded on these ships?" Arsen asked sarcastically.

"You will need all this technology with you when you get there, you will see," Alexei said.

"A hundred thousand years from now?"

"It is never too late," Alexei answered philosophically.

Arsen decided to make the trip to Moscow.

Michelle gave him the list of the members of the Committee on Biological Advancement so that he would be familiar with their names and with a résumé of their activities and civil interests.

The résumés were not very helpful. Arsen only noted that the Russian Ambassador, Olga Tolkunova, was the wife of the well known Russian space scientist. Herbert Mather, the U.S. Ambassador, had been a Baptist minister at one time but had resigned from the ministry under pressure for unspecified offenses; he had been a House Republican before he was appointed U.N. Ambassador. He might be trouble for the World Government, Arsen thought

"Find the U.S. President for me," Arsen asked Michelle over the intercom.

Arsen was wondering about Ambassador Mather and his previous Baptist ministry, which sounded like the Christian Right, deeply religious and fundamentalist.

"Mr. Secretary, it is good to hear from you," President Joseph Burns greeted Arsen. "We had a fine conversation the other day. I truly appreciated your help. What can I do for you today?"

"It occurred to me that I should ask you about Ambassador Mather."

"Yes?"

"What kind of a man is he? Southern Baptist. He used to be a Baptist minister. How difficult is he going to be on the issues of cloning and memory transfer?"

President Burns laughed.

"Do you think that I would appoint a man to such a post if his philosophy were opposite to mine? That would not be very smart, would it?"

"Pressure? Sometimes the pressures of various groups make leaders do things they would not do otherwise," Arsen said.

"Why are you so interested in his attitudes?"

"He is a member of the Committee on Biological Advancements and I am going to appear before that committee tomorrow. It never hurts to know something about the men you are going to face."

"He is conservative all right but not to a point that would hurt your survival programs. He was a forceful and rather wild man before he entered politics. He has changed. In politics you have to."

"Thank you very much, Mr. President."

"Any time."

Arsen felt better. At least one member of the Committee would not be hostile. They had to convince people.

"Doctor, your wife is on line three," Michelle announced over the intercom later in the afternoon.

"Hi," Arsen said automatically in Serbian. "How is Mom doing? How did she take the long trip?"

"Everything is under control," Nada said. "Mom had no problems in the plane. She is a bit tired."

"I will be home in another hour or so," Arsen said.

"I will probably still be up although I am tired too," Nada said. "See you soon."

Arsen was thinking of Zalev Schiff, the Israeli Ambassador, and his promise to delay the debate until Rama Chand returned from his honeymoon, when Michelle announced over the intercom that he was on the line.

"This is telepathy," Arsen said. "I was just thinking of your promise to delay the debate until Rama Chand returned."

"You wouldn't believe the pressure I have been under to start the official debate," Zalev Schiff said. "Many delegations, particularly from Catholic countries, have been pushing very aggressively. I have been under pressure myself with calls from the Orthodox groups. Don't kid yourself, these people know how to use pressure without being obnoxious about it. And they have. I had no choice, and I arranged for this committee to meet tomorrow. I refused to have anybody talk on the subject before the Assembly until Rama Chand returned. What do you think Rama Chand will propose in his speech?"

"A global referendum. Let the people decide what they want."

"How much time are we going to have for campaigning?" asked Zalev Schiff.

"Not much if I understood Rama correctly," Arsen said. "A few months. Maybe three or four months at the most."

"I better talk to my Prime Minister," Zalev Schiff said. "He will have to neutralize some Orthodox groups."

"I hope you know about the preservation problem, do you?"

"Which one?"

"The need to have a global lottery."

"Tell me."

"The problem is how many people should contribute DNA for storage on the unmanned space ships. The latest number is a thousand. How do we select these people? The decision will have to be made by a global lottery."

"Why a global lottery?" asked Zalev Schiff. "Why not ask states to assign people?"

"States will be biased and ethnic groups stand to lose their chance," Arsen said very firmly. "Who would be chosen in Israel if states had to decide? Jews?"

"Yes, I think, Jews would be chosen."

"There will be many Jews among the scientists anyway, but I don't blame you," Arsen said. "Serbs would do the same."

"I know you will give tokens to Jews and Palestinians and let them be in the lottery drum with everybody else," Zalev Schiff said.

"I must be transparent to you," Arsen said.

"You are."

"Are you still going to help resolve positively my problems in biological research," Arsen asked.

"Do I have a choice? I cannot blame you."

"As you know, Serbs are always right," Arsen said.

"Jews are always right," laughed Zalev Schiff.

This was becoming a way of saying to each other that the conversation was over. Some men were easy to deal with and Zalev Schiff was one of them, Arsen thought. He knew how to handle people right. Arsen must be biased. Not really, he knew.

Herman Wolff came to report on his conversation with Anthony Clark.

"He has not rejected the idea, which means he wants to talk to you. I think he will take the job. He will be the right man at this critical time. He knows how to handle the media and that is what we need the most now. He is superb in interpreting what other people have said, friends and foes alike. Importantly, he believes in our research goals and in the preservation of life, particularly human life. Call him at home, I have his home phone number."

"Do you think I should postpone that talk until after my visit to

England?" Arsen wondered.

"Not at all - call him now." Herman Wolff dialed the number and gave the receiver to Arsen before he left the office.

"Good evening, Mr. Clark. This is Sec. Pankovich. I hope I did not wake you up."

"Of course not. How can one sleep with so many things happening in the world? I'm glad you called. Herman Wolff has induced me to think about my own role in the present situation. Even more than that I have been thinking of the after time - after the collision threat evaporates. What then?"

"What have you concluded?" Arsen asked with interest.

"I have not," Anthony Clark said. "I'm comfortable with my Prime Minister and I'm at home. The problem is that you, Mr. Secretary, have taken the steam out of foreign affairs. From now until doomsday in 2003 - or call it the new beginning - there will be little or nothing for Foreign Ministers to do. What can we do? Make treaties among disintegrating states which would last five years at best? I wonder about that."

"We have plenty of action, if that is what you need," Arsen said.

"I know."

"Why don't you take this job and if an opportunity for you arises in London we will let you go," Arsen proposed.

"I have been thinking about such an arrangement."

"Then you accept."

"Reluctantly so," Anthony Clark said.

"Reluctantly or not you will be in New York in a week." Arsen was pleased. He needed a smooth spokesman for the Department, who would take the burden of explaining every detail to the media or anybody else who might be asking. Also, he needed someone who believed in the preservation technology, like cloning and memory capture. "We'll talk again in London."

"We are expecting you on Monday," Anthony Clark said. "Let us know of your arrival time."

Herman Wolff peeked into the office from the doorway just to inquire about the outcome of the call to Anthony Clark.

"He accepted," Arsen said. "He will take over in two weeks."

"Great!" exclaimed Herman Wolff.

Michelle walked into the office.

"Doctor, Sister Maria called to let you know she has arrived and that she'll be in the office at eight o'clock."

"Why didn't you let me talk to her?" Arsen protested.

"She didn't want to disturb you. I didn't insist. She sounded very nice on the telephone - soft pleasant voice. She's an American, from Chicago."

"Does she wear a habit?" Herman Wolff asked.

"I have no idea. We'll find out in the morning, I guess. I'll be leaving soon. Is there anything you need?"

"No. Go home and have a good evening. I will see you in the morning."

As he entered the apartment Arsen saw Nada at the kitchen door. He remembered the episode with Ursula and felt guilty and ashamed of his only extramarital excursion - even though it had been inocent. Nada noticed his chagrin and hesitation and asked him whether something was wrong.

"No, nothing is wrong," Arsen said. "Only I am a bit tired."

"Are you sure?" Nada inquired again. "Do you feel okay? Is anything wrong at the office?" She always knew when something was not right. Maybe she sensed what the trouble might be. She let him wash, and then served a well appreciated light supper of a green mixed salad and a fresh broiled chicken leg.

Slowly Arsen relaxed and forgot his secret. They talked about Belgrade after the shooting episode, and the insults leveled at him by the Serbian President. Arsen's resentment had not diminished.

"I doubt you would be welcome back in Belgrade," Nada said. "I can't even say you would be safe. The Serbian media just plain blasted you in their articles and editorials. I don't think you could find a friend even among your old friends. None of them ever called to ask about you or find out if I needed anything. Your Serbian identity is that of a traitor to the Serbian people."

"Did you talk to Stan Petkovic?"

"Only once. He called to tell me he had left the hospital."

"He has not called me either," Arsen said. "It must be politically inexpedient for him. But he should keep me informed. It makes no difference anymore; what was done had to be done. If the Kosovo problem had not been resolved radically, there would be a war by now, and blood would be spilled. For what? We accomplished three things by giving the Shiptars freedom of choice. They are now Albania's problem; we made arrangements for protection of the remaining Serbs and protection for the monasteries; and we negotiated a financial deal for the mines - particularly the very valuable Trepcha. It would have been quite different if the Serbs were in the majority. I guess the Serbs were hoping to expel the Shiptars to Albania as the Croats did to the Serbs in Krajina. That only works very rarely. Obviously, we don't belong there any more."

"Why are you so pessimistic today?"

"I have no idea," Arsen said. "I have to appear before the Committee on Biological Advancement in the morning and I need some time to prepare myself for the testimony. You must be very tired, you should go to sleep. This is the beginning of the debate. Soon it will get rough. Next week I am going to London for talks, then to Rome. The big religions are upset."

When Arsen walked into his study the phone rang.

"This is Msgr. Amato. I apologize for disturbing you, but it is urgent. Do you think we could have a meeting tomorrow with some people who approached me today?"

"I thought you were in California,"

"That is where I am - in San Francisco," Msgr. Amato said. "If the meeting can be organized, I would fly back tonight."

"Who are these people?" Arsen inquired.

"You might have heard about them. They call themselves God's Cavalry."

"Yes, I've heard about them."

"They mean trouble and they are demanding that you change your research plans," Msgr. Amato said.

"What is the hurry with that meeting?" Arsen asked, annoyed.

"They have been in New York for a while but have not been able to penetrate your office. Herman Wolff flatly refused to see them and to let them talk to you," Msgr. Amato said. "I think we should have that meeting tomorrow. At least we should show them our good will, even if we turn down their demands. I don't think we should let them wait too long. This is a good opportunity to meet them and listen to them. Perhaps there is a way to deal with them. If you ask my opinion, they are determined in their quest to have God recognized, almost the way the knights were in their crusades. This is a crusade for these people. They are not strong enough in any country yet, but they are growing."

"Maybe they are just making a lot of noise," Arsen said. "If we leave them alone and pay no attention to them they might lose their momentum and their importance might diminish."

"Maybe, but what if we were wrong," Msgr. Amato insisted. "Sometimes when such people are ignored, they become more aggressive. I think we should talk to them."

"Okay Monsignor, fly back to New York," Arsen said. "I have time in the afternoon. Oh, before you hang up, do you know Sister Maria O'Brien.?"

"Yes Sir, I surely know her and I heard she is coming to New York to work for you," Msgr. Amato said enthusiastically. "She was a star in the Vatican but reached a plateau in the hierarchy. After all, she is a woman, she could not become a Cardinal." A note of sarcasm could be felt in the Monsignor's voice as he said that. "She is a most wonderful person, a

433

straight shooter, hard working and, not the least, she is very intelligent. I know you want to know where she stands on the issues of biological technology. She is a bit like me: she believes that God comes before anything and anybody, and that people are allowed to pursue their interests and even wild ideas like cloning. God has not denied intelligence to people, and He has not forbidden this or any research by honest people who are trying to better the world and preserve life. She has also tried to reconcile her thinking with her obedience to the Church. That has not always been easy for her. She may become a force of positive thinking in the Department."

"That is quite a recommendation, Monsignor," Arsen said. "Does she wear a habit?"

Monsignor laughed heartily. "Oh, I refuse to say anything in that respect. You must see her for yourself."

"I hope her habit is not one of those black and white fan-shaped things," Arsen said with some hesitation. "I'll see you in the afternoon."

Arsen's thoughts drifted from Sister Maria's habit to the more pressing issues that would be raised at the Committee meeting in the morning. A brief statement of facts on the current research should not expose him to unwarranted attacks, Arsen thought. The rest would be up to the Committee members

CHAPTER FIFTY-FIVE

THURSDAY, 15 JANUARY 1998

A rsen walked into the office at eight o'clock. Michelle was interviewing somebody, a woman. Arsen paid no attention and walked into his office ,where he found a list of messages and a cup of coffee. Michelle was running the office very efficiently, just the way he liked it. The coffee was warm, the way he liked it, and he began to relax as the dark brown fluid flowed into his grumbly stomach. The message list was short: there was a message from Msgr. Amato which he had probably left before calling him at home last night; Song Xiaobo had a question about Zaire; Mark, Arsen's son, wanted to say hello; and Cardinal Conti had a question about the Vatican visit. The newspapers were on his desk and the front page headlines caught his attention.

DEBATE ON BIOLOGICAL RESEARCH STARTS IN UN ASSEMBLY
SISTER MARIA O'BRIEN ARRIVES FROM ROME

Arsen could not believe it. The photograph showed a beautiful woman, in her forties, well dressed in a suit. A cross hung on a chain from her neck and a smaller one was attached to the lapel of her jacket. Arsen suddenly realized this was the woman talking to Michelle. He went out to the waiting area where the two women were absorbed in conversation. A phone ringing interrupted their conversation, and Sister Maria, noticing Arsen at the door, stood up. Arsen went over to her and shook her hand.

"Sister Maria, where is your habit which we imagined to be black and white, fan-shaped at the shoulders, and generally very awkward," Arsen greeted her. "It is so good to meet you. We have a lot of work for you. Come into my office."

"Did you have a good trip from Rome yesterday?" Arsen asked her as they sat down.

"I read on the plane. That's the best way to avoid the boredom of a long trip. I've traveled extensively on business for the Vatican. It was a bit too much for me. I expect to do my business from the office not from a plane."

"You are probably right, Sister Maria," Arsen said. "It will also depend on your involvement in the politics of the biological research. Are you familiar with the goals of our research?"

"Yes, I am."

"And do you understand the problems we are facing in our insistence on continuing the research?"

"Yes, I do."

"Sister Maria, do you think you would fit into this Department and which side of the issue do you think you would take?" Arsen persisted in trying to find out her opinion and her attitude. It was important to find out if Msgr. Amato was right.

"Msgr. Amato might have told you that I take my beliefs very seriously," Sister Maria said. "I believe in God's supremacy and His divine powers. It is His desire that we live the way we do and behave as we do. Maybe it is His intention to test us by sending the celestial object in our direction, maybe not. That's the basis of my belief - among many others that are less important. Does that explain which side I'm on?"

"Not entirely," Arsen said. "How do you reconcile God's supremacy and divine powers with the progress that has been made toward achieving the triggering of life or with the notion of immortality? Isn't that contrary to Catholic doctrine and an act of interference in God's business?"

"Not at all," Sister Maria disagreed. "The issues are not properly defined and the result is confusion and conflict. In my view the issue is not human interference in God's business, but humans trying to preserve God's creations by all means available to them, using tools created with God's help. Do you know what I mean?"

"I am beginning to understand," Arsen said. "Go on."

"What I mean is that humans, and in the present situation your research people, are working on finding a way to preserve humanity - which was created by God. What's wrong with that?" Sister Maria appeared sedate; she lowered her voice. "This is not a negation of God - this is an expression of praise for Him."

"Msgr. Amato told me the same thing, but he did not come across clearly," Arsen said. "His explanation sounded as if God were agreeable with anything humans did, with a purpose or without one. You explained the conflict in the argument - the double negation in an ordinary view, maybe in the minds of Church leaders. One negation is to allow extinction of life on Earth even if it can be prevented by life-triggering, delayed cloning and other means. The other negation is to deny the existence of God and proceed with delayed life-triggering. That has been the view of the scientists. You reconciled the two apparently diametrical views by saying that God allows humanity to find a way to preserve itself and to preserve life - in effect to preserve His own creation. That is a very unusual explanation, and will likely cause heated discussions. Sister Maria, it seems to me that you may have to do some traveling, this time on behalf of the World Government."

"Does that mean I would be giving up the job you have dragged me from Rome to take?"

"That might be expedient in order for you to promote the biological research we have undertaken. I would like you to deliver a lecture on your ideas and thoughts about the current biological research."

"Where?" asked Sister Maria.

"Right here in New York City," Arsen said. "The Forum on Foreign Policy asked me to give them a second lecture on Thursday, January 22. I think your lecture would be more effective and more timely. I will talk to David Gallagher today. What do you think?"

"I traveled on business assignments for the Vatican, not on a lecture tour," Sister Maria said. "I came to New York to help you administer your department and you tell me to give lectures for which I have no inclination or ability, and positively no experience. Besides, my ideas may not be pleasing to the ears of the Curia in the Vatican."

"Cardinal Conti said that you would do what has to be done without violating your principles," Arsen said.

"He said nothing to me about giving lectures."

"Will you give the lecture if Dr. Gallagher agrees?"

"Yes I will if that's what you want," Sister Maria said obviously annoyed.

"I am glad that is settled. Let me find Herman Wolff to show you around and to get you started. This afternoon I have a meeting with the members of a group called God's Cavalry. I would like you to attend. Msgr. Amato will be at the meeting too."

The call to the Forum on Foreign Policy connected Arsen directly with David Gallagher.

"Dr. Gallagher, I have good news for you." Arsen said.

"News is not so good these days," David Gallagher said. "People don't want to talk at our meetings and members don't attend lectures. The situation at FFP is disastrous. You're going to tell me you won't give us that lecture on the twenty second, aren't you?"

"How did you guess?"

"Oh, Mr. Secretary, you're not going to do that to us, are you?" David Gallagher sounded desperate. "I was expecting good attendance."

"I have a better proposal," Arsen said convincingly. "My new Chief of Staff, Sister Maria O'Brien, has agreed to give a lecture instead of me. She has some very interesting ideas. The title of the lecture could be something like 'Dual negation in interpretation of the divine dicta on preservation and extinction.' "

"I saw her photograph in the paper," David Gallagher said. "I thought you were going to use her as a fashion model not as someone to promote your cause. She's not going to blast the biological research, is she?"

"She is from your tribe, so don't be too harsh - you may regret it," Arsen said. "You will find her smart and a believer. Talk to her about the lecture."

"Don't hang up, Mr. Secretary. What about your lecture?"

"It might not be a bad idea to postpone my lecture for a few months. By then, I might have something to say about progress in the biological research, or perhaps I will sing a requiem for the world."

"I agree as long as you promise to talk after the referendum."

Arsen felt better.

"Doctor, you have to go to the U.N. now to testify," Michelle said over the intercom. "The limousine is waiting for you."

At the U.N., Arsen went to the door of the committee room on the fourth floor and realized that this was the same room in which Alexei had testified and announced the discovery of the Demon. That had been only three months ago, but it felt like a distant memory, Arsen thought. Talk in the room quieted down as Arsen entered. The Chair of the Committee, Gabriella Variale of Italy, greeted Arsen; she was cool and distant yet courteous. The meeting started with official introductions of the members and Arsen for the record.

"Mr. Secretary, would you like to make an introductory statement before I let the members of the Committee ask you questions?" Gabriella Variale asked. "I am sure you know what the subject of this hearing is."

"Yes, I know the subject before the Committee," Arsen said. "My statement will be brief."

Arsen clearly described the purpose of his department and the goals of biological research for the preservation of life as a contingency if everything else failed.

"I would be glad to answer your questions," Arsen concluded.

Gabriella Variale assigned fifteen minutes to each Committee member, with the right to yield the allotted or remaining time to another member. Nobody wanted to yield. After Gabriella Variale asked a variety of general question on financing, on the locations of various contributing research centers and on the scientists, Olga Tolkunova asked specific questions on the research goals of the various divisions in the Department; she was followed by the Chinese, Zimbabwean, Swiss, and United States delegates along the same lines. Arsen was awaiting an attack from Panamanian, Czech or Polish delegates representing mainly Catholic populations.

The Indian delegate criticized memory capture as a new method of dependency and a tool of persecution.

"Why do you need the memory capture?" The Indian delegate, Ramesh Singh, asked. "You may want to return the memory to someone who lost it, but you will be able to discover what the content of his memory is. Isn't the privacy of the mind the last treasure left to an individual? Why don't you leave the mind alone and take the chance that there will be a few who lose their memory and never recapture it. I have no problems with your research goals but insist that you scrap the memory research."

"I understand your concerns, which have been the concerns of the Department as well," Arsen said. "The problem is survival on the distant planet. Return of the memory to an individual will facilitate his or her returning to present day functioning without having to repeat the social evolution with its attendant possibility of deteriorating in an undesirable direction."

"They will have the knowledge available to them in the computers."

"That is true," Arsen said. "But the cloned individuals will have to be able to comprehend that knowledge and to use it. There will be no teachers to instruct them individuals and no experts to use the stored knowledge. If you clone a physician his brain will have no basic medical knowledge; likewise, a clone of a scientist will not be able to understand scientific jargon. It is as simple as that. It would take years before these people could learn from the computer, even if they received the education that will be programmed in the ship's computers. They might never learn. We don't even know whether clones are capable of learning in the same way as their older twins. Perhaps they are not. Memory transfer would bypass these obstacles. We think it would be important to transfer the memory of the older twin to the younger one to avoid the identity problems which could be caused by transfers to non-related twins. We don't know the answers, and we will have no time to grow clones to find out. We have to take our chances. I think this is important."

"I see what you mean," the Indian delegate murmured and asked no further questions.

Gabriella Virale turned to the Czech delegate, "Dr. Jagr, your turn,"

"I would like to change the direction of this testimony a bit. Before we can even think about memory capture and transfer we have to decide whether it makes any sense to continue the research on *in vitro* delayed cloning. That is an enormous undertaking which will drain much of our resources and our energies and leave us poor and unprepared for life beyond the present threat from the celestial body. I deeply believe that we will weather this terrible crisis and that life will be preserved on Earth. What is your opinion Mr. Secretary?"

"I have stated my opinion on a number of occasions. I wish I knew for sure. My hopes are on Gen. Shagov and his team, but even Gen. Shagov does not know for sure."

"In your thinking, Mr. Secretary, and in your preparations for the worst, have you had any other thoughts?"

"Prayers would be an alternative to my thinking," Arsen said. "I am not sure one needs much preparation for that activity. I am sure people are praying more than ever."

"In your preservation efforts have you provided for that activity?"

"You mean praying?"

"Yes, I mean praying and other similar activities," the Czech delegate said in a challenging tone. "You could have organized an ecumenical gathering of religious leaders who would discuss our options in preparation for the apocalyptic event."

"I have not done anything like that," Arsen answered firmly. "I thought that our religious leaders would know what to do without the advice of a secularist like me. Besides, they have been discussing religious issues for so many years and they even have resources for doing it. What I have done is to appoint a Roman Catholic, Msgr. Amato, as the head of our Public Relations Section. Sister Maria O'Brien has just been appointed my Chief of Staff. I don't expect them to sabotage the present efforts of the Department, although I will not stop them from expressing their views."

"You always surprise me, Mr. Secretary," Dr. Jagr said.

"Thank you, Mr. Ambassador." Arsen said with a smile of relief; he did not anticipate further attacks that day.

Gabriella Variale looked at her watch then asked whether there were any other questions. The message was clear: time was getting late and no further questioning was appropriate. She used a gavel to conclude the session and thanked Arsen for his appearance before the Committee. She appeared even cooler and more distant than she had been at the beginning of the session, Arsen thought.

"Doctor, you have two urgent calls," Michelle said as Arsen entered the office.

"I'll take them in my office."

"Doctor, Mr. Vernier is on line two," Michelle announced over the intercom.

"I just wanted to tell you that the people who are coming to see you this afternoon, the riders in God's Cavalry, will be searched for weapons," Jean-Pierre Vernier said. "You can never tell. I have arranged for search equipment to be installed at the entrance to the building."

"You think--"

"I think we cannot take any chances anymore," Jean-Pierre Vernier interrupted Arsen. "Let me worry about that. I will see you in the afternoon. Sister Maria invited me when I met her this morning."

"Okay!" Arsen said.

Jean-Pierre Vernier hung up.

Arsen felt uncomfortable for a moment with the thought that Sister Maria might be a spy, as Herman Wolff had suggested. Impossible, he assured himself. She would be too obvious as a spy for the Vatican and they would not want to be involved in scandal or controversy. This was a genuine offer to help by Cardinal Conti, and it should be treated as such despite philosophical differences regarding the present situation.

"Doctor, Dr. Bjöstrom is on line two," Michelle announced over the intercom.

"What is so urgent in the memory business?" Arsen asked.

"Something has happened in Moscow. Gennadi Koltsov has recalled Mikhail Platov and he left New York last night. Mikhail did not even tell me he was leaving. Simply nothing. I have no idea what is happening. Gennadi did not return my call. What could be wrong?"

"I have no idea," Arsen said. "Let me call him and I will get back to you."

"Michelle, I want to talk to Gen. Shagov," Arsen said over the intercom. "Also find Gennadi Koltsov in Moscow."

"Doctor, Gen. Shagov is out of town and they are looking for him," Michelle announced over the intercom. "Dr. Koltsov is on line three."

"Gennadi, is everything all right in Moscow? Mikhail Platov left New York suddenly and mysteriously; he did not even tell Ursula that he was planning to leave. Is there reason for concern? Is there something I should know?"

"I have changed my mind about memory research," Gennadi said calmly. "We will program the equipment here in Moscow and ship it to New York. Ursula will be able to capture the memory of the individuals whose DNA will be on the ships. When we receive the memory molds we will transfer the contents onto permanent storage discs, make duplicates, and install the discs on the ships. That will simplify our operations."

"I understand," Arsen said. "I thought it was odd that Mikhail left without telling anybody anything."

"I'll find out about that," Gennadi assured Arsen. "Keep in touch."

There was nothing more to say and Arsen hung up. The whole episode was rather bizarre, Arsen thought. Even this conversation with Gennadi was bizarre. The trip to Moscow would have to be scrapped.

"Doctor, Gen. Shagov is on line four," Michelle announced over the intercom.

"Arsen, you found me on the plane. I am on the way to Tokyo. These guys are far behind Gennadi."

"I called you about Gennadi," Arsen said. "He pulled Mikhail Platov back to Moscow yesterday. Mikhail did not even leave a message for Ursula."

"That is my Gennadi," Alexei said. "He's been like that all these years. He did that to his fiancé the day before the wedding and never saw her again. He has never seen a psychiatrist though he should have. Is he crazy? I think he is. He is probably bipolar. He refuses to take medication. What are you going to do? He will rescue the world. He has made significant progress in the development of the gun. One cannot ask him anything and should not interfere. He always gets the job done. You should postpone the trip to Moscow."

"I was just wondering."

"Just don't. See you in New York after I return." Alexei hung up.

"Doctor, these people are in the conference room," Michelle said over the intercom. "Sister Maria will join you there."

As Arsen walked into the conference room the noisy conservation ceased, and the people in the room looked in his direction. Ten delegates from the God's Cavalry movement were present. To Arsen's surprise they came from all around the world: England, China, Iraq, Korea, Indonesia, Bolivia, United States, Canada, Greece and Russia. Three of them were women.

As they sat around the table Arsen asked them to present their views. A Bedouin from Iraq got up to speak. Was the Bedouin their leader? Arsen wondered. What was he going to say? How was he going to say it?

Of striking appearance and in a traditional attire this man, in his late forties, was tall, thin and erect, of dark complexion and rugged facial skin from long exposure to the sun; he addressed Arsen in fluent English with a British accent.

"We almost lost hope that we would ever see you, Mr. Secretary. If you want to hear people it should be easier to enter your door. We have been waiting around for a week.

"Let me explain the reason for our call. As you might have heard, we represent a very diverse and hardly cohesive group of people who share the same concern - a concern for God's domain. We feel that divine territory has been invaded, and we have been fighting to keep the divide. Our movement appeared spontaneously, and we have no leaders. You are probably asking who the ten of us are and how we got together if no internal organization exists. It may sound strange to you but the ten of us never met before and did not plan this meeting. We met on the streets of New York by asking a simple question: 'Have you seen the people from God's Cavalry?' The Cavalry does exist among people, but it is not regimented - not yet anyway. After ten of us met each other we decided to seek a meeting with you.

"We know you, Mr. Secretary, and some good deeds you have done. We saw you at the United Nations with Gen. Shagov and President Chand. We know who arranged for the New Year's Eve Party in Cyprus, and the reasons for it. We know about the Basques and the Cypriots, the Tamils and the Timorese, the Muslims of Mindanao and the Buddhists of Tibet and we love you for that. We love you for the happiness of the peoples who gained their freedoms with your help. We want you to know that."

The Bedouin bowed his body slightly toward Arsen, as a sign of respect.

"We are here to tell you how we feel about the research that is being done under your guidance. We are unhappy about this research. It cuts into God's domain. It works against the natural order of things, the way they were designed by God. We want to keep it that way. A great many people want to keep it that way. Why do you want to change the natural order of this world?"

The Bedouin concluded the statement with the question and sat in his chair.

Arsen was impressed by the eloquence and brevity of the Bedouin's explanation of the feelings of the group and their demand in one simple question. Don't change the natural order and don't touch God's domain.

"I couldn't have heard your message clearer or better expressed, Arsen said. "I understand your demand that we terminate the research. This very morning I was asked the same question at the United Nations. Let me define the issues before I answer your demand.

"The problem we are facing, and I say we as the human race, is simple. There is a huge celestial object in space that will collide with the Earth on 15 March 2003. That is a fact, not a speculation.

"Gen. Shagov's team is building a so-called neutrino gun. There is a good chance the gun will be able to deflect or disintegrate the celestial object. That is not a fact yet. The fact is that we are not sure.

"In the case of collision we know for sure that the human race would be annihilated. That is a fact. You can forget about Noah; this time there will be no human survivors. The question of preservation of some very primitive aquatic species like bacteria or algae is a remote possibility and at best a speculation; should they survive, it is even less likely that evolution would take the direction of recreating a human who is like, and there is a zero chance that such humans would develop the mind we now possess.

"We stand a chance of surviving as the human race by sending manned ships into space to keep the chosen few out of danger when the collision occurs. They would return to Earth to pick up the pieces if it were compatible with human life; if not, they would die in space.

"If everything fails, the only chance the human race has to survive is to send unmanned ships into space to seek a planet where human life would be sustainable. To be able to do that our biological research must go on, and it will go on until the U.N. Assembly votes to shut it down. Then I will retire to a place where I will be able to watch the end - although we may all be dead even before the impact. That is my answer to you. I have nothing to add or to retract."

"Mr. Secretary, isn't the World Government interested at all in what we are trying to get across to you - the will of God?" the Bedouin asked, his voice now raised.

"Yes Sir, the World Government is interested in the options and the desires of all people," Arsen said. "My job is to direct the research. Msgr. Amato's only daily concern is the religious aspect of this entire effort. I will let him talk with you and argue with you or even agree with you. He is well qualified to do that. I will now excuse myself."

The Cavalry riders stood up as Arsen left the meeting room. At least they had showed their respect by getting up, Arsen thought.

Once in the office Arsen remembered to call Ursula Bjöstrom. "I talked to Alexei. He feels we should let Gennadi do the job any way he wants. Alexei is not very concerned; he says Gennadi has behaved like this in the past. He is probably depressed. You will get your equipment when the time comes to store the memory. In the meantime, you should help Jean-Pierre Vernier select four hundred couples. You will have to rule on their physical and psychological fitness and Jean-Pierre will supervise the lotteries.

"Kim Bong Shik should also be involved. You might suggest a meeting. I would like to see that done so that we have people identified before we start preparation of the DNA. These people will have to provide suitable tissue specimens, which will be sent to the labs. You should also talk to Isoroku Saito who will be responsible for processing the tissues. Find out if he is ready to start and if the appropriate laboratories have been designated. You will be, so to speak, a customs and emigration officer for the ships. Kostas Cotsidis should recommend the necessary animal and plant complements. Keep me informed on a weekly basis."

"You said four hundred couples. What happens to the other two hundred places?" Ursula Björstrom asked. "Are they reserved for special people?"

"We need scientists of all kinds," Arsen said. "The most I can provide for them without cutting too much from ethnic representations is a hundred places. I must have a hundred places in reserve. Of course, we should give consideration to preserving the human genetic pool. I am not thrilled with the idea of a lottery, but we have no choice considering there are some six thousand ethnic groups. Each group should have the same chance and will be chosen by lottery."

"What if some groups are represented in greater numbers than others, like Blacks versus Indians," Ursula Björstrom asked. "What if there are no whites at all, no Europeans, no Russians, no Americans?"

"Tough luck," Arsen said. "Do we follow what Gen. Shagov said in his 'silent' speech in the Assembly or not? We repeated it often enough afterwards. Rama Chand did, I know I did, and other people did. How do we decide that Serbs are better than Nigerians or Native Americans or Koreans? Nonsense. We will deal with that when we get there, I mean I will deal with that on Planet X. In my mind that is not an issue and I will do my best to keep it out of the debate in the Assembly or anywhere else, and I will defend the equality of ethnic groups to the end. If I lose I will go to my mountain home and wait for the last scene on Earth. Come to think of it, I have been mentioning this mountain home, which does not exist. I should buy one."

Both of them laughed.

"I will start working on this right now and will let you know when you return from Europe. Have a good trip." Ursula Björstrom hung up.

Sister Maria and Msgr. Amato walked into Arsen's office.

"You must have had a fine discussion," Arsen teased them.

"Not that bad," Sister Maria said. "They're a decent group of people but they represent only themselves at this time. They don't have an organization. It's true that they had never seen each other before they arrived in New York."

"That is even more dangerous; it means their movement is spontaneous," Arsen said. "There must be thousands maybe hundreds of thousands of these God's Cavalry riders out there. If they organize themselves they will become a formidable group to deal with."

"I don't think they will form an organization," Msgr. Amato said. "You may call it a crusade, even a jihad but not a political or a religious well-organized movement. They are diverse and scattered around the globe, but not a major force anywhere. Still, we have to talk to them and deal with them. Besides, our differences are not as extensive as they may sound."

"That's true," Sister Maria said. "We disagree mainly on the potential for immortality they think might result from this research. To them that's the line in the sand, and they don't want anybody to cross it."

"I agree," Msgr. Amato said. "Is immortality just perpetuation of the body plus the soul from one clone to another? That is the question. They say it is, and I say it is not. In the view of some people the soul is resurrected in successive clones by restoration of the older twin's memory. If anything goes wrong, and something always does with anything we do - and it will happen also to a cloned individual - the cloning lineage may end sometime in the future and the soul will die with it.

"My view is that the soul is immortal. The soul is the divine product at the birth of an individual, natural or cloned, and after his or her death the soul floats in God's space. Although memory transfer may be accomplished and a clone may be given the memory of its older twin, each of the twins will possess a different soul; similar perhaps but not the same. This would be the case when the twins, the older and the younger one, live contemporaneously. Each of them would have a soul of his own not a conjoint or shared one. At their deaths their souls would fly to God's territory. The issue is, do we want to create cloned individuals, and not will we cross the line in the sand."

"I agree," Sister Maria said. "In the upcoming debate, I'm sure the line in the sand will change its location depending on the beliefs of the debaters."

"I see your point of view," Arsen said. "I am much closer to the memory view on the subject. I am sure that the debate will be vibrant. Most of all, I am glad that the decision to proceed with the research and the unmanned ships will be made by the people, in a referendum, and not by the delegates to the United Nations. At least I will feel better about the defeat."

"Doctor, Dr. Gallagher is on line three," Michelle announced over the intercom.

"You again?" Arsen asked David Gallagher.

"I know you're busy but this is an emergency. It concerns your lecture on the twenty-second."

"I thought we agreed that Sister Maria would present the lecture instead of me."

"I know that but everything was already arranged for your lecture. It seems we had sent out invitations even though we couldn't announce the topic of your talk. Several people called and expressed their anger because they had heard your talk was to have anti-Israeli if not outright anti-Jewish connotations. Others had heard that you were going to attack the Catholic Church in you quest to win approval for biotechnology research. If you send Sister Maria the confusion will be complete. We could put off her lecture for two weeks, and I know I'll get her an audience. Besides, you could introduce her during your lecture and explain what she will discuss. What do you say?"

"You got lucky; I canceled my trip to Moscow." Arsen agreed to give the lecture.

"We're all wondering what we're going to hear on Thursday," David Gallagher said.

"There is no point in explaining now - you will understand during the talk." Arsen remained mysterious about the subject.

"Thank you so much, Mr. Secretary."

"Doctor, Prof. Menguy is on line four," Michelle announced over the intercom.

"I was told you were going to call me, Professor," Arsen said.

"Things have developed and I thought you should know," Prof. Menguy said.

"Tell me."

"We have had a breakthrough in our egg development."

"Egg development? What is that?" Arsen asked.

"It is the uterus research," Prof. Menguy said. "Since we are developing an extrauterine - and obviously extracorporeal - device in a sense resembling the egg gestation of birds, we started calling it 'egg'."

"A human egg, so to speak?"

"Exactly. The problem of the placenta had to be resolved if we were to make any headway. One of my associates came up with the idea of a two-compartment egg - the inner compartment covered with the layer of autologous cloned tissue or maybe even an artificial layer, which would allow attachment of the placenta and membranes, and the outer compartment which would contain the nutrients and oxygen and provide for excretion of metabolites, something like a dialysis unit. The unit would unlock and allow the robot to remove the baby. That would also signal all systems to end the cycle. What do you think?"

"Sounds good," Arsen said and felt like a mother trying to encourage her child in writing a story or playing violin even though the progress was rudimentary and awful at best and raised the question of talent if any.

"That is not all, Mr. Secretary," Prof. Menguy exclaimed. "We would not call you about an idea - we have built the prototype of the egg and have tested it. It works, and it is not very complicated to operate. We have just seen the development of the placenta of a cloned cat. It is unbelievable. We used a synthetic coating on the inner surface since it is easiest to make and more durable, and it will last forever. If this cat survives we have the system for the ships."

"Professor that is marvelous," Arsen now said like the mother who misjudged the talent of her kid. "Hopefully the robot will be able to run such a machine."

"Of course, we expect to develop a program for the robot," Prof. Menguy said with even more enthusiasm. "We talked with Dr. Zourab Abashidze, your robot expert. We are thrilled with this success. You should have seen the staff in the lab when it was announced that the placenta had developed and was attached to the wall of the egg and that it was functioning. They expressed not only the pride of lab technicians of this Institution but the pride of Frenchmen. Come and visit us Mr. Secretary, you will be in England next week"

"Cross your fingers, Professor; you may yet lose the egg. Powerful forces are gathering on the horizon that oppose this kind of research. I am fighting for continuation of the research until the people decide in a referendum whether we have to close our shops or we'll be allowed to continue."

"Why should people have to vote for something like this?" Prof. Menguy said, obviously annoyed. "The decision must be made by scientists who know what it is all about. How can ordinary people understand? This is ridiculous. Politics and politicians always have to screw up everything. What if the Demon hits the Earth? Everybody will be dead. If we are not allowed to continue, no mechanisms will exist for the survival of the human race, let alone the preservation of life."

"My advice to you is to scrutinize all your employees to find potential saboteurs," Arsen said. "The people who will turn out to oppose this kind of research are now normal individuals, smart, knowledgeable, dedicated. They may already be opposed to this type of research, or they may be influenced to become opposed, and they may do unexpected things, like destroying your equipment. You need a back-up of everything you are doing and writing. Establish a similar lab elsewhere, maybe in Russia or China just in case."

"Is it that bad?" asked the amazed Prof. Menguy.

"Nothing is bad yet but we don't know what might develop," Arsen said. "Keep your eyes open and don't slow down on this wonderful research. Don't take any action against anybody - we cannot punish people for their beliefs. Protect your equipment and your experiments. I will talk to you again."

Arsen was very impressed with the progress in the development of the uterus. All that would have to be curtailed if the sciences lost in the referendum, Arsen thought. Hopefully not. There was no time to think with all the calls and callers he had to deal with.

"Doctor, Sabrina is on line four," Michelle announced over the intercom.

"Doctor, I'd like to talk to you," Sabrina said. "It's personal and it's important."

"Let us have dinner tonight," Arsen suggested. "Six o'clock at Circus?"

"I'll be there."

What was so urgent? Arsen wondered. It must be Alexei; the rumor was that she often slept at his apartment. That was not Arsen's business, he thought.

"Doctor, everybody's gone except for the people who stay till midnight," Michelle said, walking into his office. "I'm ready to leave unless there's something left."

"Has my trip been finalized?"

"Everything is in order," Michelle said. "You leave on Sunday afternoon. On Monday the Foreign Minister will meet you at the airport and will drive you to Downing Street to visit with the Prime Minister who will in turn take you to meet with an Anglican Bishop. In the evening there will be a dinner, and after that you fly to Rome. Cardinal Conti will take care of arrangements there.

"Thank you very much. I'll see you in the morning."

Arsen looked at his watch. It was a quarter to six. He had to rush to be on time for the dinner with Sabrina. It was only a short distance from the office, and he had to go by limousine ride. Security, Arsen thought, will become even more of a problem in the months before the referendum.

Sabrina was sitting with a double martini in her hand at a corner table when Arsen arrived. She had lost weight and looked as if she has not slept for a few nights. There were large bags under her eyes and some wrinkles Arsen had not seen before, on her forehead and cheeks. Too much make-up was obvious. She looked neat and was well dressed.

"All of us are very busy these days," Arsen said as he took the chair next to Sabrina. "We should have dinner once a month if not more often. We must remember to do that."

"I agree and drink to that," Sabrina said and sipped her martini.

"You are not drinking too much, are you?" Arsen inquired. "This reminds me of the first meeting we had at this place. You were rather low then. Are you okay now?"

"Are you guessing or does it show that much?" Sabrina asked, a surprised look on her face.

"You look tired. That's all."

"I wish I could say everything is okay, but it's not." Sabrina said. "My problems don't change, I guess."

"Alexei?"

"Yes, he's my problem," Sabrina said. "He wants to marry me."

"And you?" Arsen inquired.

"I like him. I even love him. However, I don't want to marry him. His wife should not have left him alone in New York. He is a social animal - he must have someone around who is close to him. It just happened to be me. Now he feels that he owes me something for having an affair. Why can't he just have an affair and leave his marriage intact?

"He has decided to file for divorce. That's silly in this situation. His wife knows about me I'm sure. I answered the phone once in Alexei's apartment when I was waiting for him, and Katarina was on the line. She knew who I was. She just asked me to tell Alexei to call her when he arrived. She was pleasant. She has called Alexei at the office a few times afterwards and has been just as polite and pleasant. What does Alexei want from the remaining few years?"

"He believes he will save the Earth. That is his problem." Arsen was uncomfortable with this conversation.

"What should I do?"

"Get another position in the World Government," Arsen said. "Alexei will understand."

"I don't feel like leaving him. I like the man, and he needs me in New York. If Katarina came to New York that would be different. But she stubbornly refuses to leave Moscow. Maybe she's sure he'll return to her after all this is over."

Arsen said nothing; he finished his tonic water and started his steak. Sabrina was still at her drink. They were not talking, as both of them were occupied with their own thoughts. Arsen was wondering what job he could offer to Sabrina that would not upset Alexei after she moved out of Anticollision. Something more important than her present job as Alexei's secretary. Sabrina was smart and well organized. Arsen realized that he would be looking for a replacement for Ursula Bjöstrom in the Memory Capture Division. Since Gennadi had taken over the entire project, that section would need an administrator not a scientist to make sure that memory capture was obtained from all 'souls' that would be on the ships and that the memory imprints were cataloged and stored properly on the memory discs. Sabrina would be well-suited for this position.

After the coffee had been served Arsen suggested the job to Sabrina. She was surprised and hesitant to take it.

"What do I do with Alexei? He will not like it."

"You might take him out of the hole in which he has pushed himself with the idea of marriage," Arsen said. "He may resist your leaving his office but he will eventually realize that it would be best for both of you if you took this job. Even your relationship, an affair if you wish, may become more mature without asking for major sacrifices from either of you. Is that what you want?"

Sabrina did not answer immediately; she hesitated as she was unprepared to give up her present situation, however complicated, and Arsen noticed her ambivalence. Often, he thought, people did not want to resolve their problems by resolutely making the right move because that deprived them of the pleasurable side of the mess they were in.

"Make up your mind," Arsen insisted with more intensity, as he recognized her hesitation. "You have to make the move if you really want to change your situation. Look, you don't want to get married and Alexei wants to marry you because he thinks he has to. Neither of you wants the big change, and you are at an impasse of indecision. You should make the move."

"What if he refuses to let me go and makes my life miserable?" Sabrina asked with trembling voice. "What do I do then?"

"He will let you go. You will see." Arsen was convinced that Alexei would feel rescued from a difficult spot.

"Do you think he's not serious about his intention to divorce Katarina?" Sabrina asked. "Maybe he was just pretending."

Sabrina was vacillating. She wanted Alexei to insist on their getting married, Arsen thought. Then she could leave him. 'Prove that you love me so that I can leave you.'

"Let me know by tomorrow," Arsen said and turned the conversation to memory capture and his expectations of it on Planet X. Sabrina slowly relaxed and got involved in the subject.

As they were parting after dinner Sabrina kissed Arsen and thanked him for the help.

"It's good to have a friend," she said.

Arsen insisted on walking the block from Lexington to Third Avenue on the Sixty-second Street. The Security Service agents were upset.

CHAPTER FIFTY-SIX

FRIDAY, 16 JANUARY 1998

Arsen was late in the office that morning, it was nine thirty when he arrived. It was almost unbelievable that there were no important meetings on the list. Maybe there would be time to catch up with some personal chores like shopping. Michelle confirmed that most stores opened at ten o'clock. Bloomingdale's was a few blocks up Lexington Avenue. Other stores, like Gallery Drugs, and his favorite electronic store, Franco, were nearby. Arsen thought how wonderful New York City was, where one could find within two blocks almost anything one needed, no matter what it was.

"Doctor, Sabrina is on line two," Michelle announced over the intercom.

"Doctor, I've made up my mind. I want the memory job." Sabrina was obviously determined to make changes in her life "I talked with Alexei. He protested but agreed to let me go. I'm ready to move. Do you still want me?"

"Of course we want you," Arsen said. "Would noon today be too late? I have not informed Ursula Bjöstrom of her appointment as my Deputy for Medical Affairs and of your taking her memory job. Anyway, move your staff anytime you want. Ursula will help you take over."

"Doctor, thank you very much," Sabrina said. "I would have been surprised if my appointment were to start on Monday. I'll be there after lunch."

Michelle announced Ursula Bjöstrom over the intercom.

"Dr. Bjöstrom, I wanted to tell you that you have been appointed Deputy for Medical Affairs," Arsen said. "You may not like it but I need someone to coordinate the research, which is getting more complex by the day. Besides, I will be traveling a lot in the next few months. I hope you would accept."

"Of course I accept. This is surprising, as I started the memory job only this week."

"As you know, that job now needs an administrator not a doctor," Arsen said. "Sabrina will take your job, and you are moving up here to work with Sister Maria and Herman Wolff. Expect Sabrina to move in this afternoon. Your office up here is ready for you. I should talk to you this afternoon."

The Security Service was informed about the proposed shopping and they were near panic since they had no time to make arrangements.

"What is your problem?" Arsen said to the agent, Alvin Smith, who was in charge during the day. "We have the element of surprise on our side. Who would know that I was planning to go shopping this morning? Nobody. Even you did not know."

"What if someone is waiting for an opportunity like this?" Mr. Smith protested.

"Don't we know by now who the potential assassins are?"

"Yes, we do know."

"Have they been seen around?"

"No."

"Then we go." Arsen was determined to have it his way.

Once on the street Arsen felt as if he had been let out of a cage. He had had no time to think of his confinement since he had become a Secretary in the World Government, and about the restrictions placed on his movements outside the official buildings.

The first stop was Bloomingdale's. The sidewalk was crowded with many shoppers. Arsen enjoyed the air and the open space, despite the tall buildings. Nobody noticed him and nobody recognized him. He felt like a free person and wished he could avoid returning to the Department of Human Resources. That would never again be possible, except perhaps on Planet X. Arsen laughed at the thought. He wanted two suits, which he would need on his travels around the globe. Nothing special. He stopped at the stationary section where he saw Lucite blocks with a middle slit for photographs. He wanted something like that for traveling. The sales woman was helpful in selecting the size. He settled for two blocks: a smaller and a larger one. She asked for his Social Security card and copied the number into the computer.

"You haven't been buying much recently, have you?" the sales lady asked Arsen.

"Not much."

"This will cost you forty-five dollars and you have nine fifty-five left."

"You don't need my credit card?" Arsen asked since she not not asked for one.

"Everything you buy goes on your Social Security account. You didn't know?" The sales woman looked at Arsen with surprise, if not contempt.

"What was I supposed to know?" Arsen asked, annoyed by her question.

"You really didn't know that your free upper limit was a thousand dollars, did you? Where have you been?"

"I have been busy," Arsen said, leaving the stationary section.

Arsen's next surprise was waiting for him in the men's department. He selected two suits, a dark blue and a gray one, and decided on a dark blue blazer with silver buttons. The suits and the blazer were to be delivered in a week. Again, he provided his Social Security card and again he was given the total of his remaining credit - two hundred ninety-eight dollars.

"I am not sure about this credit stuff," Arsen said. "Who is giving me this credit? I never asked for anything like that."

Again the salesman looked at him with surprise.

"You must have heard. Stores and shops have been giving set credits to people and make charges against their Social Security accounts, which are available to every taxpayer. In return the stores don't pay for the merchandise, in the amount purchased on this credit, and the factories in turn give credits to their workers instead of salaries. Nobody knows what will happen with this financial experiment, and nobody cares either, since everybody has figured out that we will be dead anyway."

Arsen almost choked. He had no idea what was happening in the world. This was shocking to one who thought he knew it all. He thanked the salesman for his help with the suits and left Bloomingdale's. He had lost interest in shopping, and went back to the office.

Michelle assured Arsen that the Social Security credit was a new trend. She had known about it for only a few days and hadn't bought anything yet herself.

"I think the idea is spreading like wild fire," she said. "Haven't you read the papers recently?"

"I had better start reading the papers again," Arsen said, somewhat disconcerted, and went to his office. "Let me talk to Goran Enstrom."

"Doctor, Mr. Enstrom is on line two," Michelle announced over the intercom.

"Goran, I was shocked in Bloomingdale's this morning by a thousand dollar gift. How did you come up with that idea?"

"It was not my idea," Goran Enstrom said.

"Whose idea was it?" Arsen implored.

"I am not sure who started it. Somebody in Europe. It came to my attention only a few days ago. It is catching on rapidly. Bloomingdale's is one of the first to offer it. I am not even sure how they arrived at the credit of a thousand dollars. One company president told me that money may become obsolete. "What do you need money for? You will be dead in a few years anyway," he said. Rather pessimistic attitude though perhaps realistic. We have no idea how this is going to work. The main concern is not the free credit but productivity. Are people going to work if everything they need costs them nothing? We talked to the Bloomingdale's people and to companies they deal with. They claim that people have agreed to work regardless of pay. It is becoming silly to talk about money which in peoples' minds means nothing and they have been spending as much as they can. Obviously, nobody is saving anymore. Live for today is the slogan you hear from many places. Strangely, the reports are that the demand for work has started to increase. We have not figured that out yet."

"Do you think money will disappear as a way of payment?" Arsen inquired.

"Nobody knows right now," Goran Enstrom said. "Social scientists have been alerted and studies are on the way but the moneyless society is still in its infancy. We will not interfere."

"Strange and interesting," Arsen mused. "I wonder who will supply poor people and poor nations?"

"We asked the same question," Goran Enstrom said. "It is too early to have any answers."

Arsen was amazed by this development. It sounded like the good old communist idea. That had never worked under communism and had not even been considered in the capitalist and socialist countries. Communists were too perfidious and selfish and outright greedy. They had managed to spend public money by pretending to be using it for government purposes. Marx had pointed out that over the ages one part of society always exploited the rest, although he had not objected to the domination of the communists over everybody else.

Who would exploit whom if wages and payments were abolished? Would people really want to work? The situation was different today, Arsen reasoned. Accumulation of money or property under the threat of annihilation in a few years would be absurd. Working also had no purpose except for survival. Therefore, survival would be the incentive to people to work and produce. Although selling tires did not mean producing survival tools it could mean providing tires for someone who needed them to drive to the factory that made survival tools or some other important item. A functioning economy and industry then became essential, and people realized it. Work became the tool of survival.

The social prospects looked surreal. This entire social experiment would not have been possible without the threat from space. World Government established, ethnic problems resolved, a different social structure evolved and major advances in genetics would be worth the suffering if the threat to the Earth were deflected.

What would happen afterwards if the collision were evaded? Sigh of relief, all right! What then? During World War Two people had worked hard under threat of the Axis. It had never been the same. The uncertainty of the unknown, and the potential for total annihilation of the human race and most of life, if not all, would take its toll on the psyche of the population. Going back to the old ways would be impossible, and accepting life as it had evolved would be difficult. It would be impractical to retain the system of no payments of salaries and no payments for purchases. Who know? His head was spinning; he had better think of something more productive, Arsen concluded.

CHAPTER FIFTY-SEVEN

SATURDAY, 17 JANUARY 1998

It was a beautiful day. Arsen was relaxed and ready to travel to London and to the Vatican.

London should not be a major problem, Arsen thought. They would ask questions and debate and avoid polarization. Their concerns would be more about the consequences of the research and of delayed cloning than about the intrusion into divine affairs. They would probably want to know about alternative applications of the techniques that were being developed, if the Demon were deflected.

The Vatican would be a hard nut to crack. They would worry about intrusion on divine territory. Asexual fertilization, the unnatural gestation environment, and not least the robot as parent would be issues that would be impossible to deal with or even to answer logically. To sell them the idea of preservation of humans by delayed cloning would be an impossible task, because they had problems accepting the idea that humans, as creatures created by God, had advanced the genetic technology because God let them. The conflict would be in the need to change the established principles and dogmas to accommodate humans instead of the other way around.

At lunch Nada inquired about the trip to Europe. Arsen asked if she would be interested in going along and attending some of the debates. She declined.

"I am sure you would like it there, and you might even like some of these sessions," Arsen said and explained some of the issues. She wanted to know about the selection procedures. Arsen explained the principles of selection and the forthcoming global lottery, and mentioned that Jean-Pierre Vernier was responsible for the preservation effort.

"What happens to the children of people who win on the lottery?" Nada asked. "Do they stay or go?"

Arsen was not sure but thought that smaller children would go with their parents.

"You mean you don't know?" Nada insisted. "How is that possible? You are supposed to set the policies. Obviously, there has to be some policy regarding children." She appeared annoyed by this lack of information.

"Why don't you talk to Jean-Pierre Vernier about your concerns," Arsen suggested. "He will probably have answers to your questions and you will be able to tell him what you think."

"I may very well do just that," Nada said.

They talked about their own children and their families and the impossible goal of taking them along.

"I would be quite comfortable staying with children to the end," Nada said. "I am not sure that being together at the collision time would be possible, with the extended families some of the children have."

"I think you would do better to leave that issue alone. The decision has to be made as to who goes and who stays. It won't be easy to separate some families, but there will be no choice. Those who decide to stay will stay and somebody else will substitute. Besides, the decision to go may also mean to be prepared to die in the manned ships if the Earth is destroyed at impact and becomes uninhabitable. The prospect of dying on a space ship might be the reason for some people to want to stay on Earth. To be doomed on a ship is a frightening thought. Alexei said that people will be able to sustain themselves on the ships for about five, maybe six years - then they will die. A rather horrifying idea. I must go in spite of everything. I wish you would come along."

"I will come along, don't worry. I am not afraid of death on the ship. Still, I am concerned about children and how to accommodate them one way or another."

"I am sure Jean-Pierre will listen to you."

"I will talk to him tomorrow," Nada promised. Arsen was pleased with her firm decision to accompany him on the space ship despite the obvious danger. He was surprised by her resolve to talk to Jean-Pierre. She was not a forceful person.

They wanted to see a movie in a theater that evening, but the idea was vetoed by the Security Service, and they settled for a video at home.

As they were getting ready to sleep Nada said that they should invite all their children for a visit and talk to them about all the problems and issues. "We've been talking about this meeting with children and nothing ever happens. We may even learn from them something we don't know. Besides, I am not sure they know that we are committed to being on these ships and going into space. I think they should know." Arsen just nodded in agreement.

CHAPTER FIFTY-EIGHT

MONDAY, 19 JANUARY 1998

Arsen slept during the overnight flight. They arrived in London early in the morning and Arsen shaved and took a shower. Breakfast was awaiting him in the dining area and the news briefs and local newspapers were on the table.

Sec. PANKOVICH IN LONDON AND VATICAN
DEBATE ON DEATH OR LIFE IS ON
LONDON IN FRIENDLY ANTAGONISM !
VATICAN OUTRIGHT HOSTILE !

Anticipation was high that the Anglican Church would try to bridge the differences in approach toward preserving a segment of humanity and of life in general. There was an extensive report on the existing situation and the options before the World Government. The report was clearly in favor of continuation of the research. Arthur Browne, the reporter, presented the scenarios facing the world and indicated that even in the worst scenario - complete destruction of the Earth, in which essentially all living matter would be destroyed - some simple life could still be preserved if water were available; maybe even some plant seeds could survive and grow.

"Of course," wrote Arthur Browne, "the chances that evolution would repeat itself and culminate in an identical Homo *Sapiens* are nil. The chances of such a sequence of events happening in a cycle of evolution have been estimated at one in a billion, although several billion years later and after several billion dead ends perhaps a new human could develop. I see no reason why nature would move in the direction of human life even after billions of years. The creation of a human would require some divine guidance, and the very existence of God would have to be doubted if He allowed the annihilation of humans at this turn."

Only an atheist would challenge God as Arthur Browne had, Arsen thought. His writing was quite powerful. They should recruit him for the staff.

Msgr. Amato came into the dinning area. He looked impressive in his new black suit; he wore a shirt with an embroidered collar, and a vest; the red belt of his order completed the appearance.

"We will deplane in about half an hour," the Monsignor said. "The Foreign Minister, Anthony Clark, will be at the airport at that time. He will take you to the Downing Street."

"Where is Dr. Rangaswamy? And Mr. McCollum?" Arsen wanted them to exit the plane in the group. "It is important that our delegation be together for the official part of the meeting with British Government offi-cials. They have to get the idea that we work together as a team, even if we have had some internal differences of opinion."

"They should be here momentarily," the Monsignor assured Arsen as they were getting ready to exit the plane.

Arsen recognized the Foreign Minister, whom he had never met. Limousines took them to 10 Downing Street where they met the Prime Minister, Kenneth Stone, who started the meeting by introducing the mem-bers of his delegation, the Ministers of the Interior and Education.

"Without further delay let me state the purpose of this meeting, as I see it," the Prime Minister said. "There have been several issues concerning the biological research that is being conducted by the World Government and that has caused certain groups and governments to complain, to protest, and in some cases to threaten outright. This is of concern to Her Majesty's Government and before further problems arise, and the situation becomes polarized, it is the belief of the Cabinet and myself that we should discuss the issues and find out where we stand. The most serious issue is the continuation of the biological research at this time: should it be stopped to allow the debate to proceed or should it continue until the referendum has been held? Mr. Secretary, we think it was a very wise move to propose the referendum. Please, tell us your views on continuation versus cessation, and the reasons for your views."

"The referendum is the product of necessity ," Arsen said. "We have a little over three years to the launch date of the space ships. This time peri-od is very short and I am not sure we will accomplish our goals. It is that simple. To stop now would be a major blow to our efforts. We don't even know how long the delay would last even if we won the mandate to con-tinue. Any delay would disrupt the production schedules. So far we have made some progress toward our goals although nothing that could not be reversed if the research has to be discontinued. I see no reason to stop now."

"Are you trying to tell us that an interruption in the research at any point could result in failure of the entire preservation effort?"

"Yes, that is what worries me the most. In order for the referendum to be meaningful it has to be preceded by an extensive debate and time has to be allowed for campaigning before the voting. In the meantime the research effort would not be idle. The damage to the preservation goals would not be done."

"Do you anticipate a long debate and protracted campaign?" Anthony Clark asked.

"I know that President Chand is intent on holding an early referendum. He was talking about two to three months. You probably know of my determination to fight any attempt to interrupt the research now. If the referendum turns against research, whenever that occurs, I will make sure that the research is terminated."

"Has there been any talk about territories where the research and preservation in technological terms would be prohibited?" asked the Prime Minister. "Of course, people from those territories wouldn't be eligible for preservation."

"At this point we see it as an all or none situation," Arsen said.

The discussion turned to the specific goals of the research - manned and unmanned space ships, cloning, DNA powder, the artificial uterus and robots as parents. The British Prime Minister listened, mostly, while three of his colleagues asked the questions.

"My God, all these projects sound like a takeover of the Divine powers," the Prime Minister said as the discussion was coming to the end.

"Not at all," exclaimed Msgr. Amato. "Not at all, Mr. Prime Minister. On the contrary, it supports the existence of God and His divine powers. We are not doing anything that would change humans. We will merely modify and adapt the fertilization and gestation processes of humans. We want humans to be preserved as they are today. There will be no genetic manipulation. No eugenic criteria will be used in the selection of people for the manned ships and for the DNA engines: a red man or a white woman, a black woman or an oriental man, a beautiful or an ugly woman, a gay or a heterosexual man, an intellectual or a plumber, a Calvinist or a Jew, a Catholic or an Islamic fundamentalist will all qualify equally.

"Only scientists will be selected on the basis of our needs and their expertise. We will be selective also in choosing healthy people to minimize medical problems, which will surface anyway. The absence of life will be only apparent since life will be preserved in the DNA configurations of humans and animals. Life will also be preserved in the seeds of plants and in the spores of bacteria. Life will not be destroyed - it will be preserved

461

and activated. Divine onset of life means life creation from nothing. We will only preserve what has been created before us." The Monsignor finished his exposition and looked at the people around him as if asking whether they found his explanation unique.

There was a long pause before the Prime Minister spoke again.

"Monsignor, you will have to find an answer for the asexual, actually parthenogenetic, development of humans that will survive the scrutiny of your Church," the Prime Minister said. "I am sure you are aware of the sexual requirement in the Catholic Church."

"I am," Msgr. Amato said quietly.

"I became aware of that after reading the statement by Dr. John Haas," Arsen said. "Dr. Haas is a known Catholic ethicist. He appeared before the Senate Committee on Labor and Human Resources on June 17, 1997. He clearly stated that only personal sexual intercourse between a man and a woman is acceptable to the Catholic Church and that cloning and parthenogenesis are unacceptable." Arsen said this in order to induce the British to express themselves.

"Nonsense," the Prime Minister exclaimed. "It is too late to talk about that in relation to humans when it has been used widely in animals. What about *in vitro* fertilization. Instillation of fertilized eggs into a woman's uterus cannot be called sexual intercourse, although the process mimics the natural steps. The natural way has often been bypassed in animals in which embryonal manipulations have been done, and cloning has been accomplished with embryonal and adult cell contents. Useful genetic changes have been created in bacteria. Eugenic methods of selection of animals have been used. What are we talking about now? Giving humans more importance sounds as if animals and plants were created by the Devil and not by the same divine power of God. Now we are working on salvaging God's creatures: humans, animals, plants and other living organisms. We must finish our work and preserve these creatures. Mr. Secretary, the British Government will support your quest to continue the research effort so long as I am at its helm."

The Prime Minister got up and shook Arsen's hand. This was an important step in the campaign to preserve the research effort until the referendum. The handshake confirmed an alliance in the common quest. The Prime Minister's initial coolness had disappeared in the ebullience of the moment.

On the way to the meeting with Bishop Smith, the Prime Minister expressed the opinion that the position of the Anglican Church and probably of the Protestant world would be sympathetic to Arsen's insistence on continuation of the research until the issue was settled by the referendum.

"I still think that people who want humanity saved should be allowed to do it on their territory and under their own terms," Arsen said.

"I am sure the opponents of the idea will insist on an all-or-none decision by the referendum, since that is the only chance they have to kill the idea of scientific salvage - which is repugnant to their thinking." The Prime Minister was confident that the referendum could be won for preservation.

They were expected at the official office of Bishop Smith. The Prime Minister was asked to see the Bishop in a short private audience. After about ten minutes Arsen was invited to enter the Bishop's office. It was a large room, with stone walls, well heated by a modern heating system. Portraits of the Queen at the beginning of her reign and of Thomas Beckett as imagined by a painter in the fourteenth century hung on the walls. The Bishop got up from behind his large mahogany desk and greeted Arsen. He invited him to sit next to the Prime Minister and positioned himself on the third chair by the coffee table. They were served tea and small nondescript dry cookies.

"Mr. Secretary, the Prime Minister has given me the abstract of your conversation this morning at his residence. I think I understand your position. The purpose of this meeting is to discuss your position on the issue of the research that is being conducted by your Department. You and your team claim that no genetic changes will be attempted during the preservation research."

"That is correct."

"Your aim is to be able to clone existing humans in space - I believe it is called delayed cloning."

"That is correct."

"How is that going to be done? What has to be developed by this research to be able to make it possible to clone people in space?" The Archbishop raised his eyebrows as he looked at Arsen for the first time during his inquiry.

"Since there will be no active life and no people to carry out fertilization, natural or artificial, we will have to depend on a substitute human - a robot. A robot will get the signal to start the process. As in the natural process we will need a medium and the DNA content, the genome, for fertilization. The fertilized material will form cells which will divide and will eventually become implanted in the wall of the artificial uterus. The rest will be the normal gestation, providing we resolve the problems of exchange of oxygen and nutrients between the fetus and the outer compartment of the uterus.

"At term the child will be removed by the robot from the uterus and brought to the outside environment. The robot will be programmed to perform repetitive actions to bring up the child. The ship will be equipped with the most sophisticated educational tools to help the child learn the basics of life. We assume existence of an environment conducive to survival of the baby. Everything we know today will be available to the clone colony on Planet X."

"Such an individual may not grow up to be what we would know as a normal child on the Earth," the Bishop said.

"This is being discussed by experts in the fields of child health and education. We have no answers to these questions at this time."

"So the main problem in accepting all this research is the issue of child development from powder to a being, to an individual child."

"That is the issue," Arsen said. "We think we are not interfering with anything divine. We are not even developing anything that would be different from what we already have. The techniques we are developing utilize human genomes the way they have already been used in cloning animals. DNA in chromosomes is the basis of life. We will not change that. We hope to develop humans who will look and behave like us although their life will start in a completely different environment."

"What about the memory capture?" asked the Bishop.

"That came about as a byproduct of neutrino research intended to produce a gun that would deflect the celestial object away from the Earth. We think that the memory content of the individual cloned on Planet X will also help in his or her mental development and in restoring humans as we know them."

"Mr. Secretary, you seem very enthusiastic about the memory capture," the Bishop said. "I hesitate to approve further development of this technique. First, the implication is that the soul of the person will be restored by memory transfer to the cloned twin. Second, the potential for abuse here on Earth, if we survive the threat that is upon us, is substantial. Third, the potential for creating humans with a single preprogrammed memory would be a disaster if they were to become the slaves of some people or group of people, such as scientists. I could go on and on in describing potential abuses."

"Potential benefits should not be forgotten." Arsen could not stop himself from expressing his optimism about humans. "There are so many human faults that we deal with daily, killing of people being the ultimate crime. Yet we find only a small percentage of people who commit such crimes. We deal with criminals as best we can. Memory capture might become a wonderful tool in the education of children and of adults; it might help develop a higher level of our civilization."

"It would take us too far from the subject that brought us together if we were to continue the discussion on uses and abuses of memory capture," the Bishop said. "The very idea of someone deciding what is good for our mental development and what we should be programmed to become makes me an opponent of memory capture. However, if survival of humans in space might be more likely if they were equipped with the memory stored for them, I would consider approving further investigation."

"We need support to continue our work until the referendum is held and the decision of the people made known. If you could be on our side at this crucial time for the World Government, I think we would have a chance to preserve the human race."

"We hope Gen. Shagov will succeed in his work on the neutrino gun," the Bishop said. "We pray for his success and for our survival."

This was the end of the audience with Bishop Smith and the Prime Minister, and Arsen left the office.

As they sat in the limousine on the way back to 10 Downing Street for lunch, the Prime Minister was relaxed, as if he had accomplished a great task. "You should understand that Bishop Smith was against the research and the whole idea of delayed cloning. To him you were the exponent of cloning, memory capture and the intrusion on God's business. I think you handled him well. He was calm and clearly receptive to your ideas. He liked the idea that humans would not be genetically changed. I could see that he liked the idea that DNA was the structure of existing life and that you had not suggested even remotely that *de novo* life was to be created by delayed cloning. I like the idea myself. It eliminates so many perplexing thoughts, as it almost provides for *status quo* in the distant future somewhere in the Universe."

"That is an idea that was generated by Msgr. Amato; I just built on it a bit. I wonder how we are going to sell the idea to the Vatican?"

"You probably won't." The Prime Minister's 'won't' was emphatic, and that was the sign that there was nothing more to discuss on the subject.

The conversation turned to the political climate in England, and the economy.

"It is hard to believe, but 'zero profit', as I call the new trend of credit assignments by corporations, is spreading faster than I anticipated," the Prime Minister said. "Obviously, the concept of profits becomes nonsensical in view of the approaching deadline in 2003. The communists would love it but for them it is too late. Socialists would flirt with it. Capitalists would have no faith in it. Survival of civilization is on people's minds, not profits. One wonders why people are looking for work."

"We think we have the answer," Arsen said. "This is analogous to the situation in Britain when Hitler attempted invasion. Everybody helped, and everybody tried to contribute to the defense. People do that during a crisis when the survival of the nation is at stake. Right now the survival of the world is at stake."

"That may not help the biological research you are fighting for, Mr.

Secretary."

"I know."

In the hotel, as he was getting ready for the dinner with the members of the British Cabinet, Arsen saw the headlines in the evening newspapers.

WHO CREATED ANIMALS AND PLANTS?
GOD OR THE DEVIL?

asked one headline and the article quoted the Prime Minister's remarks.

THE DEVIL AS A CREATOR

was the highlight of another newspaper.

The reporters were playing with the serious argument put forward by the British Prime Minister, Arsen thought. That was unfair. He would have to say something about the research at dinner.

Sec. PANKOVICH DEFENDS CLONING
AND MEMORY CAPTURE

said the third headline and the report attacked memory capture research.

Arsen arrived at dinner slightly late and instead of standing in the welcoming group with the Prime Minister and his wife, he joined the line of dignitaries.

"She's charming and friendly, and pretty, I must add," said the Prime Minister, and his wife agreed.

"Who - my wife? Is she here?"

"No, Mr. Secretary. Not your wife, your Chief of Staff - Sister Maria is here."

"She was not supposed to be here."

"She is here."

Arsen looked around and saw Sister Maria talking to Vijay Rangaswamy.

"What a surprise to find you here, Sister," Arsen greeted Sister Maria. "What did you read on the plane?"

"The Peter Principle."

"Anybody in particular reached his or her own level of incompetence?"

"Me!" Exclaimed Sister Maria. "Who else?"

"I don't want you to be idle after making a long trip," Arsen said. "After dinner I will ask you to outline the reasons for cloning and memory capture and to defend God's supremacy. Maybe you have not yet reached your level of incompetence."

"I came along to help in the conversations in the Vatican, not to give speeches."

"I need your help here tonight," Arsen said and started a conversation with the British Minister of the Interior.

At the end of dinner the Prime Minister raised his glass and welcomed Arsen to England. Arsen thanked the Prime Minister and then introduced Sister Maria.

"Sister Maria joined my staff recently as the Chief of Staff. She came to us from the Vatican, where she held many administrative functions. I asked Sister to give you an outline of our position on cloning and memory capture."

Sister Maria appeared hesitant for a moment.

"Good evening. My transition from the Vatican to New York has not even begun, and here I am in London, explaining the position of the Department and the World Government on cloning and memory capture. The issues are neither cloning nor memory capture but the implication of blasphemy, and the question 'are we playing God?'

"Our preservation effort consists of two components: cloning and memory capture.

"We will store as many individual genetic engines as possible. At our present pace, according to the scientists involved in this work, we will have enough time to process the tissues of about a thousand people. Should the process be perfected and simplified, we will take more - as many as are available.

"Memory capture is important in restoration of the mental capacities of the cloned individuals as quickly as possible, particularly of the scientific contingent. These people will be able to restore the scientific level that existed on the Earth when their memory capture was accomplished. They will be teachers of the immediate generations. They will be able to translate the information stored in the ship's computers into a form that will be practical for the development of the ingredients necessary to build industry and whatever else may be needed for the population on Planet X. The idea is that they will be able to reestablish the scientific and cultural levels of the present civilization. These people will be able to continue what they left on Earth."

"Naturally, it will be impossible to store everybody who is living on Earth today. Fifty families of scientists is all we will be able to preserve without impinging on all the ethnic groups that will be competing for a space on these ships. There will be only 450 families from ethnic groups. If more efficient preservation techniques develop we will add more people in the same proportions and using the same system of selection, except these additional people will not be represented on the manned ships, which have a fixed capacity of one thousand individuals. In discussions with Gen. Shagov and his staff we have been repeatedly told that they have made plans for a thousand people, and they are firm on that number.

"The necessary plants and animals will be stored for cloning and planting when the time comes. All the technical plans for designing these ships, and their actual manufacture are under the direction of Gen. Shagov.

"The launch date is projected to be in January of 2001. That will allow the ships to scatter in space.

"Let me now address the religious issues.

"The issue of 'playing God' is not valid.

"We plan no genetic manipulations and changes and no research on embryos.

"We will make every effort to preserve as many individual genomes as possible to enhance human diversity on Planet X. That will also apply to animals and plants.

"As for the research being conducted now on behalf of the Department of Human Resources, it is directed toward achieving the ability to clone humans and animals somewhere in space, which we call delayed cloning. Some people immediately see it as interference with divine power. We see it entirely differently. If scientists and clinicians are permitted today to do all kinds of manipulations to achieve reproduction of humans and animals and even to clone animals, and if changing of plants and animals by various techniques is acceptable, what is wrong with advancing fertilization and gestation techniques and using a robot to substitute for a humans?

"A robot is a human invention not a Divine tool, and, even if it were a Divine tool, we would still be using it to preserve the very life created by God. Besides, I believe that the robot could be considered a Divine creation by way of human skills, which were granted to humans by God.

"Our research is entirely within religious norms. We are not changing God's creation - the individual genome - we are merely trying to change the environment in which it could develop in space.

"I think our position is quite clear."

Applause followed Sister Maria's explanation. Arsen said nothing. The Prime Minister praised Sister Maria for the clarity of her statements.

Later that evening, on the plane to Rome, Arsen teased Sister Maria about the 'clarity of her statements.'

"That was quite a compliment from the British Prime Minister," Arsen said. "It seems you will need more books for your travels. People should understand what we have to say. Let us hope the Vatican will too."

CHAPTER FIFTY-NINE

TUESDAY, 20 JANUARY 1998

❪❪ Mr. Secretary, welcome to the Vatican," Cardinal Conti said, and he introduced the Secretary of State, Paul Cardinal Fiori, and the Deputy to the President of the Pontifical Council, Msgr. Franco Spinelli. "We have missed Sister Maria's wit, although she left the Vatican only last week. Msgr. Amato preferred ministering to the Romans to working for the Curia; we couldn't persuade him to work for us. Mr. Rangaswamy is well known to all of us from the time he made an extensive visit to the Vatican to study Catholicism, and also from his writings. Mr. McCollum is a journalist; we have not heard much from him."

After coffee was served Cardinal Conti invited everyone to take seats around the table.

"We meet today under difficult circumstances to discuss the research that is being conducted by the World Government, and the implications of that research. The debate on this subject has started, although I am not entirely sure what we are debating or what there is to debate. We have a clear vision of what the Catholic Church believes; in a capsule the Church is in complete agreement with the anticollision efforts of Gen. Shagov but opposed to the so called triggering of life in space. The issue is the continuation of the research that is being conducted toward the stated goal. I think the position of the Church is clear. It is up to the Assembly of the United Nations to decide whether the research should continue or be discontinued. We will do our best to persuade the member countries to vote with us against continuation of the research. That should be obvious to you."

"It is obvious all right, Your Eminence. Despite your firm stand I thought we should come to the Vatican and explain our thoughts in a direct dialog."

"Your thoughts have not been a secret," Cardinal Conti said. "Sister

Maria stated your case last night in London quite clearly. I must remind the Sister that she is out of line. Her explanations represented the views of the World Government and not of her Church."

"Your Eminence, I think you stated the case for the Church and indicated very clearly that there was nothing more to discuss," Arsen said. "Obviously the Church and the World Government have taken divergent roads, and there will be no more discussion between them. I thank you for arranging this meeting for us. We will be on our way."

Arsen bowed his head in a sign of respect to the Church officials and led his group out of the meeting room. The waiting limousines took them to the airport, and their plane took off almost immediately. They were on their way to New York.

Arsen noted the headlines in the *International Mirror* as he was changing his shirt in his bedroom

Pres. CHAND BEFORE THE U.N. ASSEMBLY: TO BE OR NOT TO BE?

President Chand had made an appeal to the Assembly not to discontinue the biological research, it was reported. He had proposed a referendum on the research in three months. He had also spoken of the importance of the manned and unmanned space ships and of delayed cloning and memory capture. The reception in the Assembly had been lukewarm.

CATHOLIC NUN FAVORS CLONING RESEARCH

That was it, Arsen thought. The W.G. and the Vatican might be on divergent roads, but the collision of forces pro and con cloning was inevitable. He decided to find out what the morale of his team was. He entered the general room, where the talk was subdued.

"The cloning battle is on," Arsen said. "You saw it in the Vatican today, it is in the news, and I feel it in my bones. It will be nasty for a while. Sister Maria how do you feel about the upcoming fight?"

"I feel terrible," Sister Maria said. "The Cardinal warned me and I got the message. It seems my career in New York will have lasted less than a week."

"You are not--"

"Yes I am going back to Rome," Sister Maria interrupted Arsen. "For good or bad. I may disagree with my Church, but I cannot work against it." Sister Maria was crying. "Sometimes I don't understand my Church."

Almost automatically Arsen looked at Msgr. Amato.

"You don't have to ask, Mr. Secretary," the Monsignor said. "I will be

470

on the same plane and for the same reasons as Sister Maria. We are servants of the Church, and we do what we are expected to do. The Church is not a democratic institution, and Her members must follow the established dogma. We will submit our resignations, pack up and return to Rome."

Arsen was stunned. He was losing two excellent individuals, after only a brief association with them, and losing their contributions to the debate on delayed cloning. It would not be the same, Arsen thought.

Arsen invited Vijay Rangaswamy to his small office, which was designed for his work and for private conversations.

"It seems that the burden of the debate will fall on your shoulders," Arsen said. "Are you prepared to carry it? You know the line of our thinking and our goals. Obviously the immediate goal is to get the approval of the Assembly for continuation of the necessary research until the referendum is held, and to explain to the people the reasons and necessity for delayed cloning. As I see it, this campaign will be primarily an educational endeavor on our part. We will also have to explain our stand concerning the unmanned project in relation to God. If I understand you correctly you are not in principle against the stand we are taking regarding religious beliefs. Is that correct?"

"Yes it is correct," said Vijay Rangaswamy. "Some of these views will have to be adapted to be understood and - hopefully - acceptable to various faiths."

"You are right about that," Arsen said. "Still, the essential stand must be the same as the one you and I understand and accept. Of course, it is easy for me, as I don't believe in God or in divine powers. I also have to accept the concept of our preaching in order to be able to function in our organization, where there will be differences of opinion. In my view there is only one difference between me, a non-believer, and the believing world, and that difference has to do with the first event ever---"

"I know," Vijay Rangaswamy interrupted Arsen. "You believe that the beginning is 'nothing' and most of us believe that the beginning is God. That is why the concept of Divine creation of everything is acceptable to you, almost as an option if 'nothing' proves not to be the beginning. On the other hand, the concept of the Divine creation of everyone and everything encompasses everything from a neutrino to the Universe and essentially does not interfere with an orderly and scientific existence of and progression of the Universe and of everything in it. The rest is just differences of opinion and differences in the way people arrived to them. That does not bother you - people can believe what they want."

"That covers it all," Arsen said. "Now we have the problem of explaining to people that delayed cloning and memory capture are just the newest inventions of the scientists. They do not deny God or His divine power -

just as the discovery of gravity or bacteria, Penicillin or electricity did not deny Him. We can use many examples of discoveries, from the existence of dinosaurs to atomic bombs. These are examples of things that are not attributed to God's initial creation of the Earth and Sun and water and people. Afterwards, God just let people discover and create what they wanted under His supporting eyes."

"We shouldn't forget the soul, which is God's creation too," Vijay Rangaswamy said.

"If you believe so," Arsen said. "We have to form a Council for Religious Affairs in the Department. The Council would appoint leaders of all religions that are interested in participating. Something like the World Council of Churches although representation would be complete. What do you think?"

"I am for a Council; but make it an independent body and not a part of the World Government. The Department of Human Resources should have a clear stand on the issue and promulgate it. We should have a public relations person who would do that."

"Would you want the job?" Arsen asked.

"No, not really," Vijay Rangaswamy said. "I would rather organize the Council and lead the discussion of the issues."

"I guess I am losing you too," Arsen said. "The Human Interrelations Division needs a new Undersecretary. Do you know somebody?"

"Your man should be a Christian as most of your problems will come from Christians. For obvious reasons a Catholic is out as he would be excommunicated for heresy if he followed the philosophy of the Department - as we saw with Sister Maria and Msgr. Amato. You need a Protestant who thinks and believes and accepts God's supremacy over everything, including delayed cloning and memory capture.

"I know just the man, a theologian from the University of Chicago. People call him Dr. Walter, although his name is Walter Herbert. He is a living encyclopedia of theology and not only of theology. He wrote a book titled *From the Beginning to the End* in which he explained his views of God, the creator of everything and of humanity with its constantly expanding knowledge and new ideas. Dr. Walter implied that God was amused by the ingenuity of humans in inventing and discovering everything over the ages, from simple tools and languages to atomic bombs and philosophes - subjects God had not even thought about at the time of creation. He was criticized for his ideas and may have toned them down to survive in the world of the infallible God. Though somewhat of an eccentric Dr. Walter is a serious thinker. You may want to call him and to talk to him."

"I will, I will," Arsen said.

There was a call from Herman Wolff.

"Arsen you remember you visit to Zagreb?"

"It is scheduled for Tuesday next week," Arsen said.

"They have not heard from you. I will let them know that you are coming. Rumors are that your visit to the Vatican was unusually short. Something must have gone wrong."

"Nothing unexpected. They just did not want to talk. Cardinal Conti said our positions were well known and antithetical to theirs. The next step is the referendum on the future of the biological research. Sister Maria and Msgr. Amato are casualties. They have resigned and will return to Rome. That is somewhat unexpected. Why did the Cardinal send Sister Maria to us at the first place? He thought she would convert us, I guess, and he was annoyed by her presentation in London." Arsen did not hide his contempt for the Cardinal although he had no problems with his beliefs. "They should have talked to us."

"Who will take their jobs?"

"Find Dr. Walter Herbert at the University of Chicago. He is a theologian. Ask him to come to New York, tomorrow if possible. I have to talk to him about the Human Relations job. We also have to find a replacement for Sister Maria. Think about it."

The flight to New York was smooth and uneventful.

CHAPTER SIXTY

WEDNESDAY, 21 JANUARY 1998

Arsen arrived at the office at eight o'clock. Sister Maria and Michelle were talking and drinking coffee.

"Michelle, please get some coffee for me," Arsen said. "Sister come to my office, I want to talk to you."

As they entered his office Arsen explained, "Sister Maria I wanted to tell you how sorry I am that you have to leave this department. I understand your reasons and in your place I would do the same thing. I have adopted a position toward the research along the lines that the Monsignor expressed - and you seemed to support - and that is the supremacy of God over everything we do and invent. It appeared logical that one who believed in God would accept this explanation and therefore find peace within her or himself when dealing with some strange experiments and goals. Think of a robot nursing a baby on a distant planet and a computer's audio system playing a lullaby. Everything else on the project is the same - strange.

"On the other hand what are the alternatives in case the Earth is hit and destroyed in a collision? The human race should survive this apocalypse, and we stand a distant chance if we continue our research and send the unmanned ships into space. The opponents of the biological research put their faith in Gen. Shagov and his team and believe that the collision will be avoided. Their real fear is having to deal with the results of this research afterward.

"My decision to go to the Vatican was prompted by the idea that we could make a deal on that issue - how to destroy the tools and results of the research in case we survive. Unfortunately, Cardinal Conti was not willing to talk."

Arsen paused for a moment.

"My problem, Sister Maria, is that I don't believe in God or anything else that is supposed to have a supernatural power. There was nothingness before the beginning of the Universe, and there will be nothingness after the Universe disappears. You may say that even nothingness was created by someone like God, but it would not be nothingness if God existed. Oh, you must feel sorry for me Sister, but don't. For me it is easier to understand and accept death as the conversion into nothingness and to become part of the Universe that will eventually also disappear into nothingness."

Arsen paused again for a moment.

"While the Universe does exist humanity should exist also. Humanity might become the victim of these times of anxiety and agitation about the collision, and might disappear forever; I don't like that. The distribution of human beings throughout the Universe would be so exciting. Imagine, Sister, that several of our unmanned ships have accomplished their missions, I mean that they have landed on habitable planets and that cloning of human individuals has taken place. That would almost assure our survival and our distribution in the Universe. There must be many planets where humans could live; they will have to be found and they will be found. If life exists out there we'll meet these living creatures. Maybe we'll meet people who were cloned on other planets. Descendants of the same DNA stock would meet millions of years hence.

"Sitting here and waiting to be hit by the celestial object is the utmost in idiotic defeatism; I cannot understand it and I don't want to understand it. I will fight for preservation with my mind and my heart and if I lose the battle in the referendum - so be it. I will join the Universe in all my nothingness when the end of life comes upon us. Too bad, Sister, that you are not willing to join the battle."

Sister Maria was listening attentively. She shrugged her shoulders and shook her head as if she were in distress after Arsen's last remark.

"I have been thinking since we left the Vatican," Sister Maria said. "It is not easy to break with something one has been associated with for many years - happy and productive years. The magnitude of the problems facing us became more apparent to me when I came to New York. I understand now what is at stake, and I cannot help being on the side of preservation of humanity at all costs. I told you that I could not work against my Church. If I remained in New York I would not be fighting my Church I would be fighting for my Church, for preservation of the people who are the children of the Church, any Church and not the least the Catholic Church. Mr. Secretary, I would like to join your team again and fight the battle for humanity."

Arsen was stunned. He was only able to say "thank you."

The news of Sister Maria's decision spread quickly.

Msgr. Amato called. No, he was not planning to remain in New York and join Sister Maria. He was worried about her and her uncertain future within the Catholic Church. Sister Maria assured him that she would be okay even if she were excommunicated."

Media were calling all day and asking for an interview with Sister Maria. They were told that she would have a press conference in the morning.

"Doctor, I wanted you to know that Dr. Walter Herbert will be here in the early afternoon, about two o'clock," Michelle said over the intercom.

"Good." Arsen had forgotten he had asked Herman Wolff to find Dr. Walter in Chicago.

Arsen called Herman Wolff to his office.

"It is about time that we have a private talk," Arsen said. "The Department is in good shape. All important appointments have been made. Sister Maria shocked me this morning with her decision to defy the Vatican and remain in her position. That is fantastic as she is a capable woman. I anticipate repercussions from the Vatican against her, possibly excommunication, and we will have to help her if that happens. On the other hand, she will symbolize a Catholic who is for research even if it means she is excluded from the Church. She is going to hold a press conference in the morning to explain her views. Make sure she says what she thinks is right not what we think is right. I presented to her my atheistic convictions, and she did not criticize me. She is a remarkable woman, don't you think?"

"I agree."

"Dr. Walter will be here this afternoon, as you know. If you talked to Vijay Rangaswamy he must have told you he would be organizing the Council on Religions, as he wants to call it. The Council should be a forum for discussion about the future of the world, whether before the collision or after it has been averted. Of course, they should discuss future societies on the distant planets if our unmanned ships ever reach one and a human is cloned."

"You will be cloned, as you know," Herman Wolff said.

"Okay. If I ever get cloned on some planet somewhere in the Universe. This council is the last institution I wanted to complete and finalize the Department. I think everybody is in place and knows what to do. Ethnic problems were initially my main task and my worry. People got the message, and the problems have steadily been getting resolved. Some new and interesting solutions have been advanced, like the Bee Sovereignty System, and in the field the people have accepted them enthusiastically. Eventually, we will have the World Court and local Mandela-Tutu Commissions in place. Corruption is on the way out, I think, as many politicians and statesmen have resigned rather than face the audits."

"Research seems to be progressing very well," Herman Wolff said.

"You are right. We have three years to produce the technology, to load the ships that will be built by Alexei, and to launch them into space. We were lucky to engage all these talented people. I am almost sure that we will have the technology we need. I can see a robot pouring the genetic engine into an egg-shaped uterus, and the hatching of a full-term baby in a much reduced time - gestation will have been accelerated by various factors. I can also visualize the development of the baby into a grown-up person - me, as you would insist, - in an environment which was programmed by the Postpartum Development Division. I have no idea what is outside that ship."

"Arsen I must tell you I am pleased and amazed by our progress," Herman Wolff said. "I work with these people constantly, and I am impressed with their intelligence and ingenuity. I think these ships will take off in January of 2001 ready to do the job."

"There is still a minor problem to be overcome, as you know: the referendum. By the way, do we know the date for the referendum?"

"15 April."

"That soon?"

"Yeah."

"Tomorrow night I will talk at the FFP," Arsen said. "I am still polishing the speech. It should be an interesting evening for me."

"People are puzzled that you refused to give the title of your talk," Herman Wolff said. "What is the mystery? Is it going to be a bombshell, like last time? Is there something in this organization that I don't know?"

"Doctor, President Chand is on line four," Michelle announced over the intercom.

"Rama, I read your speech before the Assembly and the comments in the papers. The Assembly has to be charged for action. They will do nothing until the message from the people becomes clear. We have to carry the message to the people, and the Assembly will be revived."

"As you must have heard, the referendum has been set for 15 April," Rama Chand said. "I feel three months is enough time for debate and propaganda by all sides. I think people know today what they want. They want survival of humanity. That is a natural instinct. India will vote for it."

"There are many people who find the research that is being done repugnant and they will vote against it.

"I think you are wrong," Rama Chand said. "You don't believe in people's instincts, or their intelligence."

"I will be nervous until I see the final report on the referendum."

"I hear that Sister Maria has decided to keep her job in your

Department despite the warning from the Vatican."

"I am delighted to say that is true."

"I hope your talk tomorrow night will not be another bombshell. I guess you know what you are doing. Good luck."

Arsen imagined Dr. Walter would look like a man in disarray: a strongly built man with a square face, shaggy hair, a potato for a nose, somewhat red, thick lips and decayed teeth. The surprise was complete when Dr. Walter walked into the office. He was in his fifties, tall and gracile, non-athletic, with an intelligent, refined face, smooth hair and small sad eyes.

"Dr. Pankovich people in Surgery still remember you."

"How very considerate of you, Dr. Walter, to check on me with people I once knew. I have switched professions since then."

"If you hadn't how would I be interviewed by you for this job," Dr. Walter said in his low, melodic voice. "I will accept the job if it's offered. I need some room for my own ideas. Incidentally, we're not that far apart philosophically. I'm not an atheist as you are; I believe in God. My God is not a conventional God; He is more human than divine and hardly power-wielding. This doesn't deny Him Divine power although he uses it quite rationally. That's my sin. My critics say I don't take God seriously. Dr. Pankovich I do take God seriously; if it were otherwise how could I believe in His existence?"

"I trust that you believe in God," Arsen said. "Do you understand the main purpose of your job, the job description so to speak?"

"I know that the central issue your Department faces now is the resistance by a variety of religious groups to the biological research projects that are under way. That's the issue that will be on the ballots on 15 April - biological research. How do we win this battle---"

"Honestly?" Arsen interrupted Dr. Walter.

"Yes, honestly," Dr. Walter said. "We have to take a straightforward position against accusations that we're playing God. On one front we can follow the question posed by the British Prime Minister: who created animals and plants if experiments can be done on them without the scrutiny reserved for humans - perhaps the Devil? On another front we could ask why scientists are allowed to explore anything from subatomic structures to the Universe and to develop technologies that were not created by God, like the atomic bomb used for the sole purpose of killing people? So the dilemma should be whether the preservation of humans is less worthy than killing them?

"We can claim that God created humans with intelligence and allowed them to explore the world around them, and to improve conditions in the world and save life whether on the Earth or somewhere else in the Universe. We would not be inventing life, we would just be preserving it by the delayed cloning and memory capture. It is possible - we have no way of knowing - that God would let most of the life on Earth disappear. That would be a shame, because humanity with all its faults is still a wonderful creation, and we should fight to preserve it in the Universe if not on the Earth."

"I am not quite sure why you have been criticized for your work," Arsen said. "I like your approach. Dr. Walter you can have the job."

Arsen concluded that his team was complete and ready to do the job of winning the referendum and eventually the battle for humanity. He was elated.

CHAPTER SIXTY-ONE

WEDNESDAY, 15 APRIL 1998

It was the referendum day. The campaign had ended the night before with a party given by Rama Chand for the Undersecretaries and their immediate staff. Everybody had come to celebrate what was predicted to be a victory for the biological research, and with a significant majority at that. This was the end of hard work, Arsen thought. They had traveled and talked constantly, day after day, often attending meetings late in the evening. The next day would be a reprise; only the surroundings would change a bit, sometimes not even that. They had taken no chances and worked hard to the end. A feeling of mental numbness was the best description Arsen could give for his psychological state. They would have the answer in about a week when all votes were supposed to have been counted, although the result would be apparent even today after the trends had been analyzed.

At the party Rama Chand had been cheerful and Victoria looked a bit tired, but beautiful as always. Alexei had looked tired and old and had not said much; Sabrina had not even talked to him. Sister Maria had looked exhausted and Arsen had ordered her to take a vacation somewhere in the Caribbean. Herman Wolff had been his usual self, pleasant and polite, as the campaign had not affected him much. The Enstroms had been the same - bright and cool.

Arsen was following the results on the referendum web site, which displayed a map of the world and showed voting trends in each state. The results from Japan, China and parts of India were for the research. In the Philippines the research was on the losing side. Russia was for the research. Europe was voting for the research as expected. South and Central Americas were expected to vote against it.

By the afternoon a voting mosaic in the United States was emerging and the eventual outcome was unclear. Africa was also divided. The

Muslim states were voting for the research.

The research was winning with a significant margin.

Rama Chand invited Alexei, Arsen and Goran Enstrom to a private dinner at seven o'clock at the United Nations. This sounded like a victory dinner, Arsen thought.

When they were seated Rama Chand thanked them for coming and stated the reason for the meeting.

"Gentlemen, I thought we should get together over dinner and discuss the state of the World Government. Where are we now and where are we going from now on? Alexei, tell us something about the prospects of anti-collision. Arsen, we should hear from you about the latest developments in the biological research and the present state of ethnic relations. Goran, what do people think nowadays? I know people want the biological research to proceed or at least that is how it appears from the referendum voting trends. That is obviously not all that is on people's mind.

"Anticollision worries people the most. The bottom line of people's interest is, as always, what is our chance of deflecting the Demon? Alexei, nothing very encouraging has come out your department so far.

"Arsen, ethnic problems are not of real concern to people, are they? People are concerned about survival, and they want to make sure something survives after they are gone.

"Goran, you should explain to us what is happening out there. Please tell us."

Dinner was served, and there was a pause in the conversation. Nobody ate much. Alexei was on his third vodka and Goran was sipping his wine.

"Okay Goran," Rama Chand said. "Let us hear your views."

"If I could summarize it in one sentence I would say that people are changing the old adage, 'God created his own beard first.' I thought people were getting depressed a few months ago. I was wrong. People may be psychotic, but they are not depressed. The amazing fact is that demands for work have increased, for all kinds of work. The work is the objective not the remuneration. We have studied the phenomenon, and it turns out that these people feel that any work contributes indirectly to the anticollision effort. I think they are right. People are asking for help with their basic needs, and not demanding it, and we make every effort to respond.

"You would not believe it, but the work force has increased at least ten percent, and the numbers are growing. Our administrative offices have employed many people around the globe. Anything can be done fast and efficiently, because people work harder and make sure things are done right, and there are more people to do the job. This is true for state and local offices. Companies report the same trend. The net result is that more people than ever are working, and their work is more efficient. In fact, people are not working; they are contributing. I would not be surprised if we reached total employment. The schools are not empty as was reported previously. All retired teachers are trying to get back to teaching and we are trying to accommodate them. The teaching has improved, and kids are interested. Economic growth should reach unprecedented heights.

"All religions report an increase in attendance at services and other activities. This is not because people are becoming fanatics, but because they are looking for answers to their questions.

"Crime has gone down, as the number of people working for police departments has increased significantly, but some social scientists think that even criminals have been changing their attitudes.

"Of course this is an optimistic prediction of things to come but the trends are unmistakable. I believe so and my social scientists think so. Time will tell."

"This is an amazing report," Rama Chand said. "I have read bits and pieces about it but I did not realize the magnitude of the change. Alexei, what is the progress with the neutrino gun?"

"We are working in three areas. We are researching the feasibility of the development of a neutrino gun. I know that at least theoretically it can be made. So far neutrino research has made it possible to capture memory. We are developing nuclear devices, and we will have twenty ships ready to go in the next year or two. The problems with these devices are their size and their destructive power. If we built a device powerful enough to deflect the Demon, we would have transportation problems. Also, we would have to land on the Demon, dig deep under the surface and implant the device before it is detonated. That is not possible. The alternative would be to detonate many smaller devices. I don't think that would do the job. The third area of our work is building space ships for anticollision purposes and for manned and unmanned flights. This is the easiest part of our work.

"It is still impossible to answer your question on our chances of deflecting or destroying the Demon. Our work is progressing well, but we are not yet ready to build the gun. I understand now the feelings of the scientists who worked on the Manhattan project to build the atomic bomb before Hitler did it. It was a life and death situation then, and it is the same now, although this time humanity as a whole is at stake."

"Arsen what is happening in your Department? asked Rama Chand.

"Biological research has made three significant steps. Artificial media have been developed and are now being refined. The 'egg' is feasible - that is gestation in an artificial uterus. The robot programming is progressing smoothly. We will be ready for a January 2001 launch. I just hope Gennadi Koltsov delivers on his memory capture project."

"He will deliver, don't worry," Alexei said.

"Ethnic transformation is progressing smoothly. People are cooperating better than we anticipated. That would go along with Goran's remarks."

Rama Chand's phone rang, and he talked to somebody for a few moments.

"Gentlemen, the projections by all media are that the biological research has won with a large margin. Congratulations. We should have smooth sailing from now on. I will let you know about our next meeting."

This dinner meeting left Arsen somehow cool, as if everyone was subdued and in his own sphere of thoughts. There had been too much redundancy in what had been said, as if people did not know the facts and the state of the world, World Government and the progress made by each Department. To Arsen the most interesting was Goran Enstrom's focus on people's attitudes as a consequence of the threat hanging over the world.

How could they exchange the threat for some other incentive that would induce people to behave as they had already started to behave? Money, gold and material advantages had always been the incentive. 'To live better' had been the motto of humanity. To get material advantages, people had been willing to work harder, to do things they did not like to do, to cheat, to steal and even to kill. The universal man had evolved under the threat of the collision, from the survival instinct. If the threat vanished so would the universal man.

Maybe a new civilization could be created on Planet X that would be less self-centered. Arsen would be in a position to help create it. Would he remember that he wanted to do it? How could he make a note of this in his memory capture?

CHAPTER SIXTY-TWO

WEDNESDAY, 27 DECEMBER 2000

It was nine o'clock in the morning. Michelle was talking to one of her secretaries. Arsen was alone in his office.

He had only a month left before take-off on 27 January. He was thinking about the events of the last few months. The manned ships looked good. How had they finally decided on sixty ships with twenty people on each? Anticollision had made that decision. Alexei had explained that the size was practical and they had no time to build more than sixty ships. The lottery had been a success for the minorities and for a number of obscure ethnic groups. The lottery had been an issue in the Assembly and had dominated all activities, and it had been the page one headline for several months. The Assembly had finally followed the recommendation of Jean-Pierre Vernier to establish twenty regions with separate lotteries in each to produce a list of one hundred people each. The lists had evolved by the order in which the names were selected. In the end each region had contributed sixty names. After much bickering and some serious fights Jean-Pierre Vernier had arranged the distribution of people in the ships to their satisfaction.

Religious groups had contributed to the fights more than ethnic groups had. The most notorious fight had been between the Vatican's Cardinal Conti and the Imam el-Haruni, the founder of an Islamic Seminary in Tashkent in Uzbekistan. Not far behind had been New York's Rabbi Goldman and an obscure Guru from Madras, Prakash Mehta. Arsen remembered weeks of arguments about representations of Christians and Muslims on the ships and particularly their clergy. Rabbi Goldman had wanted more Jews on the ships and Guru Mehta had wanted more Hindus. Once, in the heat of the arguments on a talk show, Guru Mehta had accused the Rabbi of pushing to colonize Planet X with Jews.

"Honorable Rabbi, it seems you are trying to create the State of Israel on Planet X. No Jews should be allowed from the peoples' pool as there are already enough Jewish scientists on these ships. We have no influence on the selection of the scientists, but you do - through your Zionist connections."

"Zionist connections, my foot," snapped back the aggravated Rabbi. "These people were selected because they were smart and they were needed on the ships and on Planet X. Do you think we should make a separate group of people who would represent the different religions?"

"Only if the major religious groups were represented, like Muslims, Christians, Jews, Buddhists - and not more than ten," Guru Mehta said. "Of course, another Jew would get on the ship."

"You are an anti-Semite," Rabbi Goldman accused Guru Mehta.

"I am a Hindu."

"Would there be time for a Catholic opinion?" asked Cardinal Conti.

"We have heard enough from Your Eminence," the Imam said.

Arsen laughed when he remembered the exchange. That was behind them now.

"Doctor, President Chand is on line four," Michelle announced over the intercom.

"Arsen our end-of-the-year meeting is scheduled for tonight at seven."

"I know about the meeting, I will be ready for any questions although you know all the answers.

"I read your interview in the newspaper. I was impressed by the number of ethnic problems that have been resolved and the workings of the Bee System in Zaire and other places. More than two thousand resolved applications! How many are unresolved?"

"Probably three thousand. Many smaller groups never applied; they were satisfied by being recognized and did not even push for autonomy. Many groups have been negotiating and will eventually make accommodations with the larger groups around them. We are pushing for recognition as the first step. Do you remember Stan Petkovic? He was my Deputy until he was shot in Belgrade during my talk at the Academy of Sciences. He talked about the importance of being recognized. Now we find it extremely important. Once recognized, people start behaving differently; you might say they become more civilized. Of course, Hegel talked about the importance of being recognized in self consciousness. That does not stop at primordial recognition; it continues to be important during one's lifetime for self-respect and in creating harmony with one's environment. Anyhow it works. "

"What happened to Stan?"

"He is in Belgrade where he represents the World Government," Arsen said. "He never wanted to return to New York."

"Some people cannot take the heat," Rama Chand said. "I had dinner with Vijay Rangaswamy a few nights ago. He is thinking seriously of returning home to India. He thinks his mission in New York is over, especially since you will soon be gone into space. The real reason I called you today was to find out who should take your job after you are gone. I wanted your opinion."

"Herman Wolff or Sister Maria. Both are excellent administrators. Herman has been my deputy, and he would be the more logical choice. You might decide to get someone from outside. Interest in ethnic problems will be more important since the research should be over, at least formally, as we promised before the referendum. I promised that to Cardinal Conti and repeatedly in my speeches."

"That is how I understand it too," Rama Chand said.

"Now I can go to my oblivion in peace," Arsen said.

"Why oblivion? We will have you in our hearts and our minds. You have done plenty for the world."

"Who will think of someone who lived a few thousand years earlier? Besides, if all of us disappear into space I will have reached my oblivion, nothingness. It could happen just the other way around, if we reach Planet X. Will we recognize ourselves or just read about our civilization? Will we ever be able to communicate with the Earth from Planet X? What if our ship finds Planet X in a hundred thousand years? We would start so far behind. You would have evolved into a different civilization, and perhaps we wouldn't even understand you."

"You sound pessimistic, Arsen," Rama Chand said. "Do you have doubts about the mission? If we collide with the Demon the people on manned ships will disappear and the only chance to save humanity will be your reaching Planet X. If the collision is eluded, you will return to Earth with the rest of the people, and the unmanned ships will be exploded in space. You should not think and worry about different civilizations."

"Screw-ups occur," Arsen said. "What if one ship fails to respond to the explosion command? Though there would be only a small chance that a single ship would reach Planet X, you never know. I cannot stop thinking."

"Why don't you think of more cheerful things? You will meet many people in the next few days and the New Year's Eve Party should be great. Be prepared to say something cheerful."

"Okay Rama."

"I'll talk to you tonight."

Sister Maria walked in.

"The end of the year is approaching quickly and the date for the launching of the unmanned ships. After your vacation in Rio you will fly

486

into space on your ship. That's the end."

"The end of what, Sister?" Arsen asked.

"The end of research and of my role in the smaller department," Sister Maria said. "Do you think the research will be discontinued?"

"I am sure it will be," Arsen said. "The President assured me just this morning that the research will stop and the information that has been accumulated will not be released."

"I'm so glad you say so. Cardinal Conti didn't believe in 1998 that the research in the Department would stop after you were gone. Maybe I should call him and tell him he was wrong?"

"I think you will be needed in New York to help Herman - or whoever - to run this Department, or to run it yourself," Arsen said. "I think Herman will get the job and you will be his deputy."

"Doctor, Mr. Wolff is on line three," Michelle announced over the intercom.

"Arsen I don't know how to start," Herman Wolff said. "It is even embarrassing."

"What is embarrassing?"

"I just talked to Rama Chand. He offered me your job after you take off into space. I am not interested, and I already have a job in Germany. What should I do?"

"What kind a job?"

"Special Assistant to the President. I will be in Berlin, among family and friends. I have been looking for a job like that for a long time. I accepted the job and was planning to start in February."

"I wish you had kept me informed," Arsen said. "Who should get my job?"

"Sister Maria is well qualified," Herman Wolff said.

"Make your recommendation and do some lobbying. You know how to do that." Arsen laughed after he said that.

"I will, I will," Herman Wolff said before he hung up.

"Sister Maria you will be the new Secretary of the Ethnic Department. Herman Wolff has a job lined up in Berlin. I am glad, and you deserve it."

Sister Maria remained silent.

"I am concerned about ethnic problems and I would like to be sure the job is done right after I am gone," Arsen continued. "Sister I would feel better if you accepted the job."

"I will do it if you want me to," Sister Maria said quietly.

"Doctor, Gen. Shagov is on line two," Michelle announced over the intercom.

"Arsen I just called to find out if I could persuade you to come to Moscow with your wife for a few days. I know you intend to go to Rio for two or three weeks. Make a short diversion. You will appreciate Rio better after the snow in Moscow. What do you say? This may be our last chance to have a day or two together."

"I'm inclined to accept," Arsen said. "Let me talk to my wife first. I'll let you know tomorrow."

"That would be fantastic. You will like Moscow and my *dacha*. We could visit Gennadi, who is crazy but an interesting person."

Arsen received many calls during the day. Many people called only to say hello or to ask unimportant questions. Arsen felt that these were farewell calls, maybe even sympathy calls, as if people wanted to say that they knew the space trip Arsen was planning to take would be final and they would not see each other again. Alexei had probably called for the same reason. This was the way people talked to a terminally ill patient. Arsen shook off that unpleasant feeling.

Arsen arrived on time at the private dinning room at the United Nations, where the annual dinner meeting was held. Rama, Alexei and Goran were already there. Alexei was drinking his vodka and Goran was sipping a scotch on the rocks. Rama was drinking a Coke and Arsen joined them with his standard tonic water. Again, Arsen had that strange feeling he had had when talking with an old friend and others who had called during the day. Were they feeling that he, Arsen, was leaving them and going to an uncertain destination of no return, or that he was leaving them behind to face a certain death? As dinner was served Arsen's thoughts drifted in the direction of the anticipated discussion of the world's affairs.

Rama Chand asked that they begin their state of the Department presentations as they were being served coffee and tea.

A litany of presentations was boring, Arsen thought; even his own. He explained all intricacies of manned and unmanned projects, and concluded with his personal thoughts.

"I tremble a bit when I try to visualize my life on Planet X. I will be alone for twenty years. Will I behave as the cave men did? Will I be self-conscious or will I need to go through the process of recognition, *à la* Hegel? I have asked myself and others many questions; the answers will have to wait until we reach Planet X.

"I will try, if I remember, to change the social structure of the cloned and naturally born people on Planet X. I will teach them to be universal not human, to be knowledgeable, economically and socially independent and tolerant. We are sending representatives of many ethnic groups. I just hope their self consciousness will not divide them as it has on the Earth.

I want to hear some cheerful thoughts from Alexei," Rama Chand demanded.

"I can tell you that we are almost there," Alexei said and made a serious face. "Almost but not exactly there. There are several critical experiments to be done before the neutrino guns can be built, loaded on the ships and transported to the main stations which will approach the Demon when it enters an orbit in our solar system. We expect to be ready for launching in about six months. Our nuclear ships are ready, and we expect to launch them within three weeks. Our men will try to land on the Demon and dig the holes for the bombs, which will be detonated after the men are at a safe distance. The chances for success for these devices are slim at best. We have to try anyway. I will keep you posted about the progress of the neutrino gun. I think it would take only one of these guns to do the job. We have planned for at least three of them."

"I wish I could inform the world that we will shoot at and deflect the Demon," Rama Chand said. "I guess I will only be able to encourage them to be patient."

Nothing further was said about anticollision and preservation.

Goran Enstrom was the last to speak.

"I know it may sound superfluous to talk at this time about social changes that have occurred in the world since our last meeting. I know how much you are concerned about the apocalypse of the approaching celestial collision. But I thought a very brief statement should be appropriate."

Nobody said anything and Goran Enstrom continued.

"You would be surprised how much people know about the progress of anticollision and preservation. The initial depressive reaction has been exchanged for ebullience. I don't think it would be an exaggeration to say that more than sixty percent of the total population are employed in some capacity and without remuneration. Our economic infrastructure has changed. It is more efficient and much less expensive and sometimes costs nothing. Our studies have shown clearly that the incentive is the desire to make the world a better place even for a short time. There is also a desire to help save the world. My problem is not what would happen to the world if the Earth were destroyed completely. There would be nobody to talk about. But I do wonder how these same people will behave if we avoid the apocalypse."

Goran completed his statement as abruptly as he had started it. Nobody made a comment.

The meeting ended in a funerary mood. Rama Chand simply said, "I will see you at the party."

Arsen left the meeting distressed. The anticollision group had failed to develop a weapon that could deflect the Demon. They were in a race with time, and soon it would be too late for them to put into orbit the ships from which they could shoot at the Demon even if they had the weapon.

Manned ships would most likely be doomed after witnessing the collision. Good God, their only chance was the hundred unmanned ships, Arsen thought, the only chance for survival of the human race.

CHAPTER SIXTY-THREE

SUNDAY, 31 DECEMBER 2000

Nada and Arsen were driven to the main entrance of the Plaza Hotel for the New Years Eve's Party. It was seven thirty.

"How many people have been invited?" Nada asked.

"All accredited Ambassadors and their wives were invited," Arsen said. "Add to that Secretaries and Undersecretaries and their wives or husbands."

"How many people is that?"

"There are now over a thousand member nations. Another two hundred people must have been invited. We will have to shake the hands of these people as they pass by us. There will be seven of us: Rama and Victoria, Alexei, you and me, and Ursula and Goran Enstrom. Alexei's wife Katarina refused to come from Moscow. You know all of them."

At the entrance a Security Service agent was waiting for them and showed them to the Grand Ball Room. Victoria and Rama were already there.

"I have recovered sufficiently after the other night to look normal," Arsen said to Rama Chand. "I fully realized the gravity of our situation. We've expected too much from Alexei's neutrino gun. Alexei has delivered everything else in perfect shape and on time. The nuclear weapons are ready to go. Memory capture is only an extra. Nobody could have done a better job. I hope you will say something encouraging tonight. You are the President, and the people expect you to give them good news. Can you?"

"Sure I can," Rama Chand said. "You are ready to go and Alexei is almost done. The nuclear bombs are also ready to go. The world is quiet."

"Quiet and awaiting the disaster."

"I disagree with you, Arsen. People are like the patient expecting to see his surgeon. He knows the news may be good or bad. He feels good, and he wants to hear good news. And he does. The surgeon tells him that there are a few hurdles on the way to recovery and that everything will be okay in the end. Then the patient is happy."

"Is the patient going to be okay?"

"I think so."

Rama Chand and his three Secretaries were ready to receive the guests. Four lines were formed. All guests were welcomed by nine o'clock.

Arsen and Nada spent the three hours before midnight mingling with the guests. Rama, Alexei and Goran must have done the same.

The last minute before the New Year was announced, and all eyes turned to the large clock ticking the seconds. Everybody counted loudly the last thirty seconds. The ball room was a very noisy place reaching a crescendo when the lights went off.

After the noise subsided, Rama Chand addressed the guests and the world.

"This is the fourth time I am addressing all of you here in the room and outside, worldwide. This is a very special year. We have just entered the first day of the third millennium officially.

"I could talk to you for a long time and tell you about the accomplishments of the World Government and of many people outside the government. I could tell you about the new attitudes of the people and the new social order that is developing. You are not interested in that tonight. You want me to tell you that the collision on 15 March 2003 will not occur. From all the information I have received, the collision will not happen on that day or on any other day."

Long applause followed Rama Chand's statement.

"My optimism is based on facts. The space ships that will carry the nuclear devices will be launched within the next two months. These are powerful weapons, and they will be delivered to the Demon and exploded on it. We should be able to see the explosions.

"The second weapon that is being designed is almost ready to be built. Three neutrino guns will be sent into space, and they will deflect the Demon or maybe even destroy it.

"I have no doubt that there will be people welcoming the first day of the fourth millennium; I strongly believe in the survival of the human race."

The applause was pandemoniac from over two thousand people in the ball room.

The world was celebrating its salvation.

Arsen was left with his doubts.

CHAPTER SIXTY-FOUR

WEDNESDAY, 3 JANUARY 2001

Nada and Arsen arrived in Florida late in the afternoon and were taken to the Kennedy Manned Space Flight Center where accommodations had been made for their stay. A junior official was asked to show them around. Activities at the Center were incredible. Twenty space ships were positioned for launching. The plan was to launch sixty ships on Thursday and forty on Friday.

At nine o'clock the Director of the unmanned flights, Dr. Leo Goodman, talked to Nada and Arsen for twenty minutes and took them to the cafeteria for dinner in a private dinning room. Two Deputies, Carl Pearson and David Korngold, joined them later. Arsen knew of them but had never met them.

As they were drinking coffee after dinner Dr. Goodman raised his cup.

"Welcome, Mr. Secretary, to the Unmanned Center. We will be sitting here on February first and getting ready to take off in the manned space ships. David will be on your ship, and I will be in another ship with a group of people from Asia. Carl will fly on yet another ship."

"Are you scared about that project?" Arsen asked. "Have you been in space before?"

"This will be my first space flight," Leo Goodman said. "I have sent many people into space and luckily they all came back. These manned missions will be different. We may or may not return. Scared? I am. President Chand talked with high optimism on New Year's Eve. I'm not sure his optimism was justified. Look at our prospects. We were told that the nuclear weapons will be on the way in a month or two. That is true but what good will that do? These weapons are baby stuff for the size of the Demon. The neutrino gun is a mystery. Nobody has seen the results or what kind of research is being done. We have heard about Gennadi Koltsov. Everybody who meets him says he's crazy. We know of his success in memory capture but we haven't seen it at work. Maybe he's a genius but most certainly a crazy one. The lead physicist in neutrino research is Prof. Isoroku Yakawa and he's still at the basic level. Whatever Gennadi is keeping up his sleeve nobody knows except for Gen. Shagov, and he's not talking. I just hope the neutrino gun is not a hoax."

"Have you ever met the General?" Arsen asked, in amazement.

"No."

"I will arrange for you to meet with the General," Arsen said. "You will change your mind after you have talked to him. I met him before he explained his discovery of the celestial object to the Space Committee. His findings had been refuted until he presented his evidence."

"I've seen his evidence," Leo Goodman said. "It was clear and straightforward. Confirmation by Hubble telescope was just a formality. The General showed the precise position of the Demon. That was brilliant."

"Do you think he has changed so much in three years?"

"I don't know. This time he has given us no information at all."

"Perhaps he has his own reasons for that," Arsen said. "I don't challenge him on matters beyond my understanding."

"He has nobody with him who could understand him or challenge him," Leo Goodman said.

"Talk to him before we take off - you will feel better," Arsen said.

"We never saw the inside of unmanned ships," Carl Pearson said.

"We only built the outside structures, the solar cells, the sensors, the engines and the landing gear," David Korngold said. "They are very well made. They are durable, and I feel confident about their mission."

"A hundred thousand years from now?" asked Arsen.

"There is nothing stronger," Leo Goodman said. "I don't know how long it can last."

"As I recall now you are the third or fourth in line to be cloned," Arsen said, changing the subject as he was very disturbed about doubts of these men. "Carl and David may be right after you."

"We're further down on the list," David Korngold said.

"I have to survive gestation and a few years afterward under the supervision of a robot," Arsen said. "Imagine being bathed by a robot or being fed by one. Then having it as the only company. I am looking forward to watching videos when I grow up. I have a chilly feeling about all that. You people will have me to talk to. That is much nicer, isn't it?"

"It depends," Leo Goodman said.

"Depends on what?"

"If we had a choice," Leo Goodman laughed.

"I will be younger then," Arsen protested and laughed, himself.

Back in their room later that evening Arsen still felt uneasy about the conversation he had had with Leo Goodman and his men. This fellow had accused Alexei of perpetrating a hoax, Arsen thought. Some of the things he had said were right. Alexei had been secretive about the research on the neutrino gun. Perhaps not so much secretive as nobody asked any questions and everybody trusted him completely; Arsen certainly had. People who worked for him were always in distant places and nobody ever came to New York. Gennadi was the only associate everybody knew and Arsen had talked to him, although only about memory capture. Even that had been quickly suppressed after Mikhail Platov was mysteriously recalled to Moscow.

The only person who had seen the machine perform was Ursula Bjöstrom when she visited Gennadi for a day in Moscow. Afterward the memory machines had been delivered from Russia and the memory contents of the people selected to be on the ships had been recorded. No one had any idea what was stored. This stuff was on the ships that would be launched tomorrow or the day after. There were too many questions to be answered. It might be too late to stop the launchings and to find out. What should he do?

Arsen asked Nada what she thought about the accusation?

"Call Rama Chand and ask him what to do," Nada said.

Arsen could not make up his mind. The accusation was outrageous, and repercussions would be enormous if an inquiry were made, even if it concluded that everything was in order. This could ruin the entire anticollision effort at a very sensitive time. The neutrino gun was the only weapon that could deflect the Demon; as Leo Goodman had put it, nuclear weapons were baby stuff. What good would an inquiry do? The unmanned ships would have to be launched with or without the memory. The cloned people on Planet X would find out about the Earth and present-day civilization from the information stored on the computers. Many people had written their life histories to help them reconstruct their previous lives. Even if memory capture were a hoax people would still be cloned and the human race preserved on Planet X.

Arsen would be himself minus his memory," he concluded. Maybe just as well to start from the beginning. If the neutrino research and the gun was just a figment of the imagination of a lunatic, finding out about it would be just as insane. People would go wild after they realized that the collision was inevitable. The world didn't need that. He had better keep this to himself."

CHAPTER SIXTY-FIVE

THURSDAY, 4 JANUARY 2001

Arsen and Nada were assigned to an observation deck from which all launchings could be observed. It was a spectacle; the launching of twenty ships one after another every five minutes. Arsen felt as though it was not only his genetic engine that was on each ship, but he, himself. His thoughts went far into the future, when one of these ships landed on Planet X. He noticed that Nada was also very excited.

"Aren't we a bit too old for this kind of excitement?" Arsen whispered to her. "How is it going to be when we take off on our ship on February first? That will be the real thing with an uncertain future."

"Don't talk about that please," Nada protested.

That evening Arsen decided to call Rama Chand.

"Arsen, we saw some spectacular liftoffs on television. You must be having a good time."

"I wish I could say so."

"Why?"

"It is hard to explain over the phone."

"I don't understand."

"It concerns Alexei."

"What about Alexei?"

"The engineers I talked to over here feel that the neutrino research may be a hoax," Arsen said.

There was a long pause before Rama Chand spoke again.

"Arsen, I hope you know what you are saying. I trust you said nothing to anybody? The implications would be enormous if this conversation became known. Let me call you back from my unlisted number."

After he called back Rama Chand continued in his worried tone.

"I am thinking and I cannot believe it. As you know, Alexei has been the authority we never questioned. Nobody has ever even suggested the possibility of a hoax. I can understand the concern of some people about the paucity of information and about the fact that there were no real break-throughs, but then we were often told that the research was progressing as expected and that the final steps were imminent. Those people said 'hoax' just like that, did they?"

"Yes they did," Arsen said. "I wondered about the memory capture too."

"I thought Ursula Bjöstrom went to Moscow and saw the actual memory capture."

"She did."

"Arsen, we will have to find out what is happening," Rama Chand said. "I could postpone the launching of one ship and have someone investigate the memory content."

"I was thinking the same as you," Arsen said. "I am not sure anything would be accomplished by finding out about the memory capture. At this point it makes no difference if the cloned people get their memory back or not. Whether or not this turns out to be a hoax, the damage would be irreparable. The same is true for the neutrino gun. You could not tell people that they had been deceived even if it were true."

There was another pause in the conversation before Rama Chand answered.

"You are obviously right but I would like to know. I will forget about this conversation and pray that your suspicion is ungrounded. Good luck to you in Moscow and Rio."

Arsen was very upset after this conversation.

CHAPTER SIXTY-SIX

FRIDAY, 5 JANUARY 2001

Friday was just as spectacular as the day before. Forty more ships were launched - or were they? Arsen thought he counted only nineteen in the last round of liftoffs.

When asked, Leo Goodman only said that there was a malfunction in the ignition process of one of the ships and it would be fixed in a few days.

Around eleven o'clock that evening Arsen received an urgent call from Alexei.

"We have a major disaster on our hands. Gennadi Koltsov killed himself. The investigators ruled out foul play and called it suicide. I went though his papers and looked over his lab. He systematically destroyed all information on memory capture and all equipment. Nothing is left. The stuff on the neutrino gun has been damaged but not so much that it is irreparable. Fortunately, I kept tabs on what he was doing. I think I will be able to restore the project and finish it myself."

Arsen was stunned and said nothing.

"Arsen, it seems that your trip to Moscow should be postponed," Alexei said. "I will be very busy for some time. I must do the salvage job and that will take all my time and energy. I will not be going to New York until the job has been done. Go to Rio, my friend, and enjoy yourself with your wife. I hope to be able to see you before your takeoff in February."

Alexei hung up abruptly without waiting for Arsen to say anything.

Nada was stunned by the news, too.

Several calls followed.

Rama Chand called to confirm the news and said nothing about the postponed launch of the one ship. Either he had ordered the 'malfunction' or he knew nothing about it, Arsen thought. There was no point in asking, as he would not get the right answer anyway. Arsen's mistrust of people had just recurred. There were too many coincidences.

He and Nada had better go to Rio in the morning, Arsen decided.

CHAPTER SIXTY-SEVEN

SATURDAY, 6 JANUARY 2001

Nada and Arsen had breakfast with David Korngold before they left for the airport.

"Too many things happened in one day to be coincidental," Arsen said. "We are going to Rio today. I don't want to know what happened and what might have happened. Coppacabana is our destination. I know I cannot change anything anymore. My schedule has been determined, and my fate sealed."

After the long flight they were driven to the Coppacabana Hotel where a suite was ready for them. The hotel was just as nice and the people just as friendly and helpful as they had been during their previous visits. Arsen and Nada were finally able to relax.

CHAPTER SIXTY-EIGHT

MONDAY, 15 JANUARY 2001

Nada and Arsen spent the morning at the pool sitting in reclining chairs and reading the books they had brought with them. The day was warm and sunny and they skipped the walk along the beach. The lunch served in the dinning area at the side of the pool was light: a sandwich and a glass of juice. After lunch they returned to their suite. Nada wanted to take a nap and Arsen read his book, *Out of Control*, by Zbigniew Brzezinski. The book was written for a super intellectual and a connoisseur of political jargon, and it contained deep substance often difficult to grasp. What irked Arsen was Brzezinski's criticism of intellectuals for embracing communism; he was saying how stupid they were. Perhaps intellectuals had been naive in accepting the communist theory literarily, apart from the less known cruel reality.

Arsen called Rama Chand; he said nothing about Alexei, nor did he bring up the malfunctioning spaceship. He was nice and asked about Nada and about the weather in Rio and whether they were having a good time and getting some rest. Arsen did not insist. There was nothing he could change anymore no matter what was going on in New York, Moscow or anywhere else. He and Nada would return to New York, Arsen thought, say goodbye to friends, and have an evening with the children. Then they would go to Florida, board their ship and take off for an uncertain mission and likely a horrific death. Period.

Nada was asleep. Arsen went to the lobby to look for the *New York Times* which was usually available in the afternoon. A concierge told him that the paper would not be delivered that day. The *International Herald Tribune* was not distributed in the hotel and to get a copy one had to take a cab ride to the place where the newspaper and magazine kiosks had on display almost every newspaper from Europe and North America. Arsen evaded the Security Service agents and hired a cab to take him there. He bought the current *New York Times*, *Time* magazine and the *International Herald Tribune*.

On the way back to the hotel, in the same cab, Arsen looked at the headlines. There was nothing of interest to him, nothing about Gennadi or about the neutrino research or about a malfunctioning spaceship. There was a cover-up, Arsen thought. They were suppressing the information.

The traffic was very light and there were only a few cars on the Avenida Atlantica. It was warm, and the back windows of the cab were rolled down. They were waiting for a traffic light to change when Arsen noticed an old Ford Mustang approaching the cab. It stopped parallel and close to the cab. Arsen saw a man in the back seat looking at him through the open window. He was white, in his thirties, with a high forehead, black hair and a prominent nose. His lips were pouting. Their eyes met. Arsen saw the handgun the man was pointing at him. He saw the man pull the trigger. The man's eyes closed for a moment. Arsen realized the bullet would be coming his way. It was too late to move.

The bullet hit his forehead and Arsen relived his entire life in one moment of agony and fell on the back seat of the cab. He was dead. The people who gathered noticed a smile on Arsen's face.

CHAPTER SYXTY-NINE

YEAR: 1 4 2 5 7 7 6 A.D.

The sunlight poured through the open doorway of the spaceship. The robot walked into the cabin, positioned itself in a corner and became immobile. The cabin was neatly organized if that was possible among the multitude of equipment taking up two thirds of the floor. Two computers were turned on. One monitor was charting values from a spectrometer attached to an egg shaped object. The other monitor showed the text from a book.

On the wall near the door a digital sign displayed the name and the year:

NAME: ARSEN PANKOVICH, M.D.

YEARS FROM TAKEOFF : 1 4 2 3 7 7 6

TAKE OFF YEAR :   2 0 0 1

In the corner opposite the robot a young man sat with a strange semicircular apparatus attached to his head. He was sitting in front of a computer and answering a questionnaire on the computer screen.

Please answer all questions:

Your full name: Arsen Pankovich

Birth year: 1425756

Have you read the manual on memory capture?

502

PRESS: 'YES'   or   'NO'

Do you clearly understand what it says?

PRESS: 'YES'   or   'NO'

Do you want to proceed?

PRESS: 'YES'   or   'NO'

If you want to transfer your captured memory

PRESS   'OK'

if not

PRESS   'CANCEL'

The young man hesitated for a moment and then clicked the 'OK' button. He remained still for thirty minutes as the instruction message had prescribed. Then the computer flashed the message:

THE INSTALLATION OF THE MEMORY
WAS SUCCESSFUL

If you wish to retain the memory

PRESS   'RETAIN'

if not

PRESS   'CANCEL' to void the transfer.

The young man hesitated again for a moment and then determinedly clicked the 'RETAIN' button. He was almost immobile for several minutes.

"My God," exclaimed the young man, "I remember Banja Luka, Belgrade, New York, the World Government and Nada and--"

The young man leaned forward and held his face with both hands - his crying was unrestrained.

Had the old soul entered his new mind?